DARKDAWN

Also by Jay Kristoff

The Nevernight Chronicle
Nevernight
Godsgrave

Lifelike Trilogy
LIFEL1K3
DEV1AT3

The Lotus War
Stormdancer
Kinslayer
Endsinger
The Last Stormdancer

Writing with Amie Kaufman
Illuminae
Gemina
Obsidio

Aurora Rising

DARKDAWN

THE NEVERNIGHT CHRONICLE
BOOK III

JAY KRISTOFF

HARPER
Voyager

Harper*Voyager*
An imprint of HarperCollins*Publishers* Ltd
1 London Bridge Street
London SE1 9GF

www.harpercollins.co.uk

First published by HarperCollins*Publishers* 2019
2

Trinity logo by James Orr

Maps by Virginia Allyn

Jay Kristoff asserts the moral right to
be identified as the author of this work

A catalogue record for this book is available from the British Library

HB ISBN: 978-0-00-818008-9
TPB ISBN: 978-0-00-818009-6

This novel is entirely a work of fiction.
The names, characters and incidents portrayed in it are
the work of the author's imagination. Any resemblance to
actual persons, living or dead, events or localities is
entirely coincidental.

Printed and bound in the UK by
CPI Group (UK) Ltd, Croydon CR0 4YY

This book is produced from independently certified FSC™ paper
to ensure responsible forest management.

For more information visit: www.harpercollins.co.uk/green

for my readers
I couldn't have done it without you, either

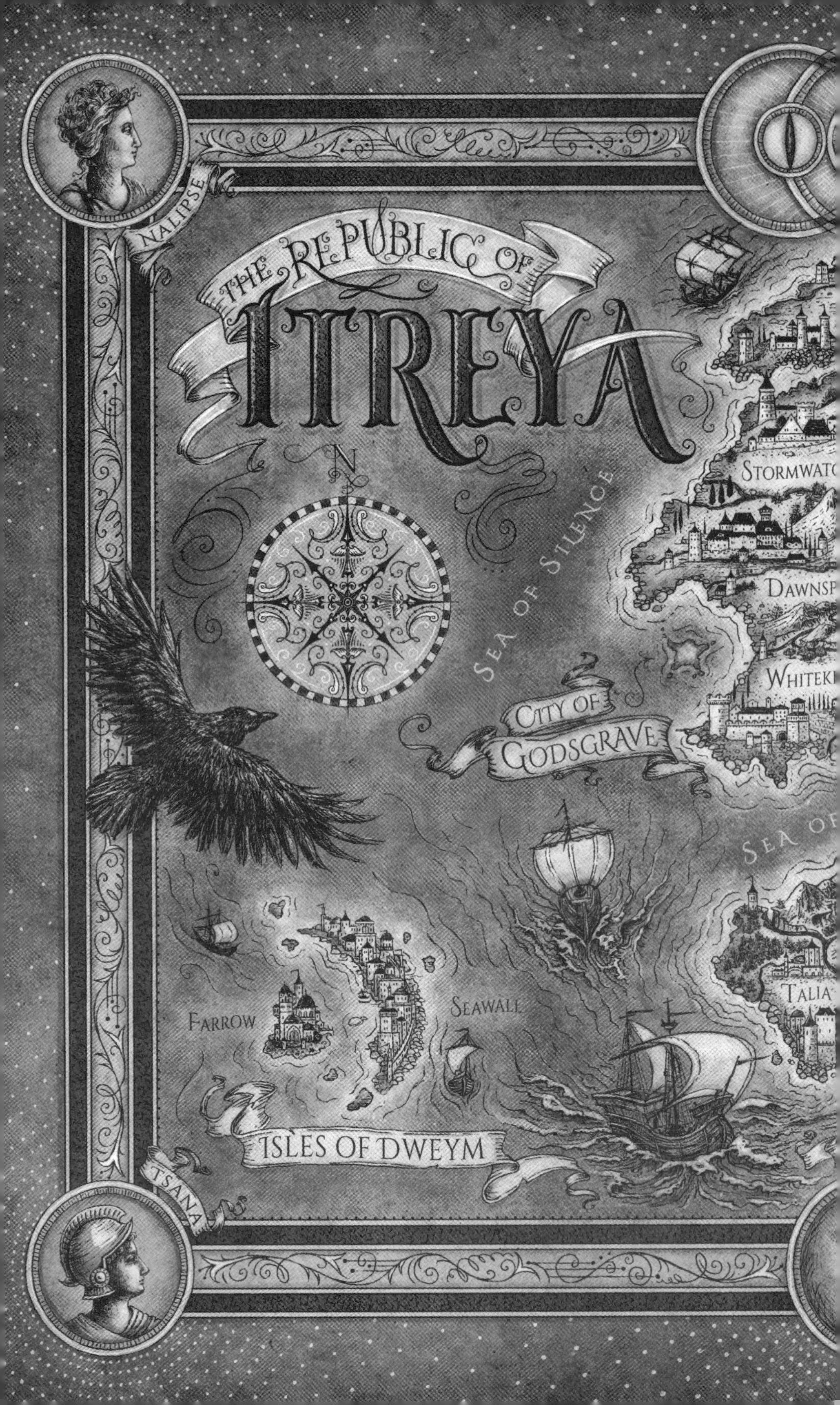

THE REPUBLIC OF
ITREYA
NALIPSE
TSANA
N
SEA OF SILENCE
CITY OF
GODSGRAVE
STORMWATC
DAWNSP
WHITEK
SEA OF
TALIA
FARROW
SEAWALL
ISLES OF DWEYM

TRELENE
UL'STAAD
VAAN
CARRION HALL
EREWOOD
SEA OF STARS
BLACKBRIDGE
ITREYA
CROW'S NEST
THE QUIET MOUNTAIN
SEA OF SORROWS
LAST HOPE
ASHKAH
GALANTE
AMAI
LIIS
TA'NISE
ELAI
KEPH

The Sword Arm
The Spine
The Heart
The Sea of Silence
Godsgrave Cathedral
Mercurio's Curios
Liisian Market
Western Nethers
The Bay of Butchers
The Bridge of Follies
IN THE REPU

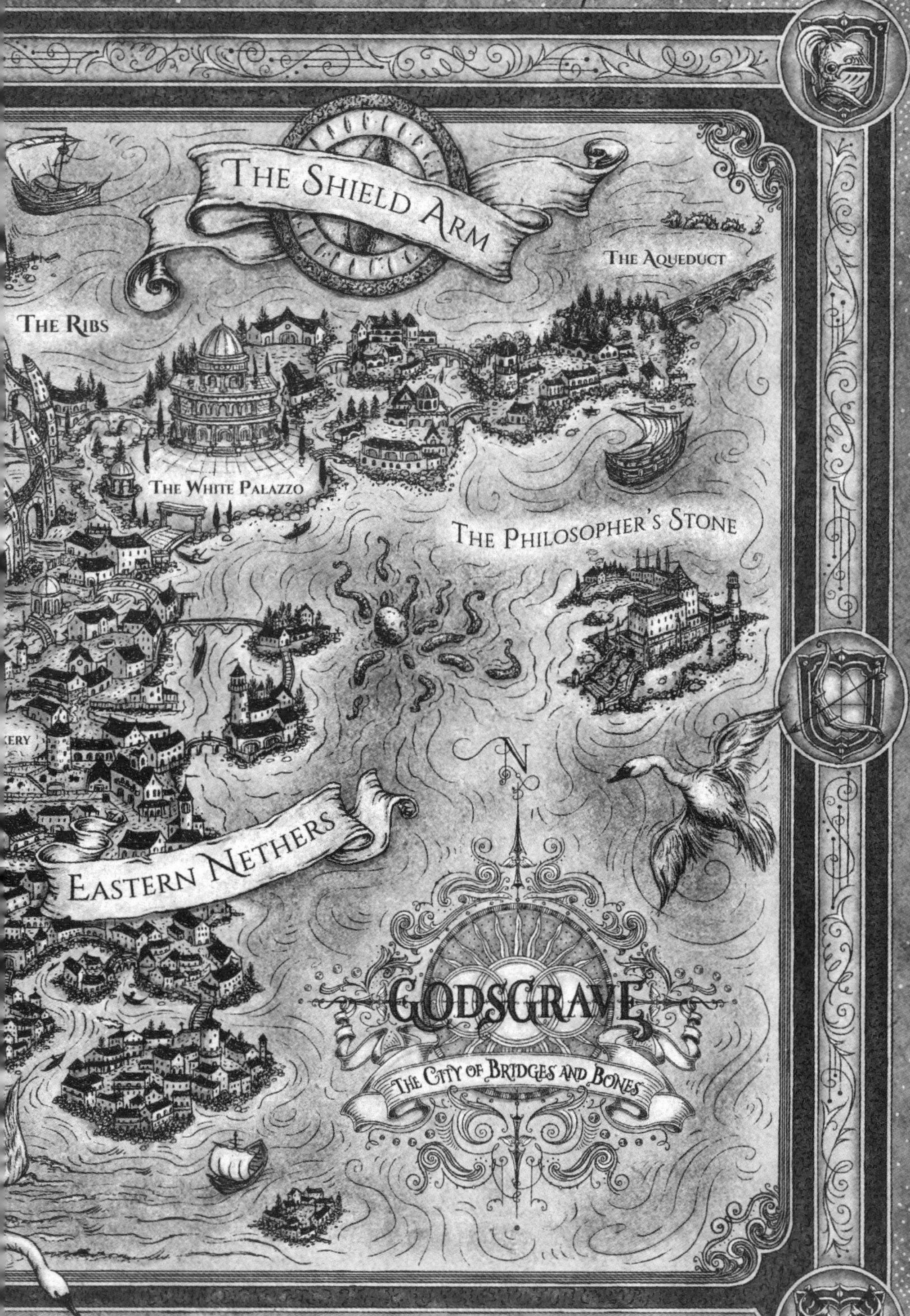

The Shield Arm
The Aqueduct
The Ribs
The White Palazzo
The Philosopher's Stone
N
Eastern Nethers
Godsgrave
The City of Bridges and Bones
IC OF ITREYA

N

Well, here we are again, gentlefriend.

I think perhaps an apology is in order. Both for the conclusion of the second part of Mia's tale, and for the state I left you in afterward. You seemed quite upset. Be assured there will be no cliff-hangers in this, our final dance together. As promised, her birth you've witnessed, her life you've lived. All that remains is her death.

But before the smut and butchery begin in earnest, allow me one final refresher for those with memories as reliable as your narrator. And then we can get on with killing our murderous little bitch, yes?

Dramatis Personae

Mia Corvere—assassin of the Red Church, gladiatii of the Falcons of Remus, and now the most infamous murderer in the Itreyan Republic. The child of a failed rebellion, Mia has spent the last eight years of her life pursuing a murderous vendetta against the men who destroyed her familia.

After discovering the Red Church had a hand in her father's murder, Mia broke ranks with the assassins and sold herself to a gladiatii stable. Upon winning the grand games of Godsgrave, Mia made several stunning discoveries in quick succession:

- Her baby brother, Jonnen, whom she presumed dead, had been stolen by her mortal enemy, Consul Julius Scaeva, and raised as his son.
- Jonnen actually *is* Scaeva's son. Meaning Mia's mother, Alinne, was sleeping with the man who would eventually oversee her husband's murder and her own death in the Philosopher's Stone.
- Like Mia, Jonnen is darkin, possessed of the ability to control shadows.

At the conclusion of the grand games, Mia assassinated Grand Cardinal Francesco Duomo. She also apparently murdered Scaeva and stole back her brother before falling to her almost-certain death in a flooded arena full of stormdrakes.

. . . Maw's teeth, that really *was* a thrilling finale, wasn't it?

Mister Kindly—Mia's companion since childhood, Mister Kindly is—depending on who you ask—a daemon, passenger, or familiar, with the ability to eat people's fear. He is made of shadows and sarcasm. Despite his acerbic wit, he obviously has a deep and abiding fondness for Mia. Just don't let him hear you say that.

He wears the shape of a cat, though like most things about him, his appearance is not entirely genuine.

Eclipse—another shadow daemon, Eclipse was passenger to Cassius, former Lord of Blades in the Red Church. She bound herself to Mia when Cassius died.

Eclipse wears the shape of a wolf, and she and Mister Kindly get along about as well as most cats and dogs do.

Ashlinn Järnheim—a former Red Church acolyte of Vaanian blood. Ashlinn betrayed the Ministry to avenge her father, Torvar, and almost brought the Red Church to its knees. After Mia foiled her plot, Ashlinn fell into the service of Cardinal Duomo, who tasked her to retrieve a map to an undisclosed location in Old Ashkah—a map of some vital import to the Red Church. Fearing betrayal, Ashlinn had the map scribed on her back with arkemical ink, which will fade in the event of her death.

Ashlinn assisted Mia with her plot to win the grand games, and the pair eventually became lovers.* After the conclusion of the games, Ashlinn was accosted by the Church Ministry and Consul Scaeva—still very much alive—who revealed Mia had only killed a doppelgänger crafted by the Flesh Weaver, Marielle, and that Scaeva had been working with the Red Church to see his rival, Cardinal Duomo, killed.

For an encore, Scaeva revealed he was also Mia's father.

Ashlinn was then attacked by Red Church assassins, but rescued by a familiar shadowy figure . . .

Tric—an acolyte of the Red Church of mixed Itreyan/Dweymeri blood, also Mia's former lover. He was murdered by Ashlinn Järnheim as part of her plot to capture the Red Church Ministry, and his corpse was pushed off the side of the Quiet Mountain.

Tric has apparently returned to life, albeit in a darker, magikal form. He accosted Mia in the necropolis of Galante and gave her several cryptic warnings without revealing his identity. He later rescued Ashlinn from Red Church assailants.

---

* Teenage hormones, gentlefriends. Quite something, neh?

How he returned from the realm of the Black Mother or why he saved the girl who murdered him is anyone's guess.

Old Mercurio—Mia's confidant and mentor before she joined the Red Church. Mercurio was a Church Blade himself for many years and was serving as bishop of Godsgrave. Despite being a terminally grumpy old prick, he assisted Mia with her plot to kill Duomo and Scaeva, fully aware his actions would incur the Ministry's wrath.

During the finale of the grand games, he was captured by the Church and taken back to the Quiet Mountain by order of . . .

Julius Scaeva—thrice-elected consul of the Itreyan Republic, known as the "People's Senator." The position of consul is usually shared, but Scaeva has maintained sole leadership of the Senate since the Kingmaker Rebellion eight years ago.

Using the rebellion as an excuse to extend his tenure, Scaeva has been working with the Red Church with the goal of claiming the title of imperator and perpetual emergency powers over the Republic. He presided over the execution of Mia's father, sentenced his lover, Mia's mother, to die in the Philosopher's Stone, stole Mia's baby brother, and ordered Mia drowned in a canal, despite knowing she was his daughter.

The word "cunt" doesn't really seem to do him justice.

But speaking of . . .

Drusilla—Lady of Blades in the Red Church and, despite her apparent age, one of the deadliest assassins in the Republic. Though she claims devotion to the Black Mother, Niah, Drusilla has been working in league with Consul Scaeva to ensure his ambition of seizing control of the Itreyan Republic.

The Lady of Blades has disliked Mia ever since the girl failed her trials as a Red Church acolyte. Presumably Mia's recent betrayals have not elevated her in Drusilla's opinions.

Solis—Revered Father and Shahiid of Songs, master in the art of steel, and surliest man alive. He is apparently blind, though he displays little impediment when wielding a sword. Solis was once a prisoner in the Philosopher's Stone and was the only survivor of a bloody cull known as "the Descent," in which the prisoners were encouraged to murder each other en masse in exchange for freedom. Solis's victory earned him his name, which in the tongue of Old Ashkah means "the Last One."

Mia cut his face during their first sparring session in the Quiet Mountain. He cut off her arm in retaliation. Solis chose to keep the scar, along with his grudge for the girl who bested him.

Spiderkiller—Shahiid of the Hall of Truth and mistress of poisons. Mia was one of Spiderkiller's most promising acolytes, but the Shahiid's fondness for the girl had all but disappeared—even *before* Mia chose to betray the Church's teachings.

If she ever offers you a glass of goldwine, I'd advise you to refuse.

Mouser—master of thievery and Shahiid of Pockets. A charming fellow with a young man's face, an old man's eyes, and a penchant for wearing ladies' underthings.

The Mouser had no enmity toward Mia before her betrayal, though presumably she's been struck off his Great Tithe gift list thanks to her recent fuckarsery.

Aalea—mistress of secrets and Shahiid of Masks. Seductive and beautiful, Aalea's tally of murders is seconded only by the notches on her bedpost.

She was actually quite fond of Mia before the girl's betrayal, but no member of the Church Ministry attained their position by being sentimental.

Marielle—one of two albino sorcerii who serve the Red Church. Marielle is a master of Flesh Weaving, a form of ancient magik practiced in the fallen Empire of Ashkah. She can sculpt skin and muscle as easily as clay, but the toll she pays for her power is terrible—her own flesh is hideously deformed, and she has no power to alter it.

In keeping with her unsettling appearance, Marielle also seems overly fond of her brother, Adonai.

Adonai—the second sorcerii who serves the Quiet Mountain. Adonai is a blood speaker who works with human vitus—he can pass messages in blood, manipulate it with but a thought, and transport people and once-living objects through the blood pools in Red Church chapels. Thanks to Marielle's arts, he is handsome beyond compare.

He murdered Ashlinn's brother, Osrik, during the Luminatii assault on the Mountain, and he owes a debt to Mia for saving his life, yet to be called in.

"Blood is owed thee, little Crow. And blood shall be repaid."

Aelius—chronicler of the Quiet Mountain. Aelius is master of the Red Church's great Athenaeum—a vast and ever-growing library of books that were destroyed, lost to time, or never even written in the first place. He also wrangles the enormous carnivorous "bookworms" that roam the dark between the shelves, and his tasks are made ever more difficult by the fact that, like everything else in the Black Mother's library, Aelius himself is dead.

Still, it's a living . . .

Naev—a Hand of the Red Church who manages supply runs in the Whisperwastes of Ashkah. After some initial difficulties, she and Mia became friends and confidants.

Naev was disfigured by Weaver Marielle out of jealousy over an affair with her brother, Adonai. But after Mia foiled the assault on the Quiet Mountain, Marielle restored Naev's beauty as a favor to her savior.

Naev keeps her face veiled, and her feelings beside.

Hush—an accomplished Blade of the Red Church. Apparently mute, Hush communicates through a form of sign language known as Tongueless.

Though he and Mia were acolytes together and he assisted her in her trials, he remains loyal to the Ministry. He attempted to capture Ashlinn at the Ministry's behest, though the girl escaped with Tric's help.

Francesco Duomo—Grand Cardinal of the Church of the Light and the most powerful member of the Everseeing's ministry. Though apparently allied with Julius Scaeva, the cardinal and the consul were in fact bitter rivals. Along with Scaeva and Justicus Marcus Remus, Duomo passed sentence on the failed Kingmaker rebels, including Mia's father, Darius.

It's safe to say Mia took the cardinal's actions personally—she trimmed his beard all the way to the bone in front of a hundred thousand screaming people.

Alinne Corvere—Mia's mother, and a fearsome politician who almost succeeded in bringing down the Itreyan Republic. Her marriage to Justicus Darius turned out to be one of friendship and political expedience—she was, in fact, lover to Julius Scaeva and bore him two children: Mia and Jonnen.

Despite her relationship with Scaeva, the consul showed no compunction in casting her aside after her husband's failed rebellion. Alinne was imprisoned in the Philosopher's Stone, where she died in madness and misery.

Mia has only recently learned her mother was not the paragon she once believed.

Darius "the Kingmaker" Corvere—the man Mia called "Father." Former justicus of the Luminatii Legion, Darius forged an alliance with his lover, General Gaius Maxinius Antonius, which would have seen Antonius crowned as king of Itreya.

However, with the assistance of the Red Church, both men were captured on the eve of battle, and Darius was hanged with his would-be king, Antonius, beside him.

To say Mia took his death badly would be something of an understatement.

Jonnen Corvere—Mia's baby brother. Thought to be dead along with his mother, Mia has recently learned the boy was raised as Scaeva's legitimate son under the name "Lucius"—Scaeva's wife, Liviana, is apparently unable to bear him children.

Jonnen has no idea about his true parentage, and was taken too young to remember his true name or sister at all.

Furian—the Unfallen, and champion of the Remus Collegium. Furian was darkin like Mia, able to bend the shadows to his will. However, he had no passenger and refused to explore his gift, believing it an abomination.

Mia killed Furian during the climax of the grand games. At the moment of his death, she was shown a brief vision of a night sky, set with a large, glowing orb, and heard the words *"The many were one. And will be again."*

After seeing this phantasm, Mia realized her shadow was dark enough for four.

Sidonius—a former member of the Luminatii who served under Darius Corvere. Sid was drummed out of the legion after he refused to participate in General Antonius's planned rebellion against the Senate. Sold into slavery, he was eventually purchased by the House of Remus and fought as gladiatii in the *Venatus Magni*.

When Mia was sold to the same collegium, Sidonius learned of her identity and took the girl under his wing, acting as a surrogate older brother to the young Blade.

He has the manners of a goat and the heart of a lion.

The Falcons of Remus—Bladesinger, Bryn, Wavewaker, Butcher, Felix, and Albanus—gladiatii of the Remus Collegium all, and Mia's friends and allies throughout the games. Though she apparently betrayed and murdered them all, Mia actually orchestrated their escape from Godsgrave.

They are currently at large somewhere in Itreya, and presumably quite drunk.

Aa—head of the Itreyan pantheon, Father of Light, also known as the Ever-seeing. The three suns, known as Saan (the Seer), Saai (the Knower), and Shiih (the Watcher), are said to be his eyes, and one or more is usually present in the heavens, with the result that actual nighttime, or truedark, in the Republic occurs only for one week every two and a half years. At the time of this tale, truelight—the moment all three suns shine in the heavens—has come and mostly gone.

Truedark approaches, gentlefriends.

Tsana—Lady of Fire, She Who Burns Our Sin, The Pure, Patron of Women and Warriors, and firstborn daughter of Aa and Niah.

Keph—Lady of Earth, She Who Ever Slumbers, The Hearth, Patron of Dreamers and Fools, secondborn of Aa and Niah.

Trelene—Lady of Oceans, She Who Will Drink the World, The Fate, Patron of Sailors and Scoundrels, thirdborn daughter of Aa and Niah, and twin to Nalipse.

Nalipse—Lady of Storms, She Who Remembers, The Merciful, Patron of Healers and Leaders, fourthborn of Aa and Niah, and twin to Trelene.

Niah—the Maw, the Mother of Night, and Our Lady of Blessed Murder. Sisterwife of Aa, Niah rules a lightless region of the hereafter known as the Abyss. She and Aa initially shared the rule of the sky equally, but, commanded to bear her husband only daughters, Niah disobeyed Aa's edict and bore him a son.

In punishment, Niah was banished from the skies by her beloved, allowed to return only for a brief spell every few years.

And as for what became of their son?

Well, gentlefriend, I believe it's time for some answers.

When all is blood,
blood is all.

—MOTTO OF THE FAMILIA CORVERE

BOOK 1

THE DARK WITHIN

CHAPTER 1

BROTHER

Eight years of poison and murder and shit.

Eight years of blood and sweat and death.

Eight years.

She'd fallen so far, her little brother in her arms, fingers still sticky and red. The light of the three suns above, burning and blinding. The waters of the flooded arena below, crimson with blood. The mob howling, bewildered and outraged at the murders of their grand cardinal, their beloved consul, both at the hands of their revered champion. The greatest games in Godsgrave's history had ended with the most audacious murders in the history of the entire Republic. The arena was in chaos. But through it all, the screams, the roars, the rage, Mia Corvere had known only triumph.

After eight years.

Eight fucking years.

Mother.

Father.

I did it.

I killed them for you.

She'd hit the water hard, the sights and sounds of Godsgrave Arena swallowed up as she plunged beneath the surface. Salt burning in her eyes. Breath burning in her lungs. Crowd still roaring in her ears. Her little brother, Jonnen, was struggling, punching, wriggling in her arms like a landed fish. She could sense the serpentine shadows of stormdrakes, cruising toward her through the murk. Razor smiles and dead eyes.

Truelight was so bright, even here beneath the surface. But even with those three awful suns in the sky, even with all the outrage of the Everseeing pouring down, her own shadows were with her. Dark enough for four now. And Mia reached toward the outflow in the arena floor—the wide spout from which all that salt and water flowed and she

Stepped

into the

shadows

inside it.

It left her dizzied and sick—she could still feel that blinding sunslight in the sky above. Mia sank like a stone in her armor, weighed down by black iron and sodden falcon's wings. Pulling Jonnen down with her, she hit the bottom of the outflow pipe with a dull *clunk*. She had only moments, only the breath she'd brought with her. And she'd not planned to have a struggling child in her arms when she did this.

Dragging herself and the boy along the pipe, she found a pocket of air inside the pressure valve, just as Ashlinn had promised. Surfacing with a ragged gasp, she pulled her brother up beside her. The boy sputtered in her arms, wailing, struggling, flailing at her face.

"Unhand me, wench!" he cried.

"Stop it!" Mia gasped.

"Let me *go*!"

"Jonnen, stop it, please!"

She wrapped the boy up, pinning his arms so he couldn't punch anymore. His cries echoed on the pipe above her head. Struggling with her armor's clasps and straps with her free hand, she dragged the pieces away, one by one. Shedding the skin of the gladiatii, the assassin, the daughter of vengeance, sloughing those eight years off her bones. It'd been worth it. All of it. Duomo dead. Scaeva dead. And Jonnen, her blood, the babe she'd thought long buried in his grave . . .

My little brother lives.

The boy kicked, thrashed, bit. There were no tears for his murdered da, only fury, rippling and red. Mia had thought the boy dead years ago—swallowed up inside the Philosopher's Stone with her mother and the last of her hope. But if she'd had any lingering doubts he could be a Corvere, that he could be her mother's son, the boy's bloody rage put them all to the sword.

"Jonnen, listen to me!"

"My name is Lucius!" he shrieked, his voice echoing on the iron.

"Lucius, then, listen!"

"I won't!" he shouted. "You k-killed my father! You *killed* him!"

Pity swelled inside Mia, but she clenched her jaw, hardened her heart against it.

"I'm sorry, Jonnen. But your father . . ." She shook her head, breathed deep. "Listen, we need to get out of this pipe before they start draining the arena. The stormdrakes will come back this way, do you understand?"*

"Let them come, I hope they *eat* you!"

"*. . . O, I LIKE HIM . . .*"

"*. . . why does that not surprise me . . .*"

The boy turned to the dark shapes coalescing on the wall beside them, the air around them growing chill. A cat made of shadows and a wolf of the same, staring at him with their not-eyes. Mister Kindly's tail twitched side to side as he studied the child. Eclipse simply tilted her head, shivering slightly. Jonnen fell silent for a moment, wide, dark eyes looking first to Mia's passengers, then to the girl who held him.

"You hear them, too . . . ," he breathed.

"I'm like you," Mia nodded. "We're the same."

The boy stared at her, perhaps feeling the same sickness, hunger, *longing*

---

*Of the three breeds of drake found in Itreyan waters—White, Saber, and Storm—the stormdrake is by far the stupidest. The beasts eat virtually anything that will fit inside their mouths, including fellow stormdrakes and their own young. A complete list of oddities found in stormdrake bellies is kept in the zoology archives of the Iron Collegium, and includes, in no particular order:

- a full suit of plate armor
- a leather chaise lounge
- a six-foot-long timber saw
- an entire family of (presumably enraged) porcupines

This habit of eating anything vaguely interesting has earned them the moniker "sewers of the sea" among Itreyan fishermen, since upon catching one and cutting it open, you're likely to find all kinds of strange . . .

Well, yes.

You get the idea.

she did. Mia looked him over, tears welling in her eyes. All the miles, all the years . . .

"You don't remember me," she whispered, her voice shaking. "You were only a baby when they t-took you away from us. But I remember you."

She was almost overcome for a moment. Tears in her lashes and a sob caught in her throat. Recalling the baby boy wrapped in swaddling on her mother's bed the turn her father died. Staring up at her with his big, dark eyes. Envying him that he was too young to know their father had ended, and all their world besides.

But he wasn't Jonnen's father at all, was he?

Mia shook her head, blinked back those hateful tears.

O, Mother, how could you . . .

Looking at the boy now, she could barely speak. Barely force her jaw to move, her lungs to breathe, her lips to form the words burning in her chest. He had the same flint-black eyes as she, the same ink-black hair. She could see their mother in him so clearly, it was like peering into a looking glass. But beyond the her in him, something in the shape of Jonnen's little nose, the line of his puppy-fat cheeks . . .

She could see him.

Scaeva.

"My name is Mia," she finally managed. "I'm your sister."

"I have no sister," the boy spat.

"Jonn—" Mia caught herself. Licked her lips and tasted salt. "Lucius, we have to go. I'll explain everything, I swear it. But it's dangerous here."

". . . ALL WILL BE WELL, CHILD . . ."

". . . breathe easy . . ."

Mia watched as her daemons slipped into the boy's shadow, eating away at his fear as they'd always done for her. But though the panic in his eyes lessened, the rage only swelled, the bunched muscles in his little arms suddenly flexing against hers. He wriggled and bucked again, slipping a hand free and clawing at her face.

"Let me go!" he cried.

Mia hissed as his thumb found her eye, whipping her head away with a snarl.

"Stop it!" she snapped, temper flaring.

"Let *go*!"

"If you'll not be still, I'll hold you still!"

Mia pushed the boy hard against the pipe, pressing him in place as he kicked and spat. She could understand his rage, but in truth, she had no time to spend on hurt feelings right now. Working at the remaining buckles on her armor with her free hand, she slipped off the long leather straps that held her breastplate and spaulders in place, dropping the armor to the floor of the valve. She kept her boots, her studded leather skirt, the threadbare, bloodstained tunic beneath. And using the straps, one each for his wrists and ankles, she bound up her brother like a hog to slaughter.

"Unhand m—*ffll-ggmm*!"

Jonnen's protests were muted as Mia tied another thong about his mouth. And gathering the boy into her arms, she held him tight, looked him hard in the eyes.

"We have to swim," she said. "I'd not waste my breath on shouting if I were you."

Dark eyes locked on hers, glittering with hate. But the boy seemed sensible enough to comply, finally dragging a deep draft into his lungs.

Mia pulled them below and swam for their lives.

They surfaced in sapphire water a half hour later to the sound of pealing bells.

With Jonnen in her arms, Mia had swum through the vast storage tanks below the arena, through the echoing dark of the mekwerk outflow pipes, catching her breath where she could and spilling finally out into the sea a few hundred feet north of Sword Arm harbor. Her brother had glared at her all the while, bound hand and foot and mouth.

Mia felt wretched at having to tie her own kin up like a spring lamb, but she had no idea what else to do with him. She couldn't possibly have left him up there on the victor's plinth with the cooling corpses of his da and Duomo. Couldn't ever have left him behind. But in all her planning with Ashlinn and Mercurio, she'd not bargained on having to wrangle a nine-year-old boy after having murdered his father right in front of him.

His father.

The thought swam behind her eyes, too dark and heavy to look at for long. She pushed it aside, focusing on getting them into shallower waters. Ash and Mercurio were waiting for her aboard a swift galley named the *Siren's Song,* berthed at the Sword Arm. The sooner they were out of Godsgrave, the better. Word would be spreading across the metropolis about Scaeva's assassination, and if they didn't know already, the Red Church would soon learn their richest and most powerful patron was dead. A storm of knives and shit was about to start raining down on Mia's head.

As she swam toward the Sword Arm docks, she saw the streets of the metropolis beyond were in chaos. Cathedrals were ringing a death knell across the City of Bridges and Bones. Folk were emerging from taverna and tenements, bewildered, outraged, terrified as rumor of Scaeva's murder uncoiled through the city like blood in the water. Legionaries were everywhere, armor glinting under that awful sunslight.

With all the fuss and bother, precious few folk noticed the bedraggled and bleeding slavegirl paddling slowly toward the shore with a boy trussed up in her arms. Picking her way carefully through the gondolas and dinghies bobbing about the Sword Arm jetties, Mia reached the shadows beneath a long timber boardwalk.

"I'm going to hide us for a moment," she murmured to her brother. "You won't be able to see for a while, but I need you to be brave."

The boy only glared, dark curls hanging in his eyes. Stretching out her fingers, Mia dragged her mantle of shadows about her and Jonnen's shoulders. It took real effort with truelight blazing above her—the sunslight scorching and bright. But even with her passengers now riding with her brother, the shadow beneath Mia was twice as dark as it had been before Furian's death. Her grip on the dark felt stronger. Tighter. Closer.

She remembered the vision she'd seen as she slew the Unfallen before the adoring crowd. The sky above her, not bright and blinding, but pitch-black and flooded with stars. And shining high above her head, a pale and perfect orb.

Like a sun, but somehow . . . not.

"The many were one. And will be again."

Or so the voice she'd heard had said. Echoing the message from that Hearthless wraith with the gravebone blades who'd saved her skin in the Galante necropolis.

Mia didn't know what it meant. She'd never had a mentor to show her what it was to be darkin. Never found an answer to the riddle of what she was. She didn't know. *Couldn't* know. But she knew this, sure as she knew her own name: since the moment Furian had died at her hands, a newfound strength was flowing in her veins.

Somehow, she was . . . *more.*

The world fell into muzzy blackness as she pulled on her shadowcloak, and she and her brother became faint smudges on the watercolors of the world. Jonnen squinted in the gloom beneath her mantle, watching her with suspicious eyes, but at least his struggles had ceased for now. Mia followed Mister Kindly's and Eclipse's whispered directions, slowly climbing a barnacle-encrusted ladder and up to the jetty proper with Jonnen under one arm. And there, in the shadow of a shallow-bottomed trawler, she curled down to wait, cross-legged, dripping wet, arms around her brother.

Mister Kindly coalesced in the shadow at Jonnen's feet, licking at a translucent paw. Eclipse melted from the boy's shadow, outlined black against the trawler's hull.

"*. . . I WILL RETURN . . . ,*" the not-wolf growled.

"*. . . you will be missed . . . ,*" the not-cat yawned.

"*. . . WILL YOU MISS YOUR TONGUE AS MUCH, WHEN I TEAR IT FROM YOUR HEAD . . . ?*"

"Enough, the pair of you," Mia hissed. "Be swift, Eclipse."

"*. . . AS IT PLEASE YOU . . .*"

The shadowwolf shivered and was gone, flitting along the cracks in the jetty's boards and off along the harbor wall.

"*. . . i hate that mongrel . . . ,*" Mister Kindly sighed.

"Aye, so you've said," Mia muttered. "About a thousand times now."

"*. . . more than that, surely . . . ?*"

Despite her fatigue, Mia's lips twisted in a smile.

Mister Kindly continued with his pointless ablutions and Mia sat cradling her brother for long minutes, muscles aching, salt water stinging in her cuts as the suns blazed overhead. She was tired, beaten, bleeding from a dozen wounds after her ordeals in the arena. The adrenaline of her victory was wearing off, leaving a bone-deep fatigue in its wake. She'd fought two major battles earlier in the turn, helped her fellow gladiatii from the Remus Collegium escape their bondage, slaughtered dozens, including Duomo and Scaeva, won the greatest contest in the history of the Republic, seen all her plans come to fruition.

An emptiness was slowly creeping in to replace her elation. An exhaustion that left her hands shaking. She wanted a soft bed and a cigarillo and to savor the taste of some Albari goldwine on Ashlinn's lips. To feel their bones collide, then sleep for a thousand years. But more, beneath it all, beneath the longing and the fatigue and the pain, looking down at her brother, she realized she felt . . .

Hungry.

It was similar to what she'd felt in the presence of Lord Cassius. Of Furian. She'd felt it when she first saw the boy on his father's shoulders at the victor's plinth. She felt it as she glanced at him now—the longing of a puzzle, searching for a piece of itself.

But what does it mean? she wondered.

And does Jonnen feel the same?

". . . i have an ill feeling, mia . . ."

Mister Kindly's whisper dragged her eyes from the back of her brother's head. The shadowcat had stopped pretending to clean his paw, instead staring out at the City of Bridges and Bones from within Jonnen's shadow.

"What's to fear?" she murmured. "The deed is done. And all things considered, nothing went too badly tits up."

". . . what difference does it make, the direction your breasts are pointing . . . ?"

"Spoken like someone who's never owned a pair."

Mister Kindly glanced at the boy he was riding.

". . . we seem to have some unexpected luggage . . ."

Jonnen mumbled something unintelligible beneath his gag. Mia had no doubts his sentiments were less than flattering, but she kept her eyes on the shadowcat.

"You worry too much," she told him.

". . . and you not enough . . ."

"And whose fault is that? *You're* the one who eats my fears."

The daemon tilted his head, but he gave no reply. Mia waited in silence, staring out at the city beyond her veil of shadows. The sounds of the capital were muted beneath her cloak, the colors naught but dull white and terra-cotta blurs. But she could still hear tolling bells, running feet, panicked shouts in the distance.

"The consul and cardinal slain!"

"Assassin!" came the cry. *"Assassin!"*

Mia glanced down to Jonnen, saw he was staring at her with unveiled malice. She knew his thoughts then, as surely as if he'd spoken aloud.

You killed my father.

"He imprisoned our mother, Jonnen," Mia told the boy. "Left her to die in agony inside the Philosopher's Stone. He killed *my* father, and hundreds more besides. Do you not remember him on the victor's plinth, throwing you at me to save his own wretched skin?" She shook her head and sighed. "I'm sorry. I know it's hard to understand. But Julius Scaeva was a monster."

The boy bucked suddenly, violently, smacking his forehead into her chin. Mia bit her tongue, cursing, grabbing her brother and squeezing him tight as he launched into another bout of struggling. He tugged against his waterlogged straps, bruising his skin as he strained to free himself. But for all his fury, he was only a nine-year-old boy. Mia simply held him until his strength ran out, until his muted cries died, until he finally went limp with a soft sob of rage.

Swallowing the blood in her mouth, she wrapped him in her arms.

"You'll understand one turn," she murmured. "I love you, Jonnen."

He flailed once more, then fell still. In the awkward quiet afterward, Mia felt a cool shiver down her spine. Goosebumps prickled on her skin, and her shadow grew darker as she heard a low growl from the boards beneath her feet.

"*. . . THEY ARE NOT THERE . . . ,*" Eclipse declared.

Mia blinked, her belly lurching a little to the left. Squinting in the glare, she peered at the murky blur of the *Siren's Song,* rocking gently at berth a few jetties down.

"You're certain?" she asked.

"*. . . I SEARCHED FROM BOW TO STERN. MERCURIO AND ASHLINN ARE NOT ABOARD . . .*"

Mia swallowed hard, her tongue thick with salt. The plan had been for Ash and her old teacher to meet each other at the Godsgrave chapel, gather their belongings, then make their way to the harbor and await Mia aboard the *Song.* With the time it took for her to swim from the arena to the ocean and out again . . .

"They should be here by now," she whispered.

"*. . . shhhh . . . ,*" came a murmur at her feet. "*. . . do you hear that . . . ?*"

". . . Hear what?"

"*. . . it appears to be the sound of . . . breasts tilting skyward . . . ?*"

Mia scowled at the jest, dragging her sopping hair over her shoulder. Her heart was beating faster, her thoughts racing. There was simply no way Mercurio or Ash would have been late—not with all their lives at stake.

"Something's happened to them . . ."

"*. . . I CAN SEARCH THE CHAPEL, REPORT BACK . . . ?*"

"No. If she . . . If they . . ." Mia chewed her lip, dragged herself to her feet despite her fatigue. "We go together."

"*. . . even our new luggage . . . ?*"

"We can't just leave him here, Mister Kindly," Mia snapped.

The not-cat sighed.

"*. . . and the tits continue to rise . . .*"

Mia looked down at her brother. The boy seemed temporarily defeated, sullen, shivering, silent. He was soaking wet, dark eyes clouded with anger. But with Mister Kindly riding his shadow, he was unafraid at least. So Mia stood, pulling Jonnen up afterward and slinging him over her shoulder with a wince. He was heavy as a bag of bricks, bony elbows and knees jabbing her in all the wrong places. But Mia was hard as nails after the months she'd spent training in the Remus Collegium, and wounded as she was, she knew she could manage him for a time. Moving slowly beneath Mia's shadowcloak, the unlikely quartet groped their way down the jetty and onto the crowded boardwalk, gentle water lapping beneath them.

Following her passenger's whispered directions, stealing past the patrols of legionaries and Luminatii, Mia slipped out into the streets beyond the harbor. Her brother's weight on her shoulders made her muscles groan in protest as she made her way through the warren of Godsgrave's back alleys. Her pulse was thumping in her veins, her belly turning slow, cold somersaults. Eclipse was prowling out ahead. Mister Kindly was still riding Jonnen. And without her passengers, Mia was left trying to fight off fearful thoughts about what might've delayed Mercurio and Ash.

Luminatii?

The Ministry?

What could have gone wrong?

Goddess, if anything has happened to them because of me . . .

Creeping through squeezeways and over little bridges and canals, the group finally reached the wrought-iron fences surrounding the city's necropolis. Mia's boots were near soundless on the gravel, one hand stretched out before her, groping blind. Almost inaudible beneath the peal of cathedral bells, Eclipse's whispers guided her through the twisted gates to the houses of the city's dead, along rows of grand mausoleums and moldy tombs. In a weed-choked corner of the necropolis's old quarter, she stepped through a door carved with a relief of human skulls. A passageway leading down to the boneyards waited beyond.

It was sweet bliss, being out of the light of those awful suns. Her sweat was burning in her wounds. Throwing aside her shadow mantle, Mia slipped Jonnen off her shoulder. He was little, but Goddess, he wasn't light, and her legs and spine practically wept with relief as she placed him onto the chapel floor.

"I'm going to free your feet," she warned. "You try to run, I'll tie you tighter."

The boy made no sound behind his gag, watching silently as she knelt and loosened the strap about his ankles. She could see the mistrust swimming in those black eyes, the unabated anger, but he made no immediate break for freedom. Looping the strap through the bonds at his wrists, Mia stood and walked on, tugging the little boy along behind her like a sullen hound on a soggy leash.

She made her way quietly through twisted tunnels of femurs and ribs—remains of the city's destitute and nameless, too poor to afford tombs of their own. Pulling on a hidden lever, she opened a secret door in a stack of dusty bones, and finally slipped into the Red Church chapel hidden beyond.

Mia crept down the twisting hallways, lined with the skeletons of those long perished. Shuffling behind her, Jonnen was wide-eyed, gazing at the bones all around them. But surrounded by the dead as he was, Mister Kindly stayed coiled in his shadow, keeping the worst of his fear at bay as they moved farther into the chapel.

The corridors were dark.

Silent.

Empty.

Wrong.

Mia felt it almost immediately. Smelled it in the air. The faint scent of blood wasn't out of place in a chapel to Our Lady of Blessed Murder, but the lingering aroma of a tombstone bomb and burned parchment certainly was.

The chapel was far too quiet, the air far too still.

Suspicion ever her watchword, Mia pulled Jonnen closer and werked her mantle of shadows back about their shoulders. Creeping onward in near blindness. Jonnen's breathing seemed far too loud in the silence, her grip on his leash damp with sweat. Her ears strained for the slightest sound, but the place seemed deserted.

Mia stopped in a bone-lined hallway, the hair on the back of her neck prickling. She knew, even before she heard Eclipse's warning growl.

". . . BEHIND . . ."

The dagger flashed from out of the darkness, gleaming silver, poison-dark. Mia twisted, damp hair whipping in a long black ribbon behind her, spine bent in a perfect arch. The blade sailed over her chin, missing her by a breath. Her free hand touched the ground, pushed her back up to standing, heart hammering.

Her mind was racing, brow creased in confusion. Beneath her cloak of shadows, she was almost blind, aye—but the world should have been just as blind to her.

Blind.

O, Goddess.

He stepped out from the dark, silent despite his bulk. His gray leathers were stretched taut across the barn-broad span of his shoulders. His ever-empty scabbard hung at his waist, dark leather embossed with a pattern of concentric circles, much like a pattern of eyes. Thirty-six small scars were etched into his forearm—one for every life he'd taken in the Red Church's name. His eyes were milky white, but Mia saw his eyebrows were gone entirely. The once-blond stubble on his head was crisped black as if burned, and the four sharp spikes of his beard were charred nubs.

"Solis."

His face was swathed in shadows, blind eyes fixed on the ceiling. He drew two short double-edged blades from his back, both darkened by poison. And, hidden as Mia was beneath her mantle, he still spoke directly to her.

"Treacherous fucking quim," he growled.

Mia reached for her gravebone dagger with her free hand. Heart sinking as she realized she'd left it buried in Consul Scaeva's chest.

"O, shit," she whispered.

CHAPTER 2

BONEYARDS

The Revered Father of the Red Church strode forward, blades raised.

"I wondered if you'd be fool enough to return here," he snarled.

Mia tightened her sweating grip on her brother's leash. Sensing movement, she glanced over her shoulder and saw a slender boy with shocking blue eyes stepping from the necropolis shadows. He was death-pale, dressed in a charred black doublet. Two wicked knives gleamed in his hands, their blades black with toxin.

Hush.

"Well?" Solis sneered. "Nothing to say, pup?"

Mia stayed silent, wondering how Solis could sense her under her shadowcloak at all. Sound, perhaps? The scent of her blood and sweat? Regardless, she was exhausted, unarmed, wounded—in no shape to fight. Sensing her fear, the spreading cold in her gut, Mister Kindly slipped from the boy's shadow into her own to quell it. And as the daemon flitted away from the dark about his feet, little Jonnen kicked Mia hard in the shins and snatched his hands from her sweating grip.

"Jonnen!" she cried.

The boy turned and bolted. Mia reached for him, hand outstretched and trying to catch him up. And Solis simply hefted his blades, lowered his head, and charged.

Mia swayed aside, the Shahiid's blade whistling past her cheek as Hush closed in behind her. Spinning swift, she threw aside her shadowcloak, werking the shadows and tangling up the boy's feet instead. He stumbled, fell, Mia slipping under another one of Solis's sweeping strikes. Glancing to the cool dark in the corridor behind the Shahiid, she saw Jonnen fleeing back the way they'd come. And clenching her jaw tight she

Stepped

into the gloom

at Solis's back

and bolted down the corridor after her fleeing brother.

"Jonnen, *stop*!"

Eclipse growled warning, and Mia twisted aside as one of Solis's short swords came whistling at her out of the black. It struck the bone wall in front of her as she reached a sharp corner, remained quivering inside some long-dead skull. Mia grabbed it as she rushed past, twisting it loose and clutching it in her left hand as she ran on.

Dashing on his little legs, Jonnen found himself overtaken quickly. As Mia pounded up the corridor behind him, he glanced over his shoulder, put on a new spurt of speed. His hands were still bound, but he'd managed to drag the gag free from his mouth, shouting as she picked him up and slung him under her arm.

"Unhand me, wench!" he cried, wriggling in fury.

"Jonnen, be still!" Mia hissed.

"Let me *go*!"

"*. . . still like him, do you . . . ?*" Mister Kindly whispered from Mia's shadow.

"*. . . LESS AND LESS WITH EACH PASSING MOMENT . . . ,*" Eclipse replied, flitting out ahead.

"*. . . well, now you appreciate how i feel about you . . .*"

"Shut it, the pair of you!" Mia gasped.

She bounced off a bone wall and stumbled around another corner, Solis and Hush close on her heels. Kicking through the tomb's doorway, Mia dashed up the crumbling stairs and back into the awful glare of those three burning suns. Despite Mister Kindly feasting on her fear, her heart was threatening to burst from her ribs.

She'd spent the entire turn fighting for her life already—she was in no shape to tackle a fully armed Blade of the Red Church, let alone the former Shahiid of Songs. Charred eyebrows aside, Solis was one of the deadliest men alive with a blade. The last time they'd tangled, he'd hacked her arm clean off at the elbow. Hush was no slouch, either, and whatever kinship Mia and the boy might have had in their turns as acolytes seemed long evaporated. She was a traitor to the Red Church in his eyes, worthy only of a slow and very painful murder.

She was outnumbered. And in her current state, outclassed.

But how the 'byss could Solis see me?

Mia Stepped through the shadows to give herself some kind of lead, but with the three suns blazing overhead and her exhaustion from the great games thickening her blood, she only managed to travel a few dozen feet. She clipped her shin on a tombstone, staggered, and almost fell. She might've pulled on her mantle again, but Solis seemed able to sense her anyway. And truth told, she was too tired to manage it all—the wriggling boy in her arms, the desperate chase, werking the dark. Wild eyes searching now for any way of escape.

She skipped up onto a low marble tomb and vaulted the wrought-iron fence of the necropolis. Hitting the ground hard, she gasped, almost falling again. She was in the grounds of a grand chapel to Aa now, built beside the houses of the dead. She could see a broad cobbled road scattered with citizens beyond the churchyard, tall tenements lining the street, flowers in the window boxes. The chapel itself was limestone and glass, the three suns on its belfry mirroring the three suns above.

Black Mother, they were so bright, so hot, so—

"... MIA, BEWARE ... !"

A dagger sailed from Hush's outstretched hand, whistling toward her back. She twisted with a cry, the blade slicing through a lock of her long, dark hair and sailing past her scarred cheek, close enough for her to smell the toxin on the blade. It was Rictus—a fast-working paralytic. One good scratch and she'd be helpless as a newborn babe.

They want me alive, she realized.

"Release me, villain!" her brother shouted, thrashing again.

"Jonnen, please—"

"My name is Lucius!"

The boy bucked and kicked under Mia's arm, still trying to free himself from her grip. He managed to drag his hand loose from the sodden leather bonds about his wrists, and with a gasp, he threw it up into Mia's face. And as if the suns were suddenly extinguished in the sky, all the world went black.

She stumbled in the sudden dark. Her boot clipped a broken flagstone, and her legs went out from under her. Mia gritted her teeth as she hit the ground, hissing in pain as she tore her knees and palms bloody. Her brother also fell, crying out as he tumbled across the gravel to a graceless halt.

The boy rose from the dirt. The boy she'd thought long dead. The boy she'd just snatched from the clutches of a man he should have hated.

"Assassin!" he roared. *"The assassin is here!"*

And fast as he could, he dashed out into the street.

Mia blinked hard, shook her head—she could hear Jonnen yelling as he ran, but she could see nothing at all. In a rush, she realized her brother had somehow werked the shadows over her eyes, completely blinding her. It was a trick she'd never learned, never tried, and she'd have admired the boy's creativity if he wasn't turning out to be such a troublesome little prick.

But the shadows were hers to werk just as much as Jonnen's, and death was running right on her heels. Mia curled her fingers into claws, tore the darkness away from her eyes just as the Revered Father and his silent companion vaulted the iron fence and dropped into the churchyard behind her.

Mia hauled herself to her feet, blinking hard as her sight returned. Her arms felt like putty. Her legs were shaking. Turning to face Solis and Hush, she was barely able to raise her stolen sword. Her shadow writhed around her long leather boots as the two killers fanned out to flank her.

"Call the guards!" Jonnen cried from the street beyond. *"Assassin!"*

The citizens turned to stare, wondering at the ruckus. A priest of Aa stepped out from the chapel doors, clad in his holy vestments. A cadre of Itreyan legionaries down the block turned their heads at the sound of the boy's cries. But Mia could pay heed to none of it.

Solis lunged at her throat, his blade a blur. Desperate, drawing on the dark new strength in her veins, she reached out, tangled up the Shahiid's feet in his own shadow before he could reach her. Solis snarled in frustration, his strike falling short. Hush hurled another knife and Mia cried out, smashing it from the air with her stolen sword in a hail of bright sparks. And then she charged the silent boy, desperate to even the scales before Solis could break loose of her shadow werking.

Hush drew a rapier from his belt, met her charge, steel on steel. Mia knew the boy from the brief comradeship they'd shared as acolytes in the halls of the Quiet Mountain. She knew where he'd come from, what he'd been before he joined the Church, why he never spoke. It wasn't because he lacked a tongue, no—it was because the owners of the pleasure house he'd been enslaved to as a child had knocked out all his teeth so he could better service their clientele.

Mia had been training in the art of the sword since she was ten years old. Hush had still been on his hands and knees on silken sheets. They'd both trained under Solis, true, and the boy had proved himself no novice with a blade. But in the last nine months, Mia had trained under the whip of Arkades, the Red Lion of Itreya—schooled in the arts of the gladiatii by one of the greatest swordsmen alive. And though she was exhausted, bleeding, bruised, her muscles were still hardened, her grip still callused, her form drilled into her hour upon hour beneath the burning sunslight.

"Guards!" came Jonnen's call. "She's *here*!"

Mia struck low, forcing Hush aside, her backswing whistling through the air. The boy stepped away like a dancer, blue eyes glittering. Mia raised her blade, telegraphing another strike. But with a deft flick of her boot, she scooped up a toeful of grit from the earth beneath them—an old gladiatii trick—and kicked it right at Hush's face.

The boy reeled back and Mia's blade sliced him across the chest, just a few inches short of splitting his ribs clean open. His doublet and the flesh beyond parted like water, but still the boy made no sound. He staggered back, one hand pressed to his wound as Mia raised her blade for the deathblow.

". . . MIA . . . !"

She turned with a gasp, barely deflecting the strike that would have split her head apart. Solis had hacked his boots away, left them wrapped in tendrils of his own shadow, and charged Mia barefoot. The big man collided with her, sent her flying, her backside and thighs shredded on the stone as she hit the ground. She tumbled back up onto her feet with a black curse, fending off the flurry of strikes Solis aimed at her head, neck, chest. She struck back, sweat-soaked and desperate, long black hair stuck to her skin, Mister Kindly and Eclipse working hard to eat her fear.

"Guards!"

This was no fresh Blade of the Church she faced now, no. This was the deadliest swordsman in the congregation. And no cheap tricks learned in the arena would avail Mia here. Only skill. And steel. And sheer, bloody will.

She struck back at Solis, their blades ringing bright beneath the burning suns. His white eyes were narrowed, fixed somewhere in the empty over her left shoulder. And yet the blind man moved as if he saw her every strike coming from a mile away. Forcing her back. Beating her down. Wearing her out.

The crowd in the street had gathered outside the chapel gates now, drawn like flies to a corpse by Jonnen's cries. The boy stood in the middle of the thoroughfare, waving at the cadre of legionaries, who were even now *tromptromptromp*ing toward them. Mia was tired, weak, outnumbered—she had only moments before this situation dissolved into a puddle of shite.

"Where's Ashlinn and Mercurio?" she demanded.

Solis's blade streaked past her chin as he smiled. "If you've a wish to see your old master alive again, girl, you'd best drop your steel and come with me."

Mia's eyes narrowed as she struck at the big man's knees.

"You don't call me girl, bastard. Not as if the word were kin for 'shit.'"

Solis laughed and launched a riposte that almost took Mia's head off. She twisted aside, sweat-soaked fringe hanging in her eyes.

"Perhaps you only hear what you want to hear, girl."

"Aye, laugh now," she wheezed. "But what will you do without your beloved Scaeva? When your other patrons learn the savior of the fucking Republic died at the hands of one of your own Blades?"

Solis tilted his head and smiled wider, stilling the heart in Mia's chest.

"Did he?"

"Halt! In the name of the Light!"

The legionaries burst through the chapel gates, all glittering armor and blood-red plumes on their helms. Hush was on his knees, the Rictus from Mia's stolen blade rendering him numb and lethargic. Mia and Solis hung still, swords poised as the legionaries spread out into the courtyard. The centurion leading them was burly as a pile of bricks, heavy brows and a thick beard bristling beneath his glittering helm.

"Put down your weapons, citizens!" he barked.

Mia glanced at the centurion, the troops around them, the crossbows aimed square at her heaving chest. Jonnen forced his way through the soldiers, pointing right at her and shouting at the top of his lungs.

"That's her! Kill her now!"

"Get back, boy!" the captain snapped.

Jonnen scowled at the man, drew himself up to his full height.*

"I am Lucius Atticus Scaeva," he spat. "Firstborn son of Consul Julius Maximillianus Scaeva. This *slave* murdered my father, and I *order* you to kill her!"

Solis tilted his head slightly, as if taking note of the lad for the first time. The centurion raised an eyebrow, looking the little lordling up and down. Despite his disheveled appearance, the grime on his face and sopping robes, it could hardly be missed that he was clad in brilliant purple—the color of Itreyan nobility. Nor that he wore the triple-sun crest of the Luminatii legion upon his chest.

"Kill her!" the boy roared, stamping his foot.

The crossbowmen tightened their fingers on their triggers. The centurion looked at Mia, drew breath to shout.

---

* Four foot, three inches.

"Lo—"

A chill stole over the scene—the legionaries, the assassins, the crowd gathered in the street beyond. Despite the blazing heat, goosebumps shivered on Mia's bare skin. A familiar shape rose up behind the soldiers, hooded and cloaked, twin gravebone swords clutched in its ink-black hands. Mia recognized it immediately—the same figure that had saved her life in the Galante necropolis. The same one who'd given her that cryptic message.

"Seek the Crown of the Moon."

Its face was hidden in the depths of its cloak. Mia's breath hung in white clouds before her lips, and despite the heat, she found herself shivering in its chill.

Without a word, the figure struck the closest soldier, its gravebone blade splitting his breastplate asunder. The other legionaries cried out in alarm, turning their crossbows upon their assailant. As the figure wove among them, blades flashing, they fired. The crossbow bolts struck home, thudding into the figure's chest and belly. But it seemed not to slow at all. The crowd in the street beyond fell to panicking as the figure wheeled and spun among the soldiers, cutting them to bloody chunks, raining red.

Mia moved swift despite her fatigue, grabbing her wriggling brother by the scruff of his neck. Solis charged across the broken flagstones toward her, and Mia brought up her blade to block his onslaught. The Shahiid's strikes were deathly quick, sheer perfection. And hard as she tried, swift as she was, she felt a blow sail past her guard and slice into her shoulder.

Mia spun aside, dropping her stolen blade as she cried out. Within seconds she could feel the Rictus in her veins, a numbing chill spreading out from the wound, flowing down her arm. With a grunt of effort, she threw up her hand, wrapped up Solis's feet in his shadow again as she tumbled onto her backside, her brother clutched tight to her chest. The Shahiid stumbled, cursed, trying to rip his bare feet free from her grip. Mister Kindly and Eclipse coalesced on the stone between them, the shadowcat hissing and puffing up, the shadowwolf's growl coming from beneath the earth.

"*. . . back, bastard . . .*"

"*. . . you will* not *touch her . . .*"

Behind Mia, the strange figure finished its grim work. The churchyard looked like the floor of an abattoir, pieces of legionaries scattered all across it, the bystanders fleeing in panic. The figure's gravebone blades dripped with gore as it stepped across the flagstones, stood above the fallen girl, leveling a sword at Solis's throat. The Revered Father of the Red Church seemed unperturbed despite the trio of shadowthings arrayed against him, lips pulled back over his teeth, white breath hanging in the air between them.

The figure spoke, its voice tinged with a strange reverberation.

"The Mother is disappointed in you, Solis."

"Who are you, daemon?" he demanded.

"You truly *are* blind," it replied. "But when dark dawns, you will see."

The figure knelt beside Mia. Her right arm was numb, she was barely able to keep her head up. But she still clung to her brother like grim death—after all the blood and miles and years, she'd be damned to come all this way and discover he lived, only to lose him again. For his part, between the presence of this strange wraith and the bloody murder it had just unleashed, Jonnen seemed frozen with fear.

The figure reached out one hand. It was black and gleaming, as if dipped in fresh paint. As it touched her wounded shoulder, Mia felt a stab of pain, ice-cold and black, all the way to her heart. She hissed as the earth surged beneath her, a frozen vertigo setting all the world awhirl.

She felt sorrow. Pain. An endless, lonely chill.

She felt she was falling.

And then she felt nothing at all.

Chapter 3

Ember

Mercurio awoke in darkness.

The pain in his head felt like the kind earned after a three-turn bender, and yet he could recall no recent debauchery. His jaw ached, and he could taste blood on his tongue. Groaning, he slowly sat upright in a bed lined with soft gray fur, hand to his brow. He had no idea where he might be, but something . . . the scent in the air perhaps, dragged him back to younger years.

"Hello, Mercurio."

He turned to his left, saw an old woman seated beside his bed. She looked to be around his age, her long gray hair bound in neat braids. She was dressed in dark gray robes, cool blue eyes pouched in deep wrinkles. At first glance, a bystander might've expected to find her in a rocking chair beside a merry hearth, a handful of grandsprogs around her, an old moggy on her knee. But Mercurio knew better.

"Hello, you murderous old cunt," he replied.

Drusilla, Lady of Blades, smiled in reply.

"You always did have a silver tongue, my dear."

The old woman lifted a cup of steaming tea from the saucer in her lap, sipped slowly. Her eyes were fixed on Mercurio as he peered around the bedchamber, breathed deep, finally understanding where he was. The song of a choir hung in the cool, dark air. He smelled candles and incense, steel and smoke. He remembered the Ministry accosting him in the Godsgrave chapel. The scratch from the poisoned blade in Spiderkiller's hand. The old man realized the blood he could taste belonged to pigs.

They've brought me back to the Mountain.

"You haven't changed your decor much," he sighed.

"You know me, love. I was never one for extravagance."

"The last time I was in this bed, I told you it really *was* the last time," Mercurio said. "But if I knew you were this hungry for a return performance . . ."

"O, please," the old woman sighed. "You'd need a block and tackle to get it up at your age. And your heart could barely stand it when we were twenty."

Mercurio smiled despite himself.

"It's good to see you, 'Silla."

"Would that I could say the same." The Lady of Blades shook her head and sighed. "You addle-minded old fool."

"Did you really drag me all the way to the Quiet Mountain for a rebuke?" Mercurio reached to his coat for his smokes and found both smokes and coat missing. "You could've just chewed my cods off back in the 'Grave."

"What were you thinking?" Drusilla demanded, setting aside her tea. "Helping that idiot girl in her idiot schemes? Do you realize what you've done?"

"I'm not fresh fallen from the last rains, 'Silla."

"No, you're the bishop of Godsgrave!" Drusilla stood, prowling around the bed, eyes flashing. "Years of faithful service. Sworn to the Dark Mother. And yet you helped a Blade of the Church break the Red Promise and murder one of our own patrons!"*

"O, Goddess, don't play the wounded devotee with me," Mercurio growled.

---

*As you might recall, gentlefriends, even the murderous bastards of the Red Church operate under a code of sorts, known as the Red Promise. Its five tenets are thus:

"It's as obvious as a beagle's bollocks that you and your nest of snakes wanted Cardinal Duomo dead. You've all been in bed with Scaeva for years. Did Lord Cassius know? Or was this something you and the others conspired to behind his back?"

"You're a fine one to speak of conspiracies, love."

"How do you think the rest of the congregation would react if they knew, 'Silla? That the Ministry was content to bend over and spread cheek for our beloved People's Senator? The hands of Niah upon this earth, become lapdogs of a fucking tyrant?"

"I should have you *killed* for your betrayal," Drusilla snarled.

- Inevitability—no offering undertaken in the history of the Church has ever gone unfulfilled.
- Sanctity—a current employer of the Church may not be chosen as a target of the Church.
- Secrecy—the Church does not discuss the identity of its employers.
- Fidelity—a Blade will only serve one employer at a time.
- Hierarchy—all offerings must be approved by the Lord/Lady of Blades or Revered Father/Mother.

It should be noted that, since its inception, the Red Promise has never been broken by a Church Blade. The cultists of Our Lady of Blessed Murder consider it Very Serious Business, and will go to extraordinary lengths to see it remain inviolate. One famous tale of dedication speaks of a Blade known only as Forde, employed to murder Agvald III, king of Vaan.

Agvald was far fonder of excess than running his kingdom, and after a lengthy session of passing the hat, his nobles managed to scrape together the coin necessary to have him professionally done in. And so, on the nevernight of the king's thirtieth birthturn, Forde infiltrated the king's bedchambers and waited there in the dark for her quarry.

Agvald had decided to celebrate his thirtieth year in style. After an extended session of drinking with his court, the king retired to his boudoir with six concubines and an entire suckling pig. During the debauchery that followed, Agvald attempted to eat a rack of ribs whilst being serviced by three of his favorites simultaneously. Sadly, the feat required rather more coordination than anticipated, and unlike his concubines, the good king inhaled when he should have swallowed.

Agvald toppled to the floor, clutching his throat and slowly turning blue. But as the royal concubines watched in amazement, Forde appeared from the shadows and proceeded to pound upon the king's back until the offending rib bone was coughed clean across the bedchamber. Forde offered the grateful king a cup of water, soothed his ruffled nerves. And once the sovereign was adequately calmed, the Blade proceeded to stab Agvald six times in the heart and cut his throat from ear to ear.

"Why?" cried one of the horrified concubines. "Why save his life only to kill him?"

The Blade glanced to the pig's rib and shrugged.

"The promise was mine."

"And yet I can't help notice I'm not dead." The old man peered under the sheets. "Or that I'm sans trousers. You certain I'm not here for an encore? I've learned a few tricks since—"

Drusilla hurled a gray robe at the old man's head.

"You are here to serve as the worm you are."

". . . As bait?" Mercurio shook his head. "You really think she's stupid enough to come after me? After all she's been through, after all she's—"

"I know who Mia Corvere is," Drusilla snapped. "This is a girl who gave up any chance at a normal life or happiness to see her parents avenged. She sold herself into slavery on a gambit that even a lunatic would consider insanity, for a single chance to strike down the men who destroyed her house. She is fearless. Reckless beyond reckoning. So if there is one thing I've learned about your little Crow, it is this: there is nothing that girl will not do for her familia. *Nothing.*"

The old woman leaned over the bed, stared into the old man's eyes.

"And you, dear Mercurio, are more a father to her than her father *ever* was."

The old man stared back, saying nothing. Swallowing the bile flooding his mouth. The Lady of Blades only smiled, leaning a little closer. He could still see her beauty beneath the scars of time. Remember the last nevernight they'd been in this bedchamber together, all those years ago. Sweat and blood and sweet, sweet poison.

"You may wander in the Mountain if you wish," Drusilla said. "I'm certain you remember where everything is. The congregation has been informed of your betrayal, but you are not to be touched. We need you breathing for now. But please, don't push the friendship by being more the fool than you've already been."

Drusilla reached under the sheet between his legs, squeezed tight as he gasped.

"A man can still breathe without these, after all."

The old woman held on a moment longer, then released her icy grip. Lips still curled in her matronly smile, the Lady of Blades took her saucer and cup back up, turned, and stalked toward the bedchamber door.

"Drusilla."

The Lady of Blades glanced over her shoulder. "Aye?"

"You really are a cunt, you know that?"

"Ever the flatterer." The old woman turned back to him, her smile vanished. "But a man like you should know exactly where flattery gets you with a woman like me."

Mercurio sat in the gloom after she left, wrinkled brow creased with worry.

"Aye," he muttered. "In deep shit."

He'd lurked in the bedchamber a few hours more, nursing his aching head and wounded ego. But boredom eventually bid him pull on the gray robe Drusilla had given him, tie the thin strip of leather about his waist. He didn't bother trying to arm himself—Mercurio knew the only ways out of the Quiet Mountain were a two-week trek across the Ashkahi Whisperwastes, out through Speaker Adonai's blood pool, or by leaping off the railings of the Sky Altar and into the shapeless night beyond.

Escape from here without help or wings was all but impossible.

He stepped from the bedchamber, leaning on the cane they'd (rather thoughtfully) left him, out into the gloom of the Quiet Mountain. Ice-blue eyes that seemed born to scowl surveyed the dark around him. The disembodied choir sung faintly, nowhere and everywhere at once. The halls were black stone, lit by windows of stained glass and false sunslight, decorated with grotesque statuary of bone and skin. Spiral patterns covered every inch of wall, intricate and maddening.

As soon as Mercurio's feet touched the flagstones outside Drusilla's room, he felt the presence of a robed figure, watching from the gloom. One of Drusilla's Hands, no doubt, tasked to be his shadow for the duration of his stay.* He ignored the figure, wandered about his way, listening to it following behind. His old knees creaked as he descended the stairs, down the wending paths and through the labyrinthine dark, until he finally stepped into the Hall of Eulogies.

He looked around the vast space, forced to admire the grandeur even after all these years. Enormous stone pillars were arranged in a circle, stone gables carved from the Mountain itself soaring above. The names of the Church's countless victims were scribed on the granite at his feet. Unmarked tombs of the faithful lined the walls.

The space was dominated by a colossal statue of Niah herself. Her black eyes seemed to follow Mercurio as he stepped closer, squinting in the false light. She held a scale and a wicked sword in her hands, her face beautiful and serene and cold. Jewels glittered on her ebony robe like stars in the truedark sky.

She who is All and Nothing.

Mother, Maid, and Matriarch.

---

*You will recall that the servants of Our Lady of Blessed Murder are divided into two main categories—Blades, who serve as her assassins in the Republic, and Hands,

Mercurio touched his eyes, his lips, his heart, looking up at his Goddess with clouded eyes. As he stood there in the hall, a knot of young folk entered from the steps below. They regarded the old bishop with wary stares as they passed, meeting his gaze only briefly. Smooth skin and bright eyes and clean hands, teenagers all. New acolytes by the look, just beginning their training.

He stared after them wistfully as they left. Remembering his own tutelage within these walls, his devotion to the Mother of Night. How long ago it all seemed now, how cold he'd grown inside. Once he'd been fire. Breathed it. Bled it. Spat it. But now, the only ember that remained was the one he kept burning for her—that snot-nosed, stuck-up little lordling's bitch who'd wandered into his shop all those years ago, a silver brooch shaped like a crow in her hand.

He'd never made time for familia. To live as a Blade of the Mother was to live with death—with the knowledge that every turn could be your last. It hadn't seemed fair to take a wife when she'd likely end a widow, nor make a child who'd probably be raised an orphan. Mercurio never thought he'd a need for children. If you'd asked him why he'd taken that raven-haired waif in all those years ago, he'd have muttered something about her gift, her grit, her guile. He'd have laughed if you'd told him he needed her as much as she needed him. He'd have cut your throat and buried you deep if you'd told him that one turn, he'd love her like the daughter he'd never had.

But in his bones, even as he ended you, he'd have known it true.

And now, here he was. A worm on Drusilla's hook. For all his bluff, he knew the Lady of Blades spoke truth—Mia loved him like blood. She'd never let him die in here, not if she thought she had a chance to save him. And with those wretched daemons riding her shadow and eating her fear, in Mia's head there was *always* a chance.

The old man peered at the granite colossus above him. The sword and scales in her hands. Those pitiless black eyes, boring into his own.

"Where the fuck are you?" he whispered.

---

who do almost everything else. Though many join the order of the Dark Mother with aspirations to do bloody murder in her name, very few have the unique blend of skill, callousness, and lunacy necessary to become professional killers.

Most folk who join the Church actually end up assisting in logistics and administration, which isn't very romantic, and hardly the stuff of sweeping epics of high fantasy. But the average life expectancy of a Blade is around twenty-five years, where most Hands live until well past retirement.

Would you rather have books written about you, or live long enough to read books about others, gentlefriends?

We seldom get to do both.

He left the hall, Drusilla's Hand lurking at a respectful distance behind as the old bishop shuffled on his way through the Mountain's maze, his cane beating crisp on the black stone. His knees were aching by the time he reached his destination—he didn't remember there being quite so many stairs in this place. Two dark wooden doors loomed before him, carved with the same spiral motif as decorated the walls. Each must have weighed a ton, but the old man reached out with one gnarled hand and pushed them open with ease.

Mercurio found himself on a mezzanine overlooking a forest of ornate shelves, laid out like a garden maze. They stretched off into a space too dark and vast to see the edges. On each shelf were piled books of every shape and size and description. Dusty tomes and vellum scrolls and famished notebooks and everything in between. The grand Athenaeum of the Goddess of Death, peopled with the memoirs of kings and conquerors, theorems of heretics, masterpieces of madmen. Dead books and lost books and books that never were—some burned on the pyres of the faithful, some simply swallowed by time, and others simply too dangerous to write at all.

An endless heaven for any reader, and a living hell for any librarian.

"Well, well," said a croaking, hollow voice. "Look what the scabdogs dragged in."

Mercurio turned to see an old Liisian man in a scruffy waistcoat, leaning on a trolley piled with books. Two shocks of white hair sprung from either side of his scalp, and a pair of finger-thick spectacles adorned his hooked nose. His back was so bent, he looked like a walking question mark. A fine cigarillo smoldered on his bloodless lips.

"Hello, Chronicler," Mercurio said.

"You're a long way from Godsgrave, Bishop," Aelius growled.

The chronicler stepped closer, squared up against Mercurio, and glowered. As they stood there, face-to-face, Aelius seemed to stand taller, his shadow growing longer. The air rippled with some dark current, and Mercurio heard the shapes of colossi moving out between the shelves. Coming closer.

Aelius's dark eyes burned as he considered Mercurio's, his voice growing harder and colder with every word.

"If I can still call you 'Bishop' at all, that is," he spat. "I thought you'd be ashamed to show your face outside your bedchamber after what you pulled. Let alone drag yourself down here. What brings your traitorous hide to the Black Mother's library?"

Mercurio pointed to the ever-present spare behind the chronicler's ear.

"Smoke?"

Chronicler Aelius hung still for a moment, eyes burning with dark flame.

Then, with a small chuckle, he unfolded his arms, clapped Mercurio on his thin shoulder. Lighting the cigarillo on his own, he handed it over.

"All right, whippersnapper?"

"Do I look all right, old man?" Mercurio asked.

"You look like shite. But it's always polite to ask."

Mercurio leaned against the wall and gazed out over the library, dragging a sweet gray draft into his lungs. The smoke tasted of strawberries, the sugared paper setting his tongue dancing.

"They don't make them like this anymore," Mercurio sighed.

"Same might be said of everything in this room," Aelius replied.

"How've you been, you old bastard?"

"Dead."*

The chronicler settled in beside him.

"You?"

"Much the same."

Aelius scoffed, breathed a plume of gray. "Still got a pulse in you from what I can see. What the 'byss you sulking about down here for, lad?"

Mercurio drew on his cigarillo. "It's a long story, old man."

"A story about your Mia, I take it?"

". . . How'd you guess?"

Aelius shrugged his bone-thin shoulders, his eyes twinkling behind his improbable spectacles. "She always struck me as a girl with one to tell."

"We might be nearing the final page, I fear."

"You're too young to be such a pessimist."

"I'm sixty-fucking-two," Mercurio growled.

"As I say, far too young."

---

*In Itreyan folklore, the dead were once sent to the keeping of Niah and held forever in her loving embrace. But after the Mother's fall from grace, it was deemed that Niah's daughter Keph would take care of the righteous dead instead. Tsana, Goddess of Fire, created a mighty hearth in Keph's domain to keep the dead warm. And there they dwell in light and happiness, until the ending to the world.

Wicked souls, however, are said to be denied a place by the fire. Known as the Hearthless, they are common figures in Itreyan folklore, blamed for almost everything that goes wrong in ordinary life. Sheep goes missing? Must've been the Hearthless. Can't find your keys? Bloody Hearthless. Last sugarcake got eaten? It wasn't me, love, it was the *Hearthless*!

Why people insist on blaming the supernatural instead of owning up to their own bullshit is one of life's great mysteries.

Still, they make for good spook stories.

Mercurio found himself chuckling, warm gray spilling from his lips. He leaned back against the wall, feeling the smoke buzz in his blood.

"How long *have* you been down here, Aelius?"

"O, a while," the chronicler sighed. "Never saw much sense in counting the years, though. It's not as though I really have a choice about when I leave."

"The Mother keeps only what she needs," Mercurio murmured.

"Aye." Aelius nodded. "She does at that."

Mercurio tilted his head back, looked out on all those dead books with heavy-lidded eyes. "Do you hate her for it?"

"Blasphemy," the old ghost scolded.

"Is it?" Mercurio asked. "If she doesn't care what we say or do?"

"And what makes you say that?"

"Well, look at what this place has become," Mercurio growled, waving his cane at the dark. "Once, it was a house of wolves. Each murder, an offering to Our Lady of Blessed Murder. Feeding her hunger. Making her stronger. Hastening her return. And now?" He spat on the flagstones. "It's a whorehouse. The Ministry feed their own coffers, not the Maw. Their hands drip with gold, not red."

Mercurio shook his head, breathing smoke as he continued.

"O, we say all the words, make all the gestures, aye. '*This flesh your feast, this blood your wine.*' But still, when all the praying is done, we drop to our knees for the likes of Julius fucking Scaeva. How can you say Niah cares, if she allows this poison to fester in her own halls?"

"Maw's teeth." Aelius raised one snow-white brow. "*Someone* woke up on the wrong side of bed this morn."

"Fuck off," the old man spat.

"What do you want her to do?" the chronicler demanded. "She's been banished from the sky for millennia, boy. Allowed to rule for a handful of turns every two and a half years. How much say over all this do you think she has? How much influence do you think she can exert in the prison her husband made for her?"

"If she's so powerless, why call her a goddess at all?"

Aelius's frown deepened into a scowl. "I never said she was powerless."

"Because you were never one to state the fucking obvious."

The chronicler looked at Mercurio hard. "I remember when you first arrived here, boy. Green as grass, you were. Soft as baby shite. But you *believed*. In her. In this. The brighter the light, the deeper the shadow."

Mercurio scowled. "I've as much need for old Ashkahi proverbs as I have for a second ballsack, old man."

"You might have more need than you know, with young Drusilla on the prowl," Aelius smirked. "Point is, you had faith, boy. Where'd it go?"

Mercurio pressed the cigarillo to his lips, thinking long and hard.

"I still believe," he replied. "The God of Light and Goddess of Night and their Four fucking Daughters. I mean, this place exists. *You* exist. The Dark Mother obviously still has some small sway." Mercurio shrugged. "But this is a world ruled by men, not divinities. And for all the blood, all the death, all the lives we've taken in her name, she's still so fucking far away."

"She's closer than you think," Aelius said.

"I swear by all that's holy, if you tell me she dwells in the temple of my heart, we're going to find out if folk can return from the dead twice."

"They can't, actually," the chronicler shrugged. "Not even the Mother has that power. You die once, you might make it back with her blessing. But cross back over to the Abyss once more? You're gone forever."

"That threat was supposed to be rhetorical, old man."

Aelius grinned, smudged his cigarillo out against the wall, and dropped the butt into the pocket of his waistcoat. "Come with me."

The chronicler leaned on his RETURNS trolley, began wheeling it down the long ramp from the mezzanine to the Athenaeum floor below. Mercurio watched the old man shuffling away, dragging on his own smoke.

"Come on, whippersnapper!" Aelius barked.

The bishop of Godsgrave sighed and, pushing himself off the wall, followed the chronicler down the ramp into the library proper. Side by side, the pair wandered through the maze of shelves, mahogany and parchment and vellum all around. Every now and then, Aelius would stop and place one of his returned tomes back into its allotted place, almost reverently. The shelves were too tall to see over, and each aisle looked much the same. Mercurio was soon hopelessly lost, and a part of him wondered how in the Mother's name Aelius made sense of this place.

"Where the 'byss are we going?" he grumbled, rubbing his aching knees.

"New section," Aelius replied. "They pop up all the time in this place. When they want to be found, that is. I stumbled onto this one almost two years ago. Right before your girl arrived here for the first time."

Out in the dark, Mercurio could hear bookworms shifting their massive bulks among the shelves. Leathery hides scraping along the stone, deep, rumbling growls reverberating through the floor. The air was dry and cool, echoing with the faint song of that beautiful choir. There was a peace to this place, no doubt. But Mercurio wondered if he'd manage an eternity in it with quite as much calm as Aelius.

They turned down a long shelf, twisting off in a gentle curve. As they walked the rows of dusty tomes wrapped in old skins and polished wood, Mercurio realized the curve was slowly tightening—that the shelf was turning in an ever-smaller spiral. And somewhere near the heart of it, out in all that dark, Aelius came to a stop.

The chronicler reached up to the top shelf, pulled down a thick book, and placed it in Mercurio's hands.

"The Mother keeps only what she needs," he said. "And she does what she can. In the small ways that she can."

Mercurio raised an eyebrow, cigarillo still smoldering at his lips as he examined the tome. It was bound in leather, black as a truedark sky. The edges of the pages were stained blood-red, and a crow in flight was embossed in glossy black on the cover.

He opened the book, looked down to the first page.

"*Nevernight,*" he muttered. "Stupid name for a book."

"Makes for interesting reading," Aelius said.

Mercurio opened the book to the prologue, rheumy eyes scanning the text.

CAVEAT EMPTOR

People often shit themselves when they die.

Their muscles slack and their souls flutter free and everything else just . . . slips out. For all their audience's love of death, the playwrights seldom—

Mercurio flipped through a few more pages, softly scoffing.

"It has footnotes? What kind of wanker writes a novel with footnotes?"

"It's not a novel," Aelius replied, sounding wounded. "It's a biography."

"About who?"

The chronicler simply nodded back to the book. Mercurio flicked through a few pages more, scanning the beginning of chapter three.

. . . dropped him into the path of an oncoming maidservant, who fell with a shriek. Dona Corvere turned on her daughter, regal and furious.

"Mia Corvere, keep that wretched animal out from underfoot or we'll leave it behind!"

And as simple as that, we have her name.

Mia.

Mercurio faltered. Cigarillo hanging from suddenly bone-dry lips. His blood ran cold as he finally understood what he held in his hands. Glancing up at the shelves around him. The dead books and lost books and books that never were—some burned on the pyres of the faithful, some swallowed by time, and others . . .

Simply too dangerous to write at all.

Aelius had wandered off down the twisted row, hands in his pockets and muttering to himself, a trail of thin gray smoke left behind him. But Mercurio was rooted to the spot. Utterly mesmerized. He began flipping faster through the pages, eyes scanning the flowing script, snatching only fragments in his haste.

"The books we love, they love us back."

"I will give your brother your regards."

"Who or what is the Moon?" she asked.

Mercurio reached the end, turning the book over and over in his hands. Wondering why there were no more pages and looking around the library of the dead in mute wonder and fear.

"I found another one, too," Aelius said, returning from farther down the row. "About three months back. Wasn't there one turn, next turn, there it was."

The chronicler handed Mercurio another heavy tome. It was similar to the one he already held, but the pages were edged in sky blue rather than blood-red. A wolf was embossed on the black cover instead of a crow. Juggling the first book into the crook of his elbow, he opened the second's cover and peered at the title.

"Godsgrave," he muttered.

"Follows on from the first," Aelius nodded. "I think I liked this one better, actually. Less fucking about at the start."

The choir sang in the ghostly dark around them, echoing through the great Athenaeum. Mercurio's hands were shaking, cigarillo falling from his mouth as he fumbled with the first tome, opening it finally to the title page.

And there it was.

NEVERNIGHT
BOOK I OF THE NEVERNIGHT CHRONICLE
by Mercurio of Liis

The old man closed the book, looked at Niah's chronicler with wondering eyes.

"Holy shit," he breathed.

Chapter 4

Gift

Arkemical globes twinkled in the arched ceilings and the music swelled in Mia's chest and all around her was pale bone and glittering gold. She stood between her father and mother, little hands clutching theirs, staring down at the dance floor in wide-eyed wonder. Elegant donas in dazzling gowns of red and pearl and black, swaying and twirling in the arms of smooth dons in long frock coats. Delicious food arrayed on silver trays and singing crystal glasses filled with sparkling liqueurs.

"Well, my dove?" her father asked. "What do you think?"

"It's so beautiful." Mia sighed.

The little girl could sense people's eyes on them as they stood there at the top of the winding stairs. The doorman had announced their arrival at the grand palazzo, and all had turned to stare. The dashing justicus of the Luminatii Legion, Darius Corvere. His lovely and formidable wife, Alinne. Her parents made their way through the marrowborn crowd, the pretty smiles, the polite nods, the faces hidden by exquisite Carnivalé masks. The palazzo's ballroom was filled to bursting, and all of Godsgrave's finest had been invited to the affair—the election of a new consul always brought out the most beautiful of people.

"Will you dance, my dear?" her father asked.

Alinne Corvere softly scoffed, one hand pressed to her swollen belly. Mia knew the baby would come soon. She hoped it would be a boy.

"Not unless you've a barrow stowed under that doublet, husband," she replied.

"Alas," Darius replied, reaching beneath the folds of his costume. "I've only this."

Mia's father presented her mother a blood-red rose, bowing low for the benefit of the onlookers around them. Alinne smiled and took the bloom, inhaling deeply as she regarded her husband. But again, she ran a hand over her belly, demurring with a glance from those dark, knowing eyes.

Mia's father turned and knelt before her.

"What about you, my dove? Will you dance?"

Mia had been feeling strange all week, truth told. Since truedark had fallen, her belly had been all aflutter, and nothing quite felt the way it should. But still, as her father offered his hand, she couldn't help but smile, caught up in the warmth of his eyes.

"Yes, Father," she lisped.

"We should give our congratulations to our new consul," her mother warned.

"Soon enough," her father nodded, offering his arm to Mia. "Mi Dona?"

The pair of them swept out onto the dance floor, the other marrowborn revelers parting to let them through. Mia was only nine years old, not yet tall or old enough to dance properly. But Darius Corvere propped her little feet upon his and led her gently to the rush and pull of the music. Mia saw the couples around them smiling, charmed as ever by the handsome justicus and his precocious daughter. She looked about her in wonder, caught up in the song and the dresses and the glittering lights above.

The three suns had sunk below the horizon over a week ago, and the Mother of Night was nearing the end of another brief reign of the sky. Mia could hear the popopopopop *of the fireworks in the city beyond, meant to frighten the Night back to the Abyss. All over Godsgrave, folk were huddled about their hearths, waiting for Aa to open his eyes again. But here, in her father's arms, Mia found she wasn't afraid at all. Instead of being frightened, she felt safe.*

Strong.

Loved.

She knew her father was a handsome man, and she was old enough to note the longing stares of the marrowborn ladies as they watched him sweep past across the ballroom floor. But despite the finest of Godsgrave's donas (and no few dons) staring after him wistfully, Mia's father had eyes only for her.

"I love you, Mia."

"I love you, too."

"Promise you'll remember. No matter what comes."

She gave him a puzzled smile. "I promise, Father."

They danced on, twirling across the polished boards to the magikal song. Mia looked to the ceilings high above her, pale and gleaming. The consul's extravagant palazzo sat at the base of the first Rib, right near the Senate House and Godsgrave's Spine. The dance floor was a revolving mosaic of the three suns, circling each other just as the dancers did. The building was carved from the gravebone of the Rib itself, same as the longsword at her father's waist, the armor he wore when he rode to war. The heart of the Itreyan Republic, chiseled from the bones of some long-fallen titan.

Mia peered through the crowd and saw her mother, speaking with a man upon a dais at the end of the room. He was resplendent in robes of brilliant purple, a golden laurel around his brow and golden rings upon his fingers. His hair was thick and dark, his eyes were darker still, and he was—though Mia would never have admitted it—perhaps a little more handsome than her father.

Mia saw her mother bow to the handsome man. An elegant woman seated on the dais looked displeased as the man kissed Alinne Corvere's hand in turn.

"Who is that, Father?" Mia asked.

"Our new consul," he replied, his eyeline following hers. "Julius Scaeva."

"Is he a friend of Mother's?"

"Of a sort."

Mia watched as the handsome man placed one hand on Alinne Corvere's swollen belly. A brief touch, light as feathers. A glance between them, quick as silver.

"I do not like him," the girl declared.

"No fear, my dove," the justicus replied. "Your mother likes him well enough for both of you. She always has."

Mia blinked, looking up at her father with black, narrowed eyes. There was a length of rope about his neck in place of his cravat now, tied in a perfect noose.

"What do you mean?" she asked.

"O, wake up, Mia," he sighed.

"Father, I—"

"Wake up."

"Wake up."

Mia felt a hard kick in her belly. A child's voice, somewhere distant.

"Wake up, curse you!"

Another kick, this time into the fresh wound at her shoulder. Mia gasped with pain and opened her eyes, seeing a silhouette leaning over her in the gloom. Without thinking, she lashed out with her good hand, seizing the figure's throat. It squeaked and thrashed, little fingers digging into her forearm. Only then, through the pain and retreating toxic haze did she recognize . . .

". . . Jonnen?"

She released the boy's neck as if his skin were scalding metal. Utterly aghast, she reached out to smooth his filthy purple toga.

"O, Jonnen, I'm sor—"

"My name is Lucius!" the boy spat, slapping her hands away.

Mia caught her breath, tried to still her thundering heart. She was horrified at herself—she'd almost hurt him without thinking. Her mind was swimming with pictures of a glittering ballroom and a truedark sky and Scaeva's hand on her mother's belly. Of an arena full of people, screaming as she buried her gravebone dagger in Scaeva's chest. Of Jonnen's face, pale and horrified as she laid his father low before him.

"I'm sorry," she repeated. "I didn't hurt you, did I?"

The boy simply scowled, his eyes as dark and bottomless as Mia's. She glanced around them, wondering where they might be. A vast black space surrounded them, lit by the glow of a single lantern on the ground beside her. The ghostly light extended only a handful of feet, and beyond that lay a darkness too deep to fathom.

The floor was uneven beneath her, and Mia realized it was made entirely of human faces and hands—stone reliefs, carved from the snow-pale bedrock itself. The faces were all female—all the same woman, in fact—her features beautiful, her tresses long and gently curled. But her expressions were all of anguish, of terror, her stone mouths open wide and silently screaming. The multitude of hands were upturned to the hidden ceiling, as if it were about to collapse.

Mia blinked hard, trying to remember how she got here. She recalled her confrontation with Solis and Hush. That spectral figure who'd rescued her in the Galante necropolis, once more saving her skin among the houses of Godsgrave's dead. She could still feel Solis's poison in her veins, though she noted the wound at her shoulder had been bound with a scrap of dark cloth. She still felt sluggish from the toxin, cold from the brittle chill around her. She felt the ache of her wounds and the tug of dried blood crusting on her skin, and somewhere distant, a nameless, shapeless anger. And looking around at that sea of frozen, terrified faces, like the sensation of sound for a man long since deafened, Mia suddenly realized she felt . . .

Afraid.

She searched the dark about her. Seeking her passengers among those stone hands and open mouths and realizing she couldn't feel them anywhere. Her skin prickled, her belly rolled, and with a hiss of pain, she forced herself to her feet.

"Mister Kindly?" she called. "Eclipse?"

No answer. Nothing but the thud of her pulse in her veins, the dreadful empty of their absence. Eclipse had walked beside her since Lord Cassius had died, Mister Kindly since her father had been hanged. She'd not been without them save by request for an age. But now, to find herself alone . . .

"Where are we?" she whispered, studying the sea of faces and hands.

"I do not know," Jonnen said, a small tremble in his voice.

Her heart softened, and she reached out to him in the dark. "It's all right, Jonnen, I'm here with—"

"My name is Lucius!" he shouted, stamping his little foot. "Lucius Atticus Scaeva! I am firstborn son of Consul Julius Maximillianus Scaeva, and I am honorbound to kill you!" He pointed an accusing finger, cheeks pink with fury. *"You murdered my father!"*

Mia withdrew her hand, studying the boy's face. The bared teeth and quivering lip. Those dark, brooding eyes, so like her own. So like *his*.

"I used to sing to you," she said. "When you were little and it stormed. You hated the thunder." She found herself smiling at the memory. "A squalling, pink-faced screamer with a pair of lungs on him that might wake the dead, you were. The nursemaids couldn't do anything to still you. I was the only one who could give you calm. Do you remember?"

She cleared her throat, croaking a rusty tune.

"In bleakest times, in darkest climes,
When wind blows cold—"

"You sound like a harpy shrieking for supper," the boy snarled.

Mia bit her lip, struggling to keep her infamous temper in check. She'd spent almost eight years plotting the deaths of the men who'd killed her kin. Six years training under the most dangerous killers in the Republic, another year in service to the Red Church, almost another year fighting for her life on the sands of Itreya's arenas, up to her armpits in blood. Never once in all that time did she learn how to deal with a spoiled marrowborn brat grieving the loss of his bastard father. But still, she tried to imagine what the boy must think. How he must feel looking at the girl who'd murdered his da.

In truth, it wasn't that hard to see his side. She remembered her own version of this moment, years past. Watching the men who hanged her own da in the forum. Her vow of vengeance ringing in her head, the hatred like white-hot acid in her veins.

Did Jonnen now feel the same way about her?

Am I his Scaeva?

"Jonnen, I'm sorry," she said. "I know this is hard. I know you're frightened and angry, that there's things you—"

"Do not speak to me, slave," he growled.

Her hand went to the arkemical brand on her cheek. The twin circles that marked her as the property of the Remus Collegium. She could feel the scar on the other side of her face. The gash cutting down through her brow, curling in a cruel hook along her left cheek—a memento from her ordeals on the sands. She thought briefly of Sidonius. Bladesinger and the other Falcons. Wondering if they'd made it to safety.

"I am no slave," she said, iron creeping into her voice. "I'm your sister."

"I have no sister," Jonnen snarled.

"Half sister, then," Mia said. "We've the same mother."

"You're a liar!" he cried, stamping his feet again. *"Liar!"*

"I'm not lying," Mia insisted, pinching the bridge of her nose to stop the ache. "Jonnen, listen to me, please . . . you were too young to remember. But you were taken from our mother as a babe. Her name was Alinne. Alinne Corvere."

"Corvere?" he scoffed, his dark eyes narrowed. "The Kingmaker's wife?"

Mia blinked. ". . . You know of the rebellion?"

"I am no gutter urchin, slave," Jonnen said, straightening his filthy robes. "I've a memory sharp as swords, all my tutors swear it. I know of the Kingmaker. My father sent that traitor to the hangman, and his harlot to the Philosopher's Stone."

"Mind your tongue," Mia warned, her finger rising along with her temper. "That's your mother you're talking about."

"I am the son of a consul!" the boy stormed.

"Aye," Mia nodded. "But Liviana Scaeva is not your mother."

"You *dare*?" Jonnen pulled his little hands into fists. "You may be the daughter of some traitor's whore, but I am no bas—"

Her slap sent him stumbling, dropping onto his backside like a brick. Mia could feel rage in her veins, swelling and rolling, threatening to swallow her whole. Jonnen blinked up at her, wide eyes brimming with tears, one hand raised to his burning cheek. He was a marrowborn lordling, heir to a vast estate, child of a noble house. Mia imagined no one had ever laid hands on him before. Especially no one with a slave brand. But still . . .

"Brother or no," Mia warned, "you don't talk about her that way."

Beneath her anger, Mia was horrified at herself. Exhausted and frightened and aching all the way to her bones. She'd thought Jonnen dead all these years, else she'd never have left him in Scaeva's keeping. She should have been throwing her arms about him for joy, not knocking him onto his pompous little arse.

Especially not for telling the truth.

Mia had learned from Sidonius that her parents' marriage was one of expedience, not passion. Darius Corvere was in love with General Antonius, the man who'd sought to become king of Itreya. The Kingmaker's arrangement with his wife was a political alliance, not a grand love affair. And it was no strange thing—such was life in many marrowborn houses of the Republic.

But of all the men Alinne Corvere could have taken as a lover, borne a child to, of all the men in all the world, how could she have chosen *Julius fucking Scaeva*?

Jonnen pawed at his eyes, at the handprint Mia had etched on his cheek. She could see he wanted to cry. But he stomped the tears down instead, clenching his teeth and turning his hurt to hate.

Maw's teeth, he really is *my brother.*

"I'm sorry," Mia said, softening her voice. "These are sharp truths I'm speaking. But your father was an evil man, brother. A tyrant who wanted to carve himself a throne out of the Republic's bones."

"Like the Kingmaker did?" Jonnen spat.

Mia swallowed hard, feeling the boy's words like a punch to the stomach. Though she tried to keep a grip on it, she could feel herself growing angry again. As if Jonnen's rage were somehow stoking her own.

"You're just a boy. You're too young to understand."

"You're a liar!" The boy climbed to his feet, his temper and volume rising along with him. "My father beat yours, and you're just mad about it!"

"Of course I'm mad about it!"

"You tricked him!" the boy shouted. "On the victor's stage! You hid that knife in your armor and you never would have touched him otherwise!"

"I did what needed to be done," she snapped. "Julius Scaeva deserved to die!"

"You don't fight fair!"

"Fair?" she cried. "He killed our *mother*!"

"You have no honor, no . . ."

The boy's voice died, the twisted snarl on his face slackening into silent wonder. Mia followed his eyeline to the floor, that tableau of wailing faces and open hands, lit by the spectral glow of their single lantern. There, on the graven stone, she could see their shadows, dark and tenebrous in the ghostly light. And they were moving.

Jonnen's shadow was slithering back, like a viper coiling to strike. Her own shadow was reaching toward his, hair flowing as if in a gentle breeze. In a blinking, Jonnen's shade lashed out at hers, wrapping its hands around its opponent's throat. Mia's shadow surged and rippled as the smaller shadow slipped hands about its neck. The shades lashed and slashed at each other, sudden violence painted in rippling black, though Mia and Jonnen both stood still and unharmed.

Mia could see the perfect fury in her brother's eyes, reflecting the war in the dark between them. It seemed as if their shadows were playing out their innermost feelings: his hatred, her affection scorned. And she knew it then, sure as she knew her own name—this boy would kill her if he could. Cut her throat and leave her for the rats. She watched those ribbons of darkness, recalling that her shadow had reacted the same in Furian's presence. Looking at her brother, she felt the same sickness and longing she'd felt near other darkin. As if she'd fallen asleep with someone beside her and woken to find herself alone. The sense of something . . . missing.

She forced calm into her voice. Willed her shadow to still itself.

"I *am* your sister, Jonnen," she said. "We're the same, you and I."

The boy made no reply, hateful stare still fixed on her. But the enmity between their shadows slowly calmed, the shades returning to their normal shapes, only faint ripples to mark anything was odd about them at all. The darkness around them was deathly silent. The wide eyes of a thousand stone faces watching them.

"How long has it spoken to you?" Mia asked softly. "The dark?"

Jonnen remained silent. Little hands curled into little fists.

"I wasn't much older than you, the turn it first spoke to me." Mia sighed, tired in her soul. "The turn your father hanged mine, ordered me drowned, ripped you from our mother's arms. The turn he destroyed everything."

The boy looked at their shadows, his dark eyes clouded.

"Eight long years it took me," she continued. "All those miles and all that blood. But it's over now. For good or ill, Julius Scaeva is dead. And we're a familia again."

"Lost," he spat, "is what we are, Kingmaker."

Mia looked about them, peering into the blackness beyond the circle of their lantern's light. From the chill in the air, the silence engulfing them, she'd guess they were far underground. In some hidden part of the necropolis, perhaps.

Why had that Hearthless one saved her life, only to abandon her down here?

Where were Mister Kindly and Eclipse?

Mercurio?

Ashlinn?

Why was she still standing here like some frightened maid?

Mia picked up the lantern. Its surface was pale and smooth as raven's claws, carved with reliefs of an odd crescent shape.

Gravebone, she realized.*

She could still feel that longing inside her. Looking at the boy, at their shadows on the floor. But there was something more, she realized. Something tugging at her out there in all that dark and all that cold. As she shifted the

* Gravebone is a curious material, found in only one place in all the Republic—the

lantern in her hand, she realized their shadows weren't moving in response to the light. Instead, they remained fixed in one direction, like iron being pulled toward a lodestone.

Mia was tired beyond sleeping. Bruised and bleeding and afraid. But the will that had kept her moving when all seemed lost, when the whole world seemed against her, when her task seemed all but impossible, bid her keep walking. She didn't know where they were, but she knew they couldn't stay. And so she held out her hand to her brother.

"Come."

"Where?"

She nodded to their shadows on the floor. "They know the way."

The boy looked at her, rage and mistrust in his eyes.

"Our familia had a saying," Mia said. "Before your father destroyed it. Neh diis lus'a, lus diis'a. Do you know what that means?"

"I do not speak Liisian," the boy growled.

"When all is blood, blood is all."

She held out her hand again.

"Blood is all, little brother," she repeated.

Jonnen looked up at her. In the dark, among those beautiful howling faces and open hands and the ghostly gravebone light, Mia could see the reflection of his father in those bottomless black eyes.

But in the end, he took her hand.

"Do you feel that?"

Mia's voice echoed in the gloom, far too loud for comfort. They'd

---

Ribs and Spine at the heart of Godsgrave. It is light as wood, yet harder than steel, and the secrets of working it are lost—or at least tightly guarded by the Iron Collegium. Even if an enterprising thief had the tools to chisel off a chunk, defacing any part of the Ribs or Spine is a crime punishable by crucifixion.

Gravebone weapons and armor are highly prized as a result. But possession of any item made of the wondrous substance is a sign of prestige and wealth, and the Itreyan nobility were infamous hoarders of the stuff. Before the rebellion that killed her husband, Queen Isabella, wife of Francisco XV, was an ardent collector of gravebone curios—it was said she was amassing the baubles in the hopes of opening a museum for "the little people," as she so fondly termed Godsgrave's citizens.

Her collection of gravebone trinkets included letter openers, shoehorns, teething rings, a multitude of hairbrushes, combs, and pins, a seventy-four-piece dinner set, and a dozen "marital aids" commissioned by at least seven different Itreyan queens.

And who said money can't buy happiness.

been walking for what seemed like miles, through a twisting labyrinth of tunnels. The walls and floor were all made of those stone hands and faces, uneven under her feet.

It felt singularly disconcerting to be walking on a surface of silent screams. Mia felt sure this was part of the Godsgrave necropolis, but nothing looked familiar, and she'd no idea why anyone would have spent years carving the walls and floors like this. The farther they walked, the more ill at ease she felt. She'd occasionally catch movement from the corner of her eye, swearing that one of the stone hands had moved, or a face had turned to follow her as she passed. But when she looked at them direct, they were motionless.

The darkness was oppressive, the air heavy, sweat burning in the cuts and gouges on her skin. That nameless, shapeless anger was budding in her chest, and she had no idea why. With every step, the feeling that had been dogging Mia since she woke in this place grew more pronounced. The pull of moth to flame.

For the time being, Jonnen's fear of the dark seemed to have overcome his hatred for her, and though he'd refused to keep hold of Mia's hand for long, he stayed close on her heels. As she led him on through the tunnels, gravebone lantern held high, she'd sometimes glance back and find him staring at her with unveiled hatred.

In complete defiance of the lantern's ghostly light, their shadows were still stretching away down the corridor, now far longer than they should have been.

With every step, the pull seemed to grow stronger.

The anger burning brighter in her breast.

"I do not like it here," Jonnen whispered.

"Nor I," Mia replied.

They walked on, pressing closer together. Mia could feel a fury, thrumming in the air around her. A sense of deep and abiding rage. Of pain and need and hunger all entwined. It was the same sensation she'd felt during the truedark massacre. The same as she'd felt during her victory in the arena.

The sense of malice in this city's very bones.

The air felt oily and thick, and Mia swore she could smell blood. The faces on the walls were definitely moving now, the ground shifting under their feet as stone hands reached toward them, stone lips mouthed silent words. Mia's heart almost leapt from her throat as she felt fingers touch hers. Looking down, she saw Jonnen taking hold of her hand again and gripping it tight, eyes wide with fear.

Hunger.

Anger.

Hate.

The tunnel opened into another chamber, too vast to see the walls. The anguished faces beneath their feet sloped downward to form a large basin, barely visible in the lantern's pale glow. The shore was all open hands and mouths, and Mia saw the basin was filled with liquid—black and velvety and still, spilling over the eyes and into the mouths of those faces closest to the edge. It looked like tar, but the reek was unmistakable. Salty and copperish and tinged with rot.

Blood.

Black blood.

And there, on that silently screaming shoreline, Mia saw two familiar shapes. Staring out at the pool of black with their not-eyes.

"Mister Kindly!" she cried. "Eclipse!"

Her passengers remained motionless as she stumbled across the faces and palms, sinking to her knees beside them. Sighing with relief, she ran her hands over their bodies, their shapes shifting and rippling like black smoke in a breeze. But neither one broke their stare from that pool of velvet darkness.

Mister Kindly tilted his head, speaking as if in a daze.

". . . do you feel it . . . ?"

". . . *I FEEL IT* . . . ," Eclipse replied.

"Mia?"

She turned at the voice, heart leaping in her chest. And there in the gloom, among the stone eyes and empty screams, Mia saw a sight more beautiful than any she could recall. A tall girl dressed in the bloodstained garb of an arena guard, another gravebone lantern in her hand, a gravebone sword at her waist. Blond hair dyed henna-red, tanned cheeks smattered with freckles, eyes the blue of sunsburned skies.

"Ashlinn . . . ," Mia breathed.

She ran. So light and fast it felt like she was flying. All the hurt and exhaustion became distant memory, even the sight of that black pool was forgotten. Stumbling over the stone faces, heart bursting in her chest, Mia flung her arms open and crashed into Ashlinn's embrace. She hit so hard, she almost knocked the taller girl off her feet. Overcome with maddening joy at seeing her again, Mia wove her fingers into Ashlinn's hair, touched her face to see if she was real, and breathless, she finally dragged the girl in for a hungry kiss.

"O, Goddess," she whispered.

Ashlinn tried to speak, her words smothered by Mia's mouth. Mia could taste blood from the reopened split in her lip, heedless of the pain, pressing her body tight against Ash's.

"I'm never letting you go again." She seized Ash's cheeks in both hands and crushed their lips together again. "Never, do you hear me? *Ever.*"

"Mia," Ashlinn protested, placing a hand on her chest.

"What?" Mia whispered.

Overcome, she lunged at the girl's mouth again, but Ashlinn turned aside, looked deep into her eyes, and pushed her gently away. Mia stared hard into that sunsburned blue, blinking in confusion.

". . . Ash, what is it?"

"HELLO, MIA."

Mia's blood ran cold as she heard the voice behind her. The temperature around them grew chill as she turned, her skin prickling. She saw a familiar figure, twin gravebone blades upon its back. Its robes were dark and frayed at the hems, its hands black, shadows writhing like tentacles at the edge of its hood.

Mia glanced at Ashlinn, saw fear swimming plain in her blue stare. She pulled herself from her lover's arms, turned to face the strange figure. Pale wisps of breath spilled from her bloody lips.

"Well," she said. "My mysterious savior."

The figure bowed low, robes rippling in some phantom breeze. Its voice was hollow, sibilant, reverberating somewhere in the pit of her belly.

"MI DONA."

"I suppose thanks are in order." Mia folded her arms, tossed her hair over her shoulder. "But they can come after introductions. Who the 'byss are you?"

"A GUIDE," the figure replied. "A GIFT."

"Speak plainly," Mia snarled, temper rising. "Who are you?"

"Mia . . . ," Ashlinn murmured, placing a gentle hand on her shoulder.

"Speak!" Mia demanded, stepping forward with clenched fists.

The figure raised those ink-black hands, drew back its hood. In the ghostly light, Mia saw pitch-black eyes and flawless alabaster skin. Dark, thick saltlocks, swaying as if they were alive. He was still achingly handsome—strong jaw and high cheekbones, once scrawled with hateful ink stains, then made perfect by the weaver's hands.

Lips she'd once kissed.

Eyes she'd once drowned in.

A face she'd once adored.

Mia looked into Ashlinn's frightened blue eyes. Back to the pools of bottomless black that passed for his.

"Black fucking Mother," she breathed.

CHAPTER 5

EPIPHANIES

"How?" Mia whispered.

She looked Tric up and down, crossing her arms over her breasts and shivering in the cold. He was different than he'd been—his once-olive skin was now carved of marble, his once-hazel eyes were pools of purest darkness. He seemed a statue in the forum, wrought cold and perfect from the stone by some master's hand and now come to life. His face was beautiful. Flawless. Pale and smooth as gravebone, cutting just as deep. Her heart could scarcely believe the tale her eyes were telling.

But there was no mistaking the boy she'd known.

The boy she'd loved?

"But she . . ." Mia turned to Ashlinn, bewildered. "You *killed* him."

Ashlinn was uncharacteristically silent, her eyes bright with fear. Mister Kindly and Eclipse were still sitting side by side on that strange shoreline, and Jonnen had joined them, dark eyes locked on that darker pool. The stone faces around them mouthed silent entreaties, stone tresses flowing as if in a wintersdeep wind. But Mia simply stood, staring at her old flame. Trying to ignore the flood of emotion rushing through her chest and simply make sense of it all.

"How can you be here if you're dead?"

Tric's black eyes glinted in the cold lantern light.

"THE MOTHER KEEPS ONLY WHAT SHE NEEDS."

Mia drew a few deep breaths, her lungs aching from the chill. She'd heard tell of wraiths returning from the Hearth to haunt the living, dismissed most of them as old wives' tales. But this was no children's fable standing before her. This was her old friend, sure as her heart was beating in her chest. The boy who'd traveled with her through the Whisperwastes of Ashkah, who'd been her ally and confidant during the Red Church trials, who'd shared her bed and chased her nightmares away during her darkest hours. Her first real lover.

Killed by her second.

Mia could feel Ashlinn behind her, close enough to reach out and touch. She could still taste the girl's lips. Smell the perfume of sweat and leather on her skin. She knew Tric must have seen them together, that he must have witnessed the passion and joy Mia had felt kissing his murderer.

"I . . ." She shook her head. Searching for some explanation. Wondering why she felt the need to explain anything at all. "I thought you were dead . . ."

Those pitch-black eyes flickered to Ashlinn.

"I AM," Tric replied.

"He saved my life, Mia," Ashlinn murmured behind her. "The Ministry ambushed me at the chapel. They took Mercurio back to the Mountain. They were set to steal me, too, but . . . Tric . . . he helped me."

Mia's stomach sank at the news of Mercurio's capture.

"Why?" she asked. "Why help you after what you did to him?"

"I don't know." Ash put a gentle hand on her shoulder. "Mia, I have to tell y—"

"What's your game, Tric?" Mia turned back to the boy, burning with curiosity and indignity. "Why save Ashlinn after she killed you? Why save Jonnen and me, then leave us to wander like rats in the dark?"

At the sound of his name, Mia's brother turned from the black pool. He blinked hard, rubbing his eyes like a boy just woken from sleep. He seemed to notice Tric for the first time, but Mia could see suspicion in his stare instead of fear. Curiosity narrowed his eyes as he looked Ashlinn up and down, and a healthy dose of hatred resurfaced as his gaze fell on her.

Tric's eyes were fixed on Mia. She realized she hadn't yet seen him blink.

"IT'S TRUELIGHT," he replied. "THE THREE EYES OF AA THE EVERSEEING BURN BRIGHT IN THE SKY ABOVE. MOTHER NIAH IS NEVER SO FAR AWAY FROM THIS WORLD AS SHE IS AT THIS MOMENT. AND IT'S ONLY THROUGH HER WILL THAT I WALK THIS WORLD AT ALL. IT TOOK ALL I HAD TO DO WHAT I DID."

"And Mister Kindly?" Mia asked. "Eclipse? Why separate us?"

"THEY WERE DRAWN HERE WHILE YOU SLEPT."

Mia looked to that darkened shore, her passengers sitting beside it. Now that the joy of seeing Ashlinn, the shock of seeing Tric, was wearing off, she could still feel the pull of this place thrumming under her skin. The black, intoxicating malice reverberating in that vast black pool. Looking down at her feet, she could see her shadow stretching toward it, despite the lantern's light. And she realized she wanted to join it.

"No more riddles, Tric," she said. "Tell me once and for all what's going on here."

"IT WILL NOT PLEASE YOU."

"Fucking *speak,* damn you!" she demanded.

The shadow of a smile curled Tric's bloodless lips. "You still have a strange way of making friends, Pale Daughter."

The words made Mia's heart ache, dispelling any lingering suspicion that this apparition wasn't her old friend. She remembered their time together, the promises they'd made each other, the way his touch had made her feel . . .

"Please," she whispered.

The Hearthless boy breathed deep, as if he were about to speak. All the air around him seemed to hush, the whispering stone faces and writhing stone hands at last falling still. His saltlocks swayed like dreaming vipers, the tattered edge of his robe danced in a wind that touched only him.

"I felt the blade." Tric glanced at Ashlinn. "When she slipped it into my chest. I felt the wind as she pushed me off the Sky Altar, down into the black beyond the Quiet Mountain. But I didn't feel the ground."

Mia sensed Ashlinn beside her, shivering as her lover reached down and took hold of her hand. She realized she couldn't feel her fingers for the chill in the air. The very world seemed to hold its breath.

"I woke in a place with no color," Tric continued. "But in the distance ahead, I saw a flickering flame. A hearth. I knew I'd be safe there. I could feel its warmth, like a lover's hands on my skin." The wraith shook his head. "But as I took my first step toward it, I heard a voice behind me, as if from far away."

"What did it say?" Mia heard herself whisper.

"The many were one," Tric replied. "And will be again; one beneath the three, to raise the four, free the first, blind the second and the third."

O, Mother, blackest Mother, what have I become?

Mia felt her belly flip, remembering the book that Chronicler Aelius had given her during her tutelage in the Red Church. She'd asked the old man for a tome about the darkin, and he'd returned with a beaten, leather-bound diary.

"Cleo's journal," she said. "Those were *her* words."

"No," the deadboy replied. "They're Niah's. She sang them to me in the dark, the music of her promises drowning out the light of that tiny hearth and all desire to sit beside it. And when her lullaby was done, the Mother showed me a path, across the dark between the stars. And through cold so fierce it burned, through a black so bleak it almost swallowed me whole, I clawed my way back."

Tric pulled up the sleeves of his robe, and Mia saw his hands and forearms were black, spattered, as if he'd dipped his arms in ink all the way to the elbows.

"And I became."

"Became what?"

"Her gift to you," he replied. "Her guide."

Mia simply shook her head in question.

"You're lost," Tric said. "It's as I once told you. Your vengeance is as the suns, Mia. It serves only to blind you."

Mia swallowed, finishing the words he'd spoken to her in the Galante necropolis.

"Seek the Crown of the Moon."

". . . The Crown of the Moon?" Ashlinn breathed.

Mia turned to the girl beside her, hearing the strange note in her voice.

"That means something to you?"

Ashlinn's eyes were still fixed on Tric. She looked as incredulous as Mia felt.

". . . Ash?"

Ashlinn blinked, focusing on Mia's face.

"The map," she said. "The one Duomo hired me to find."

Mia swallowed, remembering the first time she'd fallen into Ashlinn's bed. The sweet kisses and cigarillo smoke afterward, long red hair parting to reveal the intricate inkwerk on her lover's back. Ashlinn had been hired by Cardinal Duomo to retrieve a map from a ruin on the coast of Old Ashkah. But fearing betrayal, she'd gotten the map branded on her skin with arkemical ink that would fade in the event of her death—the same kind that was used in the slave brand on Mia's cheek. In all the chaos leading up to the *magni,* they'd never truly found time to discuss it.

"Duomo believed it led to a weapon," Ashlinn said softly. "A magik that would undo the Church. Scaeva and the Ministry must have believed it, too, or they'd never have sent *you* to steal it back, Mia. I don't know the truth of it. But I do know the map leads to a place deep in the Ashkahi wastes. A place called the Crown of the Moon."

"Where you must go," Tric said.

"Why?" Mia demanded. "What the 'byss is this Moon? And why do I give a beggar's cuss about its fucking crown?"

"You are the Mother's Chosen," Tric replied.

"O, *bollocks,"* Mia snapped. "If I'm chosen of Our Lady of Blessed Murder, why am I running for my life from her own damned assassins? If I'm so la-dee-fucking-da, why have I lived up to my neck in blood and shit for the past eight years?"

"The Red Church has lost its way," Tric replied. "And the Mother is very far from here, Mia. But she has done what she can to set you on your path. She sent you salvation as a child through Mercurio. She sent you Cleo's journal through Aelius. She sent you the map through . . ." Tric's eyes flashed as he glanced at Ashlinn. ". . . her. She sent you me. You can't imagine the struggle it took to influence this world from within the walls of her prison. But still, in what tiny way she can, she's given you all the aid she may."

"But why?" Mia demanded. "Why *me*?"

Tric steepled his black fingers at his lips, staring for long, silent moments.

"In the beginning, Niah and Aa's marriage was a happy one," he finally said. "The Light and the Night shared rule of the sky equally, making love at dawn and dusk. Fearing a rival, Aa commanded Niah bear him no sons, and dutifully, she gave him four daughters—the Ladies of Fire, Earth, Ocean, and Storms. But in the long, cold hours of darkness, Niah missed her husband. And to ease her loneliness, she brought a boychild into the world."

Tric looked to the pool of darkness at his back, sorrow in his voice.

"The Night named her son Anais."

"And Aa banished Niah from the sky for her crime," Mia said, her temper fraying. "This is children's lore, everyone knows it. What's it to do with me?"

Tric pointed one finger to the pool, the smooth black surface mirroring the ceiling above as if it were glass. And reflected in it, she could see a pale orb, hanging in the dark like smoke.

"In the empire of Old Ashkah, they knew Anais by another name."

Mia looked at the glowing orb—the same she'd seen in the moment she slew Furian in Godsgrave Arena—and felt her shadow grow darker still.

"The Moon," she realized.

Tric nodded. "He was the Eater of Fear. The Day in the Darkness. He reflected his father's light and brightened his mother's night. In the empire of Old Ashkah, he taught the first sorcerii the arts arcane. A god of magik and wisdom and harmony, worshipped above all others. No shadow without light, Ever day follows night, Between black and white . . ."

"There is gray . . . ," Mia murmured.

"He was the balance between night and day. The prince of dawn and dusk. And fearing his growing power, the Everseeing resolved to slay his only son."

The stone reliefs began moving again as Tric spoke. Graven hands shifting to cover sightless eyes. Mouths widening in horror. The orb in the pool shifted, became a sharp, crescent shape, dripping blood. In the back of her mind, Mia swore she could hear other voices. Thousands of them, just beyond the edge of hearing.

And they were screaming.

"Aa struck while Anais slept," Tric continued. "He cut off his son's head and hurled his body from the heavens. Anais's corpse plummeted to the earth, tearing the land asunder and throwing all the world into chaos. The Ashkahi Empire in the east was completely destroyed. And where his son's body lay in the west, Aa commanded his faithful to build a temple to his glory. That temple became a city, and that city became the new heart of his faith."

"The Ribs." Ash glanced at the gravebone blade at her waist. "The Spine."

"This whole place . . . ," Mia realized, looking around them.

Tric nodded. "A god's grave."

Heart hammering, mouth dry, Mia pictured the illustration she'd found at the end of Cleo's journal—a map of Itreya before the rise of the Republic. The bay of Godsgrave had been missing entirely, a peninsula filling the Sea of Silence where the Itreyan capital now stood. And in that spot, three words had been scribed in blood-red ink.

"Here he fell . . . ," she whispered.

"Here he fell," Tric nodded. "But gods don't die so easily. And the Mother keeps only what she needs. Anais's soul wasn't extinguished."

Tric drew a long, slow breath, as if before a deep plunge.

"It was shattered."

His bottomless eyes were fixed upon Mia's.

"Some pieces pooled here, in the hollows beneath this city's skin. The part of him that raged. That hated. That wished only for it all to end, just as he had." The wraith glanced at Mister Kindly and Eclipse, now watching him with their not-eyes. "In time, other shards gained a seeming of their own, crawling from the mire beneath his grave. Cut off from what they'd been, and knowing not what they were, they sought others like them. Feasting on fear as Anais had once done, and taking whatever shapes and mannerisms those they rode found comfort in."

"Daemons," Mia said. "Passengers."

Those pitch-black eyes returned to the girl's. "AND LASTLY, THE LARGEST FRAGMENTS OF THE WHOLE, THE PARTS WHICH WERE STRONGEST, FOUND THEIR WAY INTO . . ."

". . . People," Ash breathed.

"Darkin," Mia said.

Tric nodded. "BUT AT THE HEART OF YOU—DAEMONS OR DARKIN—YOU ARE ALL THE SAME. SEARCHING FOR THE MISSING PIECES OF YOURSELF. SEEKING TO BECOME WHOLE AGAIN. THE SCATTERED PIECES OF A SHATTERED GOD."

Eclipse scoffed. ". . . *THIS IS MADNESS* . . ."

". . . i mean to cause no one alarm, but i concur with the mongrel . . ."

"LOOK AT YOUR SHADOW, MIA," Tric said. "WHAT DO YOU SEE?"

Mia looked to the darkness at her feet. It was still stretching out toward that pool of black blood, just as Jonnen's was. But even with her passengers sitting on the shore across from her, it was still . . .

"Dark enough for two," she said.

"SO IT WAS WITH CLEO," Tric said. "SHE ALSO LEARNED THE TRUTH OF WHAT SHE WAS. CHOSEN BY THE MOTHER, SHE JOURNEYED ACROSS THE LANDS OF ITREYA, SEEKING TO UNITE THE SHATTERED PIECES OF ANAIS'S SOUL. SHE GATHERED A LEGION OF PASSENGERS TO HER SIDE. SEEKING OTHERS LIKE HER AND—"

"Eating them," Mia said, recalling the journal.

"TAKING THE SHARDS OF HIS ESSENCE INTO HERSELF."

Mia frowned. "So the fragment that was inside Furian . . ."

"IS NOW PART OF YOU. IN SLAYING HIM WITH YOUR OWN HAND, YOU'VE CLAIMED IT AS YOURS. MERGING TWO INTO A LARGER WHOLE. THE MANY WERE ONE. AND WILL BE AGAIN."

"But Lord Cassius died right in front of me. I didn't feel any stronger."

"CASSIUS WASN'T SLAIN BY A DARKIN. THE FRAGMENT IN HIM WAS LOST FOREVER. EVENTUALLY, EVEN GODS CAN DIE."

Mia's pulse was thumping in her veins, her belly a roiling slick of ice. She could feel the malice emanating from that blackened pool, the fury in the air around her. She understood it now, at last. It was the same fury she'd reached out and touched during the truedark massacre, the night she'd first truly wielded the power within her. Tearing the Philosopher's Stone to pieces. Storming the Basilica Grande and destroying the grand statue of Aa outside it. Embracing the black and bitter rage in this city's bones.

It was the rage of a child, betrayed by the one who should have loved it most.

The rage of a son, by his father slain.

The deadboy's bottomless eyes bored into her own.

"Cleo's journal . . . she spoke of a child inside her," Mia said.

"*. . . she was a lunatic, mia . . .*," Eclipse growled.

"This whole tale sounds like lunacy," she breathed.

"No," Tric replied. "It's—"

"*. . . destiny . . . ?*" Mister Kindly scoffed.

Tric turned bottomless eyes on the shadowcat.

"If she has courage enough to seize it."

"*. . . this is the darkest shade of nonsense . . .*"

Eclipse concurred with a sneer.

"*. . . you honestly wish me to believe this idiot moggy is a god . . . ?*"

"Anais's soul shattered into hundreds of fragments. You're no more godlike than a drop of water is the ocean. But you *must* feel you're all bound to each other? Don't you sense you are . . . incomplete?"

Mia knew what the Hearthless boy was talking about. The sickness and hunger she'd always felt around Cassius, Furian, now Jonnen. She never felt as whole as when Mister Kindly and Eclipse walked in her shadow. And she felt stronger than ever since Furian had died at her hands.

But still, it seemed sheer madness—this talk of fragmented gods and shattered souls, of restoring the balance between light and dark.

"You must make whole what was broken, Mia. You must return magik to the world. Restore the balance between night and day, like it was in the beginning. Like it was always *meant* to be. One sun. One night. One moon."

She motioned to the blackened pool. "If it's pieces of him I'm supposed to seek, that seems a good place to start."

"No," Tric said. "This is Anais's fury. This is his rage. The part of him that has lain in the dark and festered, that wants only to destroy. You must remake the world, Mia. Not undo it. This is your purpose."

Mia's eyes narrowed. "My *purpose* was avenging my familia. It was killing Remus, Duomo, and Scaeva. And I've done that, after living neck-deep in blood and shit for eight fucking years. No thanks to your precious Mother."

"Mia . . . ," Ashlinn murmured.

"The Red Church captured Mercurio, Tric. Maw knows what they want with him, but he's in their hands. They probably know he helped me murder Scaeva. I have to—"

"Mia," Ashlinn said.

She turned to her lover, saw fear swimming in that beautiful blue.

"What is it?" Mia asked.

"I have to tell you something," Ash said. "About Scaeva."

"So tell me?"

". . . You should sit down."

"Are you jesting?" Mia scoffed. "Spit it out, Ashlinn."

The Vaanian girl chewed her lip. Drew a deep and shivering breath.

"He lives."

Jonnen's eyes grew wide, his little mouth hanging open. Mia felt her heart skip a beat, an awful dread turning her gut colder than the deadboy behind her.

"What are you talking about?" Mia hissed. "I put a gravebone blade right through his ribs. I cut his fucking heart in two!"

Ash shook her head. "He was a double, Mia. An actor, fleshcrafted by Weaver Marielle to *look* like Scaeva. The consul was in league with the Red Church, and they knew our plan to win the *magni* all along. They *wanted* you to kill Duomo. Scaeva's going to use the cardinal's public murder as an excuse to exercise permanent emergency powers, claim the title of imperator, become king of Itreya in all but name."

Mia's head was swimming. Heart racing. Skin filmed with icy sweat.

Could it be true?

Could he have seen her coming?

Could she have been so blind?

Her legs felt weak. Dizzy from exhaustion, loss of blood, Solis's toxin still lingering in her veins. She glanced to Jonnen, saw the boy looking at her with triumph in his black eyes. She'd been so careful. So certain. She could remember the elation as her blade parted Scaeva's chest, the maddening joy as his blood splashed across her chin and lips, warm and thick and lovely red.

"O, Goddess . . ."

She blinked at Ashlinn, searching desperately for the lie, the ruse.

"How do you know this?"

"Scaeva told me. When they ambushed me in the chapel. And Mia . . . he told me something else besides." Ash swallowed thickly, her voice shaking. "But I don't want to hurt you. I don't want to give it voice, knowing what it will do to you."

"I thought it was finished . . ." Mia could feel bitter tears brimming in her eyes. Too tired and hurt to push them back anymore. "Eight f-fucking years, and I . . . I actually let myself believe it was done."

She sank to her knees on a sea of screaming faces, tempted to just start screaming along with them.

"What could be worse than that?"

"O, Goddess, forgive me . . ."

Ashlinn sank down on the stone beside her. Taking Mia's hands in her own, she took a deep, trembling breath.

"Mia . . ."

Ash shook her head, tears spilling down her cheeks.

"Mia . . . he's your father."

CHAPTER 6

IMPERATOR

Mia sat on a black shoreline, a war of three colors in her head.

The first was the red of blood. The red of rage. She felt it curl her hands to fists. Fill her to brimming, toe to crown. Spitting curses and fire and stomping about on those anguished stone faces. It was bliss to give in to it for a while, embracing the temper she was so notorious for. At least she knew where it came from now. Swimming in the air about her, the city above her, changing the architecture beneath her skin.

All her life.

The rage of a god laid low.

The second was cool steel gray. Suspicion, slipping into her belly like a knife, cold and hard. There was a moment where she prayed it was all a trick—manipulation from a man who'd always proved himself three steps ahead. But in her darkest depths, it all rang true. The way Scaeva had looked at her that turn in her mother's apartments. That turn he'd stretched out his hand and taken her whole world away. The gleam in his eyes as he'd looked down at her and smiled, dark as bruises.

"Would you like to know what keeps me warm at night, little one?"

And so fury killed suspicion. Drowned it beneath a scarlet flood.

But after suspicion's cool gray had come sorrow. Black as storm clouds. Turning her curses to sobs and her fury to tears. She'd slumped down on that voiceless, howling shore and cried. Like a child. Like a fucking babe. Letting her grief, her horror, her anguish spill up out of her lips and down her cheeks until her eyes were red as blood and her throat aching and raw.

Darius Corvere. Justicus of the Luminatii. Leader of the Kingmaker Rebellion. The man who'd given her puzzles for Great Tithe gifts, who'd read her tales before bedtime, whose stubble had tickled her cheeks when he kissed her goodnight. The man who'd propped her little feet upon his own and whisked her about that shining ballroom.

"I love you, Mia."

"I love you, too."

"Promise you'll remember. No matter what comes."

The man she'd adored, the man she'd grieved, the man she'd devoted the last eight years of her life to avenging. The man she'd called Father.

Nothing close.

Ashlinn sat behind her as she wept, gentle arms about her waist, forehead pressed cool and smooth against her back. Mister Kindly and Eclipse sat close by, watching silently. Jonnen looked at her with a newfound confusion glittering in those bottomless eyes. Black as crow's feathers. Black as truedark.

Just like Scaeva's.

Just like mine.

"His wife can't have children," Ashlinn murmured, her voice thick with grief. "Scaeva, I mean. I suppose that's why he took Jonnen . . . afterward . . ."

"All good kings need sons," Mia whispered. "Daughters, not so much."

"I'm sorry, love." Ash took her hand, pressed Mia's scabbed and bleeding knuckles to her lips. "Black Mother, I'm so sorry."

Eclipse drifted closer, wrapping her translucent body around Mia's waist and resting her head in the girl's lap. Mister Kindly lay across her shoulders, entwined in her hair, tail curled protectively across her chest. Mia drew comfort from their smoky chill, the whisper-light feel of their bodies against hers, Ash's arms around her. But her eyes were soon drawn back to that black pool before them, the copper stink of blood hanging heavy in the air. She looked down at her empty hands again, the passengers beside her, the shadow beneath her, darker than it had ever been.

The many were one.

And will be again?

She looked to the silent Hearthless boy standing before her. His black eyes were fixed on Ashlinn. On their fingers entwined. She remembered those eyes had been hazel once. That those fingers had touched her in places no one ever had.

His revelation still rang in her ears. The weight of the truth she'd sought all these years, now ill-fitting and crooked upon her shoulders. Part of her still found it impossible to believe—even with the memory of the truedark massacre singing in her head, the power and fury she'd wielded so effortlessly, shadows cutting like swords in her outstretched hands. She'd killed so many men, giving in to the rage that had sustained her through all the years and all the miles and all the sleepless nevernights.

It was creeping back into her now, slipping out toward her from that pool. Toxic. Narcotic. Smothering sorrow's black beneath waves of familiar, comforting red.

If she was angry, she didn't need to think.

If she was angry, she could simply *act.*

Hunt.

Stab.

Kill.

That bastard. The spider at the center of this whole rotten fucking web. The man who'd sentenced her mother to die in the Philosopher's Stone, who'd ordered her drowned, who'd used her to rid himself of his rivals, and at last, put himself within arm's reach of his bloody throne. The man who'd manipulated her from afar all these years, pushing her, twisting her, turning her into . . .

She looked down at her trembling, open hands.

Into this.

So she gave in to the rage. Let it choke the grief inside her. And into the dark, she whispered, "If a killer is what he wants, a killer is what he'll get."

Ash blinked. "What?"

Mia stood with a wince. Stretched out her hand.

"Give me the sword, Ash."

Ashlinn looked down at the longblade at her waist. She'd recovered it from Mia's chambers in the Godsgrave chapel. It was gravebone, sharp as sunslight, its hilt carved like a crow in flight. The sword had once belonged to Darius Corvere, taken from his study in Crow's Nest by Marcus Remus. Mia had killed Remus in turn—cut his throat in a dusty shithole on the coast of Ashkah, and claimed the blade as her own.

Avenging her father, or so she thought.

"I love you, Mia."

"I love you, too."

"Give it to me," Mia said.

"Why?" Ash asked.

"Because it's mine."

"Mia . . ." Ashlinn rose to her feet, caution and care turning her voice to velvet. "Mia, whatever you're thinking . . . you're exhausted. You're wounded. What Tric just told us . . . it can't be easy to—"

"Give me the *fucking* sword, Ashlinn!" Mia shouted.

The shadows flared, the darkness ringing in her voice and turning it to hollow iron. The darkness twisted about her feet, mad patterns and shapes, strobing black. The red-amber eyes of the crow on the hilt twinkled in the ghostly light. The pool behind her rippled, as if kissed by the smallest stone.

Ashlinn went pale beneath her freckles. Mia saw she was actually trembling. But she still stood her ground. Gritted her teeth and curled her hands into fists to stop the shakes. Standing up to Mia like nobody else ever dared.

"No," she replied.

Mia growled. "Ash, I'm warning you . . ."

"Warn me all you like," Ash said, taking a deep breath. "I know you're angry. I know you're hurt. But you need to *think*." She waved at the dark behind and below Mia. "Away from this cursed pool. With the blood washed off your skin and a cigarillo in your hand and a nevernight's sleep between you and all this shit."

Mia scowled, but the iron in her stare wavered.

"Give me my sword, Ashlinn."

The girl reached out and ran one gentle hand down the cruel scar on Mia's cheek. Along the bow of her lips. The look in her eyes melted Mia's heart.

"I love you, Mia," Ash said. "Even the part of you that frightens me. But you've been hurt enough for one turn. I'll not see you hurt again."

Tears welled in Mia's eyes. Black rising from beneath the red. The walls loomed about her, ready to come crashing down. Her hands fluttered at her sides as if she were desperate for an embrace, but too torn to beg for one. With a murmur of pity, a glance to the Hearthless boy watching them, Ashlinn stepped forward and wrapped her arms around Mia. She kissed her brow, pulled her in tight, Mia sinking into her arms.

"I love you," Ash whispered.

"I'm sorry," Mia breathed into Ashlinn's hair, hands roaming her back.

"It's all right."

"No." Mia's hands moved down over Ashlinn's hips, her fingers brushing the longsword's hilt. And with a flourish, Mia drew the blade from the scabbard and stepped back out of Ash's reach. "It isn't."

"You . . ." Ashlinn's eyes were wide, mouth open. "You . . . fucking . . ."

"Bitch?"

Mia flipped the sword in her hand, wiping her tears away on her grubby sleeve.

"Aye," she nodded. "But I'm a clever fucking bitch."

Mia turned to Tric, sniffed hard, and spat.

"How do I get out of here?"

"You must listen—"

"I must nothing," Mia snapped. "Julius Scaeva is in Godsgrave, do you understand that? The *real* Julius Scaeva. A hundred thousand people saw him cut down by an assassin's blade. He needs to show himself in front of the mob to assure them all is well before the city goes up in flames. And his doppelgänger is dead. So are you going to show me the way out of this fucking hole, or leave me to wander in the dark playing guess-a-game? Because one way or another, I'm going back up to the 'Grave."

"I remember the path we walked here on," came a small voice.

Mia looked to her brother, standing on the black shoreline in his grubby purple robes. The boy was watching her with his big dark eyes, obviously not quite sure what to make of her anymore. He'd not wanted to believe they were siblings, that was plain enough. But if what Ash said about his father still being alive was true, then it *all* might be true. And when Mia had been the one who killed his da, it was simple—she was an enemy, hated and feared. But now Jonnen knew his father still lived, how did he feel about the sister he'd never known?

"You do?" Mia asked.

The boy nodded. "I've a memory sharp as swords. All my tutors say."

Mia held out her hand to her brother. "Come, then."

The boy looked up at her, suspicion and hunger swimming in his eyes. But ever so slowly, he took her hand. Mister Kindly sat on Mia's shoulders, purring softly as Eclipse prowled about her ankles. She lifted the gravebone lantern and took a step into the darkness, but Tric moved to stand in front of her. Looming over her like some beautiful bloodless wraith from a fireside tale.

She could feel the chill radiating off his body, where once she'd felt a warmth that made her ache. Her eyes trailed up the alabaster line of his throat, the cut of his jaw, the soft crease of the dimple at his cheek. Pale as milk. Pale as death.

"You said the Mother sent you to be my guide," Mia said. "Show me the way."

"This isn't your path, Mia." Tric spoke softly. "Ashlinn speaks truth. You're wounded. Angry. You need sleep and a decent meal and a moment to breathe."

"Tric," Mia said. "Do you remember that time we were acolytes and you talked me out of doing something I desperately wanted by appealing to my sensible side?"

The boy tilted his head.

". . . No."

"Me either," Mia replied. "Now show me the way. Or get the fuck out of it."

The boy glanced at Ashlinn. The dark around them rang with the song of murder. The pool rippling in quiet fury. Tric looked down into Mia's eyes. Bottomless black. Utterly unreadable. But finally, he heaved a frosty sigh.

"FOLLOW ME."

"To the forum!"

The criers were on every bridge, the bellboys on every cobbled street. The shout rang up and down the thoroughfares and through the taverna, over the canals from the Nethers to the Arms and back again. All of Godsgrave ringing.

"The forum!"

Chaos had tried to take root in their time beneath the city, and Mia could smell blood and smoke in the air. But as they surfaced from the tunnels beneath Godsgrave's necropolis, she could see all-out anarchy hadn't broken loose quite yet. Luminatii and soldiers patrolled the streets, shoving folks with shield and truncheon. Gatherings of more than a dozen were swiftly broken up, along with the noses of anyone who protested too vigorously. The legion seemed to have been briefed of trouble ahead of time—almost as if the consul had anticipated chaos after the end of the games.

Always a step ahead, bastard . . .

And now the announcement was rippling through the streets. Floating up over the balconies and terra-cotta roofs and ringing across the canals. Shushing rumor and quieting unrest and promising the answers all in the city sought.

Was the cardinal really slain? The consul, too?

The savior of the Republic, laid low by the blade of a mere slave?

Mia had stolen a cloak from some washwoman's line, another strip of cloth to wrap around the scar and slave brand on her face. They made their way through the Sword Arm and down toward the Heart, Ashlinn to her left, Tric to her right, Jonnen in her arms. The boy's weight made her muscles ache, her spine groan in protest. But even if she was no longer the assassin who killed his father, she was still the abductor claiming to be his long-lost sister, and Mia didn't trust him not to make a break for it if given half the chance. Even if she didn't fear the clever little shit doing a runner, she was still loathe to let him go. She couldn't lose him now.

Not after all this.

With both Eclipse and Mister Kindly riding in his shadow, the boy seemed a little more sedate. Watching her with clouded eyes as they slipped through the Godsgrave streets, over the wending cobbles and through the grand piazzas of the marrowborn district, closer, ever closer to the forum. The crowd around them was alight with fear, curiosity, violence waiting in the wings. Mia saw the flash of hidden blades. The glint of bared teeth. The potential for ruin, just a breath and a wrong word away.

Every grudge. Every slave, every unhappy pleb, every malcontent with a bone to pick. She saw how fragile it all was—this so-called "civilization." The rage boiling at the heart of this place. Godsgrave felt like a barrel full of wyrdglass, wrapped in oil-soaked rags. Waiting for the spark that would send it all up in flames.

In the forum, a few hundred feet from the first Rib, they found the streets were simply too crowded to get any closer. The thoroughfares and bridges were packed with folk of every kind, young and old, rich and poor, Itreyan, Liisian, Vaanian, Dweymeri. Instead of trying to push on, Mia and her comrades forced their way to the base of the mighty statue of the Everseeing in the forum's heart.

The effigy towered above the mob, fifty feet high, carved of solid marble. Three arkemical globes representing the three suns were held in one of Aa's outstretched hands. In his other, he held out a mighty sword. Mia had destroyed this very statue the truedark she turned fourteen, but Scaeva had ordered it rebuilt, paying the fee from his own coffers. One more pious gesture to buy the mob's adoration.

With Jonnen in Tric's arms, the quartet climbed the statue, finding a place to rest in the great folds of the Everseeing's robes. Peering out over the mob below.

"Black Goddess, look at them all," Ash breathed beside her.

Mia could only stare. The crowd she'd fought in front of at the *Venatus Magni* had been impressive, but it seemed every citizen of Godsgrave had been ushered here for the announcement. The Ribs rose above them, sixteen gravebone arches, gleaming white and towering high into the sky. Soldiers and Luminatii shoved their way through the mob, cracking skulls and holding order by the throat. Desperation and fear hung in the air like blood-stink in a butchery. At least they had their perch to themselves—though he seemed to be struggling in the truelight as much as Mia, Tric's chill presence dissuaded other folk from climbing too close.

Mia narrowed her eyes in the truelight glare. The journey up from beneath the city had been long, silent, a hundred twists and turns. She had no idea of how long they'd trekked—time had seemed meaningless in the hollow dark below the city's skin. But now she was away from it, she longed for it again. That black pool. Those silent, wailing faces. She missed it, like she missed Mister Kindly and Eclipse when they were apart. Missed it like a part of herself had been torn away.

The many were one.

She pushed the thought aside. Focused on the rage. Her knuckles white on the hilt of her gravebone sword. None of it, the Moon, Niah, Cleo, Mercurio, Ashlinn, Tric, none of it fucking mattered.

Not until that bastard's dead.

Trumpets sounded, ringing crisp and clear in the truelight glare. The suns above were living things, beating upon her shoulders, grinding her beneath their light like a worm under a boot. The shadows in the folds of the Everseeing's robes were her only respite, and Mia clung to them like a child to its mother's skirts. But she stood taller as the fanfare sounded, squinting past the great open ring of the forum and the circle of mighty pillars crowned with statues of the Senate's finest. The Senate House itself stood to the west, all fluted columns and polished bone. The first Rib loomed to the south, the balcony of the consul's palazzo crowded with Luminatii in gravebone plate and senators in green laurel wreaths and rippling white robes trimmed in purple.

The trumpets rang long and loud, stilling the shouts, the whispers, the uncertainty brewing in the City of Bridges and Bones. Truth told, Mia had never truly considered the consequences of her scheme in the *magni* far beyond seeing Duomo and Scaeva dead. But with rumor of the consul's death running rife, all seemed on the verge of calamity.

What would happen to this place if the consul truly fell?

What truly would become of this city, this Republic, if she cut off its head? Would it simply thrash and roil for a time, then grow another? Or, like a god laid low by his father's hand, shatter into a thousand pieces?

"Merciful Aa!" came a cry from the street below. "Look!"

A shout from a rooftop behind. "Four Daughters, is it him?"

Mia felt her heart drop and thump inside her chest. Squinting in the glare toward the balcony of the consul's apartments as the Luminatii and senators stepped aside.

O, Goddess.

O, merciful Black Mother.

His purple robe was still drenched with blood, his golden laurel missing. A bandage was wrapped around his throat and shoulder, soaked with red. His face was pale, his salt-and-pepper hair damp with sweat. But there could be no mistaking the man as he stepped forward and raised his hand like a shepherd before the sheep. Three fingers outstretched in the sign of Aa.

"Father," Jonnen said.

Mia glared at her brother, wondering if he'd be troublesome enough to shout for help—but he seemed afeared enough of the Hearthless boy holding him to keep quiet for now. The crowd, however, were overcome with a wave of jubilance, a deafening, giddy roar rippling from those near enough to see with their own two eyes, out, out into the forum. Folk farther back began shouting, demanding the truth, to see, shoving and brawling. Soldiers stepped in, truncheons at the ready. The streets swayed and rolled, folk shoving and spitting and pushing each other off bridges and into the canals below, chaos budding higher, building upw—

"My people!"

The cry rang through horns scattered about the forum, amplified and echoing on the walls of the Senate House, the gravebone of the Spine. Like some kind of magik, it brought stillness to the chaos. Balance to the edge of the knife.

Though he was too far away for Mia to really see his expression, Julius Scaeva's voice was hoarse with pain. She could see Scaeva's wife, Liviana, by his side, her gown red as bloodstains, her throat glittering with gold. Mia looked down to Jonnen beside her, saw his eyes fixed on the woman who'd claimed to be his mother.

The boy glanced up at Mia. Looked away again just as swift.

Scaeva drew a deep breath before continuing.

"My people!" he repeated. "My countrymen! My friends!"

Silence fell in the City of Bridges and Bones. The air was still enough to hear the whispers of the distant sea, the gentle prayer of the wind. Mia had known the love of the crowd in the arena, sure and true. She'd brought them to their feet, roaring in adoration, made them thrill and cry and sing her name like a hymn to heaven. But never once in her time on the sands had she held them in thrall like this.

They called Julius Scaeva "Senatum Populiis"—the People's Senator. The Savior of the Republic. And though it sickened her to acknowledge, she marveled to see him still the entire city like millpond water with a mere handful of words.

"I have heard whispers!" Scaeva called. "Whispers that your Republic is beheaded! That your consul is slain! That Julius Scaeva is fallen! I have heard these whispers, and in turn, I shout my defiance before you all!" He slammed one bloody fist down on the balustrade. "Here I stand! And by God, here I stay!"

A roar. Thunderous and joyous, spreading like wildfire through the crowd. Mia could see folk below her embracing, cheeks wet with jubilant tears. Her stomach turned, her lips curled, her grip on her sword so tight her hand was shaking.

After a suitable time, Scaeva held up his hand for silence, and the hush fell like an anvil once more. He drew a deep breath, then coughed, once, twice. Hand going to his blood-soaked shoulder, he swayed on his feet before the mekwerk horn. Soldiers and senators stepped forward to aid the consul lest he fall. Dismay rippled through the mob. But with a shake of his head, Scaeva pushed his well-meaning helpers aside and stood tall again, despite his "wounds." Brave and staunch and O, so very strong.

The crowd lost their collective mind. Rapture and bliss swept through them in a flood. Even as her mouth soured, Mia had to admire the theater of it. The way this snake turned every snag and stumble to bitterest advantage.

"We are wounded!" he cried. "There is no doubt. And though it pains me greatly, I speak not of the knife blow I bear, no. I speak of the blow dealt to us all! Our counsel, our conscience, our friend . . . nay, our *brother,* is taken from us."

Scaeva bowed his head. When he spoke again, his voice was thick with grief.

"My people, it cleaves my heart to bring you tidings ill as these." The consul steadied himself against the balustrade, swallowed as if overcome with sorrow. "But I must confirm that Francesco Duomo, grand cardinal of Aa's ministry, and the Everseeing's chosen on this blessed earth . . . is slain."

Dismayed cries rang through the forum. Anguished wails and gnashing teeth. Scaeva slowly held up his hand, like a maestro before an orchestra.

"I grieve the loss of my friend. Truly. Long were the nevernights I sat in his radiance, and I shall carry the heavenly wisdom he gifted me for the rest of my years." Scaeva hung his head, heaved a sigh. "But long have I warned that the enemies of our great Republic stood closer than my brothers in the Senate would believe! Long have I warned the Kingmaker's legacy still festers in our Republic's heart! And yet not even I dared imagine that on this most holy feast, in the greatest city the world has known, the paragon of the Everseeing's faith might be cut down by an assassin's blade? In sight of us all? Before the three unblinking eyes of Aa himself? What madness is this?"

He rent his purple robe and howled at the sky.

"What madness is this?"

The crowd roared again, dismay to rage and back again. Mia watched the emotion roll up and down like waves on a storm-wracked beach, Scaeva wringing them for every drop.

The consul spoke again once the bedlam had subsided.

"As you know, my friends, to safeguard the security of the Republic, it was my intention to stand for a fourth term as consul in the truedark elections. But in the face of this assault upon our faith, our freedom, our familia, I have no other choice. As of this moment, by the emergency provisions of the Itreyan constitution, and in the face of the *undeniable* threat to our glorious Republic, I, Julius Scaeva, do hereby claim title of imperator and all powers . . ."

Scaeva's voice was momentarily drowned out by the volume of the mob. Every man, woman, and child was cheering. Soldiers. Holy men. Bakers and butchers, sweetgirls and slaves, Black Goddess, even the fucking senators up there on that awful little stage. The constitution of the Republic was being torn up in front of them. Their voices being reduced to a pale echo in an empty chamber. And still, all of them,

Every

Single

One

They didn't cry.

They didn't rage.

They didn't fight.

They fucking *cheered*.

When a babe is frightened, when the world goes wrong, who does it cry for? Who seems the only one who can make it right again?

Mia shook her head.

Father . . .

Scaeva held up his hand, but it seemed even the maestro couldn't calm the applause now. The people stomped their feet in time, chanted his name like a prayer. Mia stood, bathed in the thunder of it, sick to her bones. Ashlinn reached down, squeezed her hand. Glancing to the deadboy beside her, Mia wasn't certain if she should squeeze it back.

It seemed an age before the mob stilled enough for Scaeva to speak again.

"Know I do not take this responsibility lightly," he finally shouted. "From now until truedark, when I am certain our friends in the Senate will ratify my new position, my people, I will be your shield. I will be your sword. I will be the stone upon which we may rebuild our peace, reclaim that which was taken from us, and reforge our Republic so that it shall be stronger, greater, and more glorious than ever it was before!"

Scaeva managed a smile at the elated response, though he seemed now to be wilting. His wife whispered in his ear and he pawed his bloody shoulder, nodded slow. A centurion of the Luminatii stepped forward, began to usher him and his wife away under guard. But with one final show of strength, Scaeva turned back to the mob.

"Hear me now!"

A hush fell at his cry, deep and still as the Abyss itself.

"Hear me!" he called. "And know it true! For I speak to you now. *You*."

Mia swallowed hard, her jaw clenched and aching.

"Wherever you may be, whatever shadow has fallen over your heart, whatever darkness you may find yourself in . . ."

Mia noted the emphasis on "shadow" and "darkness." The fervor in Scaeva's voice. And though they stood hundreds of feet apart, with a hundred thousand or more between them, for a second, she felt as if they were the only two people in the world.

"I am your father," Scaeva declared. "I always have been."

He held out his hand as the crowd raised theirs.

"And together? Nothing can stop us."

CHAPTER 7

BE

The flash of a gravebone sword.

A bubbling gasp.

A spatter of red.

Another guard sank to his knees and Mia

Stepped

across

the hallway

to the second man, his eyes going wide as he saw his comrade fall. Her gravebone sword cut through muscle and bone like mist. His muscles slackened, his bladder loosed, piss and blood pooling on the polished stone floor as he sank to his knees and from there, to his end.

Mia dragged the bodies to an antechamber and crouched in the shadows, curtains of long dark hair draped about her face. Listening for footfalls. The forum outside was still awash with sound, people uncertain whether to celebrate Scaeva's speech or mourn their slain cardinal. Godsgrave was in the grip of a guilty elation, breathing easier after salvation had been snatched from calamity. Their father had defied death. Escaped the assassin's blade.

Who could now deny he was the chosen of Aa? Who better to claim the title of imperator and lead the Republic through the dangers it now faced?

Mia stole through the gravebone halls, silent and swift. She Stepped between the shadows as easily as another girl might have skipped from one puddle to another in the falling rain. It was a gift she'd practiced for years; though it seemed much simpler since Furian had died by her hand. She recalled her brother using the shadows to blind her in the necropolis, musing idly if she might learn to do the same. She wondered how much truth lay in Tric's tale of splinters of shattered god inside her. What other gifts she might discover inside herself, if she embraced them and what she was.

The walls about her were hung with beautiful tapestries, lined with statues of solid marble, lit by chandeliers of singing Dweymeri crystal. She could hear music somewhere distant—strings and a harpsichord, a touch of somberness in the shadow of the cardinal's death. The gravebone longblade in her hand was a comforting weight, the stink of blood in her nostrils a sweet perfume, the wolf made of shadows a soothing growl in her ear.

"*. . . TWO MORE AHEAD . . .*"

They fell as the last two had done, the shadows rippling, the girl coalescing out of nothingness, as if coming into focus before their wondering eyes. The men were Luminatii, gravebone armor and blood-red cloaks and feathered plumes upon their heads. The helms did wonders to smother what little sound they made as they died, and their cloaks a fine job of mopping up the mess afterward.

Her heart was hammering despite the daemon in her shadow. Her thoughts drifting to Ashlinn, Tric, Jonnen. She'd asked the former to guard the latter, watch him as if her life depended on it. *"I'm not a fucking nursemaid,"* had come the protest, and there was more waiting in the wings. But Mia's kiss had quickly silenced them all.

"Please," was all she'd said. "For me."

And that had been enough for now.

How much longer, she wasn't entirely sure.

"I'll be of no use in this," Tric had told her. "The light is too bright."

"You made short work of those soldiers in the necropolis," she'd pointed out. "Truelight or no."

"The walls between this world and the Mother's realm are thinner in the houses of the dead. And it's through Niah's will I walk this earth, no other's. I'll grow stronger the nearer we draw to truedark. But here and now . . ."

He'd looked about them, shaken his head.

"Besides, this is a foolish plan, Pale Daughter."

She'd wanted to give him a quip in reply, but hearing him call her by that name had made her chest ache instead. She'd looked at him, black hands hidden in his sleeves, black eyes hidden beneath his hood. His beautiful alabaster face, framed all in darkness. Wondering what might have been, then choking those wonderings dead.

"Please don't do this," Ash had begged.

"I have to," she'd replied. "He almost never makes public appearances anymore. That's why we struck at him during the *magni,* remember? I have to take him now before he goes to ground again."

"You're presuming that was *him* at all," Ash had protested. "Scaeva could have a dozen doubles for all we know. He's been in league with the Red Church for years. Who's to say he's still in the city? Or if he is, who's to say he's not baiting you?"

"He probably is," Mia said.

"Then what's to stop him from killing you?" Ash demanded.

"Solis and Hush both used blades poisoned with Rictus. They want me alive." Mia glanced at her brother. "Because I have something he wants, too."

"Mia, please . . ."

"Mister Kindly, stay here with Jonnen. Keep him calm."

". . . o, joyousness . . ."

"Eclipse, with me."

". . . AS IT PLEASE YOU . . ."

"You must let the past die, Mia," Tric warned.

She'd looked him in the eye then. Her voice hard and cold.

"Sometimes the past won't just die. Sometimes you have to kill it."

And she was gone.

Slipping through the forum until it grew too crowded, the soldiers too thick. Then on beneath her mantle of shadows, the world blurred shapeless, the suns blazing overhead as Eclipse guided her steps. She moved slow as she needed, quick as she dared, into the looming shadow of the first Rib. Over the wrought-iron fence, past the dozens of Luminatii posted around a heavy set of polished gravebone doors, into the consul's private apartments beyond. She had vague recollections of this place from the ball she'd attended as a child, whisked around that glittering ballroom on her father's . . .

. . . no, not her father.

O, Mother, how could you?

She stalked the shadows like a wolf on the scent of fresh blood, Eclipse scouting ahead, just a black shape on the walls. Dodging slaves and serving staff and soldiers, only a breeze on the backs of their necks, a shiver down their spines as she passed them over. All of Mercurio's and Mouser's lessons ringing in her head, her muscles taut, her blade poised, not a single movement wasted, not a whisper to her steps. Her old teacher would have swelled with pride to see her. All of it, the lectures, the practice, the pain—she could feel all of it perfectly distilled in her veins. Every choice she'd made had brought her to this moment. Every road she'd walked had led her inexorably here. Where it was always going to end.

Eclipse's whispers finally led them to a grand study. A vast oaken desk was set at the room's far end, bookshelves lining the wall, overflowing with tomes and scrolls. The floor was carved with a shallow relief and stained by some work of arkemy—a rumored hobby of Scaeva's, and one he apparently excelled at. It was a great map of the entire Republic, from the Sea of Silence to the Sea of Stars.

Mia's heart was pounding *thumpathump* against her ribs as she tossed aside her shadow mantle. Hair stuck to the sweat and dried blood on her skin. Muscles aching, wounds burning, adrenaline and rage battling exhaustion and sorrow.

And there, near the balcony, he stood.

Staring out into the dazzling sunslight as if nothing in the world were amiss.

He was just a silhouette against the glare as she stole across the room toward him, her mouth dry as dirt, her grip on her sword damp with sweat. Despite the passenger in her shadow, she'd feared he might've already been gone, that Ashlinn's words might've proved true, that the man who spoke to the adoring mob might've been just another actor wearing his face.

But as soon as she drew close, she knew.

A cool sickness in the pit of her belly. A slow horror that gave way to a sinking feeling of inevitability. The final pieces in the riddle of her life, who she was, what she was, why she was, at last clicking into place.

That feeling . . .

That O, so familiar feeling.

Mister Kindly materialized on the floor of the Philosopher's Stone beside her, his whisper cutting in the gloom. The dona Corvere took one look at the shadowcat and hissed like she'd been burned. Shrinking back from the bars of her cell, into the far corner, teeth bared in a snarl.

"He's in you," the dona had whispered. "O, Daughters, he's in *you."*

"Hello, Mia," Scaeva said.

He didn't turn to look at her. Eyes still fixed on the sunslight outside. He'd changed from his torn and bloodied costume into a long toga of pristine white. Shadow on the wall. Fingers entwined behind his back. Defenseless.

But not alone.

She saw his shadow move. Shivering as the sickness and hunger inside her swelled to bursting. And from the smudge of darkness across the study wall—dark enough for two—Mia heard a faint and deadly hiss.

A ribbon of blackness uncurled from under the imperator's feet. Slithering across the floor and rising up, thin as paper, licking the air with its not-tongue.

A serpent made of shadows.

"*. . . She has your eyes, Julius . . . ,*" it said.

The rage flared then, bright as those three suns in the cursed heavens outside. The blood in her veins, the blood that they shared, set to boiling. She didn't care in that moment, not about any of it. Mercurio or Jonnen. Ashlinn or Tric. The Red Church and the Black Mother and the poor, broken Moon. She'd have opened her wrists for the chance to drown him in her blood right then. She'd have smashed herself to pieces just to cut his throat upon the shards.

She didn't realize she was running until she was almost upon him, her blade raised high, her lips peeled back, eyes narrowed.

The serpent hissed warning.

Pulse rushing in her ears.

And, turning toward her, Julius Scaeva held up his hand.

A flash of light. A stab of pain. A blinding flare like a punch to her face, sending her sprawling backward, yowling like a scalded cat. A golden chain hung between Scaeva's fingers, and at the end of it dangled three brilliant suns—platinum, rose, and yellow gold. The Trinity of Aa, repeated on every chapel spire and church window from here to Ashkah. But this one had been blessed by a servant of *true* faith.

Eclipse whimpered, the serpent at Scaeva's feet twisted and writhed in agony. Mia was on her back, fingernails clawing the graven floor as Scaeva raised the sigil into the few feet and thousand miles between them. The light was white fire and rusty blades, lancing into the cool dark behind her eyes. Her belly roiled and her vision burned and her mouth filled with bile, that blinding, blistering, burning light reducing her to a ball of helpless agony.

"It's g-good to see you, daughter," Scaeva said.

How?

Beyond the pain, she could still feel it—the same longing she'd felt in the presence of every other like her. Scaeva was darkin, she was sure of it. But that Trinity, Black Mother, those three spheres of incandescent flame . . .

"H-How?" she managed.

"How d-do I . . . endure it?"

Julius Scaeva's voice trembled as he spoke, and through her own tears, Mia could see them welling in his eyes also. But still, the imperator of the Itreyan Republic held those awful suns up between them. His hand was shaking. His passenger coiling into knots of agony at his feet. Faint wisps of smoke snaked from between his fingers.

But still, he held on.

"The same way I just laid c-claim to a throne." Scaeva twisted the Trinity this way and that, veins standing taut in his neck, hissing through gritted teeth. "A matter of will, daughter m-mine. To claim true power, you need not soldiers . . . n-nor senators, nor servants of the holy. All you need is the *will* to do what others will n-not."

The nausea swelled in her throat, the pain of the Everseeing's flame almost blinding. But still, Mia managed to reply, her voice dripping hatred.

"I'm n-not . . . your f-fucking daughter."

Scaeva tilted his head, looked at her with something close to pity.

"O, Mia . . ."

He knelt in front of her, bringing the Trinity ever closer. Mia scrambled farther away, scuttling backward on arse and elbows like some crippled crab. Pressed back against the wall, she found herself gasping for breath, tears streaming unchecked down her scarred cheeks, hand raised against the conflagration of those three blessed circles. She could see tendons corded in Scaeva's arm, sweat glistening on his shaking fist, dripping onto the polished gravebone floor between them.

But still, he held on.

"M-May I put this away?" he asked. "Do you think . . . we have it in us to s-speak like civilized people? For a . . . m-moment at least?"

Fire inside her skull. Hatred like acid in her veins. But ever so slowly, pain-wracked and sickened, Mia nodded.

Scaeva stood at once, slipped the Trinity back out of sight in his robes. The relief was immediate, dizzying, a sob slipping up and over her lips. As Mia struggled to catch her breath, Scaeva walked away across the room, leather sandals whispering on the vast map carved into the floor. With shaking hands, he filled a small glass of water from a singing crystal carafe.

"May I offer you a drink?" he asked, his voice once more smooth and sweet as toffee. "Goldwine is your favorite poison, neh?"

Mia said nothing, glaring at Scaeva as her pulse slowed to a gallop. Watching him like a bloodhawk. Mercurio had always taught her to study her prey. And though she'd dreamed about Julius Scaeva almost every nevernight for the past eight years, this was the first time she'd seen him up close since she was ten.

The imperator was handsome, she had to admit—almost painfully so. Black curls dusted with the faintest hints of gray at his temples. Shoulders broad, bronze skin contrasting sharply with the snow-white of his robes. A wisdom earned from decades in the halls of power glittering in dark eyes.

Mercurio had taught her to sum folk up in a blinking, and Mia had ever been an apt pupil. But looking Scaeva over—this man who'd bent the Itreyan Senate to his will, who'd carved himself a kingdom in a Republic that murdered its kings centuries ago—she found herself blank. Almost all about him beyond the superficial was hidden. He was a killer. A cold-blooded bastard. But beyond that . . . he was an enigma.

With the Trinity gone, Eclipse retreated from the shelter of Mia's shadow, rippling with indignity. Scaeva's own passenger slipped free and slithered across the floor, watching the not-wolf with something close to hunger. Mia could see the imperator's shadow was moving on the wall, its robes rippling, its hands reaching out toward hers, gentle as lambs.

"Well." Scaeva turned to face her, sipping from his crystal glass. "Reunited at last. This is all rather exciting, neh?"

"Not as exciting as it's g-going to be," she said, chest still heaving.

"It *is* good to see you, Mia. You've grown into quite an astonishing young lady."

"Go fuck yourself, you unspeakable cunt."

Scaeva smiled faintly. "An astonishing young woman, then."

He poured a splash of top-shelf goldwine into a singing crystal tumbler. Padding softly toward her, he placed the glass on the floor a good safe distance away, then retired to the other side of the study. She saw a square table there, low to the ground, flanked by two divan lounges. A chessboard was embossed into the table's surface, a game in full swing. Even at a glance she could tell the white side was winning.

"Do you play?" Scaeva asked, eyebrow raised toward her. "My opponent was our good friend Cardinal Duomo. We sent runners back and forth with our moves—he didn't trust me enough to meet face-to-face in the end." The imperator motioned to the board, the golden rings on his fingers glinting. "He was close to winning this one. Poor Francesco was always better at chess than the true game."

Scaeva chuckled to himself, which served only to inflame the rage in Mia's breast. She had no knives, nothing to throw, but she still clutched her gravebone sword. Her mind was awash with all the ways she might bury it in his chest. Unperturbed, Scaeva took a seat near the chessboard, resting his glass upon the divan's crushed-velvet arm. Reaching into his robe, he pulled out a familiar gravebone dagger, a crow carved on the hilt—the dagger she'd murdered his double with just hours before. It was still bloodstained, its amber eyes sparkling as he placed it upon the table.

"What can I do for you, Mia?"

"You can die for me," she replied.

"You still wish me dead?" The imperator raised one dark eyebrow. "What in the Everseeing's name for?"

"Is this a jest?" she scoffed. "You killed my *father*!"

Scaeva looked at her with pity. "My love, Darius Corvere was—"

"He raised me!" she snapped. "I may not have been daughter of his blood, but he loved me all the same! And you murdered him!"

"Of course I did," Scaeva frowned. "He tried to destroy the Republic."

"You hypocritical shitstain, what the 'byss did you just do in the forum?"

"I *succeeded* at destroying the Republic."

Scaeva looked her in the eye with genuine amusement.

"Mia, if Darius Corvere's rebellion had triumphed, his beloved General Antonius would now be king of Itreya. The Senate House would be a ruin and the constitution in ashes. And I don't blame the man for trying. Darius gave his best. The only difference between he and I is that *his* best wasn't good enough to win the game."

Mia hauled herself to her feet, fingernails cutting into her palms. On the wall, her shadow seethed and flared, reaching toward Scaeva's, hands twisting to claws.

"This isn't a *game,* bastard."

"Of course it is," Scaeva scowled, glancing at the chessboard. "And the rules are simple: win the crown or lose your head. Darius understood the price of failure full well, and still he chose to play. So please, before you speak again of how much he *loved you,* consider he was willing to risk your life for the sake of his lover's throne."

"He was a good man," she said. "He did what he thought was right."

"As do I. As do most men, all things considered. But where Darius was set to take Antonius's throne by marching an army on his own capital, I took it with simple words . . ." He gave a small shrug. ". . . Well, perhaps a murder or three. But you cannot seriously consider me a tyrant and Darius Corvere a paragon when he was prepared to slaughter thousands and I killed only a handful. I raised you better than that."

Mia's breath was trembling in her chest.

"You never raised me! You ordered me drowned in a fucking canal!"

"And witness what you became." Scaeva breathed the words like a spell, looking her over with a kind of wonder. "When last we met, you were a snot-nosed marrowborn whelp. You had servants and pretty dresses and all you ever wanted handed to you on silver platters. Have you considered for a moment what your life would have been without me?"

Scaeva picked up the black king, moved it across the board, and knocked the white king on its side.

"Think on it a moment, Mia," he said. "Pretend that Antonius claimed his throne. That Darius stood at his right hand. And watered with the blood of a thousand innocents, all their dreams flowered to reality instead of turning to ashes on the wind."

Scaeva picked up a black pawn, held it out upon his palm.

"What would have become of you?"

The imperator let the question hang unanswered a moment. A maestro before the crescendo.

"You'd have been married off to some marrowborn fool for the sake of political alliance," he finally said. "Squeezing out pups, tending the home fires, and feeling the fire inside your own breast slowly die. Naught but a cow in a silken dress." He held the pawn up between his fingers, turned it this way and that. "Because of me, you are solid steel. A blade sharp enough to cut the sunslight in six. And still you find it within yourself to hate me."

Scaeva gave a soft, bitter chuckle as he looked her in the eye.

"All you are? All you have become? *I* gave you. Mine is the seed that planted you. Mine are the hands that forged you. Mine is the blood that flows, cold as ice and black as pitch, in those veins of yours."

He leaned back on the divan, black eyes burning into her own.

"In every possible sense, you are *my* daughter."

Julius Scaeva extended his hand, gold glinting upon his fingers. Upon the wall, his shadow did the same.

"Join me."

Mia's laughter bubbled in her throat, threatening to choke her.

"Are you fucking mad?"

"Some might say," Scaeva replied. "But what possible reason do you have left to want me dead? I killed a man who claimed to be your father. But he was a liar, Mia. A would-be usurper. A man perfectly willing to risk his familia for the sake of his own failed ambition. I killed your mother, aye. Another deceiver. Willing to share my bed and cut my throat before the sweat had even cooled. Alinne Corvere knew the stakes she wagered supporting . . . nay, *encouraging* Darius's gambit. Her life. Her son's. And yours besides. And she weighed them all lighter than a throne."

The shadowviper slithered across the ground toward Mia, licking the air. Scaeva spun the gravebone stiletto upon the table, his eyes boring into hers.

"I have never lied to you, daughter," he said. "Not once, throughout it all. When I ordered you drowned, you were worthless to me. Jonnen was young enough to claim as my own. You were too old. But now you've proved yourself my daughter true. Possessed of the same will as I: not only to survive, but to *prosper*. To carve your name with bloody fingernails into this earth. Darius sought to become a kingmaker? You can truly *be* one. The blade in my right hand. Whatever you desire will be yours. Wealth. Power. Pleasure. I can do away with those gold-grubbing whores in the Red Church and have you at my side instead. My daughter. My *blood*. As dark and beautiful and deadly as the night. And together, we can sculpt a dynasty that will live for a thousand years."

On the wall, his shadow reached out farther toward her own.

"You and your brother are my legacy to this world," he said. "When I am gone, all this can be yours. Our name will be eternal. Immortal. So aye. I ask you to join me."

Scaeva's words rang in the hollow spaces in her head, heavy with truth. Her shadow hung like a crooked portrait upon the wall. But though Mia herself remained perfectly still, slowly,

ever so slowly,

it raised one dark hand toward his.

All her life, she'd thought of her parents as flawless. Godlike. Her mother, sharp and wise and beautiful as the finest rapier of Liisian steel. Her father, brave and noble and bright as the suns. Even as she'd learned more about who they were from Sidonius in the cells beneath Crow's Nest, it never seemed to dim their reflection in her mind's eye. It hurt too much to admit they might be imperfect. Selfish. Driven by greed or lust or pride and willing to risk everything for the sake of it. And so she kept them unstained. Untarnished. Locked in a box forever inside her head.

Father is another name for God in a child's eyes.

And Mother is the very earth beneath her feet.

But now, Mia remembered that turn in the forum—the turn Darius Corvere was hanged. A girl of ten, standing with her mother above the mob, looking down on that horrid scaffold, the line of nooses swinging in the wintersdeep wind. She could still feel the rain upon her face and Alinne's arm across her breast, another hand at her neck, holding her pinned so she must look outward as they tied the noose around the Kingmaker's neck. The words Alinne Corvere whispered ringing in Mia's ears now as clear as the turn she'd first uttered them.

"Never flinch. Never fear. And never, ever *forget."*

Alinne must have known what she was making. Knew the seeds of hatred she was planting in her daughter. The vengeance that must grow from it. The blood that must flow. And all over the death of a man who—though he may well have loved her—wasn't Mia's father at all. And if she must be furious—and O, Goddess, she *was*—at Scaeva's claim that he'd made her all she was, how could she be less angry at the woman who'd stood behind her there on that windblown parapet? Forcing her to watch? Speaking the words that had shaped her, ruled her, ruined her?

Could she still love a woman like that?

And if not, could she hate the man who'd killed her?

Why *did* she hate Julius Scaeva? When all she'd based her life on was a lie? Was he so different from Alinne and Darius Corvere, save in that he'd emerged the victor? He was a killer, remorseless and cold, that much was certain. A man who'd drenched himself in the blood of dozens, perhaps hundreds, to get his way.

But wasn't that true of everyone who played this game?

Even me?

Eclipse's hackles rippled as Scaeva's serpent slithered closer. The shadowwolf's growl dragged Mia out of the darkness within, back into the burning light in that study, glinting on the black pawn in Scaeva's upturned palm.

"... STAY BACK ...," Eclipse warned.

"... *Nothing to fear, pup* ...," the serpent hissed in reply.

"... STAY BACK ..."

Eclipse took a swipe at the shadowviper with her paw, and Mia's eyes widened as she saw a fine mist of black spatter on the floor, evaporate to nothingness. The serpent reared back, hissing in cold fury.

"... *You will regret that insult, little dog* ..."

"... I DO NOT FEAR YOU, WORM ..."

The shadowviper opened its black maw, hissing again.

"Whisper," Scaeva said. "Enough."

The serpent hissed again, but held still.

"Mia means us no harm," Scaeva said, staring at his daughter. "She's intelligent enough to know where she stands. And pragmatic enough to realize that, if anything unpleasant *were* to happen to us, her dear Old Mercurio would be treated to the most gruesome of tortures before he was sent to meet his dear dark Goddess."

Mia's stomach rolled at the threat against Mercurio, but she tried to keep her face like stone. The serpent turned to regard her darkin counterpart, swaying as if to music only it could hear.

"*. . . She fears, Julius . . .*"

Scaeva gifted Mia a smile that never reached his eyes.

"So. Itreya's most infamous murderer *is* capable of love. How touching."

Mia bristled at that. Felt a soft ripple in the air, glanced toward their shadows on the wall. Where once Scaeva's had reached out as if to embrace her own, it was now poised, crook-backed and claw-fingered. Reaching toward her own shadow's throat.

"Where is your brother, Mia?"

"Safe," she replied.

Scaeva stood slowly, hand drifting to the Trinity hidden at his throat.

"You will bring him to me."

"I take no orders from you."

"You will bring him to me, or your mentor dies."

Mia's voice turned soft with menace. "If you hurt Mercurio, I swear by the Goddess you will *never* see your son again."

She saw fury boiling in his eyes then. A fury born of fear. Even with all his control, his much-vaunted will, Scaeva still couldn't quite keep it from her. She could sense it on him, sure as she could sense the suns above.

Her mind was working. Probing at the cracks in his facade, the tiny glimpses he'd given her behind his mask. He'd spoken of building a dynasty that would last a thousand years. And granted, that would be hard to do without his only son. But still, he was imperator now. He could cast off his barren wife, have any woman he wanted. Black Mother, he could take a dozen wives. Sire a hundred sons.

So why is he afraid?

Mia tossed her hair over her shoulder, glancing again at the silhouettes on the wall. Scaeva's shadow was moving now, its motion violent and sudden. Her own was responding in kind, elongating, distorting, dark shapes unfurling at its back.

"You seem awfully concerned about Jonnen, Father," she said. "And I can't bring myself to believe it's out of sentimentality. Could it be your dear wife Liviana isn't the one who can't have any more children?"

Dark eyes glanced below his waist.

"Getting soft in your old age?"

Scaeva took a step toward her, hand snaking beneath his robes. In a flash, their shadows struck each other, tangled and twisting and curling like smoke. Twice as dark as they should have been alone. Scaeva's serpent reared up as if to strike, and Eclipse bared her fangs with a black growl. Mia felt her clothes and hair moving, as if a breeze were blowing behind her. As if the world were moving beneath her feet.

"You cannot know the stakes you toy with," Scaeva said. "Do not make yourself my enemy, Mia. Not when I offer you peace. All who have stood against me now rot in the ground. *All* of them. Bring me your brother, and take your place at my side."

"You *are* afraid," she realized.

"Fear has its uses," he replied. "Fear is what keeps the dark from devouring you. Fear is what stops you joining a game you cannot *hope* to win."

He tossed the pawn toward her, and she caught it in her fist.

"If you start down this road, daughter mine, you are going to die."

She knew she couldn't touch him. Couldn't even get close. Not with that Trinity about his throat. Not with Mercurio's neck on the block. She could hear tromping feet, soft shouts in the distance—she guessed someone had found the bodies in her wake.

No more time to chat.

And so, she began to back away from him.

A single step. Then another. Farther and farther from the throat she'd sought for almost eight years. Their shadows were still entwined on the wall, strangling and seething, a knot of black rage. With effort, Mia dragged her shade back, Scaeva's clinging on.

"Bring me my son, Mia," he said, his voice soft and deadly.

She tore her shadow free, the dark about her shivering.

"I'll consider it," she said. "Father."

A rippling in the darkness.

The whispered song of running feet.

And she was gone.

He stood there for long moments afterward, still as stone and just as silent. The shadowserpent wove its way across the vast map of the Republic he now ruled, coiled in a black ribbon about his ankles.

"*. . . Do you think she will listen . . . ?*" Whisper asked.

The imperator looked to the burning light outside.

"I think she is as much her mother's daughter as mine," he replied.

The serpent sighed. "*. . . A pity . . .*"

Scaeva walked to the chessboard. He stood above the frozen battleground, the pieces arrayed in fractured rows, looking down with those cool black eyes. In one swift motion, he sat, sweeping aside the pieces with his hand. Reaching to his throat, he grasped a leather thong, snapped it free. A silver phial hung upon it, stoppered with dark wax and engraved with runes in the tongue of Old Ashkah.

Scaeva broke the seal, pouring the contents upon the board, thick and ruby red.

And, using his fingertip like a brush, he began writing in the blood.

CHAPTER 8

SCOUNDREL

If the entry under "scoundrel" in Don Fiorlini's bestselling *Itreyan Diction: The Definitive Guide* had an illustration, it probably would have looked a lot like Cloud Corleone.* But Cloud himself preferred the term "entrepreneur."

The Liisian was clad all in black: a leather vest over a finely cut shirt (unlaced perhaps a touch too far) and a pair of what could only be described as conspicuously tight pants. Emerald-green eyes gleamed beneath the brim of his feathered tricorn hat, and a perpetual three-turn growth of beard dusted a jaw you could break a shovel on. He was stood in the harbormaster's office in the Nethers docks. And he was haggling with a nun.

It had been a strange turn all told, really. It had begun eight hours earlier, when Cloud had placed a sizable and very drunken wager on the outcome of the *Venatus Magni*. In hindsight, the bet proved a less-than-sound investment of his meager funds.

O, he'd picked the winner, all right. Even the bookman who took the bet

* It did not. All plans for an illustrated second edition of *The Definitive Guide* were scrapped after Fiorlini's wife absconded with the profits from the first edition, along with their Liisian houseboy, Lorenzo, and their dog, Teacakes.

had told him he was thinking with his cock, but watching the gladiatii known as the Crow slice her former collegium mates to bloody chunks, Cloud had found himself admiring her form along with her legs. So confident had he been of the lass's abilities, he'd wagered every coin he'd won over the previous five turns of bloodsport on her victory, along with a bunch more coin he truthfully couldn't spare.

As the Crow had carved her way toward triumph in the final match, Cloud had been on his feet, hollering and howling with the rest of the mob. When she'd struck the final blow against the Unfallen, Cloud had danced a jig on the spot, grabbed the nearest comely lass and planted a kiss square on her lips (returned rather enthusiastically), which resulted in an all-in brawl with the lass's sweetheart, a dozen of his friends, half of Cloud's crew, and a hundred other punters who simply wanted a good dose of fisticuffs after a hard turn's carnage. Truthfully, it'd been absolutely marvelous.

But then along came the first dose of the unexpected.

He'd watched it happen in slow motion. The Crow drawing her hidden blade on the victor's plinth. Slicing the cardinal's throat clean through. Stabbing the consul in the chest (or so he and half the crowd had imagined, anyway). Blood flowing like cheap plonk at a Liisian wedding. And even though the rest of the crowd fell to wailing, baying, panicking, watching that greasy fucker Duomo go down in a puddle of his own shit and blood, Cloud Corleone had found himself cheering at the top of his lungs.

The next dose of the unexpected had arrived in short order.

It'd taken Cloud almost an hour to shove his way to the bookman's pits to collect his winnings, still riding high on the sight of the cardinal's messy end. It was there that the scoundrel was informed by a scowling pack of Itreyan legionaries that because a *slave* had just topped the fanciest bastards in the whole bloody Republic, all bets were null and void. It wouldn't do, you see, to profit from the death of the consul and grand cardinal at the hands of human property.

Cloud was tempted to inform the soldiers exactly what flavor of bastard the good cardinal actually was in life, but looking into their eyes, listening to the budding chaos in the city around him, he decided making a fuss would only make for further fuss. And so, with a flip of the knuckles toward the bookman's shit-eating grin, the captain and his crew headed back to the harbor with tragically empty pockets.

With all the fistfights and fuckarsery and Scaeva's announcement of his miraculous escape from the assassin's blade in the forum (Cloud could've sworn she'd stabbed him clean), it took another three hours to make it back to the *Bloody Maid*. And now, in the office of one Attilius Persius, harbormaster of Godsgrave*, the final oddity in Cloud's eventful turn had arrived in the form of the aforementioned Sister of Tsana.

Cloud had been putting the last touches on the *Bloody Maid*'s paperwork and giving Attilius a friendly heaping of shit (his wife had recently given birth to their *sixth* daughter, poor fucker) when the nun had marched into the office, shoved Cloud aside, and slapped a hefty bag of coin down on the countertop.

"I need passage to Ashkah. Swift, if it please you."

She couldn't have been more than eighteen, but she looked a few years harder. Dressed all in snow white, a coif of starched cloth and voluminous robes that flowed to the floor. Her cool blue eyes were fixed on the harbormaster, her lips pressed thin. She was Vaanian, tall and fit, what appeared to be blond hair dyed with henna peeking from the edge of her coif. Cloud idly wondered if her carpet matched her curtains.

In the doorway behind her stood a hulking fellow shrouded in dark cloth. A Trinity of Aa (of rather middling quality, Cloud thought) was strung around his neck, several suspiciously sword-shaped bulges were hidden under his robes.

Cloud shivered a little. The office seemed to have gotten cold all of a sudden.

The sister raised an expectant eyebrow at the harbormaster.

"Mi Don?"

Attilius simply stared, his stubbled jowls all awobble. "Apologies, Sister. I

---

*The harbormaster of Godsgrave is one of the most powerful titles in the entire city. Many years back, the role was appointed by the city's administratii, but the profits generated by controlling what comes in and out of the 'Grave by sea didn't escape the notice of the local braavi—the thieves, extortionists, and thugs that constitute Godsgrave's organized criminal element.

Murder was rife, and harbormasters were dropping faster than a groom's pantaloons on his wedding eve. It was Julius Scaeva who suggested the gangs themselves be allowed to appoint the role—a stroke of political genius that earned him favor with the city's merchants (who just wanted their bloody shipments to arrive on time), the braavi (who were getting rather tired of having to neck a new harbormaster every few weeks), and the administratii (who were, by that stage, having trouble finding anyone fucking stupid enough to take the job).

After discussion among the gangs, the new harbormaster was appointed, the murders stopped, and everyone settled back to the business of making barrowloads of money—including Julius Scaeva, who had, in a further stroke of genius, decided the harbormaster's office should pay a one percent tithe of all profits to the consul's chair.

You have to admire the bastard's testicles, don't you?

just . . . It's not often one sees a Sister of the Sorority of Flame outside a convent, let alone in a district as rough as the Nethers."*

"Ashkah," she repeated, clanking her coin. "This eve, if possible."

"We're headed that way," Cloud said, leaning against the counter. "Stormwatch first, then Whitekeep. But after that, through the Sea of Swords and on to Ashkah."

The nun turned to regard him carefully. "Is your ship a swift one?"

"Swifter than my heart beats looking into those pretty eyes of yours, Sister."

The nun rolled the aforementioned eyes and drummed her fingers on the countertop. "You're trying to be charming, I assume."

"Trying and failing, apparently."

"How much for our passage?" she asked.

"'Our' passage?" Cloud glanced at her hulking companion. "I didn't know it was habit for Sisters of the Virgin Flame to travel in the company of men?"

"Not that it is any of your concern," the sister replied coolly, "but Brother Tric is here to ensure nothing ill befalls me on my travels. As the murder of our beloved Grand Cardinal Duomo illustrates, Aa bless and keep him, these are dangerous times."

"O, aye," Cloud nodded. "Terrible shame about good Duomo. Cleaves the heart, it does. But you're safe aboard the *Bloody Maid,* Sister, you've no fear of that."

"No." She gave a meaningful glance to her thug. "I don't."

'Byss and blood it's cold in here . . .

"How much for passage, good sir?" she asked again.

"To Ashkah?" Cloud asked. "Three hundred priests ought to suffice."

In the background, the harbormaster almost choked on his goldwine.

"That seems . . . excessive," the sister said.

"You seem . . . desperate," Cloud grinned in reply.

The nun glanced at the big fellow behind her. Pressed her lips thinner.

---

*The Sorority of Flame is an offshoot of Aa's ministry, venerating Tsana, the Lady of Flame. Consisting entirely of women, those of the order take vows of chastity, humility, poverty, and sobriety, and generally spend their lives in chaste contemplation inside walled temples.

It should be noted however, that in addition to being a patron of women, Lady Tsana is also patron to warriors, and that along with arts such as illumination, herbalism, and midwifery, sisters of the sorority are schooled in the arts of bow, shield, and sword.

It's not only for reasons of chastity that the sisterhood is not to be fucked with, gentlefriends.

"I can give you two hundred now. Two hundred more when we reach Ashkah."

With a smile that had earned him four confirmed bastards and Daughters knew how many more besides, Cloud Corleone tipped his tricorn hat and extended his hand to the sister.

"Done."

A bigger hand engulfed his. It was stained black with what must've been ink, and it belonged to the large fellow. His grip was hard enough that Cloud could hear his knuckles grinding together. And it was cold as tombs.

"DONE," the fellow said, in a strange, oceans-deep voice.

The captain pulled his hand free, flexed his fingers open and closed.

"What name should I call you by, Sister?"

"Ashlinn," she replied.

"And you, Brother?" He glanced at the big bastard. "Tric, I heard?"

The fellow simply nodded, features hidden in the shadows of his hood.

"You have baggage?" Cloud asked. "I'll have my salts load—"

"We have all we need, Captain, thank you," the sister replied.

"Well," he said simply, snatching up the laden purse. "Best follow me, then."

He led the pair out of Attilius's office, down the crowded boardwalk, feeling the jitters in the air. He could see at least twenty other ships making ready to put out to the blue, the calls and cries of their crews echoing across the harbor. The whole city was of a mood after Scaeva's announcement—overjoyed the new imperator had taken control of the situation, but dismayed at the cardinal's murder. Cloud was glad to be leaving the city for a spell.

They arrived at the *Bloody Maid,* rocking at her berth, the deep waters of the Nethers harbor a muddy brown beneath the Everseeing's three burning eyes. The ship was a swift-cut three-masted carrack, keeled oak but planked cedar, her skin stained a warm reddish brown. Her figurehead was a beautiful naked woman with long red hair artfully arranged to preserve her modesty—or cover the most interesting parts, depending how you looked at it. Her trim and sails were blood-red, hence her name, and though he'd owned her more than seven years, the sight of her always took Cloud's breath away. Truth told, he'd lost count of the women he'd known in his life. But he'd never loved a one of them close to the way he loved his *Maid*.

"Ahoy, mates," he said as he climbed the gangplank.

"You've got a nun," BigJon said cheerfully.

"Well spotted," Cloud told his first mate.

"That's a novelty."

"First time for everything," Cloud replied.

BigJon was a littleman. Everyone in Nethers Harbor knew it. He wasn't a dwarf—he'd made that clear to the last fool who'd named him so by bashing the man's skull in with a brick. He wasn't a midget either, fuck no. He'd explained that to a taverna full of sailors as he took to some stupid bastard's crotch with his knife. Nailing the man's severed scrotum to the counter with his blade, BigJon had declared to the entire pub he preferred the term "littleman" and asked if there was anyone present who objected.

Nobody did. And nobody had since.

"Sister Ashlinn," Cloud said. "This is my first mate, BigJon."

"A pleasure." The littleman bowed, showing a row of silver teeth. "Do you leave the costume on during, or—"

"She's not a sweetgirl in a costume. She's a real nun."

". . . O." BigJon clawed at the collar of his sky-blue tunic. "I see."

"I'm taking her down to the cabins. Get us under way."

"Aye, aye, Cap'n!" BigJon spun on his heel and roared in a voice that belied his small frame. "All right, you bobtailed dung-eaters, get moving! Toliver, pull your fist from your shithole and get those fucking barrels stowed! Kael, get your eyes off Andretti's whore pipe and up into the nest before I make you wish your old man plowed your mother's earhole instead . . ."

. . . and so on.

"Apologies, Sister," Cloud said. "He's got a mouth like a sewer, but he's the best mate this side of Old Ashkah."

"I've heard worse, Captain."

He tilted his head. "Have you now?"

The sister simply stared, and the lump of beef behind her loomed a little larger, and so without further ado Cloud escorted them down the stairwell into the *Maid*'s belly. Leading the pair along the tight hallway to the portside stateroom, he opened the door with a flourish and stepped aside.

"Hammocks only, I'm afraid, but there's space aplenty. You can dine with me or alone, as it please you. I've a bath in my cabin also, if you've a need. Arkemical stove. Hot water. Your privacy will be golden, and though I'd not expect it, you get lip from any of my salts, inform myself or BigJon and we'll see it put arights."

"Your 'salts'?"

"My crew," the man smiled. "Apologies, Sister, I've a sailor's tongue. Regardless, the *Bloody Maid* is my home, and you're my guests in it."

"My thanks, Captain," the sister said, easing herself into one of the hammocks.

Cloud Corleone considered the girl carefully. Her shapeless white robes were almost loose enough to hide another nun beneath—sadly designed to leave almost everything to the imagination. Her face was pretty, though, freckled cheeks, bright eyes the color of a cloudless sky. Dragging off her coif, she released long red locks down over her shoulders, creased with a gentle curl. She looked three turns tired and in need of a good meal, but still, you'd not kick her out of bed for farting, holy virgin or no.

But something about her wasn't right.

"May I help you with something, Captain?" she asked, eyebrow cocked.

The privateer stroked his stubble. "I've a bed in my cabin, too, should the hammock grow tiresome."

"Still trying to be charming, I see . . ."

"Well." He gave a bashful schoolboy smile. "I've a thing for women in uniform."

"More out of them than in, I'd wager."

The captain grinned. "We'll be under way momentarily. North to Stormwatch, swift as sparrows, then back to Whitekeep. We'll be there by weeksend, winds be kind."

"Let us pray, then, that they are."

"Any time you want me on my knees, Sister, just say the word."

The big fellow in the corner stirred slightly, adjusting one of those suspiciously sword-shaped lumps, and the captain decided he'd learned enough for now. With a wink that could charm the paint right off the walls, Cloud Corleone tipped his tricorn hat.

"Good nevernight, Sister."

And he closed the cabin door.

Walking up the hallway a moment later, the captain muttered softly to himself.

"Nun my arse."

The balls on that slick bastard," Ashlinn whispered incredulously.

Mister Kindly coalesced above the cabin door.

". . . i wonder where he keeps his wheelbarrow . . . ?"

"I'm dressed as a *nun,*" Ashlinn said, looking about the room in indignation. "He does realize I'm dressed as a *fucking nun,* aye?"

Throwing aside her cloak of shadows, Mia faded into view in the far corner. Jonnen stood with his wrists bound, one of his sister's arms about him, her other hand clapped over his lips. He glared at the Vaanian girl as his sister removed her hand.

"You have a *filthy* mouth, harlot."

"Quiet," Mia warned. "Or it's the gag for you again."

Jonnen pouted but fell silent, his eyes on his sister's back as she crossed the cabin floor. Locking the door, Mia turned and met Ashlinn's eyes.

"I don't trust him."

In the other corner, Tric drew his hood back off his head, thin white plumes spilling from his lips as he spoke. "NOR I."

"Well, that makes three of us," Ash replied. "He might as well have the word 'pirate' stenciled on the arse end of those ridiculous pants. It's a good thing he only gets his second two hundred *after* our arrival in Ashkah."

"I didn't think the funds Mercurio gave us were still so flush."

"They're . . . not," Ash admitted. "But we can burn that bridge when we arrive at it. The *Siren's Song* already left port. This ship is sailing in our direction, and we've got nothing left to barter passage with elsewhere. So we take our chances here, or start marching across the aqueduct on foot and praying for a miracle. And considering we stole this habit of mine off a clothesline at a convent, I'm not too sure any of the divinities will be in a mood to answer nicely."

Mister Kindly began licking a translucent paw on his perch above the door.

". . . this whole endeavor would be made infinitely easier if, o, i don't know, we could somehow make ourselves unseen for the rest of the journey . . ."

Mia scowled up at her passenger. "It's truelight, Mister Kindly. I can barely manage to hide me and Jonnen with those accursed suns in the sky. But my thanks for making me feel shittier about our predicament than I already did."

". . . you are most welcome . . . ," he purred.

Mia turned her eyes to the door the privateer had left by.

"Our captain seems a clever one," she murmured.

"PERHAPS TOO CLEVER," Tric said.

"No such thing, in my experience."

Mia eased herself into one of the hammocks with a groan and a wince. She sat and chewed her lip in thought for a while, fighting a losing battle with her leaden eyelids.

"But Ash is right," she finally declared. "We don't have much left in the way of choice. I say we take our chances on the *Maid*. As long as Jonnen and I stay out of sight, and you can put up with his flirting for a few weeks, I think we're safe here."

". . . i am sure dona järnheim will loathe every minute of the attention . . ."

Ashlinn ignored the shadowcat above the door, looking at Mia with concern. The girl was slouched in her hammock, head hung low, rocking softly with the shush and whisper of the water against the hull. Mia looked about to fall over from sheer exhaustion. They could hear the *Maid*'s crew overhead, BigJon's rainbow-colored bouts of profanity, the song of sails being unfurled, the smell of salt and sea strung in the air.

Jonnen was still standing in the corner, Eclipse in his shadow.

"Did you hurt him, Kingmaker?" he asked softly.

Mia met her brother's dark eyes, the shadow of Julius Scaeva hanging in the air between them. It was long moments before she answered.

"No."

"I want to go home," the boy said.

"And I want a box of cigarillos and a bottle of goldwine big enough to drown in," Mia sighed. "We don't always get what we want."

"*I* do," he scowled.

"Not anymore." Mia ran her fingers across her eyes and stifled a yawn. "Welcome to the real world, little brother."

Jonnen simply glared back at her. Eclipse uncoiled from the dark at his feet, the shadowwolf joining the boy's silhouette on the wall, darkening it further. Without the daemon riding his shadow, he'd likely have been reduced to hysterics by now, but considering what he'd been through, the child was doing well.

Still, Ashlinn didn't like the way the boy stared at his sister.

Angry.

Hungry.

"*. . . WHAT NOW . . . ?*" Eclipse growled.

"*. . . a quick round of crumpets and strumpets . . . ?*" Mister Kindly offered.

"*. . . MUST YOU, LITTLE MOGGY . . . ?*"

"*. . . always, dear mongrel . . .*"

The shadowwolf turned its not-eyes to the rest of the room.

"*. . . AM I HONESTLY EXPECTED TO BELIEVE THIS BOORISH CUR AND ITS PREPUBESCENT HUMOR IS THE FRAGMENT OF A SHATTERED DIVINITY . . . ?*"

"Shut up, the pair of you," Ashlinn snapped.

"The 'what now' is simple," Mia said, stifling another yawn. "The Ministry have Mercurio. Until we have him back, Scaeva and I are at an impasse." She shrugged. "So we have to get him back."

"Mia, they'll have Mercurio in the Quiet Mountain," Ashlinn said. "The heart of the Red Church's power on this earth. Guarded by Blades of the Mother, the Ministry themselves, and 'byss knows what else."

"Aye," Mia nodded.

"Further, I'm sure I don't need to point out that they took Mercurio to get to *you,*" Ashlinn continued, her voice rising. "They told you they have him because they *want* you to come looking for him. If this were any more obviously a fucking trap, they'd have a row of high-priced courtesans dancing in Liisian lingerie atop it, singing a rousing chorus of 'this is obviously a *fucking trap.*'"

Mia smiled faintly. "I love that song."

"Mia . . . ," Ashlinn moaned, exasperated.

"He took me in, Ashlinn," Mia said, her smile vanishing. "When everything else had been taken away. He gave me a home and he kept me safe when he had no reason under the suns to do it." Mia looked up at the girl, eyes shining. "He's familia. More familia to me than almost anyone in this world. Neh diis lus'a, lus diis'a."

"When all is blood . . ."

"Blood is all," Mia nodded.

Ashlinn just shook her head.

"MIA—" Tric began.

"The Quiet Mountain is in Ashkah, Tric," Mia interrupted. "We have to head that way, regardless. So ease off on the destiny talk for a while, neh?"

"YOU HAVE ACCEPTED IT, THEN?"

"My mind's nothing close to made up," Mia said, stretching her legs out on the hammock with a soft groan. "But traveling in the right direction's enough for now."

"The Ministry are going to know we're coming," Ash pointed out, standing to help Mia off with her bloodstained boots. "The Quiet Mountain is a fortress."

"Aye," Mia said, wiggling her toes with a wince.

"So how in the Mother's name do you expect to get inside and rescue Mercurio?" Ash demanded, pulling off the other boot. "Let alone out alive again?"

"Front door," Mia said, sighing deep as she finally lay back in the hammock and gave in to her exhaustion.

"The front fucking door?" Ash hissed. "Of the Quiet Mountain? You'd need an army to get in there, Mia!"

Mia closed her eyes.

"I know an army," she murmured. "A little one, anyways . . ."

"What in the Mother's holy name are you babbling about?" Ash raged.

The hammock swayed and rolled with the weary girl atop it. The chaos and bloodshed of the last few turns, the epiphanies and prophecies, the promises broken and yet unfulfilled, all of them seemed to have finally caught up with her. As the lines of care in her face softened, the scar upon her cheek twisted her lip ever so slight, made it seem like she was smiling. Her breast rose and fell with the rhythm of the waves.

"Mia?" Ash asked.

But the girl already slept.

Jonnen spoke softly into the silence.

". . . What does 'prepubescent' mean?"

CHAPTER 9

SLUMBER

She dreamed.

She was a child, beneath a sky as gray as goodbye. Walking on water so still it was like polished stone, like glass, like ice beneath her bare feet. It stretched as far as she could see, flawless and endless. A meniscus over the flood of forever.

Her mother walked to her left. In one hand, she held a lopsided scale. The other was wrapped in Mia's own. She wore gloves of black silk, long and glimmering with a secret sheen, all the way up to her elbows. But when Mia looked closer, she saw they weren't gloves at all, that they dripped

dripdrip

dripdrip

on the stone/glass/ice at their feet, like blood from an open wrist.

Her mother's gown was black as sin as night as death, strung with a billion tiny points of light. They shone from within, out through the shroud of her gown, like pinpricks in a curtain drawn against the sun. She was beautiful. Terrible. Her eyes were as black as her dress, deeper than oceans. Her skin was pale and bright as stars.

She had Alinne Corvere's face. But Mia knew, in that dreaming, knowing kind of way, that this wasn't her real face. Because the Night had no face at all.

And across the infinite gray, he waited for them.

Her father.

He was clad all in white, so bright and sharp it hurt Mia's eyes to look at him. But she looked all the same. He stared back as she and her mother approached, three eyes fixed on her, red and yellow and blue. He was handsome, she had to admit—almost painfully so. Black curls dusted with just the faintest hints of gray at his temples. Shoulders broad, bronze skin contrasting sharply with the snow white of his robes.

He had Julius Scaeva's face. But Mia knew, in that dreaming, knowing kind of way, that this wasn't his real face, either.

Four young women stood about him. One wreathed in flame and another shrouded in waves and the third wearing only the wind. The fourth was sleeping on the floor, clad in autumn leaves. The wakeful trio stared at Mia with bitter, unveiled malice.

"Husband," her mother said.

"Wife," her father replied.

They stood there in silence, the six of them, and Mia could have heard her heart thumping in her chest, if only she'd had one.

"I missed you," her mother finally sighed.

The silence grew so complete, it was deafening.

"This is he?" her father asked.

"You know it is," her mother replied.

And Mia wanted to speak then, to say she wasn't a he but a she. But looking down, the child saw the strangest thing reflected in the mirrored stone/glass/ice at her feet.

She saw herself, as she saw herself—pale skin and long dark hair draped over thin shoulders and eyes of burning white. But looming at her back, she saw a figure cut from the darkness, black as her mother's gown.

It peered at her with its not-eyes, its form shivering and shifting like lightless flame. Tongues of dark fire rippled from its shoulders, the top of its crown, as if it were a candle burning. On its forehead, a silver circle was scribed. And like a looking glass, that circle caught the light from her father's robes and reflected it back, the radiance as pale and bright as Mia's eyes.

And looking into that single, perfect circle, Mia understood what moonlight was.

"I will never forgive you for this," her father said.

"I will never ask you to," her mother replied.

"I will suffer no rival."

"And I no threats."

"I am greater."

"But I was first. And I trust your hollow victory will keep you warm in the night."

Her father looked down at her, his smile dark as bruises.

"Would you like to know what keeps me warm in the night, little one?"

Mia looked down at her reflection again. Watched the pale circle at her brow shatter into a thousand glittering shards. The shadow at her feet splintered, splayed in every direction, maddening patterns surging, seething, the night-thing shapes of cats and wolves and serpents and crows and the shapes of nothing at all. Ink-black tendrils sprouted from her back like wings, razors of darkness from every fingertip. She could hear screaming, growing louder and louder.

Realizing at last that the voice was her own.

"The many were one," her mother said. "And will be again."

But her father shook his head.

"In every possible sense, you are my *daughter."*

He held up a black pawn on his burning palm.

"And you are going to die."

BOOK 2

DYING LIGHT

Chapter 10

Infidelity

Mia woke with a gasp, almost falling from her hammock.

The portholes were shuttered as they'd been for the past two turns. The cabin was shrouded in the same gloom that had filled it since they put out from the Nethers, rocking to the gentle motion of the open sea. Almost three turns after the *magni,* Mia was still aching in places she never knew she had, and still in need of about seven more nevernights' worth of sleep.

Genuine sleep, that is.

Dreams. Dreams of blood and fire. Dreams of endless gray. Dreams of her mother and her father, or things wearing their faces. Dreams of Furian, dead at her hand. Dreams of her shadow, growing darker and darker at her feet until she slipped down into it and felt it flow up and over her lips and down into her lungs. Dreams of laying on her back and staring into a blinding sky, her ribs flayed apart, tiny people crawling through her entrails like maggots on a corpse.

"More nightmares?"

The voice made her shiver, then feel guilty for doing so. She cast a furtive glance at Ashlinn, asleep in the hammock beside hers. Then back to the deadboy, sitting in that corner as he'd done since they put out to the Sea of Silence. Tric's hood was drawn back and he sat with legs crossed, gravebone swords in his lap, black hands resting flat upon the blades.

Goddess, but he was still beautiful. Not the rugged, earthen beauty he'd been before, no. There was a dark beauty to him now. Carved of alabaster and ebony. Black eyes and pale skin and a voice so deep she could feel it between her legs when he spoke. A princely beauty, wrapped in a robe of night and serpents. A crown of darkling stars on his brow.

"Apologies, did I wake you?"

"I don't sleep, Mia."

She blinked. "Ever?"

"Never."

Mia dragged her hair back from her face, swinging her legs off the side of her hammock quiet as she could. As she sat up straight, her wounds pulled and her bandages tugged at her scabs and she couldn't help but wince with the pain of it all. Conscious of those pitch-black eyes following her every move.

She was dying for a cigarillo. For fresh air. For a fucking bath. They'd been stuck in here together for two turns straight now, and the strain was wearing on all of them.

Jonnen was a knot of fury and indignity, kept in check only by Eclipse's constant presence in his shadow. He sat for hours, pouting and sullen, ripping up tendrils of his own shadow and throwing it at the far wall, just as he'd done at Mia's eyes in the necropolis. Eclipse would pounce upon the ball of shadowstuff like a puppy and Jonnen would smile, but the smile would disappear as soon as he caught Mia looking at him.

She could feel his anger at her. His hate and his confusion.

She couldn't blame him for any of it.

Ashlinn and Tric were another source of concern—the tension between them thick enough to slice up and serve with the alleged "stew" they ate each evemeal. Mia could feel the storm clouds building to a thunderhead that would black out the suns. And truth told, she had no idea what to do. She might've spoken to Tric about it once, you see. But he wasn't the same.

She hadn't known what to feel when she'd first laid eyes on him. The joy and guilt, the bliss and sorrow. Yet after a few turns in his company, she could see he was drawn with the same outline, but not filled in with entirely the same colors. She could feel a darkness to him, now—the same darkness she felt inside her own skin. Beckoning. And aye, even with Mister Kindly in her shadow, perhaps frightening.

Mia bowed her head, rivers of long black hair draping either side of her face. Silence between them thick as fog.

"I'm sorry," she finally murmured.

The deadboy tilted his head, saltlocks moving like dreaming snakes.

"For what?"

Mia sucked her lip, searching for the pale and feeble words that would somehow make this all right. But people were the puzzle she'd never managed to solve. She'd always been better at cutting things apart than putting them back together.

"I thought you were dead."

"I TOLD YOU," he replied. "I AM."

"But . . . I thought I'd not see you again. I thought you were gone forever."

"NOT THE MOST FOOLISH OF ASSUMPTIONS. SHE STABBED ME THREE TIMES IN THE HEART AND PUSHED ME OFF THE SIDE OF A MOUNTAIN, AFTER ALL."

Mia looked over her shoulder at Ashlinn. Freckled cheek resting upon her hands, knees curled up, long lashes fluttering as she dreamed.

Lover.

Liar.

Murderer.

"I kept my promise to you," she told him. "Your grandfather died screaming."

Tric inclined his head. "MY THANKS, PALE DAUGHTER."

"Don't . . ."

She shook her head, her voice failing as the lump rose in her throat.

". . . Please don't call me that."

He turned his eyes to Ashlinn. Putting one black, night-stained hand to his chest and pawing there, as if remembering the feel of her blade.

"WHAT HAPPENED TO OSRIK, BY THE BY?"

"Adonai killed him," Mia replied. "Drowned him in the blood pool."

"DID HE SCREAM, TOO?"

Mia pictured Ashlinn's brother as he disappeared beneath that flood of red the turn the Luminatii invaded the Mountain. Eyes wide with terror. Mouth filling with crimson.

"He tried to," she finally said.

Tric nodded.

"You must think me a heartless cunt," she sighed.

"YOU'D ONLY CONSIDER IT A COMPLIMENT."

Mia looked up at that, thinking him angry. But she found his lips curled in a thin, pale smile, the shadow of a dimple creasing his cheek. It reminded her so much of what he'd been for a moment. So much of what they'd had together. She looked into his bloodless face and ink-black eyes and saw the beautiful, broken boy he'd been beneath, and her heart was like lead in her chest.

"DO YOU LOVE HER?" he asked.

Mia looked to Ashlinn again. Remembering the feel of her, the smell of her, the taste of her. The face she showed the world, vicious and hard, the tenderness she showed only to Mia, alone in her arms. Melting in her mouth. Poetry on her tongue. Each a dark reflection of the other, both of them driven by vengeance to be and do and want things most wouldn't dare dream.

Wonderful things.

Awful things.

"It's . . ."

". . . Complicated?"

She nodded slow. "But life always is, neh?"

A mirthless chuckle slipped over his lips. "Try dying."

"I'd rather not, if I can help it."

"Death is the promise we all must keep. Sooner or later."

"I'll take later, if it please you."

He met her eyes then. Black to black.

"It would."

The clanging of heavy bells cut their conversation off at the knees, and both Tric and Mia looked to the *Maid*'s decks above. She heard muffled shouts, running boots upon the timbers, notes of vague alarm. Ashlinn woke from her slumber with a jolt, sitting up and dragging her forearm across her face. "Wassat?"

Mia was standing now, narrowed eyes on the boards above their heads.

"Doesn't sound good, whatever it is."

A second burst of bells. A rolling string of faint and shockingly imaginative curses. Mia stepped lightly over to the porthole and opened the wooden shutter, letting in a blinding shear of truelight. Jonnen lifted his head from his hammock, squinted around the cabin with bleary eyes. Mister Kindly cursed from his spot atop the door.

Mia blinked hard in the painful glare, joined by Ashlinn at the porthole once their eyes adjusted. Over the rolling waves beyond the glass, Mia could see sails on the distant horizon, stitched with golden thread.

"That's an Itreyan warship . . . ," Ashlinn muttered.

Mia glanced upward. "Our hosts don't seem too excited about seeing it."

". . . ON THE CONTRARY, THEY SOUND VERY EXCITED TO ME . . ."

". . . o, bravo, been practicing our banter, have we . . . ?"

". . . SOME OF US HAVE NO NEED OF PRACTICE, MOGGY. WE ARE SERVED BY WIT INSTEAD . . ."

Ashlinn dunked her face in their barrel of washwater to clear away the sleep, tied her hair back in a loose braid.

"I'll head topside for a chat."

"You'd best go with her, Brother Tric," Mia said. "I'll stay here with Jonnen."

The deadboy stood slowly. Looking at Ashlinn with bottomless eyes as he sheathed his gravebone blades beneath his robes and drew his hood up over his face.

"After you, Sister."

Ash dragged on the boots she'd been wearing since infiltrating the Godsgrave Arena, strapped her shortsword to her leg. Hauling her sorority habit over her head and pulling on her coif, she headed for the door.

"Be careful, neh?" Mia warned.

Ash smiled lopsided, leaned over, and kissed Mia's lips.

"You know what they say. What doesn't kill me had better fucking run."

The Vaanian girl slipped out the cabin door in a flurry of white robes.

Mia avoided Tric's eyes as he followed.

"Well," Cloud Corleone sighed. "As my dear old tutor Dona Elyse said the year I turned sixteen, 'Fuck me very gently, then fuck me very hard.'"

Kael Three Eyes leaned out from the Crow's Nest. "They're signaling, Cap'n!"

"Aye, I can see that!" he called, waving his spyglass. "Thank you!"

"Arse-grubbing shit queens are gaining on us, too," BigJon grunted from the railing beside him.

The captain waved his spyglass in BigJon's face. "This thing works, you know."

"Captain?" came a voice.

Cloud glanced over his shoulder, saw Her Not-So-Holiness on the deck behind him, and her six-foot attack dog looming behind her. The truelight air felt a little colder, and an involuntary shiver tickled his skin.

"Best get back down below, Sister," he said. "Safer there."

"Meaning it's not safe up here?"

"I wouldn't—"

The sister reached out and snatched Cloud's spyglass from his hand, pressed it to her eye and turned to the horizon.

"That's not regular Itreyan navy," she said. "It's a Luminatii ship."

"Well spotted, Sister."

"And it looks like they're armed with arkemical cannons."

"Again, aye, my spyglass works, thank you."

The sister lowered the glass, met his eye. "What do they want?"

Cloud pointed to the red flare the ship had sent sizzling into the sky.

"They want us to stop."

"WHY?" the big bodyguard asked.

The good captain blinked. ". . . Look, how are you doing that with your voice?"

The sister handed back his glass. "Do the Luminatii usually stop random ships in the middle of the ocean for no apparent reason?"

"Well." Cloud scuffed the deck with his bootheel. "Not usually, no."

The sister and her bodyguard exchanged uneasy glances.

BigJon whispered from the side of his mouth, "Antolini tipped them off, maybe?"

"He wouldn't do that to me, would he?" Cloud muttered.

"You plowed his wife, Cap'n."

"Only because she asked me nicely."

"That kidfiddler Flavius promised to kill you if he saw you again," the littleman mused, sucking on the stem of his drakebone pipe. "Maybe he got creative?"

"So I owe him a little coin. That's no reason to sing about me to the Luminatii."

"You owe him a little *fortune*. And you plowed *his* wife, too."

Cloud Corleone raised an eyebrow. "Do you not have things to do?"

The littleman looked around the hive of activity that were the main and foredecks, the masts above. He shrugged and showed his silvered grin.

"Not particularly."

"Still gaining, Cap'n!" Kael called above.

Cloud held his spyglass aloft. "Four Daughters, this thing fucking works!"

"Captain," the sister began. "I'm afraid I have to insist—"

"I'm sorry, Sister," the privateer sighed. "But we're not stopping."

". . . We aren't?"

"That's a Luminatii warship, Cap'n," BigJon pointed out. "Not sure the *Maid* has it in her to outrun it."

"O, ye of little faith," Cloud said. "Give the order."

"Aye, aye," the littleman sighed.

BigJon turned from the rails, roared at the crew. "Right, you jizz-gargling fuckbuckets! We're doing a runner! Hoist every inch of sail we've got! If you own a shitrag or a spunk-stained kerchief, I want it lashed to a mast somewhere, go, *go*!"

"Captain . . . ," the sister began.

"Rest easy, Sister," Cloud smiled. "I know my oceans, and I know my ship. We're sitting in the swift stream, and the nevernight winds are about to start kissing our sails the way I kissed Don Antolini's wife."

The captain lifted his spyglass with a small smile.

"These god-botherers won't lay a damned finger on us."

The first cannon shot skimmed across the water a hundred feet shy of their prow. The second one twenty feet short of their stern, close enough to scorch the paint. And the third flew past close enough that Cloud could have shaved with it.

The Luminatii warship was running parallel to the *Maid,* her gold-threaded sails gleaming. Cloud could see her name written in bold, flowing script down her prow.

Faithful.

Her cannons were ready to unleash another blast of arkemical fire—the three earlier bursts had been warning shots, and Cloud didn't fancy his chances of a fourth. Besides, considering what the *Maid* had hidden in her belly, one good kiss from old *Faithful* here would be all they needed.

"All stop," the captain spat. "Hoist the white flag."

"Stop, you useless shitwizards!" BigJon roared from the quarterdeck. "All stop!"

"O, aye," Sister Ashlinn muttered from the railing beside him. "You know the oceans and your ship all right, Captain . . ."

"You know," Cloud replied, turning to look at her, "my first impressions of you were quite favorable, good Sister, but I have to say, the more I get to know you, the less fond of you I grow."

Her bodyguard folded his arms and scoffed.

"We should have a drink sometime . . ."

The ocean was too deep for the *Maid* to drop anchor, so once the sails were stowed and their head turned to the wind, there was little for the crew to do except stand about and wait for the *Faithful* to make berth alongside. Cloud watched the massive warship cruise closer, his belly sinking lower all the while. Her flanks were bristling with arkemical cannons from the workshops of the Iron Collegium, and her decks packed with Itreyan marines.

The men were dressed in chain mail and leather armor, each embossed with the sigil of the three suns on his chest. They carried shortswords and light wooden shields, ideal for close-quarter fighting on the decks of enemy ships. And they outnumbered the *Maid*'s crew two to one.

Up on the aft deck, Cloud could see a half-dozen Luminatii in gravebone armor, their cloaks blood-red, feathered plumes of the same hue on their helms, fluttering in the sea breeze. Their leader was a tall centurion with a pointed beard, piercing gray eyes, and the expression of a fellow in desperate need of a professional wristjob.*

"Damned god-botherers," the captain grumbled.

"Aye," BigJon said, stepping up beside him. "Lady Trelene drown them all."

---

*Two copper beggars at an average dockside whorehouse, with an ale thrown in if the publican is feeling generous.

Self-care, gentlefriends. Self-care.

"We'll be fine," Cloud muttered, more to himself than his first mate. "It's well hidden. They'd have to rip the hull apart to find it."

"Unless they know exactly where to look for it."

Cloud looked at his first mate with widening eyes. "They wouldn't have . . . ?"

The littleman lit his drakebone pipe with a flintbox and puffed thoughtfully. "I *told* you not to plow Antolini's wife, Cap'n."

"And I told *you* she asked nicely." Cloud lowered his voice. "*Very* nicely, in fact."

"You think these Luminatii boys are going to be as sweet?" BigJon scoffed, watching them prepare to board. "Because they're settling in to fuck us, sure and true."

Cloud winced as the grapples were thrown, sinking into the *Maid*'s railing and splintering the wood. *Faithful*'s crew slung heavy hay-stuffed bags along her flanks to cushion the impact as the *Maid* was hauled closer by mekwerk winches, and the two ships finally came together with a heavy thump. Lines were lashed tight, and a gangplank extended from conqueror to conquered.

Centurion Wristjob glowered down from the *Faithful*'s aftercastle.

"I am Centurion Ovidius Varinius Falco, second century, third cohort of the Luminatii Legion," he called. "By order of Imperator Scaeva, I am authorized to board your vessel in search of contraband. Your cooperation is—"

"Aye, aye, come on over, mates." Cloud flashed his four-bastard smile, doffing his tricorn with a low bow. "Nothing to hide here! Just wipe your feet first, neh?"

The privateer muttered over his shoulder.

"You'd best head below to your cabin, Sister. Things will . . ."

Cloud looked to BigJon, blinking hard at the empty space where the girl and her bodyguard had stood a few moments before.

". . . Where the 'byss did they go?"

Chapter 11

Incendiary

Luminatii crawled over the *Maid* like fleas in a Liisian grandmother's chest hair.

The search was cordoned and meticulous, and Centurion Falco had obviously dealt with smugglers before—he found all three of Cloud's dummy stash spots easily. Thankfully, and despite BigJon's conspiracy theories, the boarders hadn't come close to finding the real ones, and Cloud's hidden cargo remained safe as houses. But accompanying Falco in his search and answering his questions as politely as he could, the privateer quickly came to a rather disturbing realization.

The god-botherers weren't actually interested in contraband at all—what they were looking for was people. And, acutely aware the nun he was carrying was likely no more a nun than he was a priest, the privateer was worried his sinking belly might actually start leaking out through his boots.

"And these are your only passengers?" Falco asked.

"Aye," Cloud replied, raising a fist to knock on the cabin door. "We're not usually in the business of transporting livestock."

"They came aboard where and when?"

"Godsgrave. A few turns back. Booked passage all the way to Ashkah."

The centurion gave a curt nod, and Cloud knocked loudly.

"Sister?" he sang. "Are you decent? There's a few fellow servants of the Blessed Light here who'd like to ask you some questions."

"Enter," came the reply.

Cloud opened the door and found the Vaanian girl already standing politely to one side, back against the bulkhead, hands before her like a penitent.

"Forgiveness, Sister—" Cloud began.

"Step aside, plebian," Falco said, forcing his way into the cabin.

The centurion dragged off his plumed helmet, smoothed down his sweaty mop of hair, and gave the sister a respectful bow. His steel-gray eyes flitted to the bodyguard in the corner, the muscles in his jaw tensing. The big fellow made no sound.

"Forgive me, good Sister," he said to the nun. "I am Centurion Ovidius Varinius Falco, commander of the warship *Faithful*. By order of our imperator, Julius Scaeva, I must conduct a search of this ship, and thus, your cabin."

The girl kept her eyes to the floor in a convincing show of modesty, nodding once. "No apologies are necessary, Centurion. Please, conduct your search."

The centurion nodded to his four marines. They stepped into the room, eyes to the floor out of deference, each obviously about as comfortable in the nun's cabin as a real nun would've been in a dockside fightpit. Careful not to impinge too much on the good sister's personal space, they began searching the chests, the barrels, knocking on the floors and walls in search of hollows. For his part, Falco kept his eyes on the big fellow in the corner of the room, but the figure remained motionless.

Cloud stood and watched, butterflies beating about in his belly. He could hear marines going through the other cabins farther down the ship, and none too gently by the sound. He wrapped his arms around himself, jaw clenched tight.

Colder than a real nun's nethers in here . . .

"Forgive me, Sister," Falco said suddenly. "I confess no end of strangeness in finding you in such . . . colorful company."

"I can find no fault in that, brave Centurion," the sister said, eyes still downturned.

"Might I enquire what you are doing aboard this vessel?"

"You may enquire, noble Centurion." The lass smoothed down her voluminous robes, which were blowing in the breeze from the open porthole. "But as I informed the good captain here, my task requires utmost discretion. My Mother Superior bid me speak of it to none, not even our brethren in the Light. Upon my honor, I must humbly beg your forgiveness and maintain my sworn silence."

Falco nodded, gray eyes glittering. "Of course, good Sister."

The marines finished their search, turned to the centurion.

"The boy's not here," one reported, rather needlessly.

The centurion glowered once more about the room. But seemingly satisfied, if still more than a little curious, he bowed to the sister.

"Forgive our intrusion, good daughter. Tsana guide your hand."

The sister raised three fingers with a patient smile.

"Aa bless and keep you, Centurion."

"See?" Cloud grinned ear to ear, relief melting his insides. "All shipshape and aboveboard, aye, mates? Let me show you lovely gentles out."

Falco turned on his heel, ready to leave, his men close behind. But Cloud's belly did a small flip as the man came to a sudden stop. A slight frown appeared on the centurion's brow as he stared at the girl's feet.

Gray eyes glinted in the cabin's dim light.

"My sister married a shoemaker," he declared.

The Vaanian lass tilted her head. "I beg pardon?"

"Aye," the man nodded. "A shoemaker. Four years back."

"I . . ." The girl blinked, looking bewildered. "I am . . . very happy for her."

"I'm not," Falco scowled. "He's thicker than pig droppings, my brother-in-law. He knows a great deal about boots, however. Has a contract with the Godsgrave editorii, in fact. Every guard who works the arena wears a pair of his."

The centurion pointed to the bloodstained leather toes peeking out from beneath the girl's holy vestments.

"Just like those."

Several things happened in quick succession here, each slightly more surprising than the last. First, the lass shouted "MIA!" at the top of her lungs toward the open porthole. Which, all things considered, Cloud thought rather odd.

Second, she moved, flinging a knife from inside her sleeve and drawing a shortsword she'd hidden fuck-knows-where. The knife sailed into the throat of the closest marine, and as the man fell back in a spray of red, the lass lashed out at the centurion with her blade, face twisted in a snarl.

Third, the big fellow in the corner threw back his hood, revealing a corpse-pale face, eyes like a daemon and saltlocks like . . . well, Cloud had no fucking idea, but they were *moving by themselves*. The fellow drew out his two suspiciously sword-shaped lumps from beneath his robe, which indeed turned out to be swords.

Gravebone swords.

And lastly, and probably strangest of all, as the girl aimed a scything blow at Centurion Ovidius Varinius Falco, second century, third cohort's cocky neck, a shadow shaped like a cat lunged out from beneath her voluminous robes with an unearthly yowl, followed by a rather alarmed nine-year-old boy, gagged and bound at his wrists.

For his part Falco was ready for the blow at least, drawing the sunsteel blade at his belt and speaking a prayer to Aa. The sword ignited with a shear of bright flame and he met the girl's strike, his sunsteel scoring her blade. The lass yelled "MIA!" again, the three remaining marines cried out and drew their shortblades, Cloud spat a black curse, and before he knew it, the cabin was in chaos.

The marines were well trained, obviously used to fighting in tight spaces. But as they stepped up to cut the lass down, the big lad struck, his gravebone blade cutting through chain mail like a razor through silk and slicing one man's arm off at the shoulder. Blood sprayed across the cabin and the man went down howling.

The big fellow wasn't all that spry, though—he seemed unholy strong but stumbling slow. The third marine struck back, slicing his arm deep. And with a prayer to Aa, the fourth stepped forward and skewered him straight through the belly.

The big fellow didn't fall. Didn't even flinch. With one black hand, he grabbed the marine's wrist, pulled the blade farther into his gut and the wide-eyed soldier ever closer. His other hand closed about the man's throat. And with the snap of damp twigs, he twisted the fellow's neck to breaking.

Good Sister Ashlinn and Falco were locked up, blade to blade, the bigger man pushing the lass back with his blazing sunsteel. But as he raised his sword, the sound of a thunderous explosion tore through the air from somewhere outside, shattering the other portholes and spraying glass and the bitter black stench of arkemical fire into the room. Falco realized the blast had come from the *Faithful* about the same time Cloud did, turning his head momentarily in the direction of his ship. And that moment was all the good sister needed.

Her blade tip connected with the man's throat, slicing his windpipe clean through. The centurion fell back, fountaining blood, the boy on the floor staring in wide-eyed horror as the man's not-quite-dead-yet body hit the deck. The cat shadow thing was tearing about the room yowling and spitting, the walking corpse had slammed the last marine against the wall and was choking him out barehanded, and Cloud Corleone could smell the most terrifying thing a captain aboard his own ship can imagine.

Fire.

So he did what any sensible man would have done in his boots.

"Fuck this," he said.

And he ran.

Barreling down the corridor and up onto the deck, he was momentarily overcome by the sunslight glare and the stench of smoke. The *Maid*'s deck was covered with crewmen, running to and fro at BigJon's bellowed commands.

"Cut those bloody lines! Get those grapples out, you limp-pizzled lackwits! Wet down the damned sails! Push us away, you slack-jawed nonna-fuckers! Away!"

Cloud could see the *Faithful* was on fire—both her sails and her hull. Black smoke was spewing out of her arse end, which had been somehow blown apart.

She was listing hard, taking water fast. Burning sailors and marines were diving into the sea, regular and arkemical flames were eating the wood, and her decks were in absolute chaos. And as he watched, trying to make sense of exactly what was going on aboard the stricken warship, Cloud Corleone found his jaw slackening in wonder.

"Four Daughters . . ."

He thought it a trick of the light or smoke at first. But squinting harder, he realized that among the flames and embers, he could see . . .

A girl?

She moved like a song. Weaving and spinning, all pale skin and narrowed eyes and long hair, black as crow's feathers. She held a gravebone longsword in her hand, a stolen shield in the other, drenched to the armpits in gore. As he watched, she skipped up to the aft deck toward one of the Luminatii. The man cursed and raised his sunsteel blade. A wolf made of what looked like shadowstuff flew up the stairs, mouth open and roaring. Cloud blanched as he realized he could understand what it was saying.

"*. . . RUN . . . !*" it roared, with a voice like winter. "*. . . RUN, YOU FOOLS . . . !* "

The girl raised her hand, and the Luminatii cried out, reeling back and clutching his eyes as if blinded. The lass cut the terrified man down, striking his hand off at the wrist as he fell, tossing aside her shield and snatching up his flaming sword from the deck. And as she wove among the rest of the terrified mob, that shadowwolf howling for blood, twin blades flashing in her hands, something about her form struck him as familiar. Something that put him in mind of the smell of blood and sand, the taste of a comely lass's lips, a bookman calling him a cockeyed fool as he'd placed all his winnings down on . . .

"'Byss and blood," he breathed.

Another explosion rocked the *Faithful,* her timbers cracking, her masts shattering. Cloud realized her arkemical ammunition stores must've been set ablaze, that she was tearing herself apart from the inside. Soldiers and sailors tumbled into the sea or made desperate leaps across to the *Maid,* only to be helped down into the waves by his own salts on BigJon's order. Cloud watched, gobsmacked, as the girl cut the backstays securing the mizzenmast, her gravebone blade slicing through the thick, tar-soaked ropes as if they were spidersilk. She ducked low as the wind sent the mast falling with a splintering crack toward the *Maid.* And climbing up onto the fallen timber, she dashed along it like a cat, face twisted as she took a flying leap across the widening gap between the *Faithful* and the *Maid.*

She didn't quite make it. Her gravebone blade flew from her hand and clattered across the deck at Cloud's feet as she hit the stern rail, her stolen sunsteel falling into the ocean below. She almost followed it down into the burning water, but somehow clung on, nails clawing the timber, knuckles white as she seized hold of a heavy block. Hauling herself up the pulley, her grip slippery with blood, she managed to swing one leg onto the railing and pull herself over, collapsing on the deck. Chest heaving. Coughing and sputtering.

"Fuck me very gently," Cloud murmured. "Then fuck me very hard."

Dragging a stray lock of blood-soaked hair from her lips, the lass looked up into Cloud's eyes. The captain now held her gravebone blade in his hands, its hilt sticky with red. Her shadow twisted, shifted, and the wolf that had struck such terror into the Luminatii and their men materialized on the deck between them, hackles raised, its growl seeming to come from beneath the floorboards.

"*. . . STAY BACK . . .*"

Its voice chilled his belly, the girl's stare, even more so. It was like the fear was a living thing, leaking out of the dark at her feet and into his own. Cloud heard footsteps on the stairs behind him. Felt a now familiar chill at his back. He could hear his crew forming up below, cudgels and blades at the ready, a little drunk on the carnage and maybe spoiling for a touch more. BigJon was holding them in check, but one word would be all it took for it to start again.

"Mia?" he heard a voice ask behind.

"It's all right, Ash," the lass replied, watching Cloud.

"You're the Crow," he said, his voice trembling. "Falcon of the Remus Collegium. The Bloody Beauty. Savior of Stormwatch."

Cloud licked his lips. Forced his voice to steady.

"You're the lass who murdered Grand Cardinal Francesco Duomo."

She looked at him. Her face scarred and slave-marked and smudged with blood and smoke. Eyes black as truedark, circled with shadows.

"Aye," was all she said.

Careful so as not to spook anyone, Cloud Corleone placed the gravebone sword onto the deck, gentle as if it were a newborn babe. And leaning down to the lass, he offered her his four-bastard smile along with his shaking hand.

"Welcome aboard the *Bloody Maid*."

CHAPTER 12

VERITAS

It was the most uncomfortable dinner Mia had ever attended.

The good captain was seated at one end of the table in his cabin, dressed in a fine black velvet shirt, unlaced a touch too far. His mate BigJon sat beside him, propped up on a stack of cushions. Mister Kindly was draped around Mia's shoulder at the table's other end, and Eclipse was curled up on the floor at her feet. Ashlinn was sat to her left and Tric to her right, Jonnen sitting opposite BigJon to complete the set.

Ash had shed her sorority vestments, now clad in black leathers and a red velvet shirt. Tric still wore his dark robes, though his hood was pulled back, exposing his beautiful pale face, his black eyes, his saltlocks moving in a breeze no one else could feel. Mia still wore her leather gladiatii skirt and boots, but the good captain had been nice enough to loan her one of his black silk shirts to replace her bloodstained tunic. She quickly realized the scoundrel liked his fashion low-cut, and had to bend over carefully lest uninvited guests made an unexpected visit.

The ocean whispered and shushed against the hull, the gentle rise and fall of the *Maid* on the swell setting the crockery tinkling and clinking. Sunslight streamed through the leadlight windows, the Sea of Silence spread out in azure splendor behind them.

The silence around the table wasn't nearly so pretty.

The good captain had put on a fine spread and seemed intent to impress Mia—though she'd not yet fully grasped why. After his initial fear, he'd acclimatized well to the notion she was darkin, slipping easily into the role of charming host. As the aperitifs were served, he kept the talk light, speaking mostly of his ship and his travels. His wit was so quick it might've been pure silver he was drinking. But it soon became apparent most of his audience weren't in the mood for a Charming Bastard routine. Corleone's small talk had sputtered, then died. And as the dishes were cleared in preparation for second course, the table descended into an awkward quiet.

Cloud Corleone cleared his throat. "More wine, anyone?"

"No," Ashlinn said, watching Tric.

"No," Tric said, glaring at Ashlinn.

"Fuck yes," Mia said, waving her glass.

Mia was on to her third. It was a fine vintage, dark and smoky on her tongue. And though she preferred a good goldwine—Albari if it was going, though in truth, almost any whiskey would suffice—she wasn't quite rude enough to ask the good captain if he had any. She could get drunk on red just as easily, and turns of being cooped up together in that cabin had set everyone on edge. So drunk she intended to get.

"Well," Corleone said, taking another stab. "How do you all know each other?"

Silence.

Long as years.

"We studied together," Mia finally replied.

"O, aye?" Corleone smiled, intrigued. "Public institution, or Iron Collegium, or . . ."

". . . it was a school for fledgling assassins run by a murder cult . . ."

"Ah." The captain glanced at the shadowcat and nodded. "Private tutors, then."

"SOME OF US BECAME MASTERS OF IT," Tric said, staring at Ash. "MURDER, THAT IS."

"That shouldn't surprise," she replied. "Given what we trained for."

"A KNIFE IN THE HAND OF A FRIEND IS OFTEN A SURPRISE."

"It shouldn't be, if that friend thinks to come before familia."

"Erm . . . ," Corleone stammered.

Mia drained her glass.

"Pass the wine, please?"

Corleone complied as the galley boy brought in the main and started serving. It was fine fare considering they were aboard a ship—sizzling lamb and almost-fresh greens and rosemary jus that made Mia's mouth water despite the tension in the air. As Corleone began carving, the meat almost fell off the bone.

"I saw you best that silkling at the Whitekeep games," BigJon said to her around his mouthful. "Won a strumpet's cuntful of coin on you, too. Bloody magnificent, lass."

"Four Daughters, BigJon," Cloud scowled. "Mind your cursing at table, neh?"

"Fuck," he said, biting his lip. "Apologies."

"Again?"

"Fuck. Sorry. Shit . . . *FUCK* . . ."

"No, it's all right," Mia said, leaning back in her chair and enjoying the feel of her head spinning. "I *was* bloody magnificent. I trust you spent your cuntful on something fucking marvelous."

The littleman grinned with silver teeth, raising his glass. "O, I like you."

Mia raised her glass in return, downed it in a gulp.

"What about you, young don?" Cloud said, turning to Jonnen for a change of subject. "Do you like ships, perchance?"

"Do not speak to me, cretin," the boy replied, toying with his food.

"Jonnen," Mia warned. "Don't be rude."

"I will not entertain inane chatter with this lawless brigand, Kingmaker," the boy snapped. "Further, when I am returned to my father, I will see him hanged a villain."

"Well . . ." Corleone's lips flapped a little. "I . . ."

"Don't mind him," Mia said. "He's a spoiled little shit."

"I am the son of an imperator!" the boy cried shrilly.

"But you're not above a spanking! So mind your fucking manners!"

Mia glowered at the boy, engaged in a silent battle of wills.

"Ah . . . ," BigJon tried. "More wine?"

"O, yes, please," Mia said, holding out her glass.

A more comfortable silence settled over the table as Mia got her refill and folk got down to eating. Mia had spent the last eight months dining on the various questionable broths and swills cooked up in the Remus Collegium—this was the first decent feed she'd had in as long as she could remember. She started stuffing her face, using more wine to wash her ambitious mouthfuls down. The lamb was delicious, hot, perfectly seasoned, the greens crunchy and tart. Even Jonnen seemed to be enjoying himself.

"Are you not eating, Don Tric?" Corleone asked. "I can have the galley fix something else if this displeases."

"THE DEAD HAVE NO NEED OF FOOD, CAPTAIN."

"And yet they insist on coming to the dinner table, regardless," Ashlinn muttered around a mouthful.

". . . *EXCUSE* ME?"

"Pass the salt, dwarf," Jonnen demanded.

"Oi!" Mia thumped the table. "He's not a dwarf, he's a littleman!"

"No, I am a little man," the boy said with a smug smile, pointing to Big-Jon with his fork. "*He* is a dwarf. And I will be taller tomorrow."

"That's fucking *it,*" Mia said, rising to her feet. "Go to your room!"

"I beg your pardon?" he asked. "I am the son of—"

"I give no fucks for whose son you are. You're a guest at this table and you don't talk to people that way. You want to be treated with respect, little brother? Start by treating others to it. Because it's *earned,* not fucking owed." Mia leaned forward and glowered. "Now go. To. Your. Room!"

The boy stared at his sister. His eyes narrowed. The shadows about him shivered and snapped like bullwhips, echoing the rage in his eyes. Some of the cutlery began rattling on the tabletop.

". . . Mia?" Ash asked.

". . . MIA . . . ?"

In a blinking, the shadows turned sharp and pointed like knives, lashing out at her throat. Mia scowled, jaw clenched, wresting the dark from her brother's grip with but a thought. He was furious, aye. But she was older. Stronger. Far, far deeper. Seizing control over them was literally akin to wrestling them from a child. And with a toss of her head and a whip of her will, the shadows snapped back into their usual shapes.

"I shall smile when they hang you, Kingmaker," he hissed.

"Take a number and queue up, little brother," she replied. "In the meantime, get your arse back to your cabin before I kick it."

The boy's lip wobbled as he admitted defeat. Cheeks pinking with fury. And without another word, he stormed from the room, slamming the door behind.

"Eclipse, could you keep an eye on him?" Mia murmured.

". . . AS ONLY THE EYELESS CAN . . ."

The shadowwolf rose from beneath Mia's chair and faded from sight. Mia sank back down into her seat, elbows to table, head in her hands.

"Littleman?" BigJon said into the silence following.

"Apologies." Mia waved one hand. "If that offends."

BigJon leaned forward and batted his eyes. "Will you marry me, dona?"

"Get in line, littleman," Ashlinn smiled, squeezing Mia's hand.

"JUST DO NOT TURN YOUR BACK," Tric said. "ASHLINN DISLIKES COMPETITION."

"Black fucking Mother." Ash thumped her fork down, three turns' worth of tension finally getting the best of her. "Must you take every opportunity to have a stab at me?"

"AN INTERESTING CHOICE OF WORDS, GIVEN WHAT YOU DID TO ME."

"It's called irony, Tricky," Ashlinn snarled. "Old playwright's technique. I'd have thought you an expert on drama, the way you're laying it on."

"LAYING IT ON?"

"Aye, a little thick, don't you think?"

"You *murdered* me!" Tric cried, rising from his seat.

"I did what had to be done!" Ashlinn shouted, rising along with him. "You said yourself the Red Church has lost its way! Well, I've been trying to take it down longer than *any* of you! I'm sorry you had to go, but that's just how it is! And I stabbed you friendways, in case you've forgot. In the front, not the damned back. I can't undo it, so what the fuck do you want from me?"

"A hint of regret? Some shred of remorse? For you to understand some small part of what you took from me?"

"Remorse is for the weak, Tricky," Ash said. "And regret is for cowards."

"You've got nothing inside you, do you? Not a shred of conscience or a—"

"Ah, to the 'byss with this . . ."

Ash shoved aside her plate, turned toward the door.

"Ashlinn . . . ," Mia said.

"No, fuck it," the girl spat. "Fuck this and fuck him. I'm not going to sit and eat shit for something *all* of us have done. We're all liars. All killers. 'Byss and blood, you were a sworn Blade of the Red Church, Tric. Unlike Mia, you *passed* your initiation. So don't sit there and play the fucking victim when your own victims are in the ground, too!"

The door slammed for the second time as Ashlinn left.

The room fell silent. Mia toyed with her wineglass, running her finger around the lip. Ash's words echoing in her head, along with the memory of her final Red Church trial. Called before Revered Mother Drusilla. One simple task between her and initiation.

Mia heard scuffing footsteps in the shadows. She saw two Hands swathed in black, dragging a struggling figure between them. A boy. Barely in his teens. Wide eyes. Cheeks stained with tears. Bound and gagged. The Hands dragged him to the center of the light, forced him to his knees in front of Mia.

The girl looked at the Revered Mother. That sweet matronly smile. Those old, gentle eyes, creased at the edges.

"Kill this boy," the old woman said.

For all her bravado, Mia had failed that trial. Refused to take the life of an innocent. Clinging to the few shreds of morality she had left. But Tric had been at the initiation feast when Ashlinn betrayed the Church.

Which of course meant he *hadn't* failed.

She looked up at the Hearthless Dweymeri boy. Into those bottomless eyes. Seeing his victims swimming in the dark. His hands not black, but red.

"I think I'll take some air," he said.

"You don't have to breathe," Mia replied.

"I'LL TAKE SOME ALL THE SAME."

"Tric . . ."

The door closed quietly as he left.

BigJon and Corleone glanced at each other sidelong.

". . . More wine?" the captain offered.

Mia breathed deep and sighed. "Fuck it, why not . . ."

Snatching up the bottle, she leaned back in her chair and put her feet up on the edge of the captain's polished table, taking a long, slow pull right from the neck.

"You have . . . interesting traveling companions, Crow," Corleone said.

"Mia," she replied, wiping her lips. "My name's Mia."

"Cloud," he replied.

"Is that your real name?" She squinted, suspicious.

"No," he smiled. "You don't get to know my real name."

"What'll you give me if I can guess it?"

He took in his ship with a sweep of his arm. "All you can see, Dona Mia."

The girl ran her hand across her eyes, down her face, sighing again. Her head felt too heavy for her neck. Her tongue felt too big for her mouth.

"You can drop us off at Whitekeep," she said. "Any of the two hundred silver you can refund would be appreciated. Whatever you think fair."

"You mean kick you off the *Maid*?" The privateer frowned. "Why would I do that?"

"Well, let's see," Mia sighed, counting on her fingers. "I've brought two daemons and a deadboy aboard your ship. My brother and I are both darkin, and he's also the abducted son of the imperator with what's likely the whole Itreyan Legion chasing his arse. I implicated you and your crew in the murder of a handful of Luminatii, their crew, and the destruction of their ship." She tipped her head back, guzzled the last of the bottle, and dropped it on the deck. "And I've drunk all your fucking wine."

She hiccupped. Licked her lips.

"Good wine, though . . ."

"My brother's name was Niccolino," Corleone said.

"S'a nice name," Mia said.

As if at some hidden signal, BigJon slipped down off his chair and quietly exited the room. Mia found herself alone with the brigand, save for the cat made of shadows still draped about her shoulders.

Corleone stood slowly, walked across to an oaken cabinet, and fetched another bottle of very fine red. Cutting the wax seal away with a sharp knife, he refilled Mia's glass, then retired back to his chair, nursing the booze.

"Nicco was two years older than me," he said, taking a swig. "We grew up in the 'Grave. Little Liis. Him, me, and Ma. Da got sent to the Philosopher's Stone when we were small. Died in the Descent."

Mia's eyes sharpened a little at that. "My mother died in the Stone, too."

"Small world."

"I'll drink to that," she said, swallowing deep from her glass and trying not to think about the night Alinne Corvere died.

"Ma was devout," Corleone continued after matching her swallow. "A god-fearing daughter of Aa. We went to church every turn. 'Boys,' she'd say, 'If you don't believe in him, why would he believe in you?'"

Corleone took another long, slow pull from the bottle.

"He could sing, my brother. Voice that could shame a lyrebird. So the bishop at our parish recruited him into the choir. This was twenty years ago now, mind you. I was twelve. Nicco fourteen. My brother practiced every turn." Cloud chuckled and shook his head. "His singing around the house drove me mad. But I remember my ma was so proud, she cried all through his first mass. Cried like a fucking babe.

"And then Nicco stopped singing. Like his voice just got . . . stolen. He told Ma he didn't want to be in the choir anymore. Didn't want to go to church. But she said it'd be a shame on him to waste the gift Aa gave him. 'If you don't believe in him, why would he believe in you, Nicco,' she told him. And she made him go back."

The brigand took another swig, put his boots on the table.

"One nevernight, he came home from practice and he was shaking. Crying. I asked him what was wrong. He wouldn't say. But there was blood. Blood on his bedding. I ran and got Ma. Said, 'Nicco's bleeding, Nicco's bleeding,' and she came running, asked what was wrong.

"And he said the bishop hurt him. Made him . . ."

Corleone shook his head, his eyes lost focus.

"She didn't believe him. Asked him why he'd lie like that. And then she hit him."

"Black Mother . . . ," Mia whispered.

"She couldn't grasp it, aye? Something like that . . . the shape of it just didn't fit into her world. But it's a terrible thing, Dona Mia, when the ones who should love you best leave you for the wolves."

Mia hung her head. "Aye."

"Nicco jumped off the Bridge of Broken Promises four turns later. Bricks in his shirt. He'd been in the water a week when they found him. The bishop came to his funeral. Said the mass over his stone. Embraced my mother and told her everything would be all right. That the Everseeing loved her. That he had a *plan*. And then he turned to me, and put his hand on my shoulder, and asked if I liked to sing."

Mia tried to speak. Couldn't find her voice.

Corleone looked her in her eyes.

"That bishop's name was Francesco Duomo."

Mia's belly dropped into the soles of her boots. Her mouth full of bile, lashes dewed with tears. She'd known Duomo deserved the murder she'd gifted him in the arena, but Goddess, she'd never guessed just how deeply.

Corleone stood slow, walked around the table, and, still looking into her eyes, he placed a familiar bag of coin on the table in front her.

"You stay on this ship as long as you fucking please."

CHAPTER 13

CONSPIRACY

Mercurio sat in the office of Chronicler Aelius, nose deep in **"THE BOOKS."**

That's how he thought of them in his head now. **"THE BOOKS."** Capital letters. A bold, no-nonsense script. Quotation marks, perhaps underscored—he wasn't quite sure yet. But what he *was* certain of was this: to think of these things as "some books," or "Some Books," or even **"SOME BOOKS"** was to deny, in every true and real sense, what they actually were.

Incredible books.

Impossible books.

Brain-breaking, mon-fucking-strosities of books.

"THE BOOKS."

The old man's scowl had become so permanent a fixture on his face over the past few turns, it actually hurt to change expressions now. His pale blue eyes carefully scanned his current page, every paragraph, every sentence, every word, his gnarled, toxin-stained forefinger tracking the movement of his eyes across the lines.

He was just nearing the end of the second volume, heart beating quick.

And with a final gasp, the Unfallen fell.

A hammerblow to Mia's spine. A rush of blood in her veins, skin crawling, every nerve ending on fire. She fell to her knees, hair billowing about her as if in some phantom breeze, her shadow scrawled in maddened, jagged lines beneath her, Mister Kindly and Eclipse and a thousand other forms scribbled among the shapes it drew upon the stone. The hunger inside her sated, the longing gone, the emptiness suddenly, violently filled. A severing. An awakening. A communion, painted in red and black. And face upturned to the sky, for a moment, just for a breath, she saw it. Not an endless field of blinding blue, but of bottomless black. Black and whole and perfect.

Filled with tiny stars.

Hanging above her in the heavens, Mia saw a globe of pale light shining. Like a sun almost, but not red or blue or gold or burning with furious heat. The sphere was ghostly white, shedding a pale luminance and casting a long shadow at her feet.

"The many were one."

"Crow! Crow! Crow! Crow!"

"And will be again."

Mercurio leaned back in his chair, dragging on his cigarillo.

"This is doing my bloody head in," he growled.

"Requires some mental contortions, doesn't it?"

Chronicler Aelius was hard at work, rebinding a few of the library's more beaten and worn tomes with new covers of hand-tooled leather. Occasionally pausing to take a drag on his own cigarillo and breathe a plume of strawberry-scented gray into the air, he worked with deft fingers and a needle made of gleaming gravebone. Between the pair of them smoking, the air in the office was closer to soup, the ashtray on the chronicler's graven mahogany desk piled high with lifeless butts.

"Contortions?" Mercurio scoffed. "Contortions are for circus performers and high-priced courtesans, Aelius. This is something else entirely."

"Known many high-priced courtesans, have you?" Aelius asked.

Mercurio shrugged. "In my youth."

"Got any good stories? It's been a while for me . . ."

"If it's cheap smut you're after," Mercurio sighed, tapping the first of **"THE BOOKS,"** "the tawdriness starts in volume one, page two hundred and forty-nine."

"O, I know," the chronicler chuckled. "Chapter twenty-two."

Mercurio turned his deepening scowl on Aelius. "You read those pages?"

"Didn't you?"

"Maw's fucking teeth, no!" Mercurio almost choked on his smoke, utterly horrified. "She's like my . . . I don't want to think of her getting up to . . . *that*."

The old man slumped in his chair, took a savage drag off his cigarillo. The past few turns, he'd been doing his best to come to grips with the existence of **"THE BOOKS,"** but he was having a time of it. In order to avoid suspicion from Drusilla and the Hands she had constantly shadowing him through the Quiet Mountain, he had to keep his visits to the library of Our Lady of Blessed Murder short—enough for a few cigarillos with the old chronicler, a chinwag, then out again. He didn't dare remove **"THE BOOKS"** from the Athenaeum in case they tossed his room, and so he'd been reduced to reading them in snippets. He was only just finishing the second.

It felt ghastly strange to be reading about Mia's exploits, her private thoughts, and oddest of all, his own role in her tale. Reading those pages was like watching himself in a black mirror, but the glass was propped over his shoulder instead of looking at him face-to-face. And as he read about himself, he could almost feel eyes peering over his own shoulder in kind.

"Look, how the 'byss is this even possible?" he asked, turning in his chair to face Aelius. "How can these books exist? They're telling a story that hasn't finished yet. And my name's on them, but I never wrote the fucking things."

"Exactly," Aelius replied, nodded to the Athenaeum beyond the black stone walls of his office. "That's what this place is. A library of the dead. Books that were burned. Or forgotten ages past. Or never got a chance to live at all. These books *don't* exist. That's why they're here."

The chronicler shrugged his thin shoulders, puffed on his smoke.

"Funny old place, this."

Silence descended in the Black Mother's library, punctuated by the distant roar of a single angry bookworm out in the gloom.

"You read the introduction again?" Aelius asked softly. "Carefully?"

"Aye," Mercurio muttered in reply.

"Mmm," the dead man said.

"Look, it doesn't mean a fucking thing."

Aelius tilted his head, pity in his milky blue eyes. He flipped back through the red-edged pages to the beginning of the first **"BOOK"** and started reading aloud.

"'*Be advised now that the pages in your hands speak of a girl who was to murder as maestros are to music. Who did to happy ever afters what a sawblade does to skin. She's dead herself, now—words both the wicked and the just would give an eyeteeth smile to hear. A republic in ashes behind her. A city of bridges and bones laid at the bottom of the—'"*

"I've read all that," Mercurio growled. "It doesn't mean anything."

"This is her story," Aelius replied softly. "And that's how it ends. 'A republic in ashes.' That's a good ending, Mercurio. Better than most get."

"She's eighteen years old. She doesn't deserve *any* ending yet."

"Since when did 'deserve' have anything to do with it?"

The old man lit a cigarillo with gnarled fingers, adding to the thickening fog of gray in the office. "All right, so where's the fucking third one, then?"

"Eh?" Aelius asked.

"I'm almost done with the second," Mercurio said, tapping on the black wolf cover. "And they both mention a third. Birth. Life. And death. So where is it?"

Aelius shrugged. "Buggered if I know."

"Haven't you looked for it?"

Aelius blinked. "What for?"

"So we can learn how it ends! How she dies!"

"What good will that do?" the chronicler frowned.

Mercurio stood with a dramatic sigh and, leaning on his walking stick, began pacing the room. "Because if we know what's coming, maybe we can help her so things don't turn out the way *this*"—his cane came down on the first **"BOOK"** with a dull *thwack*—"tells us they do."

"Who says you can change anything?"

"Well, who says we can't?" the old man snarled.

"You really want to see the future?" Aelius asked. "Sounds a curse to me. Better to weep for what might've been than for what you know is to come."

"We don't *know* anything," Mercurio growled.

"We know all stories end, whippersnapper. Including hers."

"Not yet." Mercurio shook his head. "I won't let it."

Aelius leaned back on the desk, exhaled a plume of strawberry-gray into the miasma above. Mercurio dragged his shaking hand through his hair.

"Reading about all this," he said. "It doesn't feel right . . . It feels . . ."

"Too big?" Aelius asked.

"Aye."

"A little like being a god, maybe?"

Mercurio folded kindling-thin arms across his thinner chest. He couldn't remember feeling as old in all his life. "Fucking gods . . ."

"You have a role to play in this," the dead man said. "The Mother brought you here for a reason. She had me find these books, show them to you, for a *reason*."

"Seems a slender fucking thread to put so much weight upon."

"It's all she can do from where she is," Aelius sighed. "A push here. A nudge there. Using what little power she gains from what little faith folk hold for her. And it's harder for her now. Once, the folk running this place actually believed. To the faithful who created it centuries back, it truly meant something. She had real power here. But now?"

"Hollow words," Mercurio muttered. "Walls painted gold, not red."

"The Mother does what little she can with what little she has. But the balance between Light and Night won't be restored by the hands of the divinities." The chronicler pointed at Mercurio's own gnarled, ink-stained hands. "It'll just be those."

"I'll not lift a damned finger if it means hastening Mia's ending."

Aelius puffed on his smoke, regarding Mercurio thoughtfully.

"First things last, young'un," he said. "You don't need to read her whole biography to know where she'll be headed now."

"Aye," Mercurio said. "Face-first into a world of flaming shit."

"So when she arrives, we'd best be ready." Aelius shrugged. "We'll not need to worry how her story ends otherwise. It'll end right here. In the halls of this mountain."

"So what can we do?" Mercurio growled, rubbing his aching arm. "I'm halfway to dead, and you're dead all the way. You can't even leave the fucking library. Between the two of us, what good can we do her?"

Aelius leaned over to the second **"BOOK"** sitting on his desk. Sky-blue edges, wolf on the cover, leather so black light just seemed to fall into it. He licked his thumb and began leafing through the pages. Finally stopping at the place he wanted, he spun the tome toward Mercurio, tapped at the text.

The old man squinted at the words, heartbeat coming quicker.

He looked down at his wizened old hands.

Such a slender thread . . .

"Righto," he sighed. "I'll go talk to them."

The room stank of blood.

Ancient and cracked to tiny black flakes, so many years between it and bleeding that its scent was just a broken promise. Old and dark, hardened to a rind in the cracks between the flagstones. A few sour splashes here and there, curled and separated like bad cream, wreathed with the stink of rot. But above it all, iron-thick and laced with salt, wafting through the open doors in invisible skeins until it permeated the entire level?

Fresh, new, ripe *blood.*

The pool was triangular, set deep in the stone, the red within it swaying and rolling like the surface of a tempest sea. Sorcerii glyphs were daubed in crimson on the wall, alongside maps of the major metropolises of the Republic—Godsgrave, Galante, Carrion Hall, Farrow, Elai. Old Mercurio could see other cities there, too. Cities ground by the heel of time into ruin and dust. Cities so old, there were few who even remembered their names. But Speaker Adonai remembered.

He was at the apex of the triangle, down on his knees. Bone-pale skin, tousled white hair, a thin red robe tossed carelessly over his smooth torso. Leather britches riding dangerously low. Barefoot.

A girl stood before him, legs slightly parted, bending backward like a sapling in a storm. Small sighs of pleasure slipped over her lips, her kohled lashes fluttering. She was dressed in a black Hand's robe, open at the front, plastered to her skin with her own blood. The ruby red spilled from a dark slice between her bare breasts, flowing down her naked belly and then lower still. She held a bloodstained knife in one hand. Her other was wrapped in his hair.

Speaker Adonai was knelt in front of her, hands clutching her buttocks, his face pressed between her thighs. Groans of bliss rose right up from the core of him as he lapped and sucked and licked. His clever tongue flickered, his smooth chest heaved, his lithe body shook. Eyes rolling back so only the pink-not-white showed. His throat moved with every deep swallow, every shivering, red mouthful. Mercurio had seen starving wolves tear apart a lamb when he was a boy. The sounds they made as they killed and the sounds coming from the speaker as he drank were much alike.

Weaver Marielle sat in the corner of the room, watching her brother feed. Dark robes draped over her hunched frame, hood pulled low over her hideous features. Wisps of bone-blond hair spilled from the shadows of her cowl, along with a thin ribbon of drool from her misshapen lips. One twisted hand was pressed to her throat. The other between her legs.

Adonai dragged his mouth away from the girl's blood-slick petals, gasping like a man near drowned. His face and teeth were smeared with crimson, red rivulets running down his throat. The girl shivered, bloody fingertips caressing Adonai's face with all the reverence of a priestess before her god. Asking no forgiveness for her sins. Preferring punishment instead.

"More," she moaned, pulling him back in.

"Am I interrupting?" Mercurio asked.

Adonai's eyes found a muzzy sort of focus, and he let out a gasping chuckle. Still shaking, swaying as if drunk, he swiveled his head like a blindworm toward the light. Finding Mercurio in the doorway, the smile fell away from his bloody lips. His gaze became a glower, a long spool of ruby spit swinging from his chin.

"Yes," he and Marielle said.

"Shouldn't have left the fucking door open, then, I s'pose," the old man replied.

He hobbled into the room, walking stick beating crisp on the moist black stone. It was uncomfortably warm down here in the sorcerii's part of the Mountain, and he knew climbing back up those stairs on his shitty knees was going to be agony. He was sweating like an inkfiend with a needle three turns dry. His legs ached like a pair of bastards. His left arm ached even worse.

"Away with you, lass," he told the bleeding, breathless girl.

Dragging her sodden robe partway closed, the Hand managed to glare at Mercurio despite looking ready to pass out from the blood loss.

"Go on," he said, waving his cane at the door. "Off with the fuck. There's at least three more of your fellows skulking on my heels. Maybe one of them has a suggestion about how better to spend your time than in the company of these fucking perverts."

The girl glanced at Adonai, and the speaker gave a small nod.

"Here, child," Marielle whispered, beckoning with twisted fingers.

The girl walked toward the weaver, a little unsteady on her feet. As she drew close, Marielle raised one misshapen hand, swayed it in the air before the girl's bleeding chest. The girl shivered. Sighed. And as she turned, Mercurio saw the bone-deep knife wound had closed as if it'd never been.

He sucked his lip, forced to admire the woman's handiwork. Despite being unable to manipulate her own hideous flesh, Marielle could mold others' like a potter with clay. There wasn't a mark on the Hand's body.

The weaver knows her work.

"Regain thy strength, sweet child," Marielle lisped through split and bleeding lips. "Then visit us anon."

With one last poison glare for the bishop of Godsgrave, the lass pulled her soaking robe closed and made her way from the room. Adonai reached out to her as she walked by, too blood-drunk to say his farewells.

Mercurio looked down the hallway she left by, saw two of the Hands that Drusilla had trailing him lurking in the gloom. Close enough to let him know they were watching. That the *Lady of Blades* was watching. But not quite brave enough to enter the speaker's chamber without invitation.

A fellow had to be quite stupid for that.

He raised the knuckles at his shadows, then slammed the door in their faces.

Adonai stood, dragging one bloody hand back through his hair and pulling his head up with it, as if it was too heavy for his neck. His robe had slipped off his shoulders, and Mercurio could see the troughs and valleys of muscle beneath. He looked a statue on a plinth outside the Senate House. Chiseled out of stone by the hands of the Everseeing himself. But Mercurio knew it was his sister's hands, not Aa's, that bestowed the blood speaker's impossible perfection. And despite the power the siblings wielded, he found that thought just about as fucked up as he'd always done.

Adonai finally rediscovered his powers of speech, eyes glinting red. "Desperate thy plight or absent thy wits must be, Bishop, to interrupt a blood speaker at his meal."

Mercurio stood at the base of the triangle, staring across the blood at Adonai.

"Well?" the speaker demanded. "Nothing to say, hast thou?"

Mercurio waved his cane in the direction of the speaker's crotch. "Just waiting for the tumescence to diminish a bit. The bulge is impressive, but a touch distracting."

"Seek ye quarrel with us, good Mercurio?" Marielle rose from her chair and stood beside her brother. "So weary of life's burden, art thou? For I swear it sure and true, more weary could I make thee afore I lifted burden from thy shoulders."

"Already thou hast ire well-earned from the Lady of Blades," Adonai said. "So common are thine enemies, thou art in need of quality? 'Pon the blood of the aged I may sup to fuel my magiks, as easily as upon the young. And I am still hungry, old man."

"Maw's teeth, you two talk a lot of shit," Mercurio growled.

Adonai curled his fingers. The pool surged, and bloody tendrils of liquid gore rose up from the surface, slick and gleaming scarlet. They were pointed like spears, semisolid, sharp as needles. They snaked slowly around the bishop of Godsgrave, blood-stink thick in the air, quivering with anticipation.

"Blood is owed thee, little Crow," Mercurio said. *"And blood shall be repaid."*

The tendrils fell still, poised a few inches from the old man's skin.

Adonai's red eyes narrowed to razor cuts in his beautiful face.

"Speak ye those words again?"

"You fucking heard me," Mercurio said. "That's what you told Mia, isn't it? Last time you saw her here in the Mountain? *'Two lives ye saved, the turn the Luminatii pressed their sunsteel to the Mountain's throat. Mine, and my sister love's. Know this, in nevernights to come. As deep and dark as the waters ye swim might turn, on matters of blood, count upon a speaker's vow, ye may.'*"

Adonai glanced at his sister. Back to Mercurio.

"Such words spake I for her ear alone," he breathed, enraged.

"None were in my chambers when troth was pledged," the weaver said. "Save I, my brother love, the darkin, and her passengers. How come ye to speak them by rote, good Mercurio, as if thou were sixth among five alone?"

"Doesn't matter how I know," Mercurio said. "But I do. You owe her a debt, Adonai. You owe her your miserable, twisted little life. You made a vow. And the water she swims now is deep and dark as it's ever been."

"Well do we know it," Marielle said.

"How?" Mercurio demanded, pupils narrowing to pinpricks.

Adonai gave a lazy shrug. "Scaeva sent a blood missive ordering the Lady of Blades to unleash every chapel in the Republic upon our little darkin's trail. A son stolen, desired returned. And for she who stole him . . ."

"Every chapel," the old man whispered.

Mercurio's belly sank, thinking about the sheer number of Blades that would now be hunting Mia. Even after the Luminatii purge and Ashlinn Järnheim's betrayal, it'd still be dozens. All schooled in the arts of death by the finest killers in the world.

"How the *fuck* can Scaeva afford that?"

"Poor Mercurio," Marielle cooed. "So silent thy turns must ring in thy room alone."

"Title of imperator, Scaeva hath claimed," Adonai said. "And all the coin in the Republic's war chests besides. 'Pon a pillow of gold, Drusilla soon shall lay her head."

The old man clenched his jaw. "That conniving bitch . . ."

"Not through kindness doth a single Blade become Lady of many, old man."

Mercurio rubbed at his left arm. His chest was aching abominably.

Mia's in deeper shit than I ever imagined . . .

"So," he finally said, meeting Adonai's scarlet stare. "Mia has the whole Church against her now. Every Blade the Ministry can find. Question is, were your words just that? Or something more? How far does your loyalty to the Church extend, Adonai? In a house of thieves and liars and murderers, how much weight does a promise carry?"

"We are no thieves," Adonai spat. "*Earned,* our magiks be. Dredged from the sands of Ashkah Old, verily, and paid for again in anguish, turn by bloody turn."

"Liars, neither," Marielle lisped, slipping her hand around her brother's waist. "Though killers, aye. That we be. Name us the former, find truth in the latter, good Mercurio. Slow and painful truth."

"As for loyalty, who can say." The sorcerii placed his arm around his sister, wiping at the gore on his mouth. "Ours be not bought with coin, that much be certain. And these walls place much stock in that since Cassius fell. But there is much danger in crossing the Ministry, Mercurio. And a vow to thy little darkin shall only carry me so far."

"And I, not at all," Marielle smiled. "My debt to thy ward be already repaid."

"We did not drag ourselves through blood and fire to wrest the secrets of the Moon from the dust of Old Ashkah, only see them thrown away on—"

"Wait, wait," Mercurio frowned. "What the fuck did you just say?"

Adonai's eyes narrowed. "Blood and fire were—"

"The Moon, you perverted fuck. The part about the Moon."

"'Twas he who taught the Ashkahi sorcery," Adonai said, head tilted, eyes glittering in the gloom. "A god dead, ages past, and all magik in this world with him."

"Our arts are but fragments of larger truths," Marielle lisped. "Forever taken from this world. Gleaned from scraps long buried beneath the sands of Old Ashkah."

The old man looked between them, his heart racing. "What if I told you Mia has something to do with this damned Moon thing? Darkin. Her passengers. What if I told you she knows the way to its crown?"

". . . What madness is this?" Marielle asked.

"Aye, mad it might just be," the old man said. "But I swear by the Black Mother, the Everseeing, and all four of their holy daughters that Ashlinn Järnheim has a map to the Moon's crown branded in arkemical ink on her back. Ink that will fade in the event she gets murdered. Say, for example, while she's protecting Mia."

The siblings looked at each other. Back to Mercurio. Red eyes glittering in the low light. The pool of blood at Adonai's back began swaying like the sea in a storm. Marielle's breath had grown so thick, she seemed almost to be wheezing.

"What do you say?" Mercurio offered his hand. "You two want to help me keep that pair alive? You've still a vow to keep, after all."

Adonai looked at the man's upturned palm. Took a deep, shivering breath. But without another word, he grasped Mercurio's hand in his, fingers slicked with gore. With no hesitation, Marielle placed her hand atop her brother's, warped and leaking pus.

The old man looked at the sorcerii and nodded.

"All right, then. Seems we've got ourselves a conspiracy."

CHAPTER 14

REUNIONS

"It's a rancid shithole," Sidonius declared.

"It's not that bad," Bladesinger said.

"It *is* that bad," Sidonius scowled. "The rats are big as dogs, the timbers are rife with mites, and one stray cigarillo and the whole shithouse will go up in flames."

"Brother," the Dweymeri woman sighed. "Considering you were locked in a piss-stained cell beneath Godsgrave Arena facing your own execution a week ago, you think you'd be more kindly disposed to the feel of the free wind upon your face."

"We're inside, 'Singer," Sidonius said, pointing to the various holes in the theater's walls. "We're not *supposed* to feel the fucking wind."

Wavewaker pushed aside a pair of moldy curtains and stomped out onto the stage. His foot went through one of the rotten timbers and he stumbled, dragging his boot free and staring at his comrades with mad joy upon his tattooed, bearded face.

"Isn't it *grand*?" he breathed.

Sidonius sighed. It seemed a lifetime ago he'd been locked under the 'Grave's Arena, not just a week as Bladesinger said. Looking back on the events of the past few months, it all felt like a dream—one he might wake from at any moment, realizing he was still gladiatii, still in chains, still a slave.

When he'd been sold to the Remus Collegium alongside Mia Corvere, he'd had no idea how that girl was set to change his life. He'd served under her father, Darius, in the Luminatii Legion, and out on the burning sands he'd sought to protect her life with his own. But in the end, Mia had been the one who saved him, and the other Falcons of Remus besides, hatching a plan that not only saw her avenged against the men who'd destroyed her familia but also freed her fellow gladiatii from their servitude.

Sid's cheek still itched from his visit to Whitekeep's Iron Collegium four turns back, where he and the other Falcons had handed over the redsheets provided to them by the slaver Teardrinker. The wizened old arkemist in the hall had poured over the *chartum liberii* for an insufferable age, and Butcher looked close to shitting his britches. But Teardrinker had owed a lifedebt to Mia Corvere, and true to her word, the slaver's papers held up under inspection.

Sid and the others had each taken their turn under the arkemist's hands, and after some swift agony, the former legionary and gladiatii found his cheek free of a slave brand for the first time in six long years.*

Three nevernights of debauched celebrations had ensued, and using some of the coin Old Mercurio had provided them, the former Falcons of Remus proceeded to get shitface drunk. Sidonius's last memory of the bender was of a smokeden somewhere in Whitekeep's brothel district, where he'd buried his face between a very fine and very expensive pair of breasts and declared he'd not emerge again until Aa himself came down and dragged him loose, while Butcher charged around the common room buck naked carrying as many sweetgirls under his arms as he could manage.†

Sid did not, under *any circumstances,* remember a discussion about buying a theater. So, on the fourth turn since acquiring their freedom, when Wavewaker woke him with an excited shake sometime after noonbells and Sid had reluctantly pried the breasts off his face, he was rather surprised to discover he had become part owner of a crooked pile of kindling by the Whitekeep docks known as the Odeum.

---

* *Chartum liberii* are the focus of any slave's existence in the Republic of Itreya. Also known as "redsheets" for the scarlet parchment they are scribed upon, they signify that the bearer has, through dint of self-purchase, a merciful master, or governmental edict, earned their freedom.

Almost impossible to forge thanks to the arkemical processes of the Iron Collegium, redsheets are an incredibly valuable commodity. A flourishing black market has arisen around their acquisition and resale, and clever purveyors of redsheets can expect to become very rich very quickly. Less clever purveyors can expect to be sold into slavery for life, along with their relatives, friends, colleagues, familia, pets, and people who owe them money. The entire Republic runs on the oil of slavery, after all.

If you fuck with the system, gentlefriends, be prepared for the system to fuck you back.

† Five, it turns out. Six if you count the one riding his back.

He was not pleased.

"We can get some carpenters in by midweek," Wavewaker was saying, his voice near trembling with excitement. "Get the stage patched up, some new doors, she'll be good as new. Then we put the word out for actors. I'll direct, Sid and 'Singer, you can work the front, Butcher has a face for backstage. Felix and Albanus can . . ."

The big man paused, scratching at his thick saltlocks.

"Where *are* Felix and Albanus, anyways?"

"Felix went home to his ma," called a still-very-drunk Bryn from the upper gallery.

"And Albanus seemed sweet on little Belle who drove us here." Bladesinger rubbed the vicious scar on her swordarm, earned during the *venatus* in this very city two months back. "I don't remember him getting out of the wagon, now I think of it . . ."

"Well, they know where to find us," Wavewaker grinned, raising his booming baritone to the rooftops. "The grandest theater the city of Whitekeep shall ever see!"

Bryn gave a drunken cheer from the gallery, dropped her half-full bottle of goldwine, hiccupped a curse, and fell backward onto her arse.

"M'allright!" she called.

Sidonius put his head in his hands, sank to his haunches, and sighed.

"Fuck me."

"I know it might seem ill-advised," Bladesinger said gently. "But you know it was always Wavewaker's dream to run a theater. Look at him, Sid." The woman nodded at the big Dweymeri, who was striding the stage and muttering a soliloquy under his breath. "Happy as a pig in shit."

"M'all—*hic*—right . . . ," Bryn called again, in case anyone was listening.

Sid dragged his hand over his stubbled scalp. "How much coin do we have left?"

"A hundred or so," 'Singer shrugged.

"Is that it?" Sidonius moaned.

"It was a very expensive pair of tits you bought yourself, Sid."

"Fuck off, don't you blame this on me," the Itreyan growled. "Six years on the sands, I deserved some cunny after that. I'm not the one who just blew a damned fortune on a decrepit armpit of a theater!"

Bladesinger winced a little. "Technically, you are."

The former gladiatii waved the bill of sale between them, and under the wine, ale, and other less-identifiable stains, Sid could make out a magnificently drunken scrawl that might have passed for his signature.

"Well, one-fifth of a fortune, anyway."

"Fuck meeeeeeeee."

"I know just the play we'll put on first, too," Wavewaker was saying. *"Triumph of the Gladiatii."*

"'Waker, will you shut the *fuck* up!" Sid roared.

"I can't feel my—*hic*—feet!" Bryn called.

Butcher rose up from the broken pews in the back row, screwed up his dropped-pie face, and looked about with bleary eyes.

". . . Is this a . . . a theater?"

"Aye," someone said behind him. "And it's a beauty."

Sidonius stood at the sound of the voice, adrenaline surging in his belly. The figure on the threshold was shrouded in a long cloak, a scarf wrapped about her face. But were he blind and deaf, Sid still would have known her anywhere. His face split into an idiot grin as Wavewaker bellowed from the stage.

"CROWWW!"

And then Sid was running, catching the girl up in his embrace, lifting her off the ground as she squealed. Bladesinger collided with the pair of them, wrapping them up in her arms, Butcher staggered over, Wavewaker arrived like an earthquake, grabbing all four of them and roaring as he lifted them off the ground and jumped in circles.

"You magnificent little *bitch*!" Sid cried.

"Let me go, you great fucking lumps!" Mia grinned.

But there was none of that. Not until they'd savored it a little more—until Bryn arrived from the gallery and joined in on the embrace, until Wavewaker dragged his nose across his sleeve and Bladesinger blinked the tears from her eyes and all of them had a chance to just stand and breathe and remember what she'd given to them.

Not just their lives.

Their *freedom*.

"'Byss and blood, how did you find us?" 'Singer asked.

"Poked my nose into the first whorehouse I saw," Mia shrugged. "After that, I just followed the trail of vomit."

Wavewaker chuckled. "What the 'byss are you doing here, little Crow?"

Her smile fell away then. She looked at the theater around them, the holes in the walls and the moth-eaten upholstery and spiderwebs, thick as blankets in the rafters. And she shook her head, smile returning as if it had never left.

"I just wanted to see if you landed on your feet."

Sidonius glanced at Bladesinger. The woman met his stare, eyes twinkling.

"So," Crow said. "Whose throat do I need to cut to get a drink around here?"

Ashlinn saw Tric on the bow, wind in his saltlocks like a lover's hands.

The *Maid*'s crew gave him a wide berth, the few who had to go near him making the sign of Aa before and after, and working as swift as any captain could ask. Ash knew Cloud Corleone had told his salts that Mia and her band were to be treated as honored guests aboard the *Bloody Maid*. But sailors were a superstitious bunch at the best of times, and the idea of a Hearthless walking among them with earthly feet was sitting about as well with the crew as it was with Ashlinn.

She could still feel it.

The slight resistance as her blade sank into his chest. The warm blood spilling over her knuckles. The tiny splash of red that spattered her cheeks as the blade slipped into his lungs, making it impossible for him to do anything but look at her in confusion

"—hrrk."

"Sorry, Tricky."

as she killed him.

"How do, Tricky?"

He glanced at her sidelong, then turned his eyes back to the vista of Whitekeep harbor. Ashlinn had returned from the market with her arms loaded, fully half their remaining coin spent on "essentials." The jetties and seawall were strung with sailors and sellswords, fishfolk and farmers, plying trade across the boardwalk. The vast archways of the aqueduct stretched over the bay, back toward the City of Bridges and Bones, and up on the hillside, Ash could see vast and winding garden mazes.* Gulls serenaded each other in the truelight sky overhead, but Ashlinn noted the glare seemed a touch less bright than yesterturn.

The larger suns, Saan and Shiih, were in descent now, the Seer's furious red and the Watcher's sullen yellow both drifting toward the horizon. Saai would remain for a time after the other two eyes of the Everseeing had com-

---

*Built by King Francisco III to entertain his many mistresses (and hide his dalliances from his bride, Annalise), the garden mazes of Whitekeep are one of the city's

pleted their descent, the Knower casting its pale blue light over the Republic. But then, sure as death and taxes, truedark would begin.

As she leaned on the railing beside Tric, Ashlinn fancied the chill off the boy's skin seemed to be dimming along with the sunslight. Perhaps it was her imagination. Perhaps some facet of the dark magik that had returned him to this life. But if she squinted hard, she could see just the faintest hint of color in his skin now. His movements had just a touch more grace. And he spoke less and less like some deathless tool of the Goddess incarnate and more like the boy she'd known.

But Ash's skin still prickled standing next to him. Her hackles still rippling.

"Wonder how our girl's faring, recruiting her little army."

"YOU SHOULD BE WATCHING JONNEN."

She nodded to the boy seated on a coil of fat rope near the main mast. He was chewing the sugartwist she'd bought him and playing shadowball with Eclipse.

"He's right there." Ash tossed her warbraids back off her shoulders. "And do me a favor, neh? I'm not a nursemaid. Don't tell me what I should be doing."

He turned to look at her then. Those pitch-black eyes like holes in his head. That bloodless pallor, painted over the pretty beneath. O, he'd been a looker when he was alive, sure and true. High cheekbones, long lashes, broad shoulders, and clever hands. Could've been a real lady-killer, if the lady hadn't got there first.

"THINK HOW MIA WOULD FEEL IF SOMETHING WERE TO HAPPEN TO HIM."

"I don't need to think how Mia feels, Tricky. I *know*."

"AND HOW DOES SHE FEEL, ASHLINN?" the deadboy asked.

"Smooth as silk," Ash said, staring into that bottomless black. "Wet as summer dew, and sweet as strawberries." Her voice grew low and sultry. "Hard as

---

treasures. The mazes extend for twisting miles, and in the years since the monarchy's fall, have become a common place for lovers to meet and bang like shithouse doors in the wind.

One infamous Minister of Aa's church, Marcus Suitonius, attempted a foray into the Senate on a platform of "moral reformation." Complaining loudly that "one can hardly throw a rock in the mazes without killing a fornicator," he vowed to put an end to the amours being so energetically conducted there. Sadly, his campaign for a "return to family values" came to a groaning halt when he was discovered buggering a sweetboy in the very mazes he proposed to clean up, and to this turn, they remain a sanctuary where every citizen of the Republic is free to fuck their tiny brains out with a partner of their choosing.

Ah, romance.

steel before she comes, and soft as clouds after. Drenched in my arms like spring fucking rain."

He moved, though still not half as fast as he'd done in the houses of the dead. His hand found her throat a full second after she brought her sword to rest against his neck, its edge poised on the place Tric's jugular should have pulsed. She had no idea how bad it'd hurt him. She'd been in that cabin when he got stabbed in his arm and belly by those Itreyan marines. Not bleeding. Not falling. She idly wondered how much of him she'd have to cut off to slow him down.

Her voice was a croak against his grip.

"Get your fucking . . . hands off m-me."

"YOU'D DO WELL NOT TO PUSH ME, ASHLINN."

"Poor choice of w-words given . . . our history . . ."

His grip tightened, saltlocks moving like snakes roused from sleep. The suns might be sinking, he might be drifting closer to what he'd been, but he was still slow out here. Goddess, he was strong, though. His fingers like cold iron on her skin. Ash pressed the blade harder against his neck. Jonnen was watching them now with dark, glittering eyes, intelligent and malevolent.

"Map," she grinned. "R-Remember?"

He held her for a moment more, then released her, his shove sending her stumbling backward. She kept her blade raised, pawing at her throat and grinning.

"You always were a fucking maid."

"THAT MAP ON YOUR BACK MIGHT FADE WHEN YOU DIE, ASHLINN," Tric said, squaring up to her. "BUT THERE'S A GREAT DEAL OF HURT CAN BE DONE TO YOU WITHOUT KILLING YOU."

"See, there you go." She gifted the boy a wink. "A little bit of spit and fire, that's what I like to see. But I'm fierier than you, Tricky. I'm quicker and I'm prettier and the girl we both adore ended up in *my* bed, not yours." She drummed her fingers on her sword hilt. "I won. You lost. So stay away from her, aye?"

"ARE YOU REALLY THIS INSECURE?" he asked. "SO AFRAID SHE MIGHT LEAVE, YOU HAVE TO STAKE YOUR CLAIM TO HER AT THE POINT OF A SWORD?"

"I've got no claim," Ashlinn snarled. "She's not mine. She's *hers*. But if you think for one second I'm not willing to bathe in blood to be the one standing by her side when all this is over, then you're insane. Do you understand me?"

Ashlinn lowered her sword and stepped closer. Her head only came up to his chest. Her voice was a deadly whisper.

"You do whatever you need to do. Moons, Mothers, I don't give a toss. But if I get a whiff of some other endgame, I get a *hint* this Anais nonsense is putting her at risk, we'll find out sure and true if deadboys can die again."

She took a step back, eyes never leaving his.

"I will rip all three suns out of heaven to keep her safe, you hear me?" Ashlinn vowed. "I will kill the fucking *sky.*"

She blew him a kiss.

Then she turned and stalked away.

The Falcons chose a smoky taverna on the edge of the docks and drank like the Black Mother was coming for them all on the morrow. Mia hunched low, hood pulled down to hide the slave brand on her right cheek, the vicious scar across her left. The part of town they were in was sharp as broken glass, but still, she was a renowned gladiatii, the girl who slew the retchwyrm, now the most wanted killer in the Republic.

It didn't do to take chances.

She drank sparingly and sucked on the shitty cigarillos they sold over the bar, listening rather than talking. Wavewaker spoke of his plans for the theater, and Bryn spoke of the *magni* and Butcher spoke about each and every sweetgirl he'd plowed since he arrived in Whitekeep. Mia laughed aloud and ached inside, and over the next few hours came to slow grips with the fact that she should never have come here. That after this eve, she'd never see any of them again.

They'd fought and given enough. She couldn't ask any more of them—let alone to follow her to the Quiet Mountain to rescue a man they'd barely met. It'd been selfish for her to even think it. So she stopped thinking it at all, simply enjoying their company instead. And when ninebells struck, she got up to use the privy, promising she'd return.

Slipping out the taverna's back door a few moments later, she pulled her hood lower against that accursed sunslight and trudged off down the alley, back toward the docks. Mister Kindly flitted along the wall beside her, quiet as dead mice.

"*. . . where are we going . . . ?*" he finally asked.

"Back to the *Maid.* She puts out at tenbells, remember?"

"*. . . we seem to be missing our army . . .*"

"We'll have to manage without them."

"*. . . mia, i know you care f—*"

"I won't do it, Mister Kindly," she said. "I thought I could, but I can't. So leave it."

"*. . . you cannot do this alone . . .*"

"I *said* leave it."

The shadowcat coalesced on the cobbles in front of her, stopping her short.

". . . if you wish a dog who simply rolls over when you growl, bring eclipse with you. but i'll speak my mind, if it please you . . ."

"And if it doesn't please me?"

". . . i'll speak it anyway . . ."

Mia sighed, pinched the bridge of her nose. "Out with it, then."

". . . i am afraid for you . . ."

Mia almost laughed, until the words sank into her skull. Ringing like cathedral bells. And then she stood there in the smell of garbage and salt, wind off the bay whipping the cloak about her shoulders, suddenly and terribly cold.

". . . i spoke to eclipse about it, but eclipse never questions, like the one she rode before you never questioned. but you have always questioned, mia, and thus, so have i . . ."

The not-cat looked back toward the harbor, the ship waiting for them.

". . . and i question what it is you want from all this, and why. i watch the part of you that made you seek sidonius and the others—full in the knowledge that you will die if you fight the mountain shorthanded—at war with the part of you that does not fear death at all. and i question if the thing we take from you is not something you need, now more than ever. because you should *be afraid . . ."*

"This isn't about me being afraid, it's about right and wrong," she snapped. "I'm not broken. Don't try to fix me."

Though the daemon had no eyes, she could almost feel them narrowing.

"You saw them, Mister Kindly. How happy they were. Black Mother, 'Waker was like a child at fucking Great Tithe. And did you see the way Bryn looked at him? They have a life now. They have a chance. Who am I to demand they give that up?"

". . . you do not demand. you ask. that is what friends do . . ."

"No," she said flatly. "We shouldn't have come here. We find another way."

". . . mia—"

"I said *no*!"

Stepping right through the shadowcat, she trudged to the mouth of the alleyway, toward the harbor's tolling bells and the smell of the sea. She dragged the last breath out of her shitty cigarillo, breathed a plume of gray into the sky and crushed it under her boot. And reaching out to the shadows with clever fingers . . .

"Leaving without saying farewell?" Sidonius asked.

She turned and there he was, leaning against the wall. Bright blue eyes, hair shaved back to stubble, skin like cast bronze. She could see the brand they'd given him when they tossed him out of the Luminatii Legion. The word COWARD burned into his chest. She couldn't recall seeing a grander lie in all her life.

Bladesinger stood behind him, her saltlocks reaching to the ground, the intricate tattoos that covered every inch of her body gleaming in the sunslight. Wavewaker loomed beside her, chest broad as a barrel, plaited beard and dark saltlocks and artful ink on his face. Bryn stood near him, tying her blond topknot and watching Mia with clever blue eyes.

Butcher was taking a furtive piss against the wall.

"Aye," Mia said. "Apologies. I lost track of time. My ship puts out at tenbells."

"Why'd you come here, Mia?" Sidonius asked.

"I told you," she said, cool as autumn breeze. "I wanted to make sure you were all right. I have and you are and that's the end of it. So I'll be off."

Mia took a step away, felt his hand on her arm. She twisted, quick as silver, slipping free of his grip. And ripping up a handful of shadows, easier and swifter than she could've done even a few weeks back, she vanished before their wondering eyes.

She squinted in the worldblur, Stepping to a shadow farther down the street,

and then another

farther still.

Her head swam from the burn of the suns above, but she stayed on her feet. And finally, content they'd not be able to follow, she began groping her way forward, blind to all the world, waiting for the familiar whispers to guide her back to the waiting *Maid*.

Except no one was whispering.

"Mister Kindly?"

She blinked, feeling about in the shadows for her friend. Realizing he'd not come with her.

"Mister Kindly?"

Mia cast aside her mantle, turned back to the alley mouth a hundred feet away. And there he sat, a ribbon of darkness at the gladiatii's feet, tail twitching side to side as he spoke. She felt a swell of rage in her chest, raising her voice in a shout.

"Don't you *dare*!"

The not-cat ignored her, and by the time she'd run back across the cobbles, the Falcons were all looking at her like she was someone new. Disappointment in their eyes. Consternation. Maybe even anger.

"Mister Kindly, shut your fucking hole!"

". . . i do not have holes, fucking or otherwise . . ."

Mia aimed a kick at the not-cat's head. It sailed harmlessly through the daemon, of course, but she tried to kick him again regardless. "What did you tell them?"

"What you were too ashamed to ask," Bladesinger scowled.

"You little shit!" she cried, kicking the cat again. "I said we'd manage!"

". . . and i said you cannot do this alone . . ."

"That wasn't your decision to make!"

". . . no, it was theirs . . ."

"You hateful fucking—"

"Mia," Sidonius said gently.

"Sid, I'm sorry," she said, looking among the Falcons. "All of you. I thought about it, but then I thought the best of it, and I never should've thought it at all. This isn't your fight, and I'd no right to drag you into it. Don't think the lesser of me, I—"

"Mia, of course I'll help," Sid said.

"Aye," Bladesinger nodded. "My sword is yours."

Bryn folded her arms and glowered. "Always."

Tears stung Mia's eyes, but she blinked them back, shaking her head.

"No. I don't *want* your help."

"Crow, you saved our lives," Bladesinger said, nodding to Mister Kindly. "And if the daemon speaks true, yours is in greater peril than ours ever were. What kind of curs would we be if we left you to swing after all you did? What kind of thanks is that?"

"What about the theater?" she demanded.

Wavewaker shrugged, gave a sad smile. "It'll be there when we return."

"No. I'll not have it."

"Mia, you risked your life for us," Sidonius said. "Everything you'd worked for danced on the edge of a knife. And still you gambled it all to see us to freedom. And now you'd stand there and tell us what we can and can't do with it?"

"Damn right I do," she snarled. "You owe me your lives? Go fucking live them. You want to give me thanks? Do it when you tell your grandchildren about me."

She spun on her heel, glaring at the shadowcat.

"We're leaving. *Now.*"

". . . as it please you . . ."

She began stalking away down the street, heard Bladesinger affect a yawn.

"You know, that last glass of goldwine just went straight to my head," she said. "Think I need to walk it off down by the harbor."

"Aye," Bryn said. "I could take a stroll on the boardwalk."

"Sea air," Sid crooned. "Think I'll come, too. Book a cruise, maybe."

Mia rumbled to a stop. Shoulders slumped.

"I hear Ashkah is lovely this time of year," Wavewaker said, strolling past her.

"Never been to Ashkah," Bryn mused, hooking her thumbs into her belt.

"Hmm," Bladesinger pouted. "Nor I, come to mention it . . ."

She watched them wander down the street toward the water, the tears back to burning in her eyes. They stopped at the end of the road, turned to look at her, slumped and scowling on the cobbles.

"Coming?" Sidonius called.

She looked at the not-cat in the gutter beside her. Betrayal like a knife in her chest. He'd always been one to question, aye, push her if he thought she was being a fool. But he'd never gone against her like this before. Never acted so contrary to what he *knew* she wanted.

"I've never been sorrier to have met you than I am at this moment."

". . . a burden i will gladly bear, to keep you breathing . . ."

She glowered down at him, shaking her head. "If anything happens to them, I fucking swear I'll not forgive you for it."

The shadowcat peered at her with his not-eyes, tail twitching.

". . . i am a part of you, mia. before i met you, i was a formless nothing, looking for a meaning. the shape i wear is born of you, the thing i became is because of you. and if i must do what you will not, so be it. at least you will be alive to hate me . . ."

She looked into the sky, the suns falling slow toward the horizon.

Another might have been afraid, then, to consider what was coming.

Turned around and run back.

But ever and always, Mia Corvere walked on.

CHAPTER 15

FINESSE

"Benino," Mia said.

"No," Cloud replied.

"Bertino, then. You look like a Bertino."

"No." Cloud frowned. "And what the 'byss does a Bertino look like, anyways?"

"Tell me the first letter," Mia demanded. "It's *B,* I'm right about that, aye?"

"No clues, Dona Mia. I told you."

"You must give me *something,*" she wheedled.

"I must give you nothing," the captain said, raising an eyebrow. "I bet my bloody ship you'd not be able to guess my name, why in Trelene's name would I help you?"

"You're sick of the sea and want to settle somewhere green?"

"Pig's arse," the privateer scoffed. "You cut these wrists, I bleed blue."

They were three turns out of Whitekeep and sailing on swift waves. Their destination lay through the Sea of Swords on the coast of Ashkah—the town of Last Hope. From that decrepit seaport, it'd be a trek across the Whisperwastes to the Quiet Mountain. Mia had no idea how Mercurio might be faring in the keeping of the Red Church, or how she might save him from their clutches. But though she'd not admit it to many, she'd loved that man more than any since her father. And now, more than any man at all. She'd be damned if she left him to rot.

The snaggletooth coastline of Liis stretched off to the south, the white cliffs of Itreya to the north, the *Maid* riding low on the rolling blue. The former Falcons of Remus kept themselves mostly to the bow, reveling in the feel of the sea upon their faces.

Sidonius struck quite a sight, his bronze skin gleaming in the sunslight, hair shaved to dark fuzz, eyes of bright baby blue. The big Itreyan always kept Mia in his eyeline if he could help it—his loyalty to Darius Corvere had seen him take Mia under his wing when they were both Falcons, and hadn't diminished one drop since. With him aboard, it felt like she had another rock to set her back against. Her little brother might be an intolerable shit. But if Mia could've had a big brother, she'd have chosen Sid.

Wavewaker wasn't shy about lending a hand on deck—like most Dweymeri islanders, he'd grown up around ships and knew the ocean like his own reflection. The former thespian towered over the crew as he worked, treating Corleone's salts to endless songs in his booming baritone. He had a voice that could make a silkling weep, and Mia still felt guilt that she'd dragged him away from his lifelong dream of owning a theater. She silently vowed to see him return to it when this was done.

Bladesinger likewise knew her way around the *Maid,* but she kept to the bow, looking out at the rolling blue with dark eyes. All Dweymeri were marked with facial tattoos when they came of age, but every inch of 'Singer's mahogany skin was covered in intricate designs—a legacy of her time studying as a priestess. Mia still found it odd to think of the woman praying in a temple somewhere. 'Singer was one of the collegium's finest warriors, a marvel on the sands. Though the forearm wound Bladesinger had earned battling the silkling still seemed to be troubling her . . .

Bryn likewise seemed troubled, and Mia knew the source—the girl's brother Byern had died on the sands but a few months back. The girl stuck close to Wavewaker, chatting and watching him work, and his presence seemed to keep the worst of her cares away. Bryn was Vaanian like Ash, hard as nails, the finest shot with a bow Mia had ever met—Mia was glad for her company. But she still feared this fool's quest might end with Bryn and the rest of her comrades in the grave beside Byern.

Of the five Falcons, only Butcher pulled up seasick—but given he'd pissed into Mia's porridge the first time they'd met, she felt that had a kind of justice to it. The big Liisian had never been the finest sword in the collegium, but what he lacked in skill, he made up for in heart, bluster, and stunning foulmouthedness. He kept near the port side, where his vomit had the least chance of blowing back into his face, cursing the goddesses and Wavewaker, too, who seemed most amused by his upset stomach.

All told, the former gladiatii seemed to be taking to life at sea quite well.

But elsewhere on deck, things weren't quite as peaceful. Ashlinn and Tric circled each other like serpents waiting to strike. Though they stayed apart from each other now that Corleone had given them their own cabins, there seemed an even deeper tension between them since they'd berthed at Whitekeep. Mia still hadn't reached a conclusion about her own feelings as far as Tric's return was concerned, but Ashlinn was clearly a knot of suspicion and open hostility.

Mia and Mister Kindly hadn't spoken to each other since they sailed from Whitekeep, either. He'd not ridden her shadow in turns.

Furious as she was about his betrayal, she missed him.

And so Mia stood with the *Bloody Maid*'s captain by the wheel, playing her new favorite game and glorying in the feel of cool wind on her face. After months in Remus Collegium or cells beneath arenas, even a breeze was a blessing. And trying to win the captain's ship off him was better than worrying about the tempest brewing aboard it.

"There's a storm headed for us," Cloud Corleone declared.

"Aye," she muttered, looking at the deck below. "I know it."

"No, I mean there's a genuine storm," he said, pointing to a glowering smear of black on the eastern horizon. "We're sailing straight into it."

Mia squinted to where he pointed. "Is it a bad one?"

"Well, it won't be breaking our backs by the look, but it'll be a rough couple of turns." The privateer flashed his four-bastard grin. "So if you want to take advantage of the bath in my cabin, Dona Mia, you'd best be about it quickly."

"I might just do that," she mused.

"Splendid, I'll bring the soap."

"Might I also suggest some splints for your broken fingers," she said, giving him a sideways smile. "And some ice for your mangled jewels."

Corleone grinned in return, doffed his feathered tricorn. He was as sly as a fox in a hens' roost and crooked as a scabdog's back leg. But despite his cheek, Mia couldn't help but like the scoundrel. Corleone seemed to enjoy a flirt, but it was clear from his playful manner that this was simply a game for him, much as trying to guess his name was for her. The tale of his brother still hung in the air with the memory of Duomo's murder, and looking into the pirate's eyes, Mia suspected she'd made an ally for life.

"I'll have the cabin boy start up the arkemical stove and run the water," Corleone winked. "If you've need of someone to wash your back, just sing."

"Go fuck yourself," she laughed, raising the knuckles.

"Alas." He pressed his hand to his heart as if pained. "That does seem the only option available, Dona Mia. For now, at least."

"In every breath, hope abides . . ." Mia grinned.

She skipped down the stairs off the aft deck and on to the quarter. Jonnen was sat to one side, playing with Eclipse at their own favorite game. The boy would gather up handfuls of shadows and toss them across the boards, and Eclipse would pounce upon them like a puppy at a bone. Jonnen sometimes moved the thrown shadowscraps to evade the daemon's jaws, and he'd laugh when she missed—though it seemed a laugh of genuine amusement, rather than derision.

He stopped playing as Mia came down the stairs, though, his smile vanishing. Drawing a deep breath, she sat down beside him, legs crossed. Ashlinn had gone to market at Whitekeep, spent most of their coin—but she'd found Mia a good set of leather britches, black and tight, and a pair of wolfskin boots. She'd tossed her leather gladiatii skirt overboard with a small prayer of thanks two turns back.

Best of all though, her girl had returned with . . .

"Cigarillos?" the boy said, eyeing her with distaste. "Must you?"

"I must," Mia nodded, propping one at her lips and striking her new flintbox.

"My mother said only strumpets and fools smoke."

"And which am I, brother mine?" she asked, sighing gray.

The boy watched her with lips pressed thin. "Perhaps both?"

Eclipse coalesced on the boards between them, placing her head in Mia's lap.

". . . YOU SHOULD NOT SPEAK TO HER SO, JONNEN . . ."

"I shall speak to her how I choose," the boy declared.

"*. . . DO YOU REMEMBER I TOLD YOU ABOUT THE LITTLE BOY I KNEW? CASSIUS . . . ?*"

"Yes," the boy sniffed, eyeing the wolf sidelong.

"*. . . HE ALWAYS SAID BLOOD STAINS DEEPER THAN WINE. DO YOU KNOW WHAT THAT MEANS . . . ?*"

The boy shook his head.

"*. . . IT MEANS FAMILIA CAN HURT YOU MORE THAN ANYONE ELSE. BUT THAT IS ONLY BECAUSE THEY* MATTER *MORE THAN ANYONE ELSE. WHEN YOU SPEAK SO, THOUGH MIA DOES NOT SHOW IT, IT WOUNDS HER . . .*"

"Good," he snapped. "I do not like her. I do not wish to be here."

Jonnen looked out to the blue waters rushing along their flanks.

"I want to go home," he said.

"We'll pass it in a week or so," Mia nodded to the Itreyan coast. "Crow's Nest."

"That is not my home, Kingmaker."

"*. . . HOME IS WHERE THE HEART IS, CHILD . . .*"

Mia tapped her breast and smiled. "Explains my empty chest."

"*. . . FOOLISHNESS . . .* ," Eclipse scoffed. "*. . . YOU HAVE THE HEART OF A LION . . .*"

"A crow, perhaps." She wiggled her fingers at the wolf. "Black and shriveled."

"*. . . YOU WILL KNOW THE LIE OF THAT BEFORE THE END OF THIS, MIA. I PROMISE . . .*"

Mia smiled and took a slow drag, reveling in the warmth of the smoke in her lungs. Looking sidelong toward Jonnen. Brother. Stranger. He was clever, that much was certain: education from the finest tutors in the Republic, coupled with the fierce intelligence of Alinne Corvere and the cunning of Julius Scaeva. Watching the way he carried himself, the way he spoke, Mia suspected he'd grow up even sharper than she was. There was a cruel streak in him, learned from his father, most like. But there was a cruelty to her, too, she supposed. Jonnen was still her blood, her familia. The only kind she had left, unless you counted the bastard she was going to kill. And after all these years without one, she found herself aching for some kind of real connection with him.

"I remember the nevernight you were born there," she told the boy. "In Crow's Nest. I was barely older than you are now. The midwife brought me in to meet you, and Mother handed you over to me and you started screaming. Just . . . screaming like the world was ending." Mia shook her head. "'Byss and blood, you had some lungs on you."

Another drag, eyes narrowed against the smoke.

"Mother told me to sing to you," she said. "She said even though your eyes were shut, you'd know your sister. So I sang. And you stopped crying. Like someone threw a lever inside your head." She shook her head. "Damnedest thing."

"My mother does not sing," Jonnen said. "She dislikes music."

"O, no, she *loved* it," Mia insisted. "She used to sing all the time, she—"

"My mother is Liviana Scaeva," the boy said. "Wife of the imperator."

Mia felt a rush of blood to her cheeks. Pulse thudding in her temple. Despite herself, she felt her brows drawing together in a scowl. Breathing smoke like fire.

"Your mother was Alinne Corvere," she said. "*Victim* of the imperator."

"Liar," the boy scowled.

"Jonnen, why would I—"

"You're a liar! A *liar*!"

"And you're a fucking brat," she snapped.

"Villain," he spat. "Thief. *Killer*."

"Like father, like daughter, I suppose."

"My father is a great man!" Jonnen cried.

"Your father's a cunt."

"And your mother a whore!"

It took everything Mia had in her not to raise her hand to him again.

". . . MIA . . ."

She hauled herself to her feet, her patience in flames. Shaking with anger. Wanting to bite her tongue but afraid the blood would just fill her mouth and drown her. Talking to the boy was like bashing her head into a brick wall. Trying to crack his shell was like fumbling at a lock with ten fucking thumbs. She'd no practice at being a big sister, no talent for it besides. And so, as was usual, frustration unlocked the door and let her temper out to run free instead.

"I'm trying, Jonnen," she said. "Maw's teeth, I am. If you were anyone else, I'd have kicked your arse over the side for what you said just now. But don't you *ever* speak like that about her again. She loved you. Do you hear me?"

"All I hear, Kingmaker," he spat, "are lies from the mouth of a murderer."

She took a deep breath. Head lowered, eyes closed.

"I hope you like storms more than you did when you were a babe," she said, looking at him again. "There's a big one headed our way. And if I hear you crying in your sleep, I'll not come singing this time."

"I *hate* you," the boy hissed.

She flicked her cigarillo over the railing, breathing smoke.

"Like father, like son, I suppose."

It wasn't a bath so much as a brass barrel.

It was bolted to the floor in Corleone's quarters—an en suite off the bedchamber, which in turn led off from the main cabin. Mia's first thought when she laid eyes on it was to wonder where exactly the brigand was supposed to fit if she'd taken him up on his offer to bring the soap. She'd be able to squeeze in there with a little effort, but it wasn't exactly palatial in scope.

This alleged "bath" had more in common with a bucket.

Still, the water in it was steaming, fed by pipes from the arkemical stove in the galley below. And as Mia stripped naked and sank into the heat, she understood why Corleone had indulged in such an extravagance.

"O, Black fucking Mother," she groaned. "That is *gooood*."

She dunked her head after some clumsy maneuvering and found if she hung her legs out over the lip, she could get most of her body submerged. Leaning back, she soaked a washcloth and draped it over her face. Lighting another cigarillo, she breathed a contented gray sigh, listening to the song of the sea outside.

"*I* could be a pirate," she mumbled, smoke bobbing on her lips. "Avast, ye lubbers. Hoist the giblets. Stow the mizzen-whatsit, you pig-loving fuckmonkey—"

"Alone at last," said a voice.

Mia dragged the washcloth away, saw Ashlinn leaning against the door. She wore a drakebone corset over her red shirt, leather leggings, and thigh-high boots. She'd bought some herbs in Whitekeep, washed the henna from her hair. It'd been let loose from her braids, rolling down her shoulders in golden waterfalls.

"Two isn't alone," Mia said.

Ash ran a finger down the doorframe. "I can leave. If you like."

"No," Mia smiled. "Stay."

Ash's face brightened and she slipped into the en suite, closing the door behind her. There was nowhere to sit, so she straddled the barrel instead. Plucking the cigarillo from Mia's mouth, Ashlinn leaned down to plant a light kiss on her lips. She remained hovering close, their noses brushing against one another, ticklish.

"Hello," Ash whispered.

"Hello," Mia replied.

Ash leaned in and they kissed again, soft and warm and altogether dizzying.

Ashlinn's lips parted, inviting, and Mia felt the girl shiver as their tongues touched, light as feathers. She sighed into Ash's open mouth, raising one hand to caress her cheek as their kiss deepened. Drowning in it, never wanting to come up for air, sucking Ash's bottom lip as they slowly pulled apart.

Opening her eyes, she saw Ash's face just an inch from hers. Their lips brushed together as the girl murmured.

"You kiss like you kill, Mia Corvere."

"And how's that?"

"With *finesse*."

Mia smirked and Ashlinn kissed her again, again, again, a dozen whisper-light touches scattered across her lips and cheeks like rose petals.

"I missed you," Mia sighed.

"How much?"

"Not entirely sure how to measure that," Mia frowned. "Couple of feet, maybe?"

"Fuck you."

"Bath isn't big enough for that."

"I hate you."

"Strange. I hate everyone *but* you."

"Sit up," Ash grinned, kissing her again. "I'll wash your back."

Ashlinn swung herself off the tub so Mia could wrangle herself upright, rest her head on her arms, and lean forward. Ash sat behind, legs slung on either side of the barrel. Mia couldn't see what she was doing, but she soon felt warm, soapy hands across her shoulders, the scent of honeysuckle and sunsbell in the air. Ash pressed her thumbs into Mia's aching muscles, kneading the knots of tension like dough.

"O, Black Mother, that's . . . fucking . . . *good* . . . ," Mia groaned.

She closed her eyes and let Ash's hands shush everything away for a moment. Her frustration at Jonnen and her anger at Mister Kindly. Her worries about Sid and the others, the thought of what was waiting for them across the ocean in Ashkah. Mercurio and the Moon and his damned crown.

Ash was keeping quiet about Tric, too, even though they could both feel the question of him hanging like frost in the air. She was too smart to bring him up. To open that door and let it ruin the first moment they'd been alone since the *magni*.

Instead, Mia felt lips on the nape of her neck, sending shivers down her spine.

"You could always get out of the bath," Ash murmured. "If it's not big enough."

"In a minute . . ." She winced as Ash's hands worked a particularly tight knot. "Goddess . . . keep doing that . . ."

"You're wound tight as mekwerk, love."

"Hard work, being the most wanted killer in the Republic."

Another kiss. A soft nibble at her ear as Ash whispered, "I can unwind you."

Mia felt Ash's hands slip around to slowly caress her breasts. Fingers running over smooth skin, setting it tingling. Mia's breath came quicker, her belly thrilled, another shiver rolling right through the core of her. Goosebumps rose over her body, a soft sigh escaping her lips as Ash's kisses tickled her neck, as the girl's hands went roaming, one teasing her hardening nipple, the other tracing a long, agonizing spiral down. Down. Over her ribs, inch by inch along her tightening belly, tracing the cusp of her navel with whisper-light circles of flickering arkemical current.

"More?" Ash whispered, lips brushing her earlobe.

Mia wondered at the rightness of it. Some lingering guilt at the presence of the Hearthless boy on deck above, perhaps, or the fight she was in with her brother or the idea she should be indulging herself at all in waters this perilous. But Ash's hand slipped below the water, and a fire rose up inside Mia, melting her misgivings as she felt the gentlest of touches between her legs.

Breathtaking.

Maddening.

"More," Mia sighed.

She felt Ashlinn's other hand rise, fingers entwining with her hair. Mia groaned as Ash pulled her back, upright, leaving her exposed, steam rising off her skin, her thighs quivering. Ash's lips found her neck again as the hand between Mia's legs began to move, firm, tight circles, strumming the tune her lover knew so well. Mia reached back, sighing, grabbing a fistful of Ash's hair and pressing her girl's lips harder against her neck. There was some illicit thrill in it; the feel of Ash pressed against her fully clothed while she was so utterly bare. A surrender that left her shaking.

"O, fuck," she breathed, hips moving in time. *"Fuck."*

"More?" Ash whispered in her ear.

Lips tickling her skin.

Teeth nipping her neck.

Fingers dancing.

"More," Mia pleaded.

She felt Ash's second hand join her first, in front and behind. Mia reached back, fingernails clawing at Ashlinn's arse, grinding back between her legs. She felt Ashlinn's fingers, stroking, kneading, singing on her lips and bud. Time frozen still and burning in the light of a black sun. Shapeless nothings spilling from her lips, eyes rolling back in her head as she was dragged ever higher by her lover's touch, flying now, every caress, every movement pulling her up toward that dark immolation.

"Yes," Ashlinn breathed.

"Yes," Mia groaned. "Fuck yes. *Yes.*"

She threw her head back as she ignited, mouth open, every muscle taut and singing, every nerve aflame. Ashlinn's hands kept moving, grinding, prolonging the shuddering, pulsing bliss. Mia cried out, pulling Ashlinn in against her, quivering and senseless, not enough air in her lungs, not enough blood in her veins.

Ash's movements slowed, working a sweet and gentle torture until Mia reached down, pressed her hands against her and held them still.

"Enough," she sighed. "Goddess . . . enough."

She felt Ashlinn's lips curling in a smile, another gentle nibble at her neck.

"Never," Ash whispered. "Not ever."

She stood up slowly, offered Mia her hand.

"Come with me, beautiful."

CHAPTER 16

TEMPEST

The storm hit a few hours later.

They lay in each other's arms in Mia's cabin, skin to skin as the thunder rolled and the oceans swelled and the *Maid* rose and crashed and rose again. Mia had been grateful for the tempest once it settled in; the thunder and wind had been loud enough to drown out Ashlinn's cries. Keeping their balance in the rising swell had proved a challenge, but through sheer determination, they'd managed it. On the floor and against the wall and in the hammock, too, finally collapsing there in a breathless, heaving tangle. The hammock swayed back and forth with the movement of the ship instead of their bodies now, timbers groaning around them.

Mia's hair was damp with sweat, Ashlinn's body slippery against hers, the girl's scent hanging in the air like the sweetest perfume. Mia could taste Ash on her lips along with the sugar of her cigarillo paper, the heady gray burn of the smoke on her tongue.

"I can't feel my legs," Ashlinn murmured.

Mia laughed around her 'rillo, dragging the smoke from her lips.

"Don't blame me. You're the one who pleaded for more."

"Couldn't help myself." Ash nuzzled closer. "And you like it when I plead."

Goddess help her, but she did. Exhausted as Mia was, just the thought of it was enough to send fresh shivers along her spine. The sweet surrender of Ash in her arms, the honeyed triumph Mia felt as she melted under her touch. She was drunk with it. Eyelashes fluttering as she smiled and breathed clove-scented smoke, the girl in her embrace hers, and only hers.

Truth was, it'd be easy to think Mia and Ashlinn were cut from the same cloth. A pair made of spit and fire, driven by vengeance, sharp and hard, aye, perhaps even cruel. But Ash was different when they were alone. She was softer here. Silk to Mia's steel. All the walls she put up for the world crumbling away to dust. There were parts of herself Ash kept just for Mia—like secrets in the dark, whispered without speaking. A language of sweet sighs and knowing eyes, of soft lips and gentle fingertips.

Lightning flashed through the porthole glass (replaced when they'd berthed at Whitekeep). Thunder rolled across the skies above, black clouds stretched over the sky. Mia could still feel the three suns waiting beyond, though, like a leaden weight on her shoulders, an ache at the base of her skull. Hate upon hate.

Mia ran her fingers up the smooth curve of Ashlinn's hips, over her back, feeling the girl shiver and sigh in her arms. She was a feast for the senses, sure and true. Beautiful, svelte, golden. But Mia found her eyes drawn to the tattoo scribed on her lover's skin. The map she'd stolen at Cardinal Duomo's behest. It showed a twisting path through a crescent mountain range, instructions in the tongue of Old Ashkah. Glancing at the inkwerk, Mia saw the map's destination between the luscious divots at the small of Ashlinn's back. It was marked with a grim and grinning skull, which didn't bode well for whatever happened on arrival at this mysterious Crown of the Moon.

This, of course, put Mia in mind of Tric, and all he'd told her as they stood beside that blackened pool beneath Godsgrave's skin. Aa and Niah. The war between Light and Night. The splinter of a dead god's soul somehow lodged in Mia's own. She thought of the deadboy sitting alone in his cabin, listening to the tempest while she locked herself in here and fucked his murderer. A cool sliver of guilt piercing her heart.

Ashlinn had risked her life for Mia countless times during her trials in the *venatus*. Aside from Mercurio and her passengers, Ash had been the only one

Mia could count on during those dark turns. And what Ashlinn had done in the Quiet Mountain after initiation—as terrible and bloody as her betrayal had been—Mia would simply be lying to herself if she said a part of her didn't understand it.

Ashlinn's father had raised his daughter to see the Red Church's corruption. And though his motives were selfish—though it was his maiming in the Church's service that led Torvar Järnheim to raise his children as weapons to bring about the Ministry's fall—Mia could understand that, too. And more, understand why Ashlinn had followed him.

He was familia.

When all is blood, blood is all.

Truth was, Mia was no different. She was no better. She wasn't a hero, driven by the cruelty and injustice of the Republic. She was a killer, driven by the pure and burning desire for revenge. Scaeva and Duomo and Remus had hurt her, and so she'd set out to hurt them back. And if others got in her way on the journey, one way or another, she moved them out of her way. Ashlinn had simply done the same.

Except one of the people she removed was Mia's friend.

Confidant.

Lover.

And a year later, Mia had fallen into Ashlinn's bed.

There was something heartless about that, Mia knew it. And it had been easy to rationalize at the time—any turn in the *venatus* could've been her last, and she'd clung to whatever comfort she could find back then. She was indebted to Ashlinn. She saw a dark kinship in Ashlinn. Goddess knew, she was attracted to Ashlinn.

And Tric was dead. Gone. Never coming back.

But now . . .

And while the press of Ash's lips left Mia feeling almost dizzy, the thought of her touch even now, laying senseless and sated, sending warm and delightful pulses up her thighs, a part of Mia—the part Mister Kindly would have filled, most likely—was still suspicious of this girl in her arms. She thought about what the shadowcat had told her in Whitekeep. Wondering if the thing he took—fear, and all the spectrum of emotions it gave birth to—were things she should cherish rather than give away.

"Where did you find it?" she asked.

"Mmm?" Ash murmured, raising her head.

"The map." Mia traced the line of Ash's tattoo with her fingertip. "Where was it?"

"Old temple," Ash sighed, sinking back onto Mia's breast. "Ashkah." She squirmed closer as Mia continued to stroke her back. "S'nice. Keep doing that."

Mia sucked on her cigarillo, breathed gray into the air. Thunder rolled outside.

"What kind of temple?"

"Ruined. Dedicated to Niah. Why?"

"Who made it? Worship of Niah has been outlawed for centuries."

Ash lifted her head again, a note of caution in her voice. "I don't know. It was old. Hidden, too. Carved out of red stone, in the northern mountains. Up near the coast."

"And you were sent by Duomo to find it, aye? With others, you told me."

Ashlinn looked at Mia a long moment before she spoke. The waves crashed against their hull, the storm swelling darker and fiercer outside.

"There were ten of us. A bishop of Aa's ministry named Valens. A pack of thugs—a Liisian named Piero, and two Itreyans named Rufus and Quintus. Can't remember the rest. I don't think Duomo trusted the Luminatii, so they were sellswords all. There was a Vaanian cartographer named Astrid, too. And me."

"What happened to them?"

"They died."

Mia took a long drag on her cigarillo, eyes narrowed against the smoke. "How?"

"What difference does it make?"

"Did you kill them?"

"Would it matter if I did?"

Mia shrugged, looking into the girl's sky-blue eyes.

"Rufus got killed by a rockadder. Valens and most of the others died in the temple." Ash looked at Mia's rising eyebrow and sighed. "There were . . . things in there, Mia. In the map chamber. Like the bookworms in the Red Church Athenaeum almost, but . . . smaller. Faster." Ash shook her head, shuddering slightly. "They attacked while Astrid was scribing the map. Piero and his sellswords tried to save the priest, they all got cut to ribbons. It was . . . messy. Only Astrid and I made it out, and then, only just."

"And what happened to Astrid?"

"I killed her," Ash said, her voice flat. "She worked for Duomo and I didn't trust her. So I cut her throat the turn I got the map scribed on my skin. Happy now?"

Lightning arced across the skies, thunder shaking the *Maid* in her bones.

"Why have you got your back up?" Mia asked. "Why so defensive?"

"Why ask me about all this now?"

"I never really had a chance before," Mia shrugged. "I want to know how all these pieces fit. If we're going to this Crown of the Moon—"

"You're not seriously considering that?" Ash asked.

Mia dragged deep on her smoke. "I don't know what I'm considering yet, Ash."

Ashlinn scowled. "I don't like it, Mia. All this talk of shattered moons and warring gods and whatnot. It stinks of rot to me. I don't trust Tric as far as I could throw him."

"You threw him all the way off a mountain, if I recall."

Ash blinked. "O, now here's a turn. Is the most infamous killer in the Itreyan Republic honestly about to lecture me on the morality of murder?"

Mia spoke slow, broaching the topic with as much care as she could muster.

"He was your friend, Ashlinn . . ."

"He wasn't my friend," Ash spat. "There *are* no friends in the Church of Our Lady of Blessed Murder. And he wasn't some lost lamb I butchered, either. He was the servant of a death cult that I was trying to burn to the ground. He killed an innocent child to take his place among Niah's Blades, Mia. And I'm not hypocritical enough to blame him for that. But just because he's got some pretty dimples doesn't mean he's not a fucking killer. Just like me. And just like *you*."

Mia looked into Ashlinn's eyes. Her walls were back up now, the softness long banished, the fire she breathed every turn of her life coming quick to her lips. For all her adoration, Ash wasn't shy about standing up to Mia when she felt the need. Pushing back where no one else dared, cutting right to the heart of it. And sure enough, she'd found her mark. The truth Mia couldn't argue with.

How can I fault her for doing what I've done a hundred times or more?

"My brother *died* in that attack on the Quiet Mountain," Ash continued. "And I never whined about it. Never once asked if you had anything to do with it."

"I didn't kill Osrik, Ash," Mia said, taken aback. "It was Adonai."

"That's not the *point*," Ash replied. "I didn't ask because it doesn't *matter*. Whatever you did, you did it because it needed to be done. Remorse is for the weak, Mia. And regret is for cowards. Whatever you did then meant you can be here in my arms now. That makes it right. And I'm not about to let some bollocks about moons and suns take that away from us."

Thunder rolled again, as if the Lady of Storms were eavesdropping at the window. Mia blinked as the lightning flickered, shadows strobing on the walls. Dragging on her cigarillo and breathing smoke into the air.

"I'm dreaming, Ashlinn," she confessed. "Every nevernight. I see my mother and father. Except they're *not* my mother and father. They're arguing. About me. And when I look at my reflection, there's someone standing behind me. A figure made of black flame, with a white circle scribed on his brow."

". . . What does it mean?"

"I've no idea. Hence my desire to see the whole board, Ash."

"I don't want to feel like I'm a piece on a board," Ashlinn said, a touch of desperation in her voice. "I don't want us to play this game anymore. I want us to get Mercurio out, get Scaeva dead, and then just get gone from all this. Someplace quiet and far, far away. You and me." Ash pouted. "I suppose Jonnen can come. If the little smart-arse learns to keep a civil tongue in his head. But he gets his own room."

"Is that how you see this playing out?" Mia asked, cigarillo bobbing on her lips. "Shacked up in some cottage? Flowers in the windowsill and a fire in the hearth?"

Ash nodded. "And a big feather bed."

"Really?" Mia dragged deep, squinting against the smoke. "Us? *Me?*"

"Why not?" Ash asked. "My da built a house on the shore of Threelakes. North of Ul'Staad. The hollyhock and sunsbell grow so thick, the whole valley smells like perfume. You should see it. The lake is so still, it's like a mirror to the sky."

"I'm . . ." Mia shook her head. "I'm not sure I'm cut out for a life like that . . ."

Ash lowered her eyes, her voice a murmur.

"You mean a life with me."

"I mean . . ." Mia sighed, trying to form her thoughts into words. "I mean I've never even *thought* about what I'll do after this. I've never imagined a moment where this wasn't my life. It's all I've been for eight years, Ash. It's all there is."

Ashlinn leaned in and kissed her, hand to her cheek, fierce and tender.

"It's *not* all there is," she whispered.

Mia looked into Ashlinn's eyes, saw them shining with almost-tears. Reflecting the lightning crawling across the dark skies outside.

"I love you, Mia Corvere," she said. "Everything you are. But there's so much more to you than this. I know you might not see a life like that for yourself, but you can have it if you want it. I'm not going to lay here and say that you deserve it. You're a thief and a killer and a hateful fucking cunt."

Mia couldn't help but smile. "Truth."

"But that's why I adore you," Ash breathed. "And the more I live it, the more I realize 'deserve' has nothing to do with this life. Blessings and curses fall on the wicked and the just alike. Fair is a fairy tale. Nothing's claimed by those who don't want it, and nothing's kept by those who won't fight for it. So let's *fight*. Fuck the gods. Fuck it all. Let's take the world by the throat and make it give us what we want."

Ash kissed her again, the taste of burning tears on her lips.

"Because I want *you*."

She didn't wait for reciprocation—Ash wasn't the kind to declare affections just to hear them parroted back. No insecurity. No bait. The girl knew how she felt, she trusted Mia enough to share it, and that was all there was to it. Mia liked that about her.

But do I love it?

Ash settled in against her side, arms wrapped around her, squeezing tight.

"There's nothing I wouldn't do for you, to keep you safe, to see you through." Ash shook her head, sniffing back her tears. "Nothing."

"I know," Mia whispered, kissing her brow.

"I want to be with you forever," Ashlinn sighed.

"Just forever?"

"Forever and ever."

Mia lay there for a long time after Ash fell asleep.

Imagining a lake so still, it was like a mirror to the sky.

Staring at the gloom above her head and picturing a pale globe shining there.

Listening to the tempest sing.

And wondering.

It was growing worse.

The *Bloody Maid* was almost a hundred and twenty feet of sturdy oak and reinforced cedar, built to cut the ocean's face like an apothecary's scalpel. But the swell was rising along with the winds, howling and gnashing about her like a wild thing at rumpus. The ship was tossed like a toy, the Ladies of Storms and Oceans both seemed in a fury. Without Mister Kindly in her shadow, each towering wave brought Mia a threefold fear—the torturous climb, an agonized, weightless quiet, and then a belly-churning drop down into the dark and an impact that felt like the whole earth was ending.

A moment's pause. And then it all would begin again.

For hours. And hours. On end.

"'Byss and blood," Ashlinn swore.

Their hammock was hung cross-ship to better sway and roll with the *Maid*'s motion, but even spent as they both were, sleep had become impossible. As the tempest grew steadily worse, the winds howling, the thunder sounding as if it were right on top of them, Mia found herself rolling out of the hammock and dragging on her leathers and boots. Belly full of butterflies. Hands shaking.

"Stay here," she told Ash.

"Where are you going?"

"Talk to Corleone. Find out what the fuck is going on."

She pushed herself through the cabin door despite her fear, staggering with the violent sway and toss. Closing the door behind, she made her way down a corridor lit by arkemical lamps, one hand pressed to either wall for balance. A crewman on his way below squeezed past her with mumbled apologies, soaked under his oilskins. She could see the floorboards were wet, seawater and rain rolling down the stairwell ahead. Passing the Falcons' cabin, she heard Butcher still puking his guts up, Bryn cursing by the Everseeing and all his daughters. She knocked on the door, Sid stuck his head out a few moments later.

"All's well in here?" Mia asked.

"F-f-fuggin' . . . m-marvelous," Butcher groaned, his battered face all but green.

"We're all right," Sid nodded, grabbing the doorway for balance as they crashed into another wave. "Butcher's got nothing left in him to puke up, poor bastard. You?"

"Still kicking. I'm headed up to talk to the captain." She licked her lips, drew a deep breath. "You can all swim, aye?"

"Aye," Wavewaker nodded.

"Aye," said Bryn and Bladesinger.

"Fuggin—*hhurrrrkkkrkk!*" said Butcher.

"I think that was a yes," Sidonius grinned.

"Keep your wits about you," Mia said. "Don't lock your door."

"We're gladiatii, Mia," the big thug smiled. "We've each of us looked death in the eye more times than we can count. No fear for us."

She clapped a hand on Sid's shoulder, cupped the side of his face. Looking around these men and women who'd fought beside her on the sands, and realizing they were her familia, too. And despite it all, just how glad she was to have them with her.

With a nod, she left them to it, staggered across the rolling floor, down to the stairwell. Seizing the railing, Mia struggled up to the deck above, fighting for balance.

The storm was deafening out here, the rain coming down like spears. Mia was awed by it—the walls of water rising ahead and behind, the sea a dark and sullen steel gray. Her heart rose in her chest as lightning tore the heavens, the wind was a mouthless, hungry howl, underscored by BigJon's bursts of blinding profanity. Looking above her head, Mia could see seamen on the rain-slick yardarms, trying to secure a sail that had come free of its ties. They balanced on thin cables, working with sodden rope and heavy, waterlogged canvas, almost a hundred feet in the air. One slip, one stumble, onto the deck or into the water, either way it would all be over.

"The fuck are you doing up here?" Corleone demanded as she climbed to the aft deck. The captain was wet to the skin, his greatcoat soaked through, the feather in his tricorn wilted in the rain. The wheel was lashed in place, and the captain was lashed to it, clinging on like a very handsome limpet.

"I thought you said this storm wasn't going to break us!" she shouted.

"I admit I may have underestimated its enthusiasm!" he yelled, grinning.

Mia couldn't find it in herself to smile back, screaming at the top of her lungs over the deafening wind. "Are we going to die?"

"Not if I have anything to say about it! We've got a full belly keeping us steady, our storm sails up, and the best salts this side of the Thousand Towers!" Corleone flashed a wink. "Besides, I might feel compelled to tell you my real name if we were about to die!"

"Is it Gherardino?" she managed to shout. "Or Gualtieri?"

"What happened to the *B* names?"

"Aha!" she roared. "So it *does* start with a *B*!"

He grinned and shook his head. "I have a confession to make!"

"So we *are* going to die?"

"The reason I didn't want to stop for those Luminatii! They were looking for you and your brother, but I thought they might be after what the *Maid*'s got in her belly!"

". . . And what might that be?"

"About twenty tons of arkemist's salt!"*

---

*Arkemist's salt is a solidified variant of the fuel that powers many of the won-

Mia's eyes bulged in their sockets. *"What?"*

"Aye," Corleone nodded.

"You're saying we're sailing with twenty tons of high explosive beneath us?"

"Well . . ." Cloud gave a small shrug. "Probably closer to twenty-one!"

"In the middle of a *lightning storm*?"

"Thrilling, neh?" Corleone laughed aloud. "Fear not, it's well stowed. The hull would have to be split apart for the lightning to touch it, and no storm is that fierce!"

"I thought only Iron Collegium brokers were allowed to freight that crap?"

Cloud looked at her a long moment. "You do realize I'm a *pirate,* don't you?"

He tossed the sodden feather from his eyes and grinned like a madman, seemingly fearless despite the power on display about him. Watching the lightning illuminate the gleam in this man's eyes, Mia knew why his men followed him. Seeing him laugh at the bedlam all around them, the danger beneath them, hands steady on the wheel, she couldn't help but stand a little taller despite it all.

"Get back below, Dona Mia!" he shouted. "Let me and my crew handle this. You go comfort that blond screamer of yours!"

". . . You heard us?"

"Four fucking Daughters, I'd have to be deaf or dead not to have heard you!" he cried. "And bravo, by the way. Quite a performance."

Mia could feel her cheeks burning under the storm's chill.

"Don't fret," he shouted. "Lad or lass, who you roll on my ship is your business. I give no fucks for who you fuck. But if you ever need company . . ."

Mia found herself grinning despite her fear. "Go fuck *yourself*!"

"Well, thanks to this storm, the good news is that's no longer my only option!"

---

drous devices in the Republic, such as War Walkers and the great mekwerks beneath the Republic's arenas, as well as mundane items like flintboxes and arkemical lanterns.

The fuel is reduced to a solid state by dangerous processes, and the salt itself is highly volatile—its production is outlawed outside the Iron Collegium. However, its yield per pound is five times higher than liquid fuel, which means smugglers have the option of earning five times the profit if they're willing to risk hauling a bomb in their bellies.

One famous incident concerns a ship called the *Iron Codger,* which had been badly loaded with forty tons of arkemist's salt in Dawnspear harbor. The nevernight before the ship was due to set out, one drunken sailor desperately in need of a tobacco fix decided to defy his captain's strict "no fucking smoking" policy by ducking down to the hold for a quick 'rillo. The resulting explosion was heard all the way up in Stormwatch.

Even in seaside taverna today, one can hear the words "lighting the *Codger*" used to describe a particularly marvelous fuckup.

Buoyed up by Cloud's confidence, Mia decided to get the 'byss out of his way. She made her way carefully down to the quarterdeck, squinting in the rain, knuckles white on the railing. The ship was swept and rocked, and Mia stumbled twice, almost falling, her heart hammering as she peered over the side into the teeth of the sea. She looked up at the men still wrestling with the loose sail on the mast above. Wondering why anyone under the suns would want to be a sailor.

And then she saw him.

He was just a silhouette against the ocean's steel gray, up past the forecastle. Almost lost under the spray as they crashed bow-first into another trough. He was stood in the bow, arms spread wide, head thrown back, long saltlocks sodden with sea.

"Tric?" she breathed.

Another wave crashed over the bow, tons of freezing seawater running down the deck and over the sides, but there he stood despite it all. Like a rock in the middle of the chaos. He was too far away for her to call, the rest of the crew seemed too intent on managing the storm to heed any lesser concerns. Mia began making her way up the deck, clinging to the railing for dear life as another wave crashed up over the deck. BigJon saw her, shouted a warning, but she ignored the man. Clawing her way on with freezing hands, her nails turning blue, her skin turning white, past the main and foremasts until she was close enough to shout.

"What the 'byss are you doing?" she cried.

He turned his head slightly, then back toward the sea, arms wide. The sleeves of his sodden robe had bunched up as he'd raised his hands, and Mia could see those strange black spatter stains, drenching him from fingers to elbows.

"PRAYING!"

"To who?" she yelled. "For what?"

"TO THE MOTHER! ASKING HER TO QUIET THE LADIES OF OCEANS AND STORMS!"

"What the fuck are you talking about?"

"THIS IS NO ORDINARY TEMPEST!" he cried. "THIS IS THE ANGER OF THE GODDESSES! THEY SENSE ME, THEY SENSE YOU, THEY KNOW WHAT YOU ARE AND WHERE YOU GO!"

"But why do they care?" she shouted over the thunder.

"THEY ARE THEIR FATHER'S DAUGHTERS! IF THE LADY OF STORMS BREAKS OUR MASTS, WE'LL BE AT THE MERCY OF THE SEA!" He turned, fixed her with those dead, black eyes. "AND THE LADY OF OCEANS HAS NO MERCY, MIA!"

He waved her off.

"Go below!" he roared. "A sharp blade and a sharper tongue are no use here! The only weapon in this war is faith, and you've none in you to fight it!"

"Are you—"

"Go!"

Mia backed away, all the confidence Corleone had instilled in her dissolved under that abyssal stare. Tric turned back to the sea, black hands spread wide again. Another wave smashed down upon the bow, and Mia stepped forward with a cry. But once the spray had cleared, he still stood there, rooted to the spot as if by some dark magik, sodden robes hanging on him like weeds wrapped about a floating corpse. She looked around them, the tiny collection of twigs and canvas that was the *Maid;* all that stood between her and death. She suddenly felt a small and frightened thing, caught up in something vaster than she could imagine. The image of that pawn on Scaeva's palm flashed unbidden in her thoughts, his words echoing in her mind.

"If you start down this road, daughter mine, you are going to die."

Blue fingernails clawing the wood, she dragged herself through the crash and the howl and the bone-deep cold, back across the deck, finally stumbling down the steps to the decks below.

"Maw's teeth," she whispered, teeth chattering.

The ship groaned in reply, her timbers in agony. She could hear Cloud roaring to BigJon, and BigJon to the crew, voices almost swallowed in the tempest. Mia made her way back down the corridor toward her cabin, sopping wet, wishing she knew where Mister Kindly was. Wondering in what dark corner or nook he might be hiding. Wanting him back to take this feeling away.

"Fear is what keeps the dark from devouring you. Fear is what stops you joining a game you cannot hope *to win."*

Stopping outside her cabin, she looked at the door opposite—Jonnen's room, closed and locked. She could see a faint light beneath, hear soft sounds under the deafening song of the thunder. Suddenly realizing what she was hearing.

Crying.

She swallowed hard. Remembering her bitter words from earlier, regret swelling in her chest. He was a hateful little shit. A spoiled brat. A rude, ungrateful snob. But he was just a little boy. He was her brother. Her blood.

A few moments' precarious work with the lockpicks in the heel of her wolfskin boots and the lock was open, the door quickly following. She dragged her sodden hair from her eyes, peered into the room. She saw her brother huddled in the corner, jammed between a heavy chest and the wall, knees up under his chin. Eclipse was sat before him, speaking softly, but it seemed even the shadowwolf wasn't enough to calm the boy's fears. Jonnen's cheeks were wet with tears, his eyes wide and afraid.

"Brother?" Mia said.

He looked up at her, jaw clenched, eyes flashing.

"Go away, Kingmaker," he snapped.

Mia sighed and stepped into the room, dripping seawater. Padding across the floorboards, she sat down in front of him. After an awkward pause, she tossed her hair from her face and reached out with chilled hands to take his. Amazingly, he didn't immediately snatch them away.

"Still frightened of storms?"

". . . I AM SORRY, MIA, HE WOULD NOT LET ME RIDE HIS SHADOW, BUT DID NOT WISH ME TO TELL YOU . . ."

Mia ran a hand over Eclipse's flanks, grateful the shadowwolf had formed so swift a bond with her brother. Though Mia herself was clearly one of Jonnen's least favorite people under the suns, the boy and the daemon were thick as thieves after only a few weeks together. Thinking about it here in the roaring storm, Mia understood why.

Eclipse misses Cassius.

And Jonnen reminds her of him.

Mia looked at her brother and nodded. He was an exceptional boy, she had to admit, no matter what enmity lay between them. She felt admiration swelling in her, that he'd chosen to face the storm without the daemon to eat his fear.

"A man has to stand on his own two feet, neh?"

The boy glared with those dark eyes of his. So like his father's. So like hers.

"But you don't have to stand alone, you know that, aye?" Mia squeezed his little hands in hers. "I'm your sister, Jonnen. I'm here for you if you need."

He licked his lips. His voice so soft she almost couldn't hear over the waves and the thunder and the driving rain. "It's . . . it's very loud."

"I know," she replied. "It's all right, brother."

"Are we going to sink?" he whispered.

The *Maid* crashed down into another abyss, shaking the ship to her bones. The timbers creaked and the oceans roared and the thunder boomed, and Mia considered telling Jonnen a lie to shush him. But though she had no practice in being one, that didn't feel like something a big sister should do.

"We might," she admitted. "I hope not."

"I . . . I cannot swim very well."

"I can." She squeezed his hand again. "And I'll not let you drown."

He stared at her, black eyes reflected with tiny pinpricks of arkemical lantern light. She could see their mother in him. Their father, too. But more than both, she could see *him*—the squalling little babe she'd held in her arms that nevernight in Crow's Nest. She could still hear her mother's voice, weary and breathless from the birth, her eyes shining as she looked at her son and daughter with an ardent, impossible love.

"Sing to him, Mia. He will know his sister."

And so, feeling every inch a fool, dipping her head so her sodden hair would hide the blood rising in her scarred and branded cheeks, Mia raised her voice and sang. The song her mother taught her. Just as she'd done back then.

"In bleakest times, in darkest climes,
When wind blows cold in skies above,
When suns won't shine, and truedark chimes,
Still I'll return to thee, my love.
Ever return to thee, true love."

Mia ran her hand across her eyes, shook her head.

"You're right," she chuckled. "I *do* sound like a harpy screeching for supper . . ."

She felt a slight pressure. A brief squeeze on her hand in his. And looking up into his eyes, she saw the boy wasn't crying anymore.

"I've a notion," she murmured, sniffling. "You want to sleep in my room? That way, if anything should happen, I'll be right there . . ."

Jonnen pressed his lips together. Clearly wanting to acquiesce and clearly too proud to do so. Mia tried another tack.

"I'm scared, too. I'd sleep easier if you were there."

". . . Well," he finally said. "If *you* are frightened . . ."

"Come on," she said, grabbing his blanket and pulling him up.

The ship rolled and shook as they made their way back to the corridor, over to Mia's cabin. She knocked on the door, poked her head in. Ashlinn was swaying in the hammock, eyes on the ceiling, concern on her face. But when she saw Mia, she smiled, threw back the blanket, and held out her arms.

"Come here, beautiful."

"Put some clothes on," Mia hissed. "Jonnen's going to sleep in here with us."

"Really?" Ash frowned, looking about her. "Shit, all right, give me a breath."

Mia shuffled her brother into the cabin as Ashlinn rolled out of the hammock, turned away from the door. The boy stood with his hands clasped before him, sneaking curious and furtive glances at the inkwerk on Ashlinn's back as the girl bent down and retrieved her slip, pulled it over her bare skin. Mia dragged off her sodden britches and shirt, down to the relatively dry slip beneath. Crawling into the hammock with Ash, she piled the blankets atop them and beckoned Jonnen.

"Come on, it's all right."

The boy was uncertain, but with his lingering fear of the storm snapping on his heels, he made his way across the boards and swung himself up into Mia's arms. She wrapped a second blanket about his shoulders, winced as he wriggled and writhed, all pointy elbows and knees. But finally, he found some kind of comfort, Eclipse curling down at Mia's feet and sighing in the gloom.

"*. . . TOGETHER . . .*"

Mia wrapped one arm about her brother, her other about the girl beside her. Ashlinn settled in against her, their bodies fitting perfectly, breathing a sigh into Mia's hair. Mia kissed her girl's brow, and after a leaden pause, risked a kiss to the top of Jonnen's head. The boy didn't react, save perhaps to breathe a touch easier, a scrap of tension easing out of his little frame.

She supposed it was a start.

Mia sighed from the bottom of her lungs. The two people she cared about perhaps most in the world, here in her arms. Her center. Her familia. The thing she'd fought and bled all this time for. Risking anything and everything.

And if she could kill for it, sacrifice everything in her life for it . . .

Could I perhaps live for it, too?

Mia looked up at the ceiling.

Imagining a lake so still, it was like a mirror to the sky.

Staring at the gloom above her head and picturing a pale globe shining there.

Listening to the tempest sing.

And wondering.

CHAPTER 17

DEPARTURES

They almost didn't make it to Galante.

The storm raged for a solid week, and though no lightning kissed the explosives in the *Maid*'s belly, the ocean still did her best to drag them all to sailors' graves. Six of the crew were lost to the deep, swept off the decks or torn from the rigging. The sails on the main and mizzenmast were split like rotten hessian, the foremast almost snapped off at the root. Through it all, Cloud Corleone had stood at the wheel, as if by sheer will he'd keep his ship together. And yet Mia suspected it wasn't the captain, but another figure up on deck who proved the difference between them all living and dying.

A deadboy.

He didn't move from the bow for seven turns. Lips moving in silent prayer to the Mother, asking she beseech her twins for respite, for mercy, for quiet. Mia didn't know for certain if the Mother listened, or if her daughters paid heed, but as the *Maid* limped into Galante harbor, torn and bleeding but somehow still afloat, Mia made her way up to the bow and leaned on the wood beside him.

He stood with those black hands on the railings, a curtain of damp saltlocks framing his face. The wind still gnashed and snapped at their heels, the water below a sea of jagged whitecaps, rain drizzling in a thin gray veil.

He was still darkly beautiful, his skin smooth and pale, his eyes black as pitch. But Mia could swear there was a little more color to him now. A faint flush of life to his flesh. A hint in the way he moved. Ashlinn had whispered to Mia of it alone in their cabin—how the closer they drew to truedark, the more . . . alive Tric appeared. It seemed a dark shade of sorcery, like nothing she'd ever heard or read about, but Mia supposed it made a kind of sense. If it was the power of the Night that returned Tric to life, he might seem more alive the closer to night it drew.

She wondered what he was exactly. The magik of him, and the mystery. And how much like the old Tric he might be by the time the suns finally failed.

"WHAT ARE YOU DOING?" he asked, glancing at her sidelong.

"Just looking," she replied.

He nodded, turning to the white jewel of Galante harbor before them. The Cityport of Churches was a curious mix of Liisian and Itreyan architecture, tall minarets and graceful domes, flat rooftop gardens and high terra-cotta roofs, hundreds of thousands milling in her streets. Cathedral bells tolled across the waves, ringing in the hour, all in time. Mia had served in the Red Church chapel here for eight months under Bishop Tenhands, and she knew the city like a boozehound knew the bottle.

"This was the place we met," she said. "Well . . . met again. I'd just killed the son of a senator, if I recall correctly."

"I REMEMBER. YOU HAD A RED DRESS ON. AND A CROSSBOW BOLT IN YOUR ARSE."

She smirked, tossing windblown locks from her face. "Not my finest hour."

"YOU LOOKED MORE THAN FINE TO ME."

The smile dropped away. Uncomfortable silence hung between them like a shroud. A lonely gull swung through the sky overhead, singing a mournful song.

"Did . . ." Mia shook her head, looking to change the subject. "What you said out there during the tempest, about the Ladies of Ocean and Storms . . . was that true? About them . . . knowing?"

"DO YOU HAVE A FLINTBOX?"

Mia blinked at the strange question. "Aye."

"GIVE IT TO ME."

Mia reached into her britches, pulled out the small slab of burnished metal. It was a simple device: flint, wick, arkemical fuel. Two silver priests at a market stall.

"Just don't drop it anywhere belowdecks, aye?"

Tric took the box in his ink-black hands, struggled a moment with the flint. Those fingers of his had once been clever as cats, deft and supple and quick. Her belly sank at another reminder that, beautiful as he was, as close to truedark as they might be drawing, out here in the sunslight, this boy still wasn't who he used to be. But after a moment, he struck the flame, lifted the flintbox toward her.

The wind was howling, the rain was spitting; the thin tongue of fire should probably have sputtered out entirely. Instead, as Tric held it between them, Mia saw the flame flicker and grow, burning hotter. And though she had the wind howling at her back, the fire stretched out toward her, reached *into* the gale. Like it . . .

. . . like it *wanted* to burn her.

"The Lady of Earth slumbers as she has done for an age," Tric said. "But so long as you seek the Crown of the Moon, Storm and Ocean and Fire will be your enemies. They are their father's daughters, Mia. Raised to hate their mother and their brother both. And thus, you."

Watching the finger of flame reaching for her, flickering and flailing, Mia felt a sliver of cold fear sink into her belly.

"All the pieces are beginning to move. And the closer you come to the Crown, the harder they will strive to stop you." Tric shook his head, pursed his lips. "I'd hoped we might make it farther undetected. But all three of Aa's eyes are still in the sky. They don't name him Everseeing for nothing."

"You're saying if we head out onto the ocean again . . ."

"The Ladies will try to stop us again."

"But Ashkah and the Quiet Mountain are through the Sea of Sorrows from here," she frowned. "We can't walk there from Liis. We need to travel by ship."

Tric looked to the harbor before them, the sea at their back.

"We could travel by land for a time," he offered. "Head east, along the coast. Have Corleone and the *Maid* sail around the Northcape without us or the Ladies' wrath, meet us in Amai. That will leave only a short journey by wave, across the Sea of Sorrows to Ashkah. We'll still risk the twins' ire, but a journey of a week is better than three."

Mia shook her head. She hadn't even made up her mind if she truly believed all this gods and goddesses nonsense. Hadn't decided if she'd even seek the Crown yet. But it seemed the divinities had decided without her, and she was becoming suddenly and painfully aware of what having a trio of goddesses stacked against her could mean.

"The closer we come to truedark," Tric said, as if reading her thoughts, "the deeper your strength will grow. You know this."

Mia nodded, remembering the power she'd wielded during the truedark massacre. Stepping across shadows in the city of Godsgrave like a little girl skipping puddles. Liquid darkness tearing down the statue of Aa outside the Basilica Grande at her whim. Mother only knew what she might accomplish now that she was older, now that the splinter that had been inside Furian resided in her.

And she could feel it. Those suns sinking toward the horizon. Slow but inevitable. The dark inside her deepening. Quickening.

Shadows at her back, waiting to unfurl in the dying light.

"But you are vulnerable now," Tric continued. "And *now* is when

THEY'LL SEEK TO STRIKE. WE MUST MOVE WITH CAUTION. OVERLAND IS OUR SAFEST ROAD."

Mia sighed but nodded. "All right, then. I'll speak to Corleone about meeting us in Amai. If you're sure they'll be safe without us aboard?"

"WHEN DEALING WITH THE DIVINITIES, NOTHING IS CERTAIN," Tric said. "BUT YOU ARE THEIR FOCUS, MIA. YOU ARE THE THREAT IN AA'S EYES."

"We'll need to buy ourselves some horses, I suppose." Mia scowled, spit on the deck. "I fucking hate horses."

Tric smiled, his dimple creasing his pale cheek. "I REMEMBER."

She looked at him then. Her voice just a whisper on the wind.

"What else do you remember?"

He tilted his head, and the look in his eyes made her chest ache.

"EVERYTHING," he replied.

"What news, Crow?"

Mia turned, saw Sidonius and Bladesinger standing behind her. Wavewaker and Bryn were at the starboard, the big man pointing to the city and giving the Vaanian girl a quick tour of the landmarks. Behind them, Mia could see Butcher bent over the railing, dry-retching into the sea. Bladesinger eyed Tric with open suspicion, and Mia wondered what the former priestess-in-training would be thinking of a Hearthless walking among them. But Sidonius's eyes were fixed on Mia.

"We have to travel overland," she told them. "In news I needed like a second arsehole, along with Aa's ministry, the Luminatii and Itreyan Legion, and the Red Church, apparently the Ladies of Storms and Oceans are also displeased with me."

"You . . . think?" Butcher managed to gasp. "I've puked up both . . . lungs and one of my fucking jewels since we g-got on this damned shit b-bucket."

"Mind your tongue, piss-weasel," came a voice. "Or I'll hack off your other nut."

BigJon scowled up at the former gladiatii, fists on hips. The first mate and his captain had joined the group on the bow as the *Maid* slipped farther toward the Cityport of Churches. BigJon was soaked through to this skin and looking salty to boot, his drakebone pipe hanging from one side of his mouth. For his part, Corleone appeared exhausted from a week of constant battle at the wheel, his clothes clinging to him like the fur on a waterlogged rat. But the fire hadn't dimmed from the man's eyes.

"Did I hear tell you're leaving us?" he asked Mia.

The girl nodded. "For a time. Being aboard is putting you and your men arisk."

"Bollocks, that was barely a breeze." Cloud stamped his foot on the deck. "Solid as the earth beneath your feet, my *Maid*."

"We should get the bloody foremast looked at, at least," BigJon said. "Got a split in it deeper than my aunt Pentalina's bosom. Bilge pumps are running like a three-legged scabdog, and we've got badger-spunk for brains if we don't re-caulk—"

"You know," Cloud sighed at his first mate, "for a fellow with a dick like a donkey, you do a remarkable impression of an old woman."*

BigJon chuckled, pipe stem clutched between silver teeth.

"Who told you I was hung like a donkey?"

"Your mother talks in her sleep."

"We'll travel overland," Mia smiled. "That'll give you a breath for repairs, and you can still meet us at Amai with plenty of time." She glanced at Tric. "Safer for all of us."

"Aye."

Corleone raised his eyebrow. "Have you ever been to Amai?"

"No," Mia answered.

"No," the deadboy replied.

The captain and his first mate exchanged an uneasy glance.

"I . . ." Butcher groaned from the railing, ". . . g-grew up there . . ."

---

* This always struck me as a peculiar turn of phrase, truth told. While a donkey's accoutrements might be of particularly impressive scope to an average littleman, according to annals in the zoology department of the Iron Collegium, a donkey's proportions simply pale in comparison to some of the other denizens of the Itreyan animal kingdom.

The whitedrake, for example, Itreya's largest ocean predator, has an average body length of twenty-five feet, and their harpoons of love can measure almost three feet long—a ratio of 10:1. Liisian blackbulls stand near seven feet tall, with a chief of staff that can measure over three and a half, a ratio of near 2:1. (Interesting fact—when slaughtering their unneeded male calves, Liisian farmers often save the penises, dry them out, and feed them to their dogs—a treat known as a "bully stick.")

The image of the flayer squid, a hooked horror that roams the Sea of Stars, can be made all the more horrifying with the knowledge that its babymaker is as long as its entire body (and yes, hooked, to boot). But the clear winner in this struggle of the ages, the sovereign of swords, the *capan de phalli capanni,* as it were, is none other than the humble barnacle, whose undersea admiral can extend to fifty times the length of its body.

To put things in proportion, that would be the equivalent of a six-foot man with a three-hundred-foot phallus.

Thank your gods, ladies and gentlefriends.

Thank your fucking gods.

"Enjoyable childhood, was it?" BigJon asked.

"Not really." The gladiatii wiped his lips, stood with a groan on unsteady legs.

"I've heard tell of it," Bladesinger said. "Rough city."

"Rough?" BigJon scoffed. "It's the blackest pit of bastards, thieves, and murderers this side of the Great Salt. Whole place is a pirate enclave. And not the Charming Bastard kind, either. The Rape and Kill Your Entire Family kind."

Corleone nodded. "High seat of His Majesty, Einar 'the Tanner' Valdyr, Blackwolf of Vaan, Scourge of the Four Seas, King of Scoundrels."

Sidonius blinked. "Pirates have kings?"

Cloud frowned. "Of course we have kings. How did you think it worked?"

"I dunno. I thought you'd be an autonomous collective or something."

"Autonomous fucking collective?" BigJon looked Sid up and down. "What kind of backward-arse shit-brained government is that? Sounds a recipe for chaos to me."

"Aye," Corleone nodded. "We work by a system, matey. Just because we're pirates doesn't mean we're lawless brigands."

Sid looked astonished. ". . . That's *exactly* what it fucking means!"*

"All right, all right," Mia sighed. "Is there any way to get from Liis to Ashkah other than crossing the Sea of Sorrows?"

"No," Corleone said.

"Is there a major port in Liis that's closer to Last Hope than Amai?"

"No," said BigJon.

"Right, well, let's stop fuckarsing about and start walking, shall we?" Mia said. "We'll deal with his majesty Einar Whatsit, Scourge of Wherever, when we get there."

---

*In actual fact, it doesn't. Like most occupations in the Republic, piracy is a highly regulated affair. The Itreyan navy is part of an impressive military machine, gentlefriends, and could crush any individual privateer with ease. But the Four Seas are very big places, and being in all of those places at once is somewhat tricky.

Truth is, gentlefriends, no matter what you have, there's always some bastard out there who's looking to pinch it. And this is especially true of fellows with a penchant for drinking grog, wearing eyepatches, and ending each sentence with the word "matey."

Since the Battle of Seawall, the idea of working together has sat rather comfortably with Itreya's freebooter population, but it was quickly realized that governance by anarchy among a pack of thieving pricks simply wasn't going to work. Give everyone a platform, and everyone will think they're entitled to voice their opinion, and yes, while everyone's technically entitled to an opinion, everyone's also technically entitled to take a shit once a day, but that doesn't mean I want to hear about it.

Monarchy, strangely enough, was discovered to be the solution. And not monar-

Mia's notion obviously didn't sit well with Corleone, but with no real alternative to offer, the privateer finally shrugged assent.

"We'll need supplies," Sidonius said. "Horses and harness. Weapons. Armor."

"We can afford the nags," Mia said. "But we'll have precious little coin left after."

"We have the kit from that Luminatii tosser and his lads killed in your cabin," Cloud offered. "Four marines plus a centurion. Steel, shields, leather, and chain."

"That could work," Sidonius said. "Posing as soldiers moving overland, we're less likely to be troubled by slavers and the like. We'll have to ditch the uniforms once we arrive, of course. But I was an officer in the legion, so I speak the language if we come across any other army folk on the way to Amai."

"Looks like you're leading us, then, Centurion," Mia said, saluting.

The group agreed, and without much more ado, set about gathering their meager possessions. By the time the *Maid* made berth in Galante, they were assembled on deck. Sidonius and the Falcons hadn't changed into their soldier's kit yet, each still dressed in the common thread they'd bought with their freedom. Ashlinn stood with Jonnen, carrying the small sack of "essentials" she'd purchased in Whitekeep over her shoulder. Eclipse stood in the boy's shadow, making it dark enough for two. Tric had finally climbed down from the bow, waiting by the gangplank.

"Daughters watch over you and yours, Mia," Corleone said, extending his hand.

"I'm hoping for exactly the opposite," she smiled, shaking it.

"We'll make our repairs, then head around the cape. I'm guessing we'll still beat you to Amai, but we'll wait for you there. Watch your step once you're inside the city, stay the fuck out of the way of other salts. Keep your head well down and yourself to yourself. Head straight to the Pub, we'll be waiting."

"I know a nice little chapel to Trelene on the foreshore, Dona Mia," said BigJon with a silver grin. "That offer of marriage is still open."

"Thank you both," she smiled. "Blue above and below."

---

chy in a "pomp and pageantry" kind of way, more monarchy in an "I am king and these fellows agree, so you will do what I say or you and everyone you ever loved will be cut into pieces and fed to the drakes" sort of way.

But with a centralized authority came a neat arrangement with the Itreyan navy. The navy accepted that a certain number of ships would be plundered each year, so long as the pirates agreed that, should this quota be exceeded, they would police their own and save the navy the trouble of hunting all Four Seas for the offenders.

Sounds a sensible solution to me, matey.

"Above and below," Corleone smiled.

"Bartolomeo?" Mia raised a finger in thought. "No, no . . . Brittanius?"

The privateer only grinned in reply. "See you in Amai, Mi Dona. Walk carefully."

The captain and his first mate set about their business. Mia's comrades marched down the gangplank one by one. Pulling her hood low, the Blade stood and looked out at the Cityport of Churches. Galante was home to a Red Church chapel—they were at risk as long as they stayed in the city. Mia was eager to get moving, thinking of Mercurio at the Ministry's mercies and praying to the Mother he was somehow well.

She felt a small shiver in her spine. A shadow-thin shape materialized on the railing beside her, licking at a translucent paw.

Mia kept her eyes on the harbor.

"Coming with me, are you?"

"*. . . always . . . ,*" Mister Kindly replied.

The wind howled in the space between them, hungry as wolves.

"*. . . are you still angry . . . ?*"

She hung her head. Thinking about who and what she was, and why. The things that drove her and the things that made her and the ones who loved her.

Despite everything.

She scowled, reached out, and ran her fingers through his not-fur.

"Always," she whispered.

Mia hated horses almost as much as horses hated her.

She'd named the only stallion she'd ever been remotely fond of "Bastard," and even though the beast had saved her life, she couldn't say she truly *liked* him. Horses had always struck her as ungainly, stupid things, and her feelings weren't helped by the fact that every horse she'd met had taken an instant dislike to her.

She'd often wondered if they could simply sense her innate disdain. But watching the horses at the Galante stable react to her brother with the same skittish nervousness they'd always displayed around her, Mia supposed it must be the touch of darkness in her veins. She was more conscious of it now than ever before. The depth of the shadow at her feet. The burn of the three suns overhead, beating on her like hateful fists even through the blanket of storm clouds. The lingering feeling of emptiness, of something missing when she looked at her brother.

She wondered if he felt the same. If that was perhaps why, ever so slow, he seemed to be warming to her.

More than this Liisian prick was warming to Bryn, anyways . . .

"I'll give you a hundred silver for the seven," the Vaanian girl was saying. "Plus the wagon and feed."

"Piss on you, girl," the stableman scoffed. "A hundred? Try three."

They were stood in a muddy stable on Galante's east side, as far from the Red Church chapel as could be managed. They'd picked up supplies in the marketplace, food and drink, and a good bow of stout ash and three quivers of arrows for Bryn. She stood with feet planted in mud and shit now, fingertips running over the bow at her back and obviously itching to use it.

The stableman stood a foot taller than Bryn. He was clad in dirty grays and a grubby leather apron hung with horseshoes and hammers. He had the lingering stare of a fellow who saw breasts as an obvious yet fascinating impediment to intelligence.

"A hundred," Bryn insisted, crossing her arms over her chest. "That's all they're worth."

"O, an expert, are we? These are Liisian purebreds, girl."

The former equillai of the Remus Collegium, and one of the greatest *flagillae* ever to grace the sands of the arena, rolled her eyes.

"*That's* a purebred," Bryn said, pointing to the largest gelding. "But he's Itreyan, not Liisian. *She's* a purebred," Bryn said, pointing to a mare, "but she's at least twenty-five and looks like she's had a bout of shinwithers in the last two years. The rest of them are racers past their prime or nags barely fit for the knackery. So hammer that purebred nonsense where the Everseeing won't shine."

The man finally dragged his stare up from Bryn's tits to her eyes.

"A hundred and twenty," she said. "Plus the wagon and feed."

The man scowled deeper but finally spit into his hand. "Deal."

Bryn snorted, hocked, and coughed an entire throatful of phlegm into her palm, then shook with a wet *squish,* staring the dullard in the eye.

"Deal," she said. "Prick."

The stableman was still wiping his hand clean as they saddled up. Mia was constantly scanning the streets about them, looking for familiar faces. She could have hidden herself and Jonnen beneath her cloak of shadows, of course, but the agents of the Red Church would likely know Ashlinn just as well as she, and Mia couldn't hide all three of them. Instead, she relied on Mercurio's training—sticking to the shadows and lurking beneath the eaves, hood pulled low as she searched the crowd. Ashlinn was stood close by, watching the rooftops. She knew as well as Mia this was a Red Church city, that Bishop Tenhands and her Blades would be hunting for them. But for all their vigilance, it seemed they'd gone unnoticed for now. With luck, they'd be out of the cityport before their fortune and this storm broke.

"Ready?" Sidonius asked.

Mia blinked, looked to their convoy. A loaded wagon, drawn by two tired draft horses. A half dozen geldings and mares, each with a former gladiatii in Itreyan military garb atop them. Sidonius led the column, looking rather resplendent in his gravebone centurion's armor, despite the rain wilting the bloodred plume on his helm. He reminded Mia of her fa . . .

. . . O, Goddess . . .

I don't even know what to call him now . . .

"Aye, sir," Mia managed to smile.

She helped her little brother up into the wagon. Ash flopped into the tray behind, propping herself against the feedbags and drawing her hood down over her face. Only Tric remained on foot, giving the horses a wide berth—Mia saw they turned wide-eyed and fitful when he strayed too near. Climbing up into the driver's seat, she settled in beside Jonnen. Thunder boomed overhead and the boy flinched, the rain coming down thicker as lightning licked the skies. Mia dragged his new cloak's hood up over his head, offered him the reins to take his mind off the tempest and hers off her sorrows.

"Want to drive us?" she asked.

He looked at her, expression guarded. "I . . . do not know how."

"I'll teach you," she said. "It'll be simple for someone as clever as you."

With a snap of the whip and a gentle nudge, the wagon began rolling. Mia and her comrades picked their way through Galante's streets, over the cobbles and flagstones, past the marble facades and fluted columns and stacked tenements, off toward the eastern gates. The road awaited them, and beyond that, Amai. And over the Sea of Sorrows, the Ashkahi Whisperwastes, her mentor, and whatever devilry the Red Church could conjure. But for now, Mia simply settled in beside her brother, instructing him gently, smiling as he began to enjoy himself. She felt Ashlinn in the wagon behind her, a light touch on her hip. Mia reached down and squeezed her girl's hand.

Eyes on the boy walking before them.

Out toward the gate, and from there, the open road beyond.

Thunder crashed again, rain beating on the tiles.

Two figures stood on a rooftop in the shadow of a chimney stack, watching the convoy set out with narrowed eyes.

The first turned to the second, hands speaking where his mouth could not.

inform tenhands

The second signaled compliance, slipped away across the rooftops.

Hush remained standing in the rain.

Blue eyes on the traitors' backs.

Nodding.

soon

CHAPTER 18

TALES

"The Lady of Storms is a hateful bitch," Mia muttered.

They were two turns into the trek, the Cityport of Churches far behind them. Working their way east along the coast, farmland to the south, raging seas to the north. The rain was growing steadily worse, the road turning to a quagmire. The horses were miserable, the riders more so. Sidonius led the column, his blood-red centurion's cloak and plumes sodden with rain. Tric walked parallel with the Itreyan, but far off to the flank where his presence wouldn't spook the horses. The first nevernight they'd made camp, the deadboy had climbed a tree to get away from them so they'd settle. Mia supposed it was a good thing he didn't sleep.

The good news was, at least for Mia, that truelight was over. While she could still feel Saai's burning blue and Saan's sullen red heat beyond the cover of clouds, she could sense by the dimming of the light, the cool relief in her bones, that Shiih had finally disappeared below the horizon, taking a third of Aa's relentless hatred with it.

One less sun beating upon her back. One sun closer to truedark.

And then . . .

"How far to Amai?" Bryn asked.

Butcher simply shook his head. "A good ways yet, sister."

"I'm wetter than a spring bride on her wedding nevernight."

Bryn's griping was met with general grumbles of assent. Bladesinger was riding beside Mia's wagon, wringing the rain from her saltlocks. Butcher's battered face looked darker than the clouds above. Everyone's spirits seemed buried in the mud beneath their hooves. But Sid had served as Second Spear in the Luminatii for years before his servitude in Remus Collegium, and Mia soon learned he knew how to keep his cohort's spirits up on the road.

"First woman I ever bedded was from Amai," he mused aloud.

"O, aye?" Butcher said, perking up.

"Do tell," Bryn grinned.

Sidonius looked around the group, met with a chorus of nods and murmurs.

"Well, her name w—"

"Wait, wait, wait . . . ," Mia said.

The girl covered her little brother's ears with her palms and pressed hard. For his part, Jonnen kept hold of the reins and simply looked confused.

"All right, out with it," Mia said. "Spare no detail."

"Her name was Analie," Sidonius said as thunder rolled overhead. "She moved to Godsgrave as a young lass. Became one of my ma's customers at the seamstry. She was a little older than me—"

"Hold now, how many years is 'a little'?" Bladesinger asked.

"Maybe . . . eight?" Sid shrugged. "Ten?"

"How old were *you*?" Wavewaker asked, incredulous.

"Sixteen."

"Braaaaah-vo!" Ashlinn said, giving Sidonius a slow clap from the wagon bed.

"Lucky little bastard," Mia grinned. "She'd have eaten you *alive*."

"Can I tell my fucking story or not?"

"Fine, fine," Mia said, rolling her eyes.

"Right," Sid said. "So, I knew she fancied me, but being green I'd no idea what to do about it. Fortunately, Analie did. I used to do deliveries for my mother, and one turn, I arrive at Analie's palazzo, and she answers the door in . . . well, basically nothing."

"Direct and to the point," Bladesinger mused, wringing her locks. "I like it."

"So she drags me inside and bends over the divan in the entry hall and demands I get to work, so being the obliging sort, get to work I do. And we're about ten, maybe eleven seconds into proceedings, and I realize I've got two pressing problems.

"Problem the first: being somewhat over enthused as most lads tend to be on their first trip into the woods, I'm about three seconds from the end of my tether. Problem the second: the front fucking door is opening. Turns out Analie is married, and her husband has come home unexpectedly."

"'Byss and blood," Bryn chuckled. "What did you do?"

"Well, more than a little flustered, I turned to face problem the second at the precise moment problem the first resolved itself."

"O, no . . . ," Mia gasped.

"O, aye." Sid smacked his hands together. "Like a shot from a crossbow, it was."

"Fuck off," Butcher gawped. "You didn't . . ."

Sid nodded. "Right in the poor bastard's eye."

Howls of amusement rang among the group, echoing along the muddy road, louder than the storm winds. A farmer toiling in a nearby field turned to stare, wondering what the fuss was about. Mia was laughing so hard she thought she might fall from the wagon seat, clinging to either side of her brother's head in desperation.

"What is so amusing?" the boy murmured.

Mia cracked the seal on his ear and whispered, "I'll tell you when you're older."

"What did you do?" Bladesinger demanded of Sidonius.

"I ran like a fucking jackrabbit, what do you think?" Sid said. "Out the door, down the road, stark naked, all the way home. Fortunately, the wolf was too spunk-blinded to give chase, so this particular rabbit lived to fuck another turn."

More laughter all round, Butcher shaking his head in disbelief as Mia wiped the tears from her eyes on her sodden sleeve.

Sid sighed. "Still the best fourteen seconds of my life, though."

"First time I ever finished a man with my mouth, it came out my nose," Bryn said.

"You fucking *what*?" Mia gasped.

"Light's truth," the girl nodded. "Nearly drowned me. I was smelling it for weeks after. We laughed about it, though. He bought me a handkerchief for Great Tithe."

Another wave of laughter crashed among the group in time with the thunder. Butcher was wheezing like he'd run a footrace, Bladesinger's locks swaying as she threw her head back and howled.

"What about you, then, 'Singer?" Bryn grinned.

"O, my first time was disastrous," the woman chuckled, pulling her sodden hood back on. "Mother Trelene, you don't want to hear about it. You boys, especially."

"Come now, out with it," Ashlinn said, thumping the wagon bed.

"Aye, come on, 'Singer," Sid laughed. "No secrets on the sands."

The Dweymeri woman shook her head. "All right, then. Don't blame me if it gives you gentles nightmares." She lowered her voice, as if she were telling a fireside spook story. The thunder cracked ominously overhead. "The boy was from Farrow. Big strapping buck named Stonethrower I'd had an eye on for a few months. Face like a picture and an arse like a poem. We were at a beach gala for Firemass, bonfires burning all down the Seawall. Beautiful. *Romantic.* He gets enough liquor in him to finally put the word on, and I've got enough in me to like the sound of his tune. So we head up into the dunes and go at it. Now, I'm nothing close to his first, he's known a few girls in his time. So he manages to last a little longer than Crossbow Sid up there."

"You wound me, Dona," Sid called from the front of the line.

Butcher whistled. "Right in the fucking *eye* . . ."

"Anyway,"'Singer said as an arc of blinding white crossed the sky. "I'm getting a little braver as we go along, so with his encouragement, I climb up on top for a ride. And we start going at it *hard,* and it's feeling really damned good, and I'm bouncing up and down with such newfound abandon that he slips right out of me on the upstroke and I land right on top of him on the downstroke and I broke his poor cock almost in half."

"O, holy fucking *GOD*!" Sid cried, wincing.

"Nooo!" Wavewaker looked at Bladesinger in horror. "That can't happen, can it?"

"Aye," the woman nodded. "Blood everywhere. Should've heard him screaming."

"Black fucking Mother," Ashlinn chuckled, covering her mouth.

"No!" Butcher cried, pointing at her. "No, that is NOT funny!"

"It's a touch funny," Mia smirked.

Bryn, meanwhile, was almost falling off her horse laughing. Wavewaker had a look of quiet horror on his face. Sid was bent over double in mock agony, shaking his head. "No, no, why the fuck did you tell us that story, 'Singer?"

"I warned you!" she cried over another thunderclap.

"I'm going to have nightmares!"

"I warned you about that, too!"

"In *half*?" Wavewaker breathed.

"Almost," she nodded. "Apparently took over a year before it straightened itself out. He never let me near it again to check, of course."

Every man in the group shifted in the saddle, while every woman guffawed.

"I can't even remember my first," Butcher said. "My da and uncle took me to a pleasure house when I was thirteen and I was too smoked to even recall the lass's face . . . Actually, come to think of it, maybe I didn't even see her face . . ."

"I broke the boy's nose my first time," Ashlinn volunteered brightly.

Mia frowned. "With your fist, or . . . ?"

"No," Ashlinn said, pointing down to her crotch. "You know . . . sitting on him . . . overenthusiastically."

"O . . ." Mia put the puzzle together in her head. "O, *right* . . ."

Ashlinn nodded. "He kept going, though. He was a trooper, that one."

"Vaanian boys," Bryn sighed wistfully.

"Mmmhmm," Ashlinn nodded.

"What about you, 'Waker?" Sid chuckled. "Any first-time catastrophes?"

"I'm hoping there won't be," the big man replied.

The whole group fell quiet, and even the tempest above seemed to still for a moment. Mia and everyone else turned to stare at the hulking Dweymeri. Wavewaker was a lump of pure beef, not at all hard on the eyes, and that voice of his hit Mia right in the sweet parts. She couldn't believe . . .

"You've not . . . ?" she asked. *"Ever?"*

He shook his head. "Waiting for the right woman."

The ladies exchanged glances—all except Bryn, who simply nudged her horse closer to Wavewaker's and gifted him a lingering smile.

"What about you, Crow?" Butcher asked.

"No real disasters, I'm afraid." Mia shrugged, dragging sodden hair from her eyes and shivering. "Though . . . I *did* go out and murder a man immediately afterward."

"Hmm," Bladesinger nodded. "Strangely enough, that fits."

More guffaws. Sidonius looked sidelong at Tric, who'd been walking alongside in silence the whole time, up to his ankles in mud. Being a good commander and not wanting the boy to feel left out, breathing or no, the Itreyan cleared his throat.

"And you?" he asked. "Any calamities on your maiden voyage?"

"No," Tric said simply.

Black eyes flickered to Mia and away again.

"NO, SHE WAS WONDERFUL."

Thunder rolled as if on cue, and at its call, the rain started coming down in earnest—a downpour heavier than Mia could ever recall. Jonnen was huddled beside her, shivering in his boots. The wind was a monster, clawing and howling, tearing their hoods from their heads and reaching beneath their sodden clothes with frozen hands. Mia found it hard to remember the sweltering heat of the arena just a few weeks back, tucking her hands into her armpits to warm them.

"This is *horseshit*!" Bryn roared, hauling out her bow and firing off an arrow at the clouds above. *"BITCH!"*

Sidonius squinted in the downpour, scanning the countryside around them.

"We could knock at one of these farmhouses," Wavewaker shouted, tapping his soldier's breastplate and the three suns embossed on it. "Declare official business and wait out the worst of it by a nice, cozy hearth."

"What about him?" Bladesinger called, motioning to Tric. "Any addle-witted peasant worth his pitchfork would be trying to burn him on a stake in a heartbeat!"

"He looks a little more lively of late," Butcher said, peering at the boy. "A bit more color to him, maybe? Or is it me?"

"There!" Sid called.

Mia looked in the direction the man was pointing. Through the blinding rain, she could see a ruin atop a distant foothill. It was a garrison tower, crumbling crenellated walls and a broken drawbridge, its stonework crushed under the hands of time. It looked like it'd been built during the Itreyan occupation, when the Great Unifier, Francisco I, first marched his armies into Liis and challenged the might of the Magus Kings. A tumbled relic of a world once at war.

"Good view of the countryside!" Sid cried. "With any luck, cellar's still dry!"

"The horses *could* use a rest," Bryn shouted. "This mud's hard work for them."

Mia looked at the road ahead, into the gray skies above.

"All right, then," she nodded. "Let's take a peek."

The tower was three stories of broken stone, crowning a spur of sharp limestone.

Long ago, Mia imagined it might've been peopled by hardened legionaries. Men who'd come across the waves under the banner of three suns with conquest in their hearts and blood on their hands. But now, centuries after the legions and the king who commanded them had crumbled to dust, the tower was finally crumbling, too. The hillside would've been cleared back in the time it'd been built, but now, nature had reclaimed the ascent and was infiltrating the building itself, prying apart stonework and tumbling walls like no warrior of the Magus Kings ever could.

It stood about sixty feet across. The wall on one side had collapsed, open to the rain and wind. But fully half the stonework was still solid, broad arches on the ground floor supporting the levels above, crumbling stairwells leading up to the reaches and down to an overgrown and, sadly, flooded cellar. An old stone cooking pit sat in the center of the floor, filled with moldering leaves.

The group huddled together on the ground floor, relatively shielded from the tempest, the horses tied up outside with the wagon. The sky was gray as lead, the sunslight dimmed, and Mia could feel the power inside her stirring a little—like her blood after too many cigarillos. Tingling at her fingertips. Numbing the tip of her tongue. She wondered what it might feel like when the two remaining suns were gone from the sky.

What she might become.

"I'll scout the surrounds," Tric declared.

"Aye," Sidonius nodded. "'Waker, go keep an eye topside."

"Two eyes," the big man nodded. "Wide open."

"I'll come with you," Bryn offered, picking up her bow.

Bladesinger glanced at Mia and Ashlinn, and the trio shared a knowing smile. They set about unpacking their gear, getting the feed someplace dry while Butcher and Sidonius searched the tower for something to burn. The timbers had rotted away long ago, but by the time the wagon was unloaded, the pair had managed to drag enough scraps and dead leaves together to fuel a small blaze in the cooking pit.

"Right," Sidonius said. "Let's see if I remember how to do this."

The Itreyan drew the sunsteel blade taken from the Luminatii centurion Mia had killed aboard the *Maid*. He held the blade in both hands, closed his eyes, muttered a prayer to the Everseeing under his breath. Mia heard a short sharp sound, like an intake of breath, and Sid's blade abruptly burst into flame.

"'Byss and blood," Butcher said, squinting against the light.*

---

*Sunsteel is the traditional weapon of the Luminatii Legion, issued to anyone ranking Second Spear or higher. The secrets of its production are tightly guarded, and Luminatii smiths must serve the legion faithfully for twenty years before being taught the art.

In theory, only the most devout of Aa's legion can ignite the steel, but truthfully, not every member of the Luminatii is a humorless god-bothering fool. Were you considering joining the legion, gentlefriends, there's no end of fun can be had with a sword that bursts into flame upon command.

Just don't let your superior officers catch you using it to dry your laundry or light a dona's cigarillo, and you'll be fine.

"Impressive,"'Singer smiled. "Keep forgetting you were bona fide Luminatii, Sid."

"Not that impressive," Sid said, thrusting the sword into the kindling they'd gathered. "Saves fuel from the flintbox, though."

The scraps and leaves caught and the fire was soon burning merrily. Butcher beckoned Jonnen, his dropped-pie face split in a wide grin.

"Come get warm, boy," the Liisian said. "Old Butcher doesn't bite."

Mia peered at the sunsteel with mild suspicion, but she'd fought Luminatii before, and their blades never had the same effect a fully blessed Trinity had on her. And so, taking her brother's hand, Mia led him over to the little blaze, now burning fierce. As she drew close, the flames on Sid's blade flickered brighter, the damp wood crackling and popping. And as she sat Jonnen down . . .

"Four Daughters," Butcher murmured. "Will you grab an eyeful of that . . ."

The fire was reaching for her. Tongues of flame stretching out from the pit and Sid's sword like grasping fingers, clawing and flickering. Mia glanced at Ashlinn, back to the blaze. She shuffled around the edge of the cooking pit, watching the flames follow, bending at her like saplings in a storm, regardless of the wind's direction.

"Fuck," Sidonius breathed.

"Shit," Ashlinn whispered.

"Aye," Butcher agreed. "Fuckshit."

Jonnen glanced about in disbelief. "You all have *filthy* mouths . . ."

Mia looked into the fire, up to the storm outside. The Ladies of Flames and Storms were letting their displeasure with her be known, and she felt a flash of anger in her chest. She'd not asked for this ire, nor to be part of this damned squabble. And here she was, drenched to the skin, unable to sail on the seas or warm herself by a happy hearth.

"I'm not afraid of a little wind and rain," she said. "Nor a damned spark, neither."

Mia reached into her britches, dragged out a cigarillo, and held it down to Sid's blade to light it. But like a serpent, the flames lashed out, bright and fierce, and she had to pull her hand back with a black curse lest she get burned.

"Steady on, Mia," Sidonius warned.

". . . perhaps we should do our best not to invoke further enmity from the daughters . . ."

Mister Kindly materialized in the arches above, head tilted.

". . . they seem quite upset with us already . . ."

"... *FOR ONCE, THE MOGGY AND I ARE IN COMPLETE AGREEMENT*...," Eclipse growled.

"... o, well, in that case, smoke all you like, mia ..."

Eclipse sighed as Sid drew his sword out of the still-burning cooking pit, slipping it into his scabbard to extinguish its flames. Mia felt her comrades' eyes on her, their slow awakening to the strangeness at work here. They'd seen their share of the world, and none of the Falcons were the kind to indulge blind superstition, but it couldn't have been easy for any of them to swallow. This was Mia's life, and she was having trouble fitting it all in her mind. Goddess only knew what was going through theirs ...

Still, with a glance to Sidonius and the pragmatism that had served her for three years on the sand, Bladesinger began stringing a rope between the archways to hang their wet clothes on. Butcher braved the rain, dragging in more wood from outside to dry by the flames, and, mumbling something about "perimeters," Sidonius waded out into the storm to go scout with Tric. Her knots in place, 'Singer gestured to Jonnen.

"Hand it over, young consul," she said. "You'll catch your death in that."

The boy mutely complied, dragging his cloak off and passing it on. Mia could see he was shivering in the chill, his sopping robes clinging to his thin frame.

"You ever swing a sword, little man?" Butcher asked.

"... No," the boy murmured.

Butcher drew his gladius, ran his eye over the edge.

"Want to learn?"

"No, Butcher," Mia said. "He's too small."

"Bollocks, I had a boy about his age. He could swing a sword."

Mia blinked. "... You have a son?"

The man glanced at his sword, shrugged once. "Not anymore."

Mia's heart sank into her belly. "Goddess, Butcher, I'm—"

"Besides, he's brother to Mia the Crow," the Liisian grinned crooked, darting around the subject with more skill than he'd ever shown on the sands. "If he wants to live up to his sister's feats in the arena, he'd best start learning now, neh?"

"I don't—"

"I am not small." The boy stood, his old imperiousness resurfacing. "I'm very tall for my age, actually. And Father said all a man needs to win is the will that others lack."

Mia sucked her bottom lip, reminded of Scaeva's words to her in his study.

That trinity spinning and burning in his hand. The imperator still standing, still speaking, while she was laid out on the ground in a shivering ball of pain.

Father . . .

"Can't argue with that, I suppose," she sighed.

Butcher's face split into his gap-toothed grin, and he beckoned to Bladesinger, who tossed him her sword. Mia watched from the corner of her eye as the Liisian began running her brother through basics of grip and stance and tactics ("When in doubt, always go for the bollocks"). She supposed it would keep Jonnen moving, at least. Keep him warm. But truth was, part of her wanted to protect the boy from this world of hers.

All the shit and hurt in it.

Ash sat by the fire, Mia a little farther away so as not to risk a burning. The flames still reached toward her, but not as fierce as when she drew close. 'Singer crouched between, stretching out her hands to warm them. Mia could see the awful scar on her swordarm, earned during their battle with the silkling at Whitekeep. The wound had almost seen her sold off by their domina, and Mia couldn't help but wonder.

"How's it healing?" she asked.

Bladesinger glanced at Mia, firelight flickering on her tattooed skin. "Slow."

"How's your swordgrip?"

The woman's lip quirked, her eyes narrowed. "No fear on that front, Crow."

Mia shook her head and smiled. "Never."

The Dweymeri watched the flames for a few moments, obviously wrestling inside.

"So, the soulless one," she finally said. "The deadboy. What's his tale?"

"He's a friend of ours." Mia glanced at Ashlinn. "Well . . . mine, I suppose."

"What do you mean soulless?" Ashlinn asked.

"I mean there's naught to him but meat and bone, lass." Bladesinger touched her breastplate. "Empty here. What's he doing traveling with you?"

"It's . . ." Mia shook her head, looking at the flames. "It's a long tale."

"What Butcher said was true, you know." Bladesinger glanced out into the rain as if she feared Tric might be listening. "I've marked it, too. There's more color to his flesh now than in Whitekeep. Less chill to the air about him."

"It's the sunslight, I think," Mia replied. "He grows stronger the weaker it becomes. Just like me. But don't fear, 'Singer. He's been sent back to help us."

'Singer raised one dark eyebrow, shook her head. "I studied seven years at the feet of the suffi in Farrow, girl. Learned about every god, every creed under the suns. And I tell you now, the dead don't help the living. They only hinder us. And they don't return lest they've business unfinished. What dies should stay that way."

Mia glanced at Ashlinn, found the girl staring back with an *I told you so* look in her eye. But Ashlinn had the presence of mind to keep silent.

"He's my friend, Bladesinger." Mia sighed. "He saved my life."

"Look at his eyes, Crow,"'Singer said. "No matter the new flush in his cheeks or the fresh spring in his step. Our eyes are the windows on our soul, and I tell you true, his look in on an empty room."

Sidonius stomped in from the storm, dripping head to feet and looking utterly wretched. He pulled off his helm and sopping cloak, shook himself like a dog.

"Four Daughters, it's falling harder than an inkfiend on the nod out there . . ."

He looked about the tower's belly, noted the strain in the air.

". . . What's amiss?"

"Nothing," Mia said. "Where's Tric?"

"Still roaming." Sid crouched by the cooking pit and stretched his hands toward the blaze. "He headed south, checking the scrubland. Sniffing the air as he went like a hound on the hunt. Strange bastard, that one."

"Aye," Ashlinn murmured, looking at Mia. "Deathly strange."

"Oi, Sid," Butcher called. "Come over here and show the boy that fancy spin move you do. The one that gutted that scythebear in Whitekeep."

"Ah, you mean the widowmaker!" Sid grinned, dragging his hand along his scalp. "I'm not sure our young consul is ready for that one."

"I can do it," Jonnen insisted. "Watch."

The boy lashed out with his gladius, one, two, his shadow dancing on the wall, his steps as clumsy as a nine-year-old with five minutes of practice under his belt.

"Impressive," Sidonius smiled. "All right, I'll show you. But you must promise not to use it unless at the utmost need. You could kill a silkling with this one."

The Itreyan stood, trudged around the cooking pit, and began running Jonnen through the move. Mia watched the pair of them for a time, a small, sad smile on her lips. Truth was, this tiny respite, these friends and familia around her—it was the closest she'd had to normalcy for eight years. She wondered what her life might have been. What she might have had before it was all taken away from her. What she would have traded to make it so again. But soon enough, she turned her eyes from the fire, out into the storm. Watching the trees sway in the grip of the wind, the flashes of lightning clawing the ocean of black cloud above.

Black like his hands.

Like his eyes.

Hazel once . . .

"An empty room," she muttered.

"What did you say, love?" Ash asked.

But Mia made no reply.

CHAPTER 19

QUIET

Bryn stood close enough to Wavewaker to feel the warmth of his body.

Wondering if she should step closer still.

She'd always had a fancy for him, truth told. Big hands and broad shoulders and a voice that just *did* things to her. But there was no opportunity for that kind of fraternization under the watchful eye of the executus in Remus Collegium, and the big Dweymeri seemed a little ambivalent to her anyways. So Bryn had always kept her feelings in a small room in the back of her skull, only letting them out when she was alone in her cell at nevernight and the desire to scratch the itch became too much to ignore.

But now . . .

. . . now they were free.

Free to do whatever they wanted.

The last two years fighting and bleeding on the sands had taught her how thin the thread holding them to this life was. The loss of her brother Byern was still a raw ache in her heart, and Bryn wondered if she'd ever truly feel whole again. But she knew only fools didn't take their chances when they could, and here her chance was, standing right in front of her. Since Wavewaker's revelation about "waiting for the right woman" earlier, the urge to tell him how sweet she thought he was burned in her chest. Too bright to ignore. Even if she wanted to.

And I don't want to.

"Can't see a damned thing in all this," the big man muttered.

His big brown eyes were on the countryside around them. The woods and rocks were draped in a gray curtain of chill and driving rain. Crystal clear droplets rolled down his smooth, dark skin, dripped from his black saltlocks and beard. The intricate inkwerk on his cheeks seemed a puzzle for the solving.

"It's a storm, all right," she agreed.

Stupid, stupid.

Think of something clever to say, woman.

"Are you cold?" she asked hopefully.

Wavewaker shook his head, eyes still on the wash of gray. Lightning crackled across the skies above the crumbling tower, illuminating the swaying greenery below, the broken stonework, the creeping ruin. The light was bright as the suns for a moment, shadows marked in black, the whole world flashing in strobe.

Bryn stepped closer, laid a gentle touch on his arm.

"*I'm* cold," she declared, in what she hoped was a sultry voice.

"You can head downstairs," 'Waker offered, turning to scan the ground to the south. "Smells like they've got the fire going. I can keep watch up here."

Bryn's eyebrows rose slowly toward her hairline. Wavewaker was utterly oblivious, looking out into the gloom and humming a soft tune in that oceans-deep baritone. She pressed her lips together, pouted in thought—or at least she *tried* to think. The vibration of those caramel-smooth tones in her loins wasn't making it easy.

All right. This calls for a frontal assault.

"'Waker," she sighed. "I don't *want* to go downstairs."

". . . No?"

"No," she said, placing her hand on her hip. "I want you to warm me up."

The big man turned to look at her. His eyebrows drew together with glacial slowness.

". . . Really?"

"Four Daughters!" she said in exasperation. "No wonder you never got your end away! Can I make this more obvious? Would grabbing you by your fucking ears and planting one on your dopey chops be of assistance in clarifying position?"

The big man gave her a shy smile. "I . . . suppose it wouldn't hurt?"

She stared up at him a moment longer. Watching his eyes dance with mirth, his grin come out to play. And then she grabbed him by his breastplate, pushed herself up on tiptoes, and crushed her lips to his.

He was laughing at first, his barrel-broad chest heaving under her hands. But soon the laughter stopped, his lips softening against hers, his chest heaving for an entirely different reason. Bryn's bow slipped from her fingers as she entwined her hands in his saltlocks, hauled herself up his body, and wrapped her legs around his waist. He pushed her back against the parapet, big strong hands beneath her arse, holding her up as if she were light as feathers. Bryn squeezed him tight between her thighs, tongue flickering against his, the warmth of his skin filling her all the way to her bones.

She sighed as he pulled his lips away from hers, the rain falling between them as if the sky were crying, her heart beating louder than the thunder.

"I didn't . . ." He blinked again, grinning for joy. *"Really?"*

"O, Daughters," she laughed. "You're going to be hard work."

"I'll try not to prove too burdensome," he vowed.

"Stop talking, you idiot," Bryn whispered, running her hand down his cheek. "There's better things you could be doing with your mouth."

"I'm not sure what you—"

The blade flashed silver, bright as the lightning above. Past the collar of Wavewaker's breastplate and down into his chest, cleaving his heart and filling his lungs with blood in a blinking. He tried to speak but only managed a cough, spattering Bryn's face with red. She drew breath to cry out just as thunder crashed overhead, the crisp ring of the second blade slipping up under her armpit lost in the rumble.

Bryn felt the steel pierce her chest. Felt herself falling. Hands caught her, slender but terribly strong, guiding her down onto the stone with all the gentleness of a mother holding her babe. She saw a figure above her as the sky kept crying. Dressed in a black doublet and britches. His lips were pursed as if he were sucking his teeth. He was one of the most beautiful boys she'd ever seen. Pale skin and sharp blue eyes.

He knelt over Wavewaker on the flagstones beside her, lifted a gleaming knife, and cut his throat, ear to ear. Simple and quick. Bryn tried to cry no, but her mouth was full of blood. Salty and thick and too much to breathe through. Let alone scream.

I'm cold.

Bubbling up over her lips.

The lips he'd been kissing just a moment before.

I'm so cold.

The beautiful boy turned to her.

I want you to warm me up.

And he raised a finger to his lips, as if wanting her to hush.

It happened in a heartbeat.

Mia was leaning back in Ash's arms, head resting on the girl's shoulders, eyelids heavy with sleep. Butcher was still instructing Jonnen, smiling encouragement as the boy ran through clumsy stances and strikes. 'Singer lay on the stone by the cooking pit and Sid stared into the flames as Mia heard the faintest of whispers upstairs.

A whisper of steel.

Mia looked up just as Sidonius did. Both of them exchanging a glance.

". . .'Waker?" Sid called.

Mia pulled herself to her feet. "Bryn?"

A tiny object fell down among the raindrops, hit the flagstones a few feet away.

Small.

Round.

White.

"Wyrdglass!"

The globe exploded with a damp *shooof,* filling the tower's lower level with a choking cloud of white vapor. Heavy, rolling thick, the arkemical tang on the tip of Mia's tongue telling her instantly what it was.

Swoon.

A sedative, brewed by Spiderkiller in the Quiet Mountain. One good breath and—

Without thinking, without breathing, Mia felt for the shadows on the ruined ground outside the tower, and in the space of a blinking, she closed her eyes and

Stepped

from the

white

and into the black and rain beyond. She tore her gravebone blade from her scabbard and turned, down in a crouch, hair streaming out behind her in the storm. She saw a figure up on the tower's broken top level, a dark-skinned arm hanging over the edge, a blond topknot, soaked in blood.

No . . .

Rage bubbling up inside her chest. The world slowing to beyond a crawl. Every second splintering into a million glittering fragments. Every raindrop falling through the gloom around her a single perfect jewel, tumbling slowly, sparkling with such sudden and astonishing clarity that each was like a diamond shot right into her mind.

More shapes, dark-clad, moving up through the scrub, stepping out from the shadows and broken stone. She recognized Remillo and Violetta from her time in the Galante chapel—they used to go drinking together with her at weeksend. Sly-faced Arturo coming around the wall—he'd borrowed her cigarillos when he was trying to quit his habit. Silent Hush atop the battlements—the boy who'd helped her pass Spiderkiller's trial during their time together as acolytes. And there, finger-thin and swift, short brown hair plastered to her brow, moving through the scrub like a drake through bloody water, came Bishop Tenhands herself.

Blades, all.

The Falcons, Ashlinn, Jonnen, each of them had fallen in the swoon already.

Five to her one, then.

No, not one.

She looked to the dark at her feet.

Many.

A flash of lightning, a tempest roar, a flicker-black shadow moving swift through the bright. She

Stepped

to Arturo first,

strongest and cruelest, skipping out from the dark at his feet and burying her blade *chu-wuffff* into his chest. A bubble of blood, a spray of crimson, gravebone cleaving skin and muscle and bone and red, red, red dancing between the rain. She twisted the blade, felt his ribs *snip-snap* as she tore it free, spinning to watch him fall.

A shapeless cry rang above, pretty Hush crouched like a bird in his bloody bower, killer-blue eyes bright in the lightning dance. She stretched her fingers into the dark at her feet, lovely deep, tearing a handful loose as she'd seen Jonnen do and reaching out through the space between them to blind that pretty blue

"*. . . behind . . .*"

whispers in her ear as the shadow who wasn't a cat became the eyes in back of her head. Moving swift, rolling forward as the knife sailed over her head, close enough to hear it cut the rain through the thunder. She spun in place as Violetta hurled another, then another, razor-sharp and poison-black, no Swoon needed now they had little Jonnen on his back and dreaming

dreaming

(of black skies and a million stars and a bright globe above)

pale fingers curled into claws and dark shadows curled up and about Violetta's boots like hungry snakes and

Mia Stepped

into the

shadow of the

tree at Violetta's

flank and plunged her longsword right into the woman's belly, sideways and twisting, shearing through outer and inner and outer again, Violetta's spine arching, mouth open as ropes of her insides, gleaming and steaming, spilled out in tangles of pink and red.

"Fucking—"

"*. . . MIA . . . !*"

Bending backward as Tenhands's blade whistled past her chin, dropping and rolling toward the tower across the dirt, hair in her eyes, sand on her tongue, the roar of arena crowds echoing in her ears

CROWCROWCROW

but that was yesterturn

when things were simple and the Moon had no name and her father was still

My . . .

Tenhands drew back her fist, filled with dark and gleaming steel, not ten but one, but O, that would be enough. Eclipse rose up roaring on the broken wall behind the woman, fear like a chill on the wind, a shape cut from a shadow deeper than Mia had ever imagined, had ever dreamed, but a shadow

a *shadow*

a SHADOW

all the same.

And Mia realized that instead of Stepping to the black at the feet of a foe, or a tree, or a stone, instead, she could just use the wolf that was shadows, too, and she stretched out her hand and

Stepped

through

Eclipse

instead

dropping out of the stone at the good bishop's back and feeling the damp *crunch* as she swung, teeth bared, spitting hate, gravebone scything between the falling rain and cleaving Tenhands's head almost off her shoulders.

Red on her hands,

on her face,

on her tongue, water-thin and copper-sweet in the downpour, deep enough to drown her and still not enough

never enough

is it?

a line of razor-white pain in her thigh, a flash of a blade, dark with venom. Mia gasped and turned, Remillo hurling another, skimming through the air she'd stood in a moment before, now empty

Stepping

into the

shadow at her feet

and out from the shadow

shaped like a cat on the ground behind him, bringing up her longsword, both hands on the hilt, ruby-red crow's eyes on the hilt watching as the blade sheared up between his legs and dropped him screaming, split clean through to the hips.

Hands slippery with blood now, smeared on her leathers, spilling from the wound he'd gifted her, poison in her racing heart, venom in her thundering veins.

Four of five fallen, but still not enough.

Too slow.

"*. . . mia . . . !*"

Turning as Hush dropped, pretty and silent

TOO SLOW.

"*. . . MIA . . . !*"

and drove his heel right into the back of her head.

White light.

Crunch.

Pain.

Thud.

Then black.

Thunder crashed again, rain beating on the stone like hammers to the anvil.

A lone figure, standing with clenched fists and narrowed eyes. Looming above the fallen girl, hair splayed like a dark and broken halo around her head. Eyelashes fluttering. Senseless and bleeding.

"*. . . stay back . . . ,*" the not-cat hissed.

"*. . . YOU WILL NOT TOUCH HER . . . ,*" the not-wolf growled, standing between them.

Hush ignored them both, stepping straight through them and seizing Mia by the hair. Face blank and pale, the boy dragged her over the rocks, back up into the shelter of the tower. He dumped her on the floor beside her unconscious comrades, taking care to crack her skull against the flagstones extra hard.

"*. . . wretched cur . . .*"

"*. . . I WILL KILL YOU, BASTARD . . . !*"

The boy glanced at the shadowwolf, his face perhaps growing a touch paler, a faint tremble in his step. He backed out from the tower, eyes on the daemons, then turned to the carnage. The other Galante Blades were scattered around the ruins, bleeding or dead. Violetta was on her knees, blood spilling in ruby rivers from between her teeth, trying to stuff her bowels back into her body. She looked up as Hush stepped lightly from the tower, over to the broken ground where Bishop Tenhands lay.

"H-Hush . . . ," she blubbed. "H-Help . . ."

The boy ignored her, too. Silent as death. Reaching down to his dead bishop, the ruin Mia's blade had made of her neck. Tenhands's head still hung by a strip of muscle and skin, her spine cleaved clean in two. Hush fished about in the human wreckage, finally grasped a leather thong and snapped it free.

At the end hung a phial of silver.

"Hu . . . ush . . . ," Violetta begged.

The boy marched back up into the tower, into the guttering firelight. Mia's passengers were stood by her body, hissing and growling, but the boy paid them no mind. Instead, he knelt by the flames, held the silver phial up to the light. Breaking the dark, waxen seal, he poured the contents onto the stone, thick and ruby red.

And using his fingertip like a brush, he began to write in the puddle.

Four Blades dead.

Boy and traitors captured.

Advise.

He glanced out into the rain as the thunder crashed, watched Violetta sinking onto her back in a pool of her own guts and shit. Shaking his head in disdain.

weak

And then the blood began to move.

Hush turned his attention to it, waiting for his instructions. The vitus belonged to Adonai—every bishop had a supply in chapel, used it to send blood missives back and forth between the Mountain. Whatever was written in the red, Adonai knew. But more, because the blood was still bound to the speaker even over impossible distances, Adonai could manipulate it as easily as the blood in his pools.

Hush watched the blood bead and shift, moving like quicksilver along the damp stone. It formed itself into letters, four in a gleaming red row.

PRAY

The pretty assassin frowned. He glanced out into the storm again, flawless brow creased as he searched for meaning in Adonai's instruction.

Pray?

What in the Mother's name was the speaker talking about?

Hush smeared the blood back across the stone and began writing again.

Do not understa

The blood moved. Forming itself into a glistening tendril and coiling around his finger. Hush pulled his hand back, but the blood moved with him, slurping around his hand like a serpent and slipping up his sleeve.

The boy stood, eyes widening in alarm as he felt the blood crawling up his forearm, shoulder, and from there, to his throat. He clawed at it, gasping on instinct as the scarlet flood crept up over his chin, his lips, and into his open mouth.

"Gnu-uuuhh!" he gurgled, lips peeled back from his toothless gums.

A bubble of blood popped in his throat, he tried to inhale, gargling and coughing instead. Clutching at his neck, staggering back and almost falling into the cooking pit, the assassin stumbled out into the rain. Hands at his throat, blood streaming from his nose and eyes back into his mouth as he choked, pale face turning red, whirling on the spot, searching for some—

The blade split his head clean apart like an axe chopping wood. Brain and skull splashed onto the ground at his feet as he fell face-first into the broken stone. Tric placed his boot on the boy's back and dragged his gravebone scimitar free, slipped his second sword into Hush's heart, and *twisted* for good measure.

Lightning tore the sky, white hands clawing at the clouds in fury.

Black hands held with palms upturned.

"HEAR ME, NIAH," the deadboy said. "HEAR ME, MOTHER. THIS FLESH YOUR FEAST. THIS BLOOD YOUR WINE. THIS LIFE, THIS END, MY GIFT TO YOU. HOLD HIM CLOSE."

". . . about time you showed up . . ."

Tric turned to the shadowcat, sitting on the broken wall and licking at its translucent paw. The wolf made of shadows peered at him from her mistress's side.

". . . A LITTLE LATE FOR A DRAMATIC ENTRANCE . . ."

"DRAMA WASN'T MY INTENT," he replied. "I KILLED HIM QUICK AS I COULD."

". . . he was already dead . . . ," the not-cat sighed.

". . . LOOK . . ."

Tric sheathed his blades, stared down at the wreckage of Hush's skull. Amid the fragments of skull and dashed brains, his eyes caught a hint of movement. A thin ribbon of blood, crawling upward in defiance of all gravity, pooling among the rain on the back of the fallen boy's leather doublet.

It struggled to hold itself together, more and more washed away in the downpour, thinned near to worthlessness. But before it lost cohesion entirely, bleeding out into the puddle of Hush's pretty ruin, the blood managed to form itself into simple shapes.

Four letters that formed a single word.

A name.

NAEV.

Book 3

A House of Wolves

CHAPTER 20

SUNDER

Cold.

That was the first sensation Mia felt. Chill seeping into her bones. Stone at her back. Cold and hard and damp.

She lifted her hand, tried to move.

Pain.

In her head. Her back. Her leg. Her fingers touched her brow and a groan escaped her lips, the light above too bright to open her eyes against.

"LIE STILL," came a voice. "YOU MAY HAVE A CONCUSSION."

Mia opened her eyes, pain be damned, saw a boy she might once have loved looming over her. Thunder rolled, stirring the ache in her skull. She winced as the lightning danced, flicker-flash, dragging her eyes closed again. The impression of the strike remained behind on her eyelids, snatches of memory shifting in the fading glow.

Shadows.

Blades.

Blood.

"Hush," she gasped, sitting up.

She felt Tric's hands on her shoulders, surprisingly warm, heard his soft murmurs bidding her lay still, but she shoved it all aside—the gentle touch, the oceans-deep voice, the glass-brittle pain—surging up to her feet and breathing deep and willing her eyes to focus. Her mind to remember.

The tower. They were still in the tower. Sid, 'Singer, Butcher, and, Goddess . . . Ash and Jonnen, all lay arranged around the cooking pit. For an awful, bottomless moment she thought they might be dead, that all of them were gone, that there was nothing and no one left. The thought was simply too terrible to manage, too dark to look at. But then she saw the gentle rise and fall of their chests, felt a shiver as Eclipse melted into the shadow at her feet and took away her fear.

"... ALL IS WELL, MIA ..."

"No," she whispered.

Her eyes found the bodies, fallen and still.

"No, it's not."

Tric had set them aside with those strong black hands of his. Apart from the others, but still under cover from the rain. The stone around them was dark with blood. Their throats cut to the bone.

"Bryn," Mia whispered, her voice cracking. "'W-Waker."

"IT WAS QUICK," came a voice. "THEY FELT LITTLE PAIN."

"O, Goddess," she breathed, sinking to her knees beside them.

Mia reached out with one shaking hand, tears burning her eyes. She touched Bryn's cheek, smoothed back 'Waker's locks. She remembered the look of joy on the big man's face as he spoke of his life in the theater, the melodies of his songs making her turns in the collegium that much easier to bear. She remembered Bryn's words about enduring the unendurable on the sands. How in every breath, hope abides.

Except Bryn wasn't breathing anymore.

"... i am sorry, mia ..."

Her eyes widened at his whisper, pupils dilating with rage. She looked up at the shape of him, coalescing on the wall in front of her. The shape of a cat. The shape he'd stolen when she was a little girl, mimicking the beloved pet Justicus Remus had murdered in front of her. The shape of something familiar. Something comforting. Something to blind her to the awful truth that he had no shape at all.

The anger felt so good.

If she was angry, she didn't need to think.

If she was angry, she could simply *act*.

Hurt.

Hate.

"You bastard," she whispered.

"... i am sorry ..."

"You fucker!" she shouted. "I told you this would happen! I told you I didn't want them here, and now look! Look what you fucking *did*!"

"... the blade that killed them was not mine ..."

"They wouldn't have been here if not for you!" she roared, rage burning brighter and hotter until it was all she was. "You selfish little shit! They're here because of you! They're *dead* because of *you*!"

". . . mia, they chose to be here . . ."

"You bastard, of course they did! They'd no sooner shirk a debt than they'd stop breathing! And you knew that, and still you had to open your fucking mouth!" She climbed to her feet, shouting over the thunder. "You always see clearer, don't you? You *always* know best!"

". . . and if they had not been here? what then? the moment's warning you had was enough to turn the battle's tide. without it, you may all be dead . . ."

"You don't know that!" she raged. "You don't know *anything*!"

". . . i know they were here because they loved you, mia. just as i do . . ."

"Love?" she spat. "You don't fucking *love me,* you don't know what love is!"

The not-cat shook his head, sorrow slipping into the velvet of his voice.

". . . that is not true. i am a part of you. and you are the all of me . . ."

"Bullshit!" she screamed, lightning tearing at the skies. "You're a leech! A fucking parasite! You love me because of what I give you, and that's all!"

". . . mia—"

"I want you gone, do you hear me?"

The not-cat tilted his head. Shivered slightly. And for the first time since the turn they met, the first time he spoke to her from the dark of her own shadow, all those years and miles and murders ago, he sounded afraid.

". . . what do you mean . . . ?"

"I mean get the fuck away from me!" she roared, spittle flying, snot spilling down her lips. "Go back to the 'Grave and crawl into the black you fucking came from. Find someone else to ride. I don't want you anywhere near me!"

". . . mia, no . . ."

She stood there with hands in fists, the blood of her friends pooling about her feet, head pounding in time with her pulse. The sight of those bodies, the memory of Bryn's laughter, the smile on 'Waker's face as he pranced about in his decrepit old theater . . . it filled her belly with broken glass, her eyes with scalding tears.

Eclipse coalesced between them, her voice low with sorrow.

". . . PERHAPS YOU SHOULD GO . . ."

". . . ah, always can we count on you, mongrel, for advice both ill-timed and unasked for . . ."

". . . SHE TOLD YOU TO LEAVE . . ."

". . . you have no right to a voice here. i have walked with her for eight years, and you, a handful of heartbeats. now silence your tongue before i rip it out . . ."

"*. . . DO NOT PUSH ME, MOGGY . . .*"

"*. . . then get out of my w—*"

"*ENOUGH!*"

Mia drew back her hand, clawed at the air between them, at the dark he was made of. The shadowcat yowled and flinched at her blow, a fine black mist spattering against the wall behind him before evaporating into nothingness. He tumbled away, disappearing and coalescing on the broken level above her head.

"Get out of here!" she roared.

"*. . . mia, don't . . .*"

"Go!"

"*. . . mia . . .*"

"*GO!*" she cried, raising her hand again.

And with one final look

A soft sigh

"*. . . as it please you . . .*"

He vanished.

Mia slumped down onto her knees again, arms wrapped around her chest to hold in the sobs. Of all the deaths she'd seen gifted or given in kind, these hurt worse than almost all of them. These were her friends. Folk who loved her. People she'd risked everything for and who'd risked everything for her in turn. All those months in the collegium together, bleeding together, living and fighting together, and in the end, this was where it finished. Some broken tower in a stretch of nowhere.

All of it had been for nothing.

She felt a gentle touch on her shoulder.

"THEY ARE BY THE HEARTH NOW, MIA," Tric murmured.

Thunder rocked the skies above. Bitter tears welled in her eyes.

"You think that makes this easier?" she whispered.

"IT IS WARM THERE. FULL OF LIGHT AND LOVE AND PEACE."

She hung her head. Face twisting as she tried to hold in the sobs. The wind was colder than she could ever remember feeling. The hands of fate, colder still. And yet, these weren't just platitudes Tric was speaking—he'd actually been beyond the veil between life and death. And if there *was* some kind of peace in it . . .

"What will they see?" she whispered, looking up at him. "What did *you* see?"

The deadboy turned to the storm above, watching the rolling gray with eyes the color of night. Thunder rumbled again, and Mia shivered in the chill. It was a long time before he answered.

"When I awoke after I fell," he said, "it was in a place with no color at all. The Quiet Mountain loomed at my back, shrouded in evernight. But before me, far in the distance, I could see a bright hearth. I could feel its warmth on my skin. And around it, I saw the faces of all those I'd loved, gone from this world." He sighed softly. "I knew I belonged there. That everything would be well when I sat beside it. And that is where they will be now. Warm and safe and far from all this. Together."

"So why . . ."

Mia sniffed hard, tried to steady her voice.

"Why didn't you stay there if it's so fucking wonderful?"

"It . . ." The boy shook his head. ". . . I shouldn't speak of it."

"Tric." Mia reached for his hand. She was surprised again to feel the warmth of it. Where once he'd been hard as stone, there was now a suppleness to his skin, his fingers pitch-black against her milk-white. "Tell me. Please."

He was still searching the sky, rain beaded on his cheeks like a beautiful statue in the forum. But finally, he looked down at her, black eyes swimming with sorrow.

"Because when I looked among all those faces," he said, "the faces of all those I'd loved, the one I loved most wasn't among them."

Mia felt her belly flip, her breath catch in her throat.

"I came back for you, Mia," Tric said, black light burning in his eyes. "That was the gift the Mother offered me. She wasn't strong enough to bring me back herself, she could only show me the way." He held out his hand, stained with black. "I had to rip my way back through the walls of the abyss itself. That was what I gave up my place by the Hearth for. Not the chance to mend the balance or restore the Moon or see the world put to right. I care for none of that." He took Mia's hand, pressed it to his chest, and she was astonished to feel a heartbeat, strong and thudding beneath her palm. "But I would strike a thousand bargains with the Night for one more moment with you. I'd die a thousand deaths and defy them all, just to hold you in my arms one more time."

All the world fell silent. All the world fell still.

"Tric, I—"

"I love you, Mia. And Night willing, I'll love you forever."

". . . Mia?"

Jonnen's voice. Tearing Mia out of the moment, back into the cold and the wet and the hurt and the blood. But she lingered in the dark pools of his eyes for one moment more. Hand pressed to the muscle of his chest. Glancing at Ashlinn, aching and wondering.

Torn in two.

"Mia?" Jonnen groaned again.

"It's all right, brother," she said, turning away from Tric. "I'm here."

She made her way across the tower, head still pounding, body aching, leg bleeding beneath the strip of dark cloth Tric had no doubt bound it in. Skirting around the fire, she watched the tongues of flame lap at her hungrily, finally kneeling beside her brother with a hiss of pain and gathering Jonnen up in her arms.

He was still groggy from the Swoon, his eyes bloodshot, face pale. But Eclipse slipped into Jonnen's shadow to calm his fears, and Mia was steeped enough in her venomlore to know he'd recover fully in an hour or so—quicker than the adults, in fact, who were only now beginning to stir.

Mia thanked the Goddess they'd all been clumped together, that the imperative to take Jonnen alive had overridden the assassins' desire to see the rest of them dead. She could remember the battle, the thunder of her blood, the power rippling in her veins. It'd never felt that way before—she'd never wielded the dark so easy, so quick. It was more than just the fact that only two suns hung in the sky now. The new fragment of the Moon inside her—once Furian's, now hers—had made her *more.*

She couldn't help but wonder about Cleo then. The woman who'd written the old journal Chronicler Aelius had found in the library's depths. Who'd given Mia the only real clues about darkin she'd ever managed to find. Who'd spent her life collecting Anais's shattered pieces, only to stumble without ever completing the puzzle Mia herself was now somehow expected to solve.

That journal had spoken of a child inside Cleo. The Mother's sins.

Might that have had something to do with her failure?

And what had become of the woman herself?

Her daughter?

Son?

Tric was watching her across the veil of rain. His declaration still ringing in her ears, louder than the storm raging above.

"How's your head?" she asked Jonnen.

"Sore," he whimpered.

"It's all right, love. I'm here. When all is blood . . ."

". . . blood is all," he murmured.

She held him tight, kissed his brow. Thinking about all that might have been, everything that could have happened, her belly cold with fear.

That unfamiliar sensation. The prickling of her skin, the churn in her gut. The absence of a cat who wasn't a cat like a hole in her chest. A missing piece of herself. But rage flooded in to replace it, and she seized hold tight, desperate, like a drowner to a scrap of driftwood. Letting the bitter, burning anger fill her to the brim.

The Red Church had thrown their dice, sent five of their best, emptied the Galante chapel to strike her down.

They'd failed. And now . . .

Now as the Goddess is my fucking witness . . .

There would be a reckoning.

Naev."

"THAT'S WHAT THE BLOOD SAID."

They were gathered around the fire, still sore and reeling from the Swoon. Wavewaker and Bryn lay still and cold on the stone. A fire burned in the eyes of the remaining Falcons, matching the one in Mia's breast.

"Who the fuck is Naev?" Butcher demanded.

"A friend of mine," Mia replied. "She's a Hand. A disciple who works in the Quiet Mountain in service to the Church. I saved her life."

Mia recalled the sight of Naev standing at the foot of her bed, drawing her knife along the heel of her hand, blood welling from the cut and spattering on the floor.

"She saved Naev's life. So now, Naev owes it. On her blood, in the sight of Mother Night, Naev vows it."

"So she's a blood worker?" Sidonius asked.

"No, that's Adonai," Ashlinn replied, her mouth twisting. "He and his sister Marielle are both sorcerii. Masters of Old Ashkahi magiks, and as fucked in the head as any pair of siblings you're like to meet." She stretched her hands out toward the fire, fingers curling. "That bastard killed my brother."

"AFTER YOU BOTH BETRAYED THE RED CHURCH," Tric replied.

"If I wanted to hear from an arsehole, I'd go use the privy, Tricky."

"Can we not?" Mia snapped, her temper rising. "Please?"

"All right," Bladesinger said. "So this blood mage Adonai is your ally, Crow?"

Mia shrugged. "I saved his life, too. He *did* say he owed me. Though I can't say he's ever struck me as the most trustworthy of bastards. Nor his sister, truth told."

Eclipse's shape flickered and shifted on the wall as the fire danced.

". . . HE KILLED HUSH, MIA. I SAW IT. WHILE YOU AND THE OTHERS WERE AT HIS MERCY, ADONAI'S BLOOD MAGIKS STRUCK THE BOY LOW . . ."

"And now Adonai's directing us toward this Naev woman," Sid said.

Mia nodded. "She does supply runs for the Church. Runs a caravan train from the Quiet Mountain to Last Hope and back. I suppose they're working together?"

"But why?" Ashlinn asked.

"I don't know," Mia sighed. "But at least I know I'm on the right path. We get to Amai, then I head across the ocean for Last Hope. From there I can ride to the Quiet Mountain and Mercurio's rescue. Just as planned."

". . . Wait," Sidonius said, a scowl forming between his dark brows. "What do you mean *you* head for Last Hope? What about the rest of us?"

"You head back to Whitekeep," Mia said. "Corleone can probably take you. Jonnen will have to come with me, and I don't suppose there's any talking Ashlinn into leaving, but you, 'Singer, and Butcher are done."

"Bollocks we are," Butcher said. "We're with you to the end."

"No," Mia said, anger creeping into her voice. "You're not. You've paid your fucking debt, all right? 'Waker and Bryn are dead because of it, and I'll not have more blood on my hands. You're leaving me in Amai."

Sid's scowl only deepened. "Mia, I might've been drummed out of the legion, but I still swore an oath to Darius Corvere. I wasn't there when your father died, but—"

"He's not my father, Sid!" she snapped, rising to her feet. "He's nothing close! I'm the daughter of Julius fucking Scaeva, do you understand that? I'm the daughter of the man who *killed* Darius Corvere!"

"'Byss and blood," Sidonius breathed.

". . . You're that bastard's *daughter*?" Butcher asked, bewildered.

"Aye," she spat. "The man I've been trying to kill for the past eight years turns out to be the man who gave me life. And if that isn't enough of a fuck-you from the divinities, I've apparently got a fragment of a dead *god* inside me that I inherited from him, too! O, and incidentally, the last boy I fucked got murdered by the last girl I fucked, then resurrected by the Mother of Night to help me with the aforementioned god problem, and the prick who just cut Bryn and 'Waker's throat used to be a personal friend of mine! I am fucking *poison,* do you see that? I am *cancer*! Whatever comes near me ends up dead. So get the fuck away from me before you get killed, too."

"You can't blame yourself for this, Mia," Sidonius said.

"Don't!" she warned. "Just *don't.*"

"It's not your fault."

"Fuck you, Sid," she spat, tears welling in her eyes. *"Look at them!"*

"Blaming yourself for another's work is like blaming yourself for the weather," he said, looking at Wavewaker's and Bryn's bodies. "And I'll mourn them as a brother and sister lost, aye. But taking a beating is part of being alive. And let me tell you something, Mia—the best brawlers I ever met were the ugliest, too. Broken noses and missing teeth and cauliflower ears. Because the best way to learn to win is by *losing*."

"I don't—"

"Pretty warriors can't fight for shit. You can't know how sweet it is to breathe 'til you've had your ribs broken. You can't appreciate being happy 'til someone has made you cry. And there's no point blaming yourself for the kickings life gives you. Just think about how much it hurt, and how much you don't want to feel that way again. And that'll help you do what you need to do the next time to win."

Sid crossed his arms and glowered as the thunder rolled.

"I give no fucks for whose cock you got spat from. I'm not leaving you."

"Nor I," Bladesinger said.

"Aye," Butcher nodded. "Neither me."

Mia hung her head, tears burning. She ran her hand across her eyes and drew a deep, shivering breath, thinking of some way she might sway them. But she knew Sid and the others well enough to know they were stubborn as mules, that a declaration like they'd just made was as solid as the stone beneath her feet. She could walk away, but they'd only follow. She could hide herself and Jonnen beneath her cloak and run, but that'd mean leaving Ash and Tric behind . . .

She slumped down, close to the firelight, not close enough for it to warm her. And mutely, she shook her head and acquiesced.

"Right," Sid nodded. "So, we find this Naev, see what she says."

"We still have to cross the Sea of Sorrows," Ash pointed out.

"Six hundred miles from Amai to Last Hope," Bladesinger murmured. "With the Ladies of Oceans and Storms trying to drown us every inch of the way."

"Well, let's burn that bridge when we arrive at it," Sid sighed, dragging his hand over his scalp. "It looks like we're going to be waiting here 'til Nalipse gets bored or the suns burn off a few of these clouds."

"You should all try and get some sleep," Mia said softly.

They all looked at her, suspicious and uncertain.

"Every Blade I knew in Galante Chapel is dead now," she said. "So I doubt there'll be anyone on our trails for a while. But Tric, can you keep watch up top, just in case?"

The boy nodded, his confession of love hanging like an unanswered question between them.

"I CAN DO THAT."

"What about you?" Ash asked. "You need to sleep, too, Mia."

"I will," she nodded. "I'll wake Sid in a few hours. Get some rest."

"You're not going to try anything foolish while we sleep, aye?" Sid asked. "Stealing off into the storm like a thief and leaving us behind?"

"You know where I'm going." She shook her head. "You'd only follow."

"Damn right we would," Sidonius scowled.

"So get some sleep, Sid."

The group were still a touch groggy from the Swoon, and ultimately it didn't take much convincing to settle them back down by the flames. Ashlinn snuggled up with her back against Mia, Jonnen was curled close by. Sid stayed awake for an hour or more, pretending to sleep but watching her through his lashes.

Mia simply watched the fire.

The wood they'd brought in earlier from the rain had mostly dried, and the blaze was burning fierce, giving out a warmth she was barely able to feel. Tric patrolled the levels above, glancing at her every now and then with those bottomless eyes.

Mia stared at the flames instead.

Stoking the fire in her own chest. Feeling it like a living thing. She was worried for her friends. Grateful that they'd chosen to stay with her despite it all. She was tired and sore and afraid. But mostly, she was just sick of this bullshit. Of Scaeva and the Church. Of others being hurt because of her. Of always being outnumbered, of constantly being on the back foot. She was headed into the fire, she knew it. Right into a house of wolves. But truth told, she welcomed the thought. Because along with the fury, she could feel the dark swelling inside her, too. Remember the anger pooled black and deep beneath Godsgrave's skin, the rage of a god laid low, a rage she'd always carried, her whole bloody life.

Anais.

The figure from her dreams, wrought of dark flame, crowned with a silver circle on his brow. Murdered by his father. His mother imprisoned in the Abyss for eternity.

Mia's father had tried to murder her, too. Locked her mother in the Philosopher's Stone to languish and die. She couldn't help but see the parallels between her and the fallen Moon. Stitched into the tapestry around her. Unfolding like destiny. But the difference was, Mia hadn't died when her father tried to kill her. Hadn't fallen to earth and shattered into a thousand pieces.

Hadn't broken. Hadn't crumbled. Instead, she'd become something harder. Not iron or glass.

Steel.

"All you are? All you have become? I *gave you. Mine is the seed that planted you. Mine are the hands that forged you. Mine is the blood that flows, cold as ice and black as pitch, in those veins of yours."*

She could see the truth of it. But that didn't mean it wasn't a truth he'd live to regret. And Mia could see the truth in Sid's words, too. Taking a beating so she knew how much it hurt, and how much she didn't want to feel that way again.

I never want to feel this way again.

And so she looked into the flames, eyes alight with her prayer.

Her vow.

Father

When the last sun falls

When daylight dies

So do you.

CHAPTER 21

AMAI

"What is that smell?" Jonnen asked, screwing up his little face.

Up at the head of the line, Sidonius pressed a finger to his nose and blew a stream of snot from each nostril.

"Sewage."

"And fish," Bladesinger nodded.

"TIMBER," said Tric. "TAR. LEATHER AND SPICES. SWEAT AND SHIT AND BLOOD."

"Quite a nose you've got there," Sidonius smiled.

Ashlinn met the deadboy's glance, saying nothing.

"We're here." Butcher stretched in his saddle and yawned. "It's Amai. You can smell it from miles away. There's a reason they call this city the Arsehole of Liis."

They'd been riding for almost two weeks, miserable and dripping the whole damn way. The Lady of Storms had calmed her temper after a turn or so, softened her howling tempest into a depressing, relentless drizzle that soaked everyone to the skin. It was as if the goddess were saving her strength, coiled and ready like a waiting serpent for the moment Mia took to the ocean again. But it made the ride easier at least.

They had no more trouble on the road—the citizens they passed stepped well out of the way of Centurion Sidonius and his tiny cohort, and the few soldiers they met simply gave bored salutes and marched on. Each nevernight they'd bed down in whatever shelter they could find, or huddle together in the lee of the wagon. Tric would prowl about on guard and Butcher would run Jonnen through his paces with the blade (the boy's form was actually quite good, and he was a frighteningly swift learner) and Mia would pace back and forth inside her head. Thinking of Bryn and 'Waker, of Mercurio and Adonai and Marielle, of that bitch Drusilla and that bastard Scaeva and all they'd taken away.

Soon, she promised herself.

Soon.

But first, there was an ocean between them to conquer.

"You said you grew up in Amai?" Mia asked Butcher, shifting her numb arse on the driver's seat. Jonnen was holding the reins, watching the road studiously.

"Aye," the man nodded. "Shipped out when I was fourteen."

"Shipped out?" Bladesinger asked. "I thought you hated ships."

"I do. But you grow up in a place like this, you've not got much choice. Fuck working in some pub or market stall. Right in the earhole."

Ashlinn frowned. "Were you a fisherman, or . . . ?"

"Fisherman?" Butcher scoffed. "I ought to box your bloody ears, girl. Could a fisherman slay Caelinus the Longshanks in single combat in front of twenty thousand people? Or gut Marcinio of the Werewood like a fish?"

"Aye," Sid said. "A fisherman could probably gut a man like a fish, Butcher."

"I was a pirate, you fucking cunts," the Liisian blustered.

"But . . ." Mia frowned. "You were *seasick,* Butcher. You spewed your guts out the entire way from Whitekeep to Galante."

"Well, I was a shitty pirate, wasn't I?" the man cried. "How d'you think I ended up a damned slave?"

"O . . . ," Mia nodded. "That . . . makes a surprising amount of sense, actually."

"Point is I grew up here," Butcher scowled. "I know this city like I know women."

Ash raised her hand—

"Don't," Mia hissed.

"Right," Sid said. "So what can we expect from the Arsehole of Liis? And they should really think of a better name for it, by the by."

"It's about as dangerous a pit of murderers, rapists, and thieves as you're ever likely to come across," Butcher said. "If you're not salted, you'd best watch your damned step. Life is cheaper than a ha'-copper sweetboy here."

"Salted?" Ash asked.

"Aye, crewed," Butcher nodded. "On a ship, like. If you're part of a crew, you're salted. If not, you're dryland scum. Pirates follow a code, see. The Six Laws of the Salt. First one's Fraternity. Let's see . . ." The man's munted face creased in thought as he tried to remember. "'*Spite him, curse him, kill him, but know he the taste of salt, your brother shall he be.*' In other words, you might hate another pirate's guts, but in harbor, you both stand head and shoulders above the freshwater plebs."

"What if it's a woman?" 'Singer asked.

Butcher blinked. "Eh?"

"If the pirate is a woman. How can a woman be your brother?"

"I don't fucking know," Butcher growled. "I didn't write the bloody things."

"How can they tell who's salted and who's not?" Sidonius asked.

"Some get inked," Butcher shrugged. "Or scarred. Others will wear a token of their ship while in harbor. The worst are just known by reputation."

"All right," Mia nodded. "What are the other rules?"

Butcher scratched his small black cockscomb of hair. "Well, there's one called Dominion. Basically what a captain says on the deck of their own ship is the word of god. And another called Allegiance, which is about chain of command. Crew follow the first mate, mate follows the captain, captain follows the king." The Liisian pouted in thought. "I always forget the name of the fourth one. Heritage or Heresy somesuch . . ."

"Still can't believe pirates have bloody kings," Sid muttered.

"Believe it," Butcher nodded. "And pray to the Everseeing and his Four fucking Daughters you never meet this bastard. Born of a jackal, they say. Drinks the blood of his enemies from a cup carved from his father's skull."

"Did his father die having sex with the jackal, or afterward?" Mia asked.

"Must've been quite a revel . . ." Ashlinn smiled.

"Scoff now, Crow," the Liisian said. "But the Butcher of Amai fears no man of woman born. And Einar Valdyr makes me want to mess my fucking pantaloons."

"Since when did you start referring to yourself in third person?" she asked. "Or wearing pantaloons, for that matter?"

"O, fuck off."*

"Einar Valdyr sank the *Dauntless,*" Jonnen said softly. "And the *Godstruth* three months after that. The *Daughter's Fire* the following summersdeep."

Mia looked at her brother, eyebrow raised.

"I studied infamous enemies of the Itreyan Republic last year," he explained. "I've a memory—"

"—sharp as swords," Mia finished, smiling. "Aye, I know."

Bladesinger sighed. "Well, Mother Trelene willing, Corleone is waiting for us at harbor. We just keep our heads down, find this pub of his, and ponder our next move."

"With a bellyful of wine," Sidonius said. "By a roaring fireplace."

"I'll drink to that," Ashlinn nodded.

"Aye," Butcher said. "The Mother of Night and all her cursed dead couldn't hold me back."

Mia looked to the silent Dweymeri boy, plodding along beside the road.

Tric didn't even flinch.

---

*All jesting aside, Einar "the Tanner" Valdyr, Blackwolf of Vaan, Scourge of the Four Seas, is the 107th king to sit upon the Throne of Scoundrels, and without a doubt, one of most brutal bastards in the history of the Itreyan Republic.

His first murder, that of his older brother, Hakon, was committed with a frying pan at the tender age of twelve, though it should be noted he hideously maimed his younger brother, Jari, at age ten by throwing him to a pack of dogs. He also reportedly beheaded his father on the same turn he cut out his mother's tongue, though the only man to ever seek confirmation of the rumor, his former first mate, Oluf Dahlman, was kept alive through three months of near-constant torture (Valdyr would drag him out at revels and beat him with hot chains for the "amusement" of his guests), and no one has dared to ask about it since.

Valdyr was sold into slavery at age sixteen and fought undefeated for two years in the gladiatii circuits around Vaan for the Wolves of Tacitus, where he first earned the name "Blackwolf." Valdyr was on his way to compete in the *Venatus Magni* in the keeping of Tacitus's son, Augustus, when their ship was attacked by a Liisian privateer named Giancarli. Valdyr killed seventeen of Giancarli's men during the attack, impressing the pirate so much that he offered the slave a berth on his crew. Valdyr agreed, slitting his former master's throat and reputedly fucking the wound while Augustus drowned in his own blood.

You read that right.

Within twelve months, Valdyr had murdered Giancarli and taken over the man's ship. He earned early infamy by sinking three Itreyan navy triremes, and fostered a reputation as a bloodthirsty combatant who favored boarding actions over cannon. It was around this time he began flaying the faces off the captains he killed, sewing them into a leather greatcoat that is now reportedly so long, he needs train-bearers to follow

---

The smell was breathtaking.

Mia couldn't describe it as a stench as such, although a stench was certainly wrapped up in the aroma somewhere. The cityport of Amai was crusted on the shores of the Sea of Sorrows like scabs on a pitfighter's knuckles. The stink of dead fish, abattoirs, and horseshit hung in the air above it, strung with notes of the ocean beyond.

But beneath the stench were other aromas. The perfume of a thousand spices: lemonmere and frankincense and black lotus.* The toast-warm scent of fresh tarts and sugardoughs. Sizzling meats, sweet treats frying in olive oil, the tang of fresh fruits and ripe berries. Because crewed by murderous privateers they may've been, but each ship in Amai's harbor had arrived with something to sell. And beyond a haven for bastards and brutes and brigands, Mia realized the city was something else besides.

A marketplace.

They'd taken off their soldier's livery—Butcher advised that entering the city wearing colors of the Itreyan Republic was just asking for trouble. Besides, Sidonius's suit of gravebone armor was worth a living fortune and would be sure to attract attentions in a city of thieves. They kept on their chain mail and swords and hid the rest in the wagon, though Mia still wore her gravebone longblade sheathed at her waist.

The city was walled, but the broad, iron-shod gates were flung open and unmanned—it seemed King Valdyr could find few fucks to give for who came and went. Making their way into the city proper, Mia was struck by the crowds. Folk of all colors and shapes and sizes: tall and swarthy Dweymeri; pale, dark-haired Itreyans; blond-haired, blue-eyed Vaanians; and everywhere, everywhere, olive-skinned Liisians with their dark curls and musical voices.

---

him wherever he walks. This habit earned Valdyr his second moniker, "the Tanner."

Within five years of taking up piracy, and at the ripe old age of twenty-three, Valdyr murdered the 106th king to sit on the Throne of Scoundrels, Saltspitter of the Seaspear clan, and claimed the title for himself. He has ruled Itreya's pirates undisputed for the past five years. The mere sight of his ebon-sailed ship, the *Black Banshee,* is enough to make the average merchantman shit his lower intestines, and recent estimates put his personal death toll somewhere in the vicinity of 423 men, women, and children.

Apologies, gentlefriends, I know I usually try to inject some humor into these footnotes. But believe me when I say this bastard is no laughing matter whatso-fucking-ever.

*Yes, I know that's only three. Use your imagination, smartarse.

"This is our mother's country," she told Jonnen. "You don't speak Liisian, do you?"

"No," the boy replied, looking around at the swell and the crush.

"Listen to it," she smiled, breathing deep. "It's like poetry."

He looked up at her then, his dark eyes clouded.

"Teach me a word, then."

Mia met his stare. "De'lai."

"De'lai," he repeated.

"That's it," Mia nodded. "Very good."

"What does it mean?"

"Sister," she smiled.

The boy turned his eyes back to the crowded streets, keeping his thoughts to himself as the wagon rolled on. Tric walked out front, the crowd instinctively parting before him as he cut them a path along the rain-soaked thoroughfare. Mia looked about them, watchful and on edge. She began to notice patterns among the throng, obvious among the colors and threads once you looked for it. Men with white kerchiefs embroidered with death's heads about their arms. Another group with mermaids inked at their throats, yet another with triangular scars etched into their cheeks. Like heraldry, or a familia's sigil. The men carried themselves as comrades would, all armed, all looking somewhere on the wrong side of dangerous.

"Salted," she murmured.

"Aye," Butcher nodded beside her. "Rulers of the roost. The ones in wolfskins are Valdyr's boys. Wulfguard. He has men all over the city."

Mia noted the group Butcher was talking about—a quartet of tall and surly-looking bucks, each with a skinned wolf across his shoulders. But though the privateers in the mobs carried themselves with swagger, there was precious little trouble for a city so allegedly rife with bastardry. A few fistfights. Some vomit and blood on the cobbles. Mia began to wonder if Butcher had overstated the case—she loved the ugly sod, but he wasn't a man to let the truth get in the way of a good yarn. Aside from having to scare off a pack of grubby urchins loitering around the wagon (Ash flashed a knife and promised to geld the first one to get too close) and a fellow flying out a second-story window as they passed, there was an almost disappointing lack of drama. Mia and her comrades soon found themselves looking down on the glittering jewel that was Amai's harbor.

Even though the Lady of Storms had drawn her veil across heaven, it was still a breathtaking sight. Ships of every cut and kind: square-rigged caravels and three-masted carracks, mighty galleys with hundreds of oars at their flanks and deadly balingers that ran under power of both oar and wind. Figureheads carved in the likeness of drakes or lions or maids with fishes' tails, sails stitched with crossed bones or grinning skulls or hangman's nooses.

Mia's eyes caught on the largest vessel at dock—one of the biggest she'd ever seen, truth told. It was a massive warship, at least a hundred and fifty feet long, with four towering masts reaching into the skies. She was painted the color of truedark, bow to stern, her name daubed down her prow in ornate white script.

Black Banshee.

"What are those?" Bladesinger asked.

The woman was pointing to two tall spires of stone, looming above the shoreline. Each was seventy feet high, pale limestone, covered in vast tangles of razorvine.

"Those are Thorn Towers," Ashlinn murmured. "They're scattered all over Liis. It's where the Magus Kings used to break their slaves. Torture their prisoners."

Butcher raised an eyebrow. "How'd you know that?"

"My father got sent on an offering in Elai." Ash's voice was low, her eyes narrowed as she looked at the spires. "He made the kill but got caught on the way out. The Leper Priests tortured him in towers just like those for three weeks. Ripped his eye out. Cut his bollocks off."

Butcher and Sidonius shifted uncomfortably in their saddles. Mia reached back and took Ashlinn's hand, saw the haunted look in her girl's eyes.

"He died there?" Bladesinger asked softly.

Ash shook her head. "He escaped. His body, anyway. But part of him stayed in there the rest of his life. It's what drove him away from the Red Church."

"I'm sorry," 'Singer said. "Must have been hard to see that."

". . . It wasn't easy."

Mia squeezed Ash's hand, entwined their fingers together. Glancing at Tric, she saw the boy watching them, his face like stone. Torvar Järnheim had raised his son and daughter as weapons to be used against the Ministry. Ashlinn's and her brother's betrayal had almost brought the Red Church to its knees. And it had cost Tric his life.

Torvar was dead now—murdered at the hands of Church assassins. Mia could see faint pain in Ashlinn's eyes as she looked down on those towers, that dark reflection of the place her father lost himself inside. Uncomfortable silence settled on the scene. But Butcher soon put paid to it, sitting taller in his saddle and squinting at the docks below.

"I can't see the *Bloody Maid,*" he murmured.

"Nor I," Sidonius said.

Mia felt an unfamiliar thrill of fear in her belly then, stamping it down with gritted teeth and trying not to think about the cat-shaped hole in her chest. She knew Cloud should've been here by now—if they'd had time to ride all the way from Galante, he'd surely have had time to sail here. But looking among the ships at berth, she saw Corleone's red-sailed beauty was nowhere in sight.

"They might be at anchor farther out in the bay," she offered. "Those berths look plenty full."

"Aye," Bladesinger said. "Let's just cleave to the plan. Where was Cloud supposed to meet us?"

"He just said he'd see us at the pub," Mia said.

Sid cast his eye over the docks below. "I don't mean to be difficult, but did the fancy bastard narrow it down at all? Because I can spy about twenty of them."

Butcher grinned and shook his head. "Follow me, gentlefriends."

Mia glanced at Tric again, but the boy was looking out at the storm-washed seas. So, giving Ash's hand one last squeeze, met with a small but grateful smile, she turned toward the harbor. Butcher led the way down to the crowded docks, the stench of old fish and new sewage mercifully thinning as the nevernight winds began blowing in off the bay. Wandering along a winding trail of inkdens, pleasure houses, and drinking holes. Shrines to Lady Trelene and Nalipse, tithed with cups of blood and animal parts and old rusted coins. Blind beggars and drunken louts and streetwalkers. And finally, they arrived at a large and somewhat well-to-do establishment on the edge of the water.

The sign hanging over the door simply read *THE* PUB.*

"I like it," Mia declared.

After a short tip from Sid, a stableboy took charge of their horses. The seven road-weary companions doffed imaginary hats to the bouncers and found themselves in the common room of a bustling, hustling taverna. The bar was wide and broad, stocked with a thousand bottles and echoing with a thousand tales. The walls were scribed with the strokes of a thousand hands—written in ink and charcoal and lead; declarations and drivel and poems and all between:

My love I left, my heart I left, with my promise to return.

Pilinius has a pizzle like a barnacle.

---

* One of the most successful taverna in Liis and indeed, the entire Itreyan Republic. The Pub's original owner, "Red" Giovanni, was a privateer who sensibly spent his ill-gotten gains on establishing the drinkhouse (rather than wasting it in someone else's drinkhouse) back when Amai was still two rotten jetties and a lean-to stable. He's

Which of you bastards took my beer?

Yes

YES

The tiger is out

"Find a table," Butcher said. "First round's on me."

"Most generous of you, Butcher," Mia smiled.

"Aye, aye," the Liisian nodded. "Listen, can I borrow some coin? I'm good for it."

Mia sighed and handed over a few beggars from her stash. Tric made his way through the throng with the group following, and just like the folks in the streets outside, the crowded commons parted before him. They found a booth on the dockside of the room, still scattered with empty mugs and small puddles that smelled suspiciously like piss, but they were so weary and cold, it mattered little. They were close to the fire and in from the rain, and after two weeks in the saddle, that was miracle enough.

They huddled into the booth, Jonnen sandwiched between them. Tric fetched a stool from the crowded bar and sat at the other end of their round table so he could better keep an eye on the room. The pub was a tangle of friendly conversations and heated debates, of drunken rebuffs and accepted advances, of tall tales and deadly truths. A trio of minstrels were sat in a corner near the fire, strumming a lyre and beating a drum and singing the bawdiest tune Mia had ever heard.*

Butcher soon returned with a tray loaded with pints of ale, slapping one down in front of each of them, including Jonnen.

"What should we drink to?" Bladesinger asked.

"The Lady of Storms?" Sidonius offered. "Perhaps she'll ease off a bit."

Butcher raised his drink. "A man may kiss his wife goodbye. The wine may

---

also credited in the annals of the Iron Collegium as a genius behind the greatest marketing campaign of all time.

Giovanni stumbled across the idea that you didn't need dancing girls or good ale or fine decor to beat out the competition—you simply needed a name that even the most piss-addled, bowlegged, slack-jawed inebriate couldn't forget.

When in doubt, keep it simple, stupid.

*An alehouse classic known as "The Hunter's Horn," in which a poacher named Ernio learns several lessons from various young ladies about the value of possessing of an enormous . . .

O, never mind.

kiss the frosted glass. The rose may kiss the butterfly, but you, my friends, can kiss my arse."

"How about to friends absent?" Mia said, raising her tankard.

"Aye," Ashlinn nodded. "Friends absent."

"TO LIVE IN THE HEARTS WE LEAVE BEHIND IS TO NEVER DIE," Tric said softly.

Mia met the boy's eyes and murmured agreement. Ash gave a grudging nod. The group hoisted their mugs and took a quaff, all save Jonnen (who eyed the drink with appropriate suspicion) and Tric (who didn't look at his drink at all).

"So where the fuck is Corleone?" Sid asked, wiping his lips.

"Is my face red?" Butcher demanded.

"Not particularly," Sid replied.

"Well, I s'pose he's not up my arse, then."

"Let's not venture too far into the realm of what's been up your arse, Butcher," Mia said.

"Speaking of, your ma says hello," the man grinned.

"Oi," Mia warned, eyebrow raised. "Leave my mother out of this."

"That's just what your da said," the Liisian chuckled.

Mia couldn't help but guffaw, raising the knuckles into the man's face. He slapped her hand away, raised his mug again. "Cheers, you beautiful bitch."

Mia blew the man a kiss, took another swallow.

"You all have *filthy* mouths," Jonnen muttered.

The group drank in silence, content to listen to the pub's hubbub and the song of the minstrels in the corner. By the time they'd reached the seventh verse* their glasses were empty. Ashlinn looked about the table wordlessly, eyebrow raised in question. And met with no dissent, she set off in search of another round.

"First time I got drunk," Sidonius ventured, "I got so sloppy I vomited on myself."

"I fell into the ocean and almost drowned," said Bladesinger.

"I got married," Butcher said.

"You win," Mia nodded, lighting a cigarillo.

Jonnen pushed his ale away with both hands.

"Good lad," Mia smiled, kissing the top of her brother's head.

"I need a bath," Bladesinger said. "And a bed."

---

*In which Ernio learns that blowing one's own horn is almost entirely . . . O, never mind.

"Aye, we should get some lodgings here," Sid said. "With good fortune, Corleone's just been delayed a turn or two."

"And with ill fortune?" Butcher asked.

Sid had no answer for that, nor Mia either. She puffed away on her cigarillo, felt the kiss of cloves on her tongue, wondering what they'd do if Corleone failed to arrive. They had coin, but not enough to book passage for seven. They'd still no answer to the problem of the Ladies of Storms and Oceans. And looking around The Pub's innards, Mia couldn't see many folk she'd trust the way she trusted the captain of the *Bloody Maid*. Now she was settled in, she could feel what Butcher spoke of, catch a glimpse of it in a silvered smile or at a knife's edge or in the bruises at the corners of a serving lass's mouth. An undercurrent of violence. A streak of cruelty in this city's bones.

Tric stood slowly, pulling his hood low, hiding those black hands in his sleeves.

"I'll walk the jetties, speak to the harbormaster," he said. "Perhaps there's some word of the *Maid* and its delay."

"Don't you want to rest?" Mia asked. "Warm yourself by the fire a spell?"

"Only one thing in this world can warm me, Mia," he replied. "And it's not a hearth in a dockside common room. I'll return."

She watched him leave, sensed the Falcons around her exchanging glances. Remembering the feel of his heartbeat under her palm. Bladesinger headed off in search of the innkeep to arrange lodgings, Butcher and Sid nursed their empty glasses. Mia smoked in silence, watching the room around her. It seemed a mix of regular citizens and salted, the pirates in their colors mixing with crew of other ships, gambling and carousing, occasionally joining in with the bawdier verses of "The Hunter's Horn." There seemed to be a birthturn revel or some other celebration up on the mezzanine. Mia heard breaking crockery and howls of laughter and . . .

"Get your *fucking* hands off me!"

Ashlinn's voice.

"Watch Jonnen," she told Sid, rising from her chair.

"What's—"

"Watch him."

Mia stalked into the crowd, pushing through the crush until she found herself in a semicircle of folk that'd formed around the bar. Ashlinn was in the middle of it, a spilled tray and empty tankards and puddles of ale about her feet. Three young men were stood in front of her, all leering grins and yellowed teeth. They wore greatcoats and leather caps and lengths of rope tied in nooses around their necks.

Salted, for certain.

Ash had her fists clenched, fury scrawled on her face as she addressed the tallest of the group—a fellow barely out of his teens with lank red hair and a monocle propped on his eye in an attempt to look lordly.

"You put your hand on me again, whoreson," she spat, "you'll be learning to toss with a stump."

The lad chuckled. "That's not very nice, poppet. We're just having a play."

"Go play with yourself, wanker."

Mia walked out into the ring of amused onlookers, took Ash's hand. Drawing attentions was in no one's interest here. "Come on, let's go."

"O, and who's this? Haven't seen you about before?" Monocle turned his stare to the twin circles branded on her cheek. "What's your name, slave?"

"Ash, let's go," Mia said, leading her away.

The two other thugs moved to cut off their escape. The crowd closed in a little tighter, obviously enjoying the sport. Mia felt a slow spark of anger in her chest, drowning out her fear. Trying to reel it in before it burst into flame. Without Mister Kindly in her shadow, she had the option to be cautious here. To let her fear have its sway. She knew starting a ruckus wouldn't end well.

Hold your temper.

"I asked you your name, girl," Monocle said.

"We seek no quarrel with you, Mi Don," Mia said, turning to face him.

"Well, you've found it all the same." The lad stepped up to her, glowering. "The crew of the *Hangman* aren't the kind to brook insult from freshwater tarts, eh, lads?"

The two behind folded their arms and murmured agreement.

Hold. Your. Temper.

"Unless . . . you can think of a way to make amends?"

A smile curled the corner of Monocle's mouth.

Hold.

Your . . .

And reaching down slow, he placed his hand on Mia's breast.

. . . All right, fuck it, then.

Her knee collided with his groin the way falling comets kiss the earth. A flock of gulls burst from a nearby cathedral spire and took to the sky, shrieking, and every male within a four-block radius shifted in his seat. Mia grabbed the lad by the noose and slammed his face into the edge of the bar. There was a sickening wet *crunch,* a horrified gasp from the onlookers, and the lad collapsed, lips mashed to mince, the splintered remains of four teeth still embedded in the wood.

One of the thugs reached for Mia, but Ashlinn punched him square in the throat, sending him reeling backward, wide-eyed and gagging. She fell atop him, snatched up one of the fallen tankards, and started pounding it into his face. The second reached for the nearest weapon that came to hand—a wine bottle, which he smashed upon the edge of the bar to craft what was colloquially known as a "Liisian jester."* But as he stepped up, Mia curled her fingers, and his shadow dug into the soles of his boots.

The lad stumbled, falling forward, and Mia helped his descent by grabbing both his ears and bringing his face down into her knee. Another ghastly *crunch* rang out as the boy's nose popped across his cheek like a burst blood sausage. Mia put a boot to his ribs for good measure, rewarded with a lovely fresh *crack*.

Ash finished up her tankard work. She turned to look at Mia, chest heaving, a savage grin on her face. Mia licked her lip, tasted blood, dragging her eyes away from the girl to the crowd around them. She pointed to her breasts with bloody hands.

"No touching save by request."

One of the scullery maids burst into applause. Folk in the crowd looked at each other, shrugging assent. The band picked up their tune and everyone turned back to their drinks. Mia grabbed Ash's hand, pulled her up off the fallen privateer. Ash pressed close, still a little out of breath, looking from Mia's eyes to her lips.

"I'd like to make a request for touching, please."

Mia smacked Ash's arse and grinned, and Bladesinger pushed her way through the mob. Sidonius and Butcher soon found them, holding Jonnen's hands. They stood together in the crowded common room, speaking in hushed voices.

"Think we've attracted enough notice for one nevernight," Sid growled.

"Should we go elsewhere?" Ash asked. "Avoid undue attentions?"

"Aye," Butcher said. "You don't fuck with the salted in this city. We should head to another inn, far from this one as we can get and still be in Amai."

"Corleone was supposed to meet us here," Sid pointed out.

"We can leave word for Tric with the doorman," Mia said. "It's not like he sleeps anyways. He can wait here and watch for when Cloud arrives."

"*If* he fucking arrives," Butcher growled.

---

*Guaranteed to make you smile from ear to ear, gentlefriends!

Mia looked at the crowd around them, caught a few sideway glances. Adrenaline was running through her veins after the brawl, her heart beating quick. Mister Kindly's absence left her empty, and Eclipse was still riding Jonnen, so she was left with her fear. Fear of reprisals. Fear for what could happen if Corleone left them hanging. Fear for Mercurio, for Ash, her brother, herself.

She looked at the bloodstains on her hands. Realized they were shaking.

"Let's get out of here," she said.

CHAPTER 22

VIPERS

Adonai was hungry.

It had only been two hours since last he fed. A deep sup from between the blood-slicked thighs of some nameless young Hand (but they were all nameless, weren't they?), listening to the lass's heart beat in time with his mouthfuls, swift as bird wings against the cage of her ribs. Her pulse thudding red upon his tongue, *lub dub lub dub,* so sweet and warm he could have swallowed the girl whole.

But he drank too much. He'd been ill afterward, spewing crimson over the bone-white planes of his palms, on his knees and shaking. The perfection of his torture never failed to amuse and outrage in equal measure, the bitterness of his curse made all the crueler by the fact he'd chosen it for himself. He knew the tithe his power would take before he claimed it. Knew the price to be paid for dredging up magiks long buried in the calamity of Old Ashkah. To have power over the blood, he must be enslaved to the blood. Just as Marielle was a slave of her flesh.

Blood was a speaker's only sustenance, but it was also an emetic. To drink too much was to know awful sickness. To drink too little was to know awful hunger. A constant, flawless sanguine torture.

What price, power?

"Any word?" Solis asked.

The Revered Father's chambers were nestled high in the Mountain, atop a twisting spiral of tightening stairs. Since he'd been given the role by Drusilla, Solis had done very little to redecorate. Arkemical glass sculpture on the ceiling, white furs on the floor, white paint on the walls. An ornate desk stacked high with papers and tomes, overflowing bookshelves lined the chamber left and right.

Behind the desk, the wall was carved with hundreds of recesses. Inside them, Drusilla had kept keepsakes from her turns as an assassin—jewelry and weapons and trinkets taken from her victims. There was still a gleam of silver to be seen there—hundreds of blood phials, sealed with dark wax. But the only trophy Solis kept from his past was a pair of rusted, bloodstained manacles, hanging on the wall above his head.

"How many didst thou slay, Lastman?" Adonai asked, a small smile on his lips.

"What?" Solis asked.

Adonai glanced at the Revered Father. Heavyset. Heavy jaw. Heavy hands. Marielle had mended his burns, but she couldn't regrow his hair—his ash blond eyebrows were mere shadows, his once-spiked beard reduced to bedraggled fluff. His dark robe strained at the muscles in his arms, drawn up around his elbows to show the scars etched on his forearm. Thirty-six deaths wrought in the Mother's name, each scribed in the smooth song of his skin. But . . .

"In the Descent." Adonai nodded to the rusty manacles. "Beating and bludgeoning thy way through the Philosopher's Stone, freedom thy goal. How many didst thou slay?" Adonai tilted his head. "And begrudge our new imperator for it, dost thou? 'Twas Julius Scaeva's notion to empty the Stone with the hands of its own occupants, neh?"

"What word from Galante?" Solis asked, ignoring the question.

"None yet," Adonai lied, the same small smile on his lips.

"None?" Spiderkiller asked.

Adonai turned from the manacles on the wall, looking to the other members of the Ministry. They were seated in a semicircle around the Lastman's desk, a trio of murderers with a tally between them that would make the Night smile.

If, of course, they had any interest in the Mother of Night at all.

Spiderkiller first. Walnut skin, saltlocks twisted into elegant curls atop her head. She was clad in her traditional emerald green, gold as always at her throat. The average Itreyan citizen would never touch a gold coin in their lives, and yet Spiderkiller dripped with it. The chains at her throat could have paid for an estate in upper Valentia. The rings on her fingers could have freed half the slaves in Stormwatch. She wore the face of the dour Shahiid of Truths well, but she hid her love of coin worst among the Ministry. She was a bower bird, decorating the nest of her own flesh. Vanity wrapped plain across expanses of dark skin.

Mouser next. Mouser with his dark, tousled hair and his young man's face and old man's eyes. Mouser, with his estates scattered all across the Republic, each one with a life-sized portrait of himself in the foyer and a dressing room full of women's underthings, deep as a forest. Adonai knew of at least seven of Mouser's wives, though he was certain there were more. Only the Mother knew how many children he'd spawned. To Mouser, immortality was best achieved through progeny. And progeny, of course, required currency.

And then, beautiful Aalea. Blood-red dress, blood-red lips, snow-pale skin. She was the closest to devout out of all of them. She'd only been the Shahiid of Masks a handful of years, ever since the death of Shahiid Thelonius*—she hadn't quite had time for the coin to totally corrupt her. But Adonai could see it beginning to. Her gowns made by the greatest seamstresses in the Republic. The pleasure houses she'd purchased in Godsgrave and Galante, the grand palazzo she kept in Whitekeep and the revels she threw there, young rock-hard slaves and bowls full of ink and acres of skin.

Power.

Corrupting.

Because they paid nothing for it, you see. No tithe. No suffering. They were not reminded, with a constant ache in their bellies or the hideousness of their own reflection, the price they paid for the power they wielded. And so they wielded it thoughtlessly. Carelessly. Believing they had served their Mother well, and now they could sit back and reap the fortunes earned by a life of servitude.

Glutted with blood money. Serenity in murder.

All of them, unworthy.

"Speaker?" Aalea asked, one perfectly sculpted eyebrow raised.

"Hmm?" Adonai asked.

"You have heard nothing from the chapel at Galante?" Dark, kohl-smudged eyes glittered in the dim light. "Bishop Tenhands set out five turns ago, did she not?"

"Aye." Adonai strolled along Solis's bookshelves, finger trailing across the spines. He thought it telling that the Lastman still kept them in here—he wanted to give the appearance of being learned, despite the fact his blind eyes couldn't read a word. "But no word from Tenhands have I heard or felt since the Cityport of Churches she left."

That was fact, at least. Aalea could smell lies with enviable skill. But Adonai could dance around the truth all nevernight and not come close to touching it.

---

*Autoerotic asphyxiation, in case you were wondering.

"Passing strange," Mouser muttered. "Tenhands is no slouch."

"Nor those who rode with her," Spiderkiller mused. "Sharp Blades, all."

"Would that we could've sent more." Solis stroked what little of his beard Ashlinn Järnheim's tombstone bomb had left him. "But we've precious few to spare."

"Would that you could have simply ended our little Crow in Godsgrave, Revered Father," Mouser said. "And saved us this trouble."

Adonai smiled as Solis's blind eyes flashed. "What did you say?"

Mouser examined his fingernails. "Only that for the leader of a flock of killers, you seem to have tremendous difficulty actually killing people."

"Careful, little Mouse," Solis warned. "Lest that tongue of yours flap itself right out of your mouth. I told you the girl had aid."

"Aye, some revenant returned from the Hearth, neh?" Mouser drummed his fingers down the hilt of his blacksteel blade.* "I confess, were I confronted with the like of our good chronicler in the streets of Godsgrave, I might shit my britches, too."

"I already told you," Solis growled, rising from his chair. "Corvere's savior was not kin to Aelius. The chronicler can't even leave the library. This thing walked where it wanted, cut a squadron of Itreyan soldiers to pieces. And one more word of dissent from you, you corset-wearing fop, and I'll show you just how much difficulty I have killing people."

"Grow up, both of you," Spiderkiller sighed.

"O, aye, advice from her favorite teacher," Solis snarled. "Wasn't it you who named Corvere top of your Hall, Spiderkiller? She was your star pupil, neh? That little whore's betrayal has cost us dearer than any in Church history, and it was *you* who made it possible for her to become a Blade."

"And I will see that betrayal put arights," the woman said softly. "I have vowed it before Mother Night, and I vow it before you now. I will have my

---

*Blacksteel, also known as ironfoe, was a wondrous metal created by Ashkahi sorcerii before the fall of their empire. The metal was said to be forged from fragments of the stars themselves, which could sometimes be seen tumbling from the night skies above the empire. Wily sorcerii hunted down these star fragments and forged the metals they contained into peerless weapons.

Blacksteel never grew dull or rusted and could be sharpened to an impossible edge. Even a fragment of the material was worth a living fortune—pound for pound it was far more valuable even than gravebone.

How Mouser got hold of an entire sword made out of the stuff is anyone's guess, but if I were the gambling sort, I'd wager he wouldn't be able to produce a bill of sale.

vengeance upon Mia Corvere. The last thing to touch her lips in this life will be my venom. Doubt it not, Solis."

"You will refer to me as Revered Father, Shahiid," Solis growled.

Adonai watched all this drama unfolding with the same small smile on his lips. So tedious. So mundane. Such was the way of things, he supposed. Vipers always turn upon each other when they have no rats to eat.

"What did Mercurio speak to you about?" Drusilla asked.

The speaker kept his face sanguine, looked to the Lady of Blades through bleached lashes. The woman stood at the head of the room, examining the hundreds of silver phials in the alcoves. Each one was filled with a measure of Adonai's blood, given out to bishops and Hands and Blades for the purpose of sending missives to the Mountain. Even standing twenty feet away, the speaker could feel every drop inside.

"Mercurio," Drusilla said again. "He came down to your chambers a week ago. Spoke to you and your sister at length, or so I am informed."

"Escape from the Mountain, good Mercurio seeks," Adonai shrugged. "And I am one such escape. Words had he also, most choice, about my . . . hungers."

Adonai watched Drusilla, pink eyes glittering. He knew where her coin went, too. Where she spent the slow fortune she was amassing since Lord Cassius perished, leaving the Church completely under her command. How much she had to lose. And why she was so desperate to cling to what she'd built.

"We should kill Mercurio and be done, Drusilla," Solis muttered.

"You catch more fish with live worms than dead ones," the Lady of Blades replied. "If our little Crow learned of his murder, we might never see her again."

"And how would she learn what happens within these walls?" Spiderkiller asked.

Drusilla shook her head. "I know not. But she seems to have a knack for it. The imperator was clear—Mercurio is not to be touched until Scaeva's heir is returned."

"Perhaps he entertains delusion his daughter will still join him?" Mouser said.

"She's no fool," Aalea said with a delicate shrug. "There's much to be gained from standing with Scaeva now. Mia may yet accept his offer."

"And you hope she will, I suppose?" Solis growled. "That her life might be spared? You always had a soft spot for that girl. And her old master."

"I have many soft spots, Revered Father," Aalea replied coolly. "And you are welcome to enquire about precisely none of them."

"Regardless, Mercurio cannot be trusted." Spiderkiller interrupted the pair, eyes on Drusilla. "We should at least lock him in his room."

"No," Drusilla said. "I want to give the old bastard enough rope to hang himself."

"All due respect, Lady," Mouser said. "But Mercurio is one of the most dangerous men in this Mountain. Are you certain that your personal feelings for h—"

"You are treading on *extremely* thin ice, Shahiid." The Lady of Blades glowered. "I would choose my next words with utmost care, were I you."

"If there be nothing else?" Adonai sighed.

"Are we boring you, Speaker?" Drusilla snapped.

"Forgive me, Lady." The speaker bowed. "But I hunger."

Drusilla aimed one last poisoned glare at the Mouser, then turned her full attention to Adonai. "I understand. And I'd not seek to keep you from your meal. But before you leave, there is one last matter to discuss."

"Pray then, Lady, let us discuss it swift."

"Since Mia Corvere so neatly did away with his last, Imperator Scaeva has need of another doppelgänger. Inform your sister we shall be in need of her services."

Adonai felt a flicker of excitement in his veins.

"Coming here, shall Scaeva be?"

"Unless the situation has changed," the Lady of Blades said. "I was informed Marielle could not create simulacra without the imperator present."

The blood speaker gave a lazy shrug. "'Tis as with any artisan. Be the model present in the room, a more accurate portrait can the artiste paint. Be my sister love's work intended to fool the Senate, or Scaeva's bride, then aye." Adonai smiled. "'Twould be prudent for the imperator to make himself available for a sitting."

"Very well," Drusilla replied. "I will inform you when he is due to arrive."

"As it please thee," Adonai said, stifling a yawn.

The speaker turned and left the Revered Father's chambers with a slow swish of red silk, taking his long and sweet time. His bare feet made no sound on the stairs as he descended into the dark, his pale lips twisted in a small smile.

He could feel Drusilla's eyes on him as he left.

Brother love, brother mine."

Adonai found Marielle in her room of faces, reading by arkemical light. She was buried in some tome from the Athenaeum, tracing her progress across the pages with twisted, seeping fingers, careful never to touch. But she looked up as her brother entered her chamber, silken robe parted from his pale, smooth chest.

Her red eyes shone with joy to see him, but she kept her smile small and tight, lest the skin of her lips split again. It had taken weeks to heal the last time.

"Sister love," he replied. "Sister mine."

Adonai gently pulled her cowl back, pressed his lips to the top of her head, locks of greasy blond spread thin over her scalp. She turned away from him, ashamed.

"Look not upon me, brother."

Adonai put his hand to her cracked and swollen cheek, turned Marielle to face him. A nightmare of wasted skin and open sores. Bleeding and seeping and rotting to the core. Perfume layered thick, but not enough to hide the dark sweetness of decay, the ruin of empires in her flesh.

He kissed her eyes. He kissed her cheeks. He kissed her lips.

"Thou art beautiful," he whispered.

She pressed her palm to the hand that still cupped her face. Smiling soft. And then he turned away, hands behind his back, looking at the faces on the walls. Empty eyes and open mouths, ceramic and glass and pottery and papier-mâché. Death masks and Carnivalé masks and ancient masks of bone and hide. A gallery of faces, beautiful and hideous and everything in between.

"What news?" Marielle lisped.

"Tenhands and her Blades all slain. Our little darkin unscathed." Adonai shrugged. "Largely, at least. And our imperator shall arrive soon from the Godsgrave, that ye may sculpt another fool to his likeness."

"Coward," Marielle sighed.

"Aye," Adonai nodded.

"That whore Naev is in readiness?"

Adonai raised his eyebrow. "She is ready. But thou hast no need of jealousy, sister mine. It becomes thee not. Naev is but a tool."

"A tool thou didst use well and often, brother love, in nevernights past."

"She pleased me." Adonai sighed. "And then, she bored me."

"Naev loves thee still."

"Then she is just as much a fool as the rest of them."

Marielle smiled darkly, drool on her lips. "Think ye Drusilla suspects us?"

Adonai shrugged. "Soon, it shall matter not. The board be set, the pieces move. The tomes in Aelius's keeping shall point the way. And when all is done, we shall have black skies and moon above, just as the chronicler promised."

Adonai ran his fingertips over the lamp on Marielle's desk—a lithe woman with a lion's head, globe held in its upturned palms. Ashkahi in origin. Millennia old.

"Think on it, sister love," he breathed. "Our magiks are but a pale sliver of what *they* truly knew. What lessons might be ours when he shines in the sky once more? What tortures might be eased, what secrets gleaned, when we leave ever-sunslit shores behind and dwell in balance again?"

Adonai smiled, his fingertips trailing down the statue's face.

"No dark without light," Marielle said. "Ever day follows night."

Adonai nodded. "Between black and white . . ."

"There is gray," they both finished.

"When the Dark Mother returns to her place in the sky," Adonai said, "I wonder what she shall make of the rot in this, her house? And all those who have profited from her without faith?"

"We shall know soon enough, brother."

Marielle threaded her fingers through Adonai's, her smile on the verge of splitting. He kissed her knuckles, her wrist. Smiling dark in return.

"Soon enough."

Aelius had never found the library's edges.

He'd looked once. Walking out into the gloom between the shelves, the forest of dark and polished wood, the rustling leaves of vellum and parchment and paper and leather and hide. He found books carved on still-bleeding skin, books written in languages never invented, books that looked back at him as he looked at them. Roaming among the aisles for turns on end, only the occasional bookworm for company, trailing a finger-thin wisp of sugar-sweet smoke behind him.

But he never found the edge. And after seven turns of searching for it, he'd finally realized the things in this library didn't get found unless they wanted to be. So he'd stopped looking altogether.

He wheeled his empty trolley up to the mezzanine, stopped outside his office to light another smoke. He saw more books piled up under the RETURNS slot, slipped back into his keeping during the nevernight by the new acolytes training within the Mountain.

Aelius sighed gray, stooping down with his creaking back and liver-spotted fingers, scooping up the books and placing them with reverence in his trolley.

"A librarian's work is never done," he muttered.

He fished about in his waistcoat for his spectacles, checked the pockets of his britches, then shirt, finally realized they were sitting atop his head. With a wry smile, he wandered into his office, drawing deep on his cigarillo.

"'A girl who was to murder as maestros are to music'?"

Drusilla looked up from the book she was reading, blood-red edges on the pages, a black crow embossed upon the cover. A mirthless smirk twisted her lips.

"Black Goddess, he really thinks a lot of his own prose, doesn't he?"

"Everyone's a critic." Aelius propped his cigarillo on his lips and shrugged at the book. "But aye, some of the metaphors are perhaps a bit much."

"Thank the Goddess he doesn't talk the way he writes. If he sounded this pretentious when he opened his mouth, I'd have had him murdered years ago."

The chronicler looked the Lady of Blades up and down. "To what do I owe this visit, young 'Silla? Haven't seen you down here for an age."

"Did you really believe I'd not know what you two were up to in here?" she asked, closing the book's cover. "Did you think me blind, or simply pray I'd not notice?"

"Wasn't sure you'd be able to see all the way down here from your high chair."

"How long have you known?" Drusilla asked.

The chronicler shook his head. "Not sure what you mean, lass."

Drusilla drew a long, wickedly sharp stiletto from the sleeve of her robe.

"What's that for?" Aelius asked. "Chest hair getting unruly again?"

Drusilla slammed the knife point-first into a stack of random histories and novels on Aelius's desk. The blade punched through the leather cover of the tome atop the pile and deep into the pages beyond. The chronicler winced, saw the wounded book was none other than *On Bended Knee,* a particular favorite of his.*

Somewhere out in the library's dark, a bookworm roared.

"I'd not do that again were I you, young lady," Aelius said.

"I believe I have made my point," Drusilla replied, withdrawing the blade.

The chronicler looked down at his hand. A hole was punched through his palm—the exact same size and shape as the wound she'd just inflicted on the

---

*The final volume in the extraordinarily popular and fabulously licentious Six Roses series, which chronicles the life, times, and jaw-dropping bedroom antics of six courtesans in the court of Francisco X. The series was biographical and named many high-ranking members of court along with the king himself.

So explosively titillating were the contents (Cardinal Ludovico Albretti was said to have suffered heart failure reading the climactic bordello scene in volume three), pub-

book. Aelius peered at the Lady of Blades through the new hole in his hand as she rested the blade's tip on another cover.

"I suppose you have," the old ghost replied.

"How long have you known?" Drusilla drummed her fingers on the crow gracing the chronicle's cover. Aelius could see she'd been leafing through the second volume, too. "About the girl. How long?"

The chronicler shrugged. "Since a little before she arrived here."

"And you didn't think to tell me?"

"So suddenly keen for my counsel, are we?" Aelius scoffed. "You haven't set foot in this place for a fucking decade."

"I am the Lady of Blades, the Red Church is—"

"Don't you fucking dare lecture me on what this place is and isn't," Aelius spat. "I know it better than *any* of you."

"I am not diminishing your contribution, Chronicler, but times have—"

"Contribution?" Aelius crowed. "I *started* this fucking place!"

"But *times have changed*!" Drusilla finished, rising to her feet. "You may have carved this church out of nothing, aye. But that was *centuries* past, Aelius. Millennia ago. The world you knew is dust, and for all your service to the Maw, she saw fit to drag you back from your place at Hearth centuries after you were dead, and for what? To make you her general? Her undying Lord of Blades to lead her flock to new and greater heights? No!" Drusilla shoved aside the stack of books on his desk, sent them spilling across the floor. "She made you her damned *librarian*."

Out in the dark, a bookworm roared again. Closer this time. Aelius drew long and deep on his cigarillo, embers sparking in his eyes, his fingers stained with ink.

"Don't fuck with librarians, young lady. We know the power of words."

"Spare me," Drusilla said. "Where is the third one?"

"Third what?"

---

lication of the fifth volume caused a major riot in the streets of Godsgrave. The series was declared illegal by Aa's ministry and, under pressure from his queen, Ilse, the king agreed to ban it—though it should be noted Francisco X was actually something of a fan and only outlawed the books under marital duress.

The author, Laelia Arrius, was imprisoned for life in the Philosopher's Stone and sadly never completed the series, hence the presence of the final volume in the library of the dead.

I've only skimmed them, myself. The politics are rather silly. The smut is top-shelf, though.

“The third volume!” Drusilla said, slamming her palm down on the first two chronicles in time with her words. “Birth! Life! Where is Death?”

“Waiting for you right outside in those shelves, you keep kicking these books around.”

“Where?” Drusilla snarled.

The chronicler tilted his head back, breathed gray into the air. “Dunno. Never looked for it. Things don’t get found in this place unless they’re supposed to be.”

“That, good Chronicler, is but the latest in a series of foolish assumptions.”

Drusilla snatched up the two Nevernight Chronicles and stalked past him, her blue eyes flashing with anger and impatience. He caught the scent of roses in her long gray hair, and underneath, the faint aroma of tea and death. Walking to the mighty Athenaeum doors, Drusilla flung them wide, glowering at the legion of Hands waiting in the dark beyond. Dozens of them. Maybe a hundred. Black-clad and closemouthed, awaiting orders like obedient lambs.

This was never how it was meant to be.

This was supposed to be a house of wolves, not sheep.

“You will search every inch of this library,” she told them. “Every shelf, every nook. Do no harm to the books, and the worms will do no harm to you. But you *will* find what I seek.” She raised the first two chronicles in her hands, displayed them before the servants. “The third in this chronicle. Mercurio of Liis the author. May the Mother be late when she finds you. And when she does, may she greet you with a kiss.”

The Hands bowed, and without a word, swarmed out into the shelves.

Drusilla turned back to Aelius, the two volumes in her hand.

“You don’t mind if I borrow these, do you, good Chronicler?”

The old ghost glanced to the Hands among the forest of dark wood, the rustling leaves of vellum and parchment and paper and leather and hide. He stubbed his cigarillo out on the wall and sighed.

“Just let me fetch you a returns slip.”

CHAPTER 23

WAR

Mia dreamed.

A sky as gray as the moment you realize you're no longer in love.

Water like a mirror beneath her, horizon to horizon beneath a forever sky.

Her breath was cold as starlight, chest rising and falling like her mother and father across the heavens. It would be nighttime soon. Time for her to ascend her throne and watch the night spread her gowns across the heavens.

She would be full tonight. And beautiful. Reflecting her father's light, bringing day to the dark, eating their fear and smiling as they walked the night, unafraid.

All in balance.

"No rival will I suffer," a voice said.

She opened her not-eyes.

Julius Scaeva stood above her, a knife in hand.

"Forgive me, child."

And the knife fell.

Mia opened her eyes.

The curtains were drawn, but she could hear heavy waves on a stony shore, wind between the rocks, mournful gulls crying in the rain. The dream was a fresh echo in her head—the same one she'd been having every never-night since Godsgrave. Her pulse was running quick, her heart thudding. She was surprised that the thump of it against her ribs hadn't woken her brother.

She turned to the boy in the bed beside her, his eyes closed, his expression serene. She brushed a stray curl from his brow and wondered what he dreamed. Envying him that he seemed to have escaped these strange visions that plagued her own sleep. If everything Tric said was true, there was a part of Anais inside Jonnen, too. And yet he slept like a babe.

She wondered why.

Could almost hear Tric's reply.

BECAUSE YOU *ARE THE MOTHER'S CHOSEN.*

She sat up in bed, dragging her hair back from her face and breathing deep. The inn they'd booked lodgings in was called Blue Maria's, and truth told, it was a little nicer than The Pub. Ash had booked the largest room they had, and the seven of them had trudged upstairs, sticking together for the sake of safety.

Sid and Butcher were on the floorboards, wrapped in piles of blankets. Ash was curled up against Mia's back in bed. A fire was burning in a small hearth, bringing a comfortable whiskey-warmth to the room. Paintings of the ocean on the walls, ships in rough wooden frames. Bladesinger was sat in a rocking chair, sword across her lap, dark eyes on the bedchamber door. She looked at Mia, her voice a soft murmur.

"You were having bad dreams."

"True dreams," Mia muttered.

"Ah. They're the worst."

Mia rubbed her face, looked the Dweymeri woman in the eye.

"What do you dream about, 'Singer?"

The woman breathed deep and sighed. "Men I've killed, mostly. Friends I've lost. The feel of arena sands under my feet. You know what it was like. You lived that life. It stays with you, even when you sleep." She looked at Mia and smiled as if sharing a secret. "But sometimes, if I try hard enough, I can change it."

"Change it?" Mia asked. "To what?"

"Instead of the sands of the arena, I think of sands on the beach of Farrow. I imagine myself walking on bright white shores and the kiss of the waves about my ankles. The smell of the ocean and crays cooking on an open fire and the feel of sunslight on my skin." Bladesinger smiled. "You should try it. Next time you sleep. Take ahold of the dream and make it what you want. It belongs to you, after all."

Mia looked around the room and sighed. "Want me to watch for a while?"

'Singer shook her head. "Sid just woke me. You should sleep."

Mia carefully extricated herself from her brother and Ash, pulled her wolf-skin boots on. She stood and stretched, slung her swordbelt over her shoulder, then padded softly toward the door. The fire reached toward her as she passed, hands of flame clawing and grasping at her heels. She spat into it.

"I'm going to have a smoke," she whispered. "If you've a need, just shout."

The Dweymeri woman nodded, rocked back in her chair, hands at rest on her blade. Mia slipped out the door, quiet as cats, her footfalls barely a whisper on the bare floorboards. She stole down the end of the corridor, through a creaking door, and out onto a balcony overlooking the docks. The wind was bitter cold, the rain still spitting, and it took three attempts to light her cigarillo. She breathed a plume of clove-scented gray, eyes narrowed against the smoke. Watching the steel-dark waters lapping against the jetties, the ships at berth, her eyes drifting past the Thorn Towers and their twists of razorvine to The Pub nestled down the boardwalk. Thoughts turning to the pale boy sitting by its hearth, patient as the dead.

"The only weapon in this war is faith."

Mia shook her head. Still unsure what to believe, or where she'd find any faith in the midst of all this. She remembered Tric's words at that ruined tower—his confession that he'd given up his place at the Hearth so he could come back for her. The thought frightened her, saddened her, and, yes, in some way, excited her. There was an allure in being so utterly wanted. To think she had such power over a boy that he'd defy death itself to stand by her side.

She remembered the feel of him inside her. The press of his hands against her. Wondering what it would be like now to touch him. Kiss him. Fuck him.

Licking her lips, she tasted sugar from the cigarillo paper, the smoke setting her tongue tingling. She pressed her thighs together, slipped one hand down the front of her britches, savoring the ache. Looking at the road ahead of her and wondering exactly where it ended. Where she might like it to. Skin like marble and eyes like truedark and clever fingers roaming all the way down . . .

"All right, enough," she growled.

She dragged the last breath out of her smoke, crushed it underheel. Tossing her windblown hair from her face, she slipped back inside, closing the door against the bitter, clawing wind. Wondering if she should head downstairs to check on—

A dark shape hit her as she turned, one hand at her neck, another grasping her wrist. She gasped, crushed back against the wall, her free hand fumbling for her sword as she felt a hard body pressed up against her, warm lips against her cheek, her throat. A flash of blond hair. A hint of lavender perfume.

"Ash?" she hissed. "'Byss and blood, I could've—"

Ash silenced her with a kiss, lips crushed to hers, hands slipping under her shirt and tracing lines of delightful featherlight fire along her hips, into the small of her back. Mia's heart was thumping from fright as Ash's hands slipped down into her britches and squeezed her arse. Mia dragged her mouth away, Ash biting her lower lip as they parted.

"What the 'byss are you doing?" Mia whispered.

"Waiting for you to sneak out for a smoke," Ash smiled, smoothing a lock of Mia's hair from her face. "Knew you'd be fiending for it. I fell asleep, though. You almost got the slip on me, bitch."

"If you wanted a snog in the hallway you could've asked."

"Not asking." Ash shook her head. "Taking."

She kissed Mia again, mouth open, deep as shadows. Mia sighed as she felt Ash's hand sliding across her belly, slipping down the front of her britches where Mia's hand had been a moment before. A soft moan slipped over her lips as Ashlinn kissed her neck, nibbling, nuzzling, setting her shivering and sinking back against the wall. Her legs parted slightly, her heart racing, and not from her fright.

Ash's lips brushed her ear. "I got us a second room."

". . . What?"

"When I booked the first. Just for us. For the night."

Mia laughed softly. "Devious bitch."

"I've been aching for you since you knocked that bastard's teeth out, Mia Corvere," Ashlinn whispered. "It gets my blood up, watching you win."

Mia groaned as Ash's fingers moved between her legs. "What about . . ."

"Your brother's with 'Singer and the others," Ash murmured, lips brushing her throat. "Safe as he can be. They can spare you for an hour or two. Goddess knows when we'll have time again."

Ash reached up under Mia's shirt with her free hand, drawing whisper-soft circles across her breasts, tightening spirals around her hardening nipples. Her breath was hot, urgent on Mia's neck, her fingers working a blinding magik between her legs.

"I want you," Ash whispered.

"O, Goddess . . ."

"I *want* you."

Mia slipped her fingers into Ash's hair, dragged her up into a breathless, aching kiss. Cheeks flushed, pressed up against the wall, she crushed Ash to her, breathing hard in the shivering dark, every thought, every foe, every fear vanishing from her mind as she sighed around their tongues.

"I want you, too . . ."

They fucked like war.

War and blood and fire.

They almost didn't make it into the room, Ash fumbling with the key as Mia pressed the length of her body up against her from behind, kissing the back of her neck, fingernails digging into her skin. They slammed the door behind them and Mia slammed Ash up against it, her laughter turning to a breathless moan as Mia lunged at her throat. Mia pressed her lips to burning skin, felt Ashlinn's pulse hammering under her teeth and tongue. Ash's hands slipped up her shirt and across her back, tickling, teasing. But Mia took hold of her wrists, pressed them back firmly against the frame, grinding up against her as she kissed and nipped her neck.

Chest heaving, lips twisted in a wicked smile, Ash thrust her away. Mia stumbled back and Ash collided with her, shoving her back onto the bed. They collapsed on the mattress in a tangle, Ash's breath coming quicker as she tore at the ties on Mia's britches, eyes glazed with lust. Mia dragged Ash's shirt up and pulled her close, kissed her breasts, licking and sucking and sighing her adoration. But Ash pushed her back down onto the bed, pressed Mia's hands against her chest to still them, finally getting her britches loose and dragging them down around her knees. Mia pushed her off and they fell to struggling, laughing and cursing and biting, flushed and panting, muscles taut, neither willing to yield. Mouth to mouth, tongues dancing against each other as they stripped each other's clothes off in a torturous, maddening battle, piece by piece, sweat rising on their skin, each boot or button a small, breathless victory.

Ash's kisses were hungry, angry, their bodies pressed together as they rolled across the bed, finally, wonderfully naked. Mia spread her legs and groaned, back arching as Ash's fingers slipped down and began to strum, hypnotic, melodic, playing a blinding symphony on her swollen lips. Mia's own hand went searching, across the swell of Ash's heaving breasts, down her drum-tight belly, through downy softness into slick, drenched heat.

"O, Goddess," Mia sighed.

"Yes," Ash breathed. "O, fuck yes."

She moaned as Mia's fingers slipped inside her, curling and coaxing, *O, Goddess, she's so warm,* lighting a fire that set her trembling. Ashlinn threw her head back and groaned, her hands matching Mia's ecstatic rhythm as she swayed and rolled her hips in time. Mia pressed her mouth to Ash's neck, fingers entwined in long, golden tresses, teeth nipping her skin, grinding against her hand. Each girl stoking the rising flames inside the other, each caress, each trembling touch, hotter, higher, more, *more,* until finally, fuck me, fuck me, *fuck me,* they set each other aflame. Ash cried out, hair strewn across her face, muffling Mia's own wordless cries as she crushed her to her breasts. Black light burst behind Mia's eyes, brighter than truelight, her head thrown back as the immolation took her, shook her, leaving her trembling and gasping for breath.

Mia's fingers retreated, tracing lines of fire across the battleground of

Ashlinn's skin. She slipped them between her lips, savoring her lover's taste, drunk with it. Ash found Mia's mouth with her own again, moaning as she tasted herself between them, the pair sinking into an endless, soul-deep kiss. Ash wrapped long legs around Mia's waist, squeezing tight, fingertips drawing arkemical spirals over her hips, across her back, up to the nape of her neck, shivers running all the way down her spine to coil thrumming and humming between her soaking thighs.

Mia wanted to possess this girl. To own and be owned, every part of her, every desperate sugared secret, every smooth curve and shadowed arc.

More.

She wanted *so* much more.

"Kiss me," Mia whispered, caressing Ashlinn's cheek.

"I am kissing you," Ashlinn sighed.

"No," Mia breathed, drawing back, looking deep into her lover's eyes. "*Kiss* me."

Ashlinn's breath came quicker, the thought making her shiver. Mia could see the want in her, the dazed, desperate, aching lust in her eyes, matching Mia's own. She kissed Mia again, tongue darting into her mouth, lips curling in a dark smile.

"Make me," she breathed.

Mia grinned, pressing Ashlinn back onto the sheets, pushing her hands up above her head. She sighed as Mia scattered a hundred lingering kisses across her lips, neck, breasts, her free hand once again slipping down between Ashlinn's legs, rolling back and forth across her soaking lips. Pushing herself up onto her knees, Mia swung around, straddling Ashlinn's face. And slowly,

ever so slowly,

"O, Goddess, yes," Ash whispered.

she lowered herself down onto Ashlinn's waiting mouth.

"O, *fuck*," she groaned, shivering as she felt Ashlinn's tongue tracing burning circles, over and around and finally inside, hands clawing her arse. Mia's hips moved of their own accord, fingers roaming across her own skin, touching and teasing, plucking at her aching nipples, her thighs shaking. Her lashes fluttered against her cheeks, head drifting back as Ashlinn's lips and tongue and fingers set her body humming, exploring her softest place, that dark, wondrous flame building inside her again.

Mia opened her eyes, looked to her lover below her, wanting not only to be tasted but to taste in kind. Ash groaned as Mia dipped her head between her parted legs, wrapped her arms around her thighs, and sank her tongue into her depths. The sweetest nectar on her tongue, their mouths moving in time now, each moan sending vibrations through Mia's whole body and making her moan in turn.

Their struggles ceased. Their battle won. They were a song, then, the pair of them. A perfect duet, old as eons, deep as the dark between the stars. Not making war, but making love, sweet and deep and perfect, hands and lips and bodies, sighs and moans and shivers, skin to skin to skin. Prolonging the honeyed, blissful torture as long as they could stand, dripping with sweat, breathless and panting and burning white-hot, each in tune. Never wanting it to end. Never or ever.

And finally,
after a blissful age,
lost utterly in time,
when they let it go and finally came,
each girl whispered the other's name.

CHAPTER 24

MAJESTY

She was still naked when they kicked in the door.

Mia woke to the ring of heavy footfalls, hackles rising down her back. But she was only reaching for her britches when the boot splintered the frame, the door smashing inward on its hinges. She was up and rolling across the floor in a heartbeat, drawing her gravebone blade from its scabbard. Ash dragged her sword from beneath her pillow, stood on the bed, freckled skin bare, weapon drawn.

Four men loomed on the threshold, each with a black wolfskin about his shoulders.

Wulfguard.

The one in front was a Vaanian almost as tall as Tric. Handsome as a four-poster bed full of top-shelf sweetboys, thick blond hair and beard parted into seven plaits. A long scar cutting down his brow and cheek wasn't enough to ruin the picture.

"This them?" he asked.

Mia looked into the hallway, heart sinking as she spied a familiar face framed by lank red hair, a monocle still propped on his blackened eye.

"Tha'sher," the lad lisped through busted lips. "Bish nogged out my fuggin' teef!"

Mia heard Bladesinger cry out from down the hall, Sidonius cursing.

Jonnen . . .

She took a step forward, naked as the turn she was born, ready to make these bastards sorry they ever had been. The men fanned out into the room, each with hands on their sword hilts. The fact that they hadn't even drawn steel yet told her they were either incredibly stupid or *extremely* confident.

The leader looked at Mia, green eyes flashing.

"His majesty, Einar Valdyr, Blackwolf of Vaan, Scourge of the Four Seas, commands your presence before the Throne of Scoundrels, girl. If you've gods, you'd best set to praying." His gaze flickered to Ashlinn, standing with sword drawn on the bed. "And if you've clothes, you'd best put them on."

"Unhand me, brigand!" Mia heard Jonnen cry. "My father will have you flayed and fed to the dogs!"

"'Singer?" Mia called, heart rising in her throat.

"Aye?" she heard the woman yell.

"Is everyone all right? Is Jonnen—"

"They have him in hand," the woman called. "But he's well."

"I am not well!" the little boy cried. "*Unhand* me, cretin, I am the son of an—"

"You want us to gut these bastards, say the word, Crow!" Butcher yelled.

"I'd not give that word," the scarred man counseled, "if I were you. That sword sits well in your hand, but you've nowhere to run. And if King Einar gets word you *tried* to run, it'll go all the worse for you." He shook his head. "You fucked up badly, girl."

Mia's mind was racing, and she was cursing herself a fool. She could kill these men, she had little doubt, but for all she knew Jonnen could be at the point of a knife. If he got hurt before she reached him, she'd never forgive herself. She was bare-arsed, her friends were outmanned, she'd no idea where Tric was or the lay of the land.

Patience, she told herself.

She looked this Vaanian fellow over, weighing him up in her mind. Easy authority. Understated confidence. Intelligence. His men were busy soaking up an eyeful, but he'd not looked away from her eyes once since she drew her sword.

"What is your name, sir?"

"Ulfr Sigursson, wulfguard and first mate of the *Black Banshee*."

"Does your king usually send his first mate out to round up troublemakers?"

"When he's bored," Sigursson replied. "And I have bad news for you, lass. He's been bored a great deal of late."

Mia glanced to Ashlinn, still standing on the bed.

This is the danger, she realized.

In having people she cared about. Familia she loved. She let her guard down around them. They made her vulnerable. Her enemies could use them against her. Mercurio. Ashlinn. Jonnen. Sid and the Falcons. If she were alone like she'd been in the beginning, she'd just be a flicker in the shadows, already gone. If she were alone, she could gut these four like spring lambs and be on her way. If she were alone . . .

But then she'd be alone.

She looked into Ashlinn's eyes.

And what would the point of it all be then?

Mia curled her hand into a claw, meeting Sigursson's stare. The shadows around the room began to move, stretching out toward the man, pointed like knives. Her hair blew about her shoulders in a cold starlit breeze that touched only her. To his credit, the brigand held his ground, but he finally drew his blade.

"Just who the fuck are you?" he asked, eyes narrowed.

"We'll come with you, Ulfr Sigursson," Mia said. "But if you or your men touch me or my friends in any unseemly fashion, I'll kill you and everyone you ever loved. Do you understand me?"

Sigursson smirked, finally looking her up and down. "My men follow my lead. And you lack the appropriate block and tackle to hoist my sail, little girl."

The man stooped and flung her britches at Mia's head.

"Put your fucking clothes on."

A stone fort awaited them at the south end of the docks.

It rose up direct from the water, its wall like a cliff face. It was limestone, round like a mighty drum, a crust of weed and mussels encircling its waterline. Cannon pointed from its battlements and guts, out across the water. From its highest tower, a green flag flew, trimmed with silver and set with the sigil of a black wolf with bloody claws. Around its wall were hung a hundred gibbets, filled with men and women. Some dead, some living, most somewhere in between.

"Fuck me," Butcher was muttering. "Fuck *me* . . ."

Sigursson walked in front, the wulfguard marching around them. Mia and her comrades had been disarmed, save the small punching dagger hidden in the heel of Mia's left boot. Sigursson was carrying her gravebone sword like a new toy. Sid had earned himself a black eye and split lip when the wulfguard charged into their room, and his chin was crusted with blood. Ash walked close beside Mia, and Mia carried Jonnen in her arms. Even with Eclipse in his shadow, she could feel the boy trembling. She squeezed him tight, kissed his cheek.

"All will be well, brother."

"I want to go *home,*" he said, on the verge of tears.

"Me too."

"You should never have brought me to a place like this."

Mia watched the keep's broad, iron-studded doors opening wide before them.

"I'm not feeling the grandest big sister in the world right now, sure and true."

She was already looking for escape routes. Shadows to Step into, moments she might slip her mantle about her shoulders and vanish. She could manage Jonnen. Maybe even Ashlinn if she tried hard enough. But Bladesinger, Butcher, and Sid . . .

Fear coiled in her belly. Fear like ice and crawling worms. Fear for those she cared about. She wanted Eclipse back to help her manage it, but that would strip Jonnen bare and Goddess knew what he'd behave like then. And without Mister Kindly—O, 'byss and blood, how she missed him now—she was forced to deal with it herself. Push through the frost and the shakes, the memory of Bryn and 'Waker lying dead on the cold stone and think, think, *think* how the fuck they were going to get through this . . .

She heard shouts and jeers ringing ahead as they walked a long hallway lined with arkemical lanterns, on through the fort's guts. More wulfguard flanked a broad set of double doors ahead. The men nodded to Sigursson and glanced at Mia and her comrades with bored expressions. The doors were oak, carved with grim reliefs of drakes and hooksquid and craykith and other horrors of the deep. The nevernight wind howled through the fort's belly like a lonely wolf, and the cold shivered Mia's skin.

"Where the 'byss is Tric?" Ashlinn whispered.

"No clue," Mia murmured in reply. "Not far, I hope."

The doors opened wide.

The room was almost two hundred feet across, circular, built similar to an amphitheater. Three concentric wooden rings rose around the edges, akin to the tiers of an arena. The rings were filled with seamen and sailors, a motley of leather caps and tricorns, greatcoats and ruffled cravats and leathers, scarred faces and silver teeth. Smoking pipes and gleaming blades and feral smiles. Pirates, all.

In the center of the room was a broad tidal pool, carved directly into the limestone floor and open to the ocean beneath. The waters were blue, slightly clouded, rippling with faint chop. Suspended above the pool was a mesh of taut steel wires, each spaced two feet apart, forming a grid six feet above the water's surface. The crowd was cheering and baying around it. And balanced atop it, two men were dueling.

A lean Dweymeri and a broad Liisian, both stripped to the waist. They fought with wooden swords, which Mia found a little odd. The weapons were edged with obsidian shards, so they could cut well enough—each man was bleeding from a gash or two, their claret dripping down into the water below. But without a direct blow to an artery, the weapons wouldn't be enough to kill.

"What is this?" Sidonius hissed.

"Affray," Butcher explained. "Fifth Law of the Salt. Trial by combat."

"Fuck the salt and its law," Ashlinn whispered. "Who the 'byss is that?"

Mia followed Ash's eyeline. At the highest tier in the circles, separate from the others, Mia saw a mighty chair. Its back was a ship's wheel with twelve broad spokes, but the vessel it came from must have been crewed by giants. The rest of the seat was crafted of bleached coral and human bones, carved and twisted into the likes of horrors from the deep. It was hung with a hundred trinkets and ornaments and curios—some Mia recognized from the salted she'd seen roaming the streets of Amai. A rope tied into a noose. A red leather glove. A white rag stitched with a death's head.

Tributes, she realized.

A man sat sprawled on the throne, one leg propped lazily on the back of a slave boy, who was bent on hands and knees before him. A chill ran down Mia's spine as she set eyes on him—an involuntary shiver she couldn't quite suppress. His eyes were rimmed with kohl, the most piercing green she'd ever seen, like emeralds shattered and sharpened into knives. His skin was tanned by years in sunslight, blond hair shaved into an undercut and running in long plaits across the top of his scalp. His beard was plaited, too, his jaw heavy, his face flecked and nicked with a dozen scars. He was built like a blacksmith, clad in leather britches, long boots. His muscular chest was bare, and over his shoulders hung a greatcoat made of cured human faces, stitched all together. The coat was so long, it trailed to the floor at his feet.

"That's Einar Valdyr," Butcher whispered, clearly terrified.

"On his Scoundrel's Throne," Mia murmured.

The wulfguard shuffled them to one side. Mia met Ash's eyes, saw she was tense and ready. As the men clashed on the wires, Mia again scanned the room, looking for the exits, shadows. There were two hundred privateers in here at least, thirty more wulfguard, Valdyr himself. Fighting wasn't an option. And as the doors slammed shut behind them, escape seemed a distant dream.

The crowd roared and Mia turned her eyes to the duel—the Dweymeri had drawn blood again, a fresh gash along the Liisian's shoulder, dripping down into the waters beneath them. The wires hummed like lyre strings as the men danced and lunged, the Dweymeri skipping across one cable to avoid his foe's sword, the Liisian's blow going wide. The smaller man lost his balance, started to wobble. The Dweymeri struck a quick blow into the Liisian's knee, almost tumbling himself. The Liisian cried out, his footing failed, and as the crowd rose up and roared, the man slipped through the cables and down into the tidal pool below with a splash.

The Dweymeri sailor bellowed in triumph. The Liisian man in the water surfaced in a panic, swimming toward the edge. Mia saw Valdyr move for the first time, rising up from his throne and stepping to the balcony's edge so he could better see. And beneath the water, Mia's belly churned as she saw the motion of a long, dark shadow.

The Liisian had made the pool's edge, but the water was low, the walls too high for him to reach the lip. He lunged upward, and Mia caught a glimpse of his face—blanched and terrified. His fingers scrabbled at the stone as the crowd stomped their feet. And as Mia watched, a long tentacle, hooked and black and glistening, rose up from the water, wrapped itself around the man's throat, and dragged him under.

*Black Mother, it's a leviathan.**

---

*The leviathan is a fearsome predator of the Itreyan oceans and natural foe to the drake. It is possessed of hooked tentacles, a razored beak, and four large, saucer-shaped eyes. The beasts can be found in deep or shallow water and are hunted for their ink, which is both an indelible pigment and a potent hallucinogenic. Dweymeri use the ink in their facial tattoos and rites of adulthood, while the rest of the Itreyan population use it to get utterly shit-faced.

Ink can be utilized as an intoxicant in three ways—drunk, inhaled, or injected. Its various effects are summarized by this lovely little poem, often sung by children around Godsgrave during games of jump rope or the like.

Quaff for the nodding,
Smoking for the high,
Needle for the bitter man,
Who'd really rather die.

Morbid little bastards, aye?

Thrashing sounds. Garbled cries. The water flushed red as the crowd howled. Up on the balcony, Valdyr clapped, throwing back his head and laughing. The faces on his coat reminded Mia of those faces beneath Godsgrave, screaming all in time. She saw his eyes were alight, that his teeth had been filed back to points.

Aye, all right. I could believe a jackal birthed this bastard.

"The Daughters have spoken!" he roared.

Quiet dropped upon the room like a hammer, and every man and woman in it fell utterly still. Valdyr stood with arms spread wide, his voice deep and booming.

"My Lady Indomitable, be you satisfied?"

A woman in her early thirties stepped forward on the second level. She had blond hair drawn back in a braid, no kohl around her eyes, no paint on her lips.

"*Indomitable* is satisfied, my king," she bowed, smiling.

"My Lord Red Liberty, be you satisfied?" Valdyr demanded.

A bearded Itreyan with a vicious scar and a red greatcoat with brass buttons bowed low, his face as sour as if he'd eaten a bowl of fresh dogshit.

"*Red Liberty* is satisfied," he said. "My king."

"Well, that *is* a fucking relief," Valdyr said, returning to his throne. The man propped his boots up on the slaveboy again, leaned back, and stroked his plaited beard. "Now, who else brings quarrel? Or can I return to my wine?"

"Majesty!" A snaggletoothed Liisian with thinning red hair and a poisonous-looking cat curled around his shoulder stepped forward with a bow. He had a noose tied about his neck like a cravat, just like the lads Mia and Ash had thrashed yestereve.

"My Lord Hangman," Valdyr replied without looking at him. "Speak."

"The matter I mentioned earlier, Majesty," the man said, glancing at Mia with an expression she could only think of as "covetous." "Your wulfguard have returned."

"Aye, aye, what news, Sigursson?" Valdyr asked.

"Six in hand, Cap'n," the man beside Mia called. "Caught them at Maria's."

"And the seventh?"

As if on cue, the doors crashed open, and a half-dozen battered and bloodied wulfguard shuffled into the hall, dragging a struggling figure. Mia's heart surged and she took half a step forward, but Ashlinn placed a hand on her arm to still her.

"Tric . . ."

He was wrapped in chains, writhing like a serpent. They'd stripped off his black, tattered robe, left him with only his leather britches beneath, the rusted iron links cutting deep into his skin. The wulfguard threw him to the floor and he snarled, his saltlocks writhing across the stone. A faint flush of rage kissed his cheeks, a spatter of blood smudged on his skin.

"Bastard killed Pando, Trim, and Maxinius," one of the wulfguard declared, his nose smashed to pulp. "Broke Donateo's legs like they were fucking kindling. I stabbed the fucker three times in the chest and he didn't fall. Barely even *bled*."

"Tric, lie still," Mia called.

"Mia . . ."

One of the wulfguard stepped forward and kicked him in the head. "Shut the fuck up, you unholy cocksucker!"

Valdyr looked down on the struggling Dweymeri boy, knife-green eyes narrowed.

"Cap'n?" Sigursson held aloft Mia's gravebone blade. "May I approach?"

Valdyr grunted assent, kicked a rope ladder over the edge of his balcony. It was then Mia realized the man's position was unassailable by anyone in the room. The only paths to his perch were a bolted door behind the Scoundrel's Throne or the ladder he'd just tossed to his first mate. Glancing around the hall, she saw at least fifty men who looked like they'd cut their own children's throats for a ha'-beggar. She could feel that undercurrent of violence again. Peering into the eyes of the folks around the room as they looked up at their king.

Not a man or woman in this room loves Einar Valdyr, save perhaps his crew.

The king of pirates holds his throne through fear . . .

Sigursson climbed the ladder, spoke in hushed tones in his king's ear, handing over Mia's gravebone sword. Valdyr's kohled eyes finally met hers, and Mia had to force herself to hold his gaze. Even near a hundred feet away, she could feel the power radiating off him. A feral, bloodthirsty intensity that made mere children of the men around him. There was an allure to him—that much was undeniable. But it was an allure bound to leave bruises on your skin, and blood on your sheets.

Valdyr stared at her for a long, silent moment, lips curling in a hungry smile.

"What say you, my Lord Hangman?" he finally called. "What tithe asked?"

"This freshwater bitch broke my boy's teeth," the snaggletoothed man said, nodding at Monocle's mangled mouth. "She's his by right. The blonde, too." He motioned to Jonnen. "And I'll take the sprog by way of the insult."

"Will you, now, Draker?" Valdyr smiled, his pointed teeth gleaming.

". . . Majesty willing, of course," the captain said, lowering his eyes.

Valdyr turned his eyes to Monocle, tongue pressed to one sharpened incisor. "You really let this slip get the jump on you, boy? I'd be shamed, were you my get."

Monocle lowered his gaze, his cheeks burning as a chuckle rippled through the hall. Valdyr hefted Mia's gravebone blade. He ran his knife-green eyes up and down the blade, then up and down Mia's body. His smile curled her belly.

"Eclipse," she whispered. "Be ready."

". . . ALWAYS . . ."

Mia glanced at 'Singer, Sid, and Butcher, whispering soft. "We head for the tidal pool, then into the ocean. That thing in the water is better than the things out here."

Sidonius nodded. "Aye."

"*Fuck* me . . . ," Butcher murmured.

King Valdyr looked down at Monocle and sneered razors.

"You'd not know what to do with trim like that if I gifted it to you, little man." He looked at Mia again. "*I'll* take the raven-haired one. You may keep the blonde, Draker. But I'd put a bit in her mouth and irons on her wrists before you let your whelp near her. You can have the boy, too, if it please you." He motioned to Tric, still laying on the stone floor. "Take that one below for Aleo to look at. Send the Dweymeri and Liisian to the Thorn Towers." A lazy wave at the tidal pool. "Give the tall one to Dona, she's not had Itreyan for weeks."

Mia's heart was racing. The shadows rippling around her.

"Hold on to me," she whispered in Jonnen's ear. "Blind anyone who comes near."

"I . . . I will try . . ."

Mia squeezed Ash's hand. "Stay close to me, love."

Mia had no idea what to do about Tric. No idea what to do about the leviathan waiting for them in that pool. No idea if they'd even make the water, or where they'd go if they reached the ocean. No weapon save the two-inch punching dagger in the heel of her boot and the shadows, writhing and rippling around her.

She felt a wulfguard grab her shoulder.

Her hand curled into a fist.

"Hold! Hold!" came a cry. "What fray is this?"

The pack of brigands near the door parted, and Mia felt a dizzying rush of relief. The newcomer flashed a four-bastard smile and dropped into a bow that would've shamed the most polished courtier of any Francisco, I all the way through to XV.

"Majesty," he said.

Cloud Corleone shot Mia a sideways wink and whispered.

"Sorry we're late."

CHAPTER 25

HERITANCE

"Well, well, my Lord Bloody Maid."

The King of Scoundrels grinned at Corleone the way drakes grin at seal pups.

"Well met, old friend."

The tone of Valdyr's voice left no illusions in Mia's mind as to whether he and Cloud were actually old friends—she could no more imagine Valdyr having friends, old or otherwise, than she could imagine a sand kraken having a pet puppy. But her relief at seeing Corleone breeze into the hall hadn't quite worn off yet.

The captain was clad in his usual kit—dangerously tight black leather pants and a black velvet shirt open a touch too far, the feather in his tricorn propped at a jaunty angle. Beside him, BigJon wore dark leathers and a bright blue shirt of Liisian silk, his drakebone pipe propped at his lips.

"My king," the captain said, sweeping off his hat and bowing again. "The heart sings to see you looking so well. Have you lost weight, perchance?"

"What the 'byss do you want, Corleone?" Sigursson spat.

"A word and then some, before you drop one of my crew in the drink."

"Crew?" Sigursson raised an eyebrow. "What are you babbling about?"

"These dogs are all salted," the captain said, gesturing to Mia and her fellow captives. "Crewed to the *Maid* afore we shipped out from Godsgrave after the games. And here you are, treating them like freshwater trout."

"Saaaaalted?" Valdyr drew the word out as if savoring it, leaning out over the railing with his chiseled teeth bared in a grin. "Is that so?"

"Light's truth, Majesty. May the Everseeing rot my toddler off if I lie."

"A tale to both confound and amaze." The king smiled wider, tongue pressed to one wicked-sharp canine. "Since the *Maid* just put into harbor this very hour, and these seven arrived in Amai yesterturn?"

"I sent them overland from Galante," Corleone said. "I had business inland."

"Bull-fucking-shit," Draker spat, dragging his thinning red hair off his brow.

Corleone tilted his head. "You mean to tell me you know who crews aboard my ship better than I, Hangman? When was the last time you set foot on my decks?"

"When I was plowing your mother," the captain growled.

"O, aye, she sends her regards, by the by," Corleone replied without skipping a beat. "She told me to tell you she hopes you're not still embarrassed. It happens even to the best of men, apparently."

Guffaws and chuckles echoed about the room as the *Maid*'s captain turned attentions back to his king.

"Majesty, these seven are my crew. Salted, every one. There's no place for them on their knees or in the pens or the pool, besides."

"Seven?" Valdyr crooked one scarred eyebrow. "Even the child, now?"

"Cabin boy." Corleone offered his four-bastard smile, sweet as honey and smooth as silk. "My last fell overboard in the Sea of Silence."

"Tragic."

"BigJon certainly thought so. He goes in for a bit of buggery recently."

The *Maid*'s first mate dragged his pipe off his lips, about to voice protest. "I do—"

"So one of your crew still knocked my boy's teeth out of his head." The captain of the *Hangman* spat on the deck. "There's tithe owed for that."

Corleone glanced at the monocle boy, flinched at the sight of his mangled snout, then leaned in for a closer look. He turned and held a finger aloft to Valdyr.

"A moment, great King, to confer with my people? I've not had a word crossways since Galante. I'm sailing a tad behind the tide."

Valdyr leaned back into his throne, hefting Mia's gravebone blade and smiling like the cat that got the cream, stole the cow, and bedded the milkmaid twice.

"By all means."

Corleone turned to Mia and her comrades, the easy smile on his face belying the deathly urgency of his tone. "Right. I'm dangerously close to being *hideously* fucking murdered here, so if you bastards would like to catch me up with what the 'byss you've been doing since you arrived, that'd be appreciated."

"Murdered?" Bladesinger frowned up at the Scoundrel King. "He's done nothing but smile since you walked in."

"The more Valdyr smiles at you, the closer you are to dead," Cloud said. "He's about two crossed words away from slitting my throat and fucking the wound."

"That's disgusting," Ashlinn hissed.

"Aye, the last man who endured it probably thought so, too."

"Tric, are you all right?" Mia asked.

The boy was still sprawled on the floor in chains, but he glanced up and nodded.

"AYE, I'M FINE, MIA."

"Look, I don't mean to sound impolite, but *fuck* him," Corleone said. "And unless you want to be as dead as he is, you need to tell me what in *Aa's name* you did."

"The twat with the monocle put his hands on my tits," Mia said flatly. "So I broke his face. And two of his friends. Ash helped."

"It was exciting," Ashlinn nodded.

Mia thumped the girl's arm to quiet her.

"Did you request said hands be placed on your . . ." Corleone's eyes drifted downward. ". . . accoutrements at any point?"

Mia raised her eyebrow and stared.

Hard.

"Right," Corleone nodded. "Had to ask."

The captain turned to the assembly, arms held wide.

"My salts tell me their ungentle treatment of Draker Junior here was warranted response to advances both unseemly and unwelcome." Corleone shrugged. "Seems a plain sailor's quarrel to me. Certainly nothing to be troubling His Maje—"

"Shuzafuggin larr!" Monocle slurred through his busted lips.

Corleone looked at him sidelong. "I beg pardon?"

"He said she's a fucking liar!" Draker spat. "I got the tale rightways from my three lads, they said this lying slip asked them for a roll then got shirty when rebuffed."

"And you believe that?" Mia blinked. "Are you a liar or a fool, sir?"

"Watch your mouth, whore."

"Call me whore?" Mia nodded slow. "Fool it is, then."

"There were witnesses aplenty," Ashlinn said. "If we—"

"Enough!"

The bellow pierced the air, sharp and bright. All eyes turned to the balcony. Valdyr was sitting up straight in the Throne of Scoundrels, Mia's longsword placed point-first in the floorboards, one scarred and callused hand at rest on the pommel.

"Draker," he said. "If you have umbrage, then call for Affray. If not, shut your fucking mouth before I make you my woman and burn your ship into the sea."

The *Hangman*'s captain took an involuntary step back, but then glared at Mia.

"Aye," the man snarled. "The *Hangman* demands Affray."

Mia whispered sidelong to Butcher. "Is that the trial-by-combat thing?"

"Aye."

Corleone raised a hand. "Now, ju—"

"I accept," Mia shouted.

A chorus of cheers and shouts went around the mezzanines, the captains and their crews clunking tankards and stamping feet and expressing general contentment at the possibility of more bloodshed.

"Shit," Corleone sighed. *"Shiiiiiiiiit."*

"What?" Mia hissed. "I already kicked the little bastard's teeth out of his head. You think I can't skip along a few of those wires and knock his arse into the drink?"

"You'll not be fighting Draker Junior," Corleone explained. "It was the *Hangman* who issued challenge. The *ship*. That means her captain gets to pick his finest salt to romance you. He's not about to send his son and heir to fight you, or you could claim Draker Junior's share of the ship through Heritance."

"Heritance!" Butcher cried, immediately lowering his voice. "*That* was it! That's the law I couldn't remember! I knew it was an *H* word."

"What the flaming blue fuck is Heritance?" Mia whispered.

"Fourth Law of the Salt," Cloud said. "Governs ownership of property acquired in pursuit of matters . . . felonious."

"Eh?"

"Booty, lass," BigJon said. "It's about booty and right of conquest. *Be it on Seas of Four, or dry of land, when you claim a man's life, you claim all he was.* You kill a man, his purse is yours. You kill a captain, his ship is yours. So you kill Draker Junior, anything his father has bequeathed him would go to you."

"Let me understand this," Sid said. "You people have codified a law that actually encourages you to murder your comrades and take their shit?"

"Well, how would you run it, then?" BigJon demanded, looking Sid up and down. "A man gets topped and any bucktoothed mongrel with a sticky set of fingers can come grab what he wants? Or the *state* takes it, maybe? Sounds a recipe for chaos to me."

"Aye," Corleone nodded. "This way, it's all kept aboveboard. I keep telling you, just because we're pirates doesn't mean we're lawless brigands."

"And I keep telling you," Sid boggled, "that's *exactly* what it fucking means!"

"Claim a man's life, you claim all he was," Mia murmured.

"Aye," Corleone said. "So the fellow they'll send to fight you won't be possessed of much. And anything he *does* own, he'll probably bequeath to his captain or mates before the battle."

Mia looked across the room and saw a mountain of a man wearing a hangman's noose who was indeed hastily scribbling a note on a scrap of parchment. He handed the note to his captain, who tucked it inside his greatcoat. The man then took the stairs down to the common floor. He was Dweymeri, as big as a small wagon, his saltlocks cut into a short, wild crop atop his head. His biceps were thicker than Mia's thighs, his face marked with beautiful inkwerk and rent with awful scars earned from a lifetime of battle.

Sigursson had climbed down from the king's balcony to stand before Mia. He held out a heavy wooden blade edged with obsidian shards.

"Mother Trelene watch over you, girl. Lady Tsana guide your hand."

"All right, then," she muttered.

Mia handed Jonnen over to Ashlinn, kissed her girl fiercely on the lips.

"Don't you die on me," Ash warned.

"Sounds a sensible plan."

"You actually have a plan?"

Mia sucked her lip and scowled. "I'm working on it."

The girls kissed again, until Corleone finally cleared his throat.

"Is there anything you'd like to bequeath to . . ."

Mia turned to look the captain in the eye, and his voice failed.

"Right," he nodded. "Had to ask."

Mia kissed Jonnen on the brow. "I'm going to need Eclipse. Just for a while, all right?"

The boy nodded slow, glanced at Mia's opponent. The man was twirling his blade through the air as if it were an extension of his own body, the air left bleeding behind it. His muscles caught the muted sunslight, gleaming like polished steel.

"Remember what Father says," the boy said.

"Aye," Mia nodded. "I remember."

"Good fortune, de'lai," he said softly.

It was the first time he'd ever called her sister. The first time he'd ever acknowledged they were familia. And even there, with death peering over her shoulder and breathing cold on her neck, Mia smiled. Blinking the burn from her eyes and feeling her love for the little bastard swelling with the lump in her throat. She hugged him, kissed his cheeks, heart melting as his arms slipped up around her neck and he hugged her back.

Turning, she drew a deep breath, took the blade from Sigursson's hands.

"Eclipse?" she said.

Sigursson's eyes grew a little wider as the daemon slipped from Jonnen's shadow. The wolf prowled once about Mia's legs, black as truedark, then vanished into the shadow at Mia's feet. Dark enough for three.

"Just who the fuck are you?" he asked.

But Mia was closing her eyes. Breathing deep. Feeling the fear melt off her bones as her passenger devoured it whole. In the space of a heartbeat, she was no longer a frightened girl dancing on razors. She was a destroyer. Shadowforged. The blood of the night flowing in her veins, and the splinter of a fallen god burning dark inside her chest.

Unbreakable.

"Eclipse, you move where I point you, aye?"

". . . AS IT PLEASE YOU . . ."

She marched across to the edge of the pool as Sigursson turned to the assembly. His voice rang out over the throng.

"Affray is called! *Hangman* has challenged, *Bloody Maid* has answered! Fight to the fall, and may the Daughters have mercy on your souls!"

Mia looked down into the water, to the dark shadow of the leviathan, coiled in the depths below the wire grid. It was thirty feet long if it was an inch—a hunter of the deep, grown fat and baleful on the blood of the men and women Valdyr threw to it.

Mia's opponent dragged off his boots and shirt. His torso rippled with muscle, every inch covered with tattoos—women and fish, mostly, though some appeared to be a combination of both. Not to be outdone, Mia stripped off her own shirt, tossed it carelessly to one side. There was some scattered applause as the audience realized she wore nothing underneath.

Eyes on my chest, bastards, not on my hands.

She pulled her boots off next, twisting the left heel as she did so, palming her punching dagger. Mia hopped up onto the cables, wrapping her bare toes around the wire for grip. The steel hummed under her feet, like the strings of some grand and terrible instrument, the first notes in a song of blood and ruin. The Dweymeri jumped up onto the cables, too, the impact of his landing running along the steel and shaking Mia where she stood. The man smiled, stomped the cable again to throw Mia off-balance, then raised himself up on one foot, arms spread, in a demonstration of perfect poise.

Mia made her way across the wires cautiously. Glancing down to the cool blue water six feet below, she saw that colossal shadow, circling, impatient. The brigands around them were baying and stomping, and she was in mind of her time in the arena. The silkling. The retchwyrm. The chaos of the *Venatus Magni*. The adoration of the mob, when their applause sang in her veins in time with her pulse, and fear . . . well, fear was something only her opponent had to worry about.

But those turns were behind her now. She didn't fight for the mob anymore.

She fought for herself. And the few she loved.

"What is your name, sir?" she called out.

"Ironbender," he replied.

Mia held out her wooden sword, dropped it into the water below them.

"Excuse me for a moment, Ironbender."

She raised her punching dagger, gleaming between her knuckles.

"Eclipse?"

She pointed to the balcony above. And the wolf who was shadows surged and vanished, and Mia

Stepped

off the wire

and up into

the shadowwolf

now coalescing in the

dark at Valdyr's feet, leaping up and straddling the big man's lap and plunging her dagger into his throat. The King of Scoundrels gasped, knife-green eyes going wide. But by the time he'd raised his hand to fend her off, the dagger had already punched through his neck three more times,

chunk

chunk

chunk,

sluices of blood arcing off Mia's blade and scything through the air as the crowd blinked in confusion at her disappearance and then realized where she was, sitting astride their sovereign, fist wrapped in his braids and hacking at his mangled throat,

chunk

chunk

chunk,

cries of terror and outrage as she worked, face twisted, teeth bared, red on her lips on her throat on her breasts, hot and thick as he gargled and spat and flailed, clawing at her neck, muscles taut and fingers curled, but the blood, O, the blood,

chunk

chunk

chunk,

already fleeing him in spurts and floods, down his bare chest and over the throne beneath them as he surged upward, fighting to the last, and yet she clung on, legs wrapped around him like a lover as he bucked, as she stabbed and stabbed and stabbed until he stopped fighting, until he stopped punching and kicking and breathing, his final exhalation a bubbling whisper, his final touch a caress as his hand fell away and his eyes rolled back and still, still she didn't stop,

chunk

chunk

chunk,

and she dragged her forearm across her eyes now, wet with sweat and blood, mouth set into a thin line as she shifted from stabbing to sawing, hand trembling with the effort, parting muscle and cartilage and bone as Sigursson roared, scrambling up the rope ladder to the aid of his captain, his lord, his king, but by the time he made the balcony Mia was done, tendons standing taut in her neck as she leaned back, damp popping, wet crunching, pulling her bloody prize from its shoulders.

Einar Valdyr's head went tumbling across the floorboards, through the balcony railing, and down to the floor below, spraying a slick of blood. It bounced once before rolling into the tidal pool and disappearing in a swirl of red. Mia grabbed Valdyr's headless corpse by the collar of his macabre greatcoat, hauled it out of the Scoundrel's Throne, and sent it to the deck with a swift kick to its arse. Valdyr's slaveboy was on his knees, utterly aghast, slipping in the thick pool of blood as he scrambled away through the mess. The onlookers in the tiers below were in equal parts horrified and awed, watching slack-jawed as Mia turned and flopped onto the throne, half-naked and covered in gore, long dark hair soaked with blood barely protecting her modesty.

She propped her bare feet up on Valdyr's headless, twitching corpse. Fished about in the arse pocket of her britches, wincing, and finally pulled out her thin, battered cigarillo box. Eclipse coalesced at her feet, black fangs bared, hackles raised.

Standing on the balcony's edge, Sigursson looked at her in utter disbelief.

"Just *who*. The *fuck*. *Are* you?" he demanded.

Mia leaned back on her throne, put a cigarillo to her lips.

"Well," she said, wiping at the blood on her face. "If I understand this Heritance thing correctly . . . I think you can call me Your Majesty?"

Chapter 26

Promises

Mia had put Valdyr's greatcoat on, but refused to wash his blood off.

She sat in a tall chair at one end of a long table, red gore crusting on porcelain skin. To her right sat Cloud Corleone and BigJon, looking like they'd each aged twenty years in the last ten minutes. Tric loomed at her right side, bare-chested, glowering. Without his robe, Mia saw fresh rends on his body: stab wounds in his belly, across the muscles in his arms, three in the flesh around his heart. She could see the flush of life plainly in his skin now, blood glittering in the new wounds, she was sure of it. But his arms were still spattered to the elbows with a black as dark as night, eyes gleaming like that pool of godsblood beneath the 'Grave.

Sid, Bladesinger, and Butcher stood around Mia's chair, and Ash sat to her left with Jonnen on her lap. When he'd first set eyes on her after she'd butchered Valdyr, her little brother had simply looked at her and smiled.

"Well played, de'lai."

At the other end of the table sat Ulfr Sigursson, a little paler beneath the handsome. Other members of the wulfguard were gathered around him, black-clad and tense as bowstrings, looking somewhere between shocked and murderous.

Mia could hear the chaos in the chamber outside. Captains howling at each other across the Hall of Scoundrels, scuffles and faint curses and breaking glass.

Mia's eyes were locked on Sigursson's, her stare cool and even. Blood was coagulating on her skin, in her hair and eyelashes and under her fingernails. All her lessons from Shahiid Aalea were ringing in her head. She knew the next sixty seconds would utterly define her relationship with this man. That, at its heart, this was a game of blink. The first person to speak was showing their weakness. Their fear. And watching the wheels turning behind this man's eyes—former right hand of the king she'd just murdered, and now ostensibly her first mate—she was damned if she'd blink first.

Claim a man's life, you claim all he was.

His ship. His crew. His throne.

She imagined being first mate to the King of Scoundrels would've been a job with certain benefits—that Sigursson had wielded power any other privateer in this city would have envied. And being part of Valdyr's crew, the rest of the wulfguard would've stood top of the pile in the dungheap that was Amai. Looking across the table at all of them, Mia knew each of these brigands was doing the math in their heads.

They accept me for now, and keep their place atop the mountain.

They reject me, and let one of the captains outside try for the throne.

Or one of them kills me.

Eclipse prowled in a slow circle around the wulfguard, black as the furs about their shoulders. The room was lit by arkemical lanterns on the walls, and Mia let the shadows curl and writhe. Stretching across the table toward Valdyr's men, her own shadow on the wall reaching out to Sigursson with translucent hands.

Tries *to kill me, at least.*

Chaos was budding outside in the hall. The shouts growing louder, the unrest rising. Each minute spent in here was another minute those flames were allowed to take root and spread. Each minute in here was another minute the wulfguard risked losing all they had. The air in the room was heavy as iron, the smell of blood thick in the air, thickest of all around Mia. Who simply sat.

And stared.

And waited.

One of the brigands finally growled, "We can't just—"

"Shut your mouth before I fuck it," Sigursson snapped.

Mia stared at the man, allowing a small smile to curl her lips.

Sigursson leaned his elbows on the table and sighed.

"Do you want your shirt back?"

Blink.

"No," Mia said, turning up the collar of Valdyr's coat. "This is warm enough."

"Your actions put us all in deep waters, girl."

"My name is Mia Corvere," she said, still unblinking. "Blade of the Red Church. Champion of the *Venatus Magni*. Chosen of the Dark Mother and Queen of Scoundrels. *Never* call me girl again."

Sigursson leaned back in his chair, leathers creaking. He glanced to the wulfguard around him, ran his hand over his chin.

"Have you ever actually crewed aboard a ship?"

"No."

"Ever attacked another vessel under a flag of piracy?"

"I sank a Luminatii warship named *Faithful* a few weeks back. But technically, they attacked us first, so I'm not certain that qualifies."

Sigursson glanced at Corleone, who nodded confirmation.

"You know how to tie a clove hitch or bowline?" the man asked. "Know a broad reach from a beam reach or a main from a mizzenmast? Can you use a sextant or trim a mainsail or read a captain's charts?"

"No," Mia admitted.

"You're not a sailor's arsehole, are you?"

"No." The dry blood on her lips cracked as she smiled. "But I *am* a queen."

"For now."

Tric leaned forward, spread his black hands on the table, and glowered. The shadows flickered and stretched, and a long, low growl came from beneath the floor.

". . . CAREFUL WITH YOUR THREATS, WULFGUARD. YOU SPORT WITH TRUE WOLVES NOW . . ."

Mia leaned back in her chair, running her fingers over her bare collarbone, down her blood-caked sternum. "I'll make you a proposition, Ulfr Sigursson."

"I await it with bated breath," he replied.

"I need to cross the Sea of Sorrows. And there's a storm coming."

Sigursson shook his head. "This is naught but a squall, it'll blow over in—"

"A storm is coming," Mia insisted. "So I need the biggest ship. The strongest ship. The ship most likely to see me through the tempest that'll crash upon my head the minute I set foot near that fucking ocean. And *Black Banshee* fits that order, neh?"

Sigursson nodded slow. "She's the mightiest ship on all Four Seas. *Black Banshee* wasn't built, she was spat from the unholy gash of the Dark Mother herself."*

"She'll be my gift to you," Mia said.

---

* The unholy nature of Niah's . . . feminine accoutrements . . . is a matter of some debate amongst theologians. Amongst most normal folk, however, the wickedness of

Sigursson's eyes narrowed.

"You get me across the Sea of Sorrows, *Black Banshee* is yours. The Throne of Scoundrels is yours." Mia's fingertips brushed her collar. "I'll even throw in this lovely leather coat, if you like. Or you can try to kill me, Ulfr Sigursson, and I can show you what it truly means to be spat from Niah's belly."

The man looked to the deadboy beside her. Eclipse, now prowling behind him. Mia's shadow reaching toward him, its hair blowing soft behind it, its hand outstretched toward him, gifting his cheek a caress that made him shiver.

He swallowed thick. "Are you accursed?"

"I am a daughter of the dark between the stars," she replied. "I am the thought that wakes the bastards of this world sweating in the nevernight. I am the vengeance of every orphaned daughter, every murdered mother, every bastard son." Mia leaned forward and looked the man in the eye. "I am the war you cannot win."

Mia pushed her seat back, stood slowly, and, content to meet him at the crossroads, she walked around the table. She let her gravebone sword trail along the ground, the tip scoring a deep runnel in the floorboards. Her oversized coat of faces dragged behind her like the train of some godsless bride. Stopping halfway down the table's length, Mia extended one bloodstained hand.

"You gift me Ashkahi shores, and I'll gift you a throne," she said. "Or you can defy me, and learn exactly what it is that makes the rest of them so afraid."

Ulfr Sigursson glanced once more to his men. Mia's eyes never wavered. And finally, slowly, the big Vaanian stood, leathers creaking, boots clomping as he walked around the table and stopped before her. Eclipse prowled around their legs, growling soft. The light flickered and the wind whispered and the shadows laughed.

Mia just stared.

I am the war you cannot win.

Ulfr Sigursson sank to one knee.

Pressed her bloody knuckles to his lips.

"Majesty," he said.

Niah's immortal lady parts is indisputable, and cursing by them is tolerated, indeed, vigorously encouraged by ministers of Aa's church.

I'm not leaving you," Ashlinn said.

"Yes," Mia replied. "You are."

Wind was blowing in off the Sea of Sorrows, cold as the fear in Ashlinn Järnheim's belly. All around her, the crew of the *Bloody Maid* were loading their gear, marching up the gangplank to their waiting ship. The Falcons were gathered at the base of the ramp, all save Butcher and Jonnen, who'd snatched a spare minute to practice with a pair of wooden swords that the man had carved with his own two hands. Eclipse bounced back and forth between them, growling encouragement to the boy. But Ashlinn only had eyes for her girl.

"Mia," she scowled. "There's no way."

"Ashlinn, there's no sense in you all shipping out with me," Mia replied. "The goddesses still want my blood. We can make our way to Last Hope separately, meet Naev there, and head out to the Quiet Mountain together. You take the *Maid* now, it'll be smooth sailing all the way to Ashkah. Trelene and Nalipse aren't interested in any of you, they want me." She glanced to Corleone. "Isn't that true, Cloud?"

"We had nary a bump on the way down here," the scoundrel nodded. "Blue above and below."

"My thanks for finally getting here, by the by," Mia said. "Were you selling some of that arkemist's salt in the *Maid*'s belly, or just taking in the sights?"

"Neither."

"Well, what took you so long?"

The man scratched the back of his head, a little bashful. "A small matter of . . ."

"Vaginas," BigJon offered. "Several, in fact."

"Good for you," Mia smiled. "Battista? Bertrando?"

Corleone just grinned, but Ashlinn felt anger swell in her chest.

"Mia, stop fuckarsing about," she said, tugging her girl's arm. "I'm serious."

"So am I," Mia replied. "The Ladies want to kill *me*. They'll save their strength for the *Banshee*. So you ship out now on the *Maid,* we'll wait six turns and follow. You'll be sunning those beautiful baps on the shores of Last Hope by the time we arrive."

"*If* you arrive."

"I have a better chance with Sigursson and his crew. *Banshee*'s almost twice the size of the *Maid*. She's made for the worst the sea has to give. But I can't bring Jonnen with me into the tempest, and I need someone to look after him while I'm not there. Who's going to do that? Butcher? Mother love him, but he's not the finest role model."

Ashlinn glanced to the former gladiatii, who'd paused his sparring with Jonnen to stick his hand down his britches, readjust his tackle, and burp louder than thunder.

"Right, get that guard up, boy . . ."

Ash shook her head, trying to make Mia see sense. "So what, you plan to cross the Sea of Sorrows on a ship full of murderous fucking cutthroats? You saw what kind of man Valdyr was. Goddess knows what kind of bastards he took for his crew."

"I think I've a notion," Mia sighed.

"You can't rescue Mercurio if these pricks cut your throat and feed you to the drakes. I'm not leaving you alone with the likes of them."

"I won't be alone. Tric's coming with me. He doesn't sleep. He doesn't eat. He can't drown. Who better to guard my back on the sea in a storm?"

If Mia's words were meant to be comforting, they had far from the desired effect. Ashlinn's eyes found the deadboy, as always looming just within earshot. He'd found himself a shirt to replace the robes they'd torn off him, leather britches, and heavy boots. He stood like a statue, gravebone blades crossed at the small of his back, constantly scanning the crowds around them. Pretty as the perfect murder. But as Ash glanced his way, those ink-dark eyes flashed right to her. Bottomless. Unreadable.

"Mia . . . ," Ashlinn pleaded. "I don't trust Tric."

"But I trust *you,* Ash," Mia said. "Jonnen's the only familia I have left who matters. And I'm asking you to look after him. Doesn't that tell you something?"

Ashlinn met Mia's eyes, tears beginning to well in her own. She could feel her walls crumbling, the iron and fire she showed the world melting away at the notion of having to leave the girl she loved behind. The thought was a stone in her belly. A knife in her chest. She threw her arms around Mia, burying her face in her hair. She kissed her lips, her cheek, her nose, resting their foreheads together as she whispered.

"Promise you'll meet me there. Promise you'll come back to me."

"Promises are for poets."

"I *mean* it. I'm not losing you."

"You know what they say," Mia smiled. "'Tis better to have loved and lost . . ."

"Whoever said that never loved someone the way I love you."

Mia met her eyes, then. Goddess, she was so beautiful. Standing there in the bitter farewell winds and sighing so soft it made Ash's heart ache.

"I've been thinking," Mia said. "The house at Threelakes you talked about. Flowers in the windowsill and a fire in the hearth."

Ash sniffled. "And a big feather bed."

"I've been thinking, and . . ."

Mia turned her eyes to the lead-gray sea.

". . . Perhaps."

Ash squeezed her hand, butterflies taking wing in her belly, a small and fragile smile curling her lips. It was more than she'd ever let herself hope for. The thought of all they might become, the dream of all they might have . . .

"Perhaps?"

Mia looked at her and nodded, a long lock of raven black tossed across her cheek, her eyes as dark and deep as the Abyss. "Look after him for me."

Ash swallowed hard, pawed away her tears.

She needs me strong now.

"I will. I promise."

Drawing a deep breath and steeling herself, Ash followed the others to the groaning gangplank, the *Maid* rocking gently in her berth. One by one, they headed up, gathering at the railing to look down on Mia and Tric. Ash and Jonnen waited 'til the last, the boy's hand clasped in hers. He stopped to look up at his big sister, lips pressed together, eyes clouded.

"Remember your manners," she told him. "Don't be a brat."

"Remember what Father said," he replied. "Don't get killed."

Mia smiled. "Good advice, little brother."

Ashlinn watched as the boy sucked his lip a moment. Staring down at his feet. And finally, he opened his arms and gifted Mia a swift hug, face pressed to her leathers. Ashlinn's heart melted to see him opening up, to see the gulf between the pair slowly closing. For a moment she was tempted to pick him up, crush them all together in an embrace, like that night they'd spent sleeping together in the storm. The thought of what they might be when all this was over surfaced in her mind's eye again. All of them together. A real familia.

But it was over almost as soon as it began. And before Mia really had a chance to hug Jonnen back, the boy was breaking away, pulling Ashlinn with him.

One last swift kiss passed between the girls, desperate and bittersweet, Ash sucking the plump swell of Mia's bottom lip as they parted. And then Jonnen was dragging her up the gangplank, nothing left to say. Ash gathered with the others at the railing, Mia blowing her another kiss, looking over her comrades in farewell.

"Look after them for me, Sid," Mia called.

The big Itreyan nodded, thumped a fist over his heart. "Never fear."

"And never forget."

They put out into the chopping blue, sails creaking overhead, BigJon's profanity like an old, familiar song. Ashlinn stayed at the railing, the wind snatching away her tears, watching her girl on the boardwalk growing smaller and smaller still. Mia held up her hand and Ashlinn waved in return. Jonnen raised his hand, too. She stooped and picked him up so he could see better, holding him tight.

"No fear, little one," she said. "Everything's going to be all right."

The boy sighed and slowly shook his head.

"No, it won't."

'Byss and blood, they're keen, aren't they?"

Mercurio stood on the mezzanine overlooking the great Athenaeum, cigarillo smoke curling on his tongue.

The Hand made no reply.

She looked to be twenty-one, twenty-two perhaps—from a crop a few years before Mia's time, at any rate. She was clad as they all were—black robes, head to foot, silent as the grave. After Drusilla's discovery and subsequent examination of the first two Nevernight Chronicles, the Lady of Blades had ordered the Hands following Mercurio to abandon all subtlety. He had three constantly behind him now—this young lass, never more than a few feet away, an older Itreyan woman perhaps in her thirties, and a Dweymeri lad, tall and silent, who usually kept the greatest distance.

They never spoke. Never responded when he asked questions. They simply followed, like voiceless, soulless shadows. He'd not heard a peep from Adonai or Marielle since Drusilla found the chronicles—the siblings had obviously decided discretion was the better part of valor with the Lady of Blades on the warpath.

He and Aelius were once more alone.

Which basically means Mia is, too . . .

"How long have they been at it now?" Mercurio asked.

Aelius called out from his office, "Almost three weeks."

"How many dead?"

"Only the two," the chronicler replied, wandering out onto the mezzanine, thumbs hooked in his waistcoat pockets. "Not sure what happened there, to be honest. Poor bastards just disappeared. Took by a bookworm, I'm guessing, though they'd have to have been fools to hurt the pages wandering about out there."

Mercurio nudged the Hand beside him with one bony elbow. "Bet you're glad Drusilla's got you dogging me instead of fucking about there in the dark, neh?"

The Hand made no reply.

Mercurio sighed smoke, watched Aelius fish another 'rillo out from behind his ear with ink-stained fingers and light it with a burnished flintbox. The chronicler's rheumy eyes were fixed out on the forest of shelves and tomes. The little pinpricks of arkemical glow moving out in the gloom. The silhouettes of Hands holding them aloft.

Their search was methodical, marking each examined aisle with a piece of red chalk, expanding out in an ever-broadening swathe. But rather than being arranged in a neat grid, the shelves of the dead library were a twisted labyrinth, more complex and nonsensical than the most fiendish of garden mazes. Where once they'd been tightly packed, the hundred or so Hands Drusilla had tasked to find the third chronicle were now spread thin—tiny lights twinkling in an endless, silent gloom. Only the Mother knew how much ground they'd covered in the last three weeks, but red chalk was certainly in short supply these turns.

"Bugger that for a job," Mercurio growled.

"Waste of time," Aelius sighed. "Nothing in this place gets found that doesn't *want* to be found. And why the 'byss would the Mother want . . ."

The chronicler's voice trailed off, a small frown forming between his snow-white and studiously unkempt eyebrows. Mercurio followed his eyeline out to the library, saw a point of arkemical light bouncing wildly, as if the person carrying it were running.

"What do you make of that?" he wondered.

Sure enough, in a few minutes, a Hand came into view, hood blown back from his head, cheeks flushed from his sprint, breathless. He rounded the shelves and dashed up the ramp to the mezzanine at a full run. Mercurio saw he was carrying a book in his hand. Bound in black leather. Pages edged in black, spattered in white, like stars across a truedark sky.

"'Byss and blood," Aelius breathed.

"You don't think that's . . . ?"

The Hand dashed through the Athenaeum doors without stopping, but Mercurio caught enough of a glimpse to see a shape embossed on the black leather cover.

A cat.

He exchanged glances with Aelius, ice-blue eyes locked with milky-gray ones.

The third chronicle.

"Shit."

The old man turned to the Hand beside him, smacked the tip of his cane on the floor. "Let's be off, shall we?"

The Hand made no reply.

Mercurio walked out of the library. Aelius watched him go, hovering on the threshold he could never cross. The old man's footsteps were swift, pulse pumping hard in his veins. Following the running Hand up the spiral of stairs, his own Hands trailing close behind, one, two, three, Mercurio hurried up into the singing dark. The ghostly choir sounded a little softer, though perhaps that was the blood now pounding in his ears, his heart struggling against his ribs. He was soon out of breath, cursing the countless cigarillos he'd smoked in his life and wondering if he couldn't have found a less-debilitating way to thumb his nose at society, propriety, and mortality in general.

Still, he followed, knees creaking, left arm aching (more often, lately), sweat rising on his liver-spotted skin. He lost sight of the running Hand in short order, but he knew exactly where the lad would be headed. Stained-glass light spilled down the stairwells, his breath rasping as he entered the Hall of Eulogies, touching brow, then eyes, then lips as he hobbled past the looming statue of the Mother.

Hope you know what you're playing at . . .

His young female Hand eventually took pity as Mercurio's struggles worsened, as his knees cried mercy, as his lungs burst into black moldering flame inside his withered chest. She slipped an arm about his waist, propped him up a little as he climbed, higher and higher, dry-mouthed, breath burning, heart afire. There were never this many stairs when he was younger, he was sure of it. The air was never this thick. But finally he stood, bent double and wheezing, outside the chambers of the Revered Father.

"Fuck me, I've got to quit smoking," he rasped.

He entered without knocking, found Solis seated at his desk, the breathless Hand who'd made the discovery standing before him. Spiderkiller was stood beside the Revered Father, clad all in emerald green and gleaming gold. The dour Shahiid of Truths was bent over the open tome and reading aloud.

"'It struggled to hold itself together, more and more washed away in the downpour, thinned near to worthlessness. But before it lost cohesion entirely, bleeding out into the puddle of Hush's pretty ruin, the blood managed to form itself into simple shapes. Four letters that formed a single word. A name.'"

Spiderkiller straightened, stabbed the page with one poison-stained finger.

"'NAEV.'"

Solis turned his blind eyes to the Hand before him.

"Have Adonai send word to the Lady of Blades immediately."

The Hand bowed low. "What word, Revered Father?"

Solis's smile glittered in his milk-white eyes.

"We have her."

The tea was a touch too hot.

Drusilla sat on a rocking chair in a rolling garden green, breathing its perfume. The sunsbells were in bloom, the lavender and candlewick wearing their dresses, too. The light of two suns was bright on the palazzo's walls, warm on her bones, banishing the Quiet Mountain's lingering chill. She could hear little Cyprian and Magnus playing nearby, their laughter like sweetest music to her ears.

But her tea was a touch too hot.

She snapped her fingers, and a tall Liisian slave in a pristine white toga stepped forward, tipping a splash of goat's milk into her cup. The old woman sipped—much better—and dismissed the girl back to the shadows with a wordless glance. She leaned back in her chair, closed her pale blue eyes, and breathed a soft, contented sigh.

She heard a shout. A distressed cry following.

"Cyprian, be nice to your brother!" she called. "Or no treats after supper."

". . . Yes, Grandmother," came the chastened reply.

"Mother?"

Drusilla opened her eyes, saw Julia standing before her, draped in red silk. A Dweymeri jeweler stood behind her daughter, carrying a velvet board studded with expensive wares. Julia held an ornate chain dripping with rubies up to her throat, then swapped it for a more austere gold circlet, studded with a single, larger stone.

"First?" Julia asked. "Or second?"

"The occasion?"

"The Imperator's Ball, of course," Julia replied.

"My dear, truedark isn't for weeks . . ."

"One can't be too prepared," her daughter replied, her tone prim. "If Valerius is to pursue his seat in the Liisian quarter, we must seek to impress."

"I hardly think your husband's senatorial ambitions will be thwarted by your choice of jewelry, my dear. The imperator tells me the seat is assured."

Julia sighed, examined each necklet in turn. "Perhaps I'll just get both."

"Have you heard news from your brother? Is he coming to dinner?"

"Aye, he'll be here. He's bringing that frightful Cicerii woman." Julia's lips turned down in distaste. "I'm afraid he'll announce their engagement soon."

"Good," Drusilla nodded. "He should be thinking toward his future at his age. Familia is the most important thing in the world, my dear. If your father and I taught you one thing, it's that."

Julia looked to the palatial gardens around them. Sighed soft.

"I miss him."

"I miss him, too. But life is for living, my love."

Julia smiled, leaned down, and kissed Drusilla's brow, then wandered back into the palazzo. Godsgrave's cathedrals began to ring in fivebells, their dulcet tones echoing through the marrowborn quarter. The old woman looked up to the third Rib towering overhead, wondering if she should purchase her son an apartment in there for a wedding gift, just as the silver phial about her neck began to tremble.

She put her hand to it, hoping she was mistaken, praying for just a few more hours' peace . . . but no, there it went again, shivering under her palm. The old woman sighed, placed her cup and saucer aside. Lifting the phial from around her neck, she broke the black wax seal, tipped the contents onto the small table beside her rocking chair. The blood welled, thick and red on the polished teak.

And of its own accord, it began to form itself into shapes.

Letters.

Drusilla pieced the letters into words. Then the words into a missive. Her old, worn pulse ran just the slightest bit quicker.

Cyprian ran up to her, breathless, his eyes alight with his smile.

"Come play with us, Grandmother."

"Another turn, my dove," she sighed.

The Lady of Blades stood slowly, leaned down to kiss his brow.

"Grandmother has work to do."

CHAPTER 27

FEED

It turned out being queen of pirates wasn't quite the job Mia imagined.

Perhaps she'd read too many tawdry ha'-beggar tales as a child in her tiny room above Mercurio's Curios, but in the thirty or forty seconds Mia had considered the role before she stabbed Einar Valdyr to death, she'd imagined being a pirate queen might involve a fair bit of . . . well, piracy. Buckling of swashes and wenches most buxom and swinging from chandeliers with a knife between her teeth. But by the second turn of her reign, Queen Mia Corvere had come to a disappointing realization.

"I'm bored shitless," she sighed.

"I did warn you," Ulfr Sigursson said. "Valdyr was half-mad with it."

"Valdyr wore a greatcoat made of human faces, Ulfr," Mia said, putting her boots up on her desk. "I don't think *half*-mad quite covers it."

"Speaking of," her first mate said, eyeing her up and down, "do you want me to find you something that fits a touch better?"

Mia glanced at her reflection in the window. She'd washed Valdyr's blood from her skin and hair, but she still wore the former monarch's greatcoat, which hung on her slender frame like a shroud. Black leathers hugged her legs and hips, wolfskin boots on her feet, her gravebone longblade sitting within easy reach. She'd bathed and combed her long black hair, trimmed her fringe into a line sharp as razors. The twin circles of her slave brand on her right cheek and the vicious scar curling across her left lent her pale features a dark cruelty. Her stare was black as coal, hard as iron. She didn't look a queen many would love.

But she did look a queen most would fear.

"No, I'm fine wearing this," she told Ulfr. "It makes people nervous."

"Would you like an undershirt, at least?" the man asked. "When you move about, you tend to show off your—"

"No," Mia said, lighting a cigarillo. "My tits make people nervous, too."

"As it please you." Her first mate sniffed. "I confess I never saw much appeal in them myself."

They were sat in the upper level of a tall limestone tower within the Scoundrel's Hall. Leadlight windows looked out across the Sea of Sorrows, and a broad, char-stained fireplace was stocked with logs of cherry-oak, burning merrily and filling the room with a perfumed warmth. The floors were covered in wolf furs, the walls with charts of the surrounding seas, the long oaken desk with parchment and scrolls and missives. Since she was abdicating her role in a handful of turns, Mia hadn't bothered acquainting herself with any of it, but from the look of things, being the Scoundrel King had involved rather more paperwork than she'd expected.

She glanced at her first mate in his black leathers and wolfskin pelt. His expression was somewhere between wary and cavalier.

"And how are my loyal subjects?" Mia asked, breathing gray.

"Well, *Obelisk* and the *Cinnamon Girl* are fermenting a rebellion against you," Ulfr sighed. "Though Marcella and Quintus hate each other like poison, so I can't imagine that coalition will last long. *Goliath, Imperium,* and

Gravedigger all spoke out against you in the Hall of Scoundrels earlier in the turn, but they're little fish. The bigger crews are waiting to see what you do next. Valdyr scared the shit right out of them. So being the bitch who hacked his head off lends you a certain . . . gravitas."

"And the wulfguard?" Mia asked, dragging on her smoke. "How fare my crew?"

"They follow my lead for now. And I follow you. Although I'm sure you know that as well as I." Sigursson stroked his blond, plaited beard. "Or did you think I'd not notice?"

Mia raised an eyebrow. "Notice?"

"My shadow, Majesty," the man said, glancing down at his boots. "It seems a touch blacker of late. I'd heard all manner of myths about darkin in my travels. Glad to see that not all of them turned out to be horseshit."

Mia leaned back in her chair and smiled.

"He's a clever one, Eclipse."

". . . YES . . . ," came the reply from the man's shadow. ". . . I LIKE THAT ABOUT HIM . . ."

"I like it, too." She looked the handsome Vaanian over. "I *like* you, Ulfr."

"Would that I could say the same, Majesty," he said with a handsome scowl.

"Well, you need only tolerate me a few more turns, and then you can be rid of me once and for all." Mia smiled wider, breathed smoke into the air between them. "But should you consider getting rid of me earlier than that, I can think of a few other myths about darkin to confirm for you."

By way of demonstration, she

Stepped

over to

the window

and watched the waves roll into the shore, crashing upon the rocks as the gulls circled in pale gray skies above. Putting her cigarillo to her lips, she breathed deep, let the shadows around the room have their head, writhing and reaching out toward her, gentle as old lovers.

"You can go," she told her first mate, not looking at him. "I'll let Eclipse know if I need you. Inform the captains of the *Obelisk* and *Cinnamon Girl* you plan to murder me at sea if you think it will quiet them. If it doesn't, I can fashion another way to silence their tongues. It's rather more permanent, though."

Sigursson turned to face her, green eyes sparkling. "Aye, aye, Majesty."

"Blue above and below, Ulfr."

The brigand gave a small, curt bow and stalked from the room. Eclipse followed without a sound. Mia remained by the window, forehead pressed against the glass and staring out at the sea. Thinking about Ashlinn's lips. Jonnen's eyes. Mercurio's scowl. Feeling the cat-shaped hole like a bleeding wound in her chest.

I wonder where he is?

If he's all right?

. . . Goddess, I miss him.

"I'm cold," she sighed.

"You could always put a shirt on," Tric said.

She turned to smile at the pale Dweymeri boy standing quiet by the fire.

"It'd ruin my Murderous Bitch aesthetic." She winced and adjusted herself beneath the coat. "But aye, perhaps. This old leather is like sandpaper on my donas."

A smile twisted the boy's lips, and he glanced at the door Sigursson had left by. "Do you trust him?"

"Not as far as I could carry him. But Eclipse is keeping watch on him. And he seems to be keeping a leash on the wulfguard. He only needs to hold things together for a handful of turns, and then he gets a free ship and a free throne. I think we can count on his greed to see us through. And if not that, his fear."

"You *are* a little frightening sometimes, Pale Daughter," Tric said, sharing their old joke. "And other times, you're just plain terrifying."

The small smile fell from his face.

"I'm sorry," he said. "I know you don't like it when I call you that."

She turned from the window to look at him. Leaning back on the sill, hands clasped behind her back.

"I *do* like it," she admitted softly. "That's why it hurts."

He stood there silently. Just watching her. That new, dark beauty, edged by the warm glow of the fire. He was still pale, his skin smooth and hard, but with truedark only weeks away, he no longer looked like a statue carved of alabaster. She fancied she could see a pulse at his neck now, beneath the curve of his jaw, the strong lines of his throat, the hint of muscle through the open neck of his shirt . . .

Mia looked away. Sucked her lip.

"I've been thinking."

"O, dear."

She smiled with him, dragged a lock of hair behind her ear. "When we reach the Mountain, getting Mercurio back is obviously our first priority. But the Blades who hit us at the tower aren't the last assassins the Red Church has to throw. They're just going to keep coming until we cut the head off the snake."

Tric turned from the fire to face her. "DRUSILLA."

"Aye," Mia nodded. "And the Ministry, too."

"STRIKE THE SHEPHERD AND THE SHEEP WILL SCATTER."

"No," she said. "Strike the shepherd and the sheep will *follow*."

Tric's eyes narrowed. "MEANING?"

"Meaning I've been thinking on it since I dragged this hideous fucking coat onto my shoulders. Folk follow leaders with the resolve to lead. It goes back to something my father said. 'To claim true power, all you need is the will to do what others won't.'" Mia dragged deep on her cigarillo, breathed gray into the air like flame. "So I'm not just going to kill the Lady of Blades. I'm going to *become* the Lady of Blades."

"YOU HAVE A GREATER DESTINY THAN THAT, MIA."

"So you keep saying. But I'll hardly fulfill it if some prick slits my throat while I'm sleeping. If I kill Drusilla and the Ministry, there's no Blade alive who'd challenge me for the role. And the Church won't be hunting me if I get to dictate who they hunt. It's like Ashlinn said. 'Nothing's kept by those who won't fight for it.' So I'm going to fight."

"ASHLINN."

The name was like a knife slicing the air. Left quivering point-first in the floorboards between them.

"You're going to have to get used to her being around, Tric."

"I CAN'T HELP BUT NOTICE YOU SENT HER AWAY. AND I'M STILL HERE."

"Don't read further into that than's warranted. She and I are together now."

He held out his arms to the room about them. "BUT YOU'RE NOT, ARE YOU?"

"You know what I mean."

"No," he said. "I DON'T. YOU NEVER ANSWERED ME WHEN I ASKED IF YOU LOVE HER."

"Because it's not your business."

She saw a flash of anger then, burning and terrible in those bottomless eyes of his. The muscles in his jaw tensed, those black hands that had once roamed her body curled tight into fists. She could sense the awful speed and strength the Mother had gifted him, etched in every hard line and beautiful curve of his body. But slowly, as he looked at her, the rage melted, the tension in his frame faded. He swallowed hard and turned to the fire. Both hands on the mantle, saltlocks draped about his face as he hung his head and stared at the flames.

". . . How can you *say* that?"

She watched him watching the fire, listening to the crackling wood, the sea singing outside, the thump of her own heart, painful and aching against her ribs.

"Do you ever think about us, Mia?" he asked.

"Of course I do."

"I mean *us*. Those times . . . Us together."

Tension crackling between them, curling the edge of her lips. She could feel it thrumming in her fingertips. Pulsing beneath her skin. Desire. Her for him. Him for her. Nothing and no one between.

"Yes," she admitted, her pulse running quicker.

"Ever wonder what might have been?"

"Weren't you the one who told me I should let the past die?"

"Weren't you the one who said sometimes it doesn't?"

"Aye," she agreed. "Aye, sometimes you have to kill it."

"Like she killed me."

Mia drew a deep breath. Pushed herself off the windowsill and walked slowly across the wolf furs scattered about the floor. She joined him near the hearth, hands clasped behind her back, watching the flames with wary eyes as they stretched toward her like grasping claws.

"She killed me, Mia," Tric said. "She took away everything I was."

"I know. And I'm sorry."

"How could you be with her after that?"

Mia looked into the flames. Her hackles were rising, her temper flaring—she didn't enjoy being questioned about who she bedded or why. Those were her choices. More than any other she'd made, they belonged to *her*. But Tric had once shared her bed, too—the first to ever do so who'd actually meant something, truth told. And given the circumstances, she could see how asking for an explanation wasn't the most outrageous request he could've made. At least he'd waited 'til they were alone.

"Ash reminds me of me," Mia declared. "She wants something, she takes it. She doesn't answer to anyone. She's fierce and she's unafraid and she's fucking beautiful. And in a world like this, that's all too rare." Mia ran a hand through her hair and sighed. "I realize the egotism at play in that. Wanting to bed yourself. But it's more than that, too. Ash stands up to me. She pushes me. She takes the world by the throat and she squeezes. But when we're alone, she reminds me of everything that's good, too. She's gentle and she's sweet and everything I'm not."

Mia put her cigarillo to her lips and sighed.

"When we first . . . with each other, I mean . . . Ash and I were both running along razor blades. Any turn could've been our last. And I thought about my life and where it'd been steered and understood I'd never really had a say in any of it. And I wanted something that could just be mine. My choice." Mia shrugged. "So I chose her."

"But you don't regret it? Even now?"

"No." Mia shook her head. "I think I *need* someone like her. Being with her . . . it shows me there's more to all this than just the blood. Because I *want* there to be. But it's so hard to remember that sometimes." Mia drew a deep breath off her smoke, savored the warm burn in her chest. "It's as if there's two halves of me, aye? Two pieces of the whole. One is just . . . darkness. Rage. She hates the world and everything in it. All she wants is to tear it down and laugh as it burns. And then there's the me who thinks there might actually be something worth fighting for in all this. And maybe something to live for after."

Mia looked into the flames—the fire ahead and behind.

"Two halves at war within me. And the one that will win is the one that I feed."

Mia stared at the fire a long time. Watching the tongues of flame consume everything before them, smoke and ashes the remainder. Wondering if that's what she was. If that was all that would be left when this was done.

She glanced toward Tric, found him gazing back at her.

"Why are you just looking at me like that?" she demanded. "Say something."

"What should I say? That I understand? That I concede?"

The boy shook his head, looking deep into her eyes.

"You say nothing's kept by those who won't fight for it? I plunged my hands into the dark between the stars for you, Mia. I turned my back on light and warmth and clawed my way through the Abyss for you. I didn't do that so I could step aside graciously and watch the girl who killed me lay claim to the girl I love."

"Well, you don't have much choice, do you?"

"Do I not?"

He turned toward her, and she could feel the want in him. Carved in the line of his lips. Smoldering in his stare. Slow as ages, long as years, he lifted his hand to her face. Mia tensed but didn't flinch, her jaw tightening as his thumb trailed down the scar on her cheek. The heat from the hearth had touched him, enriching the new flush of life in his skin, and his caress was warm as the firelight. She felt butterflies rolling in her belly, her lips parting, her breath coming a little faster.

"Don't . . . ," she warned.

"Why not?" he whispered.

"Because I said so."

"And yet you don't pull away?"

"Never flinch, Tric."

"Tell me you didn't love me, Mia."

His hand drifted down her cheek, closer to her lips, and though she knew she should stop him, every inch of skin he touched seemed to be afire.

"Tell me you don't love me, still."

He stepped closer, brought his other hand up to her face. This near to him, she could feel the fire inside him, that dark unflame burning at his heart. But strange as it seemed, wrong as it might be, she found herself *drawn* to it. Like a magnet. Like she was falling into it. The power of the goddess—the Dark Mother who'd given birth to the splinter of the god inside her, wide as the skies and deep as the oceans and black, black as the heart now thundering inside her chest. She'd thought his eyes were just empty darkness, but this close, this dangerously, wonderfully close, she could see they were filled with tiny sparks of light, like stars strewn across the curtains of night.

Beautiful.

"I denied death for you," he breathed, leaning closer still. "And I'd die for you again. Kill for you. I'd tear the stars down from the heavens to fashion you a crown. You are my heart. My queen. I'd do anything and everything you ask me, Mia."

He took hold of the collar of her greatcoat, began pushing it, inch by inch, back off her bare shoulders.

"Ask me to stop," he said.

She shouldn't, Goddess, she *couldn't* let this happen. Thoughts of Ashlinn burned in the back of her mind, but in her chest, between her thighs, a darker fire was smoldering now. She didn't know whether it was the night's kinship in them, the unearthly beauty he now possessed, the simple ache for the lover she'd thought gone forever, now standing right in front of her as if carved by the hands of the Night herself. But looking into his eyes, down to the smooth curve of his parted lips, she realized she wanted him.

O, Goddess help her, but she did . . .

The coat slipped to the floor.

"Ask me to stop."

But she didn't. She didn't breathe a word. And then he was kissing her, wrapping her in his embrace and crushing her to him, and it was all Mia could do to remember to breathe at all. She found her hands moving of their own accord, running over the smooth hardness of his arms, across his shoulders as he scooped her up off the ground. She wrapped her legs around his waist, ankles locked at the small of his back, their kiss growing deep enough to drown in. Shivers ran all the way down her spine as she felt his tongue brush against hers, the warmth of the fire and the dark flame inside him sending goosebumps thrilling over her whole body. His lips were as soft as they'd ever been, his body just as warm. His mouth tasted of smoke, his scent, the perfume of burning autumn leaves. She sighed as his lips broke away from hers, left a burning trail of kisses across her cheek, down her throat.

I can't do this . . .

His lips roamed lower, across her collarbone, like fire and ice all at once. Her skin felt alight with it, that dark flame in her chest and between her legs only growing hotter as his mouth reached her breasts, as he took one stone-hard nipple into his mouth, teasing with his tongue. Mia sighed as her head drifted back, entwining her fingers in the soft shadows of his hair and dragging him in, urging him on as she felt the soft press of his teeth, yes, yes, head spinning, chest heaving, belly filled with butterflies all at the wing.

"O, Goddess . . ."

I can't let this happen . . .

He sank down onto the furs, carrying her effortlessly. Her legs were still wrapped around him, the firelight crackling brighter beside them. She found herself atop him, half-naked, her tongue in his mouth, his hands on her waist. Goddess, she wanted to suck him. Fuck him. Feeling his pulse beneath her hands, grinding into the impossible hardness she felt at his crotch, her fingertips tracing the furrows and valleys of muscle at his chest, down his stomach. She groaned just like he did, rolling her hips, aching with the feel of him against her and the almost nothing between them. Lust inside her. Desire for the darkness inside him. A truedark hunger, born in the lightless black, so vast and empty she wondered if he could ever truly fill her. But Goddess . . .

O, sweet, merciful Goddess, she wanted him to fucking try.

She was losing herself in it. The feel of him, the taste, the familiar shapes, carved anew by the Mother of Night. Falling down into the need of him, aching from the touch of him, wanting to forget and remember and for a tiny moment, simply enjoy being lost inside it, with him inside her.

Lost.

"'Tis better to have loved and lost . . ."

"Whoever said that never loved someone the way I love you."

She heard the words in her head.

Remembered the look in the girl's eyes.

Her girl's.

Two halves warring within me.

His hands on her body, his lips on her skin.

And the one that will win is the one that I feed.

"No," she whispered.

He sat up, fingertips roaming her back, mouth roaming her breasts, his ink-black hands taking hold of her hips and helping her sway . . .

"Tric, stop," she whispered. "We have to stop."

He looked up into her eyes, his own shining with lust. Pulling apart from him felt like tearing herself in two. The want was so real, it was a physical pain. Burning like fire in her veins. The room growing hot, and hotter still.

"Mia—"

Without warning, Mia saw a flash of searing light in the hearth beside them. Felt a vicious, scorching heat. She gasped as a tongue of flame flashed out from the fireplace, lashed against her leathers, the fur they lay on. She rolled away with a black curse, the fire taking root on the fur and spreading in a blinking.

The blaze was hungry, furious, burning with an intensity fiercer than it had any right to. Streaking along the wolfskin, right toward Mia. Tric scrambled to his feet and flipped the furs over, smothering the blaze, stamping on it like serpents. Mia ran to her desk with a cry, grabbed a carafe of water. Tric stomped and kicked, finally booted the fur back into the hearth, where it curled up and blackened. With another curse, Mia dashed the water across the smoldering floorboards. And though it seethed and spat and struggled, the last of the fire drowned beneath the flood.

Black smoke and sudden silence filled the room. Mia's heart was thumping in her chest as she checked her bare skin and hair for burns. Fear rushing in to replace the lust she'd burned so brightly with only seconds before . . .

"Are you all right?" Tric asked, reaching for her, eyes full of concern.

"I'm fine," she said, backing away. "Just singed."

"Mia, I . . . "

She felt suddenly cold. Aware that she was half-naked. A clarity, cool and crystalline, breaking through the rush of desire. Stooping, she grabbed her tumbled greatcoat and threw it around her shoulders. Pulled it tight against the chill. Her pulse was thunder. Her legs were shaking.

"I think you'd best go," she said.

"Mia, tell me you don't love me," he said, stepping toward her.

"Tric, don't . . ."

"Tell me you don't want me."

"I can't!" she snarled, stepping farther back. "Because I *do*! But there's a few moments of right in that, followed by a whole lifetime of wrong." Mia shook her head, amazed to feel tears burning in her eyes. "I'm *sorry*. I'm sorry things turned out the way they did. I'm sorry we don't all get what we want. Because I want you, Tric, Goddess help me, I do. But truth is, as much as I want to have you now, I want to keep her more."

He took another step toward her, and she, another step away. He reached out to her and she looked into his eyes and saw the agony there. Saw how unfair and fucking cruel this whole tale was. She wanted to scream it. Curse the gods. Curse the life and the fate that had brought her to this moment, this awful choice. Because no matter what she did or how she chose, someone she loved was going to get hurt.

I am fucking poison, do you see that?

I am cancer . . .

Someone always gets hurt.

"I'm sorry," she said again. "But we can't do this. *I* can't do this. She means too much to me."

". . . YOU DO LOVE HER, THEN," he whispered.

"I think . . ."

Mia met his eyes, tears welling in her own.

"I think I do."

His hand fell to his side. His gaze to the floor. His shoulders slumped and his legs shook and she could almost see the heart in his chest shattering. Cleaved right in two. And her accursed hand on the blade. He closed his eyes tight, jaw clenched, shaking his head. But a single traitorous tear, black as night, still welled in his lashes. Slipping down his cheek, it trailed along the line of his dimple to his chin. Mia found herself crying, too, stepping forward with a soft murmur of pity. Wanting to make it better, to take his hurt away, to somehow make it all right.

"Don't cry," she said, fingertips brushing his cheek. "Please don't cry."

He pulled back from her touch like it burned him. Turned and walked away without a word. Not storming or stomping, not slamming the door behind him. It somehow would've been better if he were furious with her. But instead, he left calmly, quiet as the dark. The question of where they stood now and what might come between them, unanswered.

Mia was sure she could hear the flames in the hearth laughing at her.

She looked down at the fingers that had brushed his tear away.

Black like his eyes.

Like the night.

Like the heart in her fucking chest.

She slumped down before the hateful fire. Watching the tongues of flame consume everything before them, smoke and ashes the remainder.

Wondering if that's what she was.

If that was all that would be left when this was done.

CHAPTER 28

HATRED

"I don't know what the 'byss you're worried about."

Ulfr Sigursson lowered his spyglass and leaned forward over the railing, peering into the waters below. The wind at their back was brisk, the seas crested with whitecaps, pushing them onward. *Black Banshee* cut through the waters like an arrow from a master's bow, straight and smooth toward a beautiful horizon.

"Let's hope you don't find out," Mia replied.

They were two turns into the Sea of Sorrows, and the Ladies of Storms and Oceans hadn't raised their heads since they set off from Amai. *Black Banshee* had put out into the blue with an appropriate level of fanfare—many of Mia's "subjects" had gathered to see her off on her maiden voyage, and most of the city's residents had turned out to catch a glimpse of the girl who'd slain Einar Valdyr and claimed his throne.

All manner of colorful rumor had taken root in the six turns she'd locked herself away in the Hall of Scoundrels, and prowling about Amai's taverna at night, Eclipse had heard a dozen different tales about how Mia had killed the pirate king. She'd used dark magiks, they said. She'd challenged him to single combat and torn his heart from his ribs with her bare hands. Ripped out his throat with her teeth during a grand feast and eaten his liver raw.* In Mia's favorite version of the tale, she'd seduced Valdyr and cut off his manhood—which she now apparently wore around her neck for good luck.

Mia had avoided all the fanfare, however, slipping aboard the *Banshee* be-

---

*Never do this. No matter how impressive it might sound to your future col-

neath her cloak of shadows. Eyeing off the captains and crew of other ships who'd turned out to her farewell, she'd counted at least twenty who'd have cheerfully clipped their own grandmothers' throats to take a poke at her. It seemed a far more sensible option to simply appear on the deck to the whispered awe of the crowd, tricorn pulled low over her eyes, standing at the prow and looking grim as they set out to sea.

Nevernight was falling on their second turn of sailing, the two remaining suns slipping farther toward their truedark rest. Saan was close to completing its descent entirely, its red glow setting the horizon ablaze. Saii still burned above them—scarlet and azure light collided in the heavens, burning through to pale violet, breathtaking and beautiful. Mia could feel truedark clawing closer. Black light burning in her chest and in the boy standing beside her.

Tric stood his vigil, always within arm's reach. Standing guard outside her cabin door while she slept. Watching her back in the moments it was turned. Even after their quarrel, he was never more than a word away. But the truth was, they'd shared precious few words since they'd almost . . .

. . . almost.

Mia didn't know how to fix it. Didn't know what to say to make it right. In her darker moments, it infuriated her to no end that she even *had* to. She had her own problems to deal with, high enough to touch the fucking sky. But in her softer breaths, she could feel the sorrow in him, burning like that dark flame within, and she couldn't help but feel it, too. She knew how unfair this all was. How deeply he felt for her.

What she didn't know was what he'd do, now he knew she'd never be his.

Love often rusted into hate when watered with scorn.

Can I truly trust him anymore?

Can I trust him near Ashlinn?

"There's no sign of storm clouds," Sigursson reported, once more scanning the horizon. "Smooth sailing from here to Ashkah, I'd stake my ship on it."

"It's not *your* ship yet, Ulfr," Mia said. "And I'm assuring you, she's in for strife. Make sure Iacopo and Reddog have their eyes peeled when they're up top. Tell Justus to keep those galley fires unlit. Cold meals only until we make shore. The Ladies are coming for us, make no mistake. And they're bringing the Abyss with them."

---

leagues. Not only is raw meat more difficult to digest and less nutrient-rich, it's also rife with ill humors.

When feasting on the flesh of your enemies, gentlefriends, always take the time to cook it first.

The Vaanian looked his captain up and down, a soft scowl on his handsome brow. "If I might ask, my queen, what exactly did you do to irk them so?"

"That's not your concern," Tric growled. "Getting us to Last Hope is."

"Don't be telling me my concerns, boy," Sigursson said.

"Don't be calling me boy, mortal," Tric replied.

Sigursson looked Tric in his eyes. His mouth pressed thin. His shoulders square. The Vaanian was the first mate of one of the most vicious bands to sail the Four Seas—a pack of murderers and brutes who spread terror wherever they went. Now she knew them a little better, Mia could sense what a pack of ruthless bastards Valdyr had crewed his ship with. The kindest among them had probably still raped his way across all Four Seas. The worst of them likely tortured and killed children for sport.

But though the *Banshee* and her crew seemed birthed from the Abyss itself, Tric had actually *been* there. The Dweymeri boy was taller than the Vaanian man, pale and hard, one hand forever at the hilt of his gravebone blade. Eyes reflecting the Night he'd seen firsthand. As they squared up, Tric didn't blink. Didn't flinch.

If Sigursson had hoped to intimidate him, he ended up sorely disappointed.

Turning to Mia, the Vaanian finally bowed low. "My queen."

And turning on his heel, he set about his work.

Mia watched the man retreat, eyes narrowed. She'd been keeping close tabs on him over the last two turns, and she knew Sigursson had no fondness for her. Knew the razor she danced along keeping him at heel. And still, she couldn't help but admire him.

Bastards and brutes they might be, but *Banshee*'s crew knew their ship, and more importantly, they knew Mia would soon be off it. They were afraid of her, aye—she kept Eclipse in plain view at her side along with Tric to foster that fear. But they actually *liked* Sigursson. He was intense. Intelligent. Not a braggart or a buffoon. A lesser man might've lost himself in foolish pride when his captain was killed. But Ulfr knew there was little to gain by opposing Mia, and everything to lose. And so he'd swallowed that pride, biding his time and dreaming of the throne awaiting him when all this was done.

"He'll make a fine king when he returns to Amai," Mia mused.

"*If* he returns to Amai," Tric replied.

Mia turned to the boy, a soft chill in her belly.

"You know what's coming, don't you?"

Tric nodded, his eyes on the burning horizon. "These O, so pleasant

WINDS SERVE ONLY TO DRIVE US DEEPER INTO THE OCEAN. FARTHER AWAY FROM THE SAFETY OF LAND. THE LADIES ARE GATHERING THEIR STRENGTH. I CAN FEEL IT."

Mia felt her shadow shiver, the shape of a wolf stretched out dark on the timbers before her. "*. . . I FEEL IT, TOO, MIA. THEY ARE COMING FOR US . . .*"

Mia looked toward the edge of the world, wind blowing her hair across her eyes.

"DO YOU BELIEVE YET?" Tric asked. "WHAT YOU ARE? WHAT YOU MUST BECOME?"

Mia licked her lips. Tasted salt.

Truth was, she could feel it, too. Sure as she could feel the dark inside her, swelling as those suns sank ever lower. Sure as she could see the new blush in Tric's skin, feel the new strength inside herself. At the time, the tale he'd told beneath Godsgrave had seemed madness. Fantasy. Talk of slaughtered gods and fractured souls. But the malice she could sense in the sky about her, the waters below, the memory of those flames reaching out across the furs toward her, the dreams that plagued her sleep . . . all of it was becoming harder and harder to deny.

There *was* something grand at work here. She knew it now. Something bigger than any of them. Fire, Storm, Sea. Light and Dark. All of it. Mia could sense it, like a weight growing on her back. Like a shadow rising to meet her.

"THE ONLY WEAPON IN THIS WAR IS FAITH."

She'd set aside her faith years ago. Stopped praying to Aa the turn she realized that all the devotion in the world wouldn't bring her familia back. Even in service of the Dark Mother, even in the belly of the Quiet Mountain, she'd not truly held any belief for the divinities—not for divinities who might actually *care,* at least. Who knew who she was, who thought she mattered, who were more than empty words and hollow names.

And now? Moons and crowns and mothers and fathers and all of it?

Do I truly believe?

Mia shook her head, pushing thoughts of gods and goddesses away. Whatever Tric and Eclipse might feel, whatever awareness might be budding in her own chest, truth was she had more earthly concerns for now.

Mercurio needed her.

He was in danger because of her. He'd been a father when the world took her own away. When she'd prayed for Aa to help her, it had been Mercurio who saved her. But more than the debt she owed him, the simple fact was that she loved the grumpy old bastard. She missed the smell of his cigarillos. His gallows humor and foul mouth. Those pale blue eyes that seemed born to scowl, seeing right through her bullshit and into her heart.

Scaeva had claimed to have made her all she was. But in truth, if Mia owed anyone for the person she'd become, the things about herself she actually *liked,* it was Mercurio. And so she stared at the ocean between them. The hundreds of miles of blue above and below, soon to turn black with fury. At this point, it didn't matter what she believed in. Gods and goddesses. Fathers and daughters. What matter, this talk of divinities and destinies? What she might be or what she could become?

All that mattered was what she'd do.

What she'd always done.

Fight. With everything she had.

And so she leaned over the railing. Spat into the sea.

"Come for me, then, bitches."

The storm met them four turns out.

Mia had been in her cabin when she first heard the cries from the crow's nest, tossing in a fitful sleep and trying to turn her dreams as Bladesinger had said. She had the same two every nevernight—Aa and Niah wearing the faces of her parents, surrounded by their Four Daughters, arguing with each other beneath that endless sky. That scene would fade, and she'd wake to find Scaeva standing over her, knife in hand.

"Forgive me, child."

And then she'd *actually* wake. Sweating and breathless. But this nevernight, before she'd felt his knife descend, a call had cut through her dreams, dragging her upward and into her cabin's stubborn gloom. She'd rubbed the sleep from her eyes and frowned, thinking perhaps she'd imagined it. Until she heard the call again, the sound of bells—an alarm ringing across the *Banshee*'s deck.

She'd found Tric standing vigil outside her cabin as always. Together, they headed topside and found Sigursson on the aft. Black clouds had gathered at the edges of the ocean and were riding toward them like frothing horses, dragging a curtain across the sunslit skies behind. Sigursson had his spyglass up, lips parted as he watched the dark close in, faster than any storm had a right to. As he turned to Mia, she thought she caught a glimpse of worry in the piercing green of his eyes.

"Storm coming?" she asked.

"Aye," he nodded.

"Bad?"

He looked back to the black horizon. Up to the sky above.

". . . Aye."

Her first mate had marched across the deck, barking orders with a voice like iron. Mia had watched her crew set to it, moving like mekwerk, only one or two baleful glances shot her way. The wind was in their faces now, pushing them away from Ashkah, the *Banshee* tacking back and forth across the gale and crawling toward their destination. She could hear curses and songs, the swell and crash of the rising seas against their hull, the wind wailing as the sky grew steadily darker. Lightning licked the distant horizon, blinding shears of pristine white against the veil of deepening black, the waters below them slowly deepening from azure to leaden gray as whitecap fangs gnawed at *Banshee*'s hull.

And with a clap of thunder, hard enough to shake Mia's bones, the rain began.

It was bitter cold. Sharp as daggers on her skin. She pulled Valdyr's greatcoat tighter about her shoulders, the shirt beneath soaking through. The wind slapped at her tricorn, whipped her hair about her face. Her dark eyes were fixed on the eastern horizon, willing her ship onward. Eclipse was in her shadow, eating her rising fear at the power gathering about them. A ragged cry went up from the crow's nest above.

"'Byss and blood, look at that!"

Mia peered up to the lookout—saw he was pointing to the water beneath them. At first, she saw nothing save the gnashing swell, the ocean's jaws. But then, under that rolling steel-gray, she caught sight of them. Shadows. Long and serpentine. Cutting swift just below the waterline, swarming about the *Banshee*'s belly. Black eyes and razor teeth and skin the color of old bones.

"Whitedrakes," Tric said.

"Black Mother," Mia whispered.

Dozens of them. Maybe hundreds. The biggest were thirty, perhaps forty feet in length. Each one a machine of muscle and sinew with a mouthful of swords. None were big enough to hurt the *Banshee,* of course, but Mia knew whitedrakes were rogue hunters who never moved in packs. And the sight of dozens of the bastards teeming in the water all about them was enough to send a slight vibration through every man on the deck. Mia could feel it, sure as she could feel the rain now falling on her skin, the wind in her dripping hair. A sliver of fear, piercing their sailor's hearts. If the speed of the storm wasn't enough, this was a sure sign that all about this journey wasn't as it seemed. That they were all now part of something decidedly . . . unnatural.

Mia peered down into the swell. Across the water to the storm clouds rushing at them headlong. Every foe she'd faced on this road, every enemy, she'd met with a blade in her hand or a phial of poison in her palm. She'd killed men. Women. Senators and cardinals and gladiatii and Blades. Folk as different as truedark was from truelight. But each of them, *all* of them, had one trait in common.

They were mortal. Flesh and blood and bone.

How in the Goddess's name am I supposed to fight this?

"I SHOULD GO," Tric said.

"Go?" Mia felt a stab of fear in her chest, despite Eclipse. "Where?"

The boy looked at her sidelong. Even with the pain between them, the blood and years, she could see a wry amusement gleaming in those midnight eyes.

"FORWARD." He motioned to the bow. "TO PRAY."

"O," she smiled. "Aye. I understand. Will that help?"

"WE DWEYMERI HAVE A SAYING. PRAY TO THE GODDESS, BUT ROW FOR SHORE."

"Meaning we can't rely on her at all."

"MEANING WE ARE STILL A LONG WAY FROM TRUEDARK. AND THE MOTHER'S POWER HERE IS SLIGHT. BUT THEY *ARE* HER DAUGHTERS." Tric shrugged as a peal of thunder cracked the skies. "PRAYING CAN'T HURT."

"All right," she nodded. "Just be careful not to fall over the side, aye?"

He smiled, sweet and sad.

"I'LL NOT LEAVE YOU," he said. "NO MATTER WHAT. NEVER FORGET I LOVE YOU, MIA. AND GODDESS WILLING, I'LL LOVE YOU FOREVER."

He turned and trudged down the stairs, his shirt plastered to his skin, the lines of muscle etched in black velvet and leather. Mia's chest hurt as she watched him make his way down the bow and plant himself like some ancient tree, black hands raised to the sky, head thrown back. Thunder rolled and lightning flashed, the rain coming down in freezing sprays, like arrows of ice shot at *Banshee*'s black heart. Her sails were stretched and straining, her hull groaning, her shrouds and lines humming in the growing gale. The waves were building in height—not the terrifying towers of water Mia had seen aboard the *Maid,* but she knew they were on the way. There was no sign of land on the eastern horizon. They were still turns away from Ashkah. Turns of a war she didn't know how to fight. A war she couldn't wield a blade in.

Helpless.

Useless.

One of the wulfguard looked at Mia and made the warding sign against evil.

"Maybe I shouldn't have called them bitches, Eclipse," she whispered.

". . . *NO FEAR* . . . ," came the reply from her shadow. ". . . *I AM WITH YOU* . . ."

Mia dragged her sodden hair from her face, shook her head. "I wish . . ."

". . . *I KNOW* . . . ," the shadowwolf sighed. ". . . *STRANGE AS IT SOUNDS, I MISS HIM, TOO* . . ."

"Do you think he's all right? Wherever he is?"

The daemon turned her not-eyes to the horizon.

". . . *I THINK YOU SHOULD SAVE YOUR WORRY FOR US, MIA* . . ."

Mia looked to the black gathering above. Listening to her ship creak and groan and sigh. The song of the lines and sails and the men above and below, a tiny splinter adrift on a hungry sea, surrounded by fangs of water and bone.

She ran her hands over the black railing, whispered to the ship around her.

"Hold tight, girl."

Lightning, splitting the skies in two.

Rain like spears hurled from heaven's heart.

Thunder shaking her spine, like the footsteps of hungry giants.

Absolute

fucking

chaos.

They were a full turn into the storm, and the fury was like nothing Mia had ever seen. If she'd been impressed by the tempest that had hit the *Bloody Maid* in the Sea of Swords, the sheer power on display now left her near blind and dumb. The clouds hung so black and heavy, she felt she could reach up and touch them. The thunder was so loud, it was a physical sensation on her skin. The waves were like cliffs, towering, glowering faces of water, filled with whitedrakes. Taller than trees, dropping down into valleys so deep and dark they could almost be mistaken for the Abyss itself.

Each drive upward was akin to climbing a mountain, each drop was a moment of awful weightlessness, followed by a barreling rush into a bone-breaking impact in the trough below. They'd already lost four sailors in the storm—ripped from the masts by the clawing wind or dragged by the waves into the deep. Their cries were only whispers in the tempest howl, and the mouths waiting from them in the water silenced them quickly. The black roiled above them, ragged claws of lightning ripping at the sky. And there seemed no end in sight.

Mia had retired to her cabin—she'd stayed up top as long as she was able, but with no skill at sailing and nothing else to contribute, she seemed only to be in the way up above. Tric seemed immovable on the bow, but the waves crashing over the *Banshee*'s deck would surely wash Mia to her doom if they caught her. And so she found herself sitting in her hammock, tossed and rolled, listening to the timbers about her groan and creak and wondering just how much more her ship could take.

The shadows around her moved like living things. Eclipse prowled along the walls, a dark shape cut against the glow of the arkemical lanterns. Mia didn't dare smoke, didn't want to risk even a spark—with the Ladies of Storms and Oceans so enraged, who knew what the Lady of Fire would do if given opportunity. So instead, she focused on the gloom around her. The dark above and within her.

She could still feel the heat of the two suns, the cursed power of Aa beating faint upon her skin. But here below the thick black storm clouds sent by his daughter, it was almost as dark as night. The Everseeing's light was smothered. His malice waned. She was hidden almost completely from his sight. And Mia could feel power swelling inside her because of it. Not as fearsome as the power she'd wielded during truedark when she tore the Philosopher's Stone to rubble, no. But power nonetheless.

And so, she resolved to test it. To see how far it truly reached now she was hidden from Aa's eyes, and use the only weapon she could truly say was hers in this war. Her gravebone blade hung in its scabbard from a hook on the wall. The black rippled. With a gesture, she had the shadows carry it across the cabin to her waiting hand. She narrowed her eyes in concentration, and gentle as a lover, tendrils of living darkness took hold of her hammock and held it still, despite the bedlam all around her. She took hold of her own shadow, stretched it out along the floor and

Stepped

across the cabin

into it, then

into Eclipse

and back to

her hammock, all in the space of a few heartbeats. Flickering about the room like an apparition in some old fireside tale. Her breath came quicker, amazement budding in her chest and a dark joy curling her lips. These were gifts she'd used before: Stepping from shadow to shadow, or using the black as an extension of her own hands. But it had never been as effortless as this, the strength in the shadows never so potent. And yet it was becoming plain for her to see. In their attempts to kill her—in hiding their father's light—the Ladies of Storms and Oceans were also making Mia . . .

Stronger.

Still, Mia doubted her newfound power would give much comfort to her ship or crew, nor prove much worth against the tempest raging above. The *Banshee* crashed into another trough, her timbers shuddering in agony. Lightning flickered through the portholes—a new flash every handful of heartbeats—bringing a stuttering sunslight to Mia's cabin. Thunder shook the cradle of heaven again, louder than she'd ever heard, and she couldn't help but wince. She wondered if her ship would hold, if her crew could bear it, how much farther they had until they were—

Bells.

Screams.

She lifted her eyes to the decks above, wondering what was happening. A thunderous impact landed on *Banshee*'s port side, like a hammerblow from the hands of Aa himself. The ship slewed sideways, and Mia would've been flung across the room, save for the shadows cradling her in their arms. The dark kept her steady as the hull groaned, as the cries rose, as the ship listed hard and Mia finally realized . . .

Something hit us.

"Eclipse, with me."

". . . ALWAYS . . ."

With a glance, she bid the shadows fling the cabin door open and Mia

Stepped

down the

corridor and up

the ladder to the quarterdeck as the *Banshee* rocked sideways again. She heard more cries over the thunder, the crack of splintering wood, curses by Aa and all four of his daughters. She squinted through the blinding downpour, the soup-thick gloom, saw vague shapes moving on the deck below. *Banshee* rocked sideways again, a massive wave crashing over her bow and threatening to push them under as a barrage of lightning tore the clouds and lit the scene before Mia's wondering eyes.

"Black Mother . . . ," she breathed.

Tentacles. As long as a wagon train. Black above and ghostly white beneath, all suckers and scars and jagged hooks. Six of them were rising up on either side of the deck and wrapping *Banshee* in their awful embrace. Mia watched one massive limb clear a boom on the foremast with a single swipe, half a dozen sailors sent screaming to the deck and from there to the waters below.

"Leviathan!" came the roar.

She looked to the aft, saw Sigursson at the wheel, bellowing to his crew.

"Cut him loose, he'll drag us under!" he bellowed.

A few of the braver salts drew their blades and started hacking at the beast, desperate and terrified. The men were mere gnats against the creature's skin. But with Eclipse riding her shadow, Mia had no pause for fear,

Stepping

across the deck

in an instant

and bringing her longblade down in a scything, two-handed arc. The tentacle she struck was as broad as a barrel, tough as salted leather. But her gravebone sword sliced through it as if it were butter, severing it clean in two. Black blood sprayed, thick and salty, and Mia felt a shudder run through the *Banshee*'s length. The other tentacles went berserk, smashing, flailing, squeezing, splintering the railing and snapping the foremast off at the root with a deafening *craaaack*. The sailors howled as they fell, down into the thrashing waters and the mouths of the waiting whitedrakes. Lines snapped and shrouds toppled, a tangle of sails and mast crashing across the deck, *Banshee* listing hard to port as her crew's cries rose above the storm.

A massive wave crashed across their flank as Mia Stepped

again

up to the

foredeck, where

Tric was hacking away with his own gravebone blades, the leviathan's limbs writhing about him. The strength in him was astonishing, the power of the dark Goddess in him truly unleashed for the first time, and it took Mia's breath away to see him, drenched in black blood and falling rain, muscle etched in pale stone. He spun on the spot, water spraying, saltlocks streaming behind him as he brought his blades down again, again, severing another tentacle and sending it over the side with a savage kick. Tons of seawater rushed across the decks, and only the grip of Mia's shadows kept her from being swept over the side with three more of her crew, but Tric seemed immovable as a mountain. She split another tentacle in two as it rose up to grab her, rain and blood soaking her to the skin as she pressed her back against his.

"I *really* shouldn't have called them bitches!" she roared.

"Perhaps not!"

"*Banshee* can't take much more of this! So much for your prayers!"

"Row for shore, Mia!"

"Help me, then!"

"Always!"

Side by side. Back to back. The pair fought together, like in younger turns when they trained in the Hall of Songs. They were older now, harder, sadder, years and miles and the very walls of life and death between them. But still, they whirled and swayed like partners in some black and bloody waltz, and Mia was put in mind of the first time they danced together, years ago in Godsgrave. Swept up and cradled in his arms, spun and dipped and swayed as the music swelled and the world beyond became nothing. Their blades moved as one as they fought their way across the deck, hewing and slashing and spinning between the rain. The waters crashed down upon them and she leaned against him, the ship listed harder, and he pressed back against her. A pendulum in perfect balance, swinging back and forth in one shining, razored arc.

A tentacle came scything down from above, but Eclipse coalesced twenty feet across the ship, and, grabbing Tric's hand, Mia

Stepped

the pair

of them

into the shadowwolf as twenty tons of muscle and bone hooks crashed into the deck where they'd stood a moment before.

Tric's eyes were alight with the frenzy of it all, and he stood tall at her back in the chaos, wild and strong and unconquered, even by the hands of death herself. The thunder was a pounding drum, and the storm about them an endless song. Blood and rain beading on his cheeks as he looked over his shoulder and smiled just for her. And a part of Mia could have lived in that moment forever.

Sigursson had come down from the aft, hacking with his own sword, surrounded by a cadre of wulfguard. Mia's blade was quick as the lightning, Tric's swords like cleavers in an abattoir, cutting a swath across the deck and leaving it drenched in black, quickly washed away by the rain and waves. White light and thunder, the bellow of the waters and the fury of the tempest, the power of two goddesses pressing down upon them and still, *still,* it wasn't enough. And as Mia's sword split a sixth tentacle in two, as blood fell harder than the rain, the leviathan shuddered, and bucked, and finally released its grip on *Banshee*'s tortured flanks.

Another wave hit their starboard, almost sending them over. But the helmsmen bent their backs, muscles straining, *Banshee*'s spine twisted almost to breaking, and the ship managed to hold on, slowly righting herself. The oceans still thrashed, the tempest still rolled, the skies were still black as night. Mia and Tric stood back-to-back, blades dripping black on the main deck. Sigursson was gathered with a half-dozen salts, their black wolf pelts drenched, glaring at their captain and queen.

"This is no mortal storm!" one shouted.

"I told you, she's fucking cursed!" another cried.

"She's brought the fury of the Daughters down on us!"

Mia knew sailors were a superstitious bunch. Knew she stood in peril now, within and without. After four turns of punishment, of whitedrakes and leviathans and waves tall as mountains, her crew's nerve was all but gone. But she knew Einar Valdyr was a captain and king who ruled through fear, and Mia Corvere had learned the color of fear when she was but ten years old.

"I thought you lot were supposed to be the hardest crew on all Four Seas!" she spat. "And here you are, wailing like babes off the tit!"

"She'll be the death of us, Sigursson!" a tall salt yelled.

"Put her over the side," came the shout. "The goddesses will let us go!"

Tric squared up, his blades glittering as the lightning flashed and the *Banshee* shook. Mia looked her first mate in the eye, saw the malice and mutiny boiling there.

"Take hold of your jewels, Ulfr!" Mia glanced meaningfully at her greatcoat of faces. "Goddesses they might be, but Maw knows, you've far more to fear from me!"

The darkness flared around her, each man's shadow clawing and twisting along the deck. A wolf who wasn't a wolf rose up behind Sigursson, hackles raised, black teeth bared in a snarl. The Hearthless boy beside her tightened his grip on his bloody blades. The dark about Mia seethed. Lightning split the skies, catching the spray and rain and seeming to set the air about her aglow.

"Get back to your posts, you gutless bastards!" she demanded, raising her sword. "Or I'll feed you to those fucking drakes myself!"

The storm seemed to still for a moment. The thunder held its breath. Mia looked into Sigursson's eyes, saw that he *was* afraid. Of her. Of them. Of all of it.

The only question was, who did he fear more?

And then, something hit them. A colossal something. An impossible something. Rising up from beneath them, soundless and vast. Mia felt a thunderous impact. Heard the roar of the tempest and splitting timbers, the cries of the crew as they were sent flying. *Banshee* was lifted clean out of the water, and Mia only kept her feet because of the shadows holding her in place. Massive black tentacles rose up from the water, crashed about them in a deadly, crushing vise grip.

Another leviathan.

This one so big it almost beggared belief. Arms crusted in barnacles, long as years. Pale serrated hooks bigger than Mia was. A monster from the tallest tales, woken by the Lady of Oceans. Pressed by her hatred and rising up from the depths with only one intent: to drag Mia back down into the lightless black with it.

The beast's limbs crashed down on the deck, snapping the booms off the mainmast like twigs. Sails shredded as if they were damp parchment, wood cracking as if it were wafer-thin. *Banshee* groaned, stretched to breaking. Mia spun toward the beast, her shadows flaring. Tric turned also, black eyes gleaming, rain falling about them like knives.

Ulfr Sigursson dragged himself up from the deck, dripping seawater.

"Wulfguard!" he bellowed.

Mia's first mate raised his sword as lightning cracked the clouds.

"Kill this fucking bitch!"

CHAPTER 29

STANDING

Well, so much for monarchy . . .

Mia hadn't expected it to last, truth told. A tyranny will always fail when men have nothing left to lose but their lives. But she'd hoped they might've gotten a little closer to land before it finally broke them.

As Mia's former crew charged behind her and the leviathan's tentacles seethed before her, she grabbed Tric's hand and

Stepped

up on the aft deck,

landing in a crouch beside the astonished-looking helmsmen.

Sigursson turned on his heel, found her through the downpour and roared the attack. The *Banshee*'s crew seemed to have abandoned all thought of the leviathan, intent only on killing their queen in attempt to appease the Ladies. They charged up the twin stairwells, port and starboard, their blades gleaming in the lightning strikes. The beast meanwhile had wrapped four massive tentacles about the *Banshee,* squeezing like some colossal vise. The timbers along the ship's bulwarks cracked and buckled under the awful pressure. The deck rolled as if the earth were quaking, men tumbled back down the stairs or over the rails. Other mutinous wulfguard leapt over their falling comrades, desperate to put a blade to Mia and the Ladies at peace.

Tric stood atop the port stairwell, bringing one of his gravebone swords down in an overhand swing that split one man's skull clean in two, the blade plowing all the way down into the fellow's rib cage. Mia stood atop the other stairwell, plunging her sword through a sailor's chest and kicking him backward, sending the men behind him sprawling. The deck rocked again, a massive wave crashing over their bow. The *Banshee* listed dangerously, her broken masts trailing heavy in the water, adding to the weight of the leviathan beneath, all set to drag them below. As she dispatched another mutineer with a savage thrust, Mia's mind was racing, heart pounding in her chest. Fighting off her crew, she wasn't fighting off the beast, and the ship was being torn apart around them. The water was full of drakes. The waves like towers. If *Banshee* died, so did they all.

Enemies beneath. Around. Below.

Story of my life . . .

"*. . . MIA, BEWARE . . . !*"

Sigursson was charging up the stairs with his blade drawn, teeth bared. Mia caught his thrust on her longsword, turned it aside. With a gesture, she wrapped her first mate up in his own shadow, ribbons of darkness seizing hold of his arms, legs, throat, holding the Vaanian pinned and thrashing in midair.

"I warned you what would happen if you defied me, Ulfr!" she shouted.

Sigursson could only gargle, veins bulging in his neck as the shadows squeezed. Mia raised her hand, lifting him farther off the deck, fingers curling closed. Thunder shook the heavens, pressing down on her skin.

"Now you get to see what makes the rest of them so afraid!"

Mia opened her hand and Ulfr was ripped apart, pieces of him flung in every direction, blood falling like rain. The *Banshee* shook again in the leviathan's grip, the crunch of splintering timbers loud as the storm as the ship split across her middle. Tric staggered across the deck toward Mia, drenched in seawater and blood. Mia caught him in her arms, her shadows holding them steady as the aft rose out of the water.

"*. . . MIA, WE CANNOT STAY HERE . . . !*" Eclipse roared.

"I'M WILLING TO ENTERTAIN SUGGESTIONS!" the boy bellowed.

Mia could see the *Banshee* was doomed, crumbling all around her, waves rushing in over her sides, masts and spine broken. One way or another, they were going into that ocean. And even if the seas weren't crashing about them like hammers and filled with monsters from the deep, it was still an impossible distance to swim . . .

"*THE ONLY WEAPON IN THIS WAR IS FAITH.*"

Lightning flashed, that same rapid strobe turning the gloom brighter than the sunslight. The shadows were etched around her in perfect black with each strike, writhing at Mia's feet, carved deep and dark in the great valleys between the waves, miles and miles of them between her and land. But she could feel the dark above her. The dark inside her. Thinking of a line from that old Ashkahi poem,

No shadow without light . . .

and finally shouting to Tric, "Hold on to me!"

The boy obeyed, wrapping his arm tight about her waist. *Banshee* shuddered beneath them, the ocean rushing up to meet them as the leviathan dragged the ship and her murderous crew down to their dooms.

"Eclipse, you move where I point you, aye?"

". . . AS IT PLEASE YOU . . ."

"Go!"

Mia pointed across the iron-gray sea. The gnashing swell, the colossal waves full of teeth. The daemon disappeared from beside her, and holding tight to Tric, Mia

Stepped

out across the

water into the shadows

between two towering waves. She felt a moment of weightlessness, the sensation of falling, the Dweymeri boy in her arms and nothing but death beneath them both. But before they could plunge into the depths she was

Stepping again

across the hollow

storm-washed spaces

and into Eclipse,

one with

the dark, above and about and within

and from there, flicker-fast

wave

to wolf then

wolf

to wave

and back

skipping across the iron gray like a stone

Stepping the black and

dancing the shadow way

the goddesses

around her

screaming fury

the god inside her

laughing black

the power of the dark

all at her fingertips

and as the miles melted away

to nothing

as the goddesses roared

their rage

and at last

after an age

after an eon

Step

by

stuttering Step

she caught sight

of pale shores ahead

Mia found herself

laughing, too,

the shard burning black

within her

and Ashkahi sands

laid before her

and a tiny part inside her

a place she could barely see

unless she looked very hard

finally

truly

beginning

to

believe.

They fell into the sodden sand. Shallow waters rising up about her thighs. A red sliver of storm-wracked Ashkahi beach was stretched out before her. The familiar, moldering facades of Last Hope in front of her. Black clouds arrayed above her. Snarling waves rising behind her. The rain was on her skin and her hair was in her eyes and the chill was in her bones. Tric was on his hands and knees in the chopping swell, wonder and amazement in his gaze as he looked up at her.

Lightning flashed, tearing the skies in fury. The waves crashed and rolled. The Ladies of Storms and Oceans, the terrible twins, reaching out toward her with all their hatred. Mia hauled herself to her feet, Eclipse beside her, the shadows swaying like serpents. She dragged her sodden tricorn off, clawed her hair from her face, and she laughed. Her eyes alight. Her heart warmed by dark flame, burning in her chest.

All they had, they'd thrown.

All their hate, they'd given.

All their fury, spent.

Mia raised the knuckles to the sky.

"Still standing, bitches."

BOOK 4

THE ASHES OF EMPIRES

Chapter 30

Could

" "O, fuck no."

When Mia pushed open the door to the New Imperial Taverna in the town of Last Hope, she hadn't been expecting open arms or a triumphal parade. But when Fat Daniio, owner and proprietor, looked up from his shiny new countertop and saw the bedraggled and sea-soaked Blade and her Hearthless companion standing on his doorstep, Mia had actually been impressed by the sheer horror in his eyes.

"O, *fuck* no," the publican repeated.

Fat Daniio's trepidation at Mia's return was understandable: last time she was in his pub, she'd poisoned a cadre of Luminatii in his common room and burned the Old Imperial to the ground. By way of compensation, the Red Church had sponsored a rebuild, and the *New* Imperial was a rather more well-to-do affair than its predecessor. Not exactly a marrowborn villa, but at least there were no bloodstains on the floors or rats holding court in the rafters.

Still, it seemed Mia wasn't among Daniio's list of favorite people.

"Nonono," the tubby publican begged, raising his hands in surrender. "Merciful Aa, you can't come in here, I've just had the walls repainted."

"I promise to behave," Mia said, stepping over the threshold.

"Mia!"

She heard running footsteps, smelled jasmine perfume, and then Ashlinn was catching her up in a breathless embrace. Ash's lips found hers and Mia kissed her back, forgetting herself for a moment and just enjoying the simple feel of her girl in her arms again. She was soaked to the skin, freezing cold, exhausted past sleeping. But just for a heartbeat, none of it mattered.

Sidonius strode across the room and joined in on the hug, Bladesinger was quick to follow. Looking around the pub's common room, Mia saw it was full of salts from the *Bloody Maid,* talking soft and drinking hard. Cloud Corleone sat in a booth with BigJon, Butcher, and Jonnen—the trio were apparently teaching her brother how to play Kingslayer.* But all four looked up as Mia and Tric entered, amazement etched on Corleone's face.

"Fuck me very gently," he breathed.

"Then fuck you very hard?" Mia asked.

Cloud tipped his tricorn and grinned. "Good to see you, my queen."

Mia gave a slow curtsey that a marrowborn dona would envy, then looked to Jonnen and winked. Her brother climbed off his chair and, keeping his manner as lordly as he could manage, walked across the common room and wrapped his little arms around her waist in a fierce hug. She was soaked to the skin but couldn't bring herself to care, lifting him up and

---

*Perhaps the oldest drinking game in the history of the Itreyan Republic, Kingslayer was originally known as "Beggar." The rules for the game are basic—a glass is placed in the center of the table, and each player takes a turn trying to bounce a copper beggar into it. If successful, the player gets to nominate another player to take a drink.

The nominated player is allowed one chance at "revenge," by attempting to bounce the coin with their off-hand into the glass. If the revenge bounce is successful, the original nominating player must drink *twice*. However, the original player is also allowed a chance for revenge, and if successful, the drink tally doubles again.

As you can imagine, among ambidextrous players, these revenge matches can result in a rapidly escalating tally of drinks. The longest official revenge bout was recorded between Don Cisco Antolini and the newly crowned Francisco XI at a grand gala celebrating the king's own coronation. The beggar was successfully bounced back and forth between the men twenty-seven times, with the king ultimately missing the twenty-eighth bounce.

Mathematicians among you will realize this meant the new king was now compelled to drink 67,108,864 shots of goldwine.

Francisco XI wasn't the brightest king to sit on the Itreyan throne, but he *was* a man of his word. Not to see his honor besmirched in front of his entire court, and against the advice of his queen, the newly crowned monarch resolved to make an attempt. He made it to his fifty-seventh drink before he collapsed, and despite the best efforts of his apothecaries, he died the next turn.

Francisco XI's reign is the shortest in the history of the Itreyan monarchy, but remarkably, most of the citizenry found the tale of his end rather touching, and the game of Beggar was renamed Kingslayer in his honor.

When given the choice to be ruled by an honest idiot or a competent liar, most people prefer the idiot.

squeezing him tight and planting a kiss on his cheek. The boy protested, making a face as her lips touched his skin.

"You're cold."

"So they tell me," she replied.

"Unhand me, wench," he demanded.

Mia kissed him again, grinning as he wriggled in her embrace. Finally, she set him on the taverna floor and sent him on his way with a soft smack to his backside. The Falcons looked at Mia with a kind of awe. Sidonius turned to Tric, shook his ink-black hand.

"We feared you'd not make it," the Itreyan said. "That storm was a monster."

"Aye," Bladesinger said, giving a grudging nod. "Well done, lad."

"THE WORK WASN'T MINE," Tric replied. "WE'D BOTH BE AT THE BOTTOM OF THE OCEAN IF NOT FOR MIA."

"Where's the *Black Banshee*?" Butcher asked.

Mia shrugged. "Bottom of the ocean."

Tric looked at Mia with lingering wonder. "SHE TRULY IS CHOSEN OF THE GODDESS."

"Always there seemed more to her than the eye beheld," said a familiar voice.

Mia turned and saw a thin woman with her face veiled in black silk. Strawberry-blond curls. Dark, kohled eyes. Soundless as whispers and standing right behind her.

"Naev!"

Mia caught the woman up in her arms, kissed her cheeks, one after another. Naev returned the hug with fondness, a smile shining in her eyes.

"Friend Mia," the Hand said. "It is good to see her again. Speaker Adonai gave word of her coming. Old Mercurio sends his love."

"You've spoken to him?" Mia whispered, her heart swelling with joy.

Naev cast a pointed glance about the Imperial's common room, nodded to a table in a far-flung corner. Making their way past groups of Corleone's crew, the group secreted themselves at the back of the pub, squeezing into a booth around Naev. Daniio shuffled over with a round of cheap ales, his nervous stare still locked on Mia.

The girl blew him a kiss.

Once the publican had retreated, Naev spoke with a hushed voice, eyes on the door.

"Adonai sent word to Naev through the blood," the woman said, tapping the silver phial about her neck. "The speaker and weaver have aligned themselves with Mercurio against the Ministry. Chronicler Aelius stands with the company also." Naev looked at Mia. "Between them, they have pondered a way she might enter the Mountain and strike."

"But we have to move now, Mia," Ashlinn said.

"Aye," Naev nodded. "Matters are moving swift. Time is sh—"

"Hold, hold," Mia said, shaking her head. "I just fought my way across six hundred miles of storm and ocean. You're telling me the speaker and weaver have joined with the chronicler in a conspiracy to help me take down the entire Red Church Ministry. Can I at least have a fucking smoke and come to grips with this first?"

"Scaeva is headed to the Quiet Mountain," Ash whispered.

Mia's belly thrilled, her jaw tightening. "What?"

"Ashlinn speaks truth," Naev nodded. "The imperator needs Marielle to craft another duplicate to stand in his stead during public appearances. And he must be present for the weaver to craft a convincing likeness. He will be in the Mountain in a matter of turns."

"All the vipers in one nest," Ashlinn said, squeezing her hand. "This is our chance, Mia. Kill Scaeva. End the Ministry. Rescue Mercurio and be done with all of it."

Mia's skin prickled, a surge of adrenaline banishing the exhaustion, the chill. Scaeva surely wouldn't travel to the Mountain unattended. And even with their numbers culled, the Red Church was still a cult of the deadliest assassins in the Republic. But the belly of the Quiet Mountain dwelled in perpetual night—no sunslight had ever touched it. She'd be as strong within the Black Mother's halls as she'd been out there in that storm. Probably more so. And with all her enemies in the one place at the one time, just a few turns' ride across the Ashkahi Whisperwastes . . .

She looked at Naev, her voice as sharp as the gravebone at her waist.

"Tell me everything you know."

The whispers were louder than Mia remembered.

They were three turns into their trek, the heat rippling off the Ashkahi wastelands in shimmering waves. The Lady of Storms had abandoned the skies for now, the dark cloud cover peeling back to reveal a sullen purple glare above. Saan was half-hidden by the horizon, and Saai falling farther toward its rest. But out here in the desert, the temperature was still stifling.

Mia and her comrades rode inside a Red Church wagon train. The Hands who usually accompanied Naev on her supply runs couldn't be trusted to join their conspiracy, so Naev had put them down with a dose of

Swoon in their evemeals before Mia had even reached Ashkah. They were now resting in a rented room in the New Imperial, bound hand and face and foot.

Mia had told Cloud Corleone he was under no obligation to wait for her return. With the *Black Banshee* at the bottom of the Sea of Sorrows and his friendship with Mia well-known, the pirate had decided he'd sail back to Godsgrave and lie low until the succession war over the Throne of Scoundrels was settled.

As they'd made ready to trek out into the Whisperwastes, the captain had bowed low, flashed Mia his four-bastard smile, and doffed his tricorn.

"If I were the praying sort, I'd say one for you," Corleone had said. "But I'm not sure you'd welcome it anyway. And so I'll gift you this instead."

The scoundrel gently took Mia's hand, kissed her bruised and battered knuckles.

"Fortune go with you, my queen."

"You don't have to call me your queen anymore, Captain," Mia had said.

"I know it," Cloud replied. "Which is exactly why I do."

BigJon had given Mia a low bow and his silver grin. "That marriage offer still stands, Queen Mia. I'd rather fancy being a king and telling this bastard what to do for a change."

Cloud flipped his first mate the knuckles, then nodded at Mia.

"Blue above and below."

"Thank you, my friend," Mia had smiled. "Benito? Belarrio?"

Cloud had only grinned. "My loyalty only extends so far, Majesty."

The scoundrel had bowed low again and turned back to the sea.

Mia wondered if they'd ever meet again.

They'd set off soon afterward, eight camels leading a four-wagon train out into the Ashkahi wastes. Not needing to sleep, Tric sat up front in the driver's chair—they had only a few turns to reach the Mountain before Scaeva was gone, and the boy's unearthly presence served to drive their animals a little harder. Hating camels almost as much as she hated horses, Mia had given all their beasts names in her head—Ugly, Stupid, Smelly, Cockeye, Dunghead, Tosser, Bucktooth, and, for the smelliest and ugliest of the lot, Julius.

Bladesinger rode in the front wagon with Naev, watchful eyes on the horizon. Butcher stuck close by Jonnen when he could—the man still trained the boy with his wooden swords whenever they stopped for a meal—but for now he was riding with Sidonius in the rear, the pair of them taking turns at beating on a large iron contraption to keep the sand kraken away.

Mia, Ashlinn, and Jonnen rode in the middle wagon, the canvas cover shielding them from the worst of the suns. Ash sat beside Mia, hand in hers. Jonnen sat opposite, dark eyes on his sister's. Eclipse had returned to the lad's shadow, and Mia could see he was a little more at ease. But despite his tender age, Jonnen was no fool—he'd overheard enough of their talk to realize his father awaited them in the Quiet Mountain. And he knew Mia's intentions toward the imperator were less than gentle.

The boy had kept his own counsel for the first couple of turns. Practicing his bladework with Butcher and sitting quietly with Eclipse. But Mia could see it building inside him like floodwaters against a crumbling dam, until on the third turn after evemeal, he finally spoke.

"You're going to kill him."

Mia looked up into her brother's eyes. Ashlinn was dozing, head in Mia's lap. Mia had been gently reweaving the girl's warbraids, long golden locks entwined between her fingers.

"I'm going to try," Mia replied.

"Why?" Jonnen asked.

"Because he deserves it."

"Because he hurts people."

"Yes."

"Mia," the boy said softly. "You hurt people, too."

She looked into those big dark eyes, searching the heart beyond. It wasn't an accusation. Nor a rebuke. No matter what she was, the boy didn't judge her for it. Her brother was a pragmatist, and Mia liked that about him. And though he'd been slowly warming to her over the past few weeks on the road, she wondered what they truly might've been if the world hadn't ripped them apart before they could become much of anything at all.

"I know it," she finally said. "I hurt people all the time. And that's the riddle, little brother. How do you kill a monster without becoming one yourself?"

"I don't know," he replied.

Mia shook her head, staring out at the wastes around them.

"You can't," she sighed. "I'm not some hero in a storybook. I'm not someone you should aspire to be. I'm a ruthless cunt, Jonnen. I'm a selfish bitch. You hurt me, I'll hurt you back. You hurt the ones I love, I'll kill you instead. That's just the way I am. Julius Scaeva killed our mother. The man I called Father. And I don't care what they did to deserve it. I don't care that they weren't perfect. I don't even care that they were probably just as bad as him. Because truth told, perhaps I'm worse than all of them. So fuck what's right. And fuck redemption. Because Julius Scaeva still deserves to die."

"Then so do you," he replied.

"You thinking of trying, little brother?"

Jonnen simply stared. The slow trundle of the wagon rocking them back and forth, the clang of the ironsong breaking the still.

"I..."

Jonnen frowned. His lips pressed together. She could see the intelligence in him, just as fierce as her own. But in the end, he was still a child. Lost and stolen from all he knew. And she could see he was having trouble finding the words.

"I wish I had known you better," he finally said.

"So do I." Mia reached out, took his little hand in hers. "And I know I'm a shitty big sister, Jonnen. I know I'm awful at all this. But you're my familia. The most important thing in my world. And I hope one turn you might find it in yourself to love me just half as much as I love you. Because I do."

"But you're still going to kill him," Jonnen said.

"Yes," she replied. "I am."

"Please don't."

"I must."

"He's my father, Mia."

"Mine, too."

"But *I* love him."

Mia met her brother's eyes. Seeing the years lost between them, the love he felt for the man who'd taken him away from her. The wrong, rotting at the heart of that. And slowly, she shook her head.

"O, Jonnen," she sighed. "That's just one more reason he deserves to die."

They traveled on, through the Whisperwastes in what little silence Sid's ironsong spared them. And though the boy's eyes swam with questions, he gave voice to none of them after that.

Though there was always a risk of sand kraken, the Red Church had been running supplies from Last Hope for years, and Naev guided them along paths of submerged stone, broken foothills, and finally into the mountains at the wastes' northern reaches. Mia could see a black stone spire rising before them—just one of dozens in the range. It was plain. Unassuming. Capped with pale and gleaming snow. But Mia's heart beat quicker to see it. The heart of the Ministry, the temple of the Mother, the cradle of the Red Church's power in the Republic.

The Quiet Mountain.

Mia knew an ancient magik called the Discord had been placed on the peak years past—a werking to confuse unwelcome visitors. But Naev knew the words that would keep the magik at bay. Slowly, surely, their wagon train made its way through twisted gullies and broken foothills, closer to the towering granite peak. The Whisperwastes had been long left behind them—Sid and Butcher had ceased their ironsong, crawling into the middle wagon to consult with Mia and Ash about the upcoming assault. Tric had left the reins to Naev, and he and Bladesinger joined the group, gathering in a small circle around a large oaken barrel.

"Right," Mia said. "Once we get inside, we stay quiet as long as we're able. If the alarm is raised, we'll have every Blade and Hand in the place on us like flies on shite. But if we walk it right, these bastards won't even know we're there 'til it's half over."

She took a piece of charcoal, began drawing a complex map on the wagon floor.

"Tric, Ashlinn, and Naev all know their way around the Mountain, so the rest of you will follow their lead. The inside of this place is like a damned maze, so watch your step. It's easy to get turned around in the dark. Tric, you, Sid, and Bladesinger head to the speaker's chambers. Protect Adonai and cut off the blood pool. Scaeva *cannot* be allowed to escape the Mountain. Ash, you and Naev head to the Athenaeum and secure Mercurio. If you can't find him there, he'll likely be in his chambers. Guard him with your life and get him to the speaker. Butcher, you and Eclipse stay in the stables and protect Jonnen. If all goes well, I'll fetch you when it's done. If all goes to shit, you ride back to Last Hope hard as you can, get out by sea."

A stupider man might've grumbled at being left behind to babysit, but Butcher was obviously aware of the import of his task of protecting her kin, and how deeply Mia was trusting him by giving it to him.

"Aye, Crow." He thumped a fist on his chest. "I'll guard him with my life."

"And what about you?" Sidonius asked, clearly concerned.

"I'm going after the Ministry," Mia said.

"Alone?" Ashlinn asked.

Mia nodded. "Best way to do it. It'll be early morn by the time we arrive. Drusilla will probably be with Scaeva and Marielle, so I'll save them for once we're all ready. But as far as Solis and the Ministry go, I can have the head off the snake before it knows I'm there."

"... SOLIS ALMOST KILLED YOU THE LAST TIME YOU FOUGHT, MIA ...," Eclipse murmured.

"Aye," Mia nodded, smiling at Naev. "But there's not much that goes on in the Mountain that Chronicler Aelius doesn't know about. And he's given me a gift to even the scales."

She looked about the group, met each stare in turn.

"Any questions?"

Though she had no doubt every one of them was burning with them, Mia's companions kept their silence. She nodded to each, acutely aware of how much they risked for her, how deeply grateful she was to all of them. She squeezed Sidonius's hand, gave Bladesinger a fierce hug, kissed Butcher's cheek. Each donned a Hand's stolen garb as the train trundled nearer to the Mountain, hunkering down in their wagons with blades beneath their robes. The train drew closer to a blank cliff face in the Quiet Mountain's flank, and Naev rose up in the front wagon, arms spread. She spoke ancient words, humming with power.

Mia heard the sound of stone, cracking and rumbling. Felt the greasy tang of arkemical magik in the air. Bladesinger muttered beneath her breath, Jonnen gasping in wonder as a great flat stretch of stone cracked open. A faint rush of wind kissed Mia's face, a shower of fine dust and pebbles fell from above as the Mountain's flank gaped wide.

The familiar sight of the Red Church stables awaited them—a broad straw-lined oblong, set on all sides with pens for sleek horses and spitting camels, wagons and farrier's tools and bales of feed and great stacks of supply crates. The song of a ghostly choir hung in the air like smoke as Ugly, Stupid, Smelly, Cockeye, Dunghead, Tosser, Bucktooth, and Julius pulled the wagon inside. Hands in black robes walked out to guide the beasts farther in. The illumination spilling through the open door was the only sunslight the belly of the Mountain ever saw.

Mia felt her shadow surge toward the dark beyond.

She squeezed Jonnen's hand, saw the boy felt the same thrill at the dark as she did. Sidonius was tense as steel in the wagon ahead. Bladesinger still as stone. Mia could hear Ashlinn's quickened breath at her side. And finally, as a cadre of Hands stepped out of the gloom to help unload the wagon's wares, Mia and her comrades broke into savage motion.

The crisp ring of blades. The glint of arkemical light on polished steel. Mia heard several soft pops as globes of wyrdglass flew from Naev's fingertips, catching a knot of Hands in a cloud of Swoon and sending them all to the floor, senseless. The Falcons moved swift, lashing out with pommels or the flats of their blades. Hands and stable staff were sent sprawling, bleeding. Mia

Stepped

from the wagon's belly

to the stairs above,

cutting off a fleeing Hand

and catching him up in his own shadow before knocking him witless. Brief struggles. A splash of bright red. Within moments, the stables were under their control.

All was in readiness. Each of them knew their task. Eyes hard. Blades sharp. Mia nodded to each in turn. Kissed Ashlinn swift on the lips.

"Be careful, love," she whispered.

"You too," Ash replied.

She felt a dark stare on her back. Turned and met Tric's gaze.

"MOTHER GO WITH YOU, MIA," he said.

"And you," she replied.

She looked into her brother's glittering eyes. Saw the pain and uncertainty in him.

"I'll give our father your regards," she said.

And with that, Mia was gone.

Spiderkiller stalked into her Hall, wrapped in emerald green. The gold about her throat glittered in the stained-glass light, reflected in the bottles and phials and jars lining the walls. Her eyes were black, lips and fingers blacker still—stained from a lifetime of the poisoncraft she so adored. There were none in all Itreya who could match her in it. She'd forgotten more about the art of Truth than most would ever know.

The Shahiid sat at her oaken desk at the head of the Hall, pestle in hand, grinding a compound of bluespider venom and driftroot into a stone bowl. She'd been concocting a number of new poisons of late, dreaming of her vengeance against Mia Corvere. Solis's words in the last Ministry meeting had stung her more than she'd admit. It *had* been her who granted Mia her favor, allowed the girl to become a Blade. Spiderkiller would never forgive her former pupil for that. And though it couldn't be said the woman had honor to besmirch, she *did* have patience. And she knew, sooner or later, Mia would give her the chance to . . .

The Shahiid blinked. There upon the desk, she saw a shadow, leaking across the polished oak, like ink spilled from a bottle. It puddled beneath a ream of parchment, moving like black smoke and forming itself into letters. Two words that sent Spiderkiller's heart racing.

Behind you.

A gravebone longblade flashed out of the dark at her back. Spiderkiller's throat opened, ear to ear. Gasping, blood gushing from severed jugular and carotid, the woman pushed back her chair, staggered to her feet. Whirling on the spot, clutching the awful wound, she saw a girl where none had stood a moment before.

"M-muh," she gargled.

Mia stepped back swiftly as Spiderkiller drew one of the curved blades at her belt. The steel was discolored, damp with venom. But the Shahiid's face was already bleeding pale, her footsteps tottering. She sagged back against the desk, eyes wide with fear. Blood pumped rhythmically from Spiderkiller's sundered throat, covered her hands, her dress, the gold wrapped around her fingers and neck. So much.

Too much.

"I thought long and hard about how to end you, Spiderkiller," Mia said. "I thought it might be poetic to finish each Shahiid with their own mastery. Steel for Solis. Poison for you. In the end I decided you're just too dangerous to fuck about with. But I wanted you to know I killed you first because I respected you most. I thought you might draw some solace from that, neh?"

Spiderkiller toppled forward onto the stone, her eyes cold and lifeless.

"No," Mia sighed. "On second thought, I don't suppose you would."

Mouser heard a door slam somewhere out in his Hall.

He looked up from the needletrap he was loading, a frown on his handsome brow. His workshop was hidden behind one of the many doors in the Hall of Pockets, a quiet place where he puzzled with locks or played at dress-up. He was wearing women's underthings beneath his robes now, as it happened—he'd always found them more comfortable, truth be told.

Mouser rose from his desk, took up his walking stick, and limped out into his Hall. The walls were lined with dozens of other doors, leading off into his wardrobes or storerooms, or sometimes nowhere at all. Long tables ran the room's length, littered with curios and oddities, padlocks and picks. Blue stained-glass light puddled upon the granite floor, reflected in the dark eyes of the girl waiting for him.

"Mia . . . ," he said, belly running cold.

"You helped take my familia away from me, Mouser," she said. "And years later, you actually had the stomach to look me in the eye. To offer me counsel. To pretend like you were my friend. Where do stones like that come from, I wonder?"

Mouser's hand drifted to the Ashkahi blacksteel blade he always wore at his waist.

"Blacksteel can cut through gravebone, you realize."

"It's a fine sword, Shahiid," the girl agreed. "Did you win or steal it?"

As ever, Mouser's smile loitered on his lips like it was planning on pinching the silverware. "A little bit of both."

Mia smiled too. "Best not to risk it, then."

He wasn't sure where the crossbow came from—one moment the girl's hands were empty, the next, she was drawing a bead on his chest. But even with his crippled legs, the Mouser could still move quick as cats, and as Mia fired, he let go his walking stick, grasped his sword, and drew it forth with a crisp ring, sidestepping the bolt speeding toward his chest.

Or at least, that's how it played out in his head.

But as Mouser made to step aside, he found his boots affixed firmly to the floor. Too late, he brought up the blade to ward off the blow, but the bolt struck home, punching through his gray robes, the corset beneath, and into the chest beyond.

A bubble of blood popped on his lips as he stared stupidly at the fourteen inches of wood and steel now lodged in his left lung. He looked up as Mia reloaded, grunted as a second bolt thudded into his chest, wobbling him on his trapped feet and finally toppling him backward onto the stone. He hurled a fistful of throwing knives as he fell, but the girl was gone, Stepping into the shadows and reappearing a few feet to his left.

She brought her boot down on his hand as he reached for another blade, leveling the reloaded crossbow at his crotch.

"Say farewell to your stones, little mouse."

Solis opened his eyes to the sound of the choir.

Rising from his bed, the Revered Father washed his face, blinked his blinded eyes. And just as he did every morn, he picked up a wooden sword and ran himself through his practice drills. After thirty minutes, his body was dripping with sweat and he was breathing hard. Smiling at the song of his blade in the air.

Satisfied, he slipped on his robe, his scabbard. Pale eyes open and seeing nothing at all. And yet, seeing everything and more.

Imperator Scaeva and the Lady of Blades would be arriving shortly, and he knew he'd best get himself presentable. Stalking down long, dark hallways, he nodded to the Hand outside the bathhouse door, stepped silently into the empty room. Unbuckling his belt, he took a deep breath as he always did. Reaching down to run his fingers over his precious scabbard. The leather embossed with concentric circles, much like a pattern of eyes.

Slowly, he removed it from his waist, feeling all the world around him fall away into darkness. Once again blind as he'd been the turn he was born. He folded his robe neatly and placed it by the edge of the broad, sunken bath, coiling his belt and scabbard carefully on top. There were only a few in the entire Church who knew its true purpose, the magiks that coursed through it. Old Ashkahi sorcery engraved into the leather, lifting the veil on a world that would otherwise be utterly hidden to him.

Stepping down into the warm bath, Solis closed his eyes and tilted his head back beneath the water, allowing himself to float for a handful of minutes.

Deaf, dumb, and blind.

It was a habit, and the Revered Father didn't like habits—they made a man easier to ambush. But he always allowed himself this tiny moment of peace and quiet. This was the Red Church, after all. The bastion of Niah's might upon this earth.

Who could touch him here?

Solis rose to the surface, blinked the water from milk-white eyes. He smelled soap's perfume, maple burning low in the braziers, candle scent. His ears were keener than his beak, but all he heard were crackling flames, the ghostly choir out in the Church's dark. And though his own eyes were almost sightless, sensing only the absence of light, he noticed nothing odd as he sat up in the bath, save perhaps the chamber was a touch darker than usual.

Darker . . .

". . . GOOD EVE, SHAHIID . . ."

To his credit, Solis didn't flinch. Didn't even deign to look in the shadowwolf's direction. He heard a featherlight scuff of a boot on stone, caught the faint smell of sweat above the smell of maple, and . . . Spiderkiller's perfume? He knew who stood there, off to one side of the pool. Watching him with her dark, shaded eyes.

"You."

"Me," Mia replied.

A cold trickle of dread cooled Solis's belly. His hand flashed toward his robe at the bath's edge. But though his fingers found the cloth, he realized his scabbard was . . .

Gone.

"I was actually disappointed when I found out," Mia said, now speaking from farther away. "There's something quite romantic in the notion of the blind swordmaster, isn't there? But it was all lies, wasn't it, Solis? All bullshit. Just like the rest of this fucking place."

Fear turned his insides greasy cold. He reached into his robe for the dagger he kept hidden there. Not really surprised to find that gone, too. Solis rose from the bath in a cloud of steam, crouched naked at the edge. He was drawing breath to shout when—

"Your Hand is sleeping, by the by," came the girl's voice from across the room. "If you were thinking of screaming for help, that is."

"Scream?" Solis sneered. "You always did think too much of yourself, girl."

"And you too little," she replied. "Is that why you let me train here? Knowing how badly it could bite you in the arse? Did you really think I'd never find out what you all did?"

He tilted his head to better hear, straining for the sound of her footfalls. Retreating along the edge of the bath, he tried putting his back to the wall. But he heard a soft whisper of cloth over the crackling wood in the braziers, realized she was

Behind me.

He struck, hands outstretched, finding nothing but air.

"A fine lunge, Revered Father," the girl said. "But your aim. Tsk, tsk, tsk."

She was to his right, drifting away. He could feel her. Years in the dark before he'd found his Belt of Eyes, the years he'd spent locked in the Philosopher's Stone, all came rushing back in a flood now. He'd murdered a hundred men to win his freedom from that pit, all while blind as a newborn pup. He didn't need eyes to kill then. He'd not need them now.

But she's good. Quiet as death when she moves.

"It's all lies," she whispered. "The murders. The offerings. Hear me, Mother. Hear me now. All that bollocks. This place wasn't a church, Solis.

It was a brothel. You were never a holy Blade in service to the Mother of Night. You were a whore."

Keep her talking.

"And you expected something greater, is that it?" he asked. "Did you swallow the nonsense Drusilla and your Mercurio told you? 'Chosen of the Mother,' is that it?"

A soft scuff of her boot.

Left . . . ?

"I told them when you arrived we should have just ended you," he said. "I warned them this turn would come. When you learned the truth of it, and the spoiled, squalling brat you truly are showed herself. Always you thought yourself better than this place. *Always.*"

"So why didn't you kill me?" she asked.

Behind again now . . .

"Cassius wouldn't hear of it," Solis replied. "'Little sister,' he called you. Supposing some kinship in the dark between you, though he knew nothing of what he was. 'The Black Prince,' he called himself." The Shahiid scoffed. "Prince of what?"

"Why did you hate me, Solis?" she asked. "It wasn't just that scar I gifted you."

And then he saw it. The way to make her stumble. To hold her still long enough to get his fingers around her throat.

"I never hated you," he said. "I just knew it would always end this way. I knew you'd eventually discover it was the Red Church who captured Darius Corvere and handed him over to his killers. I knew Scaeva's shit would end up on our boots."

He tilted his head and smiled.

"But did you never wonder, Mia?"

"Wonder?"

Moving right. Back and forth with no pattern.

Clever.

"Wonder who it was who stole into Darius Corvere's encampment?" Solis asked. "Wonder who snatched up him and his lover and handed them over for execution?"

Solis held up his left hand. Running his fingers over the scars notched in his forearm.

"Thirty-six marks," he said. "Thirty-six bodies. In truth, I've ended hundreds. But I only branded myself with those kills I was paid for, in blood and silver. Even the ones where I never actually wielded the blade."

He ran his finger over a notch near his wrist.

"This one is General Gaius Maxinius Antonius."

He heard a scuff on the stone as she stopped moving.

"And this is Justicus Darius Corvere."

Solis turned milk-white eyes toward her soft gasp.

"You . . ."

And then he lunged.

Mia moved, slipping away quick as shadows. But not quite quick enough. His fingers closed on a lock of her hair and he seized tight, heard her yelp as he wrapped it up in his fist and dragged her in. Fingers closing around her neck. His face was twisted, rage boiling in his chest at the thought this fucking slip had blinded him, mocked him, caught him unawares.

He slammed a fist into her jaw, sent her reeling. Dragging her back in to punch her again. Slamming her like a rag doll into the wall, fingers sinking deep into the flesh of her throat. He'd gotten too soft. Too predictable. When this little bitch was dead he'd—

A blow to his chest.

Another and another.

It felt as though she were punching him, and he sneered at the thought. She was two-thirds his size, half his weight. As if her fists could hurt him . . .

But then he felt pain. Warm and wet, spilling down his belly. And he realized she wasn't simply hitting him. Her knife was just too sharp for him to feel.

Both hands were at her throat now. Blind eyes open wide as the agony started creeping in. They stumbled, falling back into the bath. As they crashed into the water, he felt her blade slip into his back half a dozen times, the pair of them sinking below the surface as he strangled for all he was worth. He'd killed a dozen men this way in his time. Close enough to hear the death rattle in their lungs, smell the stink as their bladder loosed when they died.

But the pain . . .

Rolling and tumbling beneath the water. Hard to keep his grip. Pulse rushing in his ears. Spilling from the dozen wounds in his chest, his back, his side. Arms like iron.

She's killing me.

The thought made the rage flare bright. Denial and fury. Kicking and stabbing, flailing and cursing. They surfaced, bright light in his blind eyes, gasping. The pair crashed against the edge of the sunken bath, her spine cruelly bent, his face twisted. She was still flailing at him, cursing, spitting. Stabbing his forearms, slicing his cheek, lost in her own frenzy.

He couldn't feel his hands. Was he still holding her?

It didn't hurt so much anymore. Dull impacts. Chest. Chest. Neck. Chest.

"Bastard!" she was screaming.

Is

"You!"

this

"Rotten!"

how

"Fucking!"

it

"Bastard!"

ends?

He felt his knees give out. His grip slithered away from her neck. The water was warm, but he was so cold. Hard to breathe. Hard to think. Slipping deeper, he closed his eyes and tilted his head back beneath the surface, allowing himself to float for a handful of minutes.

Would he meet her now? Gather him to her breast and kiss his brow with black lips?

Had he ever believed? Or had he just enjoyed it too much?

Mother, I . . .

Solis closed his eyes to sound of the choir.

And then he sank beneath the—"

"Enough," Scaeva said.

Drusilla looked up from the pages, one eyebrow quirked.

"Is it?" she asked.

The imperator of Itreya scowled slightly, his dark eyes on the Lady of Blades. The dozen personal guardsmen he'd brought with him were arrayed about their master, staring at the book in Drusilla's hands like it were a viper set to strike. Scaeva himself made a better show of appearing unimpressed, resplendent in his purple toga and wreath of beaten gold. But even he regarded the chronicle she'd been reading aloud from with suspicious wonder. He steepled his fingers at his lips, scowling.

"I believe you have made your point, good lady."

Flames crackled in the chamber's hearth, and Mouser shifted uncomfortably in his chair. Spiderkiller's face was blanched, even Solis looked disconcerted at the foretelling of his own murder at Mia's hands. Drusilla leaned back in her seat, closed the third Nevernight Chronicle with a gentle thump. Her fingertips traced the cat embossed in the black leather, her voice soft as silk.

"She must be stopped, Imperator," the Lady of Blades said. "I know she is your daughter. I know she has your son. But if all this tome says is true, once inside the Mountain, Mia Corvere will wield a power none of us can match."

"Mia is not the only darkin in this tale," Scaeva replied.

"O, well do I know it," Drusilla replied, patting the tome. "The results of your clash are quite spectacular, if somewhat overwritten. But they end badly for you, I'm afraid. Would you like me to read it? I have it bookmar—"

"Thank you, no," the imperator replied, glowering.

"I do not understand," Mouser said. "The first page of the first chronicle *told* us she dies."

"And indeed she does," Drusilla said, drumming her fingers on the third tome's cover. "After a long and happy life, in her bed, surrounded by her loved ones."

"I will be damned," Solis growled, "before I allow that bitch a happy ending."

"This chronicle is witchery," Aalea said, eyes on the book.

"No," Drusilla said, meeting the eyes of her Ministry. "This chronicle is a future. But it is a future we can *change*. Already we change it, here and now, by speaking as we do. These pages are not carved in stone. This ink can be washed away. And we have young Mia at disadvantage."

"O, aye?" Mouser asked.

"Aye," Drusilla said. "We know exactly how she intends to enter the Mountain. And when. And fool that she is, we know she's bringing the imperator's son with her."

All eyes turned to Scaeva.

"You should depart back for Godsgrave, Imperator," Drusilla said. "Leave your errant daughter to us. Safer for all concerned."

"And that concern is touching, Lady," Scaeva replied. "So I trust you'll forgive my honesty. But your efforts in subduing my daughter thus far have been less than impressive. And if she is bringing my son to your slaughter, I will remain to ensure that Lucius is not harmed. In *any* way."

"You may trust us on that, Imperator. But as for your daughter?"

The Lady of Blades leaned forward in her chair, staring hard.

"I know you wished her captured, Julius. I know you wished to make her your weapon, to set we gold-grubbing whores of the Red Church aside." Scaeva glanced up at that, and Drusilla met his stare, smiling. "But surely this tome demonstrates Mia is simply too dangerous to be allowed to live. The Red Church will continue to serve your imperium, just as we have always done. We will be paid for our services, just as we have always been. And Mia Corvere will die."

Scaeva stroked his chin, eyes on the chronicle. The Lady of Blades could see the wheels at work behind his stare. The plans within plans, unraveling and restitching.

But finally, as she knew he would, the imperator nodded.

"Mia Corvere will die."

A soft knock disturbed the silence of his bedchamber.

Mercurio's natural scowl deepened, and he dragged on his cigarillo, looking at the offending door in annoyance. Pulling his wire-rimmed spectacles off his nose, he set his book aside with a curse. He'd have been miffed to be interrupted reading at the best of times, but he was only two chapters from the end of *On Bended Knee*. The chronicler had been right—the politics were silly, but the smut really *was* top-shelf—and with only twenty-two pages left, he was surprisingly invested in discovering whether Contessa Sofia's evil twin really was going to marry Archduke Giorgio and—

Knock, knock.

"Fucksakes, what?" the old man growled.

He heard the key turning in the lock, and the door swung open silently. Mercurio fully expected to see one of his damned Hands poke their heads around the frame. He'd been confined to his bedchamber since the discovery of the third chronicle, and the poor sods watching him were bored shitless now. The Dweymeri lad even asked if Mercurio wanted a cup of tea yesterturn. But instead of a dispirited lackey of the Red Church, the old man found himself looking at the Lady of Blades herself.

"Since when do you knock?" he growled.

"Since I was informed about your current reading material," the old woman replied. "I'd rather not stumble into a visit from Dona Palmer and her five daughters, if it's all the same to you."

"You always were a prude, 'Silla."

"You always were a wanker, Mercurio."

The old man smiled despite himself. "Why are you here?"

Drusilla stepped inside, closed the door behind her. He could tell from her expression that despite her opening salvo, she hadn't come to jest. She sat down on his bed and he turned his chair to face her, elbows on his knees.

"What is it, 'Silla?"

"Mia is dead."

The old man felt a tightness across his chest, like iron bands constricting. His left arm ached, fingertips tingling as he felt the room begin to spin.

"What?" he managed to sputter.

Drusilla looked at him with clear concern. ". . . Are you well?"

"Of course I'm not fucking well!" he snapped. "She's *dead*?"

"Black Mother, I was speaking figuratively. The deed isn't done yet."

"Maw's fucking teeth." Mercurio massaged his chest, wincing with pain. Relief flooded over him like spring rain. "You near gave me a fucking heart attack!"

". . . Do you wish to see the apothecary?"

"No, I don't wish to see the fucking apothecary, you crusty bitch!" he snapped. "I want to know what the 'byss you're babbling about!"

"Scaeva has given approval for Mia's execution," Drusilla said. "We know exactly when and how she will enter the Mountain. Her fate is sealed, the matter is certain. I know how much you care for her, and I wished you to hear it from me first."

"You wished to fucking *gloat,* is what you mean," Mercurio snarled.

"If you believe I take pleasure in this—"

"Why the 'byss else would you have come in here?" The old man blinked hard, rubbing at the pain in his arm, his body now in a cold sweat. "Of *course* you take pleasure in it, 'Silla! You always have! You always will!"

"Know me so well, do you?"

"O, I know you, all right," Mercurio snarled, wincing as he curled the fingers on his left hand. "Better than any man b-before or since. I saw you at your best and I watched you at your worst. Why the fuck else do you think I ended it between us?"

The old woman scoffed, blue eyes glittering. "I didn't care forty years ago, Mercurio. I care even less now."

"Some of us joined this place because we believed. And some of us because it was all we had. But you?" Mercurio winced again, pawing at his shoulder. "You joined because you *liked* it. You l-like hurting things, 'Silla. You w-were always a heartless . . ."

Mercurio blinked, rising to his feet.

". . . h-heartless . . ."

The old man gasped, clutching at his chest. He staggered back against the wall, his book tumbling to the floor, a pitcher of wine knocked loose and shattering on the stone. His face twisted, he gasped again, lips moving as if he were unable to speak.

Drusilla rose to standing, eyes widening.

". . . Mercurio?"

The old man fell to his knees. A gargle of nonsense spilling over his lips, both hands pressed to his heart and twisting at the fabric of his robes. The Lady of Blades slammed her fist against the door, crying out. The Hands burst into the room as the old man fell facedown on the stone, the stink of wine and piss in his nostrils.

"Get him to the apothecarium!" Drusilla snapped.

Mercurio felt a strong grip upon his waist, the Dweymeri Hand picking him up and slinging him over one broad shoulder. He only groaned in response, eyelids fluttering. He felt the rhythmic tread of hurried footsteps, heard Drusilla barking commands above the endless dirge of the Church choir. He couldn't feel the pain anymore, thankfully. A long string of drool spilled from his lips and he groaned more nonsense. He was being carried along dark hallways and down spiraling stairs, head thumping against the Hand's backside. Drusilla was following, shaking her head.

"Stupid old fool."

The old man groaned in reply as the Lady of Blades sighed.

"This is what having a heart gets you . . ."

CHAPTER 31

WAS

Drusilla left Mercurio in the apothecarium.

Despite her better judgment, the Lady of Blades always had a soft spot for the bishop of Godsgrave. She might have lingered longer by his bedside if she were able. But sadly, she had a massacre to oversee, and the tides of time wouldn't be kept waiting by sentimentality. Drusilla had left her old lover sleeping, gray and gaunt, his thin chest rising and falling swift as a wounded bird's. She'd growled instruction that he was to be given the best of care, waving one of the chief apothecary's bonesaws in his face to impress upon him the gravity of her request. And with a cold kiss to Mercurio's damp brow, Drusilla set out to murder the girl he loved like a daughter.

She'd gathered her flock about her, all in black. Gone over proceedings one last time for safe measure. The plan was set, the path was clear. All they needed now was for the guests to arrive, and the red, red gala could get under way.

The murderers waited now in the gloom, wreathed in the stink of hay and camels. The Red Church stables lay below them in all their fetid glory. Aside from the exterior doors leading from the Mountain's flank out to the Ashkahi wastes, there were two other exits from the chamber—double doors, high up on the east and west walls. These doors led farther into the Mountain and were reached by twin sets of polished steps with heavy granite railings. Winding along the chamber's outer wall, these stairs eventually met in a single broad descent, leading down to the animal pens and storage rooms below. Drusilla stood swathed in shadow near the upper western doorway. Long knives hidden in her sleeves. Blue eyes gleaming in the dark as she pushed all thought of Mercurio from her mind.

Scaeva lurked behind her, bodyguards arrayed about him, blades drawn and ready. In his typical fashion, the imperator stood close to the exit—ready to flee back into the safety of the Mountain if things somehow went badly, but still close enough to watch the massacre unfold. Scaeva's shadow serpent was coiled about its master's shoulders, watching with its not-eyes.

Drusilla idly wondered how deep in his dark gifts the imperator stood. How dangerous he'd truly be in a place like the Mountain, where the sunslight never shone. In all the years she'd had her spies watching him, Scaeva had never once made a display of his shadow power—the lady had no idea what his true capabilities were. If not for his passenger, Drusilla would hardly believe him to be darkin at all. Those unknowns made him dangerous. Almost as dangerous as his daughter had become.

The difference being, of course, Drusilla didn't get *paid* by his daughter.

The Lady of Blades disliked the imperator, truth told. She respected his intelligence. Admired his ruthlessness. But the man was too ambitious for his own good. Too power-hungry. Too fond of the sound of his own voice. Far, far too vain. And of course, Scaeva had power over Drusilla, which made her dislike him all the more.

Coin.

It was astounding, how insidious its silvered grip was. How Drusilla's love of wealth had started with her love of familia. Whoever said money was the root of all evil had never seen the bliss in her grandsons' eyes the turn she bought them their first ponies, or heard her daughter weep with joy when Drusilla paid the full sum of her wedding without a thought.

Whoever said money couldn't buy happiness obviously never had any.

She'd amassed a fortune in the years she'd served the Ministry. Most of it from Scaeva's own coffers. But the real evil of wealth lay in the truth that too much was never really enough. No matter the sum you acquired, it seemed you always needed more. In her mind, Drusilla still needed Scaeva. When her familia's future was assured, when their wealth was absolutely unassailable, then perhaps she could reassess her relationship with the young imperator. But for now . . .

"Remember, Drusilla," Scaeva murmured behind her. "If one hair upon Lucius's head comes to harm, your grandsons shall pay the forfeit of the cost."

"We know a thing or two about killing, Julius," Drusilla replied, keeping the cold ire from her voice. "Never fear."

The viper at Scaeva's feet hissed almost too soft to hear.

". . . He never does . . ."

Over on the eastern stairwell, Drusilla could see Mouser, surrounded by two dozen of her most skilled Hands, all armed with heavy crossbows. The Shahiid of Pockets' old eyes were narrowed as he watched the outer entrance below, his hand on the hilt of his blacksteel sword.

Spiderkiller was poised at the top of the central stairwell, and a half-dozen Church Blades stood at her side. The Corvere girl was simply too dangerous to underestimate anymore, and Drusilla had called in their best, their deadliest, for her ending—Donatella of Liis, Haarold and Brynhildr from the Carrion Hall chapel, even Acteon the Black had been summoned from Godsgrave. Solis waited among their number also, twin swords in hand, blind eyes upturned, head tilted. It was a dangerous gambit, to bring the best of her remaining killers together like this. But after Tenhands's failure outside Galante, Drusilla could take no more chances. Mia was delivering herself right to the mouth of the wolves' den, after all.

It wouldn't do to have puppies waiting for her.

Only Aalea seemed to have misgivings. Lingering by Drusilla's side, the woman's dark eyes were wide, a dagger gleaming in her hand.

"Is Mercurio well? Did the apothecary sa—"

"Gird yourself, Shahiid," Drusilla whispered. "He is not your concern."

Aalea met her stare, her lips pressed thin. "He showed me kindness when I was but an acolyte in Godsgrave, Lady. If I m—"

"Silence," Solis hissed. "They come."

Drusilla's belly filled with whispering butterflies. Peering down to the stables, she heard the sound of stone. Felt the greasy tang of arkemical magik in the air. She heard Spiderkiller muttering beneath her breath, Scaeva's guards exhaling in wonder as the outer wall cracked open. A faint rush of wind kissed Drusilla's face, a shower of fine dust and pebbles fell from above as the Mountain's flank slowly split apart. About the stable, on the stairwells, dozens upon dozens of Hands and Blades stood poised, motionless, swathed in darkness. The ghostly choir was momentarily drowned out as the great doors opened wide, mekwerk rumbling and hissing.

Corvere's wagon train stood outside. The familiar sight of the Red Church stables awaited them—a broad straw-lined oblong, set on all sides with pens for sleek horses and spitting camels, wagons and carpenter's tools and bales of feed and great stacks of supply crates. But on the stairwells above, crouched in the shadows around the room, death hovered with bated breath.

It was all happening just as it was meant to.

Drusilla squinted through the garish sunslight. The camels leading Corvere's wagons snorted and spat, trudging inside and dragging their load behind them. She saw a figure in Hand's robes in the driver's seat—that half-dead Dweymeri boy, broad shouldered, head lowered. She could see more figures beneath the train's canvas coverings. Drusilla knew from reading the Nevernight Chronicle that Corvere was riding in the middle wagon with Järnheim, Scaeva's brat alongside them. If not for the presence of the boy, this would have been a far simpler affair.

Still, this wasn't exactly the Lady of Blades' first murder . . .

Drusilla looked to Spiderkiller, eyebrow raised in question. The Shahiid of Truths nodded in reply, cool and assured.

The camels leading the wagon came to a slow halt.

And at a whispered command, the assembled Blades let loose.

White globes. Small and spherical. Dozens, perhaps hundreds, like a snowstorm shimmering in the sunslight as they were flung into the stables below. They popped—*shoof! shoof! shoof!*—into great clouds of roiling white. In a heartbeat, a dense fog of Swoon had filled the lower levels, dragging anyone who breathed it down into slumber. Drusilla heard strangled groans from below, the deep *thumps* of stricken camels hitting the stone. The soft whisper of the cloud as it settled, heavy and thick.

And then she heard nothing at all.

The assembled Blades and Shahiids looked to her. The old woman waited a long and silent moment. Peering down into the pale miasma, she saw no sign of movement, no hint of danger. And finally, the Lady of Blades gave a swift nod.

The Red Church's finest assassins donned leather masks, fixing them tight behind their heads, Spiderkiller assisting with the buckles. The contraptions were designed by the Shahiid of Truths herself; the wearer's eyes were covered by glass panes, and brass nozzles filtered the air they breathed. With their masks in place, the Church Blades stole down into the poison fog. Acteon the Black was as soundless as smoke. Donatella of Liis was as sharp as the swords she carried. Solis waited at the top of the central stairs, swords drawn. Aalea stood beside Drusilla, holding her breath.

Wind was picking up from the valley outside, the Swoon was drifting out the Mountain's flank. Through the slowly thinning veil, Drusilla watched the assassins descend carefully, down the stairs toward the stable floor. She'd wondered if the dead Dweymeri boy might have proved immune to the Swoon's effects, and Mouser and his cadre of Hands had raised their crossbows, burning arrows nocked, ready to unload on the Hearthless lad. But through the lightening mist, the Lady of Blades could see the figure in the wagon driver's seat was slumped and motionless.

"Secure the imperator's son first!" Drusilla called. "End the rest."

"Bring me my boy!" Scaeva demanded.

Acteon the Black waved assent, motioning for the other Blades to fan out around the middle wagon. Solis narrowed his blind eyes, the Hands on the upper levels leaned over their crossbows as Donatella of Liis cut the ties securing the canvas to the wagon bed. Drusilla held her breath, watching the Blade take hold of the cover, and with a sharp tug drag it free.

Drusilla blinked. She could see figures in Hands' robes inside the wagon. But rather than being slumped on the floor, all were still seated. Furthermore, and stranger still, Drusilla could see a large barrel resting in the wagon's belly. It was thick oak, old and heavy and stained by salt. Bold lettering was burned into the wood.

Haarold dragged the hood off one of the sitting figures, cursing as he revealed innards stuffed with straw.

The Lady of Blades squinted at the words on the wooden barrel.

IF FOUND, PLEASE RETURN TO CLOUD CORLEONE.

IF STOLEN, WELL PLAYED, GENTLEFRIEND.

Drusilla's belly dropped into her boots.

. . . Arkemist's salt.

"Get *ba—*"

The explosion tore through the stables like a hurricane of crackling blue flame. The roar was deafening, knocking Drusilla back and staggering Scaeva's guards. The Lady of Blades shielded her eyes against the heat, watching as the wagon, Acteon, Donatella, the finest Blades left in the Red Church, were all incinerated. Solis was thrown against the wall, bleeding and scorched. Spiderkiller fell to her knees with a dark curse. Glowing ashes rose with the smoke, dancing in the air. The boom echoed around the hollow space, leaving the assembled churchmen dazed, blinded, stunned.

"Maw's fucking teeth!" Mouser coughed.

Drusilla heard Scaeva's sharp intake of breath behind. Turning to look at the imperator, she saw his eyes were wide. His shadowviper was coiled about his shoulders, licking the choking smoke with its translucent tongue.

"*. . . She is here . . . ,*" it said.

Drusilla turned back to the stables in time to see the air shiver, a black flickering un-light. A shadow cut in the shape of a wolf coalesced halfway up the eastern stairs, roaring like the winds of the Abyss. As Drusilla watched, dumbfounded, a dark shape flung itself *out* of the passenger, landing in a crouch amidst a gaggle of her staggered Hands and right beside the Shahiid of Pockets. The figure rose to her feet in the ember rain and black smoke, bringing a pale longblade around in a whistling arc.

"Mia . . ."

The girl's blade connected with Mouser's neck, the gravebone slicing clean through flesh, sinew, and bone. The Shahiid's head spun from his shoulders, old eyes open wide in surprise as it tumbled down into the charred stables below. Mia caught up Mouser's blade of Ashkahi blacksteel as it dropped from nerveless fingers, delivering a savage boot to his corpse's chest and sending it over the railings in pursuit of his bonnet. And, one blade in each hand, flickering in and out of the shadows like some awful, bloody hummingbird, she began hacking anyone carrying a crossbow to pieces.

"Black Mother . . . ," Drusilla whispered.

Aalea cursed. A shout came from the Mountain's entrance, and through the rolling smoke, Drusilla saw a handful of figures charge into the stables from the foothills outside. Sodden rags were tied about their mouths and noses to protect them from the thinning Swoon, naked swords in their hands. She recognized them all from the chronicle—the Itreyan Sidonius and the Dweymeri Bladesinger. Beside them ran the Hearthless boy, Tric, and that traitorous bitch Ashlinn Järnheim. That dullard Butcher and the treacherous Naev were in the rear, Scaeva's boy between them.

But over on the eastern stairs, Mia was cutting a swath through Drusilla's

Hands. Clearing her comrades a path into the Mountain's belly. The girl blinked in and out of seeming, like some apparition on a summersdeep eve. A poisoned knife was hurled at her chest and she simply disappeared, the blade plunging into another Hand's belly and sending him tumbling. Mia Stepped between the shadows, reappearing behind the knife thrower and cutting him down. She sliced another's legs out from under him, sending him to the stone in a spray of red, flickering aside as a blade cut the air where she'd stood and taking the swordsman's arms off at the elbows. And all the while she was looking toward Drusilla. Toward the imperator behind her. Her face was spattered with crimson. Her eyes cold and empty. As if all this blood, all this carnage, all this death, were a simple prelude to the murder to come.

Looking into Mia's eyes, Drusilla knew full well who that murder belonged to.

The eastern stairs were now empty of all but corpses, and in a flickering step, the girl was suddenly standing on the steps below Drusilla. Her comrades were rushing up the stairs behind her toward the still-stunned Solis, Sidonius and Bladesinger dashing past him and through the eastern doorway. Mia leveled her blade toward Scaeva's face, gore dripping from its razored edge.

"Father!" she roared.

Looking over her shoulder, Drusilla saw the imperator blanch. His eyes flickered from his dark daughter to his only son, silhouetted against the Mountain's entrance. Mia buried her longblade in another Hand's belly, sent the woman tumbling over the railing in a tangle of entrails. She started stalking up the stairs, flickering aside and cutting down another Hand with barely a glance. Lips pressed thin. Eyes fixed only on Scaeva.

"Corvere!"

The bellow rang through the stables. Down the stairs behind her, the Revered Father picked himself up from where the explosion had felled him. His leathers were smoldering, the wisps of beard that had survived Järnheim's tombstone bomb in Godsgrave had been burned away completely. His blind eyes were alight with rage as he leveled his swords at the deadboy and Järnheim to keep them at bay.

"Corvere!" he roared again. "Face me!"

The girl didn't even deign to glance back. Content to let her comrades cut Solis down, she kept walking up the western stair, black gaze locked with her father's. Her gladiatii were already inside the Mountain, the deadboy and Järnheim fanning out about the Revered Father, readying to cut him down and charge up the eastern stairs after Sidonius and Bladesinger. From there, they could spill out into the Mountain's labyrinthine heart, reach the speaker's chambers by any one of a dozen paths, and cut off their escape at Adonai's door.

The shadows hung about Mia's shoulders like dark wings as she drew closer. Her shadowwolf stalked before her, black fangs bared. Only Drusilla, Aalea, and Spiderkiller stood between the girl and her father now. The Shahiid of Truths drew two curved and poisoned knives from her golden belt. The Lady of Blades reached for the daggers in her sleeves, old fingers closing about the hilts. But Aalea spoke softly, her tongue sharper than any weapon in their arsenal.

"Solis killed Darius, Mia."

The girl's black eyes flickered from her father to the Shahiid of Masks. Her steps faltered, her jaw tensed. Drusilla's belly thrilled as she saw Aalea's words cut into Corvere's heart. The girl finally glanced back toward Solis, outnumbered by her fellows on the stair behind.

"*He* was the one who captured the Kingmaker and Antonius in their encampment," Aalea whispered. "He was the one who handed them over to dance on the hangman's rope for the mob's amusement. It was *Solis,* Mia."

Mia's eyes narrowed. Solis lashed out at Tric and Ashlinn, keeping the pair at bay. Scaeva was slowly retreating up the stairs, surrounded by his men. The imperator was almost close enough for Corvere to touch. Only a few dozen men stood between her and her prize. But there was a reason Aalea had been named Shahiid of Masks in the Red Church, and it hadn't been her skill in the boudoir. Even here, with Corvere's prey in sight, Aalea knew the precise words to manipulate her, beguile her, make her falter. If only for a moment.

If only for a breath.

"Face me, you cowardly little bitch!" Solis roared.

"He killed the man you called Father, Mia," Aalea whispered.

The girl's grip tightened on her blade. Her quarry was only a heartbeat away. But still, Drusilla could see that infamous temper, the rage that had sustained this girl beyond all limits of endurance, beyond all who stood in her way. Watching as that spark burst into ravenous flame inside her chest.

With Cassius's wolf riding her shadow, she had no fear of failure, after all.

She had no fear at all.

What matter, a few moments more?

Mia glanced to Drusilla, an unspoken promise in her eyes. And with a snarl, she turned toward the waiting Revered Father.

"Whoreson," she spat.

"Mia, don't . . ." Järnheim raised her blade in Solis's face. "Let me."

"LET *ME,*" Tric said.

"No." Corvere descended, eyes on the Shahiid. "This bastard's mine."

Drusilla took one step backward. Then another. She knew Solis might cut the girl down. He was a grandmaster, after all. The Lady of Blades could hear the Church bells ringing—an alarm calling all their remaining Hands and acolytes down to battle. But Mouser was already dead, along with the best of the Mountain's remaining assassins. Corvere had just slaughtered a few dozen of the faithful without a scratch. And truth told, though Drusilla was the most accomplished killer in the Red Church, her best turns of murder were behind her.

She heard retreating footsteps. Turning, she saw Scaeva's guard fleeing through the doorway and into the Mountain—true to form, the imperator had abandoned his only son as soon as his own skin was at risk. And here where the suns never shone, the Lady of Blades was damned if she'd be left behind to face his murderous daughter alone.

And so, just like Scaeva, Drusilla turned and ran.

CHAPTER 32

IS

The ash tasted like a benediction.

Mia stood on the stairs, listening to Drusilla's fleeing footsteps, the Church bells pealing their alarm. She could smell charred meat, blood and guts and shit, all of it a sweet perfume. Her eyes burned in the rising smoke and her skin was wet and sticky red and Scaeva was already beating feet back into the Mountain. Any normal girl might have been afraid he'd make good his escape in that moment. Any normal girl might have been afraid all she'd worked for might come to nothing. But not this girl.

What is the difference between courage and stupidity?

Who would you be, how would you act, gentlefriend, if you were *truly* unafraid?

Mia looked to Ashlinn and Tric, dark eyes alight.

"Go help Sid and 'Singer," she commanded them. "Cleave to the plan. Get to the speaker's chambers and cut off their escape."

Ash glanced at Solis. "Mia, are—"

"There's no time to argue, just go!"

The pair glanced at each other, bitter opposites in all but their shared love for her. Mia could see the fear in their eyes—the fear she simply couldn't share with Eclipse in her shadow. But finally they obeyed, Ash barreling up the stairwell with Tric close on her heels, following Sid and Bladesinger toward the speaker's chambers. Naev was extinguishing the fires that had started after the explosion. Butcher was standing guard over her brother.

But Mia had eyes only for the Revered Father.

Her swords were heavy in her hands, red with gore. She took two steps down toward him, his blind eyes fixed on the ceiling. He was charred, his skin pinked by her blast. But his blades were steady in his grip. His muscles gleamed, his shoulders broad as bridges, his biceps as big as her head. His lips curled with disdain as he spoke.

"So you *do* have the courage to face me. Color me astounded."

Mia glanced toward her brother, back up the stairs.

"I could kill you where you stand, Solis," she said simply. "I could bid the shadows rip you limb from limb. I could fix it so our swords never even touched."

Mia stepped closer and raised one dripping blade.

"But I *want* them to touch. Because when first we fought, I was only a novice. And when we faced each other in Godsgrave, I wasn't my best. But now? No shadows. No tricks. Blade to blade. Because you helped murder a man I loved like a father. And I'm going to kill you for that, you sonofabitch."

Whatever the Shahiid was about to say was cut off as Mia lunged. Her blade was pale quicksilver, her form blinding. The man stepped aside and struck back, blade whistling past Mia's throat. She twisted, long black hair streaming behind her, stabbing at his belly. Eclipse swirled around them, between them, snarling and growling. And there, on the bloodied steps of the Red Church, their battle joined in truth.

Most fights to the death end within moments, gentlefriends. It's a little-known fact—particularly among those of you fond of reading about sword duels, rather than actually dueling with swords. But in truth, it only takes a single mistake to spell your end when someone swings a large and sharpened bit of metal at you.

Mia knew Solis had never respected her as an acolyte, as a Blade, as an opponent. With Eclipse beside her, she was fearless. Lithe and muscled, hard as steel, Mia Corvere was every bit the champion who'd won the *Venatus*

Magni. But Solis was taller than her. His reach was longer and his experience deeper, and with his Belt of Eyes, he could see her strikes coming through that swirling rain of embers and smoke. When Mia was still a child, he was murdering hundreds with his bare hands to escape the Philosopher's Stone. He'd served for years as the greatest swordsman in the Red Church congregation. In every conceivable fashion, he thought himself her better.

"Worthless slip," he growled, blocking her strike.

He swung hard, almost taking Mia's head off her shoulders.

"Pathetic child," he spat, forcing her away.

Mia danced backward, nearly slipping on the bloody floor. She turned aside his blade, lashed out with her own. Dodge. Strike. Parry. Lunge. Her pulse was soon thumping, sweat burning her eyes. Solis's twin blades cut the air in hypnotic patterns, whistling as they came. A perfect lunge from the Shahiid almost split her rib cage in two. A second strike nearly knocked her longblade from her hand.

"Mia!" Jonnen called from below, stepping forward in fear.

". . . BEWARE, MIA . . . ," Eclipse growled at her feet.

Mia gasped for breath as Solis's lips curled in a smile.

"You disappoint me, girl," he said.

As she parried another of his punishing blows, Mia began to realize just how strong her foe truly was. Just how little her rage and her speed counted for in a match like this. The Shahiid's arms were as thick as her thighs. His hands like dinner plates. The man was made of muscle, half again her height, fully twice her weight; a single blow from him, a single mistake, would be enough to end her.

And so she had to end him first.

Mia slipped aside another of Solis's strikes, jumped up, and kicked off the stair's railing. Leaping into the air, she raised her blade in an overhead swing, throwing all her strength and fury behind it. It was an impressive move. A move that might make an audience gasp in wonder. But it was also a novice's move. A flashy and garish arena move. A move that someone in a hurry might try, in the hopes of ending a bout against a superior opponent. And Solis knew it. Because in the end, his opponent was just a worthless slip. A pathetic child. A *girl*. And he was simply stronger than her.

Fortunately, the same couldn't be said of his blades.

Solis's swords were Liisian steel, you see. The metal had been folded a hundred times, sharpened to an edge keen enough to cut the sunslight. But Mia's blade had once belonged to Darius Corvere, the man Solis helped kill. Its hilt had been crafted like a crow in flight, the sigil of the familia Solis had helped destroy. And it was made of gravebone, gentlefriend. Sharper than obsidian. Stronger than steel.

And underestimating the blade, and the one wielding it, was Solis's mistake.

The Shahiid's lips curled. He raised one sword to ward off Mia's blow, drew back his second, ready to split her guts. Their weapons met with a shuddering *rinnnng*. Edge to edge. Razored gravebone against folded Liisian steel. And the gravebone won.

Mia's sword cleaved through Solis's, sparks flying as his blade was sheared in two. Her blow found its mark, cutting into the big man's shoulder, the chest beyond, blood spraying. Solis cried out, his strike gone wide as he staggered.

"Worthless slip," Mia growled.

Dragging her blade down through his ribs, she tore it free in a slick of bright red gore.

"Pathetic child," she spat.

Spinning on the spot and opening up his belly.

"Girl," she smiled.

Solis's insides spilled out. His blind eyes open wide.

"But I'm still the one who beat you," Mia said.

She kicked him in the chest, sent him flying backward, skidding through his blood to slam against the wall. Holding in his ruptured guts, Solis tried to rise. He tried to speak. He tried to breathe. But in the end, he failed at all of it. And with a red gurgle, the Revered Father crumpled to the floor.

"Fuck yes!" Butcher bellowed from below, arms in the air. "CROWWW!"

Mia sank down into a crouch on the blood-slicked stone, one hand out to steady herself. She swallowed hard, trying to catch her breath as she clawed her hair from her eyes. Looking to the gladiatii, to Naev, she managed a ragged grin.

"Is she well?" Naev called.

"Aye," Mia managed. "But I'm not half done, yet. Look after him for me, neh?"

Naev looked to Jonnen and nodded. "With our lives."

"Never fear, little Crow," Butcher said.

"Eclipse, I want you to stay here, too," Mia gasped. "Guard my brother."

". . . AS IT PLEASE YOU . . . ," came a low growl beneath her.

The daemon parted from her shadow, coalescing on the blood-soaked stairs before her eyes. Mia looked her up and down, still struggling for breath.

". . . You're not going to warn me that I'll need you when I face him?"

The shadowwolf looked at Mia with her not-eyes, ears twitching.

"... *YOU WILL NOT NEED ME. YOU HAVE THE HEART OF A LION* ..."

"I remember you telling me that." Mia managed a tired grin. "But I have the heart of a crow, Eclipse. Black and shriveled, remember?"

The daemon stepped close, pressed her muzzle to Mia's cheeks.

"... *YOU WILL KNOW THE LIE OF THAT BEFORE THE END* ..."

The shadowwolf's fur was a whisper against her skin. Mia could almost feel it, velvet soft and cool as night. Making her shiver, even as she smiled.

"... *GO FIND YOUR FATHER, MIA* ..."

The girl nodded. And with a wince, she dragged herself to her feet.

"Mia?" her brother said, his voice faltering.

But she was already gone.

Drusilla ran.

Aalea hurried along beside her, supporting her lady with one arm. Spiderkiller followed slower, clearly torn between her vengeance against Corvere and saving her own skin. But Drusilla knew Corvere's companions would be making their way deeper into the Mountain even now, that treacherous bitch Järnheim leading them on—if they reached Adonai before Drusilla did, her only hope of escape would be lost. And so the Lady of Blades found herself running through the winding dark, as best her old legs could carry her.

"Where do we go?" Aalea asked beside her, breathless.

"The speaker," the lady replied.

"We run?" Spiderkiller demanded.

"We *live,*" Drusilla spat.

Drusilla could hear the imperator's guards ahead of them, Scaeva among them, moving swift on the winding stairs. Loyal Hands rushed past the lady and Shahiids, back down toward the stables, armed with bows and blades. Fresh-faced acolytes followed—the Mountain's latest crop of recruits and second line of defense—yelling at the Lady of Blades to run, *run*.

The Church choir seemed louder somehow, pressed with a faint urgency. Drusilla was gasping, unused to running, mouth dry as old bones.

How did it come to this?

She'd lost sight of Scaeva ahead of them now, but she knew well enough that the imperator would be headed to Adonai's chambers, too. Seeking escape through the only means now left to him, and to leave this abattoir behind him.

But none of this makes sense.

Drusilla had read the Nevernight Chronicle end to end. She'd left nothing to chance. Corvere and her comrades should've been caught entirely unaware—nowhere did the tome mention the girl carried a barrel load of arkemist's salt in her wagon, or suspected any kind of trap.

Since Drusilla had discovered their part in the plot, Adonai and Marielle were in no shape to warn Mia. Mercurio and Aelius had no means to even *speak* to her. How in Mother's name had Corvere known Drusilla planned to ambush her? If the chronicle were truly the story of her life, if the third book was truly the story of her death . . .

Drusilla could hear the clash of steel in the distance now—Corvere's gladiatii locked in a deadly dance with the Mountain's defenders. She could hear Järnheim yelling. Sidonius barking orders. The old woman's heart was thumping against her ribs. Her breath burning in her chest. Aalea was supporting her weight, long dark hair stuck to the sweat on her skin. Spiderkiller was falling farther and farther behind. Drusilla had lost sight of Scaeva's men entirely. Her knees were aching. Her old bones creaking with every step.

She was too old for this, she realized. Too tired. All her years in service to the Mother had only led her here. Leader of a Church that was coming to pieces all about her. Mistress of a Ministry torn asunder. All the plotting, all the killing, all the coin. And this was where it ended? Cut down by a monster of her own making?

They reached the Hall of Eulogies. Niah's statue towering above them. Dead names carved on the floor beneath them. Unmarked tombs all around. The ring of steel and cries of pain were growing ever closer. Drusilla realized Spiderkiller had abandoned them somewhere back there in the dark. That she and Aalea were now alone.

Almost.

"Thought you might come this way."

Drusilla dragged Aalea to a breathless halt. Mercurio stood before them in his dark robes, barring their exit from the hall. His blue eyes were soft with pity. In his right hand, he clutched an apothecary's bonesaw, dipped red with blood.

"You always were a creature of habit, 'Silla."

"You . . . ," Drusilla breathed.

"Me," the old man replied.

"But your heart . . ."

Mercurio smiled sadly, tapping his bony chest. "I'm a good liar. Not quite as good as you, I'm afraid. But then, I doubt anyone is."

"*You* did this," Drusilla realized.

But Mercurio slowly shook his head.

"I can't take much credit. It was mostly Aelius, truth told. The third chronicle was his idea. He only told me his intentions after he'd written it."

Drusilla's heart sank in her withered breast.

Aelius drew long and deep on his cigarillo, embers sparking in his eyes, his fingers stained with ink.

"Don't fuck with librarians, young lady. We know the power of words."

His fingers stained with *ink* . . .

"Things don't get found in this place unless they're supposed to be."

O, Goddess . . .

O, Mother, how could she have been so blind?

It all happened just as it was meant to.

As *he* meant it to.

That treacherous old son of a whore . . .

"Let us pass, Mercurio," the Lady of Blades hissed.

"You know I can't do that, 'Silla."

Drusilla drew one of the poisoned blades from her sleeve.

"Then you die where you stand."

The bishop of Godsgrave held his ground. He stared at Drusilla, that bloody bonesaw in his hand, a strange sadness in his eyes as he glanced over her shoulder.

"It's not me you need to be worried about."

The Lady of Blades grit her teeth, heart hammering quick. She thought of her daughter, her son, her grandchildren. Blue eyes wide with fear.

"Please," she whispered.

Mercurio only shook his head. "I'm sorry, love."

Behind her, she heard Ashlinn Järnheim and that dead Dweymeri boy step into the hall. Behind them came Corvere's gladiatii—Sidonius carrying flaming sunsteel, a breathless Bladesinger behind him. The quartet were spattered in crimson, blades dripping with the blood of the Church's faithful. All of it, finally and completely undone.

The old man glanced up to the Goddess above them and sighed.

"I'm not sure what she'll do to you, 'Silla," he said. "I'm not sure she's got much left in her anymore. But if I were you, I'd be putting down that poisoned pig-sticker and preparing to throw myself on Mia's mercy right about now."

Drusilla looked to Aalea. To Järnheim and the other bloodied swords at her back. To the old man before her and the Goddess above her and the Church falling apart all around her. The choir sang its ghostly hymn up in the stained-glass dark.

The old woman heaved a sigh.

"Well played, love," she said.

And bending slow, she placed her blade upon the floor.

"Don't be afraid, lad. Old Butcher will protect you."

Jonnen sat on the stable steps, chin on his knees and ashes on his skin. Butcher stood above him, eyes on the western doorway. Naev stood on the eastern stair, sword in her hands. The steps were smeared with blood and scattered with bodies. Smoke rose from the charred bales of feed, the roasted camel corpses. Save for the ghostly choir, all in the stable was smoke and silence.

The boy could hear the sounds of battle inside the Mountain, but they were fading now. The Church's defenders had fallen for Mia's ploy and been routed utterly. He knew somewhere up above, his sister was now stalking the darkness like a bloodhound. Cutting down all in her way in pursuit of their father.

"The battle slows," Naev called from up the stair. "Victory is at hand."

"Theirs or ours?" Butcher asked.

Naev considered that for a moment, her head tilted. Her smile was hidden behind her veil, but the boy could still hear it in her voice.

"Ours," she said.

Eclipse rode once more in Jonnen's shadow, and thus, the boy couldn't exactly be *afraid*. But still, his chest ached at the thought of what might be happening in the Mountain's belly. In truth, despite all her prowess, he didn't quite believe Mia would manage it. Their father had overcome every obstacle. Every foe. He stood triumphant in a game where to lose was to die, and all who'd opposed him already lay rotting in their tombs. In Jonnen's eyes, Julius Scaeva had ever seemed immortal.

He'd been a hard man, no doubt. Never cruel, no. But heavy as iron. Merciless as the sea. Slow with praise, swift with rebuke, fashioning his boy into a man who might one turn rule an empire. Because always, his father had made it plain—despite his parentage, the throne would be something Jonnen must *earn*.

The boy had studied hard. Seeking ever to impress. His mother's affections were always unwavering, but it was desire for his father's praise that drove Jonnen onward. Seeking only to make the man proud. Seeing in Julius Scaeva, People's Senator, consul, imperator, the man he one turn wished to become.

Until he'd met Mia.

A sister he never knew. Had never even been *told* about. At first, he'd thought her a liar. A snake and a thief. But Julius Scaeva hadn't raised a fool, and all the wishful thinking in the world couldn't hide the truth of what his sister had told him. The dark within them sang to each other. Their bond in the shadows was impossible to deny. They were kin, no doubt. And she, his father's daughter.

In recent turns, he'd even begun to think of himself not as Lucius, but Jonnen. But he missed his familia. He felt lost and alone. Eclipse made it easier, but it wasn't *easy*. He felt very small in a world that had suddenly become very big indeed.

"What was your son's name, Butcher?" he heard himself ask.

The big man looked down at him, a soft scowl on his battered face. "Eh?"

"You told Mia you had a son once," Jonnen said. "What was his name?"

The former gladiatii turned his eyes back up the stairwell. Tightening his grip on his sword. Jaw clenched. The boy heard a whisper in his shadow.

"*. . . JONNEN, BUTCHER MAY NOT WISH TO SPEAK OF SUCH THINGS . . .*"

The boy pressed his lips together. The Liisian was a thug, an ill-mannered lout, a pig. But he had a golden heart, and he'd been ever kind. Despite it all, Jonnen realized he didn't like the thought of hurting the man's feelings.

"I am sorry, Butcher," he said softly.

"Iacomo," the man murmured. "His name was Iacomo. Why do you ask?"

"Did . . ." Jonnen licked his lips, looking for the words. "Did you ever lie to him?"

"Sometimes," the man sighed.

"Why would you *do* that?"

Butcher ran his hand over his black cockscomb of hair. The sounds of battle upstairs were almost silenced now. It took a while for him to reply.

"Being a parent is no easy thing," he finally said. "We need to teach our children the truths of the world so they can survive it. But some truths change you in a way that can't be undone. And no parent really wants their child to change."

"So you lie to us?"

"Sometimes." Butcher shrugged. "We think if we try hard enough, we can somehow keep you the way you start out. Pure and perfect. Forever."

"So you lie to yourselves, too."

The big Liisian smiled, knelt beside the boy. Reaching out with one sword-callused hand, he ruffled the boy's hair affectionately.

"You remind me of my Iacomo," he grinned. "You're a clever little shit."

"If I were clever, I'd not be in this stew. I feel useless. Helpless."

Naev watched silently from above as the Liisian drew a dagger from his waist, handed it to the boy hilt-first. Jonnen took it, felt the weight of it, watched the sunslight dance on its edge. Eclipse coalesced beside him, watching with her not-eyes as the boy turned the blade this way and that.

"Feel helpless now?" Butcher asked.

"A little less," Jonnen replied. "But I'm not strong like you."

"Don't be afraid, lad. The blood you have in your veins?"

Butcher chuckled and shook his head.

"You're strong enough for both of us."

Mia flitted along darkened halls, shadows at her back.

She'd reached the Hall of Eulogies and found Mercurio standing in the doorway, bloody bonesaw in his grip. Drusilla and Aalea were in hand; the Lady of Blades standing with shoulders slumped, the Shahiid of Masks' dark eyes wide with fear. 'Singer and Sidonius were watching the pair, one crossed word away from murder. Mia met her mentor's eyes for the briefest moment, saw him smile. But she had no time for talk.

Instead, she ran on.

She reached the stairs leading down toward Adonai's chambers and Scaeva's escape. Tric and Ashlinn were both already dashing downward, Ash a little out in front. But skipping between the shadows, Mia was moving faster still. She could hear her father's guards ahead now, heavy boots ringing on the stone steps below, panic in their voices as they urged each other on. With a smack to Ash's leather-clad backside as she passed, Mia Stepped past Tric and her both

down

the winding

stair before them and

deeper into

the dark

shadows at her back

and in her hair

the black giving her wings

flying faster than

Scaeva's guards could run

reaching the slowest of them and cutting him down in an instant, the dark seizing hold of the one beside him and ripping him asunder. Looking ahead, she caught a glimpse of a purple toga among them, her heart racing quicker. The rest of the guards turned, ten remaining, blades flashing, eyes bright.

She Stepped between them, cutting through them, shadow black and silver quick. But even as she danced, her gravebone blade writing red poems in the air, she realized

She realized . . .

Something's wrong.

She couldn't feel him. The familiar sickness. That ageless hunger. The presence of another darkin crawling on her skin. Her heart sinking, she saw the purple toga she'd glimpsed had simply been slung around one of his guard's shoulders—another deception from a master of it, easy enough to believe in this gloom. Mia wondered for a moment if Scaeva might be cowering somewhere in the shadows. But even if he were hidden beneath a mantle of darkness nearby, still she'd *feel* it, sure as she could feel the fear creeping slow into her belly.

Goddess, he's not HERE.

Desperation budding in her chest, rage that she'd been duped, peeling her lips back from her teeth. She snarled and stabbed, swayed and Stepped, cutting his men into nothing, slicking the floors and walls. Standing at the end, chest heaving, wisps of ink-black hair stuck to her skin, sword dripping in her hand. Searching the dark with narrowed, burning eyes.

She Stepped on, flickering down the twisting hallway in the pulsing warmth until finally she arrived at Adonai's chambers. Lunging through the doorway, she saw the speaker knelt at the head of his blood pool, thick chains of black iron wrapped about his wrists and ankles. Crimson runes gleamed on the walls, the light was low and bloodstained. Adonai's eyes were closed and he was breathing slow, but as she entered, he looked up, pink irises on hers.

"Hello, little darkin."

"Scaeva?" she gasped.

The speaker frowned in confusion. Then slowly shook his head.

Shit.

Could he have been hiding out in the gloom while his guards led her on this merry chase? Could he know some trick of the dark? Could he have already escaped?

Could he have doubled back?

O, Goddess . . .

Mia looked back down the corridor she'd come by.

Dread certainty turning her belly to ice.

"Jonnen."

Jonnen's brow creased as his stomach rolled.

He looked up the stairs. First to the western door, past the looming form of Butcher. Then to the eastern stair, where Naev stood poised by the railing, sword raised in steady hands. Jonnen's heart was beating quicker. He could suddenly feel it—that strange, never sated hunger. That feeling of a missing piece inside him. Searching for another just like it.

"Mia?" he asked hopefully.

Naev turned at the sound of his voice, eyebrow raised. "She is returned?"

"I don't—"

The woman lurched sideways on the stair, grunting in surprise as something heavy collided with her. There was no sign of what had struck her, but still she crashed backward into the railing, gasping, arms flailing as she fought for balance. The Something struck her again, hard in the chest, smashing her back against the balustrade. The woman cried out, eyes open wide.

"Naev!" Jonnen cried.

She was struck a third time, a brutal blow right in her face. Nose bloodied, Naev bent backward, fingers clutching at nothing as she lost her balance. And with a wail, the woman fell out into the empty air. Her arms pinwheeled, robes billowing about her, veil whipped back from her terrified face as she plummeted forty feet into the stable below, hitting the stone floor with a gut-churning *crunch.*

"'Byss and fucking blood," Butcher breathed.

Eclipse growled beside him, her hackles rising.

". . . BUTCHER, BEWARE . . . !"

The gladiatii had his sword raised, stepping back into a defensive stance.

"What's th—"

A blade flashed, bright and gleaming in the dwindling light. Butcher's throat opened wide. The big man staggered, hand at his neck to hold back the flood, squinting at the vague, muddied shape now standing on the steps in front of him. The gladiatii lunged with a bubbling curse, his gladius moving swift. Jonnen heard a ragged cry, saw the shadows shiver, his father appear on the stairs. A bloody gouge was carved through the imperator's forearm, his purple toga abandoned, blood-red spattering the white robes beneath.

Whisper was coiled about his throat, the shadowviper lashing out at Butcher's face. The big man struck out on sheer instinct, slicing through the serpent's neck as he flinched back. But the creature was as insubstantial as smoke, the steel cutting nothing at all. Precious seconds and energy wasted on the strike.

Butcher gargled, hand and throat and chest drenched in blood. He fell to one knee, red teeth bared in a snarl. Jonnen saw his father retreat a few steps up the stairs, bloody dagger poised. The boy's stomach rolled, his eyes filling with tears as he saw the big gladiatii drag himself back to his feet.

"R-run, boy," Butcher wheezed.

Eclipse coalesced between the boy and his father, snarling.

"*. . . JONNEN, RUN . . .*"

The boy shuffled back down the stairs. One step. Then two. Butcher took an unsteady step forward, made a clumsy swing at the imperator. But blood was fleeing the big man's body in floods now, puddling about him, all his strength and skill for naught. His father easily avoided the strike, stepping back again as the Liisian stumbled and fell.

"Butcher!" Jonnen cried, tears in his eyes.

"Iac-como . . . ," the big man gurgled. "R-R . . ."

Eclipse glanced over her shoulder, fangs bared in a snarl.

"*. . . RUN . . . !*"

The daemon leapt over Butcher's fallen body, mouth open wide. Whisper hissed and struck, black fangs sinking into the wolf's neck. The shadows fell into a tumbling, snarling, hissing brawl, rolling down the stairs. Eclipse growled and snapped, Whisper spat and bit, black spattering on the walls and spraying like blood. Jonnen took another step back, almost slipping in Butcher's blood. Tears running down his cheeks. Horror turning his insides slick and cold.

"My son."

The passengers continued to brawl, but the boy simply froze. Looking to his father on the stairs above him. Spattered in crimson. A golden laurel upon his brow. Imperator of the entire Republic. Tall and proud and strong. Ever possessed of the will to do what others would not. Butcher lay dead on the stone before him, Naev splattered on the floor below—just two more bodies added to the pile.

"Father . . ."

The imperator of Itreya raised one red hand, beckoning.

"Come to me, my son."

Jonnen looked to their shadows on the wall. His father's was reaching out to him, both hands open and welcoming. Jonnen saw his own shadow move, reaching toward his father and catching him up in a fierce embrace.

The boy himself yet remained still. The dagger Butcher had gifted him clutched in his hands. But his eyes were drawn back to Eclipse and Whisper, still brawling on the stairs. Black blood spraying, fangs bared, hissing and growling.

"Whisper, stop it!" the boy demanded.

". . . *JONNEN, RUN . . . !*" Eclipse snarled.

Jonnen saw his father's eyes narrow. Fear rising in the boy's belly, running cold in his veins. The imperator lifted his other hand, fingers clenching. The shadows moved, sharpening themselves to points, striking at the wolf and piercing her hide.

"Don't!" the boy cried.

Eclipse howled in pain, more shadowblood spraying. Scaeva cut the air with his hand, sent the daemon sailing into the wall. Whisper struck, razored teeth sinking again into Eclipse's throat. Black coils wrapped around the shadowwolf's body, squeezing, crushing, fangs sinking in again and again.

". . . Do you regret your insult now, little dog . . . ?"

". . . *J-JONNEN . . .*"

". . . Do you fear me yet . . . ?"

"Father, make him stop!" the boy cried.

The boy could feel tears burning in his eyes. Watching Eclipse's struggles weaken. Whisper's coils squeezing ever tighter, fangs sinking ever deeper. Eclipse whimpered in pain, thrashing and rolling and biting.

"The blood you have in your veins? You're strong enough for both of us."

Jonnen raised his hands, fingers curling into claws as he used his gifts, seizing the snake's neck in an invisible grip. He smashed Whisper against the wall as the serpent flailed and hissed, tail lashing, tongue flickering.

"Lucius!" his father snapped. "Release him!"

The boy held still. Frozen with it. That voice he'd known since before he could talk. The authority he'd obeyed since before he could walk. The father he'd admired, sought to make proud, wished all his life to grow up to be.

His sister had taken him in. Showed him her world. Eclipse had lived in his shadow for months now. Kept his fear at bay. The daemon had loved him, just as fiercely as she'd once loved another boy, just as lost and afraid as he.

"... CASSIUS ...," she whimpered.

But this was the man who'd raised Jonnen. Who'd known him for *years,* not months. The man he'd feared and loved and emulated. The sun shining in his sky.

"Lucius, I said release him!" came the cry.

And so, though it tore him to his heart, though the tears scalded his cheeks to burning, Jonnen looked at Eclipse. The shadow he knew almost as well as his own. The passenger he'd carried across storm and sea. The wolf who loved him.

"I ...," he sniffled, looking at the knife in his hand. "I don't ..."

"Lucius Atticus Scaeva, I am your *father*! Obey me!"

And you may hate him for it, gentlefriend. You may think him a weak and callow wretch. But in truth, Jonnen Corvere was just a nine-year-old boy. And Father was just another name for God in his mind.

"I'm ... s-sorry," Jonnen breathed.

And slowly,

ever so slowly,

he lowered his hand.

Free once more, Whisper struck. Eclipse fell, yelping as black fangs sank deep into her hide. Again. Again. Tears burning his eyes, Jonnen heard screaming, just beyond the edge of hearing. That hunger swelling inside him. Whisper twisted and sighed, the serpent's coils roiling and tightening around the shadowwolf's body. And as Jonnen watched, horrified, Eclipse began to fade.

Growing weaker.

Paler.

Thinner.

"... J-JONNEN ..."

The wolf slowly diminishing.

"... C-CASSIUS ..."

Until only the snake remained.

Dark enough for two.

"Lucius."

Sobs bubbled in the boy's throat. Horror and grief in his chest, threatening to choke him. All the world was burned and blurred by his tears as he looked up at his father's outstretched hand. Smeared in blood. Spattered with black.

"It's time to go home, son."

His little shoulders sagged. The weight of it all too much. He played at being a man, but in truth, he was still only a child. Lost and tired and, without the wolf in his shadow, now desperately afraid. Whisper slipped across the space between them, into the dark puddled at his feet. Eating the fear, just as he'd eaten the wolf. Soundlessly, Jonnen dropped the dagger Butcher had given him.

"Imperator."

Jonnen looked up the eastern stairs at the sound of the voice. Through his tears, he saw a tall Dweymeri woman, breathless and filmed with sweat. She was dressed in emerald green, lips and eyes painted black. She wore gold about her wrists and throat, but she was stripping off the adornments, tossing them down to the stables below.

"Shahiid Spiderkiller," his father said. "You live."

"You sound surprised, Imperator," the woman replied, slipping off another bracelet. "If you've a will to leave this place, we should travel together."

"The Red Church has failed me, Spiderkiller," the imperator replied. "Why in your Black Goddess's name would I bring you with me?"

"I thought perhaps I'd bring you with *me,*" she replied with a dark smile. "And I have *failed* nothing. I swore vengeance against Mia Corvere, and vengeance now I have. So if you've a mind to see us safely down to the speaker's chambers, I'll tell the tale of how I've killed your daughter for you."

His father's eyes narrowed. Head tilted. Weighing it all in his head. His flock of assassins was all but destroyed, his daughter's bloody revenge against the Red Church all but complete. And yet, though the Ministry had failed, the imperator of Itreya wasn't one to cast aside a perfectly good hammer simply because it had bent a single nail. One killer he might make use of yet remained among Niah's faithful.

And so, almost imperceptibly, he nodded.

The Dweymeri woman descended, shedding the last of her jewelry and taking her place at his father's side. The shadows about them darkened, his father's voice darker still.

"Come here, my son."

The boy met the man's gaze. Dark and deep as his own.

The sun shining in his sky.

The god in his eyes.

"Yes, Father," Jonnen said.

And slowly, fearlessly, the boy took his father's hand.

Adonai waited in silence.

The chains about his waist and ankles made it painful to kneel, so he sat at the head of the blood pool instead. Waiting for the little darkin to return and free him. The speaker could smell fresh blood in the air, feel it flowing unchecked in the levels above—young Mia's assault was obviously going well. His eyes were closed and he was breathing slow, searching for calm. In the turns since Drusilla had learned of his treachery, he'd found very little, truth told.

When the Lady of Blades had sent emissaries to his chambers and informed him Aelius and Mercurio's conspiracy had been uncovered, he'd been dismayed. But when he'd been told that his sister had been imprisoned, that she'd be held in captivity to assure his cooperation until after Mia Corvere was dead, Adonai had been consumed with rage.

The emissaries Drusilla had sent had been drowned in his pool. The next two, who bore one of Marielle's severed ears on a velvet cushion, he'd torn to pieces with vitus spears. It was only after a turn of impotent fury that the speaker realized he had no choice but to obey. Drusilla was holding the one person in the world he truly loved to ransom. She had the one weapon that could truly be used to hurt him.

As long as Marielle was in their keeping, Adonai was in their thrall.

So he'd allowed them to bind him in irons. He'd delivered the imperator to the Mountain as commanded, the Blades that Drusilla had called to Mia Corvere's kill. He played the meek one, the frightened one. Hoping the Lady of Blades might be foolish enough to deliver herself into his clutches to gloat or goad. But she never did.

And so now, Adonai waited. A picture of perfect calm without. A tightening knot of crimson rage within. Palms pressed to his knees, legs crossed, only the ruby liquid in the pool before him to betray his agitation. Mia had arrived in his chamber, breathless and bloody, only to discover her father had outwitted her and doubled back into the Mountain. She'd fled off into the labyrinthine halls in pursuit, her comrades on her heels, sadly neglecting to take the time to free Adonai from his chains before she departed. Rather unkind, he'd mused, but sooner or later, she must—

"Speaker."

Adonai opened his eyes. Belly thrilling with fury.

"Imperator," he hissed.

Scaeva coalesced out of the shadows before him, chest heaving. A serpent made of shadows was coiled about his neck, his wounded arm bound with bloody cloth. A boy stood beside him, bleached with fear—presumably the imperator's son. Spiderkiller stood there also, the gold that usually glittered at her throat and wrists conspicuously absent. But Adonai was far more concerned with the woman sagging in the Shahiid's arms.

Sister love, sister mine . . .

Marielle was drugged senseless, eyelids drooping, hands bound. Spiderkiller held a small golden knife against his sister's throat.

Adonai narrowed crimson eyes. The blood in the pool churned to life, long whips of it uncoiling from the surface and rising like snakes, pointed like spears, weaving closer to Scaeva and his brat and the Shahiid of Truths. But Spiderkiller tightened her black grip on Marielle, pressed her dagger into his sister's neck.

"I think not, Speaker," she said.

"Thy daughter is searching for thee, Julius," Adonai said, looking at Scaeva. "She was here a moment ago. If thou wouldst take but another moment to catch thy galloping breath, I am certain she'll be back anon. Unless thou dost plan to spend the rest of the turn playing hide-a-seek with her in this dark?"

"Transit," the imperator said, ignoring his barb. "Back to Godsgrave. Now."

"The seed ye planted, come full to flower. Watered with thy hatred and now blossomed fulsome and red." A pale smile twisted the speaker's lips. "This is why I sought to make no daughters."

"Enough," Spiderkiller snarled. "Send us to Godsgrave."

Adonai turned his eyes to the woman. "Fool ye must think me, Shahiid, to send my sister love with thee to thy Grave."

"Refuse us again, and I'll deliver Marielle to hers."

"Then shall ye die."

"And your sister love will join us, Speaker. Right before your eyes."

Adonai glanced at the dagger pressed to his sister's neck, his lips curling in derision. "Think ye thy blade sharp enough to draw blood near the likes of me, little spider?"

"The littlest spiders have the darkest bite, Adonai," the Shahiid replied.

Adonai narrowed his eyes, noting the dagger pricking his sister's skin was slightly discolored. A small droplet of Marielle's blood welled on the tip, ruby bright.

"Already my venom worms its way to your sister love's heart," Spiderkiller said. "And only I have the knowing of the cure. Kill us, and you kill her besides."

The Shahiid smiled, lips black and curling. She had him at checkmate, and Adonai and she both knew it. Trapped in the Mountain, Scaeva's daughter would catch the Shahiid of Truths and the imperator eventually, no matter how many times they switched back and forth under her nose in the gloom. Their painful deaths would soon follow. The truth was, the pair had nothing to lose, and Adonai knew Spiderkiller was ruthless and vindictive enough to kill Marielle before she died just to spite him.

In truth, he'd always liked that about her.

And so, eyes still on his sister's, the speaker waved to the pool, his voice calm as millpond water.

"Enter and be welcome."

". . . *Be careful, Julius . . . ,*" the shadowviper hissed.

Scaeva's stare was fixed firmly on Adonai's, his voice cold and hard.

"No tricks, Speaker," he warned. "Or your sister dies, I swear it."

"I believe thee, Imperator. Else thee and thy get wouldst already be dead."

"Get in the pool, Lucius."

The boy glanced into the gore, obviously afraid. And yet he seemed in the end more afeared of his father, crouching beside the pool and slipping down into the red. Scaeva followed slower, gathering his boy to his side. Spiderkiller tossed her poisoned dagger out the door—nothing that hadn't known the touch of life could travel through his pools, and the damage had already been done. The Shahiid of Truths stepped down into the blood, holding a swooning Marielle in her arms.

"If never I had reason to work toward thy ruin before, I have it now," Adonai said, glaring at them both. "Sure and true."

"Enough talk, cretin," Scaeva said. "Obey."

Adonai would have dearly loved to drown him then. Sweep him away in a tide of rippling red. But Scaeva's son stood there in the crimson beside his father, and if Mia could forgive Adonai for denying her revenge against Scaeva by killing him, she'd surely not forgive him for drowning her brother in the process.

Adonai's gaze drifted to his sister.

"Marielle?" he called.

His sister stirred but made no reply.

"Always shall I come for thee," he vowed.

Spiderkiller tightened her grip, glowering at Adonai.

"My venom works swift, Speaker," she warned.

So finally, eyes rolling back in his head, Adonai spoke the words beneath his breath. The room's warmth grew deeper, the smell of copper and iron churning in the air. He heard the boy gasp as the blood began swirling, sloshing around the pool's edge, faster and faster as the speaker's whispers became a gentle, pleading song, his lips curled in an ecstatic smile, his fingertips tingling with magik.

At the last moment, he opened crimson eyes. Stared into Scaeva's own.

"I shall see thee suffer for this, Julius."

And with a hollow slurp, they disappeared into the flood.

Chapter 33

Wellspring

Mia sat on bloody stairs, head in her bloody hands.

She'd almost done it. It had almost worked.

Almost.

The Ministry were dead or defeated. The Church's best remaining Blades had been slaughtered. The Quiet Mountain—home of the most vicious cult of killers the Republic had ever known—was now in her hands.

But he'd stolen away in the chaos. Slipperier than the shadowviper about his neck, more at home in the shadows than she'd ever given him credit for. Scaeva had doubled back, then doubled back again while Mia and the others blundered about in the maze of corridors and halls and stairwells looking for him. Not only claiming his prize, but slipping out through the speaker's chambers with Spiderkiller beside him.

He'd cut Butcher's throat. Pushed Naev to her death. Goddess, Mia hadn't thought it possible, but he'd somehow murdered *Eclipse*—she knew it, she'd *felt* it, like a lance of black agony into her chest as she stumbled about in the gloom. And to compound the pain, the gaping wound he'd carved in her still-beating heart, he'd stolen back his son.

He'd taken Jonnen.

"Bastard."

She whispered to the dark, tears rolling down her cheeks.

"That fucking bastard . . ."

"We'll get him back, Mia," Ashlinn said. "I promise."

The girl sat beside Mia on the stable stairs, bloodstained hand resting on her thigh. Sidonius was knelt beside Butcher's body, closing the Liisian's eyes and arranging him in some kind of repose. Bladesinger stood close by, saying a soft prayer, spattered with the blood of the Mountain's defenders. Tric was still above with Mercurio in the Hall of Eulogies, their watchful eyes on Aalea and Drusilla.

Jonnen . . .

Mia shook her head. Feeling fear swelling in her breast and reaching out for a passenger, only to find herself empty. Mister Kindly banished. Eclipse destroyed. Her power without them was undiminished, but for the first time since she was ten years old, she was facing a solitude with no end in sight. And despite the girl beside her, the allies around her who'd fought and bled and died for her, that thought terrified her more than anything she could remember.

And so, as ever, she reached for her oldest, dearest friend.

Rage.

She looked to Butcher, dead on the stairs, and felt the spark begin to smolder. She stared at Naev, laid out on the bloody floor, and felt it kindle. She thought of Eclipse, now just a memory, and felt it burst into flame. Immolating her fear and sweeping her up on wings of smoke and embers, burning in her lungs as she gritted her teeth and climbed to her feet. Her mind turning from her father to another.

The one who'd hurt her almost as badly as he.

The one who *hadn't* escaped.

"Drusilla," she spat.

Goddess help me," Drusilla breathed.

The Hall of Eulogies was quiet as graves. The names of the dead carved on the floor beneath her. The tombs of the fallen faithful on the walls around her. A half-dead Dweymeri boy stood beside her, twin blades in his hands. Drusilla blinked as the darkness rippled in front of her, as Aalea reached down and squeezed her fingers. The lady's belly sank as she saw a dark shape step out from the shadow of the Mother's statue. Niah loomed above them, carved of polished black granite. Manacles hanging from her dress. Sword in one hand. Scales in the other.

How will she weigh me? Drusilla wondered. *How badly will I be found wanting?*

"Mia," Aalea whispered.

"Good nevernight, Mi Donas," Corvere replied.

Her longblade was crusted with gore, amber eyes on the hilt as red as the blood painting her skin. Dark hair framed her pitiless stare. Drusilla remembered the first time she'd laid eyes on the girl, here in this very hall. Young and pale and green as grass. Her shaking hands and her little bag of teeth.

"Speak your name."

"Mia Corvere."

"Do you vow to serve the Mother of Night? Will you learn death in all its

colors, bring it to the deserving and undeserving in her name? Will you become an Acolyte of Niah, and an earthly instrument of the dark between the stars?"

"I will."

This was the hall where she'd been anointed. The statue she'd been chained against and scourged for her disobedience. The floor she'd found the truth of the Church's conspiracy carved in. The heart of it all.

The old woman sighed softly.

Goddess, if only we'd known what she'd become . . .

"Good to see you again, little Crow," Mercurio said.

"And you, Shahiid," the girl replied, her eyes never leaving the Lady of Blades.

"Where's Scaeva?" the old man asked.

Mia's eyes narrowed in fury. "Not here."

So the imperator had fled.

Corvere had failed.

Aalea took a slow step forward, hands raised, all honeyed tones and beautiful, blood-red smile. "Mia, my love, we should sp—"

The darkness lashed out, pointed like a spear, sharp as a sword. It sliced through Aalea's throat, cleaving neatly from ear to ear. The woman's dark eyes grew wide, blood-red lips parted as she coughed, hand to her neck. She tottered forward, ruby red spilling over milk-white skin. Looking to the Mother's statue above, she mouthed a final prayer, tears welling in kohled lashes. And then the Shahiid of Masks toppled forward onto the bloody stone, her silvered tongue silenced forever.

Drusilla met Mia's gaze, saw what awaited her there. She reached into her robe, adrenaline and fear tingling at her fingertips as she grasped the blade she kept between her breasts—the place the Dweymeri boy had been too polite to paw at when he searched her for weapons. The boy cried out now as the steel flashed, as Drusilla flung the poisoned dagger, whistling right at the girl's throat.

Corvere raised her hand, fingers spread. The dark about her unfurled like a flower in bloom, tendrils of living shadow snatching the blade from the air. The girl lowered her chin, a small, fierce smile on her bloody lips. With a wave of her hand, the darkness carried the knife back across the room, laying it to rest at Drusilla's feet.

"So much for the Lady of Blades," she said.

"Mia . . . ," Drusilla began, her throat tightening.

"There are names missing," the girl said.

The old woman blinked in confusion. ". . . What?"

Mia motioned to the granite floor around them. A spiral, gleaming now with Aalea's blood, coiling out from the statue of Niah. Hundreds of names. Thousands. Kings, senators, legates, lords. Priests and sugargirls, beggars and bastards. The names of every life taken in the service of the Black Mother. Every kill the Red Church had made.

"There are some missing," Mia repeated.

Drusilla felt a grip on her arms. Strong as iron. Cold as ice. Looking down, she saw the shadows had caught her up, black ribbons encircling her wrists, cutting off the blood. The old woman shrieked as she was dragged along the floor, unearthly strength slamming her up against the base of the Goddess's statue. Her skull was ringing. Her nose bloodied. She dimly felt the shadows haul up her arms, bind her wrists with the manacles hanging from the Goddess's robes.

"Unhand me!" Drusilla demanded, struggling. "Let me *go*!"

Mia's reply was cold as winter winds.

"I've a story to hear, Drusilla," she said. "And no patience to cut those missing names into this floor. But I should carve something to remember them by, at least."

Drusilla felt the robes torn from her shoulders. The press of the statue's cold stone against her bare skin. Terror piercing her heart. She looked over her shoulder, saw pity in Mercurio's gaze. The deadboy's black stare. The poisoned knife she'd thrown, rising up from the floor in the grip of cold, black ribbons.

"No . . . ," the old woman gasped, pulling against her bonds. "*No!* I have a familia, I have a—"

"This is for Bryn and Wavewaker," Mia said.

Drusilla screamed as she felt the knife cut into her back. Thirteen letters, gouged with poisoned steel, deep into her flesh. Blood spilling down her skin, hot and thick. Agony seared between her shoulder blades.

"Mercurio!" she cried. "*Help* me!"

"This is for Naev and Butcher and Eclipse."

Drusilla wailed again, long and shrill, her throat cracking as she bucked against the stone. She could feel the toxin on her blade at work, worming its way toward her withered heart. But above it, she could still feel the white-hot pain of the knife carving the names of the dead into her back.

"This is for Alinne and Darius Corvere."

Warm wetness. Razored agony. Deep as years. But it was receding quickly now. A thudding ebb, slowing along with her pulse. The Lady of Blades sagged in her irons, her legs too weak to hold her any longer. The poison dragging her toward blessed blackness. She tried to think of her daughter then. Her son.

Tried to remember the sound of her grandchildren's laughter as they played in the sunslight. Eyes rolling up in her head as sleep beckoned with open arms.

"Stay with me, Drusilla," came a voice. "I saved the worst for last."

A lance of burning pain, right at the base of her spine. Dragging her back up into the hateful light for one last hateful moment. Mia stood close beside her now. A black chill spilling from the dark around her. A final caress gracing her cheek.

"This is for me," Mia whispered. "The me who never was. The me who lived in peace and married someone beautiful and perhaps held a daughter in her arms. The me who never knew the taste of blood or the smell of poison or the kiss of steel. The me you killed, Drusilla. Just as surely as you killed the rest of them."

The Lady of Blades felt a twisting stab of pain, right through her rotten heart.

A whisper, soft and black as night.

"Remember her," the girl breathed.

And then, she felt nothing at all.

The choir had stopped singing.

Mia hadn't noticed it at first. She wasn't exactly sure when the song had ceased. But trekking through the Mountain's belly, her own belly in her boots, she noticed how deathly quiet things had become. The acolytes and Hands who'd surrendered to her had been sealed inside their quarters, or locked down in the apothecarium (Mercurio had only killed two of the apothecaries during his ruse—there were still enough left to tend the others' wounds). But with no voices or footfalls or the traditional hustle and bustle in the halls, the Mountain was quiet as death.

The Athenaeum was quieter still.

The great double doors opened with the soft press of Mia's bloody fingertips. The dark that waited beyond—perfumed with parchment and ink and leather and dust—seemed more welcoming than any she'd ever felt. She walked into the library of the dead, her companions all in tow, her father's gravebone longblade and Mouser's blacksteel sword sheathed at her waist. And there, leaning against the railing of the mezzanine beside his faithful RETURNS trolley, stood the chronicler of her tale.

"Aelius," Mia said.

"Ah," the old wraith smiled. "A girl with a story to tell."

He was dressed like he always was: britches and a scruffy waistcoat. His improbably thick spectacles were balanced on his hooked nose, two shocks of white hair protruding from his balding scalp. His back was bent like a sickle's blade, a lit cigarillo dangling from his mouth. He looked about a thousand years old.

Which might not be all that far from the truth.

His smile was welcoming. Smug, even. And as Sidonius and Bladesinger looked about the Black Mother's Athenaeum in wonder, as Tric and Ash and Mercurio watched with curious eyes, Aelius reached up behind his ear, plucked his ever-present spare cigarillo free, lit it on his own, and offered it to Mia.

The girl took the smoke, placed it on her lips, and dragged deep.

"You've got some fucking explaining to do," she said, exhaling gray.

"How're Adonai and Marielle?" he asked.

"Adonai's alive," Mercurio replied. "Scaeva took Marielle to Godsgrave."

Aelius nodded, blowing a large smoke ring into the air. Mia blew a smaller one, sent it sailing through the chronicler's. Meeting his pale blue eyes with her dark ones.

"I'm waiting," she said.

"Simply put, I knew you'd charge in here half-cocked," Aelius replied. "Thinking you were good enough to gut the Quiet Mountain all on your lonesome. Say what you will about being fearless, but there's only the finest line between bravery and idiocy. And those passengers of yours tend to lead you closer to the latter than the former."

"Once, perhaps," Mia murmured. "No longer."

"Aye." The chronicler sighed a plume of smoke. "Apologies for your loss."

Mia's voice was hard as iron. Blood and tears dry on her cheeks.

"You were saying?"

The chronicler shrugged. "Given the way you were bound to burst in here, we needed a way to even the scales. Put Drusilla on the back foot, and enough Blades on the chopping block that you could gut what was left of the Church with one stroke. I figured the old bitch would come poking about the library, eventually. Find the first two parts of the chronicle. Especially with Mercurio spending all his free time down here."

Aelius patted the RETURNS trolley, the three books atop it. One had pages edged in blood-red, a crow embossed on the cover. The second was edged in blue, embossed with a wolf. The last, trimmed black and spattered white, with a cat gracing the front.

She thought of Mister Kindly then. Heart aching in her chest. Wishing she had some way to call him back, wishing she could undo what she'd—

"So I let Drusilla find the books," Aelius said. "The first two parts chronicling the story that is your life. And in the weeks that the Lady of Blades had her lackeys trawling through the dark down here for the third part . . . well, I wrote one."

The chronicler drew deep on his cigarillo, exhaled a plume of smoke.

"I had to make some of it up, of course. But among other things, it outlined your 'plan' for entering the Quiet Mountain. After Drusilla's lackeys 'found' it, all I needed to do was have Adonai warn you through Naev of the way you should *actually* approach the Church and get the drop on Drusilla's welcoming party." He squinted in the pall as he dragged on his cigarillo again. "Nice stroke with the arkemist's salt, by the way. I'd not have thought of that."

"And that's it?" Mia asked.

"It?" Aelius scoffed. "Lass, that plan was so cunning you could've painted it orange and set it loose in a bloody henhouse."

"My friends are dead," she said. "My brother is stolen by my bastard father."

"And *you,* my dear, are Lady of Blades. Who's going to refute your claim now? With the Ministry and their sharpest knives dead at your hand? The Red Church is shattered. Your nemesis is fled back to Godsgrave, licking his wounds and scooping the shite from his britches. Which means you're free to pursue the destiny you've been avoiding like the plague since I set you on this path *three fucking years ago.*"

Mia glanced at Tric. Those black eyes, burning with a million tiny stars.

"Cleo's journal," she murmured.

"Clever lass," the chronicler nodded.

"You knew," she said, narrowing her eyes as she dragged on her smoke. "The Moon's murder at the hands of the Sun. The fragments of Anais's soul. The black blood beneath Godsgrave. Darkin. All of it."

Aelius shrugged. "Aye."

"Why the fuck didn't you tell me?" she demanded.

"What did I say when you came snooping about in here last year?"

Mia sighed, remembering the last time the two of them had spoken, here in this very library. "'Some answers are learned. But the important ones are earned.'"

"I had to be sure about you," Aelius said. "I had to *know* what you were made of. Cassius didn't have it. The other darkin I've found over the years never came close. But we *have* to get it right this time, Mia. Because uniting the shards of Anais has been attempted once before, and that was so disastrous this world was almost consigned to an eternity of sunslight."

"Cleo," Mia said.

"Aye. Cleo."

Mia looked to Ashlinn. The fear she felt in her breast was reflected in her girl's eyes. Ash could feel it, sure as Mia could—the mekwerk gears of a plan countless years, perhaps *centuries* in the making, spinning all around them. For a moment, she wanted to run. To take Ash's hand and turn her back on all this blood and dark. Hide deep as they could and seek whatever happiness they could.

"Who was she?" she heard herself ask.

"Cleo?" Aelius shrugged. "Just a girl. Like any other in the newfound city of Godsgrave. Save for the sliver of Anais's soul that found its way into her heart. Married too young to a brutal man, she killed him the year she first began to bleed. Thing of it was, her husband had a shard of Anais inside him, too. Darkin were more numerous in those turns, you see—Anais's pieces were still scattered all across the Republic."

Aelius blew another smoke ring, paused a moment before he spoke again.

"Once Cleo killed her beau, Niah drew what strength she could to herself and came to Cleo in a dream. Told the girl she was 'Chosen.' That she'd restore the balance between Night and Day. The way it was in the beginning, the way it was *meant* to be. And so Cleo set out to find more darkin. Killing them. Consuming their essence and claiming their daemons and growing ever deeper in her powers. And her madness."

"She was insane?"

"She certainly went that way by the end of it all," Aelius sighed. "Set aside the messiah complex she'd been instilled with for a minute. The simple truth is you can't live a life ending the lives of others and expect to escape it unchanged. When you feed a soul to the Maw—"

"You feed it a piece of yourself, too."

"And soon, there's nothing left," Ashlinn murmured, glancing at Tric.

The chronicler nodded, exhaling strawberry-scented gray. "Cleo wandered the City of Bridges and Bones, then the wider Republic. Drawn to other darkin and consuming any she found. Urged on by Niah, amassing an ever-growing fragment of Anais's soul inside her. Problem was, there was something else growing in her, too."

"The baby she mentioned in her journal," Mia said.

"Aye," Aelius said. "And heavy with child, drenched in murder, she finally journeyed east across the Ashkahi wastes. Seeking the Crown of the Moon, where the brightest and most potent shard of Anais's soul lay in wait for her. She gave birth, right there at the Crown. Alone, save for her passengers, she brought a boy kicking and screaming into the world. Crouched over bare and bloody rock. Cutting his cord with her own teeth. Such will. Such courage."

Aelius shook his head and sighed.

"But when she learned the truth, her courage and will both failed her."

The Athenaeum was deathly still. Mia swore she could hear her own heart beating.

"I don't understand," she said.

"The Dark Mother wanted Cleo to help bring her dead son back to life," Aelius said. "But there, at the Moon's Crown, holding her own newborn son to her breast, Cleo learned the truth of what it would mean to raise Anais from the dead. She learned the body which houses the Moon's soul must perish in his rebirth. That whoever gives Anais life must give up their own to see it done."

"For the Moon to live . . ."

"Cleo had to die. But she had a son now, see. The boy she'd brought into the world with her own two hands. And she was but young herself. Her whole life ahead of her. She felt like a dupe, not a messiah. She felt betrayed rather than Chosen. And so she refused. Cursed Niah's name. There at the Crown, she chose to remain. And there she remains still. Twisted by madness. Sustained by the shards of Anais she'd gathered to herself, and refusing to let another claim them."

"Trelene have mercy," Bladesinger whispered.

"You fucking bastard," Ash spat.

Mia turned to her girl, saw her glaring at Tric.

"You knew, didn't you?" Ash said, glowering at the boy. "You *knew* this shit. Where it would lead her. What it would cost her!"

"I DIDN'T KNOW THE FULL TALE," Tric said. "I DIDN'T KN—"

"Bullshit!" Ash spat. "You've known this whole fucking time."

"Ash, stop it," Mia said.

"No, I won't stop!" Ash cried, incredulous. "You can't give the Moon life without giving up your own, Mia! That's what this crusty old prick has been planning for the last three years?" She glared at Aelius, then shoved Tric in his chest. "And this rat *bastard* has been pushing you right toward your own grave."

"DON'T TOUCH ME AGAIN, ASHLINN," Tric said. "I'M WARNING YOU."

"Warning me?" Ash scoffed. "Let's remember what happened last time we—"

"All right, stop it!" Mia snapped. "Both of you, enough!"

Silence rang through the library. Somewhere out in the dark, a bookworm roared. Mia looked Aelius up and down, the wheels turning in her head, over and over. A wraith, trapped forever in this Athenaeum. The Dark Mother's chronicler, a Hearthless soul, held for an eternity in the Church of the Lady of Blessed Murder. Helping Mia along her way. A battered journal here. A word of advice there.

"*They don't tell stories about Red Church disciples, Chronicler,*" Mia had said. "*No songs sung for us. No ballads or poems. People live and die in the shadows, here.*"

"Well, maybe here's not where you're supposed to be."

"You're him, aren't you?"

Mia peered into those pale blue eyes, realization slowly dawning.

"You're the babe she brought into the world," she said. "You're Cleo's son."

The chronicler smiled. "Not just a pretty face and a shitty attitude, are you?"

She looked around them, bewildered.

"So what the fuck are you doing *here*?"

"Fathers and daughters. Mothers and sons." The chronicler shrugged. "You're more familiar with the complexities of familia than most. My mother raised me, there at the Crown. The shadows were my only companions. I could have lived my whole life there, never knowing another soul. But as I grew older, Niah began speaking to me.

"It happened at truedark mostly. She started sending me dreams. Whispering as I slept. She told me of her husband's betrayal. Her son's murder. And over the years, she convinced me that we all have a purpose in this life, and that my mother's was to bring balance back to the skies. The Moon was inside my mother when she bore me, and that made me the Night's grandson—at least in my eyes. So I tried to convince my mother of the selfishness in what she'd done. That Aa had been wrong when he punished his bride, slew his boy. That the skies deserved some kind of harmony, and Niah, some kind of justice. But the years in solitude had only compounded my mother's delirium. There was no seeing reason for her.

"And so, after years . . . I left. Seeking another way the Night might regain her rightful place in the sky. Worship of the Black Mother had been outlawed in the years after her banishment. But I thought if I could revive faith in Niah, the power she'd glean from our devotion might be enough to break the bonds of her prison alone. And so slowly, painstakingly, I founded a church in her name."

"You were the first Blade," Mia realized.

Aelius shrugged. "It started very small. But we *truly* believed back then. There was no killing, no offerings, none of that. We operated out of a little chapel on the north coast of Ashkah. The legends of the Night and the Moon etched in the walls."

"The temple Duomo sent us to," Ash breathed. "The place I found the map."

"Aye," Aelius said. "Our first altar, carved out of stone with our own hands."

"Red stone," Ash said.

"Red Church," Mia murmured.

"It was all going well," Aelius said. "The faith was building. People still wanted to believe in the Mother of Night, despite the lies Aa's church had begun telling about her. After perhaps a decade of devotion, when truedark fell and the Mother was closest to the earth, she was strong enough to lead us to this Mountain. A place where the walls between Night and Day were thinnest. And here, we truly began to flourish. But there's a saying about all good things . . ."

Aelius dragged deep on his cigarillo and sighed smoke.

"There were those among the flock who saw differently than I, you see. Who didn't worship Niah in her guise as the Mother of Night, but instead as Our Lady of Blessed Murder. They saw a new way to run the Church. A way that might turn our devotion to hard coin and our piety into a means to earthly power."

Aelius shrugged.

"And they murdered me."

Mia blinked. "You were killed by your own followers?"

"Aye." The old man nodded, his face twisting. "Cunts."

"Goddess . . . ," Mia breathed.

"It all went to shit after that. The Church I'd begun became a cult of assassins. It grew infamous and powerful, but Niah's budding strength waned as the rot set in. Aa grew stronger as his faith spread in the wake of the Great Unifier's conquering armies. Divinities are like that, you see—they really only have the power we grant them. The Black Mother had spent so much of her strength making this place, very little remained. And as the Church became more about murder and profit, less about true devotion, she grew weaker and weaker still.

"By the time she'd gathered enough strength to bring me back to this . . . life, centuries had passed. The Church had become something else entirely. But there was still a sliver of it in the shadows. A tiny fragment of true belief she could use to play a game decades long. Making a few moves with a few pawns every truedark, just once every three years. Looking for another chosen. Seeking the one who might triumph where Cleo failed. Until finally . . . finally . . ."

The chronicler met Mia's eyes.

"Here she is."

"I'm nobody's savior," she said. "I'm no hero."

"O, *bullshit,*" Aelius spat. "You know *exactly* what you are. Look at the things you've done. The things you *do*. You've been shaping the world with your every breath for the last three years, and don't tell me you didn't feel it was for something more than vengeance." Aelius pointed at the first two Nevernight Chronicles on his little trolley. "I've read them. Cover to cover. More times than I can count. You're more than just a killer. If you open your arms to it, you're the girl who can right the fucking *sky*."

Aelius shook his head, glaring.

"But we can't afford to fuck this up again. There's so little of Anais left, and every piece of him lost brings us one step closer to ruin. The piece in me when those bastards murdered me. The piece in Cassius when he died in Last Hope. Perhaps I should have helped you more. Perhaps I should have told you earlier. But I needed to know you had the will to see this through, Mia. To the end."

The chronicler looked deep into Mia's eyes.

"The *very* end."

"Scaeva still has my brother," she said.

"Aye," Aelius said. "And by the time you reach Godsgrave, he'll probably have an army waiting for you. But if you claim the power that awaits you at the Crown, once truedark falls, you'll be able to take your brother back in a black heartbeat."

"And then I die."

The chronicler tilted his head and shrugged.

"Everybody dies sometime. Very few of us die for some*thing*. You're her Chosen, Mia. This is right. This is destiny."

"This is *bullshit*!" Ashlinn spat, glaring at the chronicler.

The old wraith sighed gray. "You've no idea what you're talking about, girl."

"Don't call me girl, you creaky old fuck," Ash snarled. "How easy is it for you to talk about what's right when you don't have to sacrifice a thing to do it?"

Aelius glowered. "Don't have to sacrifice . . . ?"

The chronicler straightened to his full height, fury burning in pale blue eyes.

"One hundred and twenty-seven years," he said. "That's what I sacrificed. Over a *century,* spent rotting in this fucking Athenaeum, bound to these pages. Not alive. Not dead. Just existing and praying for the right one to come along." He dragged his cigarillo off his lips, held it up between them. "You know how many times I thought about just tossing one of these into the stacks? Letting this place burn and me along with it? I want to sleep, girl. I want this to end.

But no, I sat here waiting in the dark because I *believed*. You be mad at life all you like. You try to protect your love as hard as you can. But don't you *dare* talk to me about fucking sacrifice. Not ever."

Mia looked about the faces of her comrades. Mercurio looked stricken, Bladesinger and Sidonius were both awed and afraid. Tric was as unreadable as stone, like the faces about the pool beneath Godsgrave's heart. Ashlinn was simply furious, smoldering, looking at Mia and slowly shaking her head.

"I need to think," Mia whispered. "I need to think about this . . ."

"The suns are falling to their rest," Aelius said, eyes returning to hers. "Truedark approaches. Niah can only breathe life into Anais while Aa's eyes are closed, and if we miss our opportunity now, who knows what the imperium will look like in another two and half years."

The chronicler crushed out his cigarillo underheel and nodded.

"So don't think too long, neh?"

CHAPTER 34

RIBBONS

Bladesinger sat in the Sky Altar, an endless night wheeling above her head.

The platform was carved deep into the Quiet Mountain's flank, open to the sky it was named for. It protruded from the Mountain's side, a terrifying drop waiting just beyond its ironwood railings. The Whisperwastes were laid out below, but above, where the sky should have burned with the stubborn light of the failing suns, Bladesinger could see only darkness. Filled with a million tiny stars.

The benches and tables around them, once peopled with assassins and servants of the Black Mother, were empty. The Quiet Mountain was living up to its name—the choir she'd heard when they'd first stormed the assassin's stronghold was still silent.

Sidonius sat opposite her, perusing the first volume of the so-called Nevernight Chronicles. He'd borrowed it from Bladesinger once she was done, flipping pages and tearing mouthfuls off a roast chicken he'd purloined from the Red Church larders. Bladesinger had only skimmed the first, and she was now halfway through the second chronicle. But she'd stopped before she reached chapter twenty-four.

Their battle with the silkling.

"'Byss and blood," Sidonius murmured, turning the page with greasy fingers.

"What part are you up to?" Bladesinger asked.

"Ashlinn just stabbed Tric."

"Ah." She nodded. "Ruthless little bitch."

"Aye," Sid said, flipping the book and looking at the cover. "You know, it's actually not a bad read. I mean, if you don't mind footnotes and a fuckload of cursing."

"Eh." Bladesinger sniffed dismissively, tossed a long saltlock off her shoulder. "You can tell it was written by a man."

". . . How's that?"

Bladesinger raised an eyebrow and peered at the big Itreyan. "You didn't think the sex scenes gave it away?"

"I actually thought some of the smut was quite good?"

"O, come off," Bladesinger scoffed. "'Aching nipples'? 'Swollen bud'?"

Sidonius blinked. "What's wrong with 'swollen bud'?"

"I've not got a fucking flower between my legs, Sid."

"Well, what would you call it, then?"

Bladesinger shrugged. "The little man in the boat?"

"Why the *fuck* would you name a part of a woman's nethers the 'little man'?"

"Something about the visual appeals?" She shrugged again. "Rowing is hard. It's nice to imagine a man actually doing some work between the sheets for a change."

Sid grinned and shook his head. "You're a fucking bitch, 'Singer."

Bladesinger laughed. "You only just noticed?"

The big Itreyan guffawed, topped up her cup of wine. Raised his own.

"What are we drinking to?" the Dweymeri woman asked.

"To Butcher," Sid declared. "An ill-mannered, foulmouthed, fuck-ugly bastard I was proud to call brother. He lived and died on his feet in a world that tried to force him to his knees. May he find his familia waiting for him by the Hearth."

"Aye,"'Singer nodded. "And may we be slow to meet him."

"I'll drink to that," Sid said, quaffing his wine.

Bladesinger downed hers, too, wincing as she placed the cup back on the table. Her swordarm ached abominably. The scar across her forearm was vicious, the tattoos that adorned her body were twisted and puckered about the wound. Sidonius pretended not to notice, but that only irked her more.

"I suppose I should give you thanks," she finally growled.

"For what?" Sid murmured, pretending to be reading.

"Fighting our way out of the stables earlier," 'Singer said. "On the second set of stairs when that big bastard came at me with the punching daggers. He'd have stuck me if not for you."

"Bollocks," Sid said. "You'd have moved. I was just being careful."

"You were just *saving my life* is what you were doing."

Sid shrugged, remaining mute.

'Singer sighed, wincing again as she stretched her swordarm.

"It's never quite healed right. Since that silkling cut me open in Whitekeep, I've not got the strength I once had. Nor the speed." She shook her head, saltlocks swaying. "The suffi named me Bladesinger when my mother presented me at Farrow. Only a few turns old, and they knew I'd be a warrior. But what song can my blade sing now?"

Sidonius waved her off with a frown. "Never fear, it'll come good."

"You *know* it won't, Sid," she snapped. "You know it's as good as it's going to get. I'm a swordswoman who can't swing a sword. A liability is what I am."

Sidonius tilted his head, peering at her with his bright blue eyes. "The finest warrior I know, is what you are. You've saved my life a score of times. You're still my sister on the sands, *and* off them, and when we follow Mia to the Crown, there's not another in this Republic I'd rather have watching her back beside me."

". . . You think she'll go, then."

"I know she will." Sidonius looked into the dark above their heads. "And she knows it, too. She's meant for more than vengeance, that one. Always has been."

"She seems frightened."

"Aye." Sid sighed, shook his head. "But not for long."

"I can't come with you. I'm as useful as balls on a priest with this arm, Sid."

"So fight with your other one," Sidonius said, looking back into her eyes. "Fighting's not just about steel. It's about heart. Wits. Guts. You stand head and shoulders above just about anyone I know on all three counts. And I hate to shatter your illusions about the Itreyan clergy, but I was Luminatii for six years, 'Singer. Priests get far more use out of their balls than you might think."

'Singer grinned and shook her head. "You're a good man, Sidonius."

The big Itreyan laughed. "You only just noticed?"

Bladesinger looked the man up and down. Battle-scarred and hard as iron.

Pretty blue eyes and a boyish charm that all the scars in the world couldn't quite cover up.

"Aye," she said softly. "I think I did."

Bladesinger refilled their wines, lips pursed in thought.

"If Mia *does* follow that crazed librarian's advice and seeks this damned Moon's Crown, you know we're like to die at it, don't you?"

"Aye, probably." Sidonius shrugged, lifted his cup. "But what can you do?"

'Singer downed her wine in a single gulp.

"Well, seems as we're like to be dead soon . . . fancy a rowing lesson?"

". . . Rowing lesson?"

Bladesinger raised an eyebrow and glanced suggestively below her waist. And gathering up the wine cup and the jug, she tossed her saltlocks back and stood.

"Coming?" she asked.

Sidonius seemed to have caught on at last. The big Itreyan set his book aside, pushed his chair back, and gifted her a wicked grin.

"Ladies first," he said.

"Hmf. We'll see about that, Crossbow Sid."

"I insist, Mi Dona."

And insist he did.

Mia wasn't thinking.

She waited in her old chambers, ensconced in a pile of pillows and soft furs. The gentle light of an arkemical lamp lit the room. The silence left by the choir's absence seemed an eternity wide. A thin gray finger of smoke drifted from the cigarillo in her fingertips. It was her fifth of the hour, the remains of her former victims piled in an ashtray beside her bed. She placed the smoke upon her lips, dragging deep, trying not to think about the Athenaeum. The Crown of the Moon. Aelius. Scaeva. Naev. Butcher. Eclipse. Poor little Jonnen.

No.

No, she wasn't thinking about it. She was lying in bed and smoking and waiting for her girl. Watching the door through long, black lashes. But the hourglass beside her had slowly drained the hour through, and Ashlinn still hadn't returned from the bathhouse. Mia was beginning to wonder if perhaps Ash intended to sleep in her old chambers in the acolytes' wing instead.

She didn't want to spend the nevernight alone.

And then the door handle turned, and her girl walked in, and Mia felt all the weight upon her shoulders vanish, as if by magik.

Ash's hair was still damp from the bath, dark blond tumbled across her shoulders. She wore a slip of black silk and a thin frown, only sparing Mia a glance as she stepped inside and closed the door. Her eyes were clouded, a troubled, storm-tossed shade of blue. But Mia's heart still beat a little quicker to see her. Watching the arkemical light playing on her skin, sharp shadows and gentle curves and legs that went all the way to the heavens.

"Hello, beautiful," she said.

Mia tossed aside the furs without ceremony. She was almost entirely naked beneath. Long dark tresses about her shoulders, rolling in black rivers down over pale skin. Cigarillo smoke drifted from her lips. A ribbon made of shadows was wrapped around her waist, a pretty bow arranged to leave just a little to the imagination.

"Like it?" Mia smiled, running her fingertips over the velvet black. "It's what all the finest donas are wearing this year."

Ashlinn looked her up and down.

"It looks chilly," she said.

Mia ran her hands down her breasts, her stomach, slipping ever lower to press between her thighs. Her back arched slightly, she breathed a little heavier.

"No, it's warm, Ash," she murmured. "It's *so* warm."

Mia didn't want to think. She wanted to feel. She wanted to fuck. Just the promise of it set her pulse racing. The thought of throwing Ashlinn down on the furs, taking and being taken in turn, of just shutting off the wheels spinning inside her head and silencing the questions and just . . .

But Ashlinn stayed where she was. Hovering by the door.

"Come here, lover," Mia whispered, opening her arms.

"No," Ash replied.

"Please," Mia breathed. "I *want* you."

Ashlinn just shook her head. "You don't want me."

"How can you—"

"You just want to avoid a conversation, Mia."

Mia looked her girl in the eye. A tiny spark of temper blooming in her chest.

"And what should we be having a conversation about, Ashlinn?"

"O, I don't know, the price of virgins in Vaan?" Ash flailed her hand, incredulous. "What the *fuck* do you think we should be talking about? I just stood and listened to that crusty old prick for an hour, and despite all his bluster and bullshit, his best-case scenario seems to be one where you end up dead! Aelius wants you to kill yourself!"

"Aelius wants to restore the balance between Night and Day."

"Because he wasn't good enough to do it himself!"

"Ever since I arrived here," Mia said. "Every step I've taken. Everything I've ever done has pointed me toward the Crown of the Moon."

"That's bullshit and you know it."

Mia rubbed her aching brow and sighed. "I don't know anything."

"I won't come with you if that's what you're thinking," Ashlinn declared. "I'll not give you the map, nor help you kill yourself. I can't."

". . . I've seen you naked enough to have the map memorized by now, Ash."

"Daughters damn you, Mia Corvere," Ashlinn hissed.

Mia sighed and snatched up her cigarillo again, dragging the covers back over her bare skin. "You know, I don't remember them ever teaching classes in it here, but you've a wonderful knack for killing the mood."

"I'm serious, Mia!"

"You think I'm not?" she shouted, her temper breaking loose. "You think I don't know what's happening? What's at stake? I've been sitting here for the past hour trying not to think about the fact that I can't conjure a single reason to actually do this!"

"Then don't!" Ash cried. "Fuck Aelius. Fuck the Moon, fuck the Goddess, fuck it *all*! We never asked for any of this! The Red Church is gutted, Scaeva's Blades are all gone, he ran from here like a whipped dog!"

Ash stormed across the room and sat on the bed. She grabbed Mia's hand, looked intently into her eyes. "We're two of the finest assassins left in the Republic. I say we head to Godsgrave, slit that bastard's throat, steal your brother back, and be done! Who gives a shit about Anais or the balance or any of it?"

"There's a piece of him inside me, Ash." Mia let out a long, heavy sigh. "Anais. I can feel him. In my heart."

"And what about me?" Ashlinn put a hand on Mia's chest. "Aren't I in there, too?"

"Of *course* you are," Mia whispered, grabbing hold of her fingers and squeezing.

"I love you, Mia."

"I love you, too."

"No, you don't." Ash shook her head. "If you did, you wouldn't be in such a hurry to say goodbye."

Mia felt tears welling in her eyes. An ocean of them waiting inside her.

"I don't want to say goodbye."

Ash caressed the slave brand on Mia's cheek. The scar cutting through her other.

"Then stay. Stay with me."

"I . . . I want to . . ."

Ashlinn lunged forward, their lips meeting in a desperate kiss. Mia closed her eyes, tasting tears, slipping her arms about Ashlinn's waist and pulling her close. They kissed like they never had before, clinging to each other as if they were drowning, two people adrift in a world of fire and suns and night and storms. All the divinities against them, trying to tear them apart.

Their kiss ended slow, Ashlinn still holding Mia as their lips parted, as if afraid to let her go. She buried her face in Mia's hair, squeezing tight, her voice a murmur.

"*Stay* with me."

Mia closed her eyes and sighed. Holding on for dear life.

"I don't know what to do," she said. "I don't know how to make this right."

Their lips met again, softer this time. Longer and sweeter and full of an aching, blissful need. Ash's fingertips caressed her cheeks and slipped through her hair, and Mia sighed as she felt her girl's tongue brush her own. Their kiss deepened as Ashlinn's hands began to roam. Down her throat to her collarbone. Skimming over her breasts and finally to the ribbon around Mia's waist.

"I want to be with you forever," Mia whispered.

"Just forever?" Ash murmured, descending.

Mia shook her head, closed her eyes.

"Forever and ever."

She dreamed.

She was the child again, beneath a sky as gray as the moment between waking and sleeping. Standing on water so still it was like polished stone, like glass, like ice beneath her bare feet. Stretching as far as she could see.

Her mother walked beside her, holding her hand and a pair of lopsided scales. She wore gloves of black silk, long and glimmering with a secret sheen, all the way up to her elbows. Her gown was black as sin as night as death, strung with a billion tiny points of light. They shone from within, out through the shroud of her gown, like pinpricks in a curtain drawn against the sun. She was beautiful. Terrible. Her eyes were as black as her dress, deeper than oceans. Her skin was pale and bright as stars.

Like always, she had Alinne Corvere's face. But Mia knew, in that dreaming, knowing kind of way, that this wasn't her real face.

And like always, across the infinite gray, her father and sisters waited for them.

He was clad all in white, so bright and sharp it hurt Mia's eyes to look at. But Mia looked all the same. He stared back as she and her mother approached, three eyes fixed on her, red and yellow and bl—

"No," *Mia said.*

"No, enough of this."

She heard Bladesinger's voice inside her head.

"You should try it. Next time you sleep. Take a hold of the shape and make it what you want. It's your dream, after all."

And so she stopped. Pushed the images of her father in his shroud of gleaming white away. She was inside the Quiet Mountain, after all—the place where the veil between the real world and the Abyss was thinnest. If she wished to speak, to learn, to know, *this then would be her best chance. And so the child balled her little hands into fists. Twisting the dream and making it hers. The scene seemed to resist her, the stone/glass/ice beneath her rippled like a millpond. But this was her place.* Her *mind. She'd never given an inch in the real world, not in all her life.*

Why the 'byss would things be different here?

The image of her father and sisters trembled, then vanished entirely. The girl was left alone in the vast emptiness with the Mother of Night, here on the border of the Abyss and the waking world. The Goddess looked down at her daughter, the black of her eyes filled with a million tiny stars. And the girl wasn't a girl anymore. She was the champion of the Venatus Magni. *The Queen of Scoundrels. The Lady of Blades.*

The war you cannot win.

"All right," *Mia said.* "We need to have a serious chat."

Niah blinked. Long as an ice age.

"Speak, child," she finally said.

"Listen, I appreciate how difficult this has been for you to manage," *Mia said.* "I appreciate you want out of your prison and your son back at your side. But you have to appreciate I don't really feel like dying for it."

The Mother tilted her head, her voice tinged with sadness.

"You fear."

The girl shook her head. "Worse. I love."

"You would deny what you are?"

"No," *she replied.* "This *is* who I am. I'm not a hero. I'm a vengeful, selfish bitch. And I've never pretended otherwise. If you wanted a savior, perhaps you should've picked a girl who believes this world is worth saving."

The Dark Mother leaned closer, looking into her eyes.

"Let us speak, then, of vengeance, little one," she said, lifting the lopsided scales between them. "Out of jealousy, out of fear, my husband slew my son while he slept. Ever I obeyed him. Only once did I defy him, and only then, out of love for him. And for that sin, he cast me into the Abyss. He killed the magik in the earth. He murdered the light in the night."

"My father's tried to murder me a dozen times," *the girl shrugged*. "Maybe your boy should've got out of bed earlier."

The Mother blinked those infinite black eyes. Impossible fury boiling inside them. For a moment, the image of Alinne Corvere trembled and shook, as if it couldn't quite hold its form, and for a second, Mia saw what lay beyond it. The monstrosity she'd seen in books as a child—the horror the Ministry of Aa preached about from their pulpits. Not the Mother of Night or even Our Lady of Blessed Murder. The soundless void between the stars. The endless black at the end of life.

The Maw.

She was tentacles and eyes and claws and open, drooling mouths. Wide as infinity. Black as eternity. But the tremors stilled and the dark subsided, and the girl looked up into her mother's face once again. Thin black lips. Hard black eyes. The face of Alinne Corvere—the woman who'd scolded her as a child, sent her to bed without supper, told her to never flinch, never fear, never forget.

"You will leave the world in the grip of tyrant?" the Goddess asked.

"No," *the girl replied*. "I'm going to *kill* a tyrant. And I can't do that if I'm dead."

The Mother frowned. "I do not speak of your petty imperator. I talk of the Ever—"

"I know who you're talking about." *The girl put her hands on her hips.* "Look, I'm sorry. I know how awful what Aa did to you and your boy was. But can't your fucked-up little familia sort out its own shit? I've got enough to deal with handling mine."

The Mother's form shifted again, the stars in her gown flickering in agitation.

"This is more important that your petty mortal concerns, child."

"It's a pity, then, that you need us petty mortals to fix it for you, Mother."

"I am a goddess. Before light, before life, there was darkness. I am the beginning and the end. I am the first divinity. I will not be denied."

"I mean no disrespect. But I'm not afraid of you. It took years and all the power you had to put a fucking book in my hands and begin touching my dreams. You don't get to threaten me. You have to *convince* me."

"This is your dest—"

"Spare me," *the girl said, raising her hand.* "I'm not a slave to your destiny. I walk my own road. I make my own mistakes. And maybe this is one of them. But I'll fucking own it. Because it's my choice. My life. *My* fate."

Sorrow and anger filled her mother's voice.

"You are as selfish as Cleo, then."

The girl stepped forward, looked deep into those burning eyes.

"I thought I'd be alone my whole life. I thought I'd never find a piece of happy. Well, I've found one now, and I want to keep it. If that's selfish, then I'll be selfish. Because at least I'll be in love. And *fuck* you for trying to take that away from me."

Niah's form rippled again, the horror of what she was flickering beneath her surface. The black of her gown growing so deep, Mia was frightened she'd simply fall in and drown.

"You dare speak so to me?"

The girl gritted her teeth and stood her ground.

"That's the difference between me and most."

Mia looked down at her feet. There in the mirror beneath her, she saw a boy cut from the darkness. His skin was black as truedark. Tongues of dark flame rippled along his body, the top of his crown, as if he were a candle burning. Dark wings were spread at his back, and on his forehead, a single perfect circle was scribed.

Pale as moonlight.

Mia looked back up into the Goddess's eyes.

"I feel for him, I really do. And I know what it's like to have a father to hate. But I can steal back my brother without your help. I don't *need* you. So you need to give me a reason to do this. Not some bollocks about destiny or justice. A *reason*. Otherwise, you can sort out your own fucking marriage."

The girl spun on her heel.

"Meantime? I'm going back to bed."

The Night stood still as stone, glaring at her back as Mia started walking toward the morning. The stars in the Goddess's gown flickered with cold fire. Her voice was as deep and dark as the void.

"I can think of a few reasons, child."

CHAPTER 35

ASHES

Ash could still taste her.

Salt and honey. Iron and blood. Eyelids heavy, she ran the tip of her tongue along her lips. Savoring it. Breathing it in. Sighing it out. Looking out over the dark expanse of nothing beyond the Sky Altar's railing and thanking whatever god or goddess or twist of fate had brought that girl into her life.

Mia.

She'd left her dreaming. Naked on the furs. Hair strewn about her head like a nimbus of black fire. Kissing her, soft as feathers, Ash had risen from their bed, pulled a black silk slip over herself. Locking their bedchamber behind her, she'd bound her long blond hair back from her face and padded barefoot down the hall in search of a drink. Her tongue was sore. Her throat was dry. Satisfying the champion of the *Venatus Magni,* the Queen of Scoundrels, and Lady of Blades, was thirsty work.

The Church was deathly silent. The ghostly choir was still missing entirely, and the captured acolytes and Hands were under lock and key and Mercurio's watchful eye. Precious few had survived the attack, truth told, and all had sworn themselves to Mia as the leader of the Church. But the new Lady of Blades had insisted they be locked up anyway—for now at least. They couldn't be too careful. Couldn't treat this as more than a minor victory. Scaeva had escaped the Mountain, Spiderkiller along with him. Jonnen was back in his father's clutches. The question of the Moon was still unresolved.

This story was far from over.

So Ash stood now on the Sky Altar, looking out over the railing to the everblack beyond. Taking a moment to breathe. Aelius had said this was a place where the walls between the world and the Abyss were thinnest. That the perpetual night now wheeling above her head wasn't really the night at all. The benches and chairs behind her were empty. The air about her, silent and still. She had a clay cup, a bottle of fine goldwine taken from the kitchen's larders—Albari, as it turned out, Mia's favorite label. Quenching her thirst with a burning mouthful and mourning the taste of her girl, dimming on her tongue. Staring out at that Abyss and wondering if it stared back. Pondering what the night might look like if the Moon ever returned to the sky.

Part of her was still afraid Mia might change her mind. Still afraid the chronicler would convince her of the madness of his plan. But the rest of Ashlinn Järnheim, the part of her that knew Mia, trusted Mia, adored Mia, knew better.

Night be damned. Suns be damned. Moon be damned.

Mia Corvere wanted to live.

With me.

Ash felt the smile curling her lips, tingling all the way to her toes. Thinking of the house her father built in Threelakes. Flowers in the windowsill and a fire in the hearth.

And a big feather bed.

Ashlinn never thought she'd have anything like she had now. Never even dreamed it. She'd been born the child of a killer, just like her brother, Osrik, and Torvar Järnheim had fashioned his son and daughter in his image. Her childhood was thievery and thuggery and the promise of a life of death in service to Our Lady of Blessed Murder. Remorse was for weaklings. Regret was for cowards.

She remembered the turn her father had returned from his captivity in Liis. The offering that ended his tenure as an assassin. The mutilations he'd suffered in the Thorn Towers of Elai had left him forever marked. Forever bitter. For even though Marielle had mended the wounds Torvar had endured during his torture, the weaver couldn't replace the pieces of him that had been cut away entirely.

His eye. His manhood. His faith.

Ashlinn's father had lost more than his bollocks and his belief on that offering. He never smiled the way he used to after he came back from it. Never kissed her mother like he used to, never hugged his children like he'd once done, never slept without waking, screaming from his nightmares. Something inside Torvar Järnheim had broken in Liis and never properly healed. And the Red Church, for all their power and all their piety, couldn't give it back.

Ashlinn had hated them for that.

So Torvar had turned his children against the Church, and his children had dived right in. The man fashioned them to be weapons against the temple that had left him a ruin. To bring down the house of the Goddess who failed him. They'd planned it well, too. She and Oz had come *so* close. They'd lied and stolen, murdered Floodcaller, Carlotta, Tric—all to get Lord Cassius and the Ministry in their clutches. And though their failure had ended in her brother's death at Adonai's hands, in the last few turns, Ashlinn had seen everything she'd worked for finally come to pass.

The Ministry shattered, and the Red Church along with them.

Torvar Järnheim would have been proud of his daughter. And if she had some unfinished business with Adonai, well, that could keep for another turn. Because truth told, much as she loved him, her big brother had been something of a prick.

And so Ashlinn stood there on the Sky Altar. Staring out into the black beyond the Mountain. The night that wasn't a night at all. The Mountain quiet as graves around her, the Ministry all sleeping in their unmarked tombs. She pulled the tie out of her hair, rivers of blond spilling over her shoulder as she shook it loose, reveling in the feeling of freedom. Pouring another cupful of goldwine, Ash raised it to the dark.

"Cheers, Da, you miserable old bastard. And cheers, Oz, you snotty little whoreson."

She drank deep, and hurled her empty cup out over the balcony.

"I got them for you."

"HELLO, ASHLINN."

Her heart stilled in her chest. Ice-cold butterflies thrilled through her belly. Ash kept her face like stone as she turned from the railing to find him behind her. Tall and strong. Beautiful as a statue, wrought by the Dark Mother's hands. Her servant. Her guide. The flush of something close to life pulsed beneath his skin now, but his eyes were still pools of truedark, shot through with pinpricks of starlight. His saltlocks moved as if in a breeze. His hands were black as murder.

The boy looked at her. The silence between them deep as centuries. Ash realized this was the last place she'd seen him alive.

This landing, this very spot, was the place she'd killed him.

"Like I said before, it's quite a nose you've got there, Tricky. And I can't have you sniffing around the entrée this eve."

*"What do y—*hrrk.*"*

"Hello, Tricky," Ash said.

"TROUBLE SLEEPING?"

She shrugged. "Sometimes."

"GUILTY CONSCIENCE?"

Ash shook her head, calculating how many steps it would take to reach the stairs. Hand slipping around the bottle of whiskey.

"Our Mia has her appetites."

"OUR MIA."

"Well," she smiled crooked. "*My* Mia."

The boy sighed, shook his head.

"YOU MAKE YOURSELF SMALLER, ASHLINN. TRYING TO RUB MY NOSE IN IT."

"I don't have to try to rub anything, Tricky," Ash replied. "I *know* you can smell her on me. Smoke and sweat and those sweet and secret places. I know you remember what it was like to visit there. And I know how bad you want to go back. That nose of yours was always more trouble than it was worth."

Tric looked out over the railing. The place she'd pushed his corpse after she'd stabbed him to his end. Ash could feel the strength radiating off him, here in this house of the dead, so close to truedark and the Abyss he'd crawled from. She'd seen him fighting during the attack on the Mountain, the dark power inside him completely and totally unleashed. Moving faster than she could hope to. Stronger than she could dream of being. Cutting down those who dared face him like a scythe to the wheat, as if he were an extension of the very Lady of Blessed Murder herself.

She felt cold. Felt what the chill in the air was doing to her body, conscious now of how thin the silken slip she wore was. She crossed one arm over her breasts, her other hand tightening around the bottle's neck.

"You play a dangerous game, Ashlinn," Tric said.

"They're the only kind worth playing, Tricky. But you're not going to kill me."

He smiled at her then, and not a hint of it reached his eyes.

"And why's that?"

Ashlinn looked him over, blue eyes glittering.

"Because deep down? Beneath the murder and shit? You've got a good heart. O, you try to hide it. But you mostly do what's right." She smiled again, tilting her head. "And murdering a girl wearing nothing but her underthings just isn't your style."

"The boy you're talking about is dead, Ashlinn."

Tric's eyes narrowed, ever so slightly.

"You killed him."

"What do y—*hrrk*."

Ashlinn blinked at the dagger in Tric's hand. The blade gleaming silver. She felt the blow to her chest. Staggering back a step and grunting. The whiskey bottle toppled, shattering on the floor. His left hand fell on her shoulder, keeping her steady. His right hand held the knife, pressed hard into the flesh above her heart.

Hilt first.

Enough to leave a bruise. Nothing more. Enough to show her he could've killed her if he meant to. His hands were warm and night black on her skin, his grip as heavy as a guilty conscience. His eyes were full of rage, dark tears welling in his lashes as his lips curled and his voice dripped fury.

"I want to kill you," he said. "Goddess help me, I do. I want to cut your fucking heart in two and hurl you into the black like you did to me. We were friends, you and I. I *trusted* you. And you ended me, without a shred of remorse or a single fucking tear."

Ash's pulse was thunder in her veins. Mouth like ashes.

"But I'd never do anything to hurt Mia. Because I love her, Ashlinn."

Tric blinked, and two black tears spilled down his pallid cheeks.

"And she loves *you*."

He released his grip. Stepped away. Turning to the railing, he leaned on it with his elbows, black hands clasped before him. His saltlocks tumbled about his face as he stared out into the dark. Beautiful and broken. Because of her.

Ash stood frozen, hands at her chest. Looking at him, she could feel it welling up inside her. Past the walls she built for the world, the battlements she hid it all behind. The thing she'd tried to kill, to stomp down with her heels until it was nothing, the life she'd tried to live, all her father's lessons ringing hollow in her head.

Remorse was for weaklings.

Regret was for cowards.

But they were lies, and she knew it.

In truth, she'd always known it.

She knew what she'd taken from this boy. She knew why. Extinguishing all he was and could have ever been. She knew how hard it must be for him, returning to a world so changed. To see the girl he loved in the arms of the girl who murdered him. And though he had every reason under heaven to hate them, to lash out in his rage and break everything around him, he remained true. Loyal to his love. Loyal to the last. That was the kind of boy he was.

That was the kind of boy she'd killed.

". . . I'm sorry," she whispered.

Tric hung his head. Closed his eyes.

Hot tears spilled down Ashlinn's cheeks, her bottom lip trembling. The heat of her anguish was like a flood in her chest, spilling up over her lips in a bitter sob. Her body was heaving as the tears took her. She slithered down onto her knees amid the broken glass, the puddled goldwine, arms wrapped about herself, walls crumbling.

"T-Tric . . . I'm s-sorry."

The Church was silent but for her sobs.

"I w-wish I could take it back," Ash said, face twisting. "I wish there had b-been another way. We were killers, Tric. Killers one, k-killers all. I did what I had to. I did it for my familia. But I w-wish . . . it wasn't you. Anyone but you. And I know it's just a f-fucking word. I know how little it muh-means now. But . . . I'm sorry."

She shook her head, closed her eyes.

"Goddess, I'm so *sorry*."

She hugged herself tight, trying to hold the grief inside. The things she'd done, the person she was . . . it was hard to believe anyone might love her at that moment. That there could be any point to this at all. The elation of her victory, so clear a moment ago, was now bitter ashes on her tongue. Because when you feed another to the Maw, you feed a part of yourself, also. And soon enough, there's nothing left.

Weakling, she heard her father whisper.

Coward.

She knew the words weren't true. She knew the shape of the lie. But there on her knees, it felt so real, so sharp, it cut her anyway. Bleeding her onto the stone beneath. How easily a parent can make a triumph of their children, gentlefriends. And how easily they can make a ruin.

Ash heard the scrape of a boot on broken glass.

Felt a warm hand on her shoulder.

She opened her eyes and found him on one knee in front of her. His pale and beautiful face framed by locks as black as the sky above. His eyes were as deep as the night itself, flecked with tiny points of brightness. She took a strange comfort in that—that even in all that dark and all that cold, a pale light still burned.

"YOU'RE A FUCKING BITCH," Tric said.

Ashlinn blinked.

". . . And you're a fucking maid," she ventured.

He chuckled then. Short and sharp, his dimple creasing his cheek. Ash found her mouth twisting into a tiny smirk, mixed with bitter sorrow, the taste of her tears still on her lips. Then she was laughing, too, and the warmth it brought to her chest went some small way toward banishing the chill around them. Wiping the tears from her eyes and letting the grief melt away. They looked at each other, there on their knees, one foot and a thousand miles apart. Both killers. Both victims. Both lovers and beloved.

Perhaps not so far apart after all.

"I do love her, you know," Ash murmured.

"I KNOW," he whispered.

"There's nothing I wouldn't do to make her happy."

"NOR I."

". . . I know."

Ashlinn slipped her arms about Tric's shoulders, pulling him into a soft embrace. He tensed at first, hard as stone. Resisting with what little rage he had left. But finally, ever so slowly, he closed his eyes, and she felt his head dip gently onto her shoulder, his arms encircle her waist. He felt warm under her touch, not the unfeeling statue he appeared, not within or without. They knelt there on the floor in each other's embrace, broken pieces all around them, the Abyss open above them.

They stayed there for an age. All about them, silence. Ashlinn kissed Tric's cheek, light as feathers, gentle on his skin. And then she pulled back to look the boy in his eyes. She could taste his tears on her lips. Black tears and the goldwine and their girl and their past and the bitter ashes between them.

"I . . ."

Bitter ashes.

On her tongue.

She winced. "I . . ."

". . . Ashlinn?"

She coughed. One hand to her mouth. A dry itch in her throat. The taste of smoke in her mouth. She frowned, pawing at her neck. Felt a pain in her belly. And then she coughed again. Feeling a sticky wetness on her hand. Looking down to her palm and seeing it, red and glistening on her skin.

"O, Goddess . . ."

And Ashlinn couldn't taste Mia on her lips anymore.

All she could taste was the blood.

Ashlinn?"

Tric caught the girl in his arms as she wilted, coughing up another mouthful of red. His eyes were wide, one black hand to her face, shaking her.

"Ashlinn!"

He looked to the broken bottle. The goldwine spattered across the floor. Leaning close and inhaling, dread certainty taking root in his gut. Fool that he was, he'd missed it. Too intent on his hurt and his rage to take a moment to breathe it in. Because he could smell it now, sure as he could smell her blood on his hands, on her lips, the death that she'd swallowed, mouthful by mouthful.

Evershade.

Tasteless. Colorless. Almost odorless. And one of the deadliest toxins in an assassin's arsenal. Tric knew even now the poison would be worming its way toward Ashlinn's heart and lungs. He had only moments. If he didn't stop it . . .

Goddess . . .

He gathered the girl up in his arms. Running from the Sky Altar, cradling her head as he ran, swift as starlight, strong as the night, boots pounding on the twisting stairs. He knew where he had to go. Sprinting through the stained-glass dark, he could only grit his teeth and pray he wouldn't be too late.

Ashlinn coughed another mouthful of blood, her face twisted in pain.

"T-Tric . . ."

He hit the landing, dashing down the hallway toward the Hall of Truths. He saw Old Mercurio sitting on a rocking chair, guarding the captured Hands and acolytes in their bedchambers, a smoke drooping lazily from the corner of his mouth. The bishop caught sight of Tric charging toward him with the bloody girl in his arms, cigarillo tumbling from his lips.

"'Byss and blood," he breathed.

"Get Mia!" Tric shouted.

"What th—"

"Get Mia!"

Snatching up his walking stick, Mercurio broke into a run, grimacing in pain. Ashlinn groaned, lips and chin smeared with crimson, coughing again and holding her stomach. Tric dashed along another corridor, down another spiraling stair, holding Ashlinn tight to his chest, light as feathers. Finally arriving at a tall set of double doors, he kicked them savagely, bursting into the Hall of Truths.

Spiderkiller's lair.

Stained windows filtered a dim emerald light into the room, the glassware tinged with every kind of green—lime to dark jade. A great ironwood bench dominated the space, lined with pipes and pipettes, funnels and tubes. Shelves on the walls were filled with thousands of different jars, thousands of ingredients within.

Tric remembered his lessons here. The venomlore taught under the Shahiid's watchful eye. He wasn't the master at it that Mia was—that girl was born to poison like a fish was to water. But Tric knew the basics. Evershade was cruel, but ultimately a simple toxin. Its properties could be neutralized by any one of a dozen reagents—milk thistle, alkalese, whiteweed, rosecream, stayleaf, crushed fawn poppy seeds, brightstone mixed with ammonia or a solution of charcoal and powdered blackthorn.

Any of them would do.

Ash coughed up more blood, moaning in agony.

"Hold on, Ashlinn, you hear me?"

He smashed the glassware implements aside with a sweep of his hand, laid her out gently on the great ironwood bench. Ash grasped his black hand with her red one, squeezing tight, groaning through bloody lips.

"Tr . . . Tric . . ."

"I'm getting the antidote, hold on."

"M-Milk th-thistl—"

"I know, I know!"

He turned to the vast shelves, the rows upon rows of ingredients—phials and jars and glasses stoppered with green wax. They were sorted alphabetically, kept in perfect order by the dour Shahiid of Truths. He ran to the *M* section, reached for the milk thistle with black hands. But the jar was empty.

"Shit . . ."

"Tric-c . . ."

"Hold on, Ash!"

Fear was tumbling inside him like a great black waterfall, his pulse thundering in his veins. He ran to the *A* section, looking for the alkalese. He found three glass vials, all neatly labeled, all of them empty. Cursing, Tric turned next to the tubes full of ammonia. But those . . .

. . . those were empty, too.

Dark heart sinking in his chest, the boy ran from shelf to shelf, trying to ignore Ashlinn's cries. Blackthorn. Brightstone. Charcoal. Fawn poppy. All of them, beakers, tubes, pots, and urns, all of them *empty.* He was hurling the spotlessly dry flask of rosecream onto the floor, glass shattering, as the doors slammed open. Mia stood on the threshold in a slip of black, eyes bright and wide, hair mussed from sleep.

Ash was curled into a ball, blood on her lips. "M . . . Mia-a . . ."

"Ashlinn?"

"She's poisoned!"

"With what?" she demanded, eyes turning to Tric.

"Evershade! Maybe half a dram!"

"Well, get the fucking milk thistle!" she shouted, dashing toward the shelves and shouldering him aside.

"It's empty, Mia!"

"Fawn poppy, then! Or—"

"Empty! All of them are empty!"

"That's impossible!" Mia spat, searching the shelves, elbow-deep in glassware. "Spiderkiller kept this place in perfect order, there's no chance she just . . ."

"O, Goddess, Mia . . ."

Tric was holding up the jar of whiteweed. The last ingredient that could save Ashlinn's life. Unlike all the others, this jar had something inside it. A dark shape, fat and hairy, peering out at him with empty black eyes. A gloating, vengeful farewell from the Shahiid of Truths.

A spider.

"O, no . . . ," Mia breathed.

Spiderkiller had poisoned the Albari goldwine in the pantry before she fled. Goddess knew what else. One last bite, one last web, hoping to catch a Crow with her favorite drink. The poison worked slow enough for them to run to her hall, only to suffer one last torture in discovering the Shahiid had taken all the antidotes away.

That evil bitch.

"M-Mia . . ."

"Ashlinn?"

Mia ran to the girl's side, lifted her up and cradled her head in her arms. Ash seized hold of Mia's hand, slick with blood, tears in her eyes.

"It h-hurts."

"O, no, *no* . . ."

Tric backed up against the wall, watching in horror. He could see the anguish on Mia's face as she searched the shelves around her. Wide, tear-filled eyes, one long strand of black hair caught at the corner of her trembling lips. He could see the wheels at work in her head, see her pondering all the venomlore she'd mastered. She'd proved herself Spiderkiller's finest pupil before her betrayal. One of the greatest poisoners the Church had ever produced. Surely there was *something* she could do . . .

"I can't . . . ," she gasped, chest heaving as she looked into Ash's eyes.

She sobbed, looking once more around the room for any kind of hope.

"There's n-nothing."

Ash grimaced in pain, even as she grinned. Teeth slicked with red.

"Bitch g-got me."

"No," Mia said. "No, don't."

Ash winced, put one bloody hand to Mia's cheek.

"I . . . I'd have k-killed the sky for you . . ."

"No, don't you *dare* say your fucking farewells to me!"

Ash squeezed her eyes shut and groaned, curling up tighter. Mia clutched her to her chest as if she were drowning and only Ash could save her, tears smudging the kohl about her eyes, running black down her cheeks. Her face was twisted in agony, in horror, pulling her girl in tight and refusing to let go.

"No," Mia said, her voice cracking. "No, no, *NO*!"

The last rose as an agonized wail. The shadows began to writhe, Tric watching as the dark in the room deepened, the jars on the shelves began to tremble. Mercurio finally arrived at the Hall of Truth, gasping and red-faced, Sidonius and Bladesinger in tow. They looked on in horror as Mia held Ashlinn and screamed, screamed, as if all her world was ending.

"Mercurio, help me!"

The old man looked about the room. Saw the empty phials. The spider's jar.

"Black Mother," he whispered.

"Someone *help me*!"

Mia's chest was heaving, grief shaking her body. She hugged Ash tighter, face twisted with helpless rage, teeth bared, fingers curled into claws. But for all her power, all her gifts, this was a foe she couldn't best. She held on to Ashlinn for dear life, the girl's head tucked under her chin, rocking back and forth.

"Forever, remember?" she pleaded. *"Forever!"*

"I'm . . . s-sorry."

"No, don't go," Mia begged. "Please, *please,* I can't *do this* without you!"

"Kiss m-me," Ash managed.

A sob.

"No."

A sigh.

"Please."

Mia's face crumpled, her shoulders wracked and shaking, a hollow keening spilling over her gritted teeth. Ashlinn pressed a trembling hand once more to Mia's cheek, smudging it with red.

"Please."

And what could Mia do, in the end?

Have her leave without saying goodbye?

And so, eyes closed, lips parted, agony and grief and endless night above, Mia Corvere kissed her love. Blood on their mouths. Tears in their eyes. A broken promise. A last caress. The shadows rolled, the darkness seethed, every jar and urn and phial on the shelves shattering as their lips met for the final time.

A lifelong heartbeat. An empty eternity.

Together once. And now alone.

Only forever?

Forever and ever.

CHAPTER 36

BAPTISM

Jonnen could still taste the blood.

It had been a full turn since they'd emerged from the pool in the Red Church chapel beneath Godsgrave's necropolis, dripping in scarlet. Fifty of the Luminatii awaiting them had given him, his father, the woman called Spiderkiller, and the sorcerii called Marielle a hasty escort through the bustling streets. The other half century had remained behind to ensure none of Mia's comrades gave pursuit.

Jonnen had wondered whether it would've been a good or bad thing. But none of them came after him at all.

Once back in their apartments in the first Rib, the Spiderkiller had taken the sorcerii away, only Aa knew where. His father had gone to bathe. Jonnen had been surrounded by slaves, thoroughly scrubbed, trimmed, and dressed in a white toga hemmed in purple. And finally, with rather more flair than he thought their ignoble retreat from the Mountain had warranted, his father had presented him to his mother.

Or at least, the woman who called herself his mother.

Liviana Scaeva had wept to see him, sweeping him up in an embrace so fierce the boy thought his ribs might have cracked. She'd praised the Everseeing, blessed his father's name, dragging him close with one hand while the other still gripped her son.

"O, Lucius," she'd sobbed. "My darling Lucius."

And though he'd not spoken, the boy still heard the words ringing in his head.

My name is Jonnen.

They'd eaten a surreal sort of dinner together. Just the three of them, like he couldn't remember them doing for an age. The table was laden with the finest fare the boy had tasted in months. No slop stews or cold porridge or dried beef. No eating in some miserable hutch or lonely ruin. No bawdy tales or cigarillo smoke. Instead, they had mouthwatering finger foods and sizzling roasts cooked to perfection and honeyed sweets that melted in his mouth. Flawless porcelain plates and silver cutlery and singing Dweymeri crystal glasses. Mother even let him have a little wine.

And all Jonnen could taste was the blood.

Poor Butcher.

Poor Eclipse.

He already missed the big Liisian and his crude talk and his wooden swords. He missed the shadowwolf's company, their games of fetch, the fearlessness he'd felt when she rode his shadow. But he'd made his choice. Loyalty to his father. Fidelity to Itreya. Allegiance to the dynasty and the throne he would one turn ascend.

He'd made his choice.

And now he must live with it.

His mother had tucked him into bed. She'd hugged him for a full five minutes, as if afeared to ever let him go again. He'd spent a sleepless nevernight on spotless sheets, staring at the ceiling and pondering what he'd done. And the next turn, his father had sent for him.

Jonnen was escorted through their apartments with a cadre of a dozen Luminatii. Heavily armed. Heavily armored. Vigilant as bloodhawks and watching every shadow. The fresh tension in the air frightened him, truth told—he'd become so accustomed to Eclipse eating his fear, he'd forgotten how to manage it. As he waited in the corridor outside his father's study, he found his hands and legs were shaking.

He honestly thought he might cry.

"Take five centuries of your best legionaries," Jonnen heard his father command. "The blood pool is to be despoiled with oil and set ablaze. Arkemist's salt set at every pillar and doorway and ignited as soon as your men are clear. I want no bone or stone of the Red Church chapel left intact."

"Your will, Imperator," a man replied.

Jonnen heard heavy footsteps, and a trio of Luminatii centurions marched out of his father's study, resplendent in their gravebone armor and blood-red cloaks. They bowed to him as they passed, hurried off at their imperator's command. Despite the fumble at the Mountain, it seemed the machinery of the entire Republic was still utterly bent to his father's will.

Soon enough, Jonnen heard his father's voice again.

"Come in, my son."

Jonnen looked to the Luminatii around him, but none of the men moved a muscle. It was clear the boy's audience with his father was to be a private one. And so, on unsteady legs, Jonnen proceeded inside.

His father was seated on the divan beside his chess set. He was dressed in a long purple toga, freshly shaved and bathed, his appearance, as ever, immaculate. But there were faint shadows beneath his eyes, as if perhaps he'd slept poorly, too.

His gaze was fixed on the only piece atop the board—a single black pawn. Beside it sat a stiletto, crafted of gravebone. Jonnen saw a crow on the hilt with red amber eyes. It seemed a little brother to the longblade Mia carried.

"Father," the boy said.

"Son," his father replied, waving to the divan opposite.

The boy trudged across the study floor, the map of the entire Itreyan region laid out at his feet. Itreya and Liis, Vaan and Ashkah—all of them now under his father's control. No longer a Republic. A kingdom in all but name.

Jonnen sat down before its ruler.

"Where is Spiderkiller?" he asked, looking about. "The sorcerii?"

His father waved the question off, as if brushing away an insect.

"I had a dream last nevernight," he said.

The boy blinked. Not quite what he was expecting.

". . . What did you dream of, Father?"

"My mother," his father replied.

"O," the boy said, not knowing how else to respond.

"She was dressed in black," his father continued, still staring at the chess piece. "As she never dressed in life. Long gloves, all the way to her elbows. And she spoke to me, Lucius. Her voice was faint. As if from very far away."

"What did she say?"

"She said I should speak with you."

"About what?" Jonnen replied.

"Mia Corvere."

Ah.

This he expected.

"You mean my sister," the boy heard himself say.

His father finally glanced up at that, and Jonnen heard a faint hiss as Whisper unfurled from the imperator's shadow. The serpent peered at Jonnen with his not-eyes, licking the air with his not-tongue. He seemed more solid than he'd once been: a deeper black, now dark enough for two.

Jonnen could still hear Eclipse whimpering as—

"She told you, then," his father said.

"Yes," Jonnen replied, his throat feeling tight and dry.

His father leaned forward, his gaze burning. "What, exactly, did she say?"

The boy swallowed hard. He met his father's eyes, but looked away just as swiftly. "Mia said she was your daughter. Sired on Alinne Corvere."

Long silence descended on the study. Jonnen's palms were damp with sweat.

"And what else?" his father finally said.

"She said . . ."

The boy's voice faltered. He shook his head.

"Whisper," his father said.

". . . Be not afraid, little one . . ."

The shadowviper snaked forward, melting into Jonnen's shadow. The boy sighed as the daemon swallowed his fear, drinking down mouthful after mouthful. Leaving him bold. Cold as steel. The boy met his father's gaze again, cool and dark and hard. But this time, he didn't look away.

"She said I was also sired on the Dona Corvere," Jonnen said, his voice firm. "She told me that my mother is not my mother."

His father leaned back on the divan, regarding Jonnen with black, glittering eyes.

"Is it true?" the boy asked.

"It is true," his father replied.

Jonnen felt his stomach turn. His chest ache. He'd *known* it. Deep down inside, he knew Mia wouldn't have told him a lie like that. But to hear it confirmed . . .

Jonnen's eyes burned with tears. He blinked them back, wretched and ashamed.

"She *is* my sister."

"I would have told you," his father said. "When you were older. I had no wish to deceive you, my son. But some truths must be earned in time. And some truths are simply matters of perspective. Though she may not have given birth to you, Liviana loves you as a son. Do not doubt it for a moment, Lucius."

"That is not the name my mother gave me."

His father's voice turned to iron. "It is the name *I* gave you."

The boy bowed his head. And slowly, he nodded.

"Yes, Father."

The imperator of all Itreya picked up the black pawn from the chessboard, though in truth, Jonnen's eyes lingered on the stiletto. His father twisted the piece in his fingers, this way and that, letting the fading sunslight glint on the polished ebony. Lips pursed. Silence lingering.

"What else did she tell you?" he finally asked. "Your dear sister?"

"Many things," the boy mumbled.

"Did she happen to speak of what she planned to do if her assault on the Mountain was successful?"

Jonnen shrugged. "Not really. But I can guess."

"Guess, then."

"She'll try to kill you again."

"And that is all she seeks? My death?"

"She *really* does not like you, Father."

His father smiled and shook his head. "What of her companions, then? The Vaanian girl? The arena slaves? The dead one, returned from the grave? What do you know of them? What do they want? Why do they follow her?"

Jonnen shrugged. "Ashlinn seems to love her. I think she follows her heart."

"And the gladiatii?"

"Mia rescued them from bondage. They follow her out of love and loyalty."

"And what of the deadboy? The Dweymeri?"

Jonnen mumbled beneath his breath.

"I cannot hear you, my son," his father said, quiet anger in his tone.

“I said, he does not follow her,” Jonnen replied. “He tries to lead her instead.”

“To what?”

The boy looked at the chess piece in his father’s hand. He felt like that, now. A little piece on a board that was far too big. His time with Mia already seemed like a dream. The way he felt about her was a tangled mess inside his head—admiration, scorn, affection, horror. Perhaps even love. She was bold and brave and twice as big as life, and he knew she was important. That she had a role to play. But he’d known her all of eight weeks. He’d known his father nine *years*. And some loyalties just don’t die quietly, no matter what the storybooks say.

“The Crown of the Moon,” Jonnen heard himself whisper.

His father blinked. Surprise in his coal-black stare. The boy savored that a moment—it wasn’t often he found his father on the back foot.

“Mother spoke that name to me,” the imperator said. “In my dream. And my old friend Cardinal Duomo sought a map to that same place last year. He was of the belief it held the key to a magik that would undo the Red Church entirely. And despite my daughter’s efforts, Ashlinn Järnheim stole it.”

“She did.”

His father leaned forward on his elbows, looking Jonnen in the eye.

“Who, or what, is the Moon, my son?”

“. . . I cannot tell you, Father.”

His father picked up the gravebone dagger from the chessboard. Staring at Jonnen as he twirled it through his fingers. He didn’t say a word. But Jonnen could feel his glower, like a truelight heat beating on his skin. With a malevolent hiss, Whisper slipped free of the boy’s shadow, and without the passenger to consume it, his fear returned. Flooding cold into his belly and making his little hands tremble. The fear of disappointment. Of anger. Of hurt. The fear that only a boy who has looked into his father’s eyes and seen what he might one night become can ever truly know.

“I cannot tell you. But . . .”

Jonnen licked at dry lips. Searching for his voice.

“I can show you instead.”

“. . . E*xtraordinary . . .*”

“It is at that,” the imperator breathed.

They stood far beneath the City of Bridges and Bones, before a black and gleaming pool. The air was oily and thick, drenched with the stench of blood and iron. Jonnen had explained something of what they might see below, and it simply wouldn't do for soldiers of the faithful to learn their imperator was darkin—thus their Luminatii guards had remained at the entrance to the catacombs.

Jonnen, his father, and Whisper had stepped inside, down stairs of cold, dark stone and into the city's underdark. The light of a single arkemical torch was all they had to see by, held high in the boy's hand. They journeyed through the twisting tunnels of the necropolis, then into the shifting labyrinth of faces and hands beyond. Jonnen led them from memory, unerringly, for what seemed like hours in the lonely gloom. Until finally, they stepped out into a vast and circular chamber.

The boy stood now at his father's side, watching their shadows stretch before them. Whisper slithered out from his master's shadow, hypnotized, just as Mister Kindly and Eclipse had been. All around them, the beautiful faces etched on the walls and the floor were moving, just as they'd done the last time Jonnen stood here. The ground shifted and rolled beneath their sandals as stone hands reached toward them, stone lips whispering silent pleas. Jonnen understood who these faces belonged to now.

Their Mother.

Their *true* Mother.

The air was alight with it. Hunger. Anger. Hate. The anguished faces sloped downward into that deep depression, at once familiar and utterly alien, barely visible in the torch's pale glow. The shoreline was all open hands and open mouths. And pooled there, gleaming dark and velvet smooth, lay the pool of black blood.

Godsblood.

"I think . . ."

His father took one hesitant step forward. He stretched out his hand, and Jonnen swore he saw the surface of the pool ripple in response.

"I think I saw this place. In my dream."

". . . *Here he fell* . . . ," the serpent whispered.

"Here he fell," the little boy replied.

"And there is more of this?" The imperator stared at the pool, finally turning to look at his son. "Awaiting her at the Crown of the Moon?"

"I do not know," the boy admitted, his voice small and afraid. "But Tric told Mia she must journey there to unite the pieces of Anais's soul."

"Why travel all the way to the ruins of Old Ashkah?" his father asked. "Why not claim the power that resides right here beneath Godsgrave?"

"The remnants in this pool will not avail you, Father," Jonnen said. "Tric warned Mia about them. They are what is left of the Moon's rage. The part of him that wants only to destroy. They have festered down here in the dark too long. Mia did not dare to touch them. Nor should you."

His father's eyes glittered in the dark. Fixed upon that liquid malevolence. His hands balled into fists. Frustration. Agitation. Calculation.

"Duomo's map." The imperator turned his piercing black stare upon his son. "The one Järnheim stole. Did you see it?"

Jonnen swallowed hard. He loved his father, he truly did. Admired him. Emulated him. Envied him. But more, and above all, he feared him.

"I . . . saw it," the boy whispered.

"Whisper," his father said.

The shadowviper remained silent, swaying before the pool.

"Whisper!" the imperator snapped.

The serpent slowly turned its head, hissing softly.

". . . Yes, Julius . . . ?"

"Since you struck down my daughter's passenger, you seem made of . . . darker stuff." Black eyes looked the serpent over. "Do you feel changed?"

". . . I am stronger since consuming the wolf, aye. I feel it . . ."

"The tale is true, then? In destroying another of these . . . fragments . . ."

". . . We claim that fragment for ourselves . . ."

The imperator looked at his son. "And my daughter *has* killed other darkin?"

The boy nodded. "At least one."

"Then she is at least twice as strong as I."

Jonnen nodded again, watching his father by the light of their lonely torch. He could see the imperator's mind at work—the cunning and intelligence that had seen Julius Scaeva lay waste to all who opposed him. To build his throne upon a hill of his enemies' bones. And ever the apt pupil, the boy found his mind working, too.

His father had two problems with his wayward daughter, the way Jonnen saw it. First, that Mia might lay claim to whatever power lay waiting at the Crown of the Moon. And second, that even if she failed to claim it, with two fragments of Anais inside her, she was still more powerful than their father was. If she returned to Godsgrave at truedark—as she almost surely would—he'd be unable to stand against her, either way.

The imperator looked out over the inky black, his face etched like pale stone in the arkemical light. Jonnen couldn't quite remember ever seeing his father wearing the expression he wore now. He seemed almost . . . afraid.

"She showed me this for a reason," he murmured. "This is the answer. No mere throne or title. No work of man, destined for dust and history. This is ageless. Undying."

The imperator of all Itreya slowly nodded.

"This is the power of a god."

". . . Yours for the taking, Julius . . ."

"It is dangerous, Father," Jonnen warned.

"And what have I told you, my son?" the imperator asked. "About claiming true power? Does a man need senators? Or soldiers? Or servants of the holy?"

"No," Jonnen whispered.

"What then, does a man need?"

"Will," the boy heard himself say. "The will to do what others will not."

Julius Scaeva, imperator of the Itreyan Republic, stood on that screaming shoreline, looking out over that ebon pool. Stone faces mouthed their silent pleas. Stone hands caressed his skin. The godsblood rippled in anticipation.

"*I* have that will," he declared.

And without another word, he stepped into the black.

". . . Julius . . . !"

"Father!" Jonnen cried, stepping forward.

No trace of the imperator remained, save a faint ripple across the gleaming black. The pool shimmered and shifted, a strange un-light playing upon its surface. The boy felt his heart thumping in his chest, taking another step closer. The stone faces had frozen still. Aa himself seemed to be holding his breath.

"Father?" Jonnen called.

A wailing beyond the edge of hearing. A thrumming in the dark behind his eyes. Jonnen blinked hard, swayed upon his feet, clutching his temples as a black pain lanced through his skull. The stone faces opened their mouths wide, the cries rising in volume until the walls themselves seemed to tremble. Whisper curled upon himself, hissing in agony. Jonnen did the same, dropping to his knees and cutting them bloody on the faces beneath him. The reverberations seemed to shake the room, the city, the very earth itself, though all in the chamber was frozen still.

Jonnen found himself screaming along, feeling a pull like some dark gravity. He looked into the godsblood and saw it trembling, perfect, concentric circles rippling out from the spot where his father had fallen. The boy's belly flipped, his heart surged as he realized the liquid was receding, like an ebbing tide, draining back down into . . .

Into what?

He couldn't move. Couldn't breathe. He'd long since run out of breath to scream, but still he tried, eyes open wide, watching the blood sink lower and lower still. He could see a figure now, crouched at the center of the basin. A man, coated in gleaming black. The blood continued to sink, leaving the stone spotless behind it, every drop and spatter being drawn into the man's very pores. His form shifted, nightmare shapes briefly twisting into being and disappearing just as swiftly. And as the screaming reached crescendo, the shape settled into something Jonnen recognized.

". . . Father?"

He knelt at the bottom of the basin. Head bowed. One knee to the spotless stone. Silence fell in the chamber like a shroud.

". . . Julius . . . ?"

Jonnen's father opened his eyes, and the boy saw they were utterly black. Despite the torchlight, the shadows around them were all being drawn toward him. Jonnen saw his own shadow, reaching out to his father's with fingers outstretched. The longing and sickness and hunger inside him was almost a physical pain.

But slowly, ever so slowly, it ebbed. Fading, like the sunslight during truedark. Jonnen could see his father trembling with effort. His every muscle taut. The veins in his neck stretched to breaking. But gradually, the black across the surface of his eyes receded, withdrawing back into his irises and revealing the whites beneath.

"The will," he breathed, his voice tinged with a dark reverberation.

The imperator raised his hands. The shadows about them came alive, writhing and twisting and seething and stretching, the black a living, breathing thing.

"The will to do what others will not."

". . . Julius . . . ?" Whisper asked. *". . . Are you well . . . ?"*

The imperator snapped his fists shut. The shadows stopped their motion, falling still like scolded children. The imperator lowered his chin and smiled.

"I am . . . perfect."

The air hummed. The shadows rippled. Whisper retreated from the pool's edge, some instinct driving the serpent to coil inside Jonnen's own shadow. But instead of the passenger lessening his fear, the boy felt his own terror double. The snake's dread bleeding into his own.

His father climbed out of the now empty basin. Jonnen looked down and saw his father's shadow was utterly black. Not dark enough for three or four or even dozens. It was a dark so fathomless that light seemed simply to die inside it. The boy could hear a faint hissing noise, like a frying pan on a hot stove.

Narrowing his eyes, the imperator reached inside his robe, pulling out a trinity of Aa hanging on a golden chain about his neck. The light from the holy symbol flared bright in the boy's eyes, sickening, blinding. Jonnen gasped, stepping back with one hand raised to blot out the awful radiance. His stomach churning, he saw his father's skin was hissing and spitting where it touched the trinity, like beef on a skillet, smoke rising up from the imperator's burning flesh.

Jaw clenched, Julius Scaeva turned his will to the golden suns in his hand. Grip tightening, veins standing taut in his forearm, he slowly curled his fingers closed. The trinity crumpled like tin in a vise, crushed to a shapeless lump in his fist. Lip curling in disdain, he tossed the ruined metal aside, off into the cavern's far-flung shadows. Eyes on the burned skin of his palm.

"We will return to the Ribs," he said. *"And you will draw me Duomo's map."*

"Yes, Father," the boy whispered.

His father looked at him then. Despite the passenger riding him, Jonnen felt a perfect sliver of fear pierce his heart. The dark about them rippled and his own shadow shivered, as if just as afraid as he was. And looking up into his father's eyes, Jonnen saw they were filled with hunger.

"It is a good thing you've a memory as sharp as swords, my son."

CHAPTER 37

AWAY

One broken and bleeding heart.

Four figures beneath the Mother's gaze.

Seven letters carved in black stone.

Ashlinn.

Mia stood in the Hall of Eulogies, looking at the letters she'd cut into the tomb. Ashlinn's body lay inside, wrapped in a beautiful white gown taken from Aalea's wardrobe. All had been silent as Mia laid her love on the stone, kissed her lips, cold as the heart in her chest. Staring down at that beautiful face forever stilled, those eyes forever closed, that breath forever stolen. Trying to convince herself she felt nothing.

She'd pushed the tomb door closed. Felt it slam on all the futures she'd allowed herself to wish for. All the happy endings she'd let herself dream.

Resting her forehead against the unyielding rock and exhaling the last of the hope inside her.

Nothing now remained.

Nothing at all.

She turned to Mercurio, and the pity in his eyes almost broke her. She looked away quickly, to Sid and 'Singer, standing close enough to touch. Sorrow in their stares, pain at seeing her pain, no comfort at all. And finally, she looked to Tric, standing still as the statue of the Mother above them, scales and sword heavy in her hand.

"To live in the hearts we leave behind is to never die," he'd told her.

But in the agony of the end, is the having worth the losing?

Mia hung her head. Face in her hands. Wondering what came next.

And then, came agony.

Black fire burning in her bloodshot eyes. Black lice crawling beneath her tearstained skin. She gasped and clutched her chest, falling to her knees, the shadows about her rolling, clawing, biting. The walls were trembling. The earth beneath her crumbling away and dragging her down into darkness. The taste of rot on her tongue. A crushing weight on her chest. The sensation of drowning in a liquid black as truedark, the stink of blood and iron. It seemed for a moment like all the world was screaming so loud her eardrums might burst.

And then she recognized the voice.

"Mia!"

Dark flame in her heart. Dark wings at her back. Dark skies above her h—

"MIA!" Mercurio cried.

She opened her eyes. Gasping and filmed in sweat. Her old mentor was crouched beside her, arms wrapped about her, holding her still. The hall about them was in chaos, the tomb doors flung open by shadowed hands, the votive candles extinguished, the great iron chain on the Goddess's scales broken in two. Her comrades were wide-eyed, pale, staring at her in fear.

"O, Mother," Mia whispered.

"It's all right, little Crow," Mercurio said. "It's all right."

"No," she breathed. "No, it's not . . ."

Mia tried to catch her breath, still her struggling heart.

"MIA?" Tric stepped forward. "WHAT IS IT?"

Mia knelt on the graven stone, her breast heaving, hair plastered to the fresh sweat on her skin. She pressed her knuckles to her temples, her skull close to splitting, black pain behind her ribs. Her heart was still thundering, her belly still full of cold dread, the shadows around her still trembling with her fear.

"Mia, what's wrong?"'Singer asked.

"He's done it," she whispered.

"Done what?" Mercurio demanded. "What are you *talking about*?"

Mia could only shake her head.

"The fucking fool has actually done it . . ."

They met in the Athenaeum again, gathering in the hungry dark.

Aelius smoking like a chimney and watching Mia intently. Sidonius and Bladesinger, eyes filled with concern, clad in their worn leathers. Adonai in his red velvet robe and Mercurio in dark bishop's garb, staring at her with pale blue eyes. Tric all in black, his skin now kissed with a faint warmth that did nothing to warm her at all.

And at the center of them all stood Mia.

Black leather britches and wolfskin boots. A white silk shirt and leather corset. A gravebone longblade slung on her back, another of Ashkahi blacksteel hanging from her waist. A burning cigarillo on her lips to smother the smell of her girl on her skin, a bottle of wine in her belly to numb the pain, and the fragments of a god long slain burning in her chest. They'd listened as she spoke of the dark tremors that had run through her, the grip of agony on her heart and the taste of black blood in her mouth.

And then she told them what it meant.

"How canst thou be sure?" Adonai asked.

"I can feel it," Mia replied, her voice cold and dead. "Sure as I can feel the ground under my feet. Scaeva's consumed the godsblood that pooled beneath the 'Grave. United the shards of Anais that rested below the city inside himself."

"THEN HE'S DOOMED," Tric said. "THE SHARDS BENEATH THE CITY OF BRIDGES AND BONES WERE A SOURCE OF POWER, AYE. BUT CORRUPTED. ROTTEN THROUGH."

"Then let the bastard rot," Sidonius growled.

Mia watched Tric with black and empty eyes, dragging on her smoke.

"You told me the pool beneath Godsgrave was made of the pieces of the Moon that wished only to destroy. All his rage, all his hatred, left to fester in the dark. What do you think will happen now that the most powerful man in all Itreya has them inside himself?"

"HE'LL GO SLOWLY MAD," Tric replied. "AND THEN, INSTEAD OF RENEWING THE WORLD, HE'LL SEEK TO UNMAKE IT. HIS RULE WILL BE ONE OF CHAOS. HATRED AND MURDER."

Mia dragged her hand through her hair. Cigarillo smoke and the wine's red hum filling the hollow nothing inside her chest.

"He has my brother," she said. "I have to find Cleo."

Mercurio scowled. "Scaeva's got nowhere to run and no one to hide behind now. We've got a sorcerii. A pair of gladiatii. Two of the sharpest assassins in the Republic and a lad who seems near unkillable. We could just head to Godsgrave and gut him where he lives."

Sidonius nodded at Mia. "Seems a better plan than your suicide to me . . ."

Bladesinger nodded. "Agreed."

Mia looked about the assembly, slowly shaking her head.

"Scaeva's beyond any of you now," she murmured. "You can't help me in this."

"You don't know that, little Crow," Mercurio said. "We haven't even *tried*."

In answer, Mia simply held out her hand, palm upward. The black around them quavered, the darkness stirred. The girl lowered her chin, closed her bloodshot eyes, her hair moving as if in a faint breeze. She slowly curled her fingers into a claw.

Sidonius cursed. Mercurio caught his breath as Adonai muttered words of power. Everyone in the room found themselves wrapped in tendrils of shadow, coiling about their waists and legs. Mia twisted her fingers like a puppeteer, and each of her comrades cursed or gasped in wonder as they were lifted gently into the air.

"The truedark I was fourteen," Mia said, "I reduced the Philosopher's Stone to ruins. I skipped across Godsgrave in the blink of an eye, cut cohorts of Luminatii to pieces with blades of living darkness, ripped the statue of Aa outside the Basilica Grande to rubble. I had *a single* fragment of Anais inside me. Goddess knows how many were in that pool of godsblood. And truedark is coming."

The darkness sighed and Mia opened her hand again. Gentle as falling feathers, her comrades were borne safely to the ground.

Her eyes were on her mentor.

"He's got Jonnen, Mercurio."

"We can still get him back, we can still—"

"Scaeva's stronger than me now. Than all of us. At truedark, he'll be stronger still." Mia shook her head, took a long and bitter drag on her smoke. "I have to even the scales. And there's only one place where that kind of power exists."

A cold silence settled on the room, until Sidonius cleared his throat.

"Crow . . ." He proffered the Nevernight Chronicles. "Have you read these?"

Mia eyed the books with disdain. "Only a wanker reads her own biography, Sid. Especially if it's got footnotes."

"The first page . . . ," Sid murmured. "It tells how your story ends."

Mia dragged on her smoke, exhaled gray.

"All right, do tell," she finally sighed.

"You reduce the Republic to ashes," Sid said.

"You leave Godsgrave at the bottom of the sea,"'Singer nodded.

"I sense a 'but' waiting in the wings," Mia said.

"You die," Mercurio said.

Mia looked to her mentor. The man who'd raised her. Who'd given her a home and love and laughter when everything else had been taken away from her. Noting the tears shining in his eyes as her father's voice echoed in her head.

"If you start down this road, daughter mine . . ."

"You die, Mia," Mercurio repeated.

She stood silent for an age. Looking out at the books below them, row upon black row. All those lives. All those stories. Tales of bravery and love, of good triumphing over evil, of joy and happy ever afters. But real life wasn't like that, was it? Thinking of eyes of sunsburned blue and lips she'd never taste again and—

"Do I get him, at least?" she asked softly. "Scaeva?"

Mercurio looked to the books in Sid's hands. Shaking his head.

"It doesn't say."

"Well. Looks like we've some suspense left after all, neh?"

Her old mentor narrowed his eyes. "So eager for an ending now, are we? Lost your girl and your hope besides, is that it? You've fought your whole life, Mia Corvere. Goddess knows you've seen times this bleak before. And you walked through. Giving all, not giving in. This needn't be the end."

Mia exhaled a plume of gray and shrugged.

"Even daylight dies."

Her comrades looked to each other. Fear in their eyes. Silence between them dark as the evernight above their heads, as the shadow now settled over Mia's heart.

The girl glanced at Aelius with flint-black eyes.

"Seems you get your way after all, Chronicler. I suppose this is farewell."

He sighed and slowly nodded.

"S'pose it is."

"Cheerio, you withered old bastard. Thanks for all the smokes." Mia's lips twisted in an empty smile. "Fuck you for the whole poisoned chalice of destiny thing, though."

"Good fortune, lass," the chronicler said sadly. "However it ends, at least you had a story to tell."

Mia crushed out her smoke underheel. Looking her old mentor in the eye. The man who'd taken her in. Who'd loved her like a daughter. Who'd been more of a father to her than any of them.

"Don't do this, Mia," he begged. *"Please."*

"I can't just leave Jonnen with him, Mercurio. What would that make me? What have the last eight years been about, if not familia?"

"But the map's gone," he said. "You don't even know the way."

She closed her eyes then. Thinking of bow-shaped lips and long tresses of golden blond. Gentle curves and sharp shadows and freckled skin on crumpled, sweat-soaked sheets. So clear in her mind she could almost reach out and touch her.

A sight she'd never forget, as long as she lived.

"I remember the way," she whispered.

Least I'm not traveling by horse," Mia sighed.

She slung her supplies onto the camel's back, shoulders aching at the strain. Mia knew trekking into the deepwastes was going to be more dangerous than sticking her face in a gorewasp's nest, so heading out by wagon was a far more sensible option.* But truth was, not enough beasts had survived

---

* O, fuck me, you were thinking. It's been a while, I wonder where all the footnotes went? Maybe the author got embarrassed by everyone in his own book taking a steaming shit on them and decided to refrain for the rest of the novel?

Well, fuck you, gentlefriends.

The gorewasp is a flying insect of the Ashkahi desert, banded in red and black and measuring around a thumb length. Though it can't compare to true horrors of the Whisperwastes like retchwyrms or sand kraken, they're still particularly nasty pricks. Their stings are incredibly painful, and, strangely, a pregnant female's venom is also imbued with psychoactive properties. Creatures stung by the mother-to-be will be thrown into frenzy by the pain, driven to self-harm or lashing out at those around them in an attempt to end their toxin-induced agony. Herd animals will be abandoned or, more frequently, killed by their fellows, and even human victims have been known to top themselves to end their own suffering.

The lady gorewasp then goes to work, laying her eggs inside the freshly killed carrion. She'll lay upward of a hundred younglings, who hatch in a burst of rancid blood and rotting meat around nine turns later. Hence their rather unimaginative name.

So there. Another footnote. And there's plenty more where that came from, you ungrateful bastards.

If you're such an expert on literature, maybe you can write your own book, neh?

her arkemist's salt explosion to haul anything of the kind. Flaming shrapnel had torn through the stables during the blast, most of the mounts had been maimed or killed. Of every beast in the Red Church pens, only one of them had miraculously escaped mostly unscathed.

The beast in question growled a complaint, staring at Mia with mud-brown eyes.

"Shut the fuck up, Julius," she growled.

Sidonius and Bladesinger stood on the stairwell, watching her load her gear.

"How long, the journey?" Sid asked.

Mia straightened, dragging her hair behind her ear. "At least two weeks across the deep Whisperwastes by my reckoning."

"Truedark will fall soon," Sid said, meeting her gaze.

"Last Hope to Godsgrave is at least eight weeks by sea," Bladesinger said. "And the Ladies of Storms and Oceans still want you dead, last we checked. Presuming we don't all die horribly out there, how are you planning on getting us back to the 'Grave in time to deal with Scaeva?"

"Who's 'us'?" Mia asked.

Bladesinger frowned as she tied back her locks. "Who do you think?"

"You're not coming with me, 'Singer. Neither you, Sid."

"Pig's arse," Sidonius said. "We're with you to the end."

"All of us," came a voice.

There on the stairs stood the last two senior members of the Red Church. Adonai was dressed in faun leather breeches and a thin robe of white silk. He also wore a broad-brimmed hat, azurite spectacles, and white gloves—obviously to spare his skin the touch of the sunslight. Beside him stood Mercurio, who'd abandoned his bishop's robes in favor of a more utilitarian tunic and britches. His walking stick beat crisply upon the stone as the pair made their way down to the stable floor.

"Where do you think you're going?" Mia asked.

"With thee, little darkin," the speaker replied.

Mia blinked. "No, you're not."

"All evidence points to the contrary," her old mentor said, shouldering his pack.

"Mercurio," Mia said, placing a hand on his arm. "You can't come on weeks-long trek into a magically polluted hellscape. You're eighty years old."

"I'm sixty-fucking-two," the old man growled.

Mia simply stared.

Mercurio put hands on hips in indignation. "Listen here, little Crow, I was slitting throats when you were knee-high to a scabdog—"

"That's my *point,*" Mia said.

The girl looked between Sid and 'Singer, Mercurio and Adonai, shaking her head.

"I appreciate the sentiment, truly. But even if I wanted you to risk yourselves, there's not enough camels to carry us all. Are you going to walk to the Crown?"

"If needs be," the old man growled.

Mia looked between the bishop and speaker. "You two are all that remains of the Church hierarchy. If I actually pull this off, if the balance is truly restored between Light and Night, we need people in charge who actually know what the Red Church is supposed to represent." Mia raised an eyebrow at Mercurio's walking stick. "And no offense, but it's been a while since any of you had to do any frontline fighting . . ."

Adonai began to protest. "Thou shalt be in need of all—"

"Am I the Lady of Blades, or am I not?"

". . . Thou art," the speaker replied.

"Then you're staying here," she said, looking at Mercurio. "If I don't return . . . If I fail, you're the only ones who can rescue Jonnen and Marielle."

"But how will we get to Godsgrave in time?" 'Singer asked.

"Aye," Mercurio asked. "Scaeva's destroyed the local chapel. And the blood pool along with it. We're cut off from the 'Grave."

Mia looked to Adonai. "The Lady of Blades never struck me as the kind of woman who wouldn't leave herself a back door."

The speaker slowly nodded. "Another pool there be. In Drusilla's palazzo."

Mia looked among her friends, her eyes finally resting on Sidonius. "I need you to do this for me. If I don't make it back . . ."

Sidonius breathed deep, his eyes shining.

"Please, Sid. Promise me."

The big man sighed. But finally, as she knew he would, he nodded. Because if Mia could've had a big brother, she'd have chosen him.

"Aye, Crow. I swear it," he said.

Mia's chest was empty. Her whole body numb. But somehow, she managed to conjure a grateful smile. Squeezing 'Singer's hand. Kissing Sid's cheek.

"I'll not leave you to face this alone," Mercurio said.

"I'm not alone," Mia said, turning to face her old mentor. "I've never been alone. You've been with me ever since that grubby, spoiled little brat stormed into your store and demanded you buy her brooch. You saved my arse that turn. And in some small way, you've been saving it ever since."

Mercurio scowled, his ice-blue eyes welling with tears.

"Never took a wife," the old man said. "Never had a familia. Didn't seem fair in my line of work. But . . . if I ever had a daughter—"

"You had a daughter," Mia said.

The girl threw her arms around the old man and squeezed hard as she could.

"And she loves you," she whispered.

Mercurio closed his eyes, tears spilling down his cheeks. He kissed the top of her head, shaking his own.

"I love you, too, little Crow."

"I'm sorry it had to end this way," she murmured.

"It's not the last chapter yet."

"Not yet."

Mia pulled back, leaving his waistcoat a little damp. She dragged her sleeve across her nose, tucked her tear-soaked hair behind her ears.

"If . . ."

She pressed her lips together, breathed deep.

"If I don't come back . . . remember me, neh? Not just the good parts. The ugly parts and the selfish parts and the real parts. Remember all of it. Remember *me*."

Mercurio nodded. Swallowed hard. "I will."

Mia looked about the Mountain's belly for the last time. There was still no whisper of the ghostly choir in the air; all was silence. But that seemed fitting somehow. She closed her eyes a moment, letting the quiet wash over her, unearthly and beatific. She felt it tingling along her skin like music, down her spine, the song of the dark between the stars. Crowning her shoulders with blackest wings. Wishing her good fortune. Kissing her goodbye. Her heart ached that another hadn't been here to do that. All the things they could've been . . .

Mia drew a deep breath. Feeling a cat-shaped hole in her chest, and all the fear and sorrow and anguish that had seeped in to fill it. But she pushed it back. Fought it down. Thinking of her brother, her father, her mother. The words she'd been taught when she was but a girl of ten. The words that had shaped her, ruled her, ruined her.

The words that had made her all she was.

Never flinch.

Never fear.

Never forget.

She kissed Mercurio's cheek, nodded farewell to Sid and 'Singer, then took hold of her camel's reins and led him out into the dying sunslight.

Giving all, not giving in.

"Farewell, gentlefriends."

Tric was waiting for her outside the Mountain.

Whisperwinds played in his long saltlocks, shifting them about his broad shoulders. His stare was fixed on the eastern horizon. His gravebone blades were crossed at his back, black leathers hugging his frame. As always, he seemed some masterwork, inexplicably placed on a rocky outcropping in a nowhere stretch of the Ashkahi wastes. Until he moved, that is, raising one ink-black hand and tucking one thick lock fallen across his face back behind his ear. His eyes were bottomless black, shot through with tiny pricks of illumination. Narrowed against the dying light.

Saan had sunk so low it was almost hidden below the horizon. Saai loitered yet in the heavens, the Knower twisting the sky into an awful, lonely violet. But truedark was near now. Tric was almost as close as he'd ever be to what he'd been. As she walked up beside him, Mia could feel the gathering dark in her bones.

"IT'S NOT FAIR," he sighed. "NONE OF THIS IS."

"I know."

"I LOVE YOU, MIA."

She sighed. "I know."

He turned to look at her. Tall and beautiful and carved of sorrow.

"CAN I KISS YOU GOODBYE?"

Mia blinked. The words like a knife in her chest. "You're . . . not coming with me?"

Tric shook his head. "YOU'D NOT HAVE ME ANYWAY, EVEN IF I OFFERED. IN YOUR HEART, YOU KNOW WHAT WAITS FOR YOU ACROSS THAT DESERT IS FOR YOU ALONE. MUCH AS I WISH TO, I CAN'T HELP YOU FACE WHAT'S TO COME. BUT I KNOW IN THE END, YOU'LL BE THE ONE LEFT STANDING."

"That chronicle seemed quite clear that I end horizontal, Tric. Not vertical."

Tric only shrugged. "NOTHING IN THIS LIFE IS CERTAIN. ESPECIALLY WHERE AND WHEN IT FINISHES. NO BOOK, NO CHRONICLER, NOT EVEN THE GODDESS HERSELF CAN SEE ALL ENDS. THIS NEEDN'T BE YOURS."

"Go on without her, is that what you mean?"

"I KNOW HOW MUCH YOU LOVED HER, MIA. I'M SORRY."

She looked at him then. This beautiful boy who'd dragged himself through the walls of the Abyss for her. The boy who loved her so much, he'd defied death to return to her side. Most would have hated the girl who'd killed them, stolen what was theirs. Most would've celebrated, not mourned her death. Seen it as a chance to worm back into Mia's affections. To plant red roses atop her lover's grave.

But not this boy.

"I know," Mia said, heart aching.

"I MEANT WHAT I TOLD YOU IN AMAI. YOU *ARE* MY HEART, MIA. YOU *ARE* MY QUEEN. I'D DO ANYTHING YOU ASKED ME, AND EVERYTHING YOU WON'T. I DON'T CARE IF IT HURTS ME. I ONLY CARE IF IT HURTS YOU. AND I'LL LOVE YOU FOREVER."

"I love you, too," she whispered.

"BUT NOT THE WAY YOU LOVED HER."

"Tric—"

"IT'S ALL RIGHT." He reached out, touched her face, gentle as first snows. "IT'S NOWHERE NEAR ENOUGH. BUT IT'LL STILL KEEP ME WARM."

"I wish . . ." Mia shook her head, pressing his hand to her cheek. Wondering how many more times her heart could splinter inside her chest. "I wish there was two of me."

"THERE ARE, REMEMBER?" The boy smiled, grim and beautiful. "TWO HALVES, WARRING WITHIN YOU. AND THE ONE THAT WILL WIN . . ."

". . . Is the one that I feed."

"DON'T GIVE YOURSELF TO SORROW, MIA. DON'T LOSE THE HOPE INSIDE. MORE THAN ANYTHING YOU ARE, MORE THAN THE COURAGE, THE CUNNING, THE RAGE, YOU'RE THE GIRL WHO BELIEVED. SO LET ME KISS YOU GOODBYE. THEN WALK ON. AND DON'T EVER LOOK BACK."

Mia breathed deep, looking up into his eyes.

"Kiss me, then."

He took her hand in his. His eyes were fathomless pools, deep as forever. He ran his thumb across her skin, scabbed and scarred, making her shiver. And eyes locked with hers, he lifted her knuckles to his lips. And he kissed them. Soft as clouds.

"GOODBYE, MIA CORVERE," he said, releasing her hand.

". . . That's it?" she asked.

"THAT'S IT," he nodded.

The wind whispered between them, lonely and longing.

"Fuck that," she breathed.

Mia grabbed his shirt in her fists. And standing up on tiptoes, she dragged him in and kissed his perfect lips. He caught her up in his arms, his body surging against her, mouth open to hers. Squeezing so hard she thought she might break. A dizzying kiss. An endless kiss. A kiss full of sorrow and regret for all the things they might have been, a kiss of love and longing for all the things they'd had, a kiss of joy for all they were, right at that moment. Forever bound in blood and ink, a part of each other's tale in a story as old as time itself.

She didn't want it to end. She didn't want it to be real. She didn't want any of this. But Mia Corvere knew, better than any, that sometimes we just don't get what we want. And so, she pulled away. Resting her forehead against his a moment longer. Cheeks wet with tears. Cupping his face and dragging an unruly lock away from those bottomless eyes and staring deep into the dark between her stars as she whispered.

"Farewell, Don Tric."

"GOODBYE, PALE DAUGHTER."

"Remember me."

"FOREVER."

She climbed onto the back of her beast, eyes on the eastern horizon.

Wiping the tears from her eyes, she rode on.

And she didn't look back.

CHAPTER 38

MOMENTUM

The whispers were growing louder.

She was seven turns into the Ashkahi wastes, a long and lonely trail of dust stretching westward in her wake. The sands were the red of rust, or old drying blood. The heavens were a melancholy indigo. Saan was only a few hours from disappearing below the worldedge now; just a sliver lightening the horizon with murderous scarlet. Saai would slink after its swollen twin soon, but for now, the smallest sun stubbornly clung to the expanse above, and the Everseeing's last eye was yet open.

Soon enough, though, Aa must relinquish his hold on the sky.

Then night would fall.

And so will he.

Mia's eyes were on the ground ahead, narrowed in the stinging winds. Her tears were long since dried on her cheeks. The earth before her was parched, a million cracks spreading out into the dead earth like black spiderwebs. She was now so deep in the wastes, she was beyond the reach of most maps of the Itreyan Republic. East across the desert lay a crescent of dark granite known as the Blackverge Mountains. The range stretched southward in jagged peaks and spires, stone fists that punched and tore at the sky. According to the map on Ash's skin, a narrow pass wound its way through the Blackverge, opening into the ruins of the Ashkahi Empire beyond.

And there lay the Crown of the Moon.

She had no idea what awaited her in that place. A woman more powerful than she was, that much was certain. A woman who'd lived with naught but shadows for company since before the rise of the Republic. A woman gripped by madness, who hated the Night and jealously guarded the very thing that could wrest Mia's brother from his plight and, at the same stroke, finally see an end to her father's twisted ambitions.

Her vengeance.

Mia's fear made Mister Kindly's absence all the more acute. She missed Eclipse like a part of her had been severed and burned at the stump. Thinking of the way the shadowwolf must have ended, falling in defense of her brother, and adding the daemon's destruction, Butcher's death, Ashlinn's murder to the ever-growing list of reasons why Julius Scaeva deserved to die.

And O, by the Black fucking Mother, die he would.

But first . . .

Cleo.

Julius spat and grumbled and complained, but Mia was feeling too hollow to pay attention to the camel's griping. Sipping from a flask of warm water, she felt Saan sinking ever lower to the horizon at her back, the light about her fading slow. She kept one watchful eye on the sands ahead—the monsters that lurked beneath the earth were ever on her mind. She knew from past experience that the beasts of the Whisperwastes were inexplicably drawn to her shadowwerking. Enraged by it. If she ran into a sand kraken or retchwyrm, her tale might end before she ever reached the Crown.

Mia wondered at that—why the predators of the Whisperwastes were so infuriated by her power. Loremasters said that the monstrosities of the deep wastes were born of the magikal pollutants left over from the Empire's destruction. But if the Ashkahi Empire fell when the Moon was struck low by his father, perhaps Anais, the fragments inside her, the horrors themselves, were all connected somehow?

Still, it could be worse. On top of the monstrosities of the wasteland she was riding toward, she might also have to worry about—

Julius bellowed again, snorting and spitting. Mia cursed beneath her breath, the noise finally breaking through the rime of numbness about her heart.

"Shut up, you ugly whoreson."

The camel bellowed again, rolling what seemed to be a full gallon of spit around in its throat. It stomped, warbled, tossed its head. Mia sighed and turned her eyes to the direction the camel was gargling in. And there, in the distance, she saw a cloud rising from the southern reaches. Smudged on the horizon in dark red.

"Storm, maybe?" she muttered. "The Ladies are still pissed at me."

A spray of white spittle came off Julius's lips, and Mia slowly nodded. She doubted the Lady of Storms was in a hurry to black out the sky again.

"Aye, you're right. This is something else."

Reaching into her saddlebags, she withdrew a long spyglass, trimmed in brass. Holding it to her eye, she peered into the rising dust. For a moment, she had trouble finding focus among the rolling curtain of red. But finally, dying sunslight glinting on their speartips, glimmering on their plumed helms . . .

"Fuck me very gently," she breathed. "Then fuck me very hard."

Itreyan legionaries. Marching north in formation, their cloaks billowing in the whisperwinds. Row upon row. She saw by their standards that they were the Seventeenth Legion out of southern Ashkah. All ten cohorts, by the look. Five thousand men. And though it could be that their commander had simply sent his fellows north into a barren stretch of nightmare wasteland for a pleasant afternoon stroll, Mia knew in her heart they were marching toward her.

Toward the Crown.

But how in the Black Mother's name . . .

"Put some clothes on," Mia hissed. "Jonnen's going to sleep in here with us."

"Really?" Ash frowned, looking about her. "Shit, all right, give me a breath."

Mia shuffled her brother into the cabin as Ashlinn rolled out of the hammock, turned away from the door. The boy stood with his hands clasped before him, sneaking curious and furtive glances at the inkwerk on Ashlinn's back . . .

"Jonnen," she breathed.

Mia had no idea how Scaeva had sent word to the Ashkahi Legion about where she was headed. But he'd taken the godsblood. The might of a fallen divinity sang in his veins. Who knows what gifts he had at his disposal now? And in the end, she supposed it didn't really matter *how*. He'd obviously done it, and she obviously had five thousand fully armed and armored cocks set to fuck her none too sweetly.

The question was, what was she going to do about it?

She looked to the Blackverge Mountains to the distant west, shot Julius an apologetic glance, and pulled out her riding crop.

"I hope you're not going to make me use this," she said.

Faster, you ugly fuck, *faster*!"

Julius was in a froth, Mia bent over her reins and riding hard, the beast's hooves thudding and thumping over the parched earth. The Lady of Blades, champion of the *Venatus Magni,* and Queen of Scoundrels had hoped she might get a good enough lead on the Seventeenth that pursuit would prove fruitless, but she hadn't counted on their cavalry cohort. She could see a group of outriders now if she squinted—twenty men on swift horses, riding up hard from the south. They might not know the camel in front of them carried the girl they sought, but they were certainly coming for a look-see. Trying to scarper as fast as Julius could gallop probably wasn't the best way to ease their curiosity, but Mia had hoped she could simply outrun them.

The problem being, of course, that horses run faster than camels.

"I never thought I'd say this," Mia gasped, "but I miss Bastard."

Sadly, the thoroughbred stallion she'd stolen from the stables in Last Hope two years ago was nowhere to be seen, and Mia was stuck riding her snarling spittle-beast. The outriders bore down on her out of the southern heat haze, dust rising behind them. She'd been thoughtful enough to pack a crossbow from the Mountain's armory, loading a bolt and drawing the string.

As the soldiers galloped closer, the lead outrider blew a long, quavering note on a silver-trimmed horn. Mia saw the men wore light leather armor, shortswords at their waists and shortbows in their free hands. Their livery and the thin crests of horsehair on their helms were stained a deep leaf-green, the standard of the Seventeenth emblazoned on cloaks dyed in the same shade.*

---

*There are a total of twenty-eight Itreyan legions under Imperator Julius Scaeva, and aside from the Bloody Thirteenth—Itreya's renowned slave legion—the soldiers of the Seventeenth are probably the most infamous.

Led by Caius "Decimus" Viridius (himself an alumnus of the Bloody Thirteenth), the Seventeenth are the legion that operate farthest from the civilization, and thus, from the jurisdiction of Godsgrave, expected to keep peace in a largely untamed land that belongs to the Republic mostly in name only. In a place so vast, the legion maintains order largely by reputation rather than physical presence. And it's not a reputation for kissing babies and helping elderly women cross the street with their market baskets.

For example, after a rise in taxation in the city of Nuuvash, the civilian populace rose in rebellion and destroyed its small garrison of Itreyan troops. Well-schooled in the art of siege warfare, the Seventeenth quickly retook the city. But Nuuvash was an

"Halt!" the leader roared. "Halt in the name of the imperator!"

"To the Abyss your imperator," Mia growled.

Mia raised her crossbow and let fly. The captain fell with a bolt in his chest, tumbling from his saddle with a grunt of pain. The other soldiers cried out in alarm, splitting up like a flock of swallows, scattering in all directions. Eight swung around behind Mia, another eight spurred their mounts ahead.

And then,

like a silent miracle at her back,

Mia felt the red sun finally slip below the edge of the world.

The sky shifted darker: moody indigo, fading through to sullen violet. Only one eye of Aa remained in the sky. Only one piece of the Everseeing's hatred holding her gifts in check. Not quite truedark yet, no. She'd not been unleashed that much.

But enough.

Looking back over her shoulder, Mia saw a legionary raising his shortbow, taking aim toward her heart. She wondered for a moment what would happen if she let the arrow strike home. If it could truly pierce what had already been broken. Picturing pretty blue eyes and a smile that made her want to cry. And then she

Stepped

from Julius's back

to the archer's horse, seizing his bow arm and turning it toward another rider. The man cursed in surprise, his arrow flew, striking his brother legionary in his neck and sending him flying off his mount. The archer cried out in alarm, let go of his bow, tried to draw his shortsword. His fellows roared warning, turned their bows on Mia. And the girl

---

important trading hub, and, unable to simply put the entire population to the sword, Viridius introduced the punishment of "redding."

The entire civilian population, men, women, and children, were divided into groups of one hundred and forced to draw stones in a lottery. Those who drew a red stone—a full tenth of the participants—were set aside. The remaining 90 percent were forced to stone the losing tenth to death, or be executed themselves.

The final death toll is unknown, but of this we *can* be certain—that until the Republic's fall, the people of Nuuvash never rebelled against Itreya again.

Stepped

to the next horse

in the line as the soldiers loosed their arrows, piercing their comrade a dozen times. He clutched at his punctured chest, a garbled scream bubbling from his throat as he tumbled to the dust.

Sitting in front of a new rider, sunslight behind him, Mia drew the longblade from her back and pushed it through his chest, gravebone splitting his chain mail as if it were dry parchment. A hail of arrows flew at her in answer, but she was already gone, Stepping to another rider's shadow, slicing as she came. A stray shot killed one of the horses, the poor wretch snapping its legs and killing its rider as it crashed to the sands. The legionaries cried out in rage and alarm, unsure how to best this unholy foe.

"Magik!" one shouted.

"Sorcerii!" bellowed another.

"Darkin!" the cry. *"Darkin!"*

Mia continued her bloody work, Stepping to three more riders and cutting them down with her blade. It was wet and brutal work. Close enough to see the fear in their eyes. To hear the bubbling in their lungs or the catch in their breath as she ended them. An old refrain. So much red on her hands already. Too much to ever wash away. She wanted to pray as she slew. The benediction to Niah ringing unbidden in her mind.

Hear me, Mother.

Hear me now.

This flesh your feast.

This blood your wine.

But in the end, she said nothing at all. Crimson hands and empty eyes. The riders scattering and shouting alarm, their horses whinnying in terror. By the time she was done, eight remained where twenty had begun. And Mia Stepped off her blood-soaked horse and back onto Julius, her face spattered with red. Wiping her blade clean and slipping it back into her scabbard, she watched as the soldiers dropped back in dismay, more than half their number wounded or slain. Mia took hold of her reins, urged her camel on harder. Looking down at her hands, sticky and wet.

Goddess, the power . . .

Mia looked up to the indigo sky, the thin wisps of cloud. The heat was failing now that Saan had fallen, the sweat cooling on her skin. The third eye of the Everseeing was yet open, the last remaining sun in the heavens looming at her back. But as sure as the world turned, Saai would soon sink to its rest.

And what will I be then?

The ring of distant horns and thunder of approaching hooves pulled her from her wonderings. Wiping her bloody hands on Julius's flanks, Mia looked off to the south. She saw the outriders had fled back to their legion, tails between their legs. But now, through the fading pall of red, Mia could see a larger dust cloud approaching. Fingers still sticky, she fetched the spyglass from her bags and peered through it.

"Bollocks," she breathed.

It seemed the Seventeenth's commander hadn't taken well to her treatment of his outriders. Galloping up from the south, Mia could see the legion's whole cavalry cohort now charging at her—heavy horsemen, clad in thick iron and leather armor, gleaming helms set with tall horsehair plumes. Each soldier was armed with a spear, shield, crossbow, and shortsword. Their mounts were clad in barding made of boiled leather, whipping up a wall of dust in their wake.

Five hundred of them.

Mia looked to the Blackverge Mountains, still at least three turns' ride away. She turned back to the boiling cloud of dust coming toward her, rising in the wake of two thousand pounding hooves. The charge was drawing closer with every breath. She was caught out in the open. Empty desert in front and behind. If she stole one of the dead scout's horses, she'd be leaving all her supplies on Julius's back. If she tried to outpace them on her camel, they'd just cut her down like scythes to the wheat.

Julius bellowed, jowls wobbling.

"Well, shit," Mia muttered.

CHAPTER 39

FATHOMLESS

Nowhere to run. Nowhere to hide.

The Seventeenth's cavalry was closing in on Mia, shaking the ground as they came. The horsehair crests on their helmets and their long cloaks were the color of forest leaves. Their mounts were black and rust-red, protected by thick sheaves of boiled leather. The glint of the last sun on their spears was like flashes of lightning. The sound of their hooves was thunder.

"Maybe the Lady of Storms isn't quite done with me yet," Mia muttered.

Saai cast a long light out of the west. Her camel's shadow was a muddy smudge stretching out across the cracked earth and rolling dunes. But Mia's was a deeper shade of black, sharper at the edges, dark enough for two. And it was moving.

It would have been simpler to cloak herself beneath her mantle of shadows, disappear entirely. But if Jonnen had given Scaeva details about the map and the Crown, the Seventeenth would know where she was headed anyway. The foot soldiers wouldn't move as swift, but she had to deal with their cavalry, one way or another. And so Mia set her shadow moving, sending it out across the wasted sands in a myriad of shapes, stretching toward that hateful sun. Calling to the dark, just as she'd done the turn she first met Naev, the turn she first fled for her life from—

Ahead.

Mia peered into the distance, saw a trail of churning earth approaching her out of the west—as if something colossal swum beneath the dirt. She glanced north, saw another two runnels converging on her.

"All right, bastards," she murmured. "Let's go give them a kiss."

Mia dragged on her reins, turning Julius toward the oncoming cavalry charge. Still twisting the shadows about her, she squinted at the oncoming horsemen. They were riding in formation, shields raised, spears pointed upward in a glittering thicket. Their line was a hundred horses wide, five deep, the leaf-green standards of the Seventeenth Legion streaming in the whisperwinds behind them.

Mia leaned over the reins, urging Julius to run faster. Ahead, someone among the cavalry blew a long note on a horn. Every man in the first and second rows lowered his spear. Another blast rang out, and Mia saw the third and fourth rows string their bows, ready to loose a volley of two hundred arrows down on her head. She glanced behind her, the shadows about her twisting and coiling, peering at the lines of boiling earth converging on her position. The closest was only thirty or forty feet behind her now, hidden beneath the storm of dust Julius was kicking up.

Closing fast.

At the sound of another horn, the archers loosed a flight of black arrows into the air. Julius bellowed as Mia grabbed him hard by the ear, steering him away from the incoming hail. And with a prayer to the Mother on her lips, Mia reached out to her shadows and wrapped them about her and the beast she rode.

The world dropped into a haze—not the black it had been beneath her cloak when two suns shone, but a blur nonetheless. Julius stumbled as he went half-blind, Mia clinging for dear life with her fingers, thighs, and teeth. But to his eternal credit, as smelly and ugly as he was, the beast didn't fall. Overcome with a panic, Julius instead broke east as the arrows began to strike. Mia heard the patter of hundreds of shots into the sands she'd rode on a moment before. Arrows piercing the earth and the thing that swam beneath it.

She heard the cavalry sound their horns again. The thunder of their hooves diminishing as they slackened their pace, dismayed at her disappearance.

And then . . .

"The fuck is—"

"Kraaaaaken!"

Mia threw off her cloak of shadows, fingernails digging into Julius's fur as she looked back over her shoulder. Rearing up out of the churned sands, she saw half a dozen massive tentacles. The appendages were dark, leathery, lined with jagged hooks of awful bone. Drawn by her shadowerking, pierced a dozen or more times by the cavalry's arrows, the enraged sand kraken dragged itself up out of the broken earth toward the men who'd hurt it. The monstrosity wrapped a hooked tentacle around the closest horse and rider, pulling them toward its hideous beaked maw.

Their horses were thrown into a frothing panic. The cavalry commander roared at his men to attack. But as another soldier cried out in fear, pointed at the two new runnels of boiling earth bearing down upon the cohort, utter chaos broke loose.

Another kraken burst from the blood-soaked sands, larger than the first. Drawn by the blood and screams, it cleaved a half-dozen riders in half with one sweep of its arms. A hail of arrows came raining down, a monstrous howl of pain shook the ground beneath Julius's hooves. Dust rose in a boiling cloud, red sands and blood spraying in all directions. Mia saw flashing steel, silhouettes dancing in the haze, heard the blast of horns as a third kraken reared up from the bloodied earth and bellowed in hunger and rage. Some horsemen broke, others charged, still more milled about in chaos and confusion. Tentacles and swords and spears cut the air, men and monsters bayed and howled, the stink of blood and iron hanging in the rising cloud of dust.

Mia turned away from the slaughter she'd unleashed, hardening her heart. Ahead, through the wind-borne dust and shimmering heat haze, she could barely make out the shadows of the Blackverge Mountains.

The Crown of the Moon awaited her beyond.

Digging her heels hard into Julius's flanks, Mia rode on.

Five turns later, Mia stood with her back to a falling sun, chewing her fingernails. In front of her, spurs of red stone rose into broken foothills and from there, into foreboding peaks. Behind her, Julius stood in a pall of dust, his jowls white with spit.

"I think this is it," Mia muttered.

The camel bellowed and dropped a few pounds of shit into the dirt.

"Look, it's not like that map was drawn by a master cartographer," Mia growled. "It was copied off the wall of a thousand-year-old temple, then copied again in some dingy alley parlor in some fuckarse nowhere town on the north coast of Ashkah. It may not have been one hundred percent accurate."

The camel warbled again, thick with disdain.

"Shut up, Julius."

This was the fifth passage through the range she'd tried in as many hours, and Mia's hope was fading. Each previous foray into the mountains had eventually finished in dead ends, or defiles too narrow to pass. Fuckarsing about with all these wasted attempts, she'd burned her lead on the Seventeenth Legion entirely. Looking to the south, she saw the soldiers were only a few hours' march away now.

"These bastards don't give up easily," she murmured.

She *had* killed a few hundred of their cavalrymen, she supposed. Even if they weren't under orders from their imperator, they'd still hunt and kill her on general principle now. But looking at the oncoming horde of legionaries, Mia could see their commander wasn't just sending his heavy horse this time. He was sending *everyone*.

Mia strode across the broken ground, grabbed her camel's rigging, and dragged herself up onto its hump. The beast bellowed a complaint, stomped its hooves, and tried to throw the girl off his back.

"O, shut the fuck *up*, Julius," Mia sighed.

She struck the beast's flanks with her riding crop, and the beast broke into a trot, leading them into a canyon between two jagged cliffs. Mia wondered if she might set an ambush at the pass for the soldiers following, but soon abandoned the notion—the gap between the peaks was wide enough to send an entire legion through abreast. Still, as she rode on, a lonely crow singing above her, she found herself frowning at the canyon walls about them.

These weren't like the cliffs around the Quiet Mountain. The rocks weren't weathered or smoothed by time. The mountains near the Church felt old, shrouded in the dust of ages, thick with history. These mountains felt . . . *new*.

The land sloped downward, as if she were headed into a depression. And riding on, Mia couldn't shake the sense of foreboding crawling on her skin.

The whisperwinds were growing louder. At times, she swore she could make out words among the shapeless babble. Voices that reminded her of her mother.

Her father.

Ashlinn.

Mia shook her head to clear it, feeling dizzy and lost. It seemed as if she were riding through a fog, though in truth, the light of the single sun was still bright at her back. She took a swallow of water from her saddlebag, wiped the sweat from her brow.

Something feels wrong here.

Magik, perhaps. The remnants of Ashkahi werkings, shattered and lost in the Empire's fall. Even after centuries, so many years beneath the burning suns, it seemed the stain lingered, like blood seeping into broken earth. But sure and true, she could at last feel it in her bones now. A certainty in her chest.

This is the right way.

She rode on, the wind scrabbling and clawing through the stones. Mia's hands and feet were tingling, a vague and muzzy feeling in her skull. An itch of sweat, dripping down her spine. She concentrated on the broken ground ahead, fancying she could hear her mother's voice again. She could feel the cool press of Tric's lips on hers as she kissed him goodbye. The touch of Ashlinn's fingertips between her legs, the girl's breath in her lungs. Unsure of what was real, what was memory. And always, ever, the whisperwinds. Close enough that she could feel soft breath brushing against her earlobe, goosebumps on her skin.

She heard crunching under Julius's feet. Looking down to the earth beneath them and seeing it was littered with old bones. Human, animal, cracking and splintering as her camel trod upon them. She frowned, blinking as a jawless skull turned toward her, staring with hollow eyes as it whispered.

"If you start down this road, daughter mine, you are going to die."

Peering at the path ahead, Mia realized it was finally narrowing. Cliffs of jagged red stone rose on either side of her. Looking to the sky above, she was struck with a sense of vertigo, realizing she had no sense of how much time had passed since she entered the fissure. Her hands were shaking. Her tongue parched. Her waterskin was almost empty, though she didn't remember drinking that much.

You are going
to die.

Ahead of her, on either side of the passage, two statues loomed. Each was carved of sandstone, humanoid in shape, details worn down by the years. The leftmost was split asunder at the waist, its ruins tumbled about its ankles. The one on the right was mostly whole—a human figure with the vaguest hint of strange writings at the base, a long headdress, the head of a cat. It reminded Mia of the lantern on Marielle's desk. She looked to Mouser's blacksteel sword at her waist—human figures with feline heads, male and female, naked and intertwined.

"Ashkahi," she murmured.

Lost to time. Lost to memory. So little of them remained. A few trinkets, scraps of knowledge. And yet, once these were a people, a civilization, an empire. Destroyed utterly in a calamity born of jealousy and rage.

She turned her eyes from the statues ahead to the path beyond. Past the broken monuments, the way was narrowing, closing to a thin defile. A crack running deep in the earth, splitting into a fork farther in, stone rising high on either side. From the map on Ash's skin, Mia knew that beyond the split in the path lay a maze of runnels and fissures, spreading across the wastelands like spiderwebs.

And beyond that . . .

Beyond that . . .

Be . . .

She could hear her mother singing. Ashlinn sighing her name. Smell Mercurio's cigarillo smoke on the air. See her father's eyes as he asked her to join him. Terror rising in her chest like a black tide, like a flood, threatening to drown her entirely.

Never flinch.

Never fear.

Her legs ached and her feet felt sore—how long had she been walking? Turns? Weeks? She couldn't remember eating, but her belly was full. She couldn't remember abandoning Julius, but the beast was nowhere to be seen. It was growing dark, she realized—as if the suns had finally sunk to their rest beyond the worldedge. For a moment she was struck with panic, thinking she'd been in here so long that truedark had fallen. But no, looking to the sky above her head, Mia could still see a thin strip of muddy indigo sunlight, feel the heat of Aa's last eye in the heavens. The Dark had yet to claim dominion of the sky.

"This is all wrong," she breathed.

She was close.

She shouldn't be here.

She should turn back while she still could.

Walking through a labyrinth of red stone and deepening shadows. She could hear faint cries behind her, trumpets blaring, wondering what had become of the soldiers who pursued her into this forsaken place. Wondering why they ever came here.

Why *she* had.

Looking down, Mia saw her shadow moving like it was black flame, licking and seething over the scattered bones. Like gentle hands, tugging at her clothes, caressing her skin. She looked toward her feet and saw the sky above her. She looked up to the sky and saw nothing at all. She felt Ashlinn naked in her arms, the girl's lips on her neck. Feeling her lover shiver as she traced the lines of her tattoo with her fingertips. The path through this place. Etched in black.

The rock around her was twisting, the shadows roiling, the light playing tricks in the nooks and crevices. It seemed as though she were surrounded by wailing faces, by grasping claws. The dark deepened, fathomless and perfect. Mia squeezed her eyes shut, realized she couldn't feel anything anymore—not the ground under her feet or the pulse in her veins or the wind in her hair. The light of the last sun seemed dim as a distant candle, though the sky at her feet was still bright.

"You're not my daughter."

"You're just her shadow."

"The last thing you will ever *be in this world, girl, is someone's hero."*

"A girl with a story to tell."

"All I hear, Kingmaker, are lies from the mouth of a murderer."

"I want you gone, do you hear me?"

"I'd have killed the sky for you . . ."

The shadows reached out toward her, stretching into the nothing she'd become. She looked down to her own shadow and saw it was black, like tar, like glue, running between her fingers like melting candle wax. She could smell faint smoke and motes of dust, the perfume of empty tombs. Something crunching beneath her feet, dry and brittle as twigs. Sharp as the screaming in her mind.

"O, Goddess," Mia breathed.

A bleakness so perfect she couldn't imagine anything before or after or ever again. No light. No sound. No warmth. No hope. Tears welling in her eyes.

"O, Goddess . . . I can *feel* her."

She pushed it aside. The fear. The sorrow. The loss and the pain. So close now, she could taste it. Reach out with trembling hands and touch it. Rip it from its cage of broken ribs and make it her own. Her birthright. Her legacy. Her blood and her vengeance. Her promise to the only one she had left.

Brother.

"I . . . I cannot swim very well."

"I can." She squeezed his hand again. "And I'll not let you drown."

The cliffs about her were fragmented now, run through with dark cracks and rife with shadows. On the broken earth beneath her, in the crumbling walls around her, she saw the faintest marks of civilization—the vague pattern of bricks here, a fragment of broken statue there. The ground she'd set her boots to sloped ever downward, and in it, she saw the faint impression of flagstones—as if this had once been a road, smashed with unspeakable fury into the shattered earth.

She was close now. That same pull she'd felt in the presence of Furian, of Cassius, of her father, now amplified a dozen-, a hundred-, a thousandfold. A black gravity. A bottomless undertow, rippling beneath the paper-thin skin of reality about her. The veil between this world and another felt thin and stretched. Something grander and more terrible was waiting on the other side. Something close to . . .

Home.

When she'd first heard tell of the Crown of the Moon, Mia had imagined something awe-inspiring. Something palatial. A fortress of gold, perhaps, glittering on an impossible mountaintop. A spire of silver, topped with a wreath of starlight. Instead, this was a desolation. A dissolution. She knew now she was walking into an enormous crater, wrought by an impact that had scoured the land of all but broken memories. Of the empire that once flourished in this place, there was almost no trace. Its legends, its lore, its magiks, its songs, and its people, all undone in an instant. A cataclysm that ruptured the very earth, leaving it forever broken.

Mia followed the slope inward. Downward. Wind curling in her hair. Whispers echoing in her ears. Vertigo swelling in her skull. She could definitely hear a woman's voice now, discernible in the shapeless, haunted babble. And through the furrowed troughs and shattered defiles, dust on her skin and steel in her eyes, she finally stepped into the heart of the Ashkahi crater and saw it laid before her in all its broken glory.

The Crown of the Moon.

She almost smiled to see it. The final answer to the riddle of her life. The last revelation in a story written in ink and blood by the light of dusk and dawning. And in the end, after all the murder and all the miles, it was so simple. She could see the city of Godsgrave in her mind, as if from above—the Sword and Shield Arms, the Nethers, the towering, ossified Ribs. Shattered isles, run through with traceries of canals, looking for all the world like a giant laid upon its back. One piece missing.

And here it was.

Not a fortress of gold or a spire of silver.

"Of course," Mia whispered.

A skull.

A colossal, impossible skull.

BOOK 5

SHE WORE THE NIGHT

Chapter 40

Fate

"The Crown of the Moon," Mia breathed.

It was hundreds of feet tall, miles across, buried to the temples in splintered earth. Its face was upturned to the sky, a circle scribed into its vast and barren brow. It was gravebone of course, just like the Ribs, the rest of Godsgrave's foundations, the blade on Mia's back. The last remnants of Anais's body, flung from the heavens by a vengeful father who should have loved him as an only son. His body had struck the earth so hard, the Itreyan peninsula was smashed beneath the sea, and there upon the ruins, Aa had commanded his faithful to build his new temple. But here, in the heart of the Ashkahi civilization, Anais's severed head had struck the ground with unthinkable force, bringing the empire that worshipped him as a god to an end.

It seemed a lonely thing. A tragic thing. Infanticide, etched in ancient bone.

Mia climbed up the broken foothills, the blasted rocks. A single crow circled above, calling to no one at all. The dust curled and danced about her feet. Mia's shadow pointed directly toward the skull, like a compass needle toward north. Fear gnawing on her stomach. Pressing on her chest. She could feel herself being pulled, stretched, a hunger like she'd never known.

It was as if all her life, she'd been unfinished, and she'd never realized until this moment. All the fragments of her brief existence seemed insignificant—Jonnen, Tric, Mercurio, Scaeva, even Ashlinn—they were only phantoms somewhere in the dark within. Because through all the years and all the blood, at last, at *last,* she was home.

No.

Mia gritted her teeth, balled her hands to fists.

This is not *my home.*

She was here for a reason. Not to sleep, but to awake. Not to be claimed, but to claim. The power of a fallen god. The legacy of a shattered line. The power of the light in the night. To tear it, beating and bleeding, from a shattered chest and wrest back her brother from the bastard who'd claimed him. To fight and die for the only thing that gave her life meaning anymore. The only thing she had left.

When all is blood, blood is all.

Mia climbed up through the open mouth, across teeth as big as cathedrals. The shadows about her were twisting and curling, a dark descending, deep as dreaming. She stole through a split in the skull's cavernous palate, up wending ways of dull gravebone, slipping out at last into a vast and lonely hall inside the skull's hollowed crown. The cavity was round like an amphitheater, wide as a dozen arenas. It was almost entirely empty, thin spears of illumination piercing the hundreds of cracks in the bone above, the last sun's dying light turning pitch-black to a dull gloom. The whisperwinds were so loud, Mia could feel them on her skin, hear the words beyond at last, here at their source—a tale of love and loss, of betrayal and butchery, of a sky torn asunder and all the land beside, a mother's tears and a son's blood and a father's shaking, crimson hands.

Mia crept forward, avoiding the tiny patches of sunlight spilling through the cracks, hidden inside the dark she'd ever called friend. Looking about that black and empty gallery, she saw nothing. And yet she knew with terrible certainty she wasn't alone. She peered into the nooks and furrows, searching for some sign of life, some source for the awful dread and hunger piercing her heart. And finally, looking up to a shelf of splintered gravebone behind her, Mia saw her standing alone.

A beauty. A horror. A woman.

At last.

Cleo.

She was tall. Willow slender. And young, O, Goddess . . . so very *young*. Mia had no idea what she'd expected—an ancient crone, an ageless husk—but Cleo barely looked older than she, truth told. Her hair was thick, black, glossy as a slick of oil, reaching past her ankles and dragging on the floor behind her. She wore a backless black gown, gossamer thin and unadorned, made entirely of shadows. The black hugged her frame, stretching all the way from her chin to her bare feet. Her arms were bare like her back, her skin the kind of pale that hadn't seen the suns in . . .

. . . well, centuries, Mia supposed.

She was beautiful. Her lips and eyelids black as ink. Utterly motionless, save for the hems of her gown, which curled and swayed as if alive. And her shadow, Goddess, it was so dark, Mia's eyes hurt to look at it. Watering as if she'd stared into the suns too long. It pooled at the woman's feet, bled out across the bone like liquid. Dripping away over the ledge she stood on and vanishing entirely before it landed.

Slow as centuries, Cleo lifted her hands, digging her fingertips into her skin. Mia saw her forearms were scratched and scabbed, her nails now laying in another score of welts. The woman's green eyes were upturned to the ceiling's vast and cracking dome, head tilted as if she were listening—save there was nothing to hear but the hush and sigh of the endless winds.

Cleo held out her hand, fingers splayed, and Mia felt something shifting in her breast. That pull again. Like gravity to earth. Like powder to naked flame. Her skin pricked with goosebumps, and the shadowed nooks and hollows about the room stirred and shivered, as if they, too, felt the woman's call.

Mia caught movement from the corner of her eye, saw a tiny black shape spring from the darkness and take to the wing. It was a passenger, she realized—a daemon, wearing the shape of a tiny sparrow. It alighted on the tips of Cleo's fingers and the woman laughed with joy, turning her hand this way and that as if to admire the daemon's dark beauty.

The sparrow trilled a tune like Mia had never heard. The notes were clear as crystal bells, ringing down the length of her spine. It was the opposite of music. An unsong, echoing there in the vast recesses of that dead god's skull. And, still smiling, Cleo stuffed the sparrow into her mouth.

Mia felt screaming across the back of her skull. That hunger swelling inside her, dark and terrifying and filling the space utterly. Cleo threw her head back, chewing as the shadows around the room shook, their fear seeping through the fragments in Mia's chest and bleeding out, cold and oily, into her belly.

This is how she's sustained herself all these centuries, Mia realized.

Gathering the pieces of Anais to herself and . . .

. . . and eating them.

Cleo lowered her chin. Oil-black locks tumbled about her face. Swallowing thickly, she looked to the alcove where Mia hid. And the woman smiled as a voice—cold and clear as a truedark sky—rang in Mia's head.

You may come out now, dearheart, sweetheart, blackheart.

Mia felt the fear spread: an icy tide, trickling out through her fingertips and down into her legs, making them shake. But she steeled herself, made her heart iron. She placed her hands on the hilts of the gravebone longblade at her back, Mouser's blacksteel at her waist. And drawing a deep breath, she stepped out onto the floor below Cleo.

The woman looked at Mia, her hair rippling with the hems of her gown. She smiled, a thin trickle of something black and sticky spilling down her chin.

"My name is Mia," the girl said. "Mia Corvere."

Cleo tilted her head.

We know.

The woman spread her arms, and the shadows in the room came alive. Bursting from the cracks and crevices, spilling from the bottomless dark at the woman's feet. Tens, dozens, hundreds of shapes, each one wrought of living, breathing darkness. Serpents and wolves and rats and foxes and bats and owls—a legion of daemons, cutting through the air or slinking across the bone or darting from shadow to shadow. A shadowviper slithered between Mia's feet, a hawk made of rippling black alighted on the ledge above her head, a mouse sat directly before her and blinked with its not-eyes. The whispers swelled, a cacophony inside her mind, speaking with one dreadful voice.

You have walked so far. Suffered so much. But you need suffer no more.

Mia narrowed her eyes, staring up at the beauty, the horror, the woman.

"How do you know what I have and haven't suffered?"

We know all about you.

Cleo smiled. Held out her hand. And from the darkness about her, a shape coalesced on her upturned palm. It was a shape Mia knew almost as well as her own. A shape who'd found her the turn her world was taken away, who walked beside her through all the miles and all the murder and all the moments until . . .

Until the moment I sent him away.

"Mister Kindly," she breathed, tears welling in her eyes.

". . . hello, mia . . ."

". . . What are you doing here?"

". . . you told me to find someone else to ride . . ."

The not-cat narrowed its not-eyes, tail whipping in anger.

". . . so i did . . ."

Walking along the pale length of Cleo's arm, Mister Kindly pushed himself into the dark locks of the woman's hair, draping himself about her throat and shoulders, just as he'd done to Mia countless times before. Cleo shivered and ran her hand over the shadowcat's fur, and he arched his back and tried to purr.

A black jealousy stirred in Mia's breast as Cleo's voice rang inside her head.

We know why you are here.

Little pawn.

Broken thing.

"You don't know anything about me," Mia said.

O, but we do. We see the bruises of their fingertips upon your throat, even now. "The many were one," yes? "Never flinch, never fear," yes? How poorly used you were, dearheart, sweetheart, blackheart, by the ones you named Mother.

Mia looked to the not-cat, her heart crawling up into her throat.

"You told her?"

". . . i knew you'd make it here eventually . . ."

Mister Kindly's tail curled about Cleo's neck, not-eyes turned to the dome above.

". . . best to be prepared for your arrival . . ."

Cleo stared at Mia with eyes as deep as centuries.

We knew you were coming. We heard you calling in the desert. The wastelings who answered your summons.

"Kraken," Mia nodded. "Retchwyrms. How can they hear us calling?"

They are all that remains of the city that once stood here. Worms and insects, twisted by the magiks that bled from this corpse that was empire.

"And why do they hate it when we werk the dark?"

They remember in their souls. They know in their blood. His fall was their ruin. And we are all that is left of him.

"Anais," Mia whispered.

Cleo's eyes narrowed at the mention of the Moon's name.

You come to claim that which is ours.

"Unless you want to give it to me."

Cleo sighed and shook her head.

Little one. Nothingling. Serf and sycophant to a power too weak to save herself. Bidding us die that her son might live. Condemning us to the grave so she might know reprieve. Asking all and giving nothing and never once questioning the right of it.

The darkness about them shivered as the woman raised her hands, palms up.

Goddess she names herself. And slaves she names us. Thinking us tiny players on a stage built of weak and hollow grandeur.

Cleo looked at Mia, black lips curling in disdain.

She offers nothing, save what she will take back. And still, you kneel before her.

"I kneel for no one," Mia spat.

Cleo's laughter echoed off the gravebone walls, rolling among the gathering of daemons like ripples through black water.

"I mean it," Mia said. "I give no fucks for gods or goddesses. I don't care about winning a war or restoring the balance between Light and Night or Niah or Aa or *any* of it. I never have. I'm here for my brother."

Cleo licked at her lips, fingertips digging into her skin. The whispers about her seemed to hush, the dark sinking deeper as she dragged broken nails down her arms again. She shivered at the pain, eyes wide and shining.

We had familia once. A boy. A beauty. All we had, we gave to him. And he left us, dearheart, sweetheart, blackheart. Left us all alone. Seek not your worth in the eyes of others. For what is given may be taken away. And what then shall remain?

"I'm not here to answer your riddles," Mia growled. "I'm not here for the meaning of life. I'm here for the power to rescue the only thing I have left that matters."

We will not give it to you.

Mia took one step closer. "Then I'll take it."

"*. . . mia, you can't win like this . . .*"

"Shut the fuck up, Mister Kindly."

"*. . . look around you . . .*," the shadowcat insisted. "*. . . look where you are, what you face. stop and think for a moment, for once in your life . . .*"

"Fuck you," she hissed, drawing her sword.

Cleo raised her arms, and the shadows erupted. Ribbons of living darkness unfurled like wings from her bare shoulders. She rose into the air, long black hair whipping and coiling, her legion of daemons swarming, swooping, swaying around her.

Mia reached into her belt, flinging a handful of red wyrdglass right at Cleo's face. Cleo's body shimmered, the glass exploded, blooms of fire flaring briefly in the gloom. But the woman was already gone, Stepping out of a shadowbat's body and hovering in the gloom above Mia with a dark smile. Cleo's long black hair formed itself into blades of shadow, flowing like liquid, sharp like steel, streaming toward Mia like spears, and Mia

Stepped

aside, reached back into her belt, flinging a handful of white wyrdglass this time. The globes exploded into a toxic cloud, but again, Cleo was simply gone, Stepping out of a shadowhawk's fleeting form, back to the air over Mia's head. The girl Stepped, up, far up, directly into the shadowed roof of this strange cathedral. Kicking off the crumbling gravebone ceiling and diving back down out of the sky, blade raised in both hands. Cleo flickered again, avoiding Mia's blow, catching her up in tendrils of liquid black. Mia slashed at the darkness,

Stepped

away like a hummingbird, flinging more red wyrdglass. Cleo simply vanished, appearing out of Mister Kindly's shape, still waiting back up on the landing.

And so they danced, the pair of them. Black smoke, echoing dark, hollow booms. Mia was silent as death, her face a grim mask, her blade flashing. Flickering around the room like a wraith. Both of them could Step where they wished, so many shadows, so dark and deep. But Cleo was simply *more.* The air was filled with her daemons, a multitude she could vanish into and out of at will. Her shadowblades seemed to be everywhere at once, hair streaming out in impossible lengths, Mia barely able to keep ahead of their edge. The whispers were deafening inside her head, the thud of her pulse drowned beneath. Her teeth were bared, eyes narrowed, face damp with sweat. And all the while, born aloft on wings of black, Cleo simply smiled.

She's playing with me . . .

A half-dozen shadowblades sliced the place Mia had stood a second before. She Stepped forward, her longblade cleaving toward Cleo's throat, only to watch the woman flicker away again. Again. Again. It was like chasing ghostlights. Like killing smoke. The woman moved too swift, more at home with the shadows than Mia could ever dream. All her training, all her will, all her desperate rage was less than worthless in the face of such impossible power.

She Stepped to the shelf beside Mister Kindly, stumbling as she landed, her blade as heavy as lead in her shaking hands. Cleo turned toward her, long black hair whipping about her. But she didn't press her attack, simply hovering in the air. Mia was drenched with sweat, smoke burning in her lungs.

Enough? Cleo asked inside her mind.

Mister Kindly appeared on the woman's shoulder, not-eyes fixed on Mia.

"*. . . look around you, mia . . . ,*" he pleaded. "*. . . you can't beat her like this . . .*"

"*. . . RELENT . . . ,*" came the whisper from the daemons around her.

"*. . . Yield . . .*"

"*. . . LOOK AROUND YOU . . . !*" the shadowcat demanded.

Cleo floated across the space between them, radiating a dark and bottomless majesty. She alighted on the bone before Mia, smiling with black lips.

You cannot defeat me, blackheart. You cannot even touch me.

Mia pawed at her burning eyes, searching for the words. Some plea or prayer, something she might say. She felt a bumbling child before the strength of untold centuries. Standing an insect high in the presence of an almost-god. The power of a fallen divinity boiled below this woman's skin. A legacy wrought of untold murders, the pieces of a shattered soul ripped from broken chests and reassembled, piece by bloody piece, inside Cleo's own.

Niah's first chosen.

What was Mia beside her?

You are nothing, the woman told her.

"I am Mia Corvere," she hissed. "Champion of the *Venatus Magni*. Queen of Scoundrels and Lady of Blades."

You are no one.

"I am a daughter of the dark between the stars. I am the thought that wakes the bastards of this world sweating in the nevernight. I am the war you—"

No, dearheart, sweetheart, blackheart.

Cleo smiled, one slender hand outstretched as if to bestow a gift.

You are afraid.

It took Mia a moment to feel the weight of it. To recognize the shape of it. Mister Kindly had walked in her shadow since she was ten years old, tearing her fears to ribbons. With Eclipse and him both inside her, she'd been indomitable. Fear had been a blurred memory, a forgotten taste, something that only happened to others. But after all those years, at Cleo's smiling behest, it had finally, truly found her. Rising on an ice-cold tide in her belly and setting her legs to buckling.

You never know what can break you until you're falling apart.

You never miss your shadow until you're lost in the dark.

Mia's sword fell from nerveless fingers.

She stumbled to her knees.

She'd been alone before, but never like this. Her brief moments without her daemons had always been tempered by the knowledge that they'd return. But now there was nothing to stand between Mia and a foe she'd never really faced. An enemy she'd never truly conquered. Her tongue was ashes and her body was lead, wide eyes searching the gloom as her breath rattled through clacking teeth.

Why had she come here? What was she doing? Who was she to script herself into prophecy, to take her place on a stage peopled with imperators and gods? One weak and frail and feeble girl, who'd only dragged herself this far with the help of the things that rode her shadow. And now, now without them . . .

You are nothing, Cleo smiled.

You are no one.

She was ten years old again. Standing in the rain on the walls of the forum. Watching her world crashing down before a howling mob. Her mother stood behind her, one arm across her breast, the other at her neck. Mia could feel her, almost see her, pale skin and long black hair and slender white arms draped about her daughter's shoulders. Claws digging into Mia's lungs. Lips brushing Mia's ears as she leaned in close enough to smell charnel breath and rusting skin. Mia closed her eyes, shook her head, trying not to listen as it hissed inside her mind.

You should have run when you had the chance, little girl.

"No," she hissed.

Beg my forgiveness.

"Fuck you."

Plead my mercy.

"Fuck. *You.*"

It was a weight, pressing on her shoulders. It was a hammer, shattering her like glass. She felt herself sinking in her own undertow, pieces drifting down into the dark. Her love was lost. Her hope was gone. Her song was sung. Nothing of anything remained. She looked for something to cling to, something to save her, something to keep her warm in a world grown so suddenly black and cold. She reached toward her vengeance and found it futile. She reached toward her anger and found it hollow. She reached toward her love and found only tears. She scrabbled in the bitter ash her heart had blossomed in, black grit beneath her fingernails, a black sting in her eyes.

Looking for a reason.

Looking for anything.

Eclipse scoffed. ". . . YOU HAVE THE HEART OF A LION . . ."

"A crow, perhaps." She wiggled her fingers at the wolf. "Black and shriveled."

". . . YOU WILL KNOW THE LIE OF THAT BEFORE THE END OF THIS, MIA. I PROMISE . . ."

And there, on her knees, the darkest night of her soul closing in around her, Mia finally saw it. A tiny spark, flickering in the black. She seized hold of it like she was freezing, like she was drowning. A strange shape, altogether unfamiliar—not the vengeance that had driven her or the rage that had sustained her or even the love that she'd set her back against. It was a simple thing, almost impossible to grasp. A tiny thing, almost impossible to see the breadth of.

Truth.

"*Never flinch,*" her mother had told her.

"Never fear."

But there, alone in Cleo's dark, Mia finally realized the impossibility of those words. Facing her fear for the first time in as long as she could remember, Mia finally saw it for what it was. Fear was a poison. Fear was a prison. Fear was the bridesmaid of regret, the butcher of ambition, the bleak forever between forward and backward.

Fear was Can't.

Fear was Won't.

But fear wasn't ever a choice.

To never fear was to never hope. Never love. Never live. To never fear the dark was to never smile as the dawn kissed your face. To never fear solitude was to never know the joy of a beauty in your arms.

Part of having is the fear of losing.

Part of creating is the fear of it breaking.

Part of beginning is the fear of your ending.

Fear is never a choice.

Never a choice.

But letting it rule you is.

And so she breathed deep. Dragged its scent into her lungs. Felt herself wanting to fly apart, to curl up and die, to lay down and litter this graveyard with her bones. Feeling it pour over her, allowing it to soak her, letting it wash her clean and knowing it would be all right. Because to be alive was ever in some way to be afraid.

And she looked up into Cleo's eyes. The press of the dark upon her lips, the press of her fingernails into bloody palms. The shadows raged and seethed, the daemons howled and roared, the dark shivered and yawned all about her. Cleo raised her hand, black claws of living darkness at the tips of her fingers. Wailing in her ears. A hunger deep enough to drown in. Teetering on the brink of the Abyss.

"*. . . LOOK AROUND YOU . . . !*" Mister Kindly cried again.

Mia's eyes flickered up, up to the pale light shining through the cracked dome above her. The single sun, waiting beyond. And at last, she heard him. She *understood* what he was telling her. Fingers closing about Mouser's blacksteel blade at her waist, its edge keen enough to slice gravebone. And shining like blood and diamonds, sharp as broken glass, she hurled the blade upward, into the ceiling above their heads.

The blade struck the cracks, pierced the ancient bone. Pale blue light streamed in through the hole, the last gasp of a falling sun, still shockingly bright in the almost-dark. A spear of brilliance, gleaming down from the dying sky, striking Cleo where she stood. The woman staggered in the sudden radiance, the shadows bending, one hand held up against the light.

Mia's fingers found the hilt of her father's sword.

The crow on the hilt watching with amber eyes.

And teeth gritted, eyes flashing, she rose up from her knees. Bringing the blade with her, whistling as it came. She felt it cleave through Cleo's chest, flesh and bone and heart beyond. The woman gasped and all the world stood still. She clutched the blade buried in her breast, palms cut to the bone on its edge. Looking into her foe's eyes, emerald green into midnight black.

"Fear was never my fate," Mia hissed.

And with one last blackened breath, Cleo fell.

Mia felt a crushing blow to her spine. Her flesh crawling. Her pulse hammering inside her veins. Her flesh felt aflame, agony, ecstasy, everything and nothing between as she swayed on her feet. A thousand screams, a thousand whispers, the black enveloping her, hundreds of daemons swarming, storming, seething about her. Her hair whipped above her as if a wind blew from below, her head thrown back, arms held out, black eyes closed. Shadows scrawled across the ground before her, through the air around her, maddened skeins of liquid black.

The hunger inside her drowned. The emptiness swallowed. Awakening and severing. Benediction and baptism and communion. All the pieces of herself, missing and lost, found at last. Every question answered. Every puzzle solved. All the world about her crumbling, flickering, shuddering, as if this were the ending of everything.

The beginning.

Face upturned to the sky, she saw it again—just as she'd done in Godsgrave Arena, the moment Furian fell beneath her blade. A field of blinding black, wide as forever. A dark infinity scattered with tiny stars, like her Black Mother's gowns.

And there above her, Mia saw a globe of pale light burning. Not red or blue or gold, but a pale and ghostly white. She knew it for what it was now. Knew its riddle, knew its purpose, knew it burned within her as surely as she knew its name. Like the circle in her dreams, inscribed into the brow of the boy in her reflection.

The boy beside her.

The boy inside her.

Anais.

"The many were one," he whispered.

The many fragments of his soul.

"And will be again."

United in me.

"One beneath the three."

One moon beneath three suns.

"To raise the four."

The Four Daughters.

"Free the first."

Niah, the first divinity.

"Blind the second and the third."

Extinguish the second and third suns.

And what then would remain?

One sun.

One moon.

One night.

Balance. As it was, and should, and will be.

She fell to her knees. Gasping. Sobbing. The totality almost too much to bear. The power burning in her chest almost overwhelming. The shadows held still, hundreds of not-eyes now watching her from the gloom. The other pieces of his soul, long kept chained here in the dark to slake a tyrant's darkest hungers.

A false messiah.

A fallen Chosen.

What now would she be?

Mia lifted her head, features framed by rivers of black.

The shadows held their breath.

"The many were one," she whispered. "And will be again."

Bloody hands outstretched. Beckoning them. The black about her shivered. Fear rippling among the fearless. And out of the trembling, hungry dark stepped a shape. A shape Mia knew almost as well as her own. A shape who'd found her the turn her world was taken away, who walked beside her through all the miles and all the murder and all the moments until . . .

Until the moment I sent him away.

"*. . . you certainly took your time getting here . . . ,*" Mister Kindly said.

She smiled, tears slipping down scarred and branded cheeks.

"Forgive me," she whispered.

The not-cat tilted his head.

"*. . . i told you before, mia. i am a part of you. and you are the all of me . . .*"

She ran her fingers through his fur. As real now as the bone beneath her feet. The part of her in him, the part of him in her, the parts of them together, many and one.

"*. . . there is nothing to forgive . . .*"

And he stepped back home. Back into the shadow he'd walked inside since the turn he found her as a child, small and frightened and alone no longer.

The others followed. Daemons of every shape: bats and cats, mice and wolves, snakes and hawks and owls. Hundreds of pieces of a shattered whole, hundreds of shadows merging with hers. A dark as deep as any she'd known now pooling at her feet, a fire as bright as any she'd felt burning inside her chest. And just for a moment, just for a breath, a dark and flickering shape was standing tall behind her. Black flame flowing over his skin, black wings at his back. A white circle was scribed at his brow, her eyes burning from within with a pale and ghostly radiance.

Moonlight.

In the distance, she could hear faint footsteps. The pulse of fearful hearts in heaving chests. The ring of steel, and prayers to the Everseeing.

Men, she realized. The soldiers of the Seventeenth who'd pursued her into the labyrinth. Five thousand of them. But the power of a god now flowed in her veins. A dark and fathomless strength no child of woman born could hope to match. Even without the legion of passengers now in her shadow, she feared no mortal man. She'd deal with them, each in kind, like moths to black flame.

Then Godsgrave.

And then . . .

Their voices rang through that broken skull, that hollowed crown.

Many and one.

"Father."

The shadows placed her bloody sword in her hand.

"We come for you."

CHAPTER 41

ANYTHING

Aelius stood in a forest of dark and polished wood in the Athenaeum, listening to the rustling leaves of vellum and parchment and paper and leather and hide.

All about him, books.

Books scribed on paper made from trees that never grew. Books written at the height of empires that never were. Books that spoke of people who never lived. Impossible books and unthinkable books and unknowable books. Books as old as he, bound to this place as he was. An inconceivable quirk of the Black Mother's magiks created, in truth, for a solitary purpose.

And now, as Aelius heard the choir begin anew in the dark around him, as he felt Niah's sigh of relief as an almost physical sensation, he knew he'd done it.

Mia had won through.

His mother was dead.

His work was finished.

The old man dragged deep on his cigarillo, savoring the taste upon his tongue. Looking about the forest of dark wood and rustling paper leaves. All those impossible, unthinkable, unknowable words. Treatises of exiled apostates. Autobiographies of murdered despots. Opuses written by masters never apprenticed. Words only he would ever know. Words he was bound to, body and soul.

He breathed gray into the dark.

And he flicked his burning cigarillo into the stacks.

It took a moment, a breath, a wisp of smoke rising from the smoldering pages. But soon, the paper caught like tinder, brittle with age, dry as dust. The flames spread quick, first out along one shelf, and then to the next, crackling and hungry. Orange fingers, trembling and tearing, leaping from cover to cover and aisle to aisle.

The Lady of Flame ever hated her Mother Night.

Aelius sat in the middle of it, watching the conflagration rise higher and higher. Listening to the bookworms roar out in the brightening gloom. Black smoke drifting into the whispering dark. Tired beyond sleeping, but wanting only that. For all her dominion over death, not even the Mother had the power to give life to the dead twice. She had no choice but to grant his wish now. Sweet, long, and dark.

Finally.

Sleep.

He breathed the smoke. Savoring the taste. Feeling the pieces of him, the pages that bound him to this earth, burning away to nothing. Smiling at the thought that, in the end, it hadn't been blades or poisons or arkemy that had brought down the murderers that took seed in this place after they struck him low. It'd been words.

Just simple words.

"Funny old place, this," he sighed.

The flames rose higher.

The dark burned bright.

And finally,

finally,
the old man slept.

Tric could still smell Ashlinn's perfume.

He stood on the Sky Altar, and it was all he could recall. Not the blood she'd coughed onto the stone, not the poisoned goldwine spilled at her feet. Staring out into the Abyss beyond the railing, all he could smell was the scent she'd worn.

Lavender.

He was glad of it. Remembering her that way. Flowers in his mind, not thorns. Forgiving her had been like lancing a festered wound. Letting go of his hatred, the weight off his shoulders, giving him wings enough to mourn her. His burden was almost lifted now. The shackles on his wrists almost broken.

Only one chain remained.

And so he thought about all he and Mia might have had. The thing they almost were. Savoring the taste on his tongue one last time before setting it aside. Throwing that last shackle off—the shackle of what might have been—and accepting what *was.*

Nowhere near enough. But perhaps enough to keep him warm.

Mia's final kiss lingered on his lips. His final promise lingered in the air.

You are my heart. You are my queen. I'd do anything you asked me.

The boy looked down at the black stains on his hands.

"And everything you won't," he sighed.

He looked out to the Abyss beyond the altar again.

And he stepped up onto the railing.

And he jumped.

CHAPTER 42

CARNIVALÉ

Words simply can't do justice to the splendor of an Itreyan sunsset.

The faintest blood-red of Saan's fallen glow, like blush on a courtesan's cheek. Saai's pale blue, like the eye of a newborn babe, falling into sleep. A magnificent watercolor portrait, glittering on the ocean's face and reaching up into the gables of heaven. Dark stains leaking across the edges of the canvas.

It takes three turns for the light to fully die. All the Republic is washed in the stink of blood as Aa's ministers sacrifice animals by the hundreds, the thousands, beseeching their Everseeing to return quick as he may. Long shadows fall across the streets of Godsgrave like funeral shrouds. As the Night creeps closer on pale, bare feet, the citizenry is gripped with a kind of hysteria. Purchasing their pretty *dominos* and fearsome *voltos* and smiling *punchinellos* from the mask makers. Fetching their finest coats and gowns from tailors and seamstresses. Hands shaking all the while. The pious flee to the cathedrals in droves to pray the long night away. The rest seek solace in the company of friends or the arms of strangers or the bottom of bottles. An endless run of soirees and salons pepper the calendar in the turns prior, as the light slowly perishes, as the citizens fight or fawn or fuck their fears away.

Then truedark falls. And Carnivalé begins.

Mercurio stared up at the night above his head. Black as the cloak across his thin shoulders. The gondola swayed and rolled along the canal under Sidonius's careful hands. Bladesinger sat at the fore, watching with dark eyes as they slipped below a crowd of revelers on the Bridge of Vows. Adonai sat beside the old man, red stare glittering in the starlight. Like Mercurio's, the blood speaker's gaze was turned to the sky above, his long and clever fingers entwined in his lap.

They'd waited for Mia to return as long as they were able, but after Saai began its final descent, the bishop of Godsgrave had decided they could wait no longer. Sidonius had promised Mia he'd rescue her brother if she failed to return, and the gladiatii took his vows to heart. Adonai had spoken of nothing save his beloved Marielle's return ever since Spiderkiller and Scaeva fled with the weaver in their clutches. Tric had simply disappeared one nevernight, and Mercurio had no idea where the boy had gone. Their numbers were thin. But who knew what was happening in the 'Grave since the imperator took the godsblood? Who knew what would remain after truedark fell? And so, as the suns failed, they'd gathered in the speaker's chambers and slipped beneath the flood.

Drusilla's palazzo had been abandoned—Mercurio presumed her familia and servants had fled at some prearranged moment when the Lady of Blades failed to return from the Mountain. They'd found weapons aplenty in the Lady of Blades' caches, though—shortswords and daggers and longblades of Liisian steel, fine and sharp. Rummaging through her familia's belongings, they purloined clothes that fit well enough, black cloaks to cover the pieces that didn't. The taste of pig's blood on his tongue, Mercurio had wandered out into the street and flagged down a runner, sent a coded message to one of his old contacts in Little Liis. Over the course of the next eight hours, word had been delivered back and forth across the City of Bridges and Bones, the old man's information network thrumming with whispers like a dusty spider's web. And finally satisfied, the bishop had led his band out to the private jetty behind Drusilla's estate and stolen the choicest of her five gondolas.

Another round of fireworks burst in the skies overhead—the noise and light meant to frighten the Mother of Night back below the horizon. In the streets beyond the canal networks, Mercurio heard the citizens whoop and cheer in appreciation. Drusilla's estate was in the heart of the marrowborn district, and they had only a short way to travel to the Ribs. But the canals were choked with boats of every shape and size, and the streets were even busier. Every taverna and pub overflowed with merrymakers, the air ringing with music and laughter, drunken shouts and bloody oaths. The citizens who passed them on the water wished them a swift truedark and a merry Carnivalé. Face hidden behind a purloined *punchinello,* the bishop of Godsgrave nodded and gave greeting in return, his old heart thudding in his chest all the while.

What had become of Mia?

What chance did they have without her?

And if she'd succeeded at the Crown of the Moon, what had she become?

"Thou had best be certain, Mercurio," Adonai murmured.

"I'm certain," the old man replied.

"If thou dost lead me on a merry chase and my sis—"

"I was bishop of this city for almost a year," he whispered. "And I brokered information for the Church for fifteen years before that out of my store. My eyes are everywhere. Scaeva hasn't moved Marielle from the first Rib since he brought her there. She's imprisoned somewhere within his estate."

"Jonnen, too?" Sidonius asked.

"Fucksakes, yes," Mercurio said. "The boy is with his father."

"Which means we have to kill his father to get him back," Bladesinger murmured.

"You're jesting, aren't you?" the old man muttered. "We'd have no chance of pulling off a miracle like that, even without that godsblood inside him. But Scaeva throws a traditional grand gala every truedark in his palazzo. The finest of Godsgrave society will be there. Senators, praetors, generals, the best of the marrowborn. If we're careful, we can work our way in through that noise and crush. Jonnen's a nine-year-old boy. He'll be abed at some stage. We wait in the dark and snatch him from his crib."

"Marielle comes not second after Scaeva's whelp," Adonai said.

"We move slow 'til we have the boy," Mercurio said. "Then you and I move quick to get Marielle while Sid and Bladesinger get Jonnen to safety."

"Not here be I for thy little Crow's brother, Mercurio," Adonai snapped. "Mia hath fallen at the Crown, for all we know. I seek my sister love, none other."

"We're not leaving without the weaver," Mercurio said. "You have my word. But there's one captain in this company, Adonai. And I'm giving the orders aboard this ship."

"Boat," Bladesinger murmured from the gondola's bow.

Mercurio sighed, tired in his bones. "Everyone's a critic."

They made berth at a busy pier near the forum. The Ribs loomed to the south, the great gravebone expanses stretching high into the night. In their hollowed innards, the marrowborn of the city made their homes—their apartments carved within the bone itself. Status was conferred by proximity to the first Rib, where the Senate and consul traditionally lived during their tenures of power. But Mercurio's rumor network had informed him that in the last two weeks, Scaeva had ordered the upper apartments vacated and the Senate relocated back to their palazzi in the marrowborn quarter; it seemed the imperator of Itreya would have none above him in his new world order. The old man had heard more disturbing rumors, too. Whispers of a shadow creeping over the metropolis, even before truedark fell. Talk of dissenters being taken in the nevernight, men and women simply disappearing, never to be heard of again. Talk of the Senate being disbanded, talk of iron fists in velvet gloves. Mercurio knew it would have been bad enough if absolute power had been handed to an ordinary man. But to give it to a man like Julius Scaeva, a man steeped in murder and brutality and now swollen with the power and malevolence of a fallen god . . .

Looking at the city around him, the old bishop shook his head.

What the fuck did they expect?

The quartet made their way through crowded streets, over the Bridge of Laws and Bridge of Hosts, under a triumphal arch and into a vast and crowded courtyard. To the south stood the Basilica Grande, the city's greatest cathedral. It was wrought in stained glass and polished marble, archways and spires lit by a thousand arkemical globes, trying in vain to banish the night above. Behind the basilica loomed one of Godsgrave's ten War Walkers. The mekwerk giant resembled an Itreyan soldier made of iron, standing silent vigil over the city below. But it was unfueled and unmanned—the ancient guardians only to be operated in times of absolute crisis.

In the courtyard's heart, surrounded by the faithful, stood a statue of almighty Aa. The Everseeing loomed fifty feet tall, his naked sword held out to the horizon, three burning globes in one upturned palm. Mia had torn that edifice to rubble during the truedark massacre, but Scaeva had ordered it rebuilt at his own personal expense.

As Mercurio led his band through the streets, the old bishop noted the countless legionaries, the Luminatii in gravebone platemail and crimson cloaks. The cobbles were packed with revelers in their beautiful masks, bright and garish and O, so loud. But there seemed an odd chill to the air. The whole city seemed on edge. Mercurio could have sworn even the shadows seemed a touch darker than usual.

The old Blade and his fellows moved quick and silent, Mercurio melting through the throng so swift that Sidonius and Bladesinger struggled to keep up. For the first time in a long time, and despite his growing trepidation, the old man felt truly alive. His knees barely ached, his arms felt strong, his grip firm. He was put in mind of past turns, when he was a younger man. A blade at his waist. A throat to slit or a fine lass to charm. All the world just his for the taking. He didn't rightly know what the night would bring, or how this story would end. But he'd made a promise to Mia, and by the Black Mother, he intended to keep it. He owed her that much.

He could see the Spine rising before them now, the Senate house, the great bibliotheca, the Iron Collegium, the halls of Itreyan power carved within. All around them, high into the truedark sky, rose sixteen great ossified towers—the Ribs of Godsgrave. To their left rose the first of them. The greatest of them. Smaller buildings were clustered around its feet, beautiful gardens hemmed in on all sides by an artful fence of wrought iron and limestone. Mercurio could see the broad front gates were flung wide, but dozens upon dozens of Luminatii guarded it with burning sunsteel blades.

The old man stopped at a sugar-floss stand on a busy corner, asked the young lass working it for four whips of strawberry. The girl smiled behind her *domino* mask and busied herself, spinning the fluffed confectionary onto long willow sticks. Mercurio waited silently, peering at the first Rib across the way. Fine coaches carrying the city's marrowborn were lined up outside the gates, spilling dazzling donas and handsome dons from within and, after a brief check of papers, into the beautiful grounds beyond.

"I favor not our chances of entering here, good Bishop," Adonai murmured.

"Aye," Sidonius said, plucking at his plain clothes. "Not dressed like this."

"You look passing fine to me." 'Singer's smile was hidden behind her *volto* but glittered in her eyes. "I'd let you through the gates if you asked nicely."

Sid chuckled. "Well, I might—"

"If you two are finished flirting?" Mercurio growled, handing out the sugar-floss.

Adonai eyed the tuft of pink confectionary with deep and abiding disdain. "No sustenance can a speaker draw from fare such as this, Bishop."

"Aye, I'm no fan of strawberry, neither," Sid said.

"Maw's teeth, just fucking follow me," the old man hissed.

Treats in hand, the quartet pushed their way through the tight-packed mob, down a broad side street. The high wrought-iron fence of the first Rib rose up on their right, the third Rib stretching up to their left. The side street was well-lit and crowded—merrymakers were making their way back and forth to their galas, servants and messengers running to and fro, and among it all, the patrols of legionaries and Luminatii were ever present. There was no chance to slip over the fence undetected.

'Singer lifted her *volto,* chewing thoughtfully on her floss.

"All right, what now?"

A loud bang sounded behind them, a shrill scream came a second after.

"Now that," Mercurio replied.

More shouts followed the first, accompanied by a series of *poppoppops*! The crowd around Mercurio and his crew turned toward the noise to see what the fuss was. A tall plume of black smoke was rising into the truedark sky, accompanied by more cries. The curious and the brave rushed for a look-see, a patrol of legionaries barreled past, shouting for folk to make way. Soon enough, a gaggle of busybodies and gawpers and fuck-all-else-to-dos were gathering in the thoroughfare behind them.

Their side street was all but empty.

"Age before beauty," the old man said.

Tossing his sugar-floss over his shoulder, Mercurio reached up to the wrought-iron fence. Straining with his own weight, legs kicking the air, he tried to drag himself up. But spry as he was, it seemed sixty-two years in the game was a little long for a bout of impromptu acrobatics. Red-faced and cursing, he hooked an arm around the fence, looked over his shoulder at Sidonius's gob-smacked mug.

"Don't just stand there like a bull's tit, give me a fucking hand."

The gladiatii came to his senses, offered cupped hands. Stepping on the big man's palms, Mercurio flung himself over the fence, dropping into a thick clump of well-manicured bushes with another curse. Bladesinger followed swiftly, saltlocks streaming. Adonai came behind, Sidonius thumping to the dirt beside him last of all.

"What the 'byss was that?" Bladesinger asked, eyes back on the thoroughfare.

"Small tombstone bomb and some black wyrdglass," Mercurio replied. "Found them in one of Drusilla's caches. I dropped them into the sugar-floss cart while the lass was making our treats."

"You blew that poor girl up?" Sid asked, aghast.

"Of course not, you bleeding nonce," Mercurio growled. "It was mostly smoke and noise. But enough for a distraction. Now, if you're done being a fucking blouse, we've got a daring rescue to undertake."

The old man dragged himself upright (with Bladesinger's help) and stole across the garden grounds, his walking stick sinking into the grass. The shrubbery was thick and lush, the fruit trees swaying in the truedark breeze. The old man knew it must have cost a fortune to maintain grounds like this, but all the greenery proved fine cover as the quartet stole toward a servant's entrance. Bringing his crew to a halt with a raised hand, Mercurio eyed the four Luminatii sentries on duty outside.

The men guarding the door were dressed in the red cloaks and gravebone armor of their order, the triple suns of the Trinity embossed upon their breastplates. They wore the kinds of dour expressions one would expect to be wearing after drawing guard duty during the most raucous piss-up on the Republic's calendar.

"All right," Sidonius said. "There's about forty feet of open ground between us and them. We need to make that distance and end them before they see us. You two stay back here, 'Singer and I will . . ."

The gladiatii blinked as Adonai drew a long knife from his belt.

"What's that for?"

The speaker ignored Sid, carving a deep furrow into his wrist. Blood welled in the wound, a long slick of it pooling along Adonai's skin. His pale brow creased in concentration, and he murmured a handful of arcane, impossible words. The blood formed itself into a long rope of scarlet, pointed like a spear, edged like a blade.

Adonai flung out his hand, sending the sluice of blood toward the Luminatii. Serpentine, glistening, it curved through the air, slicing through the throats of all four guards in quick succession. The men gasped and gargled, sinking to their knees and clutching their severed windpipes. The blood speaker wove his hands in the air like a conductor before his orchestra, and his bloodblade swung back through the air, slipping back into the wound in his wrist.

". . . Or we could do that," Sidonius said.

Bladesinger made the warding sign against evil.

Adonai smiled with bloodless lips.

Mercurio sniffed and spat. "Right, let's be off, shall we?"

The quartet hurried across the open space and into the servants' entrance. The gladiatii hid the bodies in a nearby storeroom, while with a wave of his hand and more whispered words of power, Adonai swept the spilled blood up into a long whip of red, which he promptly swallowed with a faint grimace.

"So quickly doth it cool," he said sadly.

"My heart fucking bleeds," Mercurio muttered.

The speaker glanced at him sidelong.

"Tease."

Slipping into the storeroom and locking the door behind them, the comrades stripped off the dead soldiers' armor and donned it with haste. The gravebone was light enough, but still uncomfortable on Mercurio's aching shoulders. The helmets were set with long cheekguards and tall red plumes and did a decent job of hiding the wearer's face. But still . . .

"You three don't make the most convincing legionaries," Sid said.

Looking at Bladesinger trying to squeeze the helm over her nest of saltlocks, Adonai's lithe frame wearing a suit of armor far too big for him and his own old, withered arms and walking stick, Mercurio was forced to agree.

"Look, this is the grandest gala of the Itreyan calendar," the bishop replied. "The cream of Godsgrave society is gathering out in that hall, and every servant and slave in this building has their minds on not losing their job or their heads. Walk tall, eyes front, Sidonius, you're next to me. Anyone stops us, you do the talking."

"What happens when they find those guards missing?" 'Singer asked.

"I imagine an alarm gets raised and the whole Abyss breaks loose," Mercurio said, pulling on his helm. "So we'd best get moving."

After a quick peek into the hall and a pause for a flustered serving girl to run past, the four marched out of the storeroom and into the corridor beyond. Boots tromping, red cloaks billowing about them, they marched as if they belonged, and did a passing job of appearing to do just that. Mercurio's supposition was exactly right—with the guests arriving in droves and the gala now in full swing, the servants and slaves and mistresses and minor domos they passed all seemed far too busy to even look their way. A long procession of slaves was streaming out from the many kitchens and larders, bearing carafes of the finest wines and trays artfully stacked with exotic aperitifs. It was simple enough for the quartet to slip through the brimming chaos to a quiet stairwell, and from there, to the apartments above. But still . . .

This is too easy.

Another cadre of Luminatii waited on the landing above, their centurion frowning at Mercurio as he led their small cohort up the stairs. The man's question was silenced by a wave of Adonai's hand and a bloodblade whipping through his throat, sending him and his fellows to the marbled floor. The blood speaker drank a few quick mouthfuls from the fallen centurion's neck before Sid and 'Singer dragged the bodies into an antechamber, and the quartet were soon marching through the apartment levels. Past a grand study with a grand map of the Republic laid out on the floor. What might have been a counsel room, lined with charts and shelves full of scrolls. An elaborate bathhouse trimmed in gold and peopled with beautiful statues. The old bishop couldn't shake the trepidation from his shoulders, the feeling that something simply wasn't—

"Where's Jonnen's room?" Sidonius asked.

"How the fuck should I know?" Mercurio muttered.

"Because you were bishop of this city for almost a year?" Bladesinger whispered incredulously. "And you brokered information for the Church for fifteen years before and your eyes are fucking everywhere?"

"Well, not *everywhere*, obviously," Mercurio said.

"'Byss and blood," Sid hissed. "So we just stumble about until we find it?"

A bald man in expensive servant's livery and the triple circles of an educated slave branded into his chubby cheek walked out of a washroom, wringing his hands. At the sight of the four mismatched Luminatii before him, the fellow came to a stop, looking somewhat confused. Mercurio shrugged.

"We can ask him?"

In a quiet blinking, Sidonius had slammed the servant up against the wall, palm clapped over his mouth, knife to his groin.

"Make a squeak, I'll cut your fucking jewels off, tubby," the gladiatii growled.

Bladesinger sighed, pinching the bridge of her nose. "He's a eunuch, Sid."

"O . . ." Sidonius glanced downward, then lifted the knife to the bald man's throat. "Apologies."

"Nw wpwujzz mwssussuwuh," the eunuch replied.

Sidonius lifted his palm away. "What did you say?"

"No apologies necessary," the man whispered.

"I presume you want your insides to stay inside you?" Sid asked.

"O, most assuredly," the eunuch nodded.

"Then you can tell us where the young master of the house sleeps."

One detailed explanation, one sharp blow to the head, and one slumbering eunuch stuffed into a washroom later, and the comrades were making their way upstairs. Mercurio could hear a multitude of voices from the ballroom below now, the beautiful notes of a string orchestra. Another Luminatii patrol was swiftly dealt with by Adonai's blood magiks, and finally, all too miraculously, the bishop of Godsgrave found himself outside Jonnen's bedchambers with the alarm as yet unraised. A quick peek inside showed a large empty bed with crisp white sheets, rich tapestries on the walls, toy soldiers, long shadows cast by a single arkemical globe. Mercurio stole inside, the others following, Adonai closing the door with a soft click.

Fear sat on the old man's shoulder, ice roiling in the pit of his belly.

Far too easy . . .

"Right, it's after tenbells," he said. "The boy will be abed soon enough. We hide in here, snatch the little bastard when he hits the sheets, then get the fuck out, aye?"

"First we seek Marielle," the speaker said, unbuckling his gravebone greaves.

"That eunuch said she's down in the basement cells." Sidonius watched Adonai slough off his breastplate. "You might need armor in quarters that tight."

"Love be my armor." Adonai tossed white hair from blood-red eyes, flung his vambraces onto the bed. "Devotion my blade."

". . . *Touching* . . . ," came a whisper.

Mercurio wished he could have at least felt surprised. But as he turned and saw the dark shape of Scaeva's daemon slithering out of the long shadows, all he felt was a sinking inevitability. The serpent licked the air with its translucent tongue, peering at Adonai and hissing soft.

". . . Most touching, Speaker. Your sister sang much the same when we put the hot irons to her . . ."

Adonai stepped forward, dagger raised. "If thou hast done her harm . . ."

". . . You may be most assured we have, Adonai. You threatened my master, after all . . ."

"No threat, daemon, but a vow," the speaker replied. Whipping his blade across his other wrist, Adonai let two long gouts of crimson spill forth. "And on matters of blood, count upon a speaker's vow, ye may."

Mercurio's heart sank as he heard boots tromping in the hall outside. He glanced over his shoulder, saw at least two dozen Luminatii assembling just outside the room. Ornate suits of gravebone armor. Blazing sunsteel blades setting the shadows dancing. Scarlet cloaks edged in purple.

Scaeva's elite guard.

Sidonius drew his sword with a curse, Bladesinger beside him, each setting their backs against the other. But Mercurio only glanced at them and shook his head.

"This is no time for heroics, children."

The bishop of Godsgrave turned rheumy eyes to the shadowviper.

"How long have you known we were coming?"

". . . Since first you set foot in one of Godsgrave's shadows, old man . . ."

Mercurio sighed, reached into his cloak, and retrieved a cigarillo from his wooden case. Striking his purloined flintbox, he lit the smoke, breathed gray into the air.

"So what now?"

". . . My master, Julius Scaeva, People's Senator and imperator of the Itreyan Republic, requests the pleasure of your company at his grand gala this eve. However, I must insist you abide by the dress code . . ."

"Dress code?" Sidonius growled.

Half a dozen of the elite stepped into the room, eyes on Adonai, sunsteel burning in their hands. One held out a set of heavy manacles as Whisper hissed.

". . . Iron is in fashion this season . . ."

CHAPTER 43

CRIMSON

Mercurio could smell the fear as soon as he walked into the room.

On the surface, it was a picture of opulent splendor. The finest of Godsgrave society, perhaps a thousand dons and donas, filling the great hall to brimming. A kaleidoscope of color and sound, of shimmering silk and glittering jewels. The ballroom itself was gravebone and gold, ringed with statues of Aa and his Four Daughters. Graven pillars rose to the high ceiling like the trunks of ancient elms, vast chandeliers of singing Dweymeri crystal glittered like stars in the high gables overhead. The dance floor was a revolving mekwerk mosaic of the three suns, inlaid with gold. The long tables were set with delicacies from every corner of the Republic—sizzling meats roasting over open coals, the sweetest treats laid out on silver platters. A twenty-piece orchestra played on a mezzanine above, the beautiful notes of a sonata drifting over the throng like smoke.

The guests were all arrayed in their finery, like songbirds in a jeweled cage. They hid their faces behind a multitude of astonishing masks—*dominos* of finest porcelain, *voltos* of black glass, masks made of peacock plumage and carved coral, of glittering crystal and flowing silks, smiling, frowning, laughing. Slave-marked servants wore gladiatii helms and suits of armor decorated with gold filigree—perhaps some nod to Scaeva's miraculous survival at the *Venatus Magni.* They carried silver trays set with Dweymeri crystal glasses, overflowing with the finest vintages, the most precious goldwines. Candied treats and spiced fruits. Cigarillos and needles loaded with ink.

But Mercurio could still smell the fear.

The doors were sealed and locked behind them, heavy bolts sliding into place. The elite legionaries marched forward, leading their prisoners on, Mercurio, Sidonius, Bladesinger, Adonai stalking last of all, hands manacled behind their backs. The guests parted before them, some watching with curious eyes. But most still looked to the far end of the room, to the dais where the consuls' chairs had once stood.

At its heart, the Itreyan Republic had been founded on a single simple principle—all tenure of power was shared, and all tenure of power was short. A senator could sit as consul only once, and even then, that senator shared their role with another. Consuls were supposed to be elected during truedark—during the very Carnivalé going on around them. But instead?

Since the Kingmaker Rebellion, Julius Scaeva had been twisting that fundamental truth, worming through the Republic's constitution as if it were rotten fruit. Loudly and publicly refusing the ever-increasing responsibilities he'd orchestrated for himself, accepting them only reluctantly for the "security of our glorious Republic."

Before the uprising that ended their monarchy, the kings of Itreya had worn a gravebone crown on their brows. After the insurrection that finished them, that crown was kept in the Senate House, still stained with the blood of the last king who wore it. The plinth it rested upon was engraved with the words *Nonquis Itarem.*

"Never again."

Julius Scaeva had been ever careful to avoid the perception he was becoming the kind of king the Itreyans had rid themselves of long ago. Ever the circumspect leader, the hesitant figurehead, counseling against his increases in power even as he grasped for more. But now, approaching the dais when the man himself waited, Mercurio saw the imperator was ensconced on what could only be called . . .

A throne.

Austere in design—nothing too garish or flamboyant. But a throne nonetheless. Gold and velvet, fashioned with the motifs of Aa, his Four Daughters, the three circles of the Trinity. Mercurio couldn't help but note the second consul's chair was set to one side, sat upon by little Jonnen, the boy watching Mercurio with his dark eyes.

Scaeva was using the first consul's chair as a footrest.

Liviana Scaeva stood beside her husband, clad in a beautiful corseted gown—the purple silk of Itreyan nobility. Her mask was crafted in the likeness of Tsana, Goddess of Flame, a fan of shimmering firebird feathers about her eyes. But no mask could cover the fear in her eyes as she gazed at her husband.

There was a large bloodstain before the throne. It was smeared across the revolving mosaic floor, halfway up the wall. Mercurio had no idea who'd made it—there were no bodies to be seen. But the multitude of servants floating about the room had obviously been instructed to leave the stain where it was, gleaming and wet on the tiles.

Julius Scaeva watched Mercurio approach, one foot propped on the old consul's seat. The imperator of Itreya was dressed in spotless white, hemmed with purple. Mia's gravebone dagger hung at his waist—Mercurio recognized the crow at the hilt instantly. Scaeva's mask was a representation of the Light God, Aa. Three faces, three guises: the Seer, the Knower, the Watcher. Glancing at the shadows in the room, the shadows through which Scaeva now apparently saw all, Mercurio alone fancied he got the joke.

Everseeing.

The old man could feel the power thrumming beneath Scaeva's skin. Something akin to what he'd felt inside Mia when he found her after the truedark massacre, bleeding and weeping and alone. But there was a wrongness to the radiance spilling from the imperator's throne. Something unwholesome that permeated the room, crawled on the skins of the guests, set every trembling note played by the orchestra above just a fraction off-key.

Perhaps here, too late to do anything about it, Godsgrave's finest had caught a glimpse of the monster they'd helped create.

Jonnen sat at his father's right hand. The boy watched Mercurio approach, face hidden behind a mask fashioned like the Trinity of suns. He was dressed all in white like his father, fear swimming in his dark eyes. Mercurio noted Spiderkiller lurking in the shadows at the back of the hall, close by one of the exits. The Shahiid of Truths was clad in brilliant emerald green, her throat and wrists encircled with gold, lips as black as her fingertips. Her eyes followed Mercurio as he was marched into the hall, but occasionally they drifted toward Scaeva. And in them, the bishop of Godsgrave could see it, sure as he saw it on every face in this room.

They're all terrified of him.

The music seemed to quiet as their little band was marched before the imperator's throne. Scaeva's beautiful mask didn't cover his lips, and he greeted them with a warm and handsome smile.

"Ah," he said. "Is there any pleasure so fine as unexpected guests?"

Sidonius took a breath, readying himself to step in with some smartarsery, but a glare from Bladesinger was enough to explain the rhetorical nature of the question. The gladiatii wisely kept his mouth shut, his muscles tense as iron.

"Mercurio of Liis," Scaeva said, dark eyes turning toward him. "Your reputation precedes you, I'm afraid."

"Nice to see you again, Julius," Mercurio nodded.

"Apologies," the imperator said, shaking his head. "But we've never met."

"No, but I've seen you. Watched you. It's what I do." The old man sniffed, looking the imperator up and down. Scaeva's skin was filmed with a sheen of sweat. White-knuckle grip on the arms of his throne. Muscles trembling. "You look like shit."

"Mmm," Scaeva smiled. "Now I see where our Mia learned her dazzling wit."

"O, no, that's all hers, I'm afraid."

Mercurio nodded to the smear of gore across the floor.

"Shaving accident?"

"A disagreement with three of our esteemed senior senators," the imperator replied. "On matters of constitution and the legality of my claim as imperator."

"They do say the only good lawyer is a dead one."

The imperator smiled wider. "These ones are quite good indeed."

The bishop tilted his head, staring at Scaeva hard. Summing him up in a blinking as he'd always taught Mia to. The man was in pain, that much was obvious. His muscles rigid, his skin gleaming. It seemed Tric had spoken true—

taking the godsblood had pushed Scaeva very close to some hidden edge. The tapestry of him unraveling almost before Mercurio's eyes. The old man wondered how many threads he might pluck loose before he ended as another stain on the floor.

"Having trouble holding it in, are we?" he asked.

"Whatever do you mean?" Scaeva replied.

"There's a tithe to be paid for power," Mercurio said. "Sometimes it's measured in conscience or coin. Sometimes we pay with pieces of our own souls. But whatever we owe, this much is true—sooner or later, the debt always comes due."

"You *do* think an awful lot of your own prose, don't you?"

"Do you even know what you've got inside you?" Mercurio shook his head, lip curling. "What you've become?"

The shadows in the room seemed to darken at that, to tremble like water with a stone dropped within. A murmur rippled among the guests, and for the first time Mercurio noticed the fathomless black pooled about Scaeva's feet. A chill spread over the gala, all the life and breath sucked out of the ballroom. The orchestra fell silent, notes dying as if someone had slowly choked them. The fear on the old man's shoulders seemed a leaden weight, trying to force him to his knees.

Scaeva blinked, and Mercurio saw his eyes had become a complete and bottomless black, edge to edge. The veins at the imperator's throat were corded as he closed his eyes, his jaw clenched tight. Jonnen looked toward his father, lower lip trembling. Liviana Scaeva placed a hand on her husband's shoulder, fear and concern in her gaze. But finally, the imperator hung his head, breathed deep, summoning some hidden reserve of will. And when he opened his eyes again, they were normal—dark as his daughter's, aye, but edged once more in white.

"I know full well what I am," he said, turning his eyes to the mezzanine above. "And I said keep *playing*!"

The musicians picked up their tune again, strained notes ringing in the chill.

"Enough of this," Adonai snarled, stepping forward. "Where be my Marielle?"

Scaeva turned toward the speaker, swallowing hard. His posture straightened, his pain seemed to ease a little. That handsome smile curled his lips once more.

"Your sister is an honored guest of the Itreyan Republic."

"Thou shalt bring her unto me now," Adonai glowered.

Scaeva smirked at Adonai with faint amusement. "You break into my house. Murder my men. Attempt to steal my son and assassinate me among my guests. And then you have the temerity to beg favor of me?"

"I beg nothing," Adonai spat.

Scaeva shook his head sadly, glanced to his elite.

"Your position seems unsuitable for making demands, Speaker."

Adonai narrowed crimson eyes, seemingly helpless in his restraints and surrounded as he was by Scaeva's thugs. But behind his back, Mercurio saw the speaker had reopened the slashes at his wrists by working his flesh against his manacles. His blood was flowing free from the wounds now, thin ribbons working at the bolts that held his bindings closed, the locks that held them tight.

"I warn thee, Julius . . . ," he said.

"You warned me once before, if memory serves."

"No third time shall there be."

With a tiny click, the manacles at Adonai's wrists slithered loose. With a fluid, poetic grace, the speaker flung his arms out, blood streaming from his self-inflicted wounds, humming beneath his breath. Long whips of gore flowed from his wrists, glittering sharp. They sliced through half a dozen Luminatii throats in as many seconds, the men clutching at their sundered necks as jets of crimson fountained into the air.

The crowd screamed, surging back, pressing against the sealed doors. Even Sidonius and 'Singer retreated a few steps, eyes wide in horror. Adonai wove his hands about himself, singing a song of ancient magik beneath his breath. The blood from the murdered legionaries rose up off the floor, scything and arcing through the air in a crimson storm at the speaker's command.

Adonai glared at Scaeva, lowering his chin.

"Thou shalt bring my Marielle unto me," he spat. "*Now.*"

The smile on Scaeva's face never faltered. He glanced at another of his elite, nodding slightly. A small bell rang somewhere distant, and soon enough, a fresh cohort of Luminatii marched into the ballroom, a sagging figure between them. Mercurio's jaw tightened at the sight, Adonai's breath slipping over his lips in a hiss of perfect hatred.

They'd dressed her in a beautiful ball gown, strapless, backless: the height of daring fashion. But what might have been dazzling when worn by a beautiful young dona seemed only tragic about the body of the weaver. Her puckered and bleeding skin, usually kept hidden beneath her robes, was now exposed. Open sores and pus, cracks running through her flesh like fissures in parched earth. Her lank hair was shrouded about her face, too thin to cover it. The wound where Drusilla had cut off her ear had been opened anew, and her face showed signs of a beating—eyes black, lips split and swollen. Her hands were encased in iron, and she was only half-conscious, groaning as the Luminatii cast her onto the bloody floor before the throne.

Mercurio's heart swelled with pity. Adonai's eyes smoldered with rage.

"Sister love," he breathed.

Marielle whispered through bleeding lips. "B-Brother mine."

The speaker turned burning eyes on Scaeva.

"Vile coward," he spat. "Bastard whoreson."

The imperator's smile slowly faded as the crowd backed farther away.

"Still your rage, Adonai," Scaeva said. "This was but a well-earned reminder to your sister of her place in my order. You and Marielle served me well for many years, and I am not a man who squanders gifts such as yours. There is a place for you at my side. So take your knee. Swear your allegiance. Beg my forgiveness."

The shadows at Scaeva's feet rippled.

"And I will grant it."

Adonai's eyes flashed, the blood storm about him swirling, seething.

"Speak ye of *gifts*?" he spat. "As if I found them in a pretty box on Great Tithe?" Adonai shook his head, long pale hair come loose from its ties and draped about crimson eyes. "*Paid for* my power be, bastard. With blood and agony. But thou art thief of a power unearned."

He narrowed his eyes, pointing at Scaeva.

"Usurper, I name thee. Wretch and villain. Already I see how thy theft takes its tithe upon thee. But I have not the patience nor desire to await the descent of fate's cold hand. I promised thee suffering, Julius."

Adonai raised his bone-white hands, fingers spread.

"Now I gift it thee."

The blood storm exploded, a hundred blades of glittering crimson streaking outward from Adonai's hands. A wail of terror rang through the assembled guests, the crowd surged backward again, the doors groaning. The remaining guards were cut down like spring grass, dropping to the tiled floor in sprays of red. Liviana Scaeva shrieked and grabbed her son, tumbling to one side as Adonai's blades sped toward the imperator's chest. And in a blinking, Scaeva disappeared.

The throne was punctured, torn, cut to pieces. Adonai wove his hands like a grim conductor, the blood from the freshly murdered Luminatii rising up off the floor, the storm of crimson about him thickening. Sidonius and Bladesinger backed away, Mercurio between them. Their hands were still bound in iron, but Mercurio had some lockpicks hidden in his bootheel, sinking to his knees and working them free.

The blood speaker stood in the center of the dance floor, standing protectively over his wounded sister. He reached up and tore his robes away, exposing his smooth, muscled chest, long hair billowing about him, lithe arms open wide. The blood of two dozen murdered men moved about him as if caught in a tempest, swirling, slashing, seething. A red wind roared in the vast hall.

"Face me, usurper!" he roared.

The shadows in the room came alive, forming into long, pointed spears. Whipping toward Adonai's chest, Marielle's back. With a flick of his hand, the speaker sent his blood crashing upward like a wave on a storm-wracked sea. The wall of gore crashed upon the razored shadows, foiling the thrust, crimson besting the black.

"Coward!" Adonai roared. *"Face me!"*

Again, the shadows struck at the speaker, again the wave of blood defeated the strike. Adonai's eyes were alight as he turned in a circle, arms spread, his beautiful face twisted with rage. Mercurio felt his manacles click loose, rubbing his wrists and turning to work on 'Singer's bonds with his lockpicks. Glancing across the hall, he saw the marrowborn guests, all those highborn senators and praetors and generals now battering on the sealed doors in a frenzy. He couldn't see Spiderkiller anywhere—the Shahiid of Truths had apparently made good her escape already.

But Adonai seemed in no mood to run.

"Where art thou, Julius?" he roared. "Thou dost prove thyself the cur I name thee!" He turned in another circle, arms spread. "Hide then, in thy shadows! Thou wouldst strike at my familia? Thine own, then, shall pay thy tithe to me!"

Adonai turned his bloody eyes to Liviana Scaeva, cowering with her son beside the shattered throne. Jonnen stood in front of his mother, little fists clenched.

"Adonai!" Mercurio warned. *"Don't!"*

"No!" Sidonius cried.

The speaker flung out his arms toward the woman and boy. Ribbons of blood scythed through the air at them both. Sid was dashing forward, bellowing at Adonai to stop. But Mercurio knew he'd be too late.

Too late . . .

With a whispered roar, a shape coalesced between the boy and the incoming blood—a man in a white robe, trimmed in purple. Julius Scaeva held up his hands, cried out as the blood struck him, burst through him. He staggered, gasping, eyes widening. Clutching his chest, the man turned slow, one hand held out to his boy.

"Father?" Jonnen breathed.

"M-my son . . ."

And with a bubbling sigh, the imperator of Itreya toppled to the floor.

Silence reigned—the guests' panic stilled, the storm of blood around the speaker cutting lazy, broad arcs through the air. Taking no chances, Adonai curled his fingers again, lances of gore piercing Scaeva's body dozens of times. The flat sound of splitting meat rang in the hall. The speaker's beautiful face was turned hideous by the fury in his eyes.

Chunk.

Chunk.

Chunk.

Curling his fingers into fists, the blood about Adonai finally stilled. It splashed to the ground, lifeless, spatter-mad patterns coating the dance floor in a gleaming slick.

Mercurio's heart was thunder in his chest as he whispered. "'Byss and blood, he fucking did it."

Jonnen took one step toward the imperator's corpse, tears shining in wide eyes.

". . . Father?"

Adonai spat on the floor. Eyes on Scaeva's body.

"*Earned* my power be."

The speaker knelt beside his sister, knees in the blood, wrapping her up in his arms. Marielle slipped her manacled hands over his bare shoulders, seized hold of him tight, eyes closed against her tears.

"I feared the worst," she whispered.

"Always shall I come for thee," he murmured. "Always."

Adonai pulled back from her embrace, brushed tapered fingertips over her bruised eyes, her split lips. Marielle turned away, putting her chained hands to her breast as if to cover the wasted skin and weeping sores. But Adonai cupped her cheeks with bloody hands, turned her to face him.

"How many times must I tell thee, sister love, sister mine?" he whispered.

Adonai kissed her eyes. He kissed her cheeks. He kissed her lips.

"Thou art beautiful."

The shadow punched through his chest. Black and gleaming and sharp as broken glass. Adonai gasped, red eyes wide. Marielle screamed, her brother's blood spattering on her face. Another blade of shadows pierced the speaker's chest, another, another, the weaver wailing again as her brother's body was torn from her arms, up into the air. Adonai's beautiful face was twisted, blood spilling over his lips as he clutched the shadows piercing his flesh. Eyes on Marielle as she reached toward him.

Mercurio looked to Scaeva's body, watching in horror as the imperator placed one palm on the bloody floor, pushed himself upright. Liquid darkness was leaking from the holes in his flesh as he stood, his shadows writhing. Whisper slithered up from the dark at his master's feet, coiled about his shoulder. Scaeva looked at the pinioned speaker with eyes black as the skies above.

"I have the blood of a god inside me, Adonai." The imperator shook his head. *"How could you possibly think to harm me with the blood of men?"*

Scaeva closed his fist.

And Adonai was torn to pieces.

Marielle's scream of rage and horror rang on marbled walls and singing Dweymeri crystal. Another wave of panic hit the crowd and they surged again, finally breaking through the ballroom doors and streaming out into the palazzo beyond. Mercurio could hear their cries, their panic, the thunder of their retreating footsteps, staring in disbelief at Adonai's remains.

Sidonius was less awestruck. The big gladiatii had stolen across the bloody floor at Scaeva's back, snatching up a fallen sunsteel sword. Bladesinger had already gathered Jonnen in her arms, dragging a dumbstruck Liviana Scaeva to her feet. Mercurio beckoned them, hoping to slink back into the dark and flee for their lives.

Except the dark could see everything he did now.

The shadows lashed out, snatching Jonnen from 'Singer's arms and smashing her into the far wall. Sidonius roared and raised his sunsteel, the sword bursting into flames. A shadowblade punched through his belly and the gladiatii gasped, staggering. Another black blade flashed, sending the big Itreyan skidding across the bloody floor and crashing into one of the tall, fluted pillars.

"Sidonius!" Jonnen cried.

The imperator of Itreya staggered on his feet, clutching his head, dragging his hands back through his hair. He screamed once, mouth open wide, his tongue black and gleaming. The room trembled, as if in an earthquake. His shadow swelled about his feet, burst like a bubble, spilling out across the floor in a hundred shapeless rivulets. Scaeva tore at his robes, roaring again as black vomit gushed from his mouth.

"Julius!" Liviana wailed with horror at the sight of her husband. *"Julius!"*

The shadows around the room whipped and thrashed, spilling out over the tiles at Scaeva's feet in a bottomless flood. A wind had picked up from nowhere, howling through the hall with a tempest's fury. Liviana staggered toward her husband, eyes narrowed in the gale, hand outstretched.

"Julius!" she cried. "I beg you, *stop this*!"

Scaeva screamed again, clutching his temples. The shadows lashed about in blind fury, clawing great gouges through the walls, ripping upward through the ceiling. Mercurio crouched low as the mezzanine level shuddered and collapsed, the entire structure shaking. A vast chandelier overhead broke free, crashing to the floor and crushing the imperator's wife before shattering into a million glittering shards.

"Mother!" Jonnen cried.

Scaeva clutched his temples again, roaring so hard his voice broke.

"FATHER!"

Scaeva's eyes were filmed with black. Tearing off his mask of three suns, he cast it to the floor with a snarl of hatred. Black tears running down his cheeks, he lifted his foot and smashed it under his heel. Laughing. Arms about himself and groaning. And staring into those bottomless black eyes, Mercurio could see the fury of that fallen god was breaking loose inside him now. All the rage, all the pain, all the perfect hatred of a son betrayed, wishing only to destroy the temple to his betrayer.

Scaeva held out his arms as the room shuddered again. Wings of liquid darkness sprouted from his shoulders, lifting him into the air. Marielle dragged herself away from his dark fury, taking shelter against the pillar where Sidonius lay clutching his sundered belly. Black winds roared in the hall, almost forcing Mercurio to the floor. The burning coals in one of the cookfires had spilled, setting the tablecloths ablaze. Staggering across the bloodstains, heart thundering in his chest, the old man took hold of Bladesinger's tunic and dragged her unconscious body to shelter near the weaver.

The old man worked at Marielle's manacles with shaking hands, the lockpicks clicking as her irons slithered free. The scent of smoke was rising in the unholy wind as the flames spread. Mercurio gestured to Jonnen, now pressed back against the wall near Scaeva's shattered throne.

"We need to snatch the boy and get the fuck out of here!" he bellowed.

Their pillar was ripped apart, the gravebone splintering like old, rotten wood. Mercurio cried out, the companions scattered and tumbled across the blood-soaked floor. The bishop felt ribbons of black seize his throat, wrap about his waist, strong as iron, cold as graves. He was dragged up into the air, gasping, flailing, clutching the bands of darkness squeezing his throat.

He found himself floating before the thing that had been Julius Scaeva. Pale cheeks smudged with black tears. Lips smeared with darkest blood.

"But . . . ," he gurgled.

Looking death in the face. Death smiling back.

"But . . . w-who writes the . . . third book?"

Black blades reared up, wicked sharp, gleaming dark. Ready to cleave his chest and heart in two. But with a hissing sigh, the thing that had been Scaeva suddenly turned his pitch-black eyes to the ceiling. Pale fingers curled into fists. The winds quieted for a moment, a tiny, fractured breath within the breaking chaos.

And into that silence, the godling breathed.

"She comes."

CHAPTER 44

DAUGHTER

She wore the night.

Her gown was silken black. The jewels at her throat, darkling stars. Long skirts billowed out from her waist, flowed down to her bare feet, a corset of midnight cinched tight across ghost-pale skin.

White powder on her cheeks.

Black paint on her lips.

Legions in her eyes.

She alighted on the stony shore of the Nethers, a city of bones laid before her. A blade of the same in her hands. The black velvet wings at her back were vast as open skies, tips brushing the piers, the cobbles, the buildings beside her as she stalked up from the crusted waterline. The city's shadows sighed at her coming, caressed her face with loving hands, welcoming her home.

The merrymakers. The hucksters. The beggars and the priests and the whores. All of them felt her before they saw her. Their music falling silent, their laughter falling still. A chill brushed the backs of their necks. A stillness deeper than death. Bringing to the pious and the sinner alike, a whisper.

A warning.

A word.

Run.

The fear spread out from her feet like a black tide. The suns had never seemed so far away, the night above never so dark, and they felt it, those mortals—felt it in their chests and in their bones. She was a reckoning. A ruin. The vengeance of every orphaned daughter, every murdered mother, every bastard son. Her father awaiting her, ahead and above.

Many waiting to become one.

And so they ran. The cobbles emptying before her. Rats flooding up from the sewers, fleeing as if she were dark flame. Folk scattering for their lives, not just back to the comfort of hearth and home, but down to the waterline, across the aqueduct, like the vermin all about them. Panic, pure and black, rippling before her. The city about her trembling, this tomb of a fallen divinity too long profaned by the tread of mortal feet. The grave of a fallen god, set now to become the grave of an empire.

She stalked the emptying streets, the deserted thoroughfares, on toward the forum. Pausing beside an upturned cart, she opened one pale hand. The shadows lifted a fallen mask, leafed in gold, placing it over her eyes. It was shaped like a crescent. Like a moon not yet full. The dark was alive about her. Inside her.

Pale and beautiful, she walked on.

She wore the night, gentlefriends.

And all the night came with her.

CHAPTER 45

LOVER

Spiderkiller closed her eyes.

The truedark breeze was cool on her skin.

The sky above as empty as the place her heart had once been.

The city was in chaos, growing deeper all the while. Somewhere behind her, the marrowborn fools who'd gathered for Scaeva's gala were finally spilling out of the first Rib in a wailing multitude. The entire archipelago was trembling as if in the grip of an earthquake, great rents splitting the cobblestones or cracking the facades of the buildings about her. Black clouds had gathered above, choking the starlight and filling the air with thundersong. Somewhere in the warehouse district, the quakes had started a fire, black smoke rising into the dark. A wave of rats was streaming up from the Nethers, tumbling and squealing as they came. Spiderkiller could hear a growing mob of terrified citizens following on the rodents' tails.

Godsgrave was coming to pieces all about her.

The Shahiid of Truths had known throwing in her lot with Scaeva was a gamble, but truthfully, it wasn't one she'd bet heavily on. Before she was an acolyte of the Dark Mother or a member of the Red Church Ministry, Spiderkiller had been a survivor. She'd made her way in a world that had seemed ever set to end her, and she'd not only lived, but prospered. A woman didn't last long in a world like hers by risking her entire stake on a single throw of the dice. No matter how sure the wager.

The Shahiid took a deep breath, calmed herself, opened her eyes again. She was well north of the forum, the chaos rising to the south and bleeding toward her. But she was ahead of it for now, making her way over the little bridges and whispering canals, shouldering her way through the good-hearted and the fatally curious who were making their way back *toward* the clamor.

She could understand that—the impulse to tread closer to the cliff to peer over the edge. The need to skip ahead a few chapters and learn how the story ends. But Spiderkiller herself had no desire to know how the tale of Itreya's first imperator finished. Only that she be alive to read about it afterward.

Scaeva's men had destroyed the Red Church chapel in the necropolis, but Spiderkiller knew of at least one cache of coin and weaponry he'd left untouched. Furthermore, the Church had a half-dozen boats moored at the Sword Arm docks, and at least two were small enough for her to handle alone. She may have grown into one of the deadliest assassins the Church had ever produced, but Spiderkiller was born a daughter of the Dweymeri Isles. Her father had been a shipwright, her older brother beside him. She knew oceans almost as well as she knew poisons.

The thoroughfares were becoming crowded now, the panic behind her swelling as Godsgrave shook again, again, like a diorama in the grip of a hateful child. People were spilling from their homes and taverna, out into the piazzas, bewildered, drunken, afraid. Screams and smoke were rising from the south, fear spreading through the streets like evershade through a bottle of Albari goldwine. The Shahiid kept to the back ways, crossing the Bridge of Threads and softly cursing the long, elaborate hems of her gown. She drew one of her poisoned blades from her waist, gilt with gold, carefully cutting a long slit into her dress so she might run better. And then, run she did.

The city shook again. Vermin streaming about her feet. Spiderkiller could see the gates of the necropolis ahead, fences of wrought iron silhouetted against the storm sky. She was only a few blocks from the waterline now, and from there, escape. Picking up her pace, she wiped sweat from her eyes, one long saltlock coming loose from the artful coils atop her head. The lightning above glittered on the gold at her throat and wrists, gleamed on her black lips as she entered the houses of Godsgrave's dead.

Making her way through the graveyard, she stopped to steady herself against the cache—hidden in the tomb of some long-dead senator. She cast one dark eye over the inscription while she waited for the tremor to subside. The name was worn away with time, the features of the marble bust smoothed by years.

"Food for worms, all of us," she murmured.

Black lips curled in a smile as she gazed to the night above.

"But not tonight, Mother."

A chill stole over her, dark and hollow. Goosebumps rippling on her skin. Lightning flashed overhead, etching the necropolis shadows in black. A shape rose up before the Shahiid of Truths, hooded and cloaked, swords of what could only have been gravebone in its hands.

"Maw's teeth," she whispered.

It wasn't human. That much was clear. O, it was shaped like one beneath that cloak. But though the night wasn't all that cold, the figure's breath hung in white clouds before its lips, Spiderkiller's body shivering at the chill.

"Greetings, Shahiid."

"'Byss and blood," Spiderkiller breathed.

The thing peeled back its hood. Pallid skin. Ink-black fingernails. Long braids writhing like living things. Dark and bottomless eyes, alabaster wrought anew by the Mother's hand. But even in truedark, all the city around her falling to chaos, Spiderkiller would have recognized her face anywhere.

The light of a thousand stars glittered in the girl's gaze.

Empty as the Abyss she'd crossed to return here.

". . . Ashlinn?"

"He couldn't be here himself," she said, black tears gleaming in her eyes. *"Not even the Mother has the power to gift life to the dead twice. So he could only show me the way back. He was willing to give that much for her. That was the kind of boy he was. But Tric told me to tell you hello, Spiderkiller."*

The gravebone swords rose up in her hands.

"And he asked me to give you these."

The truedark breeze was cool on her skin.

The sky above as empty as the place her heart had once been.

And Spiderkiller closed her eyes.

Chapter 46

Father

The shadows loosed their grip on his throat, and Mercurio fell to his knees.

The wind was a funeral dirge, howling and clawing at his skin. The fire was spreading from the spilled coals across the fallen furniture, smoke on his tongue. The thing that had been Julius Scaeva lowered his gaze from the ceiling to the entrance of the great hall as every door blasted inward with the sound of thunder. The shadows in the room warped and stretched, the entire Rib trembling. The dark seemed to deepen, the light of the few working arkemical globes suffocated. Mercurio felt a weight on his shoulders, pressing on his chest, crushing out his breath. A chill descended on the room, the scent of cloves and fallen leaves, the air thrumming with a tempest song. He lifted his head, old eyes turned toward the door.

And there she was. In all her glory.

"Mia," he whispered.

Goddess, she was beautiful. The weight of years and blood and sacrifice, spread at her shoulders like dark wings. The scars of her trials etched on her skin and in the hollows of her chest, mirrored in her eyes. But nothing, no one, not the broken hearts or the shattered dreams or the simple tragedy of being alive and breathing had ever been enough to stop her. Larger than life, she was.

A girl with a story to tell.

She was dressed all in black: a corset and long skirts flowing like a river about her feet. A gravebone longblade waited in her hands. A golden mask covered her face, black paint on her lips, parting now as she spoke with a voice that shook the world.

"Father," she said.

"Yes?" Mercurio answered.

She looked at him then. All the years between them became nothing at all. He was back in his little store, before it all began. Just the two of them, alone together. She was eleven years old, sitting at his feet as he showed her how to sweet-talk a padlock. She was thirteen, flint-black eyes glittering as she demanded to know why boys didn't bleed. She was fifteen, borrowing his cigarillos and telling him some bawdy joke, a skinny, scrappy thing with a crooked fringe, not yet grown into her own skin. And it struck him in that moment just how much a part of him she was, just how much she meant, just how deeply she'd changed him, forever and always. This girl who'd dared where others had failed, who had never *ever* seen the world the way others did.

Nor had he, really.

Goddess, how he loved her . . .

She smiled at him. Just for a heartbeat. Black eyes gleaming with tears she'd never allow to fall in a place like this. And it struck him then, just how much she loved him back.

"I didn't mean you," she whispered sadly.

And she turned her dark, shaded eyes to the man behind him.

"I meant *you,*" she breathed.

Julius Scaeva looked at Mia with a stare as black as the blood inside him. He hovered perhaps twenty feet above the ground, dark, translucent wings rippling in the air about him, liquid black dripping from his fingertips. It was easy to see the thing inside him, the godling howling and smashing itself against the cage of his flesh. But the imperator of all Itreya seemed to have remembered himself for this last dance—some small part of what he'd been dragging itself back up to a thin and cracking surface. Enough at least to bare his teeth in a ghastly parody of a smile.

"It's good to see you again, daughter," he said.

"Mia!"

Mercurio and Mia both looked to the ruins of Scaeva's throne, where young Jonnen was still crouched among the wreckage. His eyes were wide with fear, little hand outstretched toward his sister. But the shadows rose up from the floor like razored teeth, barring the way between the girl and her brother.

"Let him go, Father," Mia said. "This is yours and mine now."

"He is *my* son." Scaeva's face was twisted, black on his teeth. "*My* legacy."

"He's a nine-year-old boy! Let him go, you fucking *cunt*!"

"Your mother called me that once." Scaeva smiled faintly, frowned at the ceiling as if lost in memory. "I believe I took it as a compliment."

Mia shook her head, looking around at the wreckage of the room. The shattered throne. The spreading flames. The bloodstains of brave senators and loyal soldiers and beloved brothers smeared upon the floor. The remains of Scaeva's own bride crushed under glittering glass. Everything he'd wrought, everything he'd lied and stolen and killed for, and it had all come to this. Black blood boiling in his belly. Spilling from his eyes and bubbling on his lips. She looked on the man with a sort of awful pity.

"You thought you were building. And all this time, you were only digging." She shook her head. "Now look what you've made of yourself. All for fear of me."

"What *I* made of myself?"

Scaeva laughed, strings of black drool between his teeth. He opened his hand. And there in his palm sat a pawn, carved of polished ebony. Spattered with tar black and blood-red. The imperator's hand was shaking, veins stretched like rusted chains under his skin. The black began spilling from his mouth again as he spoke, too much of the broken god inside him now to hold it all in.

"I warned you about joining a game you cannot hope to win. Do you see this, daughter? This is what you've made of us both. Mere pieces in a game of gods."

"Take heart then, bastard. Because the game ends tonight."

The shadowviper coiled around Scaeva's neck bared its fangs.

". . . Do you still not see what your precious Goddess has made you . . . ?"

Mia didn't even meet the snake's stare.

"Whisper, if you speak one more word to me," she warned it softly, "I promise things will go very badly for you."

The serpent narrowed his not-eyes, hissing softly.

". . . I do not fear you, little girl. You should never have come here. Least of all alone . . ."

Mia looked at him, then. Eyes glittering like polished jet.

"O, but Whisper," she sighed. "I am not alone."

Mia spread her arms, and the dark erupted. A many, a horde, a *legion* of daemons, bursting from the shadow at her bare feet, from within the black of her gown. They streamed past her on black wings, pounced forward on black paws. Dozens, hundreds, a roiling, furious multitude.

They wore the shapes of night-things: bats and cats and wolves and owls and mice and crows, all the shapes of all the darks the world had ever known. Drowning out the winds with their snarls and roars and cries. They gnashed their teeth and curled their claws and crashed into Scaeva like a flood, falling upon the serpent about his throat and ripping Whisper from his master's shoulders.

The shadowviper hissed in fury, tumbled among the countless other shapes, biting and spitting and flailing. He was darker than the rest of them—dark enough for two—the taste of a murdered not-wolf still fresh on his not-tongue.

But the many tore at him, relentless, the hunger burning inside them, pieces of him spattering black upon the floor as he cried out to his master.

"*. . . Julius, help me . . . !*"

"Release him!" the imperator roared.

Scaeva's hand cut the air, the dark turned sharp as knives. But though he stabbed them, bled them, scattered them across the hall like the rising smoke, Mia's daemons were simply too many. Tumbling and tearing at Whisper as his cries grew piteous, his form grew thin, trembling and fading. All of them feasting on him until not even a shadow remained.

All save one.

He sat on Mia's shoulder, wearing the shape of a cat. Paper-flat and semi-translucent, black as death, his tail curled around her throat. His not-eyes were fixed upon Scaeva's serpent as it perished, as if savoring his screams.

"*. . . that . . .*," Mister Kindly whispered, "*. . . is for eclipse . . .*"

"You dare . . . ," came the trembling growl.

Scaeva turned on his daughter, fingers curled into claws, black fury bubbling over his lips as he roared at the top of his lungs.

"YOU *DARE*?"

Mia's lips curled in an ice-cold smile.

"How does it feel to lose something you love, bastard?"

Lifting one pale hand, Mia pointed to the gravebone stiletto he wore at his waist. The dagger gifted to her years before by the shadowcat now riding her shoulder. The dagger that had saved her life. The dagger she'd buried into the heart of a doppelgänger and dared to dream all this might end another way. Its eyes were red amber, twinkling in the gloom. Its hilt was fashioned into the likeness of a crow with wings spread—the sigil of the familia this man had so utterly destroyed.

"That belongs to me," she said.

"Nothing belongs to you," Scaeva spat, black tears bleeding from his eyes. "Do you not yet understand? Everything you have, *everything* you are, you owe to me."

"I owe you nothing, Father."

Mia raised her longblade between them.

"Nothing except this."

Scaeva's shadow boiled. Black eyes fixed on his daughter. Black drool on his chin. The darkness deepening between them until nothing else remained. He glanced to the place Whisper had perished, lips peeling back from his teeth as the pure and perfect rage inside him spilled upward and outward, finally and forever taking hold.

"Come give it to me, then," he whispered.

Mia vanished without a sound, reappearing a second later in the air above and descending with her sword raised high. The shadows warped, curling into grasping hands, slicing through the air. But instead of vanishing, stepping aside, Scaeva reached up with a roar and caught her by the throat. And with titanic strength, he spun with her momentum and slung her backward onto the floor.

A thunderclap sounded, the marble and gravebone splitting asunder as she struck the ground. Mercurio flinched away from the shards cutting the air, the boom ringing white inside his skull. In a heartbeat, a black shape flashed up from the ruins, a dark phoenix rising, striking Scaeva in the chest and driving him upward into the gables. The ceiling shattered like ice as they struck it, great shards of gravebone falling about them as they crashed back down to earth. Mia's longblade skidded across the floor, coming to rest among the rubble.

Mercurio could see Mia's body was shrouded in shadow now. Ink-black tendrils sprouted from her shoulders like wings, ribbons of razor-sharp darkness springing from her fingertips. The old bishop could barely recognize the daughter he loved as the power inside her finally and completely broke loose. Her hair was longer, flowing about her like serpents. Her skin seemed aflame. He saw a pale circle burning at her brow as if it had been inscribed into her skin. She seemed more shadow than flesh, growing in size, filling the hall. Scaeva loomed larger also, the pair of them colliding with another clap of thunder and flash of moonlight. Mirrored fragments of a murdered god, the two halves within him at war now with themselves and ripping all to ruins. The air was a storm of daemons, a choir of black screams, all the Abyss breaking loose.

The city about them shuddered, thunder crashing in the sky above, the wind like a hurricane. Mercurio had crawled away from the brawl, back to the edge of the room. He found Sidonius clutching his butchered belly among the wreckage, soaked in blood. The gladiatii was holding his intestines in with one hand, trying to drag an unconscious Bladesinger to some kind of safety. Mercurio saw Marielle crouched in the shadows nearby, pressed by the howling wind, lank hair plastered to her tortured skin.

It seemed the whole world was coming to an end. All their stories along with it. And there, amidst all the chaos, all the sound, all the fury, a thin black shape appeared on the cracking floor beside him, tail twitching side to side.

". . . you must lead them away from here, mercurio . . ."

"I'm not leaving her!"

". . . you will always be with her. and she with you. but it is time to let her go, old man . . ."

"No! She doesn't end like this, I won't let her!"

". . . you promised to remember her. not just the good parts. the ugly parts and the selfish parts and the real parts, too. all of her, mercurio. who can do that, if not you . . . ?"

The old man looked at the not-cat as the black storm raged all about them. The love they both bore her as real and sharp as broken glass, cutting him to the bone. But he knew the shadow spoke true.

". . . remember her . . ."

Ever since he began, he'd known how this story would end.

We all did, didn't we?

"Marielle!" he bellowed, turning to the weaver.

The woman seemed almost comatose, lost to her grief, to the chaos around them. Leaning against the wall and staring at titans clashing and waiting for death.

"*Marielle!*" Mercurio roared again.

She blinked blood-red eyes. Looked at the old bishop.

"Can you walk?" he shouted.

The weaver flinched as Mia and Scaeva collided with the far wall, tearing a mighty fissure through the gravebone. The remains of the ceiling shuddered, more cracks spreading through the support pillars as Mia's legion shrieked and howled about them. The island shook so violently, Mercurio was tossed onto his knees. Sidonius covered Bladesinger's body with his own, prayers on his bloody lips.

"Can you fucking walk?" the old man bellowed again.

"Aye." Marielle blinked the shadow of her brother from her eyes. "Walk I can."

"Help Sidonius! We have to move!"

The weaver grit her teeth, crawled across the bucking floor. Reaching the wounded gladiatii, she held out one twisted hand, whispering beneath the roaring winds. Sidonius gasped, clutching his sundered gut. But before his wondering eyes, his innards crawled back up inside him, his wound sealing closed as if it had never been.

"'Byss and blood . . . ," he breathed.

"The weaver knows her work!" Mercurio yelled. "Now get the fuck up!"

Sidonius swayed to his feet, staggering as the shadow titans smashed into another wall. Mercurio's eyes were narrowed against the sight, as if the dark they shed were somehow too bright to look at. Mia and Scaeva were almost entirely unrecognizable now, looming black figures with translucent wings and bodies rippling like shadowflame, crashing against each other like tidal waves amidst a storm of howling passengers. Only Mia's long, writhing hair and that circle scribed at her brow served to tell the pair apart.

"Merciful Aa," Sid breathed. "Look at her . . ."

"Where shall we go?" Marielle demanded. "Without Adonai—"

"We've got to get off these fucking islands!" Mercurio shouted. "A republic in ashes behind her, remember? A city of bridges and bones laid at the bottom of the sea by her hand! We all know what's going to happen here!"

"What about Jonnen?" Sid yelled.

Mercurio looked to the boy, crouched and terrified near the wreckage of Scaeva's throne. He was sealed behind bars of solid shadow, eyes wide, cheeks wet with tears as he watched his father and sister collide.

". . . the boy must remain . . ."

Mercurio looked to Mister Kindly, sitting calmly on the broken ground and licking at one ink-black paw.

". . . he also has a story to tell . . ."

The avatars crashed into another pillar, ripping it out by the root. The walls of the Rib split again, hurling them all to their knees. Mercurio gasped, breath ragged, his whole body shaking. Gravebone dust on his tongue, his shadow twisting beneath him. Mister Kindly appeared in front of him, not-eyes wide.

". . . go . . . !" he shouted. *". . . head to the nethers now . . . !"*

Sidonius grabbed Mercurio by his collar, hauled him to his feet. "Come on!"

Helping Marielle up, the big Itreyan slung Bladesinger over his shoulders and pushed the weaver out through a gaping new split in the wall. The city beyond was in flames. Storm howling. Earth shaking. Oceans swelling. All Four Daughters, arisen. Mercurio looked back into the room, watching the pieces of the Moon crash and burn. Looking for whatever remained of the girl he'd loved. And knowing what he had to do.

Sid roared over the tempest, "Mercurio, *come on*!"

The old man pressed his fingers to his lips, held them out to her.

"I'll remember you," he whispered.

He turned and ran.

Chapter 47

All

Dark flame burned inside Jonnen's chest as he watched them crash against each other, shattering the world around them. Each of them part of a god unleashed, the moon made manifest beneath their Mother's sky. They were giants now, the dark about them growing and flaring. Their wings brushed the edges of the broken hall, the dark flames burning at their crowns were tall enough to scorch the ceiling. But if he squinted hard enough, through the storm of black, the bodies wrought for them of living shadow, the boy fancied he could still see faint impressions of the people they'd once been.

His father. His world. The man he'd dreamed of being. The god he'd worshipped, now taken on the guise of a true divinity, corrupted and rotten through. Rage and hatred and misery, seeking only to hurt the way it had been hurt in kind. The boy could understand it. Because looking from his mother's broken body to the thing his father had become, he knew what it was to hate the one who'd made you.

But his sister. His de'lai. A girl he'd never met until a few months ago, and yet had somehow always known. Brave in a way he'd never been. Dark and bloodstained and scarred to the bone. She had every reason in the world to be nothing but rage and hatred and misery. But he knew, as much as she tried to hide it, she hadn't let life turn her cold. She loved with a heart as fierce as lions. Gave in a way that left her bleeding, but never broken. Because even with all she'd lost, all she'd sacrificed, all the hurt heaped upon her shoulders, she'd still come back.

She still came back for me.

He could feel it, burning out in that storm of rage and shadows. The love she felt for him. Too bright to smother, even beneath the power of a god.

But a fragment of that power burned inside him, too. He could feel it reaching toward the other pieces of itself, even now, longing to be made whole. A hunger filled him, scorched him, bottomless and ravenous. He wanted to join them, he realized. Be swept up in the totality, many made one, ascending to his rightful throne in the sky.

He tore at the shadows that hemmed him in, tried to bend them to his will. His father and sister ripped at each other, shaking the first Rib about them, all the darkness howling. Mia's daemons tore through the air like a hurricane, smashing themselves against his father's skin. Her claws cut great gouges through him, black spraying upon the walls. But the longer the battle wore on, the more they tore off each other, the more Jonnen realized they were equals. Each a dark opposite of the other. It was like watching someone fighting their own reflection—every inch claimed was also lost, every hurt inflicted was another gained.

They were so alike in so many ways, the two of them. O, Goddess, the things they could have done if he'd loved her like a father. But there was too much between them now—too much blood, too much hate, too much darkness. And so each railed against the other, tearing and cursing and gaining nothing at all. All about them, the dark whispered a prayer, a plea, ringing in the dark inside his heart.

The many were one.

THE MANY WERE ONE.

But Godsgrave was being torn to pieces.

The earthquakes were almost constant now, keeping Jonnen on his knees. Lightning split the skies above, waves crashed upon the jagged shorelines, the red glow of an inferno was blazing in the streets beyond. All Four Daughters had woken at their brother's fury, battering at his grave in the hopes of keeping him inside it. Jonnen was terrified in a way he'd never known, his whole body shaking, tugging at the bars about him and searching within for some fragment of the steel he saw in her. Turning his will onto the shadows and trying to make them his own, eyes narrowed in concentration.

"Bend, curse you," he whispered.

And there in the darkness, he caught a flash of gold amidst the crushing gloom. Looking to the broken double doors, Jonnen's heart stilled in his chest as he saw a pale figure on the threshold, dressed in a white gown, smudged with dirt and blood. Her hands clutched twin gravebone blades, her fingertips stained black. Her eyes were black, too, her face beautiful and pale, long blond braids moving across her shoulders as if they had minds of their own.

"Ashlinn?" he whispered.

Her dark eyes were turned up to the shadow titans, swirling and clashing across the shattered hall. Grip tightening on the hilts of her swords. But the storm of daemons swept over her, past her, through her, whispering with a hundred not-voices.

". . . the boy . . ."

"*. . . THE BOY . . .*"

"***. . . THE BOY . . .***"

She turned to him then. Eyes darker than the place she'd dragged herself from, lips parted as she whispered his name.

"Jonnen."

A horrifying blow from his sister drove his father down through the floor, into the twisted mekwerk and the cellars beyond. He tore upward like a black spear, wings streaming behind, the pair of them cleaving through the broken levels above with a deafening crash. The gravebone shattered, shrieking glass, splintering timbers, the noise so loud, Jonnen was forced to cover his ears as the entire top half of the first Rib began to shear away from the base. The mighty tower held a moment longer, inertia fighting a ponderous battle with gravity and finally losing. Thousands of tons of gravebone toppled and fell, crashing into the third Rib and ripping it free with an ungodly *booooom.*

"Jonnen!"

The boy blinked in the blinding dust, opening his eyes and looking into darkness, shot through with the light of a million stars. Ashlinn's hands were pressed against the bars, trying in vain to bend them.

"Stand back!"

Ashlinn hefted her gravebone swords, hacking at the black hemming him in. Jonnen wondered at the futility of it. But his eyes widened as the blades sank deep, splitting the shadows asunder. Ashlinn struck again, swinging as though she were chopping wood, more of the dark sheared away. And Jonnen saw the truth of it all then. How all of it fit together. The bones. The blood. The city about him and the titans above him and the fragment inside him—all of it was connected.

All of it was One.

So he opened his hands toward the darkness. Entwined with the black around him, within him, a single fragment of the greater whole. His fingers curled as he took hold, cold and slick beneath his grip. And teeth gritted, face twisted, he tore the bars apart, the shadows shattering about him.

Ashlinn caught him up in her arms, slinging him onto her hip with one hand, the other still holding a bloody sword. They looked up through the broken rib into the truedark sky as two black shapes streaked overhead, crashing into the cobblestones outside and splitting the island down to its foundations. Ashlinn staggered, even the strength of the grave barely enough to keep her upright. The tremors shook them, the City of Bridges and Bones thrashing in its death throes. Jonnen saw water rushing in through the cracked wall now, covering the street outside, its scent heavy in the air.

"The ocean," he whispered.

"Never fear," the girl replied, kissing his brow. *"I'll not let you drown."*

He'd heard those words before. Aboard the *Bloody Maid,* as the tempest roared and the lightning flashed and the Ladies of Storms and Oceans tried to drag them down to their doom. He remembered Mia sitting across from him, cross-legged and soaked to the skin. He'd hated her, back then. With all he had to give. And still she'd squeezed his hand and sang to him in the dark and promised not to let him sink.

Ashlinn was making her way through the broken wall now, ankle-deep in the rising seas, cradling him with one arm. Beyond, the city was burning, splintering, crumbling. The streets were all but deserted as they staggered out into the thoroughfare. To the south, toward the Basilica Grande, Jonnen heard screaming darkness, the rage of godlings at war. To the north lay the rubble of the forum, and beyond, the harbors of the Sword and Shield Arms.

Ships.

Escape.

Ashlinn looked into the boy's eyes. A question swimming amidst that starlit black. Divinities only knew what she'd been through to return here. The strength it had taken to drag herself back from the Abyss. He'd heard her swear to Tric that she'd kill the sky to be the one standing beside Mia at the end. But meeting Ashlinn's gaze, he knew she understood how much he meant to the one they both loved. Knew that, if he asked it, she'd turn her back and get him to safety first.

But the boy pressed his lips together. Looking past the fear, the chaos, the hunger, the pain, seizing hold of what mattered most and holding tight.

He looked into Ashlinn's eyes and shook his head.

"When all is blood, blood is all."

"You scat-loving fuckweasels, pull them in before I toss you over!"

Cloud Corleone reached over the railing, dragging another sodden child to safety. The lass was shivering, terrified, dripping wet. Beside him, his crew were hauling up their ropes and dragging more folk in from the thrashing oceans. Not being much help in matters of physicality, BigJon was up on the quarterdeck, bellowing obscenities at his salts in the hope it'd further motivate them.

As if witnessing the end of the entire fucking Republic wasn't enough.

Cloud pulled the little girl into his arms, handed her off to Andretti behind him. Dragging his sleeve across his soot-stained cheeks and pressing his spyglass to his eye, the captain took a moment to look back out across the City of Bridges and Bones. Smoke was pouring from the warehouses, flames spreading across the laden silos in the Nethers, cinders falling like rain.

The blaze had started in the southern 'Grave, and most folk had fled north across the aqueduct or to the harbors in the Arms. But there was still no shortage of people who'd taken to the closest waters they could find. The storm-wracked ocean around them was filled with rowboats, gondolas, dinghies, wine barrels, and planks of wood laden with men, women, and bawling children—every kind of craft capable of floating and some that weren't. Itreyans, Liisians, Vaanians, 'byss and blood, a countless horde of dogs, rats, even horses. Name the creed or kin and there they were, paddling away from the dying city, clinging to the *Maid*'s flanks or grasping at the ropes his crew threw down or simply swimming for their lives fast as they were able. The ocean was lit red by the raging firelight. The winds about them cut to the bone.

"We can't take on many more, Captain!" BigJon yelled over the rolling thunder, steadying himself against the rails. "We're close to overcrowded as is!"

"Keep bringing them aboard until we're well past close!" Corleone yelled.

Cloud had already ordered his holds emptied to make room for more hapless passengers—he knew exactly how many his *Maid* could take before she floundered. But before you mistake him for a lovable scoundrel rather than a mercenary bastard, you should know he was as keen as his first mate to take his leave from the dying metropolis. But alas . . .

"I can't see them anywhere!" BigJon shouted.

"I keep telling you, this thing fucking works!" Corleone waved his spyglass. "But the shadowcat said they'd be coming, and we're not leaving 'til they're aboard!"

"I didn't know we'd started taking orders from daemons, Cap'n!"

"I didn't know you'd traded in your balls for a vagina, either, but here we are!"

"You know, I've never understood that!" BigJon called. "I mean, women squeeze *babies* out of those things, why are they considered—"

"There they are!" Kael cried from the crow's nest.

Cloud turned his eyes to the water, squinting through the smoke and cinders, wincing as thunder crashed again. He saw a gondola cutting the rolling waters, familiar bedraggled figures inside it. Sidonius was at the bow, arms gleaming in the firelight as he paddled with a broken board. Cloud could see some misshapen crone shrouded in a dark cloak, sitting beside an old man who could only be Mia's mentor, Mercurio. Bladesinger sat aft, looking a little worse for wear but still paddling hard. The quartet had picked up a dozen passengers in their flight, men and women hanging on to the sides, children crowded about them in the gondola's belly.

"Throw a line!" Cloud bellowed.

His salts scrambled to obey, tossing a rope over the rails into the thrashing seas. Sidonius snatched it up, dragged them in. The big gladiatii helped the children up first, going so far as to toss a few of the smaller ones up to his crew's waiting arms like toys. The misshapen woman followed with a helping hand from Bladesinger, clutching her cowl about her neck, head bowed low. 'Singer followed and then came Sidonius, reaching down and roaring at Mercurio to climb.

The old man looked back toward the City of Bridges and Bones, his face pale and drawn. The capital of the Itreyan Republic was crumbling, hungry waters rushing in, the smaller islands already beginning to sink below the waves. He had tears in his eyes, glittering with the glow of the flames before them and the lighting arcing above.

"Mercurio, come on!" Sidonius bellowed.

The old man shook his head. But finally he took hold of the rope, the big Itreyan hauling him aboard.

"All right, make sail, you two beggar fuckstains!" BigJon bellowed. "Toliver, get your worthless hide aloft before I skin it off you! Andretti, move your arse before I kick it over the side! Away, you nonna-fuckers, away!"

As his crew scurried to obey, Corleone helped Mercurio to steady himself. Wiping the sweat and soot from his face, the privateer peered into the old man's eyes.

"Where's Mia?" he asked.

The old man looked back into the doomed city, letting his tears fall.

"Gone," he whispered.

A moonlit eon burned inside her.

The life that was hers before this one.

Mia remembered all of it. What it was to sail across the velvet black above this mortal plane. To sit astride a throne of silver, bringing magik to the world and light to the darkness. To be a child. To be a god. To be worshipped and feared, to be alive, to be dead, to be somewhere and forever in between.

To love and live.

To hate and die.

Fury boiled in her veins and crackled in her father's eyes as they crashed to the earth, splitting the flagstones to rubble. Their impact shattered a thousand windows across the forum, blasting doors from their hinges and ringing bells in their teetering towers. The city that had been their body groaned and bled and burned and drowned, and they tore at each other in their rage, heedless of it all. Mia could feel it—all the years and miles and blood and wrong between them. There wasn't a hole in creation deep enough to bury it all. So she'd bury him instead.

Father.

But Scaeva was her match. Just as strong. Just as swift. Just as sharp. Slamming her backward into the Senate House, steps paved with the skulls of Darius Corvere's legions. Toppling the body of a mighty War Walker, the metal giant crashing onto the Iron Collegium and shattering it like glass. Marble pillars falling, stone rent asunder, lightning arcing in the heavens overhead. Their forms, black and vast now, the god inside them breaking loose, choking itself inside its own grave.

They crashed against each other like waves on a broken shore. Ripping each other and the city around them to splinters. She tore at his face. He gouged at her eyes. He hurled her into the sky. She smashed him into the earth. The buildings collapsed and the cathedrals fell and the Ribs toppled, the oceans rose and the fires burned, and above them, high above them, their Mother bit her lip and hoped that all she'd done wouldn't prove to be for naught.

Father and daughter. Creator and destroyer. Two halves at war, without and within. Dark and light. Silence and song. Earth and sky. Sleep and waking. Serenity and rage. Water and blood. Mia had no idea which half would win.

"You should have joined me when I asked," he hissed.

"You should have killed me when you had the chance," she spat in reply.

They slammed against the towering statue of Aa, three arkemical globes still burning in the Everseeing's outstretched hand, his mighty sword raised to the horizon. Scaeva looked to the shattered metropolis around them, smiling black.

"Is this what you wanted, daughter?"

"All this," she hissed. *"And just one thing more, Father."*

Her hands closed around his throat, sinking into black skin.

"Die for me."

A legion of daemons tore and clawed the air about them, dark winds howling with the rage of a hurricane. He smashed her away from him, the blow like thunder, the blood like rain.

"You cannot kill me," her father said.

His lips twisted in a dripping smile.

"You are *me."*

The words stilled her. Struck her. Shook her to her core. Because wasn't it true? Wasn't *that* the half she'd fed? The half that must win in the end? What was Mia Corvere, if not murder and rage? What had driven her from the dark of her past? Sustained her when all else failed? So many buried in their graves by her hand. Soldiers and senators and slaves. Could she remember their faces? She'd never even *known* their names. And how much sleep had she lost over it, truly? How many women had she widowed? How many children orphaned?

Had she stopped to think, for a single moment, who they might be? Had they been people to her at all? With hopes and lives and dreams? Or had they simply been obstacles in the way of her ambitions? An annoyance to be removed, just as Julius Scaeva removed Darius and Alinne Corvere? Because at the last, if she were honest with herself, in the long quiet hours of the nevernight without her passengers, alone with her heart, Mia Corvere's greatest fear wouldn't have ever been failing to kill her father.

It would have been becoming him.

But how many Mias had she helped create?

After all of it, all the blood and death?

How can I hate him?

When I'm so much like him?

And then she saw them.

Two tiny figures, golden in the darkness.

Two burning truths, shining in the night.

They seemed so small amidst all that sound and fury. Jonnen clutched Mia's gravebone dagger in his hands. Ashlinn held the boy in her arms, fingers spattered black by her return through the walls of the Abyss. Together, they struggled through the raging tempest, step by step through the howling gale. Not away, but toward. Around the base of Aa's statue, across the shattered stone, inching ever closer to her father's back.

Her brother and her girl.

Her blood and her beloved.

The difference between him and me.

Mia fixed black eyes on her father. The statue of the Everseeing behind him, the pale sword gleaming in its hand. The darkness around them shivered. Black wings unfurled at her back. She remembered what it was to sail across the dark above this world. The burning shards swelling inside her, longing to return.

She could see her loves, even now, forcing their way through the storm. Ashlinn's golden blond, whipping in the winds, Jonnen's eyes narrowed against the tempest. The night burned bright above her, her heart ached for all she'd be leaving behind. But this was good, she realized. This was right. A republic in ashes behind her. A city of bridges and bones laid at the bottom of the sea by her hand.

That was a better ending than most.

She spread her arms wide, as if to embrace him.

He readied himself for her blow.

"Goodnight, Father," she said.

And cradled in Ashlinn's arms, Jonnen struck. A pinprick really. A needle into the heel of a titan. But beyond anything else it might have been, the blade was gravebone. Crafted from a body that had plummeted to earth a millennium ago, still imbued with some tiny fragment of the power of the god it belonged to.

And in the end, who can cut you deeper than yourself?

The blade sank through the shadows.

Black blood flowed.

Scaeva screamed.

Arms open wide, Mia collided with him. Driving him back onto the Everseeing's outstretched blade. The statue's sword pierced his chest, burst through her back, gleaming white as lightning licked the skies. A tremor hit the island, the earth splitting beneath them. Black winds roared and thunder crashed and she raised her hands and seized his face, forcing him back farther onto the blade as her thumbs found his eyes. She pushed through, black bursting, agonized wails bubbling in the howling night. The shards burning white-hot inside her, all the world collapsing around her, a deafening voice screaming inside her.

The many were one.

THE MANY WERE ONE.

Mia felt the ground crumble away beneath her feet. The warm infinity waiting beyond. Birth and death. Day and night. Crushing him in her hands, enfolding him in her arms, kissing him goodbye. A rushing swell, deeper than oceans, than the black between the suns, than the dark at all light's ending. All the pieces inside her catching fire, a billion tiny points of light, a shattered totality begun now anew.

They were everything.

They were nothing.

Ending.

Beginning.

A universe about them, warm and red and barely a hand's width wide. A dark pressure all around them, forcing them out, inviting them in. Gravity dragging them from weightlessness, down, down toward an earth that must, in the finish, reclaim us all. The source abandoned, amniotic warmth left behind. Cold air on bloody skin, noises too sharp and real, new eyes closed tight against awful brightness, the violence of their becoming. A severing, stripping them from their core, cutting them off from all they'd known and leaving them alone, alight, alive.

A howl spilling from their virgin throats.

And then?

And then, the shelter of strong arms. The cushion of a warm breast. The perfect joy of her kiss upon their fevered brow and the promise that all would be well in the end.

"Mother?" they asked.

"I love you, my son."

The many were one.

Burning in the eyes of the sun.

Beginning anew what was undone.

The many were one.

THE MANY

ARE

ONE.

CHAPTER 48

TITHE

The sky was as gray as the moment you realize you can never go home again.

Anais walked on water so still it was like polished stone, like glass, like ice beneath his bare and burning feet. It stretched as far as he could see, flawless and endless.

His mother walked to his left. Beautiful and terrible. But though she'd tried to, he wouldn't allow her to hold his hand. He was angry with her, you see. At her meddling and machinations. Though her visitation to the little imperator's dreams had proved the spur to prick the Chosen's skin, to have her embrace the destiny that was hers, he was keenly aware of how badly it all could have gone wrong. And of the tithe that had been paid for his rebirth.

His mother carried her scales instead, black gloves up to her elbows, dripping on the eternity at their feet, like blood from an open wrist. Niah's gown was black also, strung with a billion tiny points of light. Her eyes were as dark as her prison had been, and her smile was vengeance, one thousand years wide.

Across the infinite gray, he waited for them.

Father.

He was clad all in white. Tall as mountains. But Aa didn't burn so bright as Anais remembered. His three eyes, red and yellow and blue, were all closed now. His radiance dimmed. The dark about them swelled, his mother looming at his shoulders, black as the truedark skies gleaming below the gables of heaven.

The Moon's sisters stood arrayed about their father. Tsana wreathed in flame and Trelene shrouded in waves and Nalipse wearing only the wind, Keph sleeping on the floor, clad in autumn leaves. They watched him approach with unveiled malice, but he could see they feared him. He could see why. His domain was the sky, after all. Higher than all of them.

Perhaps that was why they had hated him.

"Husband," Niah said.

"Wife," Aa replied.

"Sisters," Anais nodded.

"Brother," they bowed, each in turn.

They stood in silence as long as years. A millennium of suffering and rage and sorrow between them. And finally, the Moon turned to the Suns. Though his three eyes were closed, Anais knew Aa saw him. The Everseeing saw everything, after all.

"Father," he said.

The reply came then, like a knife in the dawn.

"You are no son of mine."

It hurt to hear him say it. Even after all these centuries. The wrongness of it was total—to be loathed by the one who should have loved you best. The silence grew deafening, the Moon's mind filled with a thousand If Onlys *and* Why Couldn't You*s.*

They were futile and he knew it. But even gods bleed.

Anais looked downward, saw himself reflected in the mirrored stone/glass/ice at his feet. His form shivered and shifted like lightless flame. Tongues of dark fire rippled from his shoulders, the top of his crown, as if he were a candle burning. On his forehead, a circle was scribed. And like a looking glass, that circle caught the light from his father's robes and reflected it back, the radiance pale and bright. He hesitated then, even then, *wondering at all that might have been.*

But standing at his back, he saw a figure cut from the darkness.

A girl.

Pale skin and long dark hair draped over her shoulders and eyes of burning black. Fierce and brave and quick and clever. He knew her then. What she'd sacrificed. What she'd lost. He knew that unlike his own sisters, she'd loved her brother with all she had to give. And most of all, he knew her name.

Mia.

She put her hands on his shoulders and leaned close. His mother frowned as the girl spoke, lips brushing featherlight against his ear. Her touch was ice on his skin, and her voice, fire in his heart.

"Never flinch," *she whispered.*

And the Moon looked up then. To the Suns who should have loved him. Fingers closing into fists as he spoke.

"You gave me life, but that does not give you power. And though you left me shattered, that does not make me broken. The pieces of me you left behind are sharp as knives. Sharp as truth. So hear it now, and know.

"You struck at me when I was but a child. You lay me low when I was sleeping. But I am a child no more, Father.

"And I am awake."

He was clad all in white, but not so bright that the Moon couldn't see. He was tall as mountains, but not so high that the Moon couldn't reach. And Anais stretched out his hands toward his father, cupping his face. The Suns tried to pull away. But it was truedark now, and with Night beside him, the Moon was stronger.

His sisters held their breath as he leaned close.

He kissed his father's brow, just above the first of his eyes.

And with his thumbs, he put out the second and the third.

The Suns screamed. His sisters wailed. His mother smiled. He felt those orbs of red and blue give beneath the pressure, felt the hard, warm arc of the sockets beneath. How easy it would have been to push farther then. To feel the bone splinter, to reach up and tear out the last, plunge the world below into cold and black unending.

But again, he felt the girl's hands on his shoulders. Slipping about him in a cool embrace. Her cheek was pressed against the back of his neck, and all the rage, all the hate, all the bitter sorrow and regret, the worthless Could Have Been*s and* If Only*s melted away at the sound of a single word.*

"Enough," *Mia said.*

He turned and met her gaze, black as truedark skies.

She kissed his lips, resting her brow against his as tears spilled from her eyes.

"It's finished," *she sighed.*

And she was gone.

His father was on his knees, bleeding from the places his eyes should have been. His sisters knelt before him, their heads bowed low. His mother spread her gowns across the heavens, the bonds of her prison forever broken.

And Anais ascended his throne.

One sun.

One night.

One moon.

Balance.

"All is as it should be," the Night declared. "The scales weigh even at last."

The prince of dawn and dusk looked to the infinity above them.

He shook his head.

"One tithe remains," he said.

And with black and burning hands, he reached for a piece of forever.

CHAPTER 49

SILENCE

Mercurio stood in the dark of the Athenaeum, the scent of ashes in the air.

The shelves remained untouched, but the books were all gone. Memoirs of murdered tyrants. Theorems of crucified heretics. Masterpieces of geniuses who ended before their time. The chronicler's blaze had claimed them all, just as they'd claimed Cleo's son himself. The shelves before the old man were empty now, the Dark Mother's library gutted.

Not a single page remained.

"Marielle is looking for you upstairs," the boy said.

The Lord of Blades patted his robe, searching for his cigarillos. Finally finding one behind his ear, he struck his flintbox and breathed gray into the singing black.

"Let her look," he replied.

Jonnen peered out over the railing, his eyes on the gloom. The ghostly choir sang in the stained-glass dark about them, and Mercurio wondered what exactly the boy saw. The shadows around Jonnen rippled and sighed, pooling thick about his feet and whispering with voices the old man couldn't quite hear.

"Have you any word from Ashlinn?" the boy finally asked.

"Not since we hauled you two from the ocean that night," Mercurio replied. "Somehow I think I'll not be hearing from her again."

"A message arrived for us in Last Hope," Jonnen said. "From Bonifazio."

"Who?" Mercurio blinked.

"Cloud," the boy replied. "Corleone."

"Ah," he nodded. "And what did the King of Scoundrels and Tight Leather Pants have to say for himself?"

"He wanted to know if we wished safe passage to Whitekeep."

". . . What for?"

"Sidonius. Bladesinger."

The old man blinked.

"The *wedding,*" Jonnen sighed.

"O," Mercurio scowled. "Fuck that. I'll send something fancy. I'm too busy to go traipsing over the Four war-torn Seas just for a piss-up."

"And too old."

"Mind your fucking manners."

The boy looked out at the dark with eyes that belied his youth. "We may not need the seas soon."

"Lessons coming along, then, little Speaker?"

The boy looked up at him. A small smile on his lips.

"Marielle says it's not to be toyed with, but . . ."

The boy reached down, drawing the gravebone stiletto he kept at his belt. The crow on the hilt seemed to peer at Mercurio with its amber eyes as the boy raised the blade and pricked his fingertip.

Blood welled from the wound, a tiny bead of scarlet against the boy's pale skin. Jonnen frowned, whispering beneath his breath. As Mercurio watched, the blood lifted off the boy's fingertip, up into the air. It shaped itself into the likeness of a tiny crow, flapping little wings as it performed a slow circuit of the old man's head.

"Impressive," Mercurio said.

"Magik died when Anais did," the boy said. "It was reborn with him, too."

Jonnen shrugged his thin shoulders.

"And part of him is alive in me."

If he squinted, Mercurio fancied he could see a moonlight radiance on the boy's skin. A power, thrumming just beneath his surface. It had been strange enough raising a girl with the fragment of a dead god inside her. He had no idea how he'd manage someone with the shard of a *living* god inside him. But in truth, last darkin or no, he liked Jonnen. He could see the Corvere in him. The *her* in him. And Daughters knew there was no one else he'd trust to raise a demigod with as much lip as this one had . . .

"Here thou art," came a voice behind them.

Jonnen started, and the droplet of blood fell, spattering upon the floor. Mercurio turned to the Athenaeum doors, saw a beautiful woman swathed in black. Her hair was bone blond, rolling in thick waves about her shoulders. Her skin was albino pale, perfect as the statues that had stood in Godsgrave's forum. Pink irises and blood-red lips.

It made sense she'd use her magiks upon herself as soon as she realized how much they'd grown after the Moon's rebirth. But still . . .

"The weaver knows her work," he sighed.

"A pity, then," Marielle replied with a beautiful scowl, "that the Lord of Blades doth not. The king of Vaan awaits reply to his missive. The four factions at war in Itreya's ruins all seek suit from us. I have heard whisper that a new Magus King has arisen in Liis. All the lands are chaos. Dawn and dusk now stand but twelve hours apart, the Moon ascends his new throne every night, the Mother is freed from her prison. And we have not even decided what shape her new Church shall take."

Mercurio dragged his hand back through his hair. Drawing deep on his cigarillo, he sighed a plume of gray. "I'm too old for this shite . . ."

"I concur," Jonnen said.

"Well, the joke's on you, you little bastard." The Lord of Blades waggled his smoke, rubbed his aching arm. "Odds are good I'll be dead soon."

"I think you will be here for a while," the boy replied, watching him with eyes deeper than his nine years should've rightly allowed. "You have much work to do."

Mercurio glanced to the dark above. The library around them.

"You think she'd . . ."

Jonnen shrugged. "The Mother keeps only what she needs."

The Lord of Blades looked to the weaver and sighed. "We'll speak on it after evemeal. You have my word."

Marielle pursed her lips and bowed. "As it please thee."

She left with a silken swish of night-black robes.

Mercurio turned to the echoing dark, cigarillo hanging from his lips. Listening to the choir and breathing the gray and savoring the ache in his heart. Finally noticing the boy still looking at him from the corner of his eye.

Jonnen nodded to the empty shelves. "What will we fill them with?"

"Do you not have lessons to attend?" the old man asked.

"Do you not have a walking stick to find?"

"I mean it, you little bastard. Off with the fuck."

"What have you been doing, spending all your time down here alone?"

Mercurio looked out to the empty shelves and dragged on his smoke.

"Keeping a promise," he finally said.

The boy nodded, eyes downturned. Toes scuffing, he made his way over to the mighty double doors leading out to the Mountain proper.

"I miss her, too," he said.

"Out," Mercurio growled.

Jonnen faded into the shadows on soundless feet.

Mercurio turned to the chronicler's old office, shuffled inside trailing a thin finger of smoke. He sat down at the mighty oaken desk, rubbed at his rheumy eyes. And taking one last drag, he crushed his smoke and tugged out a stack of white parchment from a thick leather folio. The topmost was marked with his bold, flowing hand.

NEVERNIGHT
BOOK 1 OF THE NEVERNIGHT CHRONICLE
by Mercurio of Liis

The old man leafed through the pages until he found his place. He sighed, gray smoke spilling from his lips and into the dark above.

"I remember," he said.

And he began to write.

CHAPTER 50

SILVER

A house sat on the shore of Threelakes.

It stood alone beneath an endless sky, the valley all about it wrapped in perfect silence. It was made of good oak, high gables and broad verandahs and tall windows looking out over the water at its back.

A girl sat on the shoreline, watching the sunset.

It was strange now, with only one sun in the sky. Stranger still to track its movement across the heavens in a handful of hours, watching it fall to its rest with her black and naked eyes. Aa and Niah shared dominion of the sky once more. Dark and light forever changed. Dawn the gateway to waking, and dusk the door to sleeping. All the world about her was trying to come to grips with the balance. Wondering what to make of the pale orb that waxed and waned in the new night sky.

But Ashlinn knew they'd soon remember.

He was rising, now the sun had fallen. Anais ascending his dark throne, the stars glittering like diamonds and steel all about him. He was beautiful, she had to admit. Casting a glittering light across the lake, turning all to quicksilver. But it struck Ashlinn as sad somehow, to watch him burning up there by himself.

He was alone, just like she was.

She didn't know how to die. Didn't even know if she could. She'd followed Tric's directions, treading the path he'd already torn with his bare hands, his farewell kiss still burning on her brow. Her fingertips forever blacked from clawing her way through, her skin forever paled from that lightless path, her breath forever stolen by the endless dark. She had no regrets—she'd promised to kill the sky to be the one standing by Mia in the end. And looking to the Moon above, the swiftly turning night, she supposed in some strange way, she had. But Ashlinn had never stopped to wonder what she'd be when it was over. Or how she might endure forever without her.

"Mia."

The name was a prayer on her lips. A kiss to alabaster skin. A question without an answer. Because what had become of her? Where was she now? Curled up warm beside the Hearth with those she cherished while Ashlinn lingered here, ageless, deathless, loveless? Wandering with divinities on some empyrean shore? Or had she simply been annihilated, consumed with all those other fragments so that the Night might regain her crown, and the Moon reclaim his throne?

An immortality alone didn't seem a fair tithe to pay for that.

And yet she'd pay it all again. Because it seemed if she tried hard enough, Ash could still taste her. Salt and honey. Iron and blood. Running the tip of her tongue along her lips. Breathing it in and sighing it out. Looking out over the smooth expanse of silver beneath the Moon's unblinking gaze and thanking whatever god or goddess or twist of fate had brought that girl into her life.

If only briefly.

Mia.

And then, across the silver, she saw a figure.

Walking on water so still it was like polished stone, like glass, like ice beneath her bare feet. She was pale and she was beautiful, draped in a gown made of shadows. Her scars were healed, her brand gone, the marks of her trials vanished like smoke. Long black hair streamed about her bare shoulders, her kohled eyes deep as the hole she'd filled inside Ashlinn's chest.

"Mia?" she asked, not daring to hope.

Ash's eyes were wide as she took a halting step out into the water. Ripples shimmered across the silver, and Ash feared Mia might be dispelled like an illusion, a fever dream, some desperate mirage born of impossible hope. But her girl walked on, across the glass, close enough now to see the black of her eyes, the curl of her lips. And then Mia was in her arms, her flesh as pale and real as Ashlinn's own. Their bones colliding, their bodies entwined. She'd thought Mia's eyes were just empty darkness, but this close, this dangerously, wonderfully close, she could see they were filled with tiny sparks of light, like stars strewn across the curtains of night above.

Just like hers.

Beautiful.

They kissed. Sweet as clove cigarillos. Deep as midnight. A kiss that spoke of blood spilled and battles won, of reborn moons and blinded suns, of the dark within and the light without and the shadows of the past burned away in the glow of the new dawn. They kissed like it was the first time, like it was supposed to be, like nothing, not gods or goddesses or flames or storms or oceans would ever come between them again.

Their lips parted, their brows pressed together, their noses brushing against one another, ticklish. Staring into each other's deathless eyes and understanding the meaning of Always.

"How?" Ashlinn whispered.

Mia's shadow stirred, and a shape melted onto the dark shore beside them. Looking to the orb of silver above their heads with its not-eyes. It wore the shape of a cat, though truthfully, it was nothing close to a cat at all.

"*. . . one tithe remained . . . ,*" it whispered. "*. . . now repaid . . .*"

Ashlinn sobbed. Mia smiled. They kissed again, black tears on their lips.

"I love you, Mia."

"I love you, too."

All was silence about them, perfect and whole and deep. And they sat side by side on the shoreline's gentle curve and watched Anais rise higher in the sky. Arm in arm, skin to skin, alabaster and onyx and gold. Two girls beneath one moon, one sun, one night, one heart. All and everything in balance.

"*. . . beautiful . . . ,*" the not-cat sighed.

The hollyhock and sunsbell were so thick, the whole valley smelled like perfume.

The lake was so still, it was like a mirror to the sky.

"I'm going to be with you forever," Mia whispered.

"Just forever?" Ashlinn murmured.

Mia smiled in the silver light.

"Forever and ever."

Dicta Ultima

The deed is done.

The war is won.

And at the last, gentlefriend, her song is sung.

I suppose you can say you know her now, at least as well as I did. The ugly parts and the selfish parts and the everything in between. A girl some called Pale Daughter. Or Kingmaker. A Queen of Scoundrels. A Lady of Blades. I like little Crow best of all. A girl who never knelt, who never broke, who never, *ever* allowed fear to be her fate.

A girl I loved as much as you did.

Look now upon the ruins in her wake. As pale light glitters on the waters that drank a city of bridges and bones, and a Republic's ashes dance in the dark above your head. Stare mute at the broken sky and taste the iron on your tongue and listen as lonely winds whisper her name as if they knew her, too. I gave you all I promised, gentlefriend. I gave it to you in spades. And if her death didn't unfold in the way you dreaded, I hope you'll not name me liar for it. She did die, just as I said she would.

But even the Moon loved our girl too much to let her die for long.

The ink is drying upon the page. The tale is ending before your eyes. And if you feel some sorrow at this, our last farewell, know your narrator feels it, too. We are not made more by the stories we read, but by the stories we share. And in this, in *her,* I think we've shared more than most.

I shall miss it when it's gone.

But to live in the hearts of those we leave behind is to never die. And to burn in the memories of our friends is to never say goodbye. So let me say this instead.

Goodnight, gentlefriend. Goodnight.
Never flinch.
Never fear.
And never, ever forget.

FIN

N
here he fell

ACKNOWLEDGMENTS

Thanks as deep as the Dark to the following:

Amanda, Pete, Jennifer, Paul, Joseph, Hector, Young, Steven, Justin, Rafal, Cheryl, Martin, Bethany, and all at St. Martin's Press; Natasha, Jack, Katie, Emma, Jaime, Dom, and all at Harper Voyager UK; Rochelle, Alice, Sarah, Andrea, and all at Harper Australia; Mia, Matt, LT, Josh, Tracey, Samantha, Stefanie, Steven, Steve, Jason, Kerby, Megasaurus, Virginia, Vilma, Marc, Molly, Tovo, Orrsome, Tsana, Lewis, Shaheen, Soraya, Amie, Jessie, Cat, all my ladies in the Bitch Posse, Ursula, Andrea, Tori, Caz, Piéra, Nan Fe, Lesya, Iryna, Mona, Niru, TJ, Morgana, Cira, Holly, Rin, Zach, Daphne, Marie, Nael, Marc, Tina, Maxim, Zara, Ben, Clare, Jim, Weez, Sam, Eli, Rafe, AmberLouise, Caro, Melanie, Barbara, Judith, Rose, Tracy, Aline, Louise, Adele, Jordi, Kylie, Joe, Julius, Antony, Antonio, Emily, Robin, Drew, William, China, David, Aaron, Terry (RIP), Douglas (RIP), George, Margaret, Tracy, Ian, Steve, Gary, Mark, Tim, Matt, George, Ludovico, Ronnie, Chris, Antony, Briton, Philip, Randy, Oli, Maynard, Pete (RIP), Marcus, Tom (RIP), Trent, Winston, Tony, Kath, Kylie, Nicole, Kurt, Jack, Max, Poppy, and every reader, blogger, vlogger, bookstagrammer, and bookpimp who helped spread the word about this series. These books are what they are because of you. I love you, stabbykids.

This book was written all over the world, from New York to Zurich, LA to Sydney. But at least half of it was written in the city of Venice. Wandering those windswept streets and walking alongside those winter canals, I discovered the story *Darkdawn* would become. I'll owe the people and city of Venezia a debt forever, but special mention must go to Ola, the incredible folks at Sullaluna for their daily hospitality, the wonderful signore del caffè at Caffè del Doge, and the staff at Torrefazione Cannaregio and L'Angolo della Pizza for helping me not starve to death.

Lastly, I have to thank you, my amazing readers. This series, more than any other I've worked on, has resonated with people in a way I'm still coming to grips with. It's humbling and it's astounding and I'll be eternally grateful for the way you've embraced my murderous little bitch of a daughter. Thank you for your letters. Thank you for your art. Thank you for your tattoos and your stories and your passion. Thank you for letting Mia into your heads and your hearts. I hope, in some small way, she helps.

The dream I live is because of you.

The life I have is because of you.

I'll never forget it.

JK